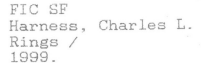

Rings

Charles L. Harness

edited by Priscilla Olson

The NESFA Press
Post Office Box 809
Framingham, MA 01701
1999

FIRST EDITION
December 1999

International Standard Book Number:
1-886778-16-7

Publication Information

The Paradox Men (a.k.a. *Flight into Yesterday*)
>> Bouregy & Curl, 1953
>> Ace, 1955 (bound with *Dome Around America* by
>>>> Jack Williamson)
>> Faber & Faber, 1964
>> UK SFBC 1966
>> Four Square, 1967
>> New English Library, 1976
>> *Space Opera*, ed. by Brian W. Aldiss, Orbit, 1974
>> Crown, 1984
>> Easton Press, 1992

The Ring of Ritornel
>> Gollancz, 1968
>> Berkeley, 1968; Panther, 1974

Firebird
>> Pocket Books, 1981
>> Science Fiction Book Club, 1981

Drunkard's Endgame
>> First publication

All stories appear by permission of the author and the author's agent, Linn Prentis.

Contents

Rings

On Rings of Power

Rings . . . ?
Circles . . . ?
Cycles . . . ?

We all know that space is curved—but what Charles Harness can *do* with that fact is downright vertiginous . . . !

The extravagantly symmetrical selections in this omnibus were chosen to spotlight his dazzling "ring" stories. These powerful works display the momentous themes spoken of in NESFA's previous Harness collection, *An Ornament to His Profession*—transformation, change, transcendence, evolution . . . destruction and rebirth, death and transfiguration . . . grand beginnings and epic endings . . . .

Rings contains three previously-published novels that loop through space-time, and a new one that accomplishes the same dizzying feats as its predecessors. Together, they'll take you on an exhilarating roller-coaster ride through space-time (and beyond?)

Read, and enjoy—and remember (as Arkady Darell once noted) that "a circle has no end . . ."

Priscilla Olson, 1999

CHARLES L. HARNESS:
WIELDER OF LIGHT

This volume is an event: a collection of novels by the legendary Charles L. Harness. Among these are the classic *The Paradox Men* and an entirely new novel. What riches!

It is unusual for any writer to have a collection of his novels published. It sometimes happens when a writer is long established and held in high esteem. In the case of Harness this esteem is now decades old and still growing, having begun with praise from Arthur C. Clarke, James Blish, Brian Aldiss, Damon Knight, Michael Moorcock, Robert Silverberg, Ian Watson, and many others, with several of these praising him during the first decade of his career. All the current major science fiction reference works and encyclopedias echo the same high praise. But much more enduring is what has gone on between Harness and his readers, where it all began. This love affair has made him a revered author, but too often his publishers were the last to know, leading to his being tucked away between the self-fulfilling prophecies of profit and loss statements, which in true Heisenbergian fashion actually hinder the very sales they are meant to describe.

This collection illustrates once again the cyclic pattern of rediscovery of Harness's works, driven by merit and reader acclaim rather than vast sales pressures. Once every few years, the wit, intelligence, and ingenious invention present in Harness's works shines through into a reader's mind. And if that reader happens to have an editorial voice, the question arises, "Why is this wonderful book out of print?"

NESFA Press, a visionary house run by readers, which for some time now has been reclaiming science fiction's past, has shown a gratifying presence with the design and sales of its books. The press offers desirable books and keeps them in print—in modest numbers, to be sure—but numbers have a way of adding up, and availability of an author's work is the only chance it has to live across the generations. Too many fine works are all locked up in private libraries.

There are a number of features to this collection that deserve to be emphasized. *The Paradox Men* is one of the two novels for which Harness is best known (the other being *The Rose,* now happily available in NESFA's collection of Harness stories, *An Ornament to His Profession,* 1998, in its only definitive, corrected version. The collection also includes more information about Harness's life and work). *The Paradox Men* appears here

13

in its author-restored and corrected text of 1984, now long out of print. It's some 4000 words longer than the book version published as *Flight Into Yesterday* in 1953 and as *The Paradox Men* in the Ace Double of 1955.

The novel received a "guilty pleasure" kind of recognition in *Science Fiction: The 100 Best Novels, 1949-1984* by David Pringle, in 1985. Pringle lists it between Arthur C. Clarke's *Childhood's End* and Ward Moore's *Bring the Jubilee.*

In "Extrapolation", the MLA/SFRA publication, Norman L. Hills wrote about *The Rose, The Paradox Men,* and *The Ring of Ritornel,* and concluded that ". . . in his three major works, Harness attempted three different things and that within the frame of reference of these forms, he created close to the epitome of that form . . ." ("Charles L. Harness: The Flowering of Melodrama" by Norman L. Hills, May 1978, pp. 147-148). Although this is a somewhat critical piece, it does permit Harness's attractions to shine through. For an academic piece, it does have the virtue of introducing the psychology of reader involvement that is almost always ignored by academic literary critics: the actual experience of reading a particular author and what the emotional reaction might be. This is where most academic criticism fails, since reading and taste involve issues of human biology, psychology, and the personal history of the reader. Our ignorances in these areas are still so deep that to acknowledge them would dispute all purely rational analysis. We can only describe the phenomenal experience of reading, and fall short of explaining it. "All three of the major works of Harness are enjoyable to read," writes Hills, but it's not enough. Reread Harness and you'll learn that it's never the same book twice.

Little did I know when I came up as a writer that I would have any contact with my boyhood gods of SF, or that some of them would become my friends. It would have astounded me to know that I would, as editor, publish new works by them or shepherd unavailable works back into print. I selected *The Paradox Men* for my 1980s ten-volume "Classics of Modern Science Fiction" from Crown, and wrote the introduction for the 1992 Easton Press leatherbound "Masterpieces of Science Fiction." So when NESFA asked me to introduce this collection of Harness novels, including a new novel, I looked forward to being transported into the rapt state so easily induced by reading Harness.

Let me try to describe what I mean. His stories shine from within, with a strange, glittering pleasure of bitterness and wise but happy acceptance of their characters. It is as if one has opened up a beautiful gold watch, only to find a mechanism of gems and mysterious motion. And at the center, instead of a spring or battery, one finds that the whole artifice is driven by an emotional core of thought and memory.

A few minutes after I had written the above paragraph, I called up Charles Harness and asked what he thought of these four books today. What a wonder such a call would have been to my teenage self!

"Well, George," he said, "I think the four novels can be considered as tributes to certain people. By 1948 I had sold several stories. The time had come to try a novel. It would be a tribute to A. E. van Vogt. I had been awed with his incomparable *Slan*, *The World of Null-A,* and *The Weapon Makers*. All overflowing with action, mystery, suspense, and superhumanity. His worlds unfolded before us with multidimensional clarity. I tried to figure out how he did it. Fifty years later I'm still trying."

"And *The Ring of Ritornel?*" I asked.

"This one is a tribute to my brother, Blandford Bryan Harness, who died in 1932 of a brain tumor. He was twenty-six, nine years older than I, and a fine artist. He's Omere in the novel; I'm Jimmie. The cosmic background here is straight out of Fred Hoyle: a steady-state universe, expanding but with constant density, maintained by the creation of new hydrogen atoms. Those new hydrogens offered all sorts of SF possibilities. Against this background I took a look at two major forces that seem to control our lives: our deliberate free-will designs (Ritornel) and random chance (Alea)."

"What about the way in which the chapters are numbered?" I asked.

"The numbering of the chapters has excited comment. Halfway through the story I noted that the sequences were beginning to replicate, but with opposite meanings. With this, the numbering of the chapters fell irresistibly and thematically into place."

"I was not disappointed by *Firebird*," I said, confessing that I had not read this novel before. "It continues to develop your characteristic themes and is filled with ingenuities and clever moments, as well as a lot of feeling."

"*Firebird* explores a different cosmic scheme," he said with his usual modest immunity to direct praise. "It's the oscillating universe, where gravitation eventually halts the expansion and pulls matter back to the starting point, and we get the Big Crunch, to be followed by the next Big Bang . . . and so on, forever and ever."

"I particularly liked the effort at cosmic engineering," I said.

He replied, "The mythic name says it all, and blends neatly with the theme of the legendary lovers, Tristan and Isolde. He dies, she lives, and it all happens again and again, forever and ever. My tribute to Richard Wagner."

"I just saw a 1943 film by Jean Cocteau, 'The Eternal Return,'" I said. "It's a modern retelling of the story. At one point Tristan, played by Jean Marais, picks up Isolde in a Ford automobile. In your novel it was a starship. And the old woman who brings the love potion is just an old woman, but in your novel she's someone special."

"Don't give it away, George."

"What can you tell me about the new novel?" I asked.

"*Drunkard's Endgame* explores two features mentioned in *The Ring of Ritornel* and in *Firebird:* the so-called 'Drunkard's Walk', and 'Omega'—the latter involving the flight of a seed pair to dead Earth. This novel is a tribute to several people—to the men and women of good will who we hope and trust will avert the doom on which the book is premised, and to Isaac Asimov, who showed us that robots are people."

I don't want to say too much more about this novel. It deserves to be presented without preconceptions to regular Harness readers, and discovered by new ones.

I envy Charles Harness his peace of mind. Unless it is called to his attention, he has been innocently unaware of the growing favorable opinion of his stories and novels, which presents him today as an established master of a certain kind of SF. This lack of concern sometimes produces a writer who is unproductive, or one who creates only a small body of work. But not so with Harness. The way that he has pursued the writing of what has been described as the "widescreen baroque" kind of space opera—with personal satisfaction in the writing emerging from deep feeling for the autobiographical wellsprings of his characters—has created a body of work worthy of any full-time author in the field; but he has done so without the strain of the full time professional.

His work has been influential, both technically, in the example of his plotting, and in the aesthetics of SF's imagery. Although he was influenced by van Vogt, one can clearly see Harness's influence in Alfred Bester, in Philip K. Dick, even in Kurt Vonnegut's *The Sirens of Titan,* and perhaps even in the "Endymion" novels of Dan Simmons. I clearly see van Vogt and Charles Harness in my own "The Omega Point Trilogy."

Harness wields light in the poetry of his constructions and in the beauty of his dramatic situations. These are the qualities, along with masterful plotting, that make his works memorable, and spur his readers to pass on the beauty. Some of this has been stated in print; much passes by word of mouth. What happens is that his out-of-print copies are sold and resold countless times, in both hardcover and paperback, and one wishes that more copies had been available and kept in print from the start.

If you are coming to read Harness for the first time, I have only one piece of advice.

Pass on the beauty.

George Zebrowski, Delmar, NY, August 1999

THE PARADOX MEN

PROLOGUE

He had not the faintest idea who he was.

And he didn't know why he was treading the cold black water so desperately.

He didn't know either why a great battered shining thing was sliding into the moonlit waves a dozen yards in front of him.

A vision of vast distances traversed at unimaginable velocities flicked across his numbed understanding but was instantly gone again.

His head ached horribly and he had no memory of anything.

Suddenly a blinding shaft of light swept the waters ahead of him and came to rest on the broken flank of the rapidly sinking wreckage. Along the top of the broken hull he thought he could see a tiny, great-eyed animal whose fur was plastered to its shivering sides.

Almost immediately a sleek, brass-trimmed boat whirled to a halt beside the fast-disappearing hulk, and he knew, without knowing why he knew, that he must not linger. Making sure that the thing he clasped in his left hand was safe, he turned toward the distant river shore lights and began a slow, silent breast stroke. . . .

1. NOOSE FOR A PSYCHOLOGIST

Masked eyes peered through the semi-darkness of the room.

Beyond the metal door ahead lay the jewels of the House of Shey—a scintillating pile that would buy the freedom of four hundred men. A misstep at this point would bring hell down about him. Yet, in the great city outside, dawn was breaking and he must act quickly. He must tiptoe to the door, hold the tiny voice-box to the center of the great bronze rosette, pillage a fortune and vanish.

The slender black-clad figure leaned against the gold-and-platinum-tapestried wall and listened intently, first to the tempo of his strange heart, and then to the world about him.

From across the room, some six meters away, rose and fell the faint, complacent snoring of Count Shey, sometime Imperial Psychologist, but famed more for his wealth and dilettantism. His ample stomach was doubtless finishing off pheasant and 2127 burgundy.

Below his mask, Alar's lip curled humorlessly.

Through the doorway behind him he detected the rattle of a card deck and muffled voices—a roomful of Shey's personal guards. Not broken-spirited slave servants, but hard-bitten overpaid soldiers of fortune with lightning rapiers. His hand tightened subconsciously on the hilt of his own saber and his breathing came faster. Even a trained Thief such as he was no match for six of the guards that Shey's fortune could afford. Alar had been living on borrowed time for several years and he was glad this assignment was dry-blade.

He glided with catlike silence to the bronze door, drawing the little cube from his waist-pouch as he did so. With sensitive fingers he found the center of the rosette with its concealed voice-lock. Pressing the cube to the cold metallic cluster, he heard a faint click, then the shrill recorded words, almost inaudible, of Shey, stolen from him, one by one, day by day, over the past weeks.

He replaced the cube in his waist-pouch and waited.

Nothing happened.

For a long moment Alar stood motionless. Perspiration began to gather in his armpits and his throat grew dry.

Either the Society had given him an outdated voice key, or there was an additional, unaccounted-for variable.

21

And it was then that he noticed two things. The first was an ominous quiet in hall and guardroom. The second was that the gentle snores from the bed had ceased. The next moment stretched endlessly toward its breaking point.

His incorrect signal had evidently activated some unseen alarm. Even as his mind raced in frantic fury he visualized briefly the hard alert faces of half a thousand Imperial Police, who would be wheeling patrol jets about, then hurtling toward the area.

A faint hesitant scrape of sandals came from the hall. He instantly understood that the guards were puzzled, uncertain as to whether their entry would endanger their master.

He knew that soon one of them would call out.

In a bound he was at the bedroom door that opened to the guard annex and slammed it noisily behind electronic bolts. He listened momentarily to the angry voices on the other side.

"Bring a beam-cutter!" came a cry.

The door would be down in short order.

Simultaneously a heavy blow struck him in the left shoulder and the bedroom sparkled with sudden light. He whirled, crouching, and appraised coolly the man in bed who had shot him.

Shey's voice was a strange mixture of sleepiness, alarm and indignation. "A Thief!" he cried, tossing the gun away as he realized that lead-throwers were no good against a Thief's body-screen. "And I have no blade here." He licked pudgy lips. "Remember," he giggled nervously, "your Thief code forbids injuring an unarmed man. My purse is on the perfume table."

Both men listened to the blend of distant police sirens and the muffled curses and grunts coming from beyond the bedroom door.

"You will open the jewel room," said Alar flatly.

Shey's eyes widened.

"My jewels!" he gasped. "You shall not have them!"

Three sirens sounded very close. As Alar listened one of them choked off suddenly. I.P.'s would be swarming out of a patrol jet and setting up semiportable Kades in the street, capable of volatilizing him, armor or no armor.

The bedroom door was beginning to vibrate in resonance with the beam-cutter.

Alar strode almost casually to the bed and stood over Shey's heavy face, which was upturned in trembling pallor. In a startling snakelike movement the Thief seized his host's left eyelid between thumb and forefinger.

Shey chuckled horridly, then raised his head painfully and reluctantly. He found himself sitting on the edge of his bed, then standing beside it. And when he attempted to grasp the slender throat of his tormentor, a knife seemed to stab into his eyeball.

Sweat was pouring down his face when, a moment later, he stood before his beloved treasure room.

All the sirens had ceased wailing. A hundred or more jets must be waiting for him outside.

And Shey knew it too.

A cunning grin stole over the psychologist's mouth.

"Don't hurt me any more," he giggled. "I'll open the jewel room."

He put his lips to the rosette and whispered a few words. The door rolled noiselessly into the wall.

He staggered back and rubbed his eye gingerly as the Thief leaped into the treasure alcove.

With methodical speed Alar tore open the teakwood drawers and scooped their glittering contents into his pouch. A less experienced Thief would not have known where or when to stop but Alar, even in the act of reaching for a beautiful choker worth forty men, jerked back his hand and drew his pouchthong tight in a single motion.

He was at the portal in a bound, just in time to see the bedroom door crash inward beneath a dazzling mass of rapiers. Even as his own blade whipped from its scabbard and disarmed the foremost guard, he knew that the odds were too great, that he must be wounded and perhaps killed before he could leap from the mile-high window. This was so because, before he could leap, he must tie his coiled shock cord to some immovable object. But to what? Shey's bed was no antique. It had no bedposts. Suddenly he knew the answer.

By a miraculous coordination of concentration and skill he had remained unscathed during his retreat to the open window. The guards, unaccustomed to such mass attacks on a single opponent, were thrusting ad lib instead of simultaneously and he was able to parry each thrust as it came. But now, probably by accident, two guards lashed at him from either side. He attempted an intricate level-blade parry for both thrusts, but the angle of approach of the two rapiers was too wide.

However, even as his blade was losing contact with that of the guard on his right, his left hand was drawing a noose of shock cord from the coil case on his chest, and as the blade seared into his side, he was throwing, left handed, a lasso towards the wet, balding face of Shey, who was crouching on the other side of the bed.

And then the Thief, without waiting to see whether the noose had seized Shey's neck, flung himself backward. The sword in his side did not pull free. Instead it was wrenched from the startled guard's hand. With the sword imbedded in his side, Alar plunged out of the window into space.

Somewhere in the first thirty meters, while he counted off the quarter seconds, he felt his side. The wound was not bad. The blade had sliced the flesh, was held now by his clothing. He tore the sword from his side.

The line would gradually grow taut at the fourth second, assuming that the noose had tightened about Shey's neck and that all the guards would be grasping at it with their bare hands for the better part of a minute before one of them should have the presence of mind to sever it with his sword. And by that time Alar would have cut it himself.

He suddenly realized that the whirling, crashing fifth second had come and gone, and that he was now plummeting in free fall.

The noose had not caught.

He noted almost curiously that he was beyond panic and fear. He had often wondered how death would come, and how he would meet it. He would not live to tell his companion Thieves that his reaction to imminent death was simply a highly intensified observation, that he could see individual grains of quartz, feldspar, and mica in the granite blocks of the wall of the great building as it hurtled up and past. And that everything that had happened to him in his second life flashed before him in almost painful clarity. Everything, that is, except the key to his identity.

For Alar did not know who he was.

As the mill of death ground away he relived the moment when the two professors had found him, a young man of about thirty. They had found him wandering adaze along a bank of the upper Ohio River.

He relived their searching tests of those far-off days. They were sure at the time that he was a spy planted by the Imperial Police, and for all he knew he might have been. His amnesia had been complete. Nothing of his past life had seeped through to suggest to him—or to his two new friends—what he might have been.

He remembered their astonishment at his voracity for knowledge, recalled in detail the first and last university class he had attended and how he had fallen into a polite doze after the instructor's fourth inaccuracy.

He remembered vividly how the professors, after they had finally become convinced that his amnesia was unfeigned, had bought false indicia of his educational history. With the papers, he became, overnight, a Doctor of Astrophysics on sabbatical leave from the University of Kharkov and a substitute lecturer at the Imperial University, where the two professors taught.

Then came the long walks at night, his arrest and beating by Imperial Police, his growing awareness of the wretchedness about him.

Finally, he saw the foul-smelling battered van clatter through the streets in the early morning with its wailing burden of aged slaves.

"Where were they being taken?" he had asked the professors later. "When a slave is too old to work he is sold," was all he could get from them.

But he had finally discovered the secret. The charnel-house. The cost had been two bullets in his shoulder from the guard.

Of all nights that he could remember that was the most revelatory. The two professors and a third man, a stranger with a black bag, were waiting for him when he crept blindly into his room in the early morning. He recalled vaguely the painful probings in his shoulder, the white bandages and finally the momentary nausea that followed the flow of something tingling from his scalp to his toes—Thief armor.

By day he had lectured on astrophysics. By night he had learned the gentle arts of climbing a smooth wall with his fingernails—of running a hundred yards in eight seconds—of disarming three lunging Imperials. In his five years as a member of the Society of Thieves he had looted the wealth of Croesus, and the Society had freed tens of thousands of slaves with it.

Thus had Alar become a Thief, thus was he now fulfilling an unpleasant maxim of the Society of Thieves—No Thief dies a natural death.

Suddenly he felt a blasting blow on his back that tore his black vest off, and he realized that the shock cord, now tight as a steel wire, had jerked him back against the building.

His lungs filled to the bursting point in the first breath he had drawn during the fall.

He would live.

His descent was gradually being broken. The noose must have caught on Shey, after all. He smiled at the struggle that must now be going on far above him—six burly men holding a thread-like cord with their bare hands to keep their source of revenue alive. But within a matter of seconds one of them would think to cut the cord.

He looked below. He had not fallen as far as he had thought. It was now evident that he had counted the quarter seconds too rapidly. Why did time linger so in the presence of death?

Now the dimly-lit street was rushing up to meet him. Tiny lights scurried around below, probably I.P. armored cars with short-range semi-portable Kades as well as shell-throwers. He was certain that half a dozen infrared beams were bathing this side of the building, and knew that it was just a question of time before he was spotted. He doubted that the I.P.'s could score a direct shell hit on his body, but the shock cord was highly vulnerable. A flying metal fragment could easily sever it.

The lights below were now forbiddingly large. Alar lifted his hand to the cord case, ready to engage the decelerator. About one hundred feet above the ground he jammed home the gear lever and almost blacked out under the abrupt deceleration. And then he was stumbling dizzily to his feet, cutting the cord and starting up a street barely alight with the fast-coming dawn.

Which way to run? Would police cars with Kades guns be waiting for him when he turned the corner? Were all the streets blocked?

The next few seconds would have to be played very accurately.

A shaft of light stabbed at him from the left, followed by the stamp of running feet. He whirled in alarm to see a glittering sedan chair carried on the shoulders of eight stalwart slaves, whose sweating faces reflected the growing redness in the east. A woman's slurred voice floated to him, and then the chair was past.

Despite his growing peril he almost laughed. Now that nuclear-powered jet cars were available to all, the carousing nobility could distinguish themselves from the carousing bourgeois only by a return to the sedan chair of the Middle Ages. The padding feet died away.

Then, the shock of what she had said hit him, "The corner to your left, Thief."

The Society must have sent her. But he really had no choice. He swallowed hard and ran around the corner—and stopped.

Three Kades guns immediately swiveled in three I.P. cars to cover him. He threw up his hands and walked slowly towards the car on the left.

"Don't shoot!" he cried. "I surrender!"

He gulped with relief as Dr. Haven dismounted from the impostor car, rapier drawn, and pretended to advance cautiously to meet him. A pair of handcuffs was gripped in one hand.

"The reward goes three ways!" called an I.P. from the middle car.

Dr. Haven did not turn, but held up a hand in acknowledgment.

"Easy, boy," he whispered to Alar. "Thank the gods you came this way. Lost a bit of blood? Surgeon in the car. Can you make it to your lecture?"

"I think so, but in case I pass out, the jewels are in my pouch."

"Beautiful. That gives us four hundred freemen." He seized Alar by the belt roughly. "Come on, you scum! You've got a lot of questions to answer before you die!"

A few minutes later the Thief car lost its escorts, changed its insignia and sped toward the University.

2. THE LADY AND THE TARSIER

The woman sat before the mirror, quietly brushing her black hair. Under the glow of the vanity lamp, the long strands were lustrous and fine, shimmering with blue highlights. The thick richness of her hair was a striking frame for her face, accentuating the whiteness of her skin, the cheeks and lips that were barely pink. It was a face as calm and cold as the hair was vibrant and warm. But the eyes were different. They were large and black and brought the face alive to harmonize with the hair. They, too, sparkled in the glow of the lamp. She could not dull those eyes as she could her face. She could only mask them, partially, by keeping her dark lashes low. She was keeping her eyes that way now, for the benefit of the man who stood behind her.

"You might be interested to learn of the latest offer," Haze-Gaunt said. He seemed to be toying idly with the emerald tassels on the vanity lamp, but she knew his every sense was strained to catch her faintest reaction. "Shey offered me two billion for you yesterday."

A few years ago she might have shuddered. But now . . . she continued to brush her black hair with long even strokes, and her quiet black eyes sought out his face in the vanity mirror.

The face of the Chancellor of America Imperial was like no other face on earth. The skull was smooth-shaven, but the incipient hairline revealed a broad high forehead beneath which were sunk hard intelligent eyes. The pupils were dark, immense. The aquiline nose showed a slight irregularity, as though it had once been broken and reset.

The man's cheeks were broad, but the flesh was tight-fitting, lean and seamless except for one barely visible cicatrix across the jutting chin. She knew his dueling philosophy. Enemies should be disposed of cleanly and without unnecessary risk, by specialists in the art. He was courageous but not naïve.

The mouth, she decided, might have been described in another man as firm; on him, however, it seemed vaguely petulant. It betrayed the man who had everything—and nothing.

But perhaps the most remarkable thing about him was the tiny, huge-eyed ape-thing that crouched in eternal fright on the man's shoulder, and which seemed to understand everything that was said. The warlock and his familiar, thought Keiris. What grotesque affinity had joined them?

Unsmiling, Haze-Gaunt asked, "You aren't interested?" He lifted his hand in an unconscious gesture and stroked his shrinking little pet.

He never smiled. Only a few times had she known him to frown. An iron discipline defended his face from what he seemed to regard as puerile emotional vanities. And yet he could never hide his feelings from her.

"Naturally, Bern, I'm interested. Have you entered a binding agreement for my disposal?"

If he was rebuffed, he gave no sign of it beyond an imperceptible hardening of his jaw muscles. But she knew he would have liked to rip the jeweled tassel from its enchased foundation and hurl it across the room.

She continued to brush her hair in unperturbed silence, her expressionless eyes looking calmly at his mirrored ones.

He said, "I understand that you called to a man on the street early this morning when the chair slaves were bringing you in."

"Did I? I don't remember. Perhaps I was drunk."

"Some day," he murmured, "I really shall sell you to Shey. He loves to experiment. I wonder what he would do to you?"

"If you want to sell me, then sell me."

His mouth barely curled. "Not yet. You are, after all, my wife." He said it unfeelingly, but there was that faint trace of a sneer at the corner of his lips.

"Am I?" She felt her face grow warm and saw in the mirror the deepening shade of pink on her cheeks surging toward her ears. "I thought I was your slave."

Haze-Gaunt's eyes flickered in the mirror. He had noticed the flush of color on her skin, and she secretly raged that he did. These were his moments of satisfaction against her husband—her true husband.

"It's the same thing, isn't it?" he said. The faint sneer had subtly altered into a faint smirk.

She was right: he had scored and found his pleasure. She tried to twist the direction of the conversation. "Why bother to mention Shey's offer? I know I afford you far too much pleasure to exchange for a bit more wealth. More money won't satisfy your hatred."

The curl in his lips faded away, leaving only the sharp line of his mouth. His eyes locked with hers in the mirror.

"There is no one I need hate now," he replied.

What he said was true, she knew, but it was an evasive truth. He did not need to hate her husband, for he had destroyed her husband. He did not need to hate, but he still did. His bitter hatred and envy of the achievements of the man she loved was as strong as ever. It would never be quenched. That was why she was enslaved. She had been the beloved of the man he hated—she was a means for revenge against the dead.

"That has always been true," she said, holding his gaze steadily with her own.

"There is no one," he repeated slowly, "I need hate now." He bore down on the final word just enough for her to catch the stress. "You cannot escape the fact that I have you."

She deliberately made no reply. Instead she lazily shifted the brush from one hand to the other, attempting to make the movement an insolent gesture. She told herself, "You think I cannot escape, that I remain with you because I must. How little you know, Haze-Gaunt!"

"Some day," he muttered, "I really shall sell you to Shey."

"You said that before."

"I want you to know that I mean it."

"Do it any time you like."

The curl came back to his lips. "I will. But not yet. All things in due time."

"Just as you say, Bern."

The televizor buzzed. Haze-Gaunt bent over, snapped the "Incoming" switch and was welcomed immediately by a nervous giggle. The screen, in the intimacy of the boudoir, had a manually operated button which required continuous fingertip pressure for a two-way image. Haze-Gaunt thumbed the button. The screen remained blank.

"Ah," said the caller's voice, followed by some throat clearing. "Bern!" It was Shey.

"Well, well. Count Shey." Haze-Gaunt glanced at the woman. She had dropped the brush to her lap and straightened her dressing gown as he had reached for the switch. "Perhaps he's calling to increase his already generous offer for you, Keiris. But I will remain firm."

Keiris said nothing. Shey, at the other end, was making some querulous croaks, more over the unexpected greeting, probably, than from embarrassment. She knew, however, the subtle point behind Haze-Gaunt's remark. It served more than merely to drive another barb into her; Shey had been informed that she was present and, therefore, to be discreet.

"Well, now, Shey," Haze-Gaunt said abruptly. "What prompts your call?"

"I had an unfortunate encounter during the night."

"Yes?"

"With a Thief." Shey paused for the dramatic effect of his words, but Keiris noticed that there wasn't a flicker of a muscle in the face of the Imperial chancellor. His only reaction was a series of quick, rough strokes across the fur of the little animal on his shoulder. The tiny ape-thing shivered, wild-eyed, more frightened than ever.

"My throat was lacerated," Shey continued, when it became obvious that no comment was forthcoming. "My personal physician has been administering to me all morning." There was a sigh. "Nothing serious, no interesting pain, just soreness. And, of course, some bandages which only serve to make me look ridiculous." There was the reason, thought Keiris with secret amusement, for the blank screen—Shey's vanity.

The details of the attack and escape by the Thief came out swiftly. Plainly Shey's throat had recovered enough not to hamper his smooth flow of words. He concluded his narration by asking the chancellor to be sure to meet him a little later in the Room of the Meganet Mind.

"Very well," agreed Haze-Gaunt and turned off the vizor.

"Thieves," the woman said and began to brush her hair again. "Criminals."

"The Society of Thieves," mused Keiris, "is about the only moral force in America Imperial. How strange! We destroy our churches and feast our souls on robbers!"

"Their victims rarely report a spiritual awakening," returned Haze-Gaunt dryly.

"Which is hardly unexpected," she retorted. "Those few who wail over their trifling losses are blind to the salvation which is brought to the many."

"No matter how the Society uses its loot, remember, it is still made up of common thieves. Simple police cases."

"Simple police cases! Just yesterday the Minister of Subversive Activities made a public statement to the effect that if they weren't obliterated within another decade—"

"I know, I know," Haze-Gaunt said impatiently, trying to cut her off.

Keiris refused to be interrupted. "—if they weren't obliterated within another decade the Thieves would destroy the present 'beneficial' balance between freeman and slave."

"He's perfectly right."

"Perhaps. But tell me this: Did my husband really found the Society of Thieves?"

"Your *ex*-husband?"

"Let's not quibble. You know who I mean."

"Yes," he agreed, "I know who you mean." For a fleeting moment his face, though completely immobile, seemed transformed into something hideous.

The man was silent for a long time. He said finally, "That's quite a story. Most of it you know as well as I."

"Perhaps I know less about it than you think. I know that you and he were bitter enemies as students at the Imperial University, that you thought he deliberately tried to excel you and defeat you in campus competitions. After graduation everyone seemed to think his researches were a shade more brilliant than yours. Somewhere along about then there was something about a duel, wasn't there?"

It had always struck Keiris a little odd that dueling had come back, complete with deadly weapons and a rigid etiquette, to a civilization so coldly scientific as the present one. Of course, it had been rationalized by many. The official attitude was one of resignation; there were laws against it, naturally, but what could the government do when the people themselves persisted in the ridiculous practice? Underneath that legal attitude, however, Keiris knew that it was secretly encouraged. She had heard many officials openly boast of their duels and explain smugly that it was instilling a healthy, vigorous spirit into the aristocracy. The age of chivalry, they maintained, had returned. Yet beneath it all, rarely voiced

by anyone, was the feeling that dueling was necessary for the preservation of the state. The Society of Thieves had brought back the sword as
a basic instrument for survival—the last defense of the despots.

Her question had not been answered, so she persisted, "You challenged
him to a duel, didn't you? And then you disappeared for a few months."

"I fired first—and missed," said Haze-Gaunt shortly. "Muir, with his
characteristic insufferable magnanimity, fired into the air. The I.P.'s were
watching and we were arrested. Muir was released on probation. I was
condemned and sold to a great orchard combine.

"An underground hydroponic orchard, my dear Keiris, is not the
country idyll of the nineteenth century. I didn't see the sun for nearly a
year. With thousands of tons of apples growing around me I was fed
garbage a rat wouldn't touch. The few of my companion slaves who tried
to steal fruit were detected and lashed to death. I was careful. My hatred
sustained me. I could wait."

"Wait? For what?"

"Escape. We took turns, laid the plans carefully and were frequently
successful. But, on the day before my turn was due, I was bought—and
freed."

"How fortunate. By whom?"

"By 'a party unknown,' the certificate said. But it could only have been
Muir. He had been scheming, borrowing, and saving for months to fling
this final gesture of contemptuous pity in my face."

The little ape-creature sensed the icy savageness in the man's voice and
ran fearfully down his jacket sleeve to the back of his hand. Haze-Gaunt
stroked his pet with a curled index finger.

The only sound in the room was the soft luxurious meeting of brush
and black hair as Keiris continued her silent task. She marveled at the
insane bitterness evoked by a simple act of humanity.

Haze-Gaunt stated, "It was not to be borne. I then decided to devote
the remainder of my life to the destruction of Kennicot Muir. I could
have hired an assassin, but I wanted to kill him myself. In the meantime
I entered politics and advanced quickly. I knew how to use people. My
year underground taught me that fear gets results.

"But even in my new career I could not escape Muir. The day I was
appointed Secretary of War, Muir landed on Mercury."

"Surely," Keiris said, carefully filtering the sarcasm out of her words,
"you don't accuse him of deliberately planning the coincidence?"

"What does it matter how it happened? The point is, it did happen.
And such things continued to happen. A few years later, on the eve of the
elections that were to make me chancellor of America Imperial, Muir
returned from his trip to the sun."

"That was certainly an exciting time for the world."

"It was an exciting time for Muir, too. As if the trip alone wasn't enough to stir the populace, he announced an important discovery. He had found a way to beat the tremendous solar gravity by the continuous synthesis of solar matter into a remarkable fission fuel via an anti-grav mechanism. Again he was the toast of imperial society—and my greatest political triumph was ignored."

Keiris did not marvel at the bitterness in these words; she could too easily understand the resentment Haze-Gaunt must have felt at that time, was feeling even now. He had become a successful politician at the precise moment Muir had become a public hero. The contrast had not been flattering.

"But," he continued, his eyes narrowing, "my patience was finally rewarded. It was almost exactly ten years ago. Muir finally had the temerity to differ with me on a strictly political matter, and I knew then that I must kill him quickly or be eclipsed by him forever."

"You mean, have him—" She spoke the word without flinching. "—killed."

"No. I myself, personally, had to do it."

"Certainly not by dueling?"

"Certainly not."

"I didn't know Kim ever went in for politics," murmured Keiris.

"He didn't view it as a political question."

"What was the argument?"

"Just this: After establishing the solar stations Muir insisted that America Imperial follow his own policy in the use of muirium."

"And," Keiris continued to probe, "just what exactly was that policy?"

"He wanted production to be used to regenerate the general world standard of living and to free the slaves, whereas I, Chancellor of America Imperial, maintained that the material was needed for the defense of the Imperium. I ordered him to return to Earth and to report to me at the chancellory. We were alone in my inner office."

"Kim was unarmed, of course?"

"Of course. And when I told him that he was an enemy of the state, and that it was my duty to shoot him, he laughed."

"And so you shot him."

"Through the heart. He fell. I left the room to order his body removed. When I returned with a house-slave he—or his corpse—had vanished. Had a confederate carried him away? Had I really killed him? Who knows? Anyway the thefts began the next day."

"He was the first Thief?"

"We don't really know, of course. All we know is that all Thieves seemed invulnerable to police bullets. Was Muir wearing the same type of protective screen when I shot him? I don't suppose I'll ever know."

"Just what is the screen? Kim never discussed it with me."

"There again we don't know. The few Thieves we've taken alive don't know, either. Under Shey's persuasion they indicated that it was a velocity-response field based electrically on their individual encephalographic patterns, and was maintained by their cerebral waves. What it really does is spread the bullet impact over a wide area. It converts the momentum of the bullet into the identical momentum of a foam rubber cushion."

"But the police have actually killed screen-protected Thieves, haven't they?"

"True. We have semiportable Kades rifles that fire short-range heat beams. And then, of course, plain artillery with atomic explosive shells; the screen remains intact but the Thief dies rather quickly of internal injuries. But you're fully acquainted with the main remedy."

"The sword."

"Precisely. Since the screen resistance is proportional to the velocity of the missile, it offers no protection against the comparatively slow-moving things, such as the rapier, the hurled knife or even a club. And all this talk of rapiers reminds me that I have business with the Minister of Police before meeting Shey. You will come with me and we'll watch Thurmond at rapier practice for a few minutes."

"I didn't know your vaunted Minister of Police required practice. Isn't he the best blade in the Imperium?"

"The very best. And practice will keep him that way."

"Just one more question, Bern. As an ex-slave I should think you'd favor the abolition of slavery rather than its extension."

He replied sardonically, "Those who struggle mightily against enslavement can best savor their success by enslaving others. Read your history."

The tarsier stared fearfully at her from the shelter of Haze-Gaunt's shoulder. She could see the faces of man and beast together. There was something . . . As she studied the animal, she thought, In nightmares, I know you. You fascinate, you horrify. Yet you seem so harmless. Aloud she said, "Wait up, I'm coming."

3. THE MIND

An obsequious house slave in the red-and-gray livery of the Police Minister led them down the arched corridor to the fencing rooms. At the threshold of the chamber the slave bowed again and left them. Haze-Gaunt indicated chairs and they seated themselves unobtrusively.

Thurmond noted their arrival from the center of the gym, nodded briefly and immediately resumed a quiet conversation with his fencing opponent.

Keiris ran her eyes in grudging admiration over the Police Minister's steel-chiseled face and gorgeously muscled torso, clad lightly in a silken jacket and flowing trunks. A metallic indomitable voice floated to her.

"Do you understand the terms?"

The opponent replied thickly, "Yes, excellency." His face was covered with perspiration, and his eyes were wide and glazed.

"Remember then that if you are still alive after sixty seconds you will have your freedom. I paid nearly forty thousand unitas for you and I expect a good return for my money. Do your best."

"I shall, excellency."

Keiris turned to Haze-Gaunt sitting stiffly in the chair next to her, his arms folded across his chest. "Tell me, Bern, frankly: Doesn't it strike you that dueling nowadays is just a perverted sport? Hasn't the honor in it been lost?" She kept her voice low, away from the ears of the others.

He searched her with his hard, intelligent eyes to see if her questioning was serious. He found that it was; this was no attempt to irritate him.

"Times have changed things," he said. He decided to answer her flatly. "Yes, the traditions have been for the most part lost. The primary motivation is no longer one of 'cowardice and courage.'"

"Then it has degenerated into a mere barbaric rite."

"If it has, you can thank the Thieves for that."

"But was it ever more than that?"

"It once commanded great respect." He watched Thurmond and his opponent choosing their weapons. "Although dueling prevailed in antiquity, the modern private duel grew out of the judicial duel. In France in the sixteenth century it became very common after the famous challenge of Francis the First to his rival Charles the Fifth. After that every Frenchman seemed to think that he was called upon to use his sword in defending his honor against the slightest imputation."

"That was Europe, though," Keiris insisted, "in the old days. This is America."

Haze-Gaunt continued to watch the two men preparing for their combat. He seemed to forget the woman beside him, his reply sounding more like a recital for his own benefit. "In no part of the world was dueling so earnestly engaged in as in America. Combats were held under all sorts of conditions, with every conceivable variety of weapon. And most of them were fatal. That's what brought about laws which stamped it out until the establishment of the Imperium." He turned to look at her. "It's not remarkable that it has been revived."

"But now it has lost all moral respectability," she said. "It's just an invitation to legalized murder."

"We have laws," he replied. "No one is forced to duel."

"Like that poor fellow," said Keiris, pointing toward the center of the gym, and her black eyes flashed.

"Like him." Haze-Gaunt nodded soberly. "Now be quiet. They are ready to begin."

"En garde!"

Thrust, parry, feint, thrust, parry . . .

The tempo increased rapidly.

Thurmond's blade had the enchanting delicacy of an instrument that was part of its wielder. The man was incredibly light on his feet, balancing effortlessly on tiptoe —an extraordinary stance in a fencer—while his bronzed body rippled and flashed, itself a rapier, in the soft light of the chamber. His eyes were heavy-lidded, his face an expressionless mask. If he was breathing, Keiris could not detect it.

She transferred her study to the slave fencer and noted that the man had cast aside his despair and was defending himself with savage precision. So far his new owner had not scratched him. Perhaps in free life he really had been a dangerous duelist. Then a tiny trickle of red appeared magically on his left chest. And then one on his right chest.

Keiris held her breath and tensed her fists. Thurmond was touching each of the six sections into which a fencer's body is arbitrarily divided—a demonstration that he could kill the other at will.

The doomed man's jaw dropped, and his efforts passed from science to frenzy. When the sixth cut appeared on his lower left abdomen he screamed and sprang bodily at his tormentor.

He was dead before his disarmed blade clattered to the floor.

A gong sounded, indicating that the minute was up.

Haze-Gaunt, erstwhile pensive and silent, now arose and clapped his hands twice. "Bravo, Thurmond. Nice thrust. If you're free I'd like you to accompany me."

Thurmond handed his reddened blade to a house-slave and bowed over the corpse.

Within the transparent plastic dome the man sat trance-like. His face was partly obscured from Keiris's view by a cone-shaped metal thing that hung from the globe's ceiling and that was fitted at its lower extremity with two viewing lenses. The man was staring fixedly into the lenses.

His head was large, even for the large body that bore it. His face was a repulsive mass of red scar tissue, devoid of definable features. His hairless hands were similarly scarred and malformed.

Keiris shifted uneasily in her seat in the semicircle of spectators. On her left was Thurmond, silent, imperturbable. On her right Haze-Gaunt sat immobile in his chair, arms crossed over his chest. It was clear that he was growing impatient. Beyond him was Shey, and beyond Shey was a man she recognized as Gaines, Undersecretary for Space.

Haze-Gaunt inclined his head slightly toward Shey. "How long will this go on?" His furry pet chattered nervously, ran down his sleeve, then back to his shoulder again.

Shey, his face wreathed in perpetual smiles, raised a pudgy hand in warning. "Patience, Bern. We must await the end of the present net runs."

"Why?" asked Thurmond with mixed curiosity and indifference.

The psychologist smiled benignly. "At present the Meganet Mind is in a deep autohypnosis. To expose him to unusual exterior stimuli would rupture some of his subconscious neural networks and his usefulness to the government as an integrator of disconnected facts would be seriously impaired."

"Facts?" said Thurmond distantly. "What are these facts? Please explain."

"Of *course*," replied the rotund psychologist with amiable eagerness. "At the outset, let me say that here in this room all we have is the terminal. There's a lot you don't see: logic circuits, memory, current input, and associated hardware. All of that is located far underground, to minimize radiation damage. Memory is comprehensive, with ten to the fifteenth bytes. We access all items in all libraries: some three billion books and documents, in all languages. We have all graphics: maps of villages and galaxies. We get data from several hundred spy satellites. The Mind designed the whole thing. The logic and memory are combined into one superchip. Not really a chip, though. More of a polymeric, grapefruit-sized blob, traced out by electronmicroscope. The Mind selected the tri-di shape deliberately. It permits complete memory access in a matter of nanoseconds. The entire data output is integrated into a series of microscopic networks and fed into a viewer, to form a meganet. Each of the Mind's eyes is observing a different net projection, and each projection passes through the viewer at a speed of forty frames a second.

"One-fortieth of a second is the approximate reversal rate of the visual purple of the retina and this represents the upper limit at which the Meganet Mind can operate. His actual thought processes, of course, are much faster."

"I begin to see," murmured Haze-Gaunt, "how the Mind can read an encyclopedia within minutes but I still don't understand why he must work under autohypnosis."

Shey beamed. "One of the main traits of the human mind that distinguishes it from, for example, that of your pet is its ability to ignore trivia. When the average man sets about solving a problem he automatically excludes all that his conscious mind considers irrelevant.

"But is the rejected matter really irrelevant? Long experience tells us we can't trust our conscious mind in its rejections. That's why we say, 'Let me sleep on it.' That gives the subconscious mind an opportunity to force something to the attention of the conscious mind."

"What you're saying," said Haze-Gaunt, "is simply that the Meganet Mind is effective because he functions on a subconscious level and uses the sum total of human knowledge on every problem given him."

"Exactly!" cried the psychologist with pleasure. "How clever you are, Bern!"

"I believe the viewer is being retracted," observed Thurmond.

They waited expectantly as the man within the globe slowly sat erect and stared at them, still half-unseeing.

"Do you notice his face and hands?" burbled the psychologist. "He was burned badly in a circus fire. He used to be a mere entertainer before I discovered him. Now he's the most useful instrument in my whole collection of slaves. But look, Bern, he's going to discuss something with Gaines. Listen and judge for yourself whether you want to ask him some questions."

A transparent panel rolled aside in the dome. The Mind addressed Gaines, a tall, cavern-cheeked man.

"Yesterday," said the Mind, "you asked whether the Muir drive could be adapted for use in the *T-twenty-two*. I think it could. The conventional Muir drive depends upon the fission of muirium into americium and curium, with an energy output of four billion ergs per microgram of muirium per second.

"However, when Muir synthesized muirium from americium and curium in his first trip to the sun, he failed to realize that the element could also be synthesized from protons and energy quanta at a temperature of eighty million degrees. And the reverse is true.

"If the muirium nucleus is disrupted at eighty million degrees, the energy developed would be over forty quintillion ergs per microgram, which would be power enough to accelerate the *T-twenty-two* very quickly to a velocity beyond the speed of light, except for the theoretical limiting velocity of the speed of light."

Gaines looked dubious. "That's too much acceleration for a human cargo. Ten or eleven G's is the limit, even with a pressure-packed abdomen."

"It's an interesting question," admitted the Mind. "Like slow freezing, a few G's could be expected to rupture and destroy cell life. On the other hand, a few *million* G's administered *ab initio* with no transition from low to high acceleration, might be comparable to quick freezing in its preservation of body cells.

"However, the analogy ends there, for while freezing inhibits cell change, gravity stimulates it. Observe the effect of only one G on a plant. It causes certain of the plant cells slowly to accumulate skywards to constitute a stalk, and certain others slowly to accumulate earthward to form the rhizome structure.

"Several million G's would undoubtedly cause drastic but unpredictable micro- and macropathologic geotropic transformations. Check with the scientists working on the Geotropic Project. I can only suggest that you try various biota as passengers in the *T-twenty-two* before human beings make the trip."

"You're probably right. I'll install a Muir drive with the proper converting system at eighty million degrees."

The conversation ended perfunctorily. Gaines bowed to the group and left.

Shey turned a delighted face up to Haze-Gaunt. "Remarkable chap, this Mind, isn't he?"

"Really? I could do as well myself by mixing some old newspaper reports with a little pseudoscience and mumbo-jumbo. What can he do with something only *I* know about?" He caressed the little animal on his shoulder. "My pet here, for example?"

The Mind was not addressed directly. Yet he replied immediately in his factual monotone. "His excellency's pet appears to be a spectral tarsier."

"*Appears?* You are already lost in speculation."

"Yes, he appears to be a *tarsius spectrum.* He has the great eyes, large sensitive ears and elongated heel bone that help the tarsius in detecting insects at night and in jumping to catch them on the wing. He has the small platyrrhine nose, too.

"Structurally he appears, like the spectral tarsier, higher in the evolutionary tree than the tree shrews and lemurs, lower than the monkeys, apes, and man. But appearances are deceptive. *Tarsius* is at most an arboreal quadruped. Your pet can brachiate, the same as the primates. His thumbs are opposable and he can walk erect on his hind legs for short distances."

"All that would be obvious to a keen observer," said Haze-Gaunt. "I suppose you'd say he's a mutated lemur evolving toward the primates?"

"I would not."

"No? But surely of terrestrial stock?"

"Very likely."

The chancellor relaxed and tweaked his pet's ears idly. "Then you can learn something from me." His voice was ominously cold. "This creature was recovered from the wreckage of a ship that almost certainly came from outer space. He is the living proof of an evolving biota remarkably parallel to our own." He turned languidly to Shey. "You see? He can do nothing for me. He's a fraud. You ought to have him destroyed."

"I know about the wreckage referred to," interjected the Mind quietly. "Despite its interstellar drive, as yet unknown on Earth—with the possible exception of the mechanism I just explained to Gaines for the *T-twenty-two*—there is other evidence that points to the terrestrial origin of the ship."

"What evidence?" asked Haze-Gaunt.

"Your pet. Instead of being a tarsioid reaching toward primatehood, he is more likely of human stock that has degenerated into a tarsioid line."

Haze-Gaunt said nothing. He stroked the little animal's sleek head, which peeped fearfully over his shoulder toward the Mind.

"What is the Mind talking about?" whispered Shey.

Haze-Gaunt ignored him and looked down at the Mind again. "You realize I cannot permit such inference to go unchallenged." The edge on his voice was growing sharper.

"Consider the whale and porpoise," said the Mind unhurriedly. "They seem to be as well as or better adapted to the sea than the shark. And yet we know they are not fishes but mammals, because they are warm-blooded and breathe air. From such evolutionary residua we know that their ancestors conquered dry land and later returned to the water. And it's the same with your pet. His ancestors were once human, perhaps even higher, and dwelled the earth—*because he can speak English!*"

Haze-Gaunt's lips were pressed together in a thin white line. The Mind continued relentlessly. "He talks only when the two of you are alone. Then he begs you not to go away. That's all he ever says."

Haze-Gaunt addressed Keiris without turning his head. "Have you eavesdropped?"

"No," she lied.

"Perhaps you do have some extraordinary power of factual synthesis," Haze-Gaunt said to the Mind. "Suppose, then, you tell me why the little beast keeps begging me not to 'go away' when I have no intention of leaving the Imperium?"

"He can foresee the future to that extent," stated the Mind tonelessly.

Haze-Gaunt gave no sign of either believing or disbelieving. He rubbed his lower lip with his thumb and regarded the Mind thoughtfully. "I am not ignoring the possibility that you may be a fraud. Still, there is a question that has been troubling me for some time. On the answer to this question my future—even my life—may depend. Can you tell me both the question and its answer?"

"Oh, come now, Bern," interrupted Shey. "After all—"

He was interrupted in turn. "The Imperial American government," intoned the Mind, "would like to launch a surprise attack on the Eastern

Federation within six weeks. The chancellor wishes to know whether factors unknown to him will require the postponement of the attack."

Haze-Gaunt was leaning forward in his chair, body tense. Shey was not smiling.

"That's the question," admitted the chancellor. "What is the answer?"

"Factors that may require postponement of the attack do in fact exist."

"Indeed? What are they?"

"One of them I do not know. The answer depends on data presently unavailable."

"I'll get the data," said Haze-Gaunt with growing interest. "What's necessary?"

"A competent analysis of a section of a certain star chart. Four years ago the Lunar Station began sending me microfilm plates of both celestial hemispheres by the square second. One of these plates is of particular interest, and I feel that what it shows may have a bearing on the future of civilization. It should be analyzed immediately."

"What sort of bearing?" demanded Haze-Gaunt.

"I don't know."

"Eh? Why not?"

"His conscious mind can't fathom his subconscious," explained Shey, fingering his rich robes. "All his conscious mind can do is bring to light the impressions of his subconscious mind."

"Very well. I'll put the lunar staff to work on it."

"A routine examination will prove worthless," warned the Mind. "I could recommend only two or three astrophysicists in the system capable of the necessary analysis."

"Name one."

"Ames has recently been attached to the staff of Undersecretary Gaines. Perhaps Gaines could be persuaded to lend—"

"He'll do it," said Haze-Gaunt succinctly. "Now, you mentioned 'factors'—in the plural. I presume the star plate isn't the only one."

"There is another factor of uncertainty," said the Mind. "It involves the personal safety of the chancellor as well as the ministers and consequently bears on the question of postponing the attack."

Haze-Gaunt looked sharply at the man in the globe. The Mind returned the stare with emerald-basilisk eyes. The chancellor coughed. "This other factor—"

The Mind resumed placidly, "The most powerful creature—I hesitate to call him a man—on Earth today is neither Lord Chancellor Haze-Gaunt nor the Dictator of the Eastern Federation."

"Don't tell us it's Kennicot Muir," said Haze-Gaunt sardonically.

"The creature I have in mind is a professor at the Imperial University named Alar—possibly so named because of his winged mind. He is very likely a Thief, but that's of minor consequence."

At the word "Thief," Thurmond looked interested. "Why is he dangerous? Thieves are limited to defense by their code."

"Alar seems to be a mutant with potentially great physical and mental powers. If he ever discovers he has these powers, considering his present political viewpoint, no human being on earth would be safe from him, code or no code."

"Just what are his potentialities?" queried Shey. "Is he a hypnotist? A telekineticist?"

"I don't know," admitted the Mind. "I can only offer my opinion that he is dangerous. *Why* is another matter."

Haze-Gaunt appeared lost in thought. Finally, without looking up, he said, "Thurmond, will you and Shey be in my office in one hour? Bring Eldridge of the War Office with you. Keiris, you will return to your rooms in the company of your bodyguard. It will take you all evening to dress for the Imperatrix's ball tonight."

A few minutes later the four left the room. Keiris, taking a last look backward, met the enigmatic, unblinking eyes of the Mind and was troubled. He had been telling her at various intervals during the interview, by the code they had worked out long before, that she must be prepared to receive a Thief in her rooms tonight and protect him from his pursuers.

And Haze-Gaunt would be expecting her at the masked ball simultaneously.

4. THE RAID

From his seat at the grand piano Alar peered over the music sheets toward his two friends, Micah Corrips, Professor of Ethnology, and John Haven, Professor of Biology, who were huddled in complete absorption over their voluminous manuscript.

Alar's dark, oversized eyes glanced at the two savants briefly; then his gaze went past them, by the disordered stacks of books and papers, beyond the mounted row of human and semi-human skeletons, past the urn of coffee gradually boiling dry near the street window and out over the university campus, where a large black truck was pulling up quietly in the late afternoon behind a hedge of Grecian junipers. It simply stopped. Nobody got out.

His pulse was climbing slowly. He sounded a certain chord on the piano keyboard. Two men heard him, he knew, but did not seem alarmed.

"Now, Micah, read what you have there," said Haven to the ethnologist.

Corrips, a large vigorous man with friendly blue eyes and a classroom manner so seductive that the great university auditorium had been assigned to him as a lecture room, picked up the preface and began to read.

" 'We may imagine, if we like, that early one afternoon in the year forty thousand B.C. the advance group of Neandertals reached the Rhone Valley, about where Lyons now stands. These men and women, driven southwest from their hunting grounds in Bohemia by slowly encroaching glaciers, had lost nearly a third of their number since crossing the frozen Rhine the previous January. There were no longer any children or very aged people in the group.

" 'These men from eastern Europe were not handsome. They were squat, massive, almost neckless, with beetling brow ridges and flattened nostrils. They walked with bent knees, on the outer edges of their feet, as do the higher anthropoids.

" 'Even so, they were tremendously more civilized than the brutish Eoanthropus (Heidelberg man?) into whose territory they were marching. Eoanthropus's sole tool was a crude piece of flint, chipped and shaped to fit his hand, which he used to grub at roots and occasionally to strike at reindeer from ambush.

" 'He passed his short dim-witted life in the open. Neandertal, on the contrary, made flint spearheads, knives and saws. For these he used large flintflakes rather than the core of the flint. He lived in caves and cooked over a fire. He must have had some idea of a spirit world and a life in the hereafter, for he buried his dead with weapons and artifacts. The group leader—' "

"Excuse me, gentlemen," Alar broke in quietly. "I register one fifty-five." His fingers continued to ripple on through the second movement of the "Pathétique." He had not taken his eyes from the music sheets since he had first looked across the room and through the window in response to the warning acceleration of his strange heart.

" 'The leader,' " continued Corrips, " 'gray, grizzled, ruthless—paused and sniffed the air moving up the valley. He smelled reindeer blood a few hundred yards down the draw, also another, unknown smell, like yet unlike the noisome blend of grime, sweat and dung that characterized his own band.' "

Haven arose, tapped his pipe gently on the ash tray lying on the big table, stretched his small, wiry frame with tigerish languor and walked slowly toward the coffee urn by the window.

Alar was now well into the final movement of the "Pathétique." He watched Haven carefully.

Corrips droned on resonantly without the faintest change of inflection, but Alar knew the ethnologist was watching his collaborator from the corner of his eye.

" 'The old man turned to the little band and shook his flint-tipped spear to show that the spoor had been struck. The other men held their spears up, signifying that they understood and would follow silently. The women faded into the sparse shrubbery of the valley slope.

" 'The men followed the reindeer path on down the gully and within a few minutes peered through a thicket at an old male Eoanthropus, three females of assorted ages and two children, all lying curled stuporously under a windfall of branches and debris that overhung the gully bank. Blood still drained sluggishly from a half-devoured reindeer carcass lying under the old man's head.' "

Alar followed Haven with narrowed eyes. The little biologist poured a cup of coffee of the consistency of mud, added a little cream from the portofrij and stirred it absently, the while looking out of the window from the shadows of the room.

" 'Some sixth sense warned Eoanthropus of danger. The old male shook his five-hundred-pound body and convulsed into a snarling squat over the reindeer, searching through nearsighted eyes for the rash interlopers. He feared nothing but the giant cave bear, *Ursus spelaeus*. The females and children scurried behind him with mingled fear and curiosity.

" 'Through the green foliage the invaders stared thunderstruck. It was immediately evident to them that the killers were some sort of animal, pretending to be men. The more intelligent of the Neandertals, including the old leader, exchanged glances of wrathful indignation. Without more ado the leader broke through the brush and raised his spear high with an angry shout.

" 'He was seized by the conviction that these offensive creatures were strange, hence intolerable, that the sooner they were killed the more comfortable he would feel. He drew back his heavy spear and hurled it with all his strength. It passed through the heart of Eoanthropus to protrude half a foot beyond the back.' "

Haven was frowning when he turned away from the window. He lifted the cup of coffee to his mouth and, just before he drank, his lips silently formed the words, "Audio search beam."

Alar knew that Corrips had caught the signal, even though the latter continued to read as though nothing had happened.

" 'The brute-mind behind that hurtling spear, faced with the problem of an alien people, arrived at a solution by a simple thalamic response uncomplicated by censorship of the frontal lobes—kill first, examine later.

" 'This instinctive reaction, a vestige perhaps from the minuscule mental organization of his insectivore ancestor (Zalambdolestes?), dating probably back to the Cretaceous, has characterized every species of Hominidae before and since Neandertal.

" 'The reaction is still strong, as two World Wars bear horrible witness. If the man with the spear could have reasoned first and hurled second, his descendants might have reached the stars within a very few millennia.

" 'And now that fissionable materials are being mined directly from the sun's surface in enormous quantities by America Imperial, the Western and Eastern hemispheres will not long delay another attempt to contest the superiority of their respective cultures. This time, however, neither side can hope for victory, stalemate, or even defeat.

" 'The war will end, simply because there will be no human beings left to fight—if we except a hundred or so animal-like creatures huddling in the farthest corridors of the underground cities, licking their radiation sores and sharing with a few rats the corpses that lie so well-preserved everywhere (there being no putrefying bacteria remaining to decompose the dead). But even the ghouls are sterile and in another decade—' "

There was a knock at the door.

Haven and Corrips exchanged quick glances. Then Haven put down his coffee and walked toward the foyer. Corrips looked quickly about the room, reaffirming the positions of their sabers, which hung with innocent decorativeness from straps among the Hominidae skeletons.

They heard Haven's voice from the hallway. "Good evening, sir—? Why, it's General Thurmond. What a delightful surprise, general! I recognized you at once but of course you don't know me. I'm Professor Haven."

"Mind if I come in, Dr. Haven?" There was something chilling and deadly in that dry voice.

"Not at all! Why, bless my soul, we're honored. Come in! Micah! Alar! It's General Thurmond, Minister of Police!"

Alar knew that the man's effusiveness covered unusual nervousness.

Corrips timed his approach so that the group would coalesce about the Hominidae. Alar, following close behind, observed uneasily that the ethnologist's hands were twitching. Were they so afraid of just one man? His respect for Thurmond was increasing rapidly.

Except for a piercing appraisal of Alar, Thurmond ignored the introductions. "Professor Corrips," he rasped gently, "you were reading something very peculiar just before I knocked. You know, of course, that we had a search beam on the study?"

"Did you? How odd. I was reading from a book that Dr. Haven and I are writing—*Suicide of the Human Race*. Were you interested?"

"Only incidentally. It's really a matter for the Minister of Subversive Activities. I shall report it, of course, for whatever action he deems best. But I'm really here on another matter."

Alar sensed the tension mount by a full octave. Corrips was breathing loudly—Haven, apparently, not at all. Thurmond's feral eyes, he knew, had not missed the cluster of sabers dangling with the Hominidae.

"What," asked the officer abruptly, "is the Geotropic Project?"

"Surely not a question of subversion, general?" said Corrips. "We understand the project was recommended by the Meganet Mind himself."

"Irrelevant," said the visitor calmly. "Please summarize it briefly."

The two professors exchanged glances. Corrips shrugged. "The project investigates the effects of high velocities and accelerations on living organisms. In the general case we used an extremely fast centrifuge, providing a gravity gradient developing from one G to several million over a period of weeks."

"Results?" said Thurmond.

"Results varied. And are still not understood."

"Examples?" said the visitor.

"Well, in one case obelia, a sea-dwelling primitive polyp-feeder, evolved forward into the sea anemone. On the other hand, radiolaria, a silica-secreting protozoa, evolved backward to limax amoeba—which doesn't secrete anything. In another case, euglena, the first of the one-celled protozoa to possess chlorophyll, as well as being the first plant-like form, fell back down the evolutionary ladder to become a simple flagellate."

"Higher forms?" asked Thurmond.

"Various," said Corrips. He did not elaborate.

The general lifted his hand indolently, as though to indicate it didn't matter. "I understand that the project is staffed largely with persons with—impediments," he said coldly.

"Yes," said Corrips. The word faded into a whisper.

"They work for you?"

"We direct and assist them in their work," explained Haven.

"You control them," said Thurmond flatly.

No one answered. Haven wiped perspiring hands on the sides of his coat.

"May I see the personnel register?" asked Thurmond.

The two professors hesitated. Then Corrips stepped to the desk and returned with a black book. He gave it to Thurmond, who leafed through it idly, examining two or three of the photographs with gloomy curiosity. "This chap with no legs," he said. "What does he do within the project?"

Alar's pulse beat had climbed to one hundred seventy a minute.

Corrips cleared his throat. "The Gemini . . ." The words were garbled. He coughed and tried again. "The Gemini Run."

Thurmond looked at him with thinly veiled amusement. "Which is?"

"Two tree shrew fetuses in the centrifuge. Extraordinary gravities, recorded under strobe lights at picoseconds. One went up the scale, to become the fetus of what looked like a lemur. The other retrogressed to a lizard-like form. Just before it died it looked rather like a dog fish."

"He can't carry a gun, can he?"

"Who? Oh, the Gemini scientist?"

Alar watched the six black-shirted I.P.'s ease quietly into the room behind Thurmond.

"Of course not," snapped Corrips. "His contributions lie in an altogether different—"

"Then the government can't be expected to continue his support," interjected Thurmond. He ripped the sheet from the book and handed it to the officer who stood just behind him. "And here's another," he said, frowning at the next page. "A blind woman. No use at all in a factory, is she?"

"Her mother," said Haven tightly, "collaborated with Kennicot Muir in determining the Nine Fundamental Equations that culminated in the establishment of our solarions on the surface of the sun. This child, in her own right, is one of the most brilliant minds in the Geotropic Project. For instance, she has fed all our data into the computer, and she has put the question, 'What would be the effect on a human being?' "

"The answer?"

Haven clenched his fists. "I—we—we need more work."

"But what does it look like so far? What effect on human beings?"

The professor sighed. "It would be a bit like the Gemini Run. According to the computer, two samples of the same species would have to be associated together to show the effect. In the hypothetical case, one would *e*volve, the other would *de*volve."

"And this girl programmed the computer for *that?*"

"Yes."

"Most unscientific, Professor Haven. In fact, it's downright ridiculous." Thurmond studied the registry sheet. "If that's the best this girl can do, you'll never miss her. More to the point, she's incapable of precision labor and her mother was an associate of Muir, a known traitor." He ripped the sheet out and passed it back to a young officer.

"Just what does the lieutenant intend doing with those sheets?" asked Haven with a rising voice. He moved his hand carelessly to the clavicle of the Cro-Magnon skeleton, a few inches from the sabers.

"We're going to take all your research staff away, professor."

Haven's mouth opened and closed. He seemed to shrink where he stood. Finally he said hesitantly: "For what reason, sir?"

"For the reason I have said. They are useless to the Imperium."

"Not really, sir," Haven said slowly. "Their usefulness must be evaluated in terms of the long-range good they will do for humanity—and, of course, the Imperium. . . ."

"Perhaps," Thurmond said unemotionally. "But we shall not take that chance."

"Then," Haven asked cautiously, "then you plan to . . . ?"

"Do you insist that I be precise?"

"Yes."

"They will be sold to the highest bidder—probably a charnel-house."

Alar found himself licking pallid lips. It could not be happening but it was happening. Twenty-two young men and women, some of the most brilliant minds in the Imperium, were going to be snuffed out with casual brutality—*why?*

Corrips's voice was hardly a whisper. "What do you want?"

"Alar," stated Thurmond icily. "Give me Alar and keep the others."

"No!" cried Haven, staring white-faced at Thurmond. He turned to Corrips and found confirmation there.

Alar listened to his voice. It seemed that of another man. "I must go with you, of course," he said to Thurmond.

Haven shot out a restraining hand. "No, boy! You haven't the faintest idea what it's all about. You're worth far more than any two dozen minds on Earth. If you love humanity do as we tell you!"

5. THE PROJECTION

Thurmond called a quiet command over his shoulders. "Shoot them!"

Six blasts of lead, urged by the titanic pressures of fission-generated steam, bounced harmlessly off the three men and ricocheted about the walls.

The sabers were no longer hanging from the Hominidae.

And Thurmond's blade was lunging for Alar's heart.

Only the tightest breast parry saved the Thief. The lieutenant and his men, evidently hand picked, were forcing the two older men back down the wall.

"Alar!" cried Haven. "Don't fight Thurmond! The trapdoor! We'll cover you!"

The Thief flung an anguished look toward the professors. Haven broke free from the wall and joined Alar, who was as yet miraculously unbloodied. They immediately crashed into the wing of the grand piano.

The floor dropped from under them.

Alar's last view of the study was Corrips's body at the foot of the wall with his face cut away. With a shriek of grief he flung his sword futilely at Thurmond, and then the trap wings closed over his head.

As he careened through the tunnel his nostrils were assailed by the musty, mysterious smell of earth. His face broke spider webs. The little eight-leggers must live on smaller, blundering insects, he thought. He and Haven dashed by algae growing in vague green circles around the dim intermittent lights. A couple of tiny winged insects flew off in alarm. A diminutive underground ecosystem. Predators and prey. He deeply sympathized. Like rabbits, he and his friend were fleeing through the emergency exit burrow. The wolves behind them would break down the entrance trapdoor in another sixty seconds. Time enough. Unless more wolves awaited them at the exit. Keep running. No choice. Not now. Too late for anything else. Far too late. He could have—*should* have—saved Corrips.

In the semi-darkness he accosted Haven bitterly. "Why didn't you let me go with Thurmond?"

"Do you think it was easy for Micah and me, boy?" panted the professor brokenly. "You'll understand some day. Right now we've got to get you to a safer place."

"But what about Micah?" insisted Alar.

"He's dead. We can't even bury him. Come along, now."

They hurried silently to the end of the tunnel, half a mile away, where it opened into a dead-end alley from behind a mass of debris.

"The nearest Thief rendezvous is six blocks up the street. You know the one?"

Alar nodded dumbly.

"I can't run as fast as you," continued Haven. "You've got to make it alone. You simply must. No questions. Off with you, now."

The Thief touched the older man's bloody sleeve silently, then turned and ran.

He ran swiftly in the center of the streets, easily, rhythmically, breathing through dilated nostrils. Everywhere were the thin, weary faces of free laborers and clerks returning from the day's work. Peddlers and beggars, dressed in drab cast-off garments but not yet slaves, dotted the sidewalks.

Three hundred meters above him twelve or fifteen armed helicopters followed leisurely. He sensed that a three-dimensional net was closing in on him. Road blocks were probably being set up ahead as well as on the side streets.

He had two squares to go.

A trio of searchlights stabbed down at him from the darkening skies like an audible chord of doom. To attempt to dodge the beams was futile.

Still, explosive shells would follow within seconds and a near hit could kill him.

Subconsciously he noted that the streets had suddenly become empty. When Thief-hunting, the I.P.'s fired their artillery with fine disregard of careless street dwellers. He would never make the Thief underground station. He must hide now or never.

With flashing eyes he looked about him, and found what he wanted, an entrance to the slave underworld. It was fifty yards away, and he sprinted toward it frantically.

Above him, he knew, some thirty narrowed eyes were squinting into gun sights, trigger fingers with cool, unhurried efficiency were squeezing. . .

He flung himself into the gutter.

The shell struck ten feet in front of him. He was up instantly, coughing and stunned, but invisible in the swirling dust clouds. Pieces of brick and cobblestone were falling all about him. Two of the spotlights were roving nervously over the edge of the cloud nearest the underworld entrance. The other was playing rapidly and erratically around the periphery of the cloud. He couldn't even make the slave entrance. He waited for the spotlight to pass, then dashed for the nearest tenement door.

The door was boarded and locked. He pounded frantically.

For the first time he felt—hunted. And with that cornered feeling time slowed down and finally crept. He knew that his senses had simply accelerated. He noted several things. His ears caught the heavy grinding of an armored car churning around the corner on two wheels, with headlights that swept the entire street.

He saw that the dust had settled and that two of the 'copter searchlights were combing the area methodically. A third beam had settled motionless on the underground stairway entrance. That beam was the only real obstacle. It was a neat problem in stimulus-response physiology. Stimulus—observer sees object enter white circular field ten feet in diameter. Response—pull trigger before object leaves field.

Like a frightened deer he leaped between the two converging beams of the armored car and sped toward the brilliantly lighted stairs. He was struck twice by small-arm fire from the car but his armor absorbed it easily. The turret computer would need only milliseconds to train the gun on him. But that was all the time he needed.

He was in the lighted area of the stairs now, hurtling downward toward the first landing. He had tried desperately to clear all the steps, and he did. He crashed to the concrete platform and immediately stretched out flat as a shell shattered the entrance.

He was up again instantly, tearing down the remaining flights to the first underground level of the slave city. It would take his pursuers a few seconds to pick their way through that wreck of muck and rubble. He would need the delay.

He eased out of the stairway cautiously, leaned against the wall and peered about him, sucking in the foul air gratefully. On this level lived the higherclass slaves, those who had sold themselves into bondage for twenty years or less.

It was time for the night shifts to be leaving the slave compounds, accompanied by bullet-browed squad masters. They would be transported to the fields, mines, mills or wherever the slave contractor ordered them sent. There they would work out the nameless fraction of their lives that they had sold.

By crossing through these grim work parties he should be able to make his way to the ascending stairs *behind* the armored car and resume his flight to the Thief hideaway.

But not a person was moving in the silent substreets.

The row on row of slave compounds, up and down the narrow streets, were shut up tightly. That could not have been done within a few minutes. It bespoke hours of preparation by Thurmond. It must be that way on every level, even to Hell's Row, where diseased and manacled wretches labored in eternal gloom. He whirled in alarm. An armored car was rolling through the darkened street toward him.

He understood then that most of the small mobile artillery available to Thurmond from his own police forces, as well as a considerable contingent borrowed from Eldridge of the War Department, had been placed strategically on all slave levels, hours before, just to kill him.

They had driven him underground to finish him.

But why? Why was it so important to kill him? Not because he was a Thief. The government harbored a vengeful bitterness against Thieves, but this was a turnout of force on a scale for suppressing revolution.

What gigantic danger did he represent to Haze-Gaunt?

Haven and Corrips must have known more about him than they had ever admitted. If by some remote chance he ever saw Haven again, he would certainly have some questions to ask him.

Down the street to the left another armored car was rumbling up. Almost simultaneously searchlights shot from both cars, blinding him. He dropped to the ground and buried his face in the crook of his arm. The two shells exploded on the steel wall behind him and the concussion threw him into the center of the street between the oncoming cars.

His coat was ripped to shreds and his nose was bleeding. His head was spinning a bit, but otherwise he was undamaged. For the moment he decided to lie where he had fallen.

One of the spotlights was playing over the dust cloud. Alar watched the beam glowing above him like the sun attempting to burn its rays through an overcast sky. As the dust began to settle the light, too, was dropping closer to him. He knew that it was marking time, waiting to reveal a corpse—his corpse. The other spotlight was darting nearly everywhere along the street where he lay. They were taking no chances that the shot had not been fatal.

Alar examined the ground around him. There was some rubble now, covering the rough macadam-topped cobblestones, and a layer of dust, but there were no holes to slide into, no depressions or objects large enough to hide behind. The street was open around him, with the distant cars and buildings boxing him in. He estimated his chances of escape by springing erect, and saw immediately that he had none. He could only crouch there and hope. Hope for what? In a few seconds the accusing finger of light must point at him and the grim game would continue.

It would not be a long game.

As he lay there in the foul humid dirt, he wished fervently that he had the legendary lives of the cat, and that one of them would emerge from the luminous cloud of dust. He could see himself staggering through the settling fog surrendering one life after another to the firing guns. Buying enough time to—

What was that?

He blinked and stared. He *was* seeing a figure. A man with a tattered coat very much like his own stumbled through the haze. *Who?* It didn't matter—in seconds the figure would be struck down, blasted into lifelessness. But the man was conscious of the danger. He looked up the street both ways, noting the armored cars, now very near, then began to run quickly along the steel wall that paralleled the street from the entrance stairway.

While Alar stared, thunderstruck, the farthest car, now about abreast of the stranger, fired point blank. At the same time the other pursuing car passed within a few inches of the Thief and sped on to the chase.

Now if the stranger emerged unscathed from the sure hit . . . ! And he did! Hugging the wall, the shadowy form continued to run up the street.

Two more explosions came, very close together.

Even before he heard them, Alar was running down the dark street in the opposite direction.

Within forty seconds, if he were lucky, he would reach the stair formerly guarded by the first car and would be "upstairs" again. There he would have time to wonder about the man who, perhaps unwittingly, had saved his life.

Had some fool blundered through the police blockade at the head of the stairs into the blossoming shell dust? He rejected that immediately, not only because he trusted the I.P.'s to maintain a leakproof watch over the entrance above, but also because he had recognized the face.

Yes, he had finally recognized the face when the lights had blazed squarely upon it. He had seen it many times before: the slightly bulging brow, the large dark eyes, the almost girlish lips—yes, he knew that face well.

It was his own.

6. IMPERIAL REFUGE

An hour later Alar—poised statue-like on the marble sill, balancing on one knee with steel fingertips extended to the cold stone surface—*stared.*

The woman was about his own age, dressed in a white evening gown of remarkable softness and luster. Her long blue-black hair, interlaced with inconspicuous gold netting, was gathered in a wide band over her left breast.

Her head seemed unusually large, rather like his own, with large black eyes that studied him carefully. The expertly rouged lips were in odd contrast to the pale, utterly expressionless cheeks. She was not standing straight, but with her left hip slightly dipping, so that the left thigh and knee were sharply defined beneath her gown.

The whole impression was one of alert hauteur.

Alar was conscious of a growing, indefinable elation.

He slipped noiselessly down to the floor and moved to the side of the window, where he was invisible from the courtyard, and turned to face her again—just as something flashed by his face and buried itself in the wall paneling at his ear.

He froze.

"I am glad you are logical," she replied quietly. "It saves time. Are you the fugitive Thief?" He saw the flashes in her eyes and evaluated her character quickly: self-contained and dangerous.

He made no answer.

The woman took several quick steps toward him, simultaneously raising her right arm. The movement drew the white gown across the front of her figure and emphasized her curves. In her upraised hand was a second knife. It gleamed wickedly in the soft light.

"It will be to your advantage to answer truthfully and quickly," she said.

He still made no answer. His eyes were opened wide now and boring into hers, but those large eyes with their black fire within were steady, unflinching.

A short laugh burst unexpectedly from her lips. "Do you think you can stare me down?" she asked. The knife waggled suggestively above her fingers. "Come, now. If you are the Thief, produce your mask."

He gave an ironic grin, shrugged his shoulders and pulled out the mask.

"Why didn't you go to your Thief rendezvous? Why did you come here?" She lowered her arm, but kept the knife firmly in her hand.

He peered at her narrowly. "I tried. All paths were blocked for miles. The weakest protection led here, to the chancellory. Who are you?"

Keiris ignored the question. She moved a step nearer him, scrutinizing him from his soft shoes to his black skull cap. Then she scanned his face and a faint, slightly puzzled frown gathered between her eyebrows.

"Have you seen me before?" he asked. There was something in her expression which bothered him. It added mysteriously to the elation building within him.

She ignored that question, too. She said, "What shall I do with you?" The query was solemn, demanding a serious answer.

He almost said, facetiously, "Call the I.P.'s, they'll know what to do." Instead he said simply, "Help me."

"I must leave," she mused. "Yet I can't desert you. These rooms will be searched before the hour is out."

"Then you will help?" He immediately felt stupid for his words. Usually he met the unexpected in complete possession of himself—it disturbed him to find that this woman could disturb him. To recover his balance, he added quickly, "Perhaps I can leave with you?"

"I have to put in an appearance at the ball," she explained.

"Ball?" The Thief considered the possibilities rapidly, accepting her help now as a matter of fact. "Why can't I come along? I'll even escort you."

She studied him curiously. Her rouged lips had parted just enough for him to see the whiteness of her teeth. "This is a masked ball."

"Like this?" He pulled on the Thief mask coolly.

Her eyes widened imperceptibly. "I accept your invitation."

If he had not, one short hour ago, lost all sense of probability and proportion, he might have toyed briefly with such words as fantastic, preposterous and insane, and wondered when the whistle of the coffee urn would awaken him.

He bowed ironically. "It is my pleasure."

She continued without humor, "You intend, of course, to leave the festival rooms at the first opportunity. Let me assure you that it would be very dangerous. You are known to be in this vicinity, and the palace grounds are swarming with police."

"So?"

"Wander through the ballroom and assembly room for a while and then we'll try to arrange your escape."

"We?" he asked with mock suspicion.

She smiled at this, with just the slightest twist at one corner of her mouth to make it particularly provocative to him. "The Society, of course. Who else?" She glanced down to place the knife on a small end table. Her lashes, he noticed, were long and black, like her hair, and emphasized the unusual paleness of her cheeks. He found he had to exert himself to concentrate on her words. Was she teasing him?

"So! You're the beautiful Thief spy within the palace walls!" His own mouth was mirroring her smile.

"Not at all." She was suddenly cautious and her smile flickered away. "Will you do as I say?"

He had no choice and nodded his head. "Tell me this," he said. "What do the newscasters say about the affair at the Geotropic Project?"

She hesitated for time first time, but seemed to lose none of her poise. "Dr. Haven escaped."

He sucked in his breath. "And the staff?"

"Sold."

He leaned wearily against the wall, and gradually became conscious of sweat dripping in irritating rivulets down his legs. His armpits were soaking, his face and forearms were stinging with an odorous melange of perspiration and grime.

"I'm sorry, Thief."

He looked at her and saw that she meant it. "It's over, then," he said heavily, walking to her vanity dresser and peering into the mirror. "I shall need a shower and depilatory. And some clothes. Can you find some for me? And don't forget a saber."

"I can provide everything. You'll find the bathroom over there."

Fifteen minutes later she took his right arm and they walked sedately down the hall toward the broad stairs that coiled in one beautiful sweep to the great reception chamber. Alar fussed nervously with his mask and eyed the magnificent tapestries and paintings that lined the cold marble walls.

Everything was in exquisite taste, but he got the impression that it was the hired taste of a decorating firm—that the people who passed their brilliant, insecure days in these rooms had long ago lost their ability to appreciate the subtle sunlight of Renoir or the cataclysmic color-bursts of Van Gogh.

"Leave your mask alone," whispered his companion. "You look fine."

They were descending the stairs now. He couldn't seize the whole picture—just isolated scraps. This was existence on a scale he had never expected to experience. Solid gold stair handrail. Carpets with pile that seemed to come up to his ankles. Intricately sculptured Carrara balusters.

Luminous alabaster lighting everywhere. The vista of the reception chamber rushing up to them. A thousand unknown men and women.

It was all strange, but he felt that he had known it all forever, that he belonged here.

From time to time the brightly uniformed reception master announced the names of late-comers through the public address microphone. Here and there, among the sea of heads, were eyes staring up at him and the woman.

And suddenly they were at the foot of the stairs, and the reception master was bowing deeply and saying:

"Good evening, Madame."

"Good evening, Jules."

Jules eyed Alar with apologetic curiosity. "I'm afraid, excellency—"

The Thief muttered coldly, "Dr. Hallmarck."

Jules bowed again. "Of course, sir." He picked up the microphone and called smoothly: "Dr. Hallmarck, escorting Madame Haze-Gaunt!"

Keiris ignored the shocked look the Thief threw at her. "You don't have to wear your mask all the time," she suggested. "Just when you see someone looking suspicious. Come along; I'll introduce you to a group of men. Work yourself into an argument and no one will pay any attention to you. I'm going to leave you with Senator Donnan. He's loud, but harmless."

Senator Donnan threw back his barrel chest impressively. "I run a free press, Dr. Hallmarck," he said to Alar. "I say what I want to. I print what I want to. I think even Haze-Gaunt would be afraid to close me down. I get on people's nerves. They read me whether they want to or not."

Alar looked at him curiously. The stories he had heard of the Senator had not left an impression of a Champion of the Downtrodden. "Indeed?" he said politely.

The Senator continued. "I say, treat the slaves as though they were once human beings, just like ourselves. They've got rights, you know. Treat 'em poorly, and they'll die on you. The slaves in my printing shops used to complain of the noise. I gave them relief."

"I heard about that once, Senator. Very humane. Removed their eardrums, didn't you?"

"Right. No more complaints, now, about *anything*. Hah! There's old Perkins, the international banker. Hiya, Perk! Meet Professor Hallmarck."

Alar bowed, Perkins nodded sourly.

Donnan laughed. "I killed his Uniform Slave Act in the Senate Slave Committee. Old Perk is unrealistic."

"Most of us thought your proposed Slave Act rather striking, Mr. Perkins," said Alar suavely. "The provision for the condemnation and sale of debtors particularly interested me."

"A sound clause, sir. It would clear the streets of loafers."

Donnan chuckled. "I'll say it would. Perk controls eighty percent of the credit in the Imperium. Let a poor devil get a couple of unitas behind in his installment payment and *bang*—Perk has himself a slave worth several thousand unitas, for almost nothing."

The financier's mouth tightened. "Your statement, Senator, is exaggerated. Why, the legal fees alone . . ." He moved away mumbling.

Donnan seemed vastly amused. "All kinds here tonight, professor. Ah, here comes something interesting. The Imperatrix, Juana-Maria, in her motorchair with Shimatsu, the Eastern Fed Ambassador, and Talbot, the Toynbeean Historian, on either side of her."

Alar watched the approaching trio with great interest.

Her Imperial Majesty . . . impossible, yet inevitable, given all the circumstances.

During the previous century, fear had jelled the loose system of hemispheric treaties, mutual defense pacts, and alliances into a cumbersome confederacy. A subsequent series of emergencies (including a devastating misfire in a silo near Moscow) had buried ancient mistrusts under strata of threatened holocaust, and so the final irrevocable step had been taken: during this period, called The Crises, all countries of the Western Hemisphere had united under the hegemony of what had once been the United States of America. The Latins had proposed a figurehead imperial family for the new superstate. Imperial America? At first, Washington had laughed. On the other hand, why not? Rich, powerful families, enduring as any Egyptian dynasty, authenticated by periodic assassinations, had long controlled the United States. It but remained to formally ennoble them.

Alar joined the group in a deep bow as the trio drew near and regarded the titular ruler of the Western Hemisphere curiously. The Imperatrix was an old woman, small and twisted in body, but her eyes sparkled and her face was mobile and attractive, despite its burden of wrinkles.

It was rumored that Haze-Gaunt had caused the bomb to be planted in the Imperial carriage that had taken the lives of the Imperator and his three sons. That bomb had also left the Imperatrix bedridden for years and consequently incapable of vetoing his chancellorship. By the time she had been able to get about in a motorchair, the reins of the Imperium had passed completely from the House of Chatham-Perez into the hardened palms of Bern Haze-Gaunt.

"Gentlemen, good evening," said Juana-Maria. "We're in luck tonight."

"We're always lucky to have you around, ma'am," said Donnan with genuine respect.

"Oh, don't be idiotic, Herbert. A very important and dangerous Thief, a Professor Alar at the University—can you imagine?—escaped a strong police trap and has been traced to the palace grounds. He may be in the palace at this very moment.

"General Thurmond is seething in his quiet way, and he's thrown up a perfectly tremendous guard around the grounds and is having the whole palace searched. He is taking personal charge of our protection. Isn't it thrilling?" Her voice seemed dry and mocking.

"Glad to hear it," commented Donnan with sincerity. "The rascals looted my personal safe only last week. Had to free forty men to get the stuff back. It's high time they caught the ringleaders."

Alar swallowed uncomfortably behind his mask and looked about him covertly. There was no sign of Thurmond yet, but several men that his trained eye identified as plainclothes I.P.'s were filtering slowly and attentively through the assembly. One of them, several yards away, was studying him quietly. Finally he passed on.

"Why don't you yourself do something about the Thieves, your majesty?" demanded Donnan. "They're ruining your Imperium."

Juana-Maria smiled. "Are they really? But what if they are?—which I doubt! Why should I do anything about it? I do what pleases me. My father was a politician and a soldier. It pleased him to fuse the two Americas into one during the Crises. If our civilization survives a few hundred years longer, he will undoubtedly be accorded his place as a maker of history.

"But it pleases me merely to observe, to understand. I am purely a student of history—an amateur Toynbeean. I watch my ship of empire founder. If I were my father I would patch the sails, mend the ropes and beat out to clearer waters. But, since I am only myself, I must be satisfied to watch and to predict."

"Do you predict destruction, your majesty?" queried Shimatsu behind narrowing eyes.

"Destruction of what?" queried Juana-Maria. "The soul is indestructible, and that's all that's important to an old woman. As to whether my chancellor intends to destroy everything else . . ." She shrugged her fragile shoulders.

Shimatsu bowed, then murmured, "If your new super-secret bomb is as good as our agents say, we have no defense against it. And if we have no defense we must meet the attack of Haze-Gaunt with our own attack as long as we are able. And we have two advantages over you imperials.

"You are so certain that you have an overwhelming balance of force that you have never troubled to evaluate the weapons that may be used against you. Also, you have assumed that we must wait politely and let you choose the moment. May I suggest, your majesty, and gentlemen, that the Imperium is run, not by the famed 'wolf pack' but by credulous children?"

Donnan laughed uproariously. "There you have us!" he cried. "Credulous children!"

Shimatsu picked up the bear cape that he had been carrying over one arm and threw it around his shoulders in a gesture of finality. "You are amused, now. But when your zero hour draws close, prepare for a shock." He bowed deeply and passed on.

Alar knew that the man had issued a deadly warning.

"Now isn't that an odd coincidence?" observed Juana-Maria. "Dr. Talbot was telling me only a few minutes ago that the Imperium stands at this moment with the Assyrian Empire as of Six Hundred and Fourteen B.C. Perhaps Shimatsu knows whereof he speaks."

"What happened in Six Hundred and Fourteen B.C., Dr. Talbot?" asked Alar.

"The world's leading civilization was blasted to bits," replied the Toynbeean, stroking his goatee thoughtfully. "It's quite a story. For over two thousand years the Assyrians had fought to rule the world as they knew it. By Six Hundred and Fourteen B.C. the Assyrian ethos dominated an area extending from Jerusalem to Lydia. Four years later not one Assyrian city remained standing. Their destruction was so complete that when Xenophon led his Greeks by the ruins of Nineveh and Calah two centuries later, no one could tell him who had lived in them."

"That's quite a knockout, Dr. Talbot," agreed Alar. "But how do you draw a parallel between Assyria and America Imperial?"

"There are certain infallible guides. In Toynbeean parlance they're called 'failure of self-determination,' 'schism in the body social' and 'schism in the soul.' These phases of course all follow the 'time of troubles,' 'universal state' and the 'universal peace.' These latter two, paradoxically, mark every civilization for death when it is apparently at its strongest."

Donnan grunted dubiously. "Amalgamated Nuclear closed at five hundred and six this morning. If you Toynbeans think the Imperium is on the skids you're the only ones."

Dr. Talbot smiled. "We Toynbeans agree with you. Yet we don't try to force our opinions on the public, for two reasons. In the first place Toynbeans only *study* history—they don't make it. In the second place nobody can stop an avalanche."

Donnan remained unconvinced. "You long-haired boys are always getting lost in what happened in ancient times. This is here and now— America Imperial, June Sixth, Two Thousand One Hundred Seventy-seven. We got the Indian sign on the world."

Dr. Talbot sighed. "I hope to God you're right, Senator."

Juana-Maria said, "If I may interrupt . . ."

The group bowed.

"The Senator may be interested in learning that for the past eight months the Toynbeeans have devoted themselves to but one project—a re-examination of their main thesis that all civilizations follow the same inevitable sociologic pattern. Am I right, Dr. Talbot?"

"Yes, your majesty. Like other human beings we want to be right. But in our hearts we hope rather desperately that we'll be proved wrong. We grasp at any straw. We examine the past to learn if there weren't some instances where the universal state was not followed by destruction.

"We search for examples of civilizations that endured despite spiritual stratification. We look at the history of slavery to see whether the enslaving society ever escaped retribution.

"We compare our time of troubles—the Crises—with the Punic Wars that reduced the sturdy Roman farmer class to slavery and we study the Civil War of our North American ancestors over the slavery question. We consider then how long the Spartan Empire continued after the Peloponnesian War ground its once proud soldiery into serfdom.

"We seek comparisons in the past for our divided allegiance between the ancestor-worship taught our boys and girls in the Imperial Schools and the monotheism followed by our older people. We know what a divided spiritualism did to the Periclean Greeks, the Roman Empire, the budding Scandinavian society, the Celts of Ireland and the Nestorian Christians.

"We compare our present political schism—the Thieves versus the Government—with the bitterly opposed but unrepresented minorities that finally erased the Ottoman Empire, the Austro-Hungarian League and the Later Indic society, as well as various other civilizations.

"But we have found no exceptions to the pattern so far."

"You mentioned the institution of slavery several times as though it were undermining the Imperium," objected Donnan. "How do you arrive at that conclusion?"

"The rise of slavery in the Imperium precisely parallels its rise in Assyria, Sparta, Rome and all the other slave-holding empires," answered Talbot carefully. "No culture can aggrandize its ruling classes generation after generation without impoverishing its peasantry. Eventually these wretches are left with no assets except their own bodies.

"They are swallowed up by their richer brethren under contracts of bondage. Since their produce is not their own they have no means to better the lot of their numerous progeny and a perpetual slave class is born. The present population of the Imperium is over one and a half billion. One third of these souls are slaves."

"True," agreed Donnan, "but they don't really have such a hard lot. They have enough to eat, and a place to sleep—something a great many freemen don't have."

"That, of course," observed Juana-Maria dryly, "is a great recommendation for both free enterprise and for the slave system. To buy bread for his starving children, their father can always sell them to the highest bidder. But we're getting off the main track. Will there be a Toynbee Twenty-two?"

"We hope, your majesty. But, of course, a mere historian can make no guarantees."

"If there is to be a Twenty-two," she continued, "how would it differ from, say, our present Toynbee Twenty-one?"

"We think Twenty-two would successfully challenge our present drive to suicide," said Dr. Talbot simply.

"Interesting. To take it a little further, let us look back a bit. The Egyptaic Society was brought in by Imhotep, the Sinic by Confucius, the Andean by Viracocha, the Sumerian by Gilgamesh, the Islamic by Mohammed, and so on. Will a specific person usher in Twenty-two?"

The savant's eyes sparkled with admiration. "Your majesty is well read. But the answer isn't clear cut. Some civilizations are 'brought in,' as you say, by a given person. But many of them were not. Many are clearly group efforts."

"So we're back to groups," said the old woman. "How do you evaluate a given group, Dr. Talbot? How do you determine what cultural samples to take and what weight to give each?"

"The historian can evaluate his own society only as a weighted synthesis of its microcosmic components," admitted Talbot, tugging again at his goatee. "He can establish at best a probability as to the stage it has reached in the invariant pattern for civilizations. However, when he studies group after group, as I have, from the noblest families—your pardon, your majesty—right down to the bands of escaped slaves in the waste provinces of Texas and Arizona—"

"Ever studied the thieves, Dr. Talbot?" interrupted Alar.

7. THE WOLF PACK

The Toynbeean studied the masked man curiously. "The Thieves are unapproachable, of course, but the Society is just a rubber stamp of Kennicot Muir and I knew him well some years before he was killed. He realized all along that the Imperium was living on borrowed time."

"But how about our tiny settlements on the Moon, Mercury and the Sun?" insisted Alar. "There you ought to find enough vaulting optimism to negate the whole of the fatalism you've found here on Earth."

"For our Lunar Observatory Station I expect that's true," agreed Talbot, "assuming that you consider them as an independent society separate from the lunar fortifications. The morale of the few hundred men there should be high, owing to the flood of knowledge that continues to flow into the two-hundred-meter reflector.

"The Mercury station is of course purely derivative of the solar stations and stands or falls with them. Your suggestion is interesting, because it so happens the Toynbeeans have finally received permission from Minister of War Eldridge to let one of our staff visit a solarion on the sun for twenty days, and I have been selected to go."

"How delightful!" exclaimed the Imperatrix. "What do you expect to find?"

"The very apotheosis of our civilization," replied Talbot gravely, "with all pretense and indirection thrown to the winds. Our present-day phase of civilization, you know, we refer to as Toynbee Twenty-one. It is, of course, an attempt to categorize an extremely complex situation with the exclusion of irrelevant factors. But the solarions are unique. They are most directly a product purely of our own day. Specifically, I expect to find in Solarion Nine the distilled essence of Toynbee Twenty-one—thirty madmen hell-bent on suicide."

Intriguing, thought the Thief, but academic as far as he personally was concerned. He never expected to visit a solarion. "Could we take it one step further," he said. "What is the absolute minimum sample for a highly restricted zone? Say—a space ship?"

"We've worked it out on the computer," said Talbot. "According to the extrapolations, three is the minimum that would demonstrate significant societal change."

"Change to what?" persisted Alar.

"One degenerates, one progresses."

"The third?"

"The third dies."

Alar heard the last few words only perfunctorily, because his heartbeat was accelerating alarmingly. Shey, Thurmond, and a man he took to be Haze-Gaunt were passing by his elbow. He turned his back and shrank toward the wall.

The three paid him no attention whatever but walked rapidly toward the orchestra pit. From the corner of his eye Alar saw Thurmond say something to the conductor. The music stopped.

"May I apologize for this interruption, my lords and ladies?" came the chancellor's rich baritone over the speakers. "A very dangerous enemy of the Imperium is believed to be in the ballroom at this moment. I must ask, therefore, that all men who have not already done so remove their masks in order that the police may apprehend the intruder. This need not mar nor delay our festivities! On with the dance!" The chancellor nodded to the conductor and the great orchestra crashed into *Taya of Tehuantepec.*

An excited buzz sprang up everywhere as the bright-plumaged males began removing their masks and looking about the room. Gradually the couples were reabsorbed on the dance floor. As Alar slid along the wall his hand went to his mask, then dropped slowly. His strange heart began to beat even faster.

Several things were clamoring for his attention. The dancers were now taking notice of him even in the shadowed portion of the tapestried wall where he leaned. From the air, it seemed, several men in gray with I.P. service sabers crystallized a few feet from him on either side.

They were just standing there quietly, seemingly absorbed in the whirling gaiety. Two more leaned unobtrusively against a great column some twelve feet ahead. Alar's brown Thief mask was about as inconspicuous here as a red rag in front of a bull. He must have been mad to wear it.

His tongue worked dryly in his mouth. He carried an unfamiliar blade. He was exhausted—living on pure nervous energy. Even if his roving eyes could spot an exit opening on the gardens, he wasn't at all sure he could break out unscathed.

"*Your mask, sir?*"

It was Thurmond—standing squarely before him, hand on rapier pommel.

For a long, horrid moment the Thief thought his legs would give way and drop him to the marble flagging. At best he could not avoid the reflex action of licking his lips.

The police minister's feral eyes missed nothing. His mouth curled faintly. "Your mask, sir?" he repeated softly.

The man must have approached him from behind the column, and made one of the shadowy catleaps for which he was famous—and feared. He was drawing his blade slowly, seeming to take an almost sensuous pleasure in the Thief's rapid breathing.

"*Faut-il s'éloigner le masque? Pourquoi?*" asked Alar huskily. "*Qu'êtes-vous?*"

The barest shadow of doubt crossed Thurmond's face. But his blade was now out. Its point flashed even in the subdued light of the ballroom. "The chancellor would still like a conference with you," continued Thurmond. "If I can't arrange that, I'm to kill you. Conferences are just so much idle chatter and you might get lost on the way. So I'm going to kill you. Here. Now."

Alar finally got a deep breath.

There were other flashes of steel around him now. The gray men along the wall had drawn their blades and were sidling toward him. Two or three couples had stopped dancing and were staring in fascination at his approaching murder.

A blur! And Thurmond was suddenly one step closer. It was simply impossible for a human being to move so fast. It was clear now why poor Corrips—no mean swordsman—had lasted but seconds before the slashing wizardry of Giles Thurmond. And yet the man held back. Why? That phony diplomatic French must have removed his one-hundred-percent certainty. Thurmond evidently did not intend to kill him until the mask was off.

"Vous m'insulte, tovarich," clipped Alar. *"Je vous demande encore, pourquoi dois-je déplacer le masque? Qu'êtes-vous? Je demande votre identité. Si vous désirez un duel, més séconds—"*

Thurmond hesitated. *"Il faut déplacer le masque,"* he said curtly, *"parceque il y a un énémi de l'état au bal. C'est mon devoir, de l'apprendre. Alors, monsieur, s'il vous plaît, le masque—"*

The police minister had now taken care of the one-in-a-million possibility that Alar was actually a visiting dignitary who had not understood the chancellor's announcement. He was now ready to kill the Thief whether or not he removed his mask.

Alar's mind began to float in that curiously detached way that ignored time. His heart, he noted, had leveled off at 170. Within one or two seconds he would be impaled by Thurmond's blade against the thick tapestries, writhing like an insect. That was no way for a Thief to die.

"Madame, messieurs!" he bowed in utter gratitude. Keiris had rounded the column with the chancellor and Ambassador Shimatsu on either arm. Thurmond's blade, an inch in front of his heart, wavered.

"Madame," continued the Thief smoothly, *"voulez-vous expliquer à cet homme mon identité?"*

Keiris's eyes were wide with something nameless. This moment, one that she had dreaded for years, had finally come. If she saved the life of the Thief her double life must soon be discovered. What would happen to her then? Would Haze-Gaunt sell her to Shey?

She said quietly, "You have made a grave mistake, General Thurmond. May I introduce Dr. Hallmarck, of the University of Kharkov?"

Alar bowed. Thurmond sheathed his weapon slowly. It was clear that he was unconvinced.

Shimatsu, too, was studying Alar dubiously. He started to speak, then hesitated, finally said nothing.

Haze-Gaunt fixed hard eyes on the Thief. "We are honored, sir. But as a matter of courtesy, it might be well to—"

"Comment, monsieur?" Alar shrugged his shoulders. *"Je ne parle pas l'anglais. Veuillez, madame, voulez-vous traduire?"*

The woman laughed artificially and turned to the chancellor. "The poor dear doesn't know what it's all about. He has this dance with me. I'll get his mask from him. And you really ought to be more careful, General Thurmond."

She was talking before they were well away. "I doubt that you can escape now," she said hurriedly. "But your best chance will be to do exactly as I say. Remove your mask immediately."

He did so, placed it in his jacket pocket. She had maneuvered him carefully, so that he faced away from the chancellor's group.

His arm was around her now and they glided in a slow whirl across the room. To have her so close, with her body continuously touching his, reactivated the tantalizing memory syndrome of the balcony—only now it was doubled, redoubled.

He was not much taller than she and his nostrils once got buried in the fine black hair at her temple. Even its odor was exasperatingly familiar. Had he known this woman at some time in his phantom past? No way to tell. She had given no hint of recognition.

"Whatever you have in mind," he urged nervously, "do it quickly. As we left them Shimatsu was telling Haze-Gaunt that I spoke English. That's all Thurmond needs."

They were through the milling crowd now and in the shadowed fountain gallery.

"I can't go any further, Alar," said the woman rapidly. "At the end of this corridor is a refuse chute. It will drop you into one of the incinerator pits in the bowels of the palace. The incinerators will be fired at any moment but you'll have to take the chance. You'll find friends in a great vault adjoining the incinerators. Are you afraid?"

"A little. But who are these 'friends'?"

"Thieves. They're building a strange space ship."

"The *T-twenty-two?* But that's an imperial project. It's guarded tighter than a drum. The Undersecretary for Space, Gaines, is in charge himself."

"Two I.P.'s are coming up the hall," she countered quickly. "They're sure about you now. You'll have to run for it."

"Not yet. They think I'm cornered and they'll wait for reinforcements. In the meantime, what about you? Haze-Gaunt isn't going to like this." His hands were on her shoulders. They looked at each other silently a moment, bonded by their unknown and dangerous features.

"I'm not afraid of *him*. It's Shey, the psychologist. He knows how to hurt people so that they will tell him whatever he wants to know. Sometimes I think he tortures just for the sake of seeing suffering. He wants to buy me—

_or that—but so far Haze-Gaunt hasn't let him touch me. Whatever you do, avoid Shey."

"All right, I'll keep away from him. But why are you doing this for me?"

"You remind me of someone I used to know," replied the woman slowly. She looked behind her. "For God's sake, hurry!"

His fingers tightened insistently on her shoulders. "Who is this person I remind you of?" he cried harshly.

"Run!"

He had to.

Within seconds he was at the chute-door, flashing frantic fingers over it. There was no handle. The rush of feet sounded just behind him. Of course there was no handle—the thing was hinged inward.

He plunged into the narrow blackness and was swirled around and around as he shot down. If he crashed into a pile of anything solid at this velocity, he would certainly break both legs. In the very act of trying to slow his descent by turning out his knees and elbows, he hurtled through the darkness into a mass of something foul and yielding. Nothing was hurt but his dignity. He was on his feet almost before the clouds of dust began to rise.

The blackness was complete, save for a beam of light from one side of the incinerator that was his prison. It was apparently the operator's peep-hole in the charging door. He stumbled over to the peephole, blinked and peered out.

The great room was deserted.

He rattled the door cautiously, and tried the iron drop-latch.

It was locked from outside.

The Thief wiped his forehead with his sleeve, drew his saber and pried tentatively at the lock mechanism. It was too solid.

The soft grate of steel on steel echoed mockingly within the narrow confines of the incinerator as he replaced the weapon.

He had begun to feel his way slowly around his prison when he heard footsteps on the concrete floor outside.

The furnace door opened and a mass of flaming rubble sailed past his horrified eyes.

The door clanged shut just as he leaped to smother the torch with his chest.

The shaft of light was gone. A slave janitor was probably peering into the darkness, and wondering.

The Thief heard a muffled curse, then the sound of fading footsteps. He was at the door instantly.

The slave ought to be back in a minute or two.

And he was. This time the ignition wad was larger. The peephole was closed a long time as the slave made sure the charge was burning properly. Finally he went away. The Thief removed his saber point from the lock engagement and eased the door open. Cold air rushed into his scorched lungs and over his blistered face.

He was on the floor instantly, and forced himself to take time to close and relock the door. Precious seconds were gone, but it might delay his pursuers if they had to look in every incinerator for him.

He vanished, wraithlike, between the bulge of two furnaces, heading toward the west wing and the fabulous *T-twenty-two.*

Was the brilliant Gaines really a Thief? If he were, did that mean that Haze-Gaunt's government was riddled with members of the Society?

Two things were certain. The wolf pack knew a great deal about him. To them he was something more than *a* Thief. And the Society of Thieves had placed an incredible value on his life. Furthermore, Haven knew as much, or more, about him than the wolf pack. He had some pressing questions to ask him if ever he saw his friend again.

He opened the door to the great vault chamber a quarter of an inch and peered along the inner wall. Nothing moved. From far away, toward the center of the chamber, he heard the hiss of the nucleic welders.

Very quietly he slipped inside the door—and sucked in his breath sharply.

Even in the dusky gloom the *T-twenty-two* shimmered with a pale blue haze. Her sleek, sheer flanks shot fifty meters into the air, but she was less than three meters in diameter at her waist. A great moon freighter would make several hundred of her.

But the thing that troubled him, the thing that seized his mind and blanked out the trip-hammering of his heart, was this—He had seen the *T-twenty-two* before—*years* before.

Even as the sandbag crashed into his head, and even as he clawed futilely toward consciousness, he could only think—*T-twenty-two*—*T-twenty-two*—where—when?

8. DISCOVERY THROUGH TORMENT

"He's regaining consciousness," sniggered the voice.

Alar sat up on one knee and peered out from aching eyes.

He was in a large cage of metal bars, barely tall enough for him to stand. The cage stood in the center of a large stone-walled room. All about him was a raw, musty odor. The rawness, he realized with quivering nostrils, was blood. In these rooms the imperial psychologist practiced his inhuman arts.

"Good morning, Thief!" burbled Shey, rising up and down on tiptoe.

Alar tried in vain to swallow, then struggled to his feet. For the first time in his life he was thankful that he was utterly exhausted. In the long hours that would follow he could faint easily and frequently.

"It has been suggested to me," chirped Shey, "that with proper stimulation you might demonstrate powers not before known in human beings—hence the iron cage that now holds you. We would like to see a good performance—but without danger to ourselves or the risk of losing you."

Alar was silent. Protests would avail him nothing. Furthermore, it would not improve things for Shey to recognize the voice of the Thief who had so recently robbed him.

The psychologist drew closer to the cage. "Pain is a wonderful thing, you know," he whispered eagerly. He rolled up his right sleeve. "See these scars? I held hot knives there as long as I could. The stimulation—ah!" He inhaled ecstatically. "But you'll soon know, won't you? My difficulty is that I always release the knife before I attain maximum stimulation. But with someone else to help as *I* shall help *you*—" He smiled engagingly. "I hope you won't disappoint us."

Alar felt something cold crawl slowly up his spine.

"Now," continued the psychologist, "will you hold out your arm and let the attendant give you an injection or do you prefer that we crush you between the cage walls to administer it? Just a harmless bit of adrenalin so you won't faint—for a long, long time."

There was nothing to be done. And in a way he was even more curious than Shey as to what would happen. He thrust out his arm in grim silence and the needle jammed home.

The phone buzzed. "Answer that," ordered Shey.

"It's from upstairs," called the attendant. "They want to know if you've seen Madame Haze-Gaunt."

"Tell them no."

Additional attendants wheeled up a heavy hinged case, opened it and began to take things from it and to lay them on the table. Still others rolled the cage walls together, flattening the Thief like a bacillus between microscope slides.

Alar listened vaguely to the sweat plashing from his chin to the stone floor, providing an insane obbligato to the strumming of an adrenalin-fed heart. From behind him somewhere wafted the odor of red-hot metal.

At least Keiris had got away.

It was twilight and, because there was no longer any pain, he thought for a moment that he was dead. Then he stood up and looked about him in wonder. In this world he was the only moving thing.

He was suspended in space near a silent, winding column. Gravity was banished here. There was no up, no down, no frame of reference for direction, so the column was neither necessarily vertical nor horizontal. He rubbed his eyes. The physical contact of palm to face seemed real. This was no dream. Some enormous soul-shaking thing had happened to him that he could not fathom. Here there was no movement, no sound, nothing but the column and vast brooding silence.

Gingerly he reached out to touch the column. It had a strangely fluid, pliant quality, like a ray of light bending. And it had a strange shape. The part that he touched was a five-finned flange that extended from the central portion of the column.

If he had a power saw, he thought, how simple it would be to saw out innumerable arms with hands and fingers. Touching the flange lightly, he floated around the column to the other side, where he found an identical five-finned arrangement. He frowned, perplexed. Farther around the column were leg-like fins.

His eyes brightened as he realized that a cross-section of this column would resemble very closely the vertical cross section of a human being. Looking about, he discovered that the column appeared to go on indefinitely.

He then floated along it in the opposite direction for some minutes, noting that it gradually grew smaller in cross section. The cheek outline was thinner, the bones more prominent. The outline might be that of a skinny youth. Even farther on, the column was still smaller, and, by straining his eyes, he thought he could see where it shrank to a thread in the distance.

The Thief believed his life depended on the solution to this mystery, but cast about as he might, the answer eluded him.

He returned slowly, pensively, and studied the column at approximately the point where he had found himself when he recovered consciousness. He knotted his jaws in exasperation.

Perhaps the interior of the column held an explanation. He thrust an arm into it slowly, and noted with interest that some plastic force seemed to draw his fingers into the five-finned portion of the column. He stuck in his right leg. That fitted perfectly.

Tentatively, he eased the rest of his body into the column.

And then something immense and elemental seized him and flung him—

"He's regaining consciousness," sniggered the voice.

Alar sat up on one knee and peered out from aching eyes.

His head was whirling. He was in the center of the cage, not crushed between the walls. There was no blood on him anywhere and somehow his shirt and coat had got back on him. Everything—the position of the men, the table, the instruments—were in the same places as when he first awakened in the cage an infinity ago, before the injection and the pain.

Had the pain really been just a nightmare, topped off by that queer episode of the man-shaped column? Was it just an illusionary *déjà vu* to expect Shey to rise up and down on tiptoe and burble—

"Good morning, Thief!" burbled Shey, rising up and down on tiptoe. Alar felt the blood draining from his face.

He understood one thing very clearly. Through means utterly incomprehensible to him he had, for a time, left the time stream and had re-entered it at the worst possible locus. He knew that this time his resolution would falter—that he would talk and that his comrades would die. And he had no weapon, no means to prevent this catastrophe that was finally upon him.

Except—his heart bounded in fierce joy and he listened to his calm icy voice. "I think that you will release me very soon."

Shey shook his curly head in rare good humor. "That would spoil everything. No, I won't release you for a long time. I might even say—never."

Alar's lips compressed in a chill confidence he was far from feeling. Speed was utterly essential. He must get in his point before the telephone rang. Yet he must not seem hurried or anxious. Shey was sure to recognize his voice but that couldn't be helped.

He folded his arm across his chest and leaned against the back bars. "I am perhaps overvalued by the Society of Thieves," he said shortly. "Be that as it may. Still, certain precautions have been taken against my capture and I must warn you that if I do not leave the palace safely within ten minutes the corpse of Madame Haze-Gaunt will be delivered to the chancellor tonight."

Shey frowned and studied his quarry thoughtfully. "That voice— Hmm. You're lying, of course—just trying to gain time. Her excellency is still on the ballroom floor. Your shortened breathing, narrowed pupils, dry voice—all point to a deliberate lie. I won't even check on it. Now, will you hold out your arm, please, for a little shot of adrenalin?"

Wasn't the phone ever going to ring?

His continued calm exterior amazed him. "Very well," he murmured, thrusting out his arm. "We three die together." The needle jabbed in and struck a nerve. Alar's face twitched faintly. The attendants rolled the cage walls together, flattening the Thief spread-eagle fashion.

The odor of heating metal was strong behind him. His head was beginning to spin. Something was wrong. But for the bars crushing him he knew he would drop. Wet circles of sweat were spreading slowly from the armpits of his jacket.

Two burly attendants wheeled up the instrument chests. Alar forced himself to watch them casually as they opened it and handed a strange-shaped pair of pliers to Shey.

A shudder of nausea crept up Alar's throat as he remembered his bloody nail-less hand-things from—that other time.

"Do you know," chuckled Shey as he fixed a coy eye on Alar, "I believe you're the chap that called on me a few nights ago."

The phone buzzed.

Shey looked up absently. "Answer that," he ordered dreamily.

Time ground slowly to a halt for the Thief. His chest was heaving in great gasps.

"It's from upstairs," called the attendant hesitantly. "They want to know if you've seen Madame Haze-Gaunt."

Shey waited a long time before answering. His look of introspection died away slowly. Finally he turned around and carefully replaced the nail pullers in the chest.

"Tell them no," he said, "and get the chancellor on the phone for me instantly."

Alar was left at the busy downtown intersection as he had demanded and, after an hour of careful wandering to elude possible I.P. tailers, he walked via alley and cellar to the door of the Society rendezvous. Before he slept, ate or even got a new blade, he wanted to lay before the Council the incredible occurrences in the slave underground and in Shey's torture chamber.

Something sharp jabbed into his side. He raised his hands slowly to find himself surrounded by masked Thieves with drawn blades. The man wielding the nearest saber stated, "You are under arrest."

9. WILD TALENT

"You are now under a sentence of death," intoned the masked man on the dais. "In accordance with the laws of the Society the charges against you will be read, and you will then be given ten minutes to present your defense. At the end of that time, if you have failed to refute the charges against you beyond a reasonable doubt, you will be put to death with a rapier thrust through your heart. The clerk of this tribunal will read the charge."

Alar could not free his brain of a numbing dullness. He was too tired even to feel bewildered. Of all the Thieves here he recognized only Haven, whose stricken eyes peered out at him through a brown mask.

The masked clerk arose from a desk near the dais and read gravely. "Alar was captured by government operatives in the imperial palace approximately four hours ago, taken to the lower chambers and delivered into the custody of Shey.

"A few minutes later he was escorted unscathed from the palace to the street and there released. In view of his unbroken skin it is presumed that the prisoner disclosed confidential information concerning the Society. The charge is treason, the sentence death."

"Fellow Thieves!" Haven sprang to his feet. "I object to this procedure. The burden of proof of betrayal ought to be on the Society. In the past Alar has risked his life for the Society many times. I now urge that we give him the benefit of the doubt. Let us presume him innocent until we have proved him guilty."

Alar studied the sea of masks confronting him. The judge listened to several men who bent toward him and whispered. Finally the judge straightened up. Alar's nails dug into the wooden rails. He knew he could prove nothing.

"Number eighty-nine," said the judge slowly, "has proposed a radical innovation in trial procedure. In the past, the Society has found it necessary to liquidate Thieves who have been unable to free themselves from suspicion. Trial boards of the Society unanimously agree that by this method we destroy more innocent men than guilty.

"That price, I feel, is small, if it ensures the continuation of the Society as a whole. The question now is—are there any special circumstances that indicate the ends of the Society will best be served by a reversal of the burden of proof?"

Alar listened to his pulse-rate mount slowly. One seventy-five . . . one eighty . . .

"There are unusual, even strange, circumstances in this case," continued the judge, leafing slowly through the brochure before him. "But all of them"—he transfixed Alar with steely eyes and hardening voice—"all of them indicate that we should redouble our care in dealing with this man, rather than lessen it.

"He is unable to account for his life prior to one night five years ago when, as an ostensible amnesiac, he found shelter with two members of this Society. And we must keep in mind that Chancellor Haze-Gaunt would be sufficiently ingenious to attempt to plant an agent provocateur among us by just such a ruse.

"When Alar emerged safely from the clutches of Shey we were entitled to suspect the worst. Does the defendant deny that he stands here among us with a whole skin when by rights he should be dead or dying?" The voice was faintly ironic.

"I neither deny nor affirm anything," replied Alar. "But before I begin a defense, I would like to ask a question. Since the sentence is death and I cannot leave this room alive, perhaps the judge will be willing to tell me why the Society protected me when I was a helpless amnesiac and why, after permitting me to lead the dangerous life of a Thief, Dr. Haven and Dr. Corrips suddenly decided my life was more important than some twenty-odd brilliant minds in the Geotropic Project at the University. Without regard to what has—or has not—happened since, you must admit the stand is inconsistent."

"Not necessarily," replied the judge coldly. "But you may form your own opinion. Five years ago a strange space ship crashed into the upper Ohio River. Certain flotsam was recovered from the wreckage that indicated it must have come from outer space. Two living things were recovered from it. One was a strange ape-like animal later captured by the River Police and given to Haze-Gaunt. The other was—you. We immediately got a note from Kennicot Muir concerning your disposition."

"But he's dead!" interjected Alar.

The judge smiled grimly. "He is thought to be dead by the Imperial Government and by the world outside. As I say, we got a note from him to the effect that you were to be enrolled in the Society as soon as your emotional pattern was stabilized. You were to be given routine assignments involving but little physical danger, and you were to be studied.

"It was Muir's opinion that possibly you were a species of man of rather special properties—that your ancestral line had evolved beyond homo sapiens into something that could be of immense help to us in averting the impending Operation Finis that Haze-Gaunt may launch at any hour. Very early we discovered that your heart accelerates before you consciously detect danger.

"We know now that your subconscious mind synthesizes impressions and stimuli of which your conscious mind is unaware, and prepares your body for the unseen peril, whatever it is. This was good but not good enough for us to place you beyond homo sapiens or to absolve you completely from suspicion as a planted spy.

"We waited for other manifestations of your possible ultra-humanity but nothing more was forthcoming. And after your probable treachery tonight, your threat to the existence of the Society outweighs its desire to continue studying you."

So his earlier life would soon be sealed forever. Did no one know? He demanded, "Is Muir present now? Does he agree to my death?"

"Muir is not present, and as a matter of fact none of us has seen him in the flesh since his disappearance. But you can be sure he knows of this trial. So far he has not disagreed. Do you have any more questions? If not, the time for your defense must begin to run. You have ten minutes."

With pale face Alar studied his executioners. Many of them must have shared perilous adventures with him but would now kill him willingly to save the Society. His heartbeat was mounting steadily. Two hundred. It had never been so high.

"Any defense"—his coolness amazed him—"that I might bring forward would be so implausible and incredible from the point of view of most of you that it would be a waste of precious minutes to attempt any explanation whatever. If I have ten minutes to live—"

"Nine," corrected the clerk firmly.

"Then I intend to use them to save my life. John!"

"Yes, boy?" Haven's voice shook a little.

"John, if you believe that I am innocent, please explain this to me—what is the chemical basis of eyesight?"

The biologist looked startled but instantly recovered his poise. Blood began to flood back into his cheeks. "It is generally agreed," he declared, "that photons reflected from the thing being viewed enter the pupil of the eye and are focused as they pass through the vitreous and aqueous humors to the retina, where an image is formed.

"There they impinge upon the visual purple, which then gives off a substance to which the retinal rods and cones are sensitive. The rods and cones pass the stimulus on to the retinal nerve endings, which gather finally into the great optic nerve and register the image in the crevasses of the optic lobe at the base of the brain."

"Would you say that it is quite impossible for the reverse of that process to occur?"

"Reverse? You mean, where the brain conceives an image, passes it along the optic nerve to the retina, and the visual purple is so stimulated that it releases photons that are focused by the eyes' refractive fluids to project an image? Do you mean to ask whether your eyes may be capable of projecting an image as well as receiving one? Is that what you mean?"

"Precisely. Is it impossible?"

The men strained forward in puzzled attention.

"You have three minutes," reminded the clerk sharply, looking from Alar to Haven and back again.

Haven fixed eyes wide with surmise on his protégé. "Visual projection has been predicted for the creature that may follow homo sapiens in the evolutionary scale. This power may evolve within the next fifty or a hundred millennia. But now, in modern man? Highly improbable.

"However"—he raised a warning hand in a gesture full of hidden meaning—"if someone *were* able to project light beams from his eyes—if he were able to do that he ought to be able to reverse other stimulus-response systems. For example, he should be able to turn the tympanum of the ear into a speech membrane, by activation of the cochlear nerves with the cerebral auditory tract. In a word, he should be able to reproduce aurally—not orally—any sound he can imagine!"

Alar stole a glance at the dim fluorescent tube in the ceiling fixture. A warm flush crept quickly up his throat. He knew now that he would live and not die—that he would live to unravel the gray net that enshrouded his past—that he would leave the Thieves and that he would henceforth search for himself in earnest. But there was much to be done yet, and he was far from being out of danger. He awakened to the voice of the judge:

"What did you hope to accomplish by that senseless discussion with Dr. Haven? Only thirty seconds of time remain for your defense."

Around him there was the eerie sliding of finely wrought steel on steel. All the Thieves except Haven had drawn their blades and were watching him with feline intentness.

Alar stared upward at the ancient fluorescent light. It reminded him of the searchlight beam glowing through the dust cloud when he was trapped that time in the slave underground. There was no more mystery now about his escape then. He knew the explanation for the figure in the tattered coat, the figure that appeared to be his own. The figure had indeed been his own. It had been an image of his own body projected on the settling dust. He had not known the extent of his ability to reverse his stimulus-response system, and yet, subconsciously, with the wish to see himself escape he had created a photic image of himself—and the wish had been fulfilled.

He closed one eye and concentrated feverishly on the dim tube in the ceiling, trying to reawaken his wonderful power. This time it might save him again, although in a different way. If he could only impinge enough photons of the proper quanta and frequency on the fluorescent coating of the lamp, he believed he could fill in the troughs of the emitted photonwaves and throw the room into darkness.

The light seemed to flicker a little.

His breath was like that of a panting dog and sweat was streaming into his open eye. A few feet in front of him a Thief raised his blade level with Alar's heart and sighted along it coolly.

Haven's nervous whisper rasped behind him. "Fluorescent light is higher on the spectrum. Raise your frequency a little."

The executioner lunged at him.

The room went dark.

Alar held his left hand over the nasty cut in his chest and slipped away a few feet. Not far—he had to stay in the open in order to control the lamp. Life now would depend on the boldest improvisation.

No one had moved. All around him came the accelerated expectant breathing of the men who wanted to kill him—as soon as they could distinguish his dark form from themselves.

Then—

His right ear heard sounds coming from his left ear:

"Let no one move! Alar must still be in the room. We'll find him as soon as we have a light. Number twenty-fourteen, go immediately to the outer office and obtain emergency lighting." It was a reasonable facsimile of the judge's voice. The danger was, did the judge think so too?

Alar backed off quickly two paces and said in muffled tones, "Yes, sir."

How soon would it take someone to remember that Number twenty-fourteen was stationed down the corridor?

Again the tense silence as he edged backward towards the door. It was a fantastically difficult task to avoid cutting off his view of the lamp. He pushed fellow Thieves apologetically out of the way as he stumbled ever backwards. But only one man need walk in front of his line of vision and his control of the lamp would vanish in a blaze of light. A dozen blades would cut him down.

He sensed the door now beside him, the guard in front of it.

"Who is it?" The guard's tense question shot from the dark, a bare foot away.

"Twenty-fourteen," Alar whispered quickly. He could feel warm blood trickling down his leg. He must find bandages soon.

A heated, sibilant argument was in progress somewhere in the room. He caught the word "twenty-fourteen" once.

"Your honor!" called someone nasally.

He listened to the guard hesitate in the very act of sliding back the bolts. His hoax would be exposed in seconds. "Hurry up!" he whispered impatiently.

"You have the floor!" called the judge to the nasal Thief.

The guard stood motionless, listening.

"If Alar escapes because of your delay," hissed Alar to him, "you'll be responsible."

But the man stood immobile.

Again that nasal voice from the other side of the room—"Your honor, some of us are of the understanding that Number twenty-fourteen is actually stationed at the far end of the exit corridor. If this is so your orders that he leave the room must have been answered by Alar!"

It was out.

"*My* orders?" came the astounded reply. "*I* gave no orders. I thought it was the sergeant of the guard! Door guard! Let no one whatever leave the room!"

The bolts clanged shut before him with grim finality. With a last despairing blast of mental effort Alar reactivated the dampened fluorescent bulb with a shaft of dazzling blue light.

Pandemonium broke loose.

A split second later he had knocked down the blinded guard, drawn the bolts and was out while a score of men groped inside. But their retinal over-stimulation would wear off quickly and he must hurry. He looked up the corridor. Number twenty-fourteen and his detail blocked that path. He knotted his fists, then turned to study the dead end of the corridor behind him—and his hand flew futilely to his empty scabbard.

Someone was standing there in the cul-de-sac.

"You can escape this way."

"Keiris!" he exclaimed softly.

"You'd best come quickly."

He was immediately beside her. "But how—?"

"No questions now." She pushed open a narrow panel in the wall, and they stepped behind it just as the trial room burst open. They listened to the muffled but grim voices from beyond the panel.

"Don't underestimate them," whispered the woman, pulling him up the dark passage by the hand. "They'll question the guard up the corridor, then scour this end. They'll find the panel within sixty seconds."

Soon they were in a dim-lit alley at the first street level.

"What now?" he panted.

"My coupé is over there."

"So?"

She stopped and looked up at him gravely. "You are free for a little while, my friend, but your reason must tell you that you can expect to be caught within a matter of hours. The I.P.'s are combing the city for you, block by block, house by house, room by room.

"All roads from the city are closed. All non-police aircraft are grounded. And the Thieves are looking for you too. Their methods will be less gross but even more efficient. If you try to escape without a plan or without assistance the Thieves will certainly recapture you."

"I'm with you," he said shortly, taking her arm. They got into the coupé silently.

The gloomy alleyway began to race by them as the atom-powered rotors gathered speed.

"You'll find antibiotics and astringents in the first-aid kit," said the woman coolly. "You'll have to dress your wound yourself. Please do it quickly."

He ripped off his coat, shirt and underwear with blood-slippery fingers. The antibiotic powder stung and the astringent brought tears to his eyes. He slapped adhesive gauze over the wound.

"You'll find more clothes in the bundle beside you."

He felt too weak to bring up the question of propriety. He unwrapped the bundle.

"You are in the process of assuming the identity of one Dr. Philip Ames, Astrophysicist," Keiris informed him.

Alar zipped up his new shirt in silence, then loosened his belt and changed his trousers.

"Actually," continued the woman tersely, "Ames doesn't exist except in certain Government transcripts. The wallet in your inside coat pocket contains your new personal papers, a ticket for the next lunar flight and your sealed orders from the Imperial Astrophysics Laboratory, counter-signed by Haze-Gaunt."

There was some tremendous fact staring at him that he couldn't quite grasp. If only he weren't so tired. "I assume," he said slowly, "that the Imperial Laboratory knows that Haze-Gaunt is sending a man to Lunar, but doesn't know who is being sent. Otherwise, I would be exposed immediately as an impostor.

"I must assume, too, that Haze-Gaunt, if he has thought about it at all, believes he is sending an Imperial Astrophysicist whose identity is known only to him. Such double deception must have been planned and executed by a third person."

Now he had it!

And he was just as much in the dark as ever. He turned to the woman accusingly. "Only one intellect could have calculated the probability of my escape from Shey and where my trial by the Society would be held. Only one man could have controlled Haze-Gaunt's course of action in selecting 'Ames'—The Meganet Mind!"

"It was he."

Alar took a deep breath. "But why should he try to save the life of a Thief?"

"I'm not sure, but I think it's because he wants you to discover something vital at Lunar, something in a fragment of sky map. It's all in your orders. Besides, the Mind is a secret Thief sympathizer."

"I don't understand."

"Nor I. We weren't supposed to."

Alar felt completely lost, out of his depth. A few minutes before the world consisted neatly of Thieves and Imperials. Now he felt vividly the impact of a brain that treated both factions as children—an inconceivably deep brain that labored with infinite skill and patience toward—what?

"That's Lunar Terminus ahead," said his companion. "Your luggage has already been checked aboard. They'll examine your visa carefully but I don't think there'll be any trouble. If you want to change your mind this is your last chance."

Haze-Gaunt and the Imperial Laboratory would eventually get together and compare notes. A brief vision of being cornered by hard-bitten I.P.'s in the tiny Lunar Observatory settlement flashed into Alar's mind and his saber hand twitched uneasily.

And yet—just what *was* on the star plate? And why had the Meganet Mind picked *him* to discover it? Could it throw any light on his identity?

Of course he would go!

"Goodbye, then, Keiris," he said gently. "Incidentally there's something I ought to warn you about. It's known at the chancellory that you're missing right now. Don't ask me how I know. I just do. It will be very dangerous for you to return. Can't you come with me?"

She shook her head. "Not yet—not yet."

10. THE QUESTIONING

As she hurried up the secret stairway to her chancellory apartment, Keiris's calm exterior belied the tumult within her—the same tumult that had been raging from the moment Alar's lithe form had dropped over her window sill earlier in the evening. The armor that she had carefully built up around her since Kim's disappearance (was he really dead?) had fallen about her in ruins.

Why should an unknown Thief affect her this way?

His unmasked face had provided no clue. That was disappointing, because she never forgot a face. And yet her first glimpse of that rather broad soft face with the incongruously hard dark eyes, instead of dismissing the problem as nonexistent, had accentuated it.

She knew that she had never seen that face before. She also knew that he was utterly familiar—as much a part of her as the clothes she wore. Was that disloyal to Kim? It depended on how she meant it.

As she stood before the panel opening into her bathroom, she found herself blushing.

She shrugged her shoulders. No time now for analysis of personal feelings. Haze-Gaunt would be waiting for her in her bedroom, wondering where she'd been. Thank heaven for his fantastic jealousy. He'd only half-believe her anyway, but it provided a queer sort of security for her—a status quo consistently defined by its very insecurity.

She sighed and started sliding the panel back.

At least she'd have time to take a shower and have her women rub her down with rose petals. That would give her more time to invent answers for the questions that Haze-Gaunt would certainly ask. And then she'd squeeze into that low-necked—

"Have a pleasant outing?" asked Haze-Gaunt.

She would have screamed if her tongue hadn't stuck to the roof of her mouth. But she gave no exterior sign of shock. She got a full deep breath into her lungs and it was over.

She looked at the three intruders with outward calm. Haze-Gaunt was staring at her in gloomy uncertainty, legs spread, hands locked behind his back. Shey was beaming in happy anticipation. The deep lines in General Thurmond's face were, on the whole, noncommittal. Possibly the parentheses enclosing his small dash of a mouth looked a little harder, a little crueler.

Her heart beat faster. For the first time since Haze-Gaunt had placed her in his quarters she felt a thrill of physical fear. Her mind simply refused to accept the implications of Haze-Gaunt accompanied by the two most merciless monsters in the imperium.

She had planned her most plausible line of defense even as Haze-Gaunt's question left his lips. Smiling wryly, she closed the panel behind her. "Yes, I had a pleasant outing, Bern. I go out whenever I can. Slaves have the vices of slaves, don't they?"

"We'll come back to that," rejoined the chancellor grimly. "The main question is, what do you know about Alar? How did you meet? Why did you let him escort you to the ball instead of turning him over to the palace guards?"

"Bern," she said, "is my bathroom the place for an inquisition? And it's really rather late. Perhaps in the morning."

She could have bitten off her tongue. This defense was not ringing true. She could sense the little psychologist anticipating her every word—knowing almost exactly what she would say next. Perhaps the diabolical little man had even forewarned Haze-Gaunt of what she could be expected to say if she were hiding something from them.

"Oh, very well," she said wearily, stepping away from the wall. "I'll tell you what I know, though I can't see why it's so important. Alar climbed up on my balcony this evening. I threw a knife at him but I wasn't a very good shot. I missed and in the next instant he had me by the wrist.

"He said he'd kill me if I didn't take him into the ballroom. What could I do? My maids were gone. It's really your fault, Bern, for not providing at least a minimum of protection for me."

She knew it was no good, but at least they'd take a few moments to pick it to pieces. Meanwhile, she would be thinking. She walked casually to the wash basin, as though she had made her final contribution to the discussion, and studied her face in the mirrors a few seconds. She was spraying her face with a perfumed water-palm oil emulsion when Haze-Gaunt spoke again.

"Your friend seems to have taken a shower in here and borrowed some of my clothes—not to mention the Italian saber. Were you bound and gagged during all that?"

Keiris stopped rubbing her oiled face and reached languidly for the water-alcohol spray knob. "It has always been my understanding that my apartment was wired with concealed microphones. I assumed that every word that passed between the Thief and me would be heard by the guards and that Alar would be captured in this very room."

"By a remarkable coincidence," Thurmond murmured, "your knife severed the wire."

The water-alcohol spray stung her cheeks sharply. She rubbed her face briskly with a deep-napped towel, then faced the three again with a shell of poise that was growing thinner by the minute.

Shey was still smiling. Once, he seemed almost to chuckle.

"I'll give you the benefit of the doubt on that," said Haze-Gaunt coldly. He unlaced his fingers from the small of his back and folded his arms on his chest as he sauntered toward them. "And I'll even assume, for the time being, that the next phase of your story is true—that you believed we knew all along that the Thief at the ball was Alar, and that we were biding our own good time in taking him. We'll let that go.

"You may or may not know that after his capture Alar was given to Shey for examination and that Alar somehow knew that you were missing from the palace grounds an hour ago, just before Shey was to have begun his experiments. Alar obtained his release by telling Shey that you were being held as a hostage by the Thieves. You must have told him that you would be missing at that moment, and that he could use the knowledge to effect his release. Do you deny that?"

Keiris hesitated and looked at Shey for the first time. The pain-dabbler was eyeing her in rapt anticipation. She knew that her face must be very pale. For nearly a decade she had thought she could face death with calm. But now that the probability was crystallizing before her very eyes it became horrible.

What was it about death that frightened her? Not death itself. Only the hour of dying—the hour that Shey knew how to prolong indefinitely. And she would talk. She knew that Shey could make her talk. She would have to tell about the Meganet Mind and a potent weapon would be lost for Kim's Thieves.

Somewhere, somehow, Kim might still be alive. What would he think when he learned of her betrayal? And incidentally, just how had Alar known that she had been waiting for him at the Thief rendezvous during his brief imprisonment in Shey's chambers? There were too many questions, and no answers.

She wondered just how much pain she could take before she became talkative.

"I deny nothing," she said finally. "If you want to think that I provided the Thief with the means for his escape you may certainly do so. Does my background lead you to expect an overwhelming loyalty to you, Bern?" She watched his face closely.

Haze-Gaunt was silent. Thurmond shifted his feet restlessly and glanced at his wrist radio.

"Haze-Gaunt," he clipped, "do you realize we're letting this woman hold up Operation Finis? Every second is vital if we are to achieve surprise, but we can do nothing until we evaluate Alar. I urge that you turn her over to Shey immediately. Her actions show something more than a generalized sympathy with a subversive organization that she identified with her late husband.

"There was something special between her and Alar. We must pull it out of her. And what about these incessant leaks of high secrets to the Thieves? You always thought you knew every move she made, every word she said. Where," he concluded tersely, "has she been for the last hour?"

"I have been with Alar." She found it incredible that her voice could be so calm. She watched for the effect of the statement on Haze-Gaunt. The barest flicker of anguish passed over his eternally immobile mouth.

She had been abandoned.

Shey giggled and spoke for the first time. "Your answers are so clear that they completely obscure—what? You point with sweeping gestures to a wide-open highway but it is the camouflaged path that we seek.

"Why are you so eager to imply that you have been activated all along by a simple emotional attachment for a man—even if he is a gallant swash-buckling Thief—whom you never saw before? I ask this, not because I expect answers here and now but so that you will understand the necessity, from our point of view, for what must follow."

Keiris finally knew the shape of physical despair. It was a leaden numbing thing that seized one nerve after the other and made her rotten with fear.

"What do you—they—want to know, Bern?" she said. It was not a question but rather an admission of defeat. Her voice sounded oddly plaintive in her ears.

Haze-Gaunt nodded to Shey, who stepped up and swiftly strapped a disc-like thing to her arm—a portable verigraph. The needles that circulated venous blood through the instrument stung sharply; then the pain was gone. The thing's eye blinked green at each heartbeat. She rubbed her arm above the instrument.

They would make her own body betray her. They would program it with their insidious drugs, and then they would feed questions to it, just as though they were talking to a computer, and the answers would flash out as colors on that incorruptible little crystal, just like lines slavishly jumping out on a CRT. Green for truth, red for lies. Destroyed by a needle prick. She couldn't even claim they had broken her under torture. It was bitterly unfair. She suppressed a whimper.

Haze-Gaunt waited a moment for the scopolamine to take effect. Then he asked, "Had you ever known Alar before tonight?"

"No," she replied with what she believed perfect truth.

To her utter amazement and wondering surmise, the blinking green eye of the instrument turned slowly red.

"You have seen him before," observed Haze-Gaunt grimly. "You should know better than to try to deceive the verigraph on the first question. You know well enough that it is effective over a three-minute period."

She sat down dizzily. The instrument had said she had lied—had said that she really *had* known Alar before. But where? When?

"Perhaps a glimpse somewhere," she murmured faintly. "I can't account for it otherwise."

"Have you carried information to the Thieves before?"

"I don't know." The light flashed a vivid yellow.

"She isn't sure," interpreted Shey smoothly, "but she thinks she has occasionally betrayed information in the past, evidently through anonymous intermediaries, and she believes it reached the Thieves. We have only two minutes before the 'graph becomes ineffective. Let's hurry on."

"In these matters," Thurmond asked her harshly, "do you act independently?"

"Yes," she whispered.

The light immediately flashed red.

"A categorical lie," sniggered Shey. "She's working for someone. Who directs you?" he demanded.

"No one."

Again the red light.

"Is it a cabinet member?" demanded Thurmond.

Even in her near-stupor she marveled at his eternal suspicion of treachery in high places.

"No," she whispered.

"But someone in the palace?"

"The palace?"

"Yes, here in the chancellory palace?"

The light was blinking green steadily. She groaned with relief. The Meganet Mind was quartered within the imperial palace, not the chancellory palace.

"The imperial palace, then?" suggested Shey.

She didn't answer but knew the light was burning crimson.

The three men exchanged glances.

"The Imperatrix?" asked Thurmond.

The light turned green. The police minister shrugged his shoulders.

She realized dully that she must faint, but that she could not.

And it came. Haze-Gaunt displayed once again the flash of dazzling intuition that had brought him to the leadership of his wolf pack. He asked:

"Do you receive orders from the Meganet Mind?"

"No."

It was no use. She knew without looking at the light that it must surely have betrayed her.

Oddly, she felt only relief. They had got it out of her without pain. She couldn't blame herself.

Then "Barbellion?" asked Thurmond dubiously, naming the Colonel of the Imperial Guards.

She froze. The three minutes had passed. The verigraph was no longer registering. The light must not have turned red on the name "The Meganet Mind."

"We've run over the time a little," interposed Haze-Gaunt, frowning. "Her blood is buffered again, and her reactions for the last questions were meaningless. We'll have to wait six or seven days for another try at the truth."

"We can't wait," objected Thurmond. "You know we can't wait."

Shey stepped up and disconnected the verigraph. Keiris felt the stab of another needle, and her head was horridly clear again by the time she realized what Haze-Gaunt had replied.

"She's yours, Shey."

11. RETURN OF KEIRIS

"Dear, dear Keiris," smiled Shey. "Our rendezvous here was as inevitable as death itself."

From where she lay, strapped to the operating table, the woman sucked in her breath and looked with wide eyes about the room. There was nothing there but the gleaming whiteness, the pans of strange instruments—and Shey, swathed in a white surgical gown.

The psychologist was speaking again, his words interspersed with giggles.

"Do you understand the nature of pain?" he asked, leaning over her as far as his rotundity would permit. "Did you know that pain is the finest of the senses? So few people do. In the gross animality of most of mankind pain is used solely as a notice of physical injury.

"The subtler overtones are missed entirely. Only a few of the enlightened—such as the Hindu fakirs, the Penitentes, the Flagellants—appreciate the supreme pleasures that may be obtained from our sadly neglected proprioceptive system.

"Look!" He pulled back his sleeve deftly, exposed a pulpy raw spot on his inner arm. "I peeled off the epidermis and let flaming drops of ethanol fall there for fifteen minutes, while I sat in my box at the opera, enthralled by the Imperial Ballet's rendition of *Inferno*. In the whole audience I alone completely appreciated it." He paused and sighed. "Well then, let us begin. You can talk any time you wish. I hope not too soon."

He wheeled up a dial-clustered box and unreeled two needle-tipped wires from it. One needle he jabbed into the palm of her right hand, then strapped it down to the palm with adhesive tape. The other was similarly applied to her right bicep.

"We start with the elementary, and advance to the complex," explained Shey. "You will appreciate the stimuli more fully if you understand their effect. Observe the oscillograph." He pointed to a circular glass panel of dull white, split horizontally by a luminous line.

She cried out involuntarily as a sharp pain shot up her arm—and stayed there, throbbing rhythmically.

Shey giggled. "Nice appetizer, eh? See the cathode beam? It shows that impulses travel up that particular nerve trunk in several speeds. There's the sudden flashing pain—the peak on the cathode tube, traveling about thirty meters a second. Then several slower impulses come up, with speeds down to half a meter a second. They make up the dull ache that follows stubbing your toe, or burning your finger.

"These impulses are gathered into larger and larger nerve fibers that eventually pass into the spinal cord and are carried to the thalamus, which sorts out the various stimuli of pain, cold, warmth, touch, and so on, and routes the messages to the cerebrum for action.

"The post central convolution lying just behind the fissure of Rolando seems to get all the pain impulses." He looked up cheerfully and adjusted the needle in her upper arm. "Bored with the monotonous old stimulus? Here's another."

She braced herself but the pain was not nearly so sharp.

"Not much, eh?" said the psychologist. "Just barely above threshold. After stimulation the fiber can't be stimulated again for four-tenths of a millisecond. Then for fifteen milliseconds it goes the other way—hypersensitive—and then it's subnormal again for eighty milliseconds, then normal from then on. It's that fifteen-millisecond hypersensitive period that I find so useful—"

Keiris screamed.

"Splendid!" crowed Shey, shutting off the switch on the black box. "And that was on only one nerve in one arm. It's perfectly fascinating to add one pair of electrodes after another until the arms are covered with them, even though the subject generally dies." He turned to the box again.

Somewhere in the room a radiochron was ticking out the seconds with mocking languor.

Alar stared in slow wonder at the bearded starveling in the mirror.

What hour?

What day?

A sharp glance at the chronocal told his incredulous eyes that six weeks had passed since he had locked himself in the study here beneath Lunar Station, in a frantic race against the moment when the combined might of the Thieves and the Imperials would search him out and kill him.

Had he really succeeded in solving the mystery of the star plate?

He didn't know.

He thought he had discovered the identity of that luminous wheel in the lower right-hand corner of the negative. He had discovered some very interesting aberrations in the nebulae in the intervening space and had considered several explanations, none of which were entirely satisfactory. He wondered if the Mind knew the answer. He rather suspected he did.

Everyone seemed to know all the answers except him. There was almost a comical injustice in that he, the possessor of the miraculous ear and eye, who had skirted the fringe of godhood that night in Shey's evil chamber, knew so little of himself.

And now this strange and wonderful star plate—it held something that the Mind wanted him to know. But what?

He scratched absently at his beard while his eyes toured the study. From the ceiling lamp dangled a small three-dimensional model of the galaxy. It seemed to apologize for the preposterous scenery beneath, which consisted of—books, gigantic, minuscule, gaudy, modest, in all the tongues of distant Earth.

They swarmed over floor, chairs and tables, half-way up the four walls, a rugged landscape drained here and there by valleys made by Alar as he walked the floor during the past weeks. The valleys were carpeted by a forlorn detritus of discarded scribblings.

In a glaciated cirque of the book-Matterhorn that arched over his work-desk, his electron microscope was enshrined, surrounded by a gray talus of negatives.

His roving eye next caught the glint of the tube of depilatory peeking at him from between the pages of Muir's *Space Mechanics*. A moment later he was again before the mirror, rubbing his beard away by degrees, followed by curious inspection, as men invariably do when they depilate after a long absence from civilization.

But when the stubble was all gone he was appalled at the pinched pallor of his face. He tried to remember when he had last slept or eaten. He couldn't place either event precisely. He vaguely recalled devouring frozen cubes of vegetable soup with his bare fingers.

He walked to the porthole and looked out into the blackness toward a ridge of wild lunar mountains, silver-tinged by the setting sun. Crescented Terra hung in gigantic splendor just above the ridge. He would like to be there now, asking questions of the Mind, of Haven—of Keiris. How long would it be before Earth would again be safe for him? Probably never, with both Thief and Imperial searching. It was a miracle that his imposture here at the observatory had not been detected.

He reflected. Am I here for a purpose? Do I have a destiny? For good? For evil? Shall I share the doom of that wretched Earth? Or can I change those hapless creatures? Ridiculous thought! As John Haven once pointed out, someone would have to go back into the time of dawn man and work an impossibly intricate bit of genetic engineering on their genes and chromosomes. The Neandertals and others before and after them would have to be changed from unreasoning killers to men willing to recognize the brotherhood of men. Toynbee Twenty-two. And forget it.

He shook his head gloomily. What he needed was a brisk walk along the sparse streets of Selena—the lunar settlement that housed the observatory staff and their families. He strode toward his shower room.

Alar had been wandering through the streets about an hour when he saw Keiris.

She was standing alone on the steps of the Geographical Museum, regarding him gravely. A light cape was thrown about her shoulders and she appeared to hold it together with the fingers of her right hand, or possibly a barely visible metal clasp.

The lamps on the museum porticoes threw an unearthly blue light over her bloodless face. Her translucent cheeks were drawn and lined, and her body seemed very thin. There was now a streak of white in her hair, which was knotted unobtrusively at the side of her neck.

To Alar she was completely lovely. For a long time he could only stare, drinking in the moody, ethereal beauty of the composition of light and blue shadow. His torturing frustration was forgotten.

"Keiris!" he whispered. *"Keiris!"*

He walked quickly across the street and she descended the steps stiffly to meet him.

But when he held out both hands to her, she merely lowered her head and seemed to swirl her cape closer. Somehow, he had not expected so cool a reception. They walked silently up the street.

After a moment he asked, "Did Haze-Gaunt give you any trouble?"

"A little. They asked some questions. I told them nothing." Her voice was strangely husky.

"Your hair—have you been ill?"

"I have been in a hospital for the past six weeks," she replied evasively.

"I'm sorry." After a moment he asked, "Why are you here?"

"A friend of yours brought me. A Dr. Haven. He's waiting in your study, now."

Alar's heart leapt. "Has the Society reinstated me?" he asked quickly.

"Not that I know of."

He sighed. "Very well, then. But how did you meet John?"

Keiris studied the dim-lit flaggings of the street. "He bought me in the slave market," she said quietly.

Alar sensed the outline of something ominous. What could have angered Haze-Gaunt to the point of selling her? And why had the Society bought her? He couldn't talk to her about it. Perhaps Haven would know.

"There's really nothing mysterious about it," she continued. "Haze-Gaunt gave me to Shey. When Shey thought I was dead he had me sold to what he thought was a charnel-house buyer, only it turned out to be a surgeon sent by the Thieves. They kept me in their secret hospital for six weeks and as you can see I didn't die. And when Dr. Haven came I told him where you were. We slipped through the blockade last night."

"Blockade?"

"Haze-Gaunt grounded every planetary and spacejet immediately after you left. The Imperials are still combing the hemisphere for you."

He stole a cautious look behind them. "But how could a Thief ship enter Lunar Station? The place is swarming with I.P.'s. You've been spotted, surely. It was insane of Haven to come. The only reason both of you weren't arrested when you landed was that the I.P.'s hoped you'd lead them to me. Well, we're being tailed right now."

"I know but it doesn't matter." Her voice was quiet, with a soft huskiness. "The Mind told me to come to you. As for Dr. Haven, I question none of his acts. As for you, you'll be safe for several hours."

"Suppose the guards at the landing locker *did* identify Dr. Haven and me, and suppose that I *have* called their attention to you and suppose we *are* being followed. If we don't try to leave Selena they won't do anything, at least not until Thurmond arrives and perhaps Shey. Why should they? They think you can't escape."

He started to make a sarcastic retort, then changed his mind. "Does Haven really think he can get me off the moon?" he queried.

"A high government official, a secret Thief, will plant his bribed guard at the exit port at a certain hour and all of us can escape then." She compressed her lips, gave him a strange side look, and then said without expression: "You won't die on the moon."

"Another prediction of the Meganet Mind, eh? Incidentally, Keiris, who *is* the Mind? Why do you think you have to do everything he says?"

"I don't know who he is. It's said he was once a common circus performer who could answer any question if the answer had ever appeared in print. Then about ten years ago he was in a fire that left his face and hands disfigured.

"After that he couldn't make any more public appearances, and became a clerk in the data banks of the Imperial Science Library. That's where he learned to absorb a two-thousand-page book in less than a minute and that's where Shey discovered him."

"Go on." He felt a twinge of guilt at pressing her for details about a life she must long to forget. But he had to know.

"About that time Kim disappeared and Haze-Gaunt—took me. I got a note in Kim's handwriting asking me to do whatever the Mind requested. So—"

"Kim?" Something sagged within the Thief.

The woman said quietly: "Kennicot Muir was my husband. You didn't know?"

A great deal was suddenly incisively, painfully clear.

"Keiris Muir," he muttered. "Of course! The wife of the most fabulous, most elusive man in the system. In ten years he hasn't appeared in person to the Society he founded or to the woman he married." He said abruptly, "What makes you think he's alive?"

"Sometimes I wonder myself," she admitted slowly. "It's just that on *that* night, when he left me to go to his fatal interview with Haze-Gaunt, he told me he'd get through and come back for me. A week later, when Haze-Gaunt had installed me in his personal quarters, I received a note in Kim's handwriting asking me not to commit suicide. So I didn't.

"The next month I got another note telling me about the Meganet Mind. About once a year since then there have been other notes in what looks like his handwriting, telling me that he looks forward to the day we can be together again."

"Have you considered that they might be forgeries?"

"Yes, they might be. He may be dead. Perhaps I am naïve for thinking him alive."

"Is that the only evidence you have?—those notes in his handwriting?"

"That's all." Keiris nodded solemnly. "And yet, I think it's significant that none of the wolf pack thinks he's dead, either."

"That includes Haze-Gaunt?"

"Oh yes, Haze-Gaunt is almost certain Kim is in hiding, perhaps overseas."

To Alar that was the strongest possible indication that Muir was indeed alive. The hard, practical chancellor would be certain to hide his secret fears if he thought them baseless.

"But," Alar said, "what about the Mind? What is his connection with the Society?"

"A secret agent, I suppose. His access to the Imperial Science Library is probably of considerable value to the Society."

Alar smiled humorlessly. Keiris's intimacy with greatness had apparently blinded her to the probability that the Society was a mere catspaw of the Mind. You, I, all of us, he thought, caught in the omnivorous meshes of that mysterious net. Ah, Mind with the Meganet, you are well named!

And the comparison led to a startling possibility.

"You say," he began slowly, studying her closely, "that Kennicot Muir disappeared about the same time that the Mind put in his appearance. Does that seem significant to you?"

Her eyes widened, but she didn't say anything.

"Have you considered," he persisted, "that the Meganet Mind might be your husband?"

She was silent for a moment before she replied.

"Yes, I've considered it." Her dark eyes searched his face eagerly. "Have you learned something?"

"Nothing specific." He saw the sudden disappointment reflected in her eyes. "But there seems to be an inordinate number of coincidences connected with the two men."

"The only resemblance between them is in their over-all size. Otherwise they're utterly different."

"The Mind is disfigured, so that would be a perfect disguise. More important is the rise to prominence of the Mind after your husband's disappearance. Note his influence with the Society." Alar watched her carefully. "And he treats you like a special ward."

"They can't be the same man," she said without conviction. There was doubt, now, in her eyes.

"What proof do you have that they *aren't?*" Alar said gently.

"Proof?" She obviously had no answer to his question.

"You said," he continued, pursuing the point which formed the basis for her doubt, "that you've weighed the possibility. What made you discard it?"

"I don't know," she replied, beginning to be upset as she felt her confidence fading away. "I just did." She shook her head almost desperately. "I have no proof, if that's what you mean."

He was being cruel, he knew, with his questioning. She wanted to be objective, to face the situation, but the pain within could not be controlled. He hunted frantically through his brain for a final question to settle the doubts in both their minds.

Suddenly he had it. "Has Haze-Gaunt also considered the possibility?"

"Why, yes! Yes, he has!" Her eyes were very wide now.

"To what effect?"

"He rejected the idea completely! I know he did!"

"So!" Alar said and sighed. That was importantly significant—that was negative proof as good as one might expect to find. The interrogation was over. He looked abruptly at the luminous dial on his wrist radio.

"It's four now. If Thurmond left immediately—and we must assume he did—he'll be here with troops by midnight. We have eight hours to complete the solution to the star plate and to blast off. Our first step is the Galactarium, then back to my study and John Haven."

12. Search for Identity

The wizened curator unlocked the door, and Alar led the woman into the great dark chamber of the Galactarium. The door closed quietly behind them, and their eyes strained forward in the cold gloom, sensing rather than seeing the vastness of the place.

"A gallery circles the interior," whispered Alar. "We'll take a moving platform to the necessary point."

He led her down the ramp and they were soon speeding around the dark periphery of the great room.

Within a few seconds the platform slowed to a stop in front of a vaguely lit control-board. Keiris smothered a gasp as Alar's hand flew to his saber pommel.

A tall somber figure stood by the panel station. "Good evening, Mrs. Muir, Alar!"

The Thief felt his stomach turn over slowly.

The tall man's laughter welled in ghastly echoes out into the blackness, circling and sodden. His face was that of Gaines, Undersecretary of Spaceways. The voice was that of the Thief judge who had condemned him to death.

Alar was silent, wary, speculative.

The man seemed to read his thoughts. "Paradoxically, Alar, your escape from us was the only thing that could have reinstated you in the Society. It confirmed your ultrahumanity as no number of words could have done. As for me, if you're wondering, I arrived on the sun-bound *Phobos* last night, and I am here now to provide for your safe passage home and to ask if you have discovered the secret of the star plate. Our time is growing very short."

"Why do you want to know?" queried Alar.

"I don't, particularly. The important thing is that *you* know."

"That's easily answered, then. I don't know—or at least I don't know the whole story." Alar had a stubborn impulse to maintain a strict silence until he learned more about his role in this fantastic drama. Still, for ill-defined reasons, he trusted this man who had once wanted his life. "Look out there," he said simply, pointing into the man-made space before them.

The three of them stared into the silent vastness while Alar flicked a switch on the panel. Even Gaines seemed subdued.

Sol with his ten planets sprang into glowing three-dimensional view before them. Cerberus, the newly discovered trans-Plutonian planet, was nearly a mile away, barely visible. Expertly the Thief manipulated the dials and the system began rapidly to shrink. The three picked up opera glasses from the panel pockets and watched. Finally, Alar spoke.

"Our sun is now about the size of a very small speck of luminous dust, and even with our magnifiers we can't see Jupiter." He quickly began to activate more switches. "That's Alpha Centauri, a visual binary, over two hundred yards away from the sun on the present scale. The bright one on the other side is Sirius. And there's Procyon. They're accompanied by dwarfs too faint to see.

"Within this mile-diameter Galactarium there are now about eighty of the stars nearest the sun. On this scale the galaxy would fit in a space about as big as the moon. So we'll have to shrink the projections still more to see any substantial part of the galaxy."

He turned more dials and a great glowing wheel with spiraling spokes began to form before them "*The* galaxy—our local universe," he said softly. "Or at least ninety-five percent of it, scaled down to a mile across and one-tenth of a mile thick. It's just a haze of light now—the Milky Way.

"The main identifying features are the two Magellanic Clouds. For more accurate identification we can refer to the positions of the spiral arms, the hundred globular clusters and the configuration of the star cloud in the center of the galaxy. Now watch."

The wheel and its Magellanic satellites shrank quickly. "The Galactarium is now on a diametric scale of five million light years. Far off to the right, about seven hundred and fifty thousand scale light years away, is our sister galaxy, M thirty-one in Andromeda, with her own satellite clusters M thirty-two and NGC two hundred and five. Below are two smaller galaxies, IC one thousand six hundred and thirteen and M thirty-three. On the other side is NGC six thousand eight hundred and twenty-two. The universe-fragment you now see," he concluded simply, "is exactly what I found on the star plate."

"But this is old stuff," protested Gaines in heavy disappointment.

"No," interjected Keiris. "Alar means that he has seen our own galaxy *from outside.*"

"That's right," said the Thief. "For two centuries astronomic theory has predicted that our own galaxy would be visible as soon as a telescope were constructed capable of penetrating the thirty-six-billion-light-year diameter of the universe."

"So!" Gaines said. "From the outside!" He beat a faint tattoo with his opera glasses against the panel pocket. "Then we're peering clear across the universe!" He seemed immensely impressed.

"Well," Alar said, giving a fleeting wry smile, "that's not very much to my credit. When the Lunar Observatory was finished it was just a question of time before my discovery was made. So my contribution in *that* direction is largely routine."

Keiris glanced sharply at him.

"Have you discovered something else, then?" she asked.

"Yes. In the first place, light from the Milky Way, passing in a closed circuit across the universe, should return only after thirty-six billion years, so that what we now see on the plate should be our galaxy as of thirty-six billion years ago, on the very eve of its formation from cosmic dust. Instead, the plate shows the Milky Way as of now—today—just as you see it out there."

"But that's impossible!" exclaimed Gaines. "There ought to be a thirty-six-billion-year lag!"

Smiling, the Thief said, "It should be impossible, shouldn't it? But the positions of the galactic spiral arms, the peripheral velocity of the nebula as a whole, the positions of the globular clusters, the spectral age of our own sun, even the positions of the planets, including Terra, prove otherwise."

"Then how do you explain it?" asked Keiris.

"Here is my hypothesis: According to Einstein, time multiplied by the square root of minus one is equated to Euclidean space. That is, a light year of distance equals a year of time multiplied by the square root of minus one. So if space is finite, so must time be. And like space, time curves and bends back on itself, so that there is no beginning and no end.

"Our galaxy moves simultaneously along time and space coördinates like this." He held up two pencils crossed at right angles. "Let the x-axis be time, the y-axis space, our galaxy located at the intersection. Now I move the y-pencil to the right, and simultaneously push it up. Anything at the intersection will be moving in both coördinates."

He offered the two pencils to Keiris, but with a toss of her head she deferred the honor to Gaines. The Undersecretary took the two slim implements and, holding them together at right angles, moved them back and forth and up and down. His lips were pursed and his eyes were intent. Keiris was concentrating on the demonstration, too.

Alar watched the two of them adjusting themselves to the concept. He leaned towards them and touched the pencils.

"Now," he said, "suppose you substitute two hoops for the pencils, so that the hoop frames intersect each other at right angles like the frame of a toy gyroscope. Let one hoop be equivalent to thirty-six billion light-years of space and the other equivalent to thirty-six billion years of time, with our galaxy always at their intersection.

"I'll assume further that for any given time-space intersection there can be but one distribution of matter, with the corollary that, when the same intersection recurs, the same matter will be there. So, after the hoops have made one-half revolution, the intersection does recur, and it follows that our galaxy is in two places at once, or to be more precise, in the same space at the same time.

"But space and time have vanished and rematerialized across the poles of the universe and, when they did, our galaxy materialized with them. The joker in my illustration is that we are tempted to view the rotation of the hoops in Euclidean space, while they're really associated only through the square root of minus one via the fourth dimension. Only their inter-sections—just two geometric points—have mutual Euclidean values."

He took back the two pencils Gaines was offering.

"And, since the two intersections are diametrically opposite in the space-time cycle, one should always be thirty-six billion years ahead of the other, so that when light starts from the 'future' intersection and travels across the poles of time and space to the lagging intersection, it arrives at the other thirty-six billion years later, to be received by the same space-time-matter continuum from which it originated. That's why the 'mirror' galaxy was the same age as ours now is, when its light began that long journey."

The three were silent a moment. Finally Gaines said, almost diffidently, "What do you think it means, Alar?"

"Standing by itself, it means nothing. But viewed in the light of another peculiarity appearing on the plate it might mean a great deal. For example, it seems to suggest the possibility of traveling backward in time. We can talk about it after I've seen John Haven and asked him some questions."

Alar dropped his opera glasses back into the pocket and moved close to the control panel. He spun the dials back to neutral, flipped the power switch. The light points in the huge room dwindled rapidly into nothingness. For a moment the three of them stood there silently in the heavy darkness which had come with the disappearance of the starry projection. "We'd better leave now," he said.

As their eyes grew accustomed to the faint wall lights which had reappeared, Alar stepped on the moving platform, Keiris and Gaines moving in step behind him.

The platform carried them quietly around the great curving edge of the room to the ramp. They started up the ramp toward the entrance hall beyond the gallery. Near the top, Alar suddenly halted.

"A guard," he said. He could see an I.P. officer standing near a huge steel column, hands on hips, talking in a low voice to a second man.

Keiris was huddled against Alar's back, Gaines at his side, a firm left hand on his shoulder.

"We should have nothing to fear," Gaines said. But the tone of his voice was not quite so positive.

"It will be best if we're cautious," Alar replied. He studied the thin, shriveled figure of the second man. It was the curator. "You wait here. I'll check out with the curator and inform him we'll leave by the side exit." He pointed to the deeper shadows to his left, where a dim red bulb was barely visible. "I'll meet you there."

Before Keiris or Gaines could reply, Alar stalked off toward the two figures.

Keiris watched him approach the others, anxiety drawing lines on her face. The I.P. officer stepped back a pace, then followed the curator and Alar as they wandered toward the Galactarium office, conversing as they went.

"Come," Gaines whispered and led her toward the red light.

The minute that it took Alar to rejoin them seemed like an hour to her. Her fears were completely swept away when he paced up to her, relaxed and confident.

"Everything all right?" Gaines asked hoarsely.

"We're in no immediate danger, I'm certain," Alar replied. He caught the swift look from Gaines. "Let's go away from here first and I'll explain further."

They pushed open the exit, stepped outside. The door swung shut behind them, locking itself. They stood for a second on the side passageway, facing the main corridor fifty feet away.

"The I.P. asked me to identify myself," the Thief said. "I gave him my credentials as Dr. Philip Ames and he was satisfied. Then he asked me where the rest of the party was."

Gaines frowned, continuing to peer down the passageway toward the main corridor.

"I explained that I just left you two in the gallery. He asked me, then, what your names were."

Keiris sucked her breath in sharply. Gaines turned his head and asked softly, "What did you say?"

Alar smiled slightly. "I told him the truth."

"You did?" Gaines said incredulously.

"It was the best way. If the I.P. really knew my true identity, nothing would be served by lying. And if he didn't, then the truth would allay his suspicions."

"But he'll report our get-together to his superiors," Gaines pointed out. "No one knows we've just arrived on the moon. In a couple of hours there'll be I.P.'s swarming all over us."

"I'm afraid," Alar said ominously, "that they already know. The non-chalance of that I.P. at the mention of your names gave it away to me."

After a moment of shocked silence, Gaines said, "I suppose it was too much to expect to hide our arrival. We'll just have to keep out of sight and not provoke them and hope that they'll wait until they get direct orders from Thurmond." Gaines was frowning again. "What do you think, Alar? Should we dodge around a bit in the back passageways or split up?"

The Thief reflected for a moment. The three of them together would find it more difficult to escape from trouble if it arose, but if they stayed together they would stand a better chance to avoid it.

"Let's take a back way," Alar said. He looked at Keiris, whose eyes had widened in alarm and whose body seemed to have shrunk within her swirling cloak. He glanced at the streak of white which ran across her head and into the knotted bun at the side of her slender neck. She still looked ill. He wished she could be spared all the tension that was being forced into her life. He patted her shoulder briefly. "Don't worry, Keiris. They don't have us on the run—we're just playing it safe."

Gaines stalked off, away from the main corridor, without a backward look. As Alar and Keiris started to follow, she exchanged a penetrating glance with him. Her look was so full of tenderness and concern for him—and he involuntarily returned it so forcefully—that he was for the moment emotionally shaken.

Then she was ahead of him, close behind Gaines.

They weaved through corridors, criss-crossing the main ones, for nearly half an hour.

"I'll try to answer your last question first, my boy," said John Haven. The biologist studied his protégé warmly as he lit his pipe and took a few experimental puffs. Finally he settled back in his chair. "Do you know what 'ecstasy' means?"

Keiris and Gaines were following avidly.

"You may assume that I know the dictionary definition, John," answered Alar, absorbing the older man with keen eyes.

"That isn't enough. Oh, it tells you it's from the Greek verb 'existani,' meaning 'to put out of place.' But out of place from what? Into what? What is this peculiar mental state known as 'ecstasy'? All we know is, that it may be attained through alcohol, drugs, savage dancing, music, and in various other ways.

"During your encounter with Shey, in your moment of greatest need, you probably passed into—or beyond—the state we are discussing. In so doing you burst from your old three-dimensional shell and found yourself in what was apparently a new world.

"Actually, if I have followed your description accurately, it was simply an aspect of your eternal four-dimensional body, which has three linear dimensions and one 'time' dimension. The ordinary human being sees only three dimensions—the fourth, time, he senses intuitively as an extra dimension.

"But when he tries to imagine the shape of a thing extending through the time dimension, he finds that he has simply lost a space dimension. He imagines his body extending through time just as your body did during your experience. In this new world the three dimensions visible to you were two linear and one of time, which combined to give an appearance of regular three-dimensional solidity."

"You are saying," said Alar slowly and thoughtfully, "that I viewed my four-dimensional body through three new dimensions."

"Not three *new* dimensions. They were all old. Height and breadth were the same. The only apparently new dimension was time, substituting for depth. The cross section of your body simply extended with changing time until it became an endless pillar.

"And you stepped out of your pillar when the pain became unbearable. The difference in your ecstasy and that of the Greeks was that you didn't have to go back into time at the same moment—or place—that you left."

"John," said Alar with gloomy, almost exasperated surmise, "do you realize that I could have stepped back into time at a period prior to my amnesia? That I could have solved my personal mystery with utter ease? And now—I don't know how to get back, except perhaps through that unutterable hell of pain." His chest lifted in vast regret. "Well, then, John? About my other question—who am I?"

Haven looked toward Gaines.

"I think I'd better try to answer that one," interposed the Undersecretary. "But there isn't any answer, really. When you crawled up on the river bank five years ago you were clutching something in your hand—this." He gave Alar a small leather-bound book.

The Thief studied it curiously. It was water-stained, and the cover and pages had shriveled and warped during drying. The cover was stamped in gold:

T-22, Log.

He was breathing considerably faster when he sought Gaines's eyes. But the Undersecretary simply said, "Look inside."

Alar folded back the cover and read the first entry:

" 'July 21, 2177 . . . ' "

His eyes narrowed. "That's next week. There's an error in the date."

"Finish the entry," urged Haven.

" 'July 21, 2177. This will be my only statement, since I know where I am going and when I shall return. There is little now to be said and, as perhaps the last living human being, I have no inclination to say it. Within a few minutes the *T-22* will be traveling faster than light. Under more cheerful circumstances I should be exceedingly interested in following the incredible evolution that has already started in my companion.' "

That was all.

"The rest of the book is blank," said Haven shortly.

Alar ran nerveless fingers through his hair. "Are you saying that I'm the man who wrote that? That I was on the ship?"

"You may or may not have been on the ship. But we are certain you didn't make the log entry."

"Who did?"

"Kennicot Muir," said Gaines. "His handwriting is unmistakable."

13. VISITOR FROM THE STARS

Alar's eyes opened a trifle wider and fastened hawklike on the Space Undersecretary. "How," he asked, "can you be so sure I'm not Kennicot Muir?"

"He was a larger man. Furthermore, the fingerprints, eye capillaries, pupil chroma, blood type, age and dental and skeletal characteristics are different. We've considered the point very carefully, hoping to find points of identity. There aren't any. Whoever you are, you're not Kennicot Muir."

"And yet," Alar said, with a grimace which was almost a grin, "is that necessarily conclusive evidence?"

"Why—what do you mean?" Gaines was honestly puzzled. Haven's eyes had been almost completely closed in thought, now he opened them wide.

"It would appear," Alar said, "that the trip might have caused some very peculiar changes. Isn't it possible that, as Muir, my body was distorted? Enough so that I am a completely disguised Kennicot Muir? Disguised so well that I can't even recognize myself?"

Gaines's mouth opened and closed several times before he replied: "I think it's impossible."

"Perhaps not impossible," Haven said slowly, "but improbable, shall we say. As a theory, there is nothing to support it except that a lot of our puzzling questions could be glibly answered by it."

"Well, then," Alar continued, turning first from Gaines to Haven and then back to Gaines. "What about the Meganet Mind?"

"The Mind?" Gaines repeated, rubbing his chin. "You think Muir might be the Mind?"

"Yes, I think it's possible."

Gaines chuckled. "It would be a very, very fascinating development if it were true. Unfortunately it isn't. The only resemblance between the Mind and Muir is in the over-all size of their bodies. There have been investigations several times—that possibility has been discarded."

"Investigators can be bribed," Alar said. He stretched his fingers over the front ends of the arm rests of his chair, shifting his glance briefly to them and then back to the two older men. "Records can be destroyed or forged. Facts can be hidden."

"That may be true," Gaines said flatly. "But I know personally that the Meganet Mind existed long before Muir ever disappeared. Not as the Mind, *per se,* of course, but even then showing the potential of what he would eventually become."

Haven made a clicking noise with his pipe stem against his teeth. "The chances of you, Alar, being Muir," he said thoughtfully, "as small as they are, are still better than that of the Mind being Muir."

During this time Keiris had not taken her eyes from Alar's face.

The Thief sighed. "Well, then, that's that. But what about the date of the entry? July twenty-first, two thousand one hundred and seventy-seven is only a few days off. Since the book is at least five years old Muir must have made a blunder in the date."

"We don't know the answer," admitted Gaines. "We thought you might."

The Thief smiled humorlessly. He said:

"How could Muir return in the *T-twenty-two* before it was even built?"

The room slowly grew quiet. Nothing was audible except Keiris's suppressed jerky breathing. Alar felt a nerve throbbing restlessly in the small of his back. Haven pulled placidly at his pipe but his eyes missed nothing.

"The non-Aristotelians at their wildest never suggested that time could be traversed negatively unless—" Alar rubbed the side of his cheek in deep thought. The others waited.

"You said the pilot panel of the crashed ship indicated the possibility of speeds beyond the velocity of light?" he asked Gaines.

"So it seemed. The drive proved to be virtually identical with that designed for the *T-twenty-two.*"

"But by elementary Einsteinian mechanics transphotic velocities are impossible," remonstrated Alar. "Nothing can exceed the speed of light—theoretically, at least. The fact that I may have been aboard a ship similar to the *T-twenty-two* means nothing to me. In fact the very name *T-twenty-two* seems meaningless. Where did our *T-twenty-two* get its name?"

"Haze-Gaunt adopted the name on a suggestion from the Toynbeean Institute," replied Gaines. "It is simply an abbreviation of 'Toynbeean Civilization Number Twenty-two.' The great historian gave each civilization an index number. The Egyptaic was Number One, the Andean Number Two, the Sinic Number Three, the Minoan Number Four, and so on. Our present civilization, the Western, is Toynbee Number Twenty-one.

"The Toynbeeans secretly theorized that an interstellar ship might save Toynbee Twenty-one by launching us into a new culture—Toynbee Twenty-two—in the same way the sail launched the Minoan thalassocracy, the horse the nomadic cultures, and the stone road the Roman Empire. So *T-twenty-two* is more than just the name of a ship. It may prove the life-bridge, linking two destinies."

Alar nodded. "Quite plausible. There's no harm in hoping." But his thoughts were elsewhere. The *Phobos* that had brought Gaines was sunward bound. In the solarions would be men who had known Muir intimately. And then this question of negative time. How could a space ship land before it took off?

Keiris broke into his reverie. "Since we've come to a standstill on solving your identity," she suggested, "suppose you tell us the rest of your star plate discovery. In the Galactarium you said there was more to come."

"Very well, then," agreed Alar. He plunged abruptly into his theme. "Ever since the completion of Lunar Station, we have assumed that it would be just a question of time until we penetrated the whole of space and found our own galaxy at the opposite pole of the universe.

"That was predictable and my discovery simply bore out the prediction. But there were some other developments in that section of the sky that were not so easily predictable.

"Let us go back a bit. Five years ago, as any student of astronomy knows, a body of incalculable mass, apparently originating at a point in space near our own sun cluster, possibly quite near our own solar system, sped outward into space.

"It passed near the M Thirty-one galaxy, disrupted its outer edge with assorted novae and star collisions and then, apparently traveling at a speed greater than light, disappeared about eighteen billion light years out. By 'disappeared' I mean that astronomers were no longer able to detect its influence on galaxies near the line of hypothetical flight.

"The reason they couldn't was that they were no longer looking in the right direction. The body had passed the midpoint of the universe, with respect to its point of origin, and had begun to return. Naturally it was approaching in the opposite direction, which is of course the same direction in which the lunar reflector must be collimated to pick up our galaxy.

"In the six weeks that I have studied this sky-sector I have watched the effect of the unknown body on galaxies near its line of return and I have computed its path and velocity, with considerable accuracy. The velocity, incidentally, is decreasing very rapidly from its outer-space peak of two billion light years per year.

"Six weeks ago, when I first began my observations, it had almost completed its circuit of the universe and was returning to our own galaxy. Yesterday it passed so close to the Magellanic Clouds that its attraction drew them toward one another in what may be a collision course. In the Lesser Cloud I have already counted twenty-eight novae."

He concluded tersely. "This body will land on Earth on July twenty-first."

A hush fell over the group. The only sound for several minutes was the rasping from Haven's empty pipe.

"The queer thing," mused Gaines, "is its varying mass. The disruption of the stars of our own galaxy in Andromeda is an old story, as Alar said. But the Andromeda star cluster was acted upon by something traveling just below the speed of light and with a mass of some twenty million galaxies concentrated at one point.

"But by the time that body reached the M Thirty-one galaxy some three weeks later, its velocity was many times that of light and its mass was incalculable—possibly bordering on the infinite if such a thing is permissible. I have no doubt but that Alar found the same conditions obtaining for its return—a gradual diminution of velocity and mass until, by the time it reaches Earth, it again has very little mass or velocity, at least none capable of affecting this system. Alar has supplied the final piece in the jigsaw puzzle that has driven astronomers crazy for five years. And now the assembled puzzle is even more incomprehensible than its parts."

"You said this body will 'land' on the earth," said Haven. "You think then—"

"It will prove to be another intergalactic ship."

"But even the biggest lunar or solar freighters don't exceed a mass of ten thousand tons," objected Gaines. "The ship that crashed five years ago was really rather small. Even the largest interstellar ship couldn't possibly have a detectable gravitational effect on a planet, let alone on a whole galaxy."

"Objects traveling at trans-photic velocities—even though such velocities are theoretically impossible—would approach infinite mass," reminded Alar. "And don't forget, the mass of this object increased with increasing velocity. Its mass at rest is probably relatively small. But it needn't be large if its velocity is trans-photic. I suspect that a mere gram weight hurled past the M Thirty-one nebula at a velocity of several million c's would do damage comparable to our own hypothetical intergalactic ship."

"But no intergalactic ships were known in the solar system five years ago," protested Keiris, yawning sleepily. "And you said that it *left* our system five years ago and passed M Thirty-one at many times the velocity of light. Do you mean there are two intergalactic ships? One that arrived five years ago from parts unknown and a second one that left here five years ago and is due to return next week?"

Alar laughed harshly. "Insane, isn't it? Especially when there were no intergalactic or even interstellar ships in existence in the solar system five years ago."

"Maybe the Eastern Federation furnished it," suggested Haven. "I have a suspicion that Haze-Gaunt has consistently underestimated them."

"Not likely," said Gaines. "We know they've got a tremendous plutonium production network, but that's just talcum powder compared to muirium. And they'd have to have muirium for an interstellar drive and they don't have it—yet."

Alar began pacing the floor. Two intergalactic ships. One crashed five years ago and he must have been on it. Another was due to arrive on July 21—next week—bearing whom? Furthermore, on earth, the *T-twenty-two* was due to blast off in the early morning of July 21. Again—with whom?

By the river that bore him, that made *three* ships! He groaned and gnawed at his lip. It seemed that the answer was within his grasp, that it lay on the tip of his tongue. That if he solved this riddle he would know who he was. He knew Haven and Gaines were watching him covertly.

How strange that he, the apprentice, had grown so in stature within the past few weeks. And yet he had no sensation of development. It seemed that the others were growing dull, slow-witted. The genius, he knew, never appears particularly intelligent to himself.

He stopped and looked at the woman.

Keiris seemed to be asleep. Her head had fallen forward on her right shoulder, and her lock of gray hair had dropped over her right eye. Her face had assumed the same waxen pallor that had characterized her since her arrival at the observatory. Her chest rose and fell rhythmically under her enveloping cape.

As he stared at her closed and sunken eyes, the conviction seized him that he had seen her thus before—*dead*.

The Thief blinked. The hallucination was undoubtedly the result of overwork and sleeplessness. With his nervous system thus deranged he could endanger the lives of all of them.

"Gaines," he whispered, "your guard won't relieve the regular I.P. officer at the landing docks for another two hours. Let's all take a nap until then."

"I'll stand watch," volunteered Haven.

Alar smiled. "If they want to kill us, finding out about it in advance won't do us any good. I'll wake us up in plenty of time."

Haven patted a yawn. "All right."

Alar got down on the cold metal tiles just in front of Keiris's chair, forced his mind to become blank, and was instantly asleep.

After a quarter of an hour Keiris listened carefully to the steady breathing of her three companions, then opened her eyes and studied the man asleep at her feet. Her eyes soon came to rest on his upturned face.

It was a strange, unworldly face—yet attractive and gentle. A deep peace lay about the eyes. As she watched him, the lines in her own cheeks softened a little.

She crouched forward slowly, her moody, half-opened eyes fixed on the man's closed ones, and then got out of her chair entirely and stooped beside him.

She stiffened, then relaxed. Across the room Gaines mumbled fitfully and shifted in his chair.

Again she bent over the sleeping Thief until her eyes were but a few inches from his face. After a brooding pause, she eased back into the chair, slipped the sandal from her right foot with the toe of her left and flexed her toes luxuriously over the material of Alar's left sleeve. Her right foot reached hesitantly toward his hand, then quickly withdrew.

She took a deep breath and clenched her teeth, and the next instant her long toes, like fingers, were caressing the man's hand, barely touching the skin. She let her foot rest against the back part, across the knuckles and fingers, so much like an awkward hand gently holding his.

For a while she remained that way. Then she withdrew her foot and knelt forward. Her eyes, once more inches from his own closed ones, studied him. Satisfied that he was deeply asleep, she tilted her head and laid her cheek to his. She could feel the faint stubble of a new beard, the firm, angular cheekbone. Her spine tingled as his uncombed black hair brushed her forehead and pressed against her own. Her face was flushed and hot, and she had a curious feeling that time was standing still.

14. ESCAPE FROM THE MOON

Toward the end of the second hour Alar quickened his breathing. She drew herself back silently, thrust her foot into the sandal just before he opened his eyes and looked at her.

His eyes roved somberly over her body, which was completely hidden from throat to knees by her cape, then returned to her face. He said quietly, "You have no arms."

She turned her face away.

"I should have guessed. Was it Shey?"

"It was Shey. The Thief surgeons told me there wasn't enough left of them—that they had to amputate to save my life."

"Some remarkable prosthetics are available."

"I know. The thieves fitted me with computerized arms. I could never get used to them. I let them go. But it isn't too bad. I can wash my face, thread a needle, hold a knife—"

"You know that Thieves are not permitted to kill even in self-defense, Keiris?"

"I don't want you to kill Shey. It doesn't matter any more."

The Thief lay on the cold floor, his eyes soft and thoughtful. Then he pushed himself to his knees, reached out, grasped her around the waist gently and lowered her to the pillow beside him. She sat there, silently, feet tucked under, as he curled himself in front of her, close to her.

"Keiris," he said, keeping his hands at her waist. "It matters to me. It matters to me how you feel, whether you can be happy now." His face was near to hers and he caught that exasperatingly familiar scent which came from her. Again he wondered if he had known this still beautiful woman in his phantom past. Several times there had seemed to come from her the faintest hint of recognition.

She just stared at him. Not wild-eyed, but calmly, almost tenderly, as though she too sensed the bond between them and accepted it. The lines in her face had loosened and the increase of moisture in her large black eyes magnified the unfathomable emotion in them. Unrouged to the extent she usually was, yet there was a warm color in her face now.

"I don't know what it is," he said simply, "but I feel a kinship toward you. Something unexplainable." He felt her body tense beneath his hands.

"I know what you feel, my dear," she said. "And neither can I explain it. I have always loved Kim, I always shall love him. But I know that to love you too will not be disloyal." She turned her head sharply away and her hair swung softly against her neck.

Alar thought back into the vanished hours. He recalled how he had met this woman, and how they had gone to the great ball together, and how they had parted there. He relived that final terrible scene in his mind. Aloud, he mused: "You said I reminded you of someone you used to know. It was Kennicot Muir, wasn't it?"

"Yes."

"And yet I am not Muir. There's not the faintest resemblance."

She raised her head. She was not crying, though her eyes were sparklingly wet. "True," she said. "You are completely different from him—and yet I felt when we first met that I once before had seen your face, with those oh so intense dark eyes."

He took his hands from her waist and cupped them around her face.

"Keiris," he said, the name a caress on his lips, "one day, not so long from now, we will know who I am." He put his hands in his lap. "We must not give up until we find that day."

"We won't," she said.

Alar lay his head on her knees, hiding from her the hard concentration in his eyes.

He remained in that twisted position for many minutes, unable to relax.

At last the woman spoke, her cheek briefly stroking his ear. "Gaines's guard is probably on duty by now."

"Yes, I know." He got heavily to his feet and wakened the others.

Gaines rubbed his eyes and stretched. "The three of you will have to stay here a moment until I check out clearance with my man," he warned.

He stepped into the corridor, and the panel wound shut quietly behind him.

Alar was grateful for the delay. Ever since he had learned that the *Phobos* had docked, en route for the sun, he had been making calculations. Even now, despite the trauma wrought within him by what Shey had done to Keiris, his thoughts were sunward.

On the sun would be station masters who had served under Muir. If he could meet just one who knew Muir's whereabouts—just one who could explain why he, Alar, had been found with the Log of the *T-twenty-two* in Muir's handwriting . . .

On the other hand, a quasi-safety awaited him on Terra, under the protection of the Society. There he could pursue his personal mystery in relative peace and quiet. And there he could be with Keiris, who really needed him now.

"Gaines ought to have been back before now," he said to Haven shortly. "Something may have gone wrong with his plan. I'd better reconnoiter."

Haven shook his head. "No, boy. I'll go."

Apparently Haven still viewed him as nonexpendable. On the other hand he knew from his past experience with danger that he would be more likely to come back alive than Haven.

"You'd better stay with the girl," urged the biologist persuasively.

Against his better judgment Alar let the older man through the panel and watched him as he walked slowly up the corridor. At the first intersection Haven turned left toward the passenger docks. His head jerked once, and, leaning awkwardly against the intersection corner, he tried to turn around. Then he slumped to the floor.

Keiris watched Alar's body grow rigid. "What's wrong?" she whispered tensely.

The Thief turned an ashen face to her. "He has just been killed with a poison dart." Stricken eyes looked into hers and beyond. He had to breathe several times before he could speak again. "You stay here. I'm going out there."

But she followed him closely as he stepped through the panel, and he knew it was futile to insist that she remain. Together they walked slowly up the corridor.

The Thief could not take his eyes from the sprawling body of the man who had walked into death—for him. He could not think but knew he must think, and quickly.

He paused a few feet before the intersection and looked at the face of his dead friend. It was a craggy, noble face, almost beautiful now in its final peace.

While he gazed, the misty stupor that numbed his mind evaporated and he had a plan. He licked his lips and cleared his throat. His scheme required that the killers show themselves, but to lure them out he would have to expose himself in the intersection, with the probability that they would shoot first and ask questions later. It was a risk he had to run.

"I am unarmed," he called. "I wish to surrender."

The military heart, he knew, longed for recognition. The capture of a man who had eluded even the great Thurmond might bring a transfer to Terra and rapid promotion. He hoped an imaginative officer was in charge of the detail.

He stepped into the intersection.

Nothing happened.

Around the corner he could see Gaines's body sprawled out lifeless. A wicked metal sliver protruded from his neck. His bribed guard had evidently been discovered.

"Put your hands up, Alar—slowly," said a tense voice behind him. "You too, sister."

"I will do so, but madame has no arms and cannot raise her hands," said Alar, concealing the rising excitement in his voice. Arms high, he turned slowly and saw a young I.P. officer covering him with a snub-nosed gun, apparently powered by compressed air, or by a mechanically wound spring, to give a muzzle velocity of a hundred or so meters a second—just slow enough to penetrate Thief armor.

"You're right," said the officer grimly, noting Alar's rapid survey of the weapon. "It's not accurate beyond fifty yards, but its poison darts kill faster than bullets. Fourteen of these guns are covering you from peepholes at this instant." He pulled a pair of handcuffs from his pocket and approached the two cautiously.

The icy exterior of the Thief's face concealed a frantically racing mind. Both eyes were focused on the radioreceptor button on the guard's right shoulder, directly below the ear, that connected all guard personnel with the central police room. Alar's eyes were growing beady and feverish but nothing was happening.

He knew he was capable of emitting photic beams in the infra-red with a wave length of at least half a millimeter. The U.H.F. intercom band certainly shouldn't exceed a meter. Yet his eyes were pouring out the electromagnetic spectrum from a few Angstroms to several meters, without raising a squeak in the receptor button.

Something had gone wrong. He was aware of Keiris's body shivering near his side.

In another instant the I.P. would step around to slap the handcuffs on him from behind, and he would lose precious visual contact with the receptor disc.

A bead of perspiration slid down Alar's cheek and dangled at his stubbled chin.

"A.M." said Keiris quietly.

Of course! Amplitude modulation, unheard of since the earliest days of radio, could be used here, where there was virtually no static.

Suddenly the button whistled. The officer stopped uncertainly.

"Instructions for Gate Eleven," intoned the receptor button. "It has been decided to permit the Alar group to 'escape' in their ship. No further attempt shall be made to kill or capture members of the party. End."

Although modified by the liaison neural network that integrated his larynx, optic lobe and retina, further disguised by the imperfections of the one-inch speaker cone on the officer's shoulder, it seemed to Alar that the other could not fail to recognize the voice of the man he was about to manacle.

"You heard Center, mister," said the officer harshly. "Get going. Carry this stiff with you; I'll have the other sent out." His face was knotted in a hard smile. Quite evidently he expected the great lunar guns to open up on the tiny craft immediately after it had blasted off.

The Thief knelt without a word and gently gathered Haven's body into his arms. The body of the older man seemed curiously shriveled and small. Only now did Alar realize what stature the bare fact of being alive contributed to flesh and bone.

Keiris led the way and opened the panels for them. The little spacer was just ahead. To one side of it lay a larger freighter, the *Phobos*. Someone was on the landing platform and calling into the sunbound ship. "No word yet. We'll give him three minutes."

Alar's heart skipped a beat. Slowly he climbed the ramp to the Thief spacer, stooping as he entered.

His lifeless burden he placed on one of the rear bunks.

A puffing guard dragged Gaines in behind him, left the body on the cabin floor and departed without a word.

Alar looked up pensively, and after a few seconds realized that he was gazing into Keiris's somber eyes.

"My hypothesis was wrong," he said.

"You mean about the two—or was it three—intergalactic ships?"

"Yes. I said that one left the earth five years ago, crossed the universe and is due to return in a few days—on July twenty-first."

She waited.

"It can't be returning," said Alar, still seeming to stare through her, "because it hasn't left yet."

The cabin was utterly silent.

"To travel at a velocity greater than light," continued the Thief, "*seems to require that the Einsteinian equation for the equivalence of mass and energy be overthrown. But the conflict is only apparent. The mass of a Newtonian body may be restated in terms of an Einsteinian body through a correction factor thus*—"

He wrote the formula on a bulkhead with a pencil:

$$\frac{mc}{\sqrt{c^2 - v^2}} = M$$

"Here c is the velocity of light, v the velocity of the moving body, m is Newtonian mass and M is Einsteinian mass. As v increases, of course, M must grow. As v approaches c, M approaches infinity. Heretofore we have considered a limiting velocity. Yet it can't be, because something— my hypothetical intergalactic ship—has crossed the universe in only five years, less than one-billionth the time required by light. So v *can* be greater than c.

"But when v is greater than c, it would seem that Einsteinian mass M must be meaningless, involving as it does the square root of a negative number. But such a conclusion is inconsistent with the observed effect of the ship on galactic matter during the whole of its flight.

"Now the alternative to meaningless M is negative v, which would make v-square positive, and the equation then follows the usual pattern for the determination of M. But v is simply a ratio of distance to time. Distance is a positive scalar quantity, but time can be either positive or negative, depending on whether it stretches into the future or the past."

He looked at her in triumph. "What I'm saying is, that it is a necessary and sufficient condition for trans-photic velocities that the ship move backward in time."

"Then," she said wonderingly, "a ship traveling faster than the speed of light would land before it ever blasted off. So there never were three or even two ships *but only one.* The ship that brought you to earth five years ago—"

"Really is the *T-twenty-two,* which won't be launched until July twenty-first."

The woman leaned dizzily against the curving cabin wall.

Alar continued with bitter amusement. "Do I hop into the *T-twenty-two* next week for a five-year cruise backward in time? Is the original unwitting Alar walking the earth at this moment, planning on the same thing? Will he take the original of that little ape of Haze-Gaunt's as a mascot?" He laughed unsteadily. "Why, it's the damnedest thing I ever—" He broke off abruptly. "I'm not returning to Earth with you."

"I know. I'm sorry."

Alar blinked. "You mean, you knew just now, after I told you."

"No. The *Phobos* is en route to the sun. You think you'll be able to find some of my husband's old friends who can tell you something about yourself. The Meganet Mind said you'd try to go if the opportunity arose."

"He did?"

"He further stated that you'd discover your identity there."

"Ah!" The Thief's eyes flamed up. "Why didn't you tell me before?"

The woman studied the floor. "Life in a solarion is dangerous."

His laughter was soft, brittle. "Since when has danger been a determining factor with either of us? What's the real reason for holding back?"

She turned up her quiet eyes to his. "Because when you learn about yourself, the information will be useless. The Mind said that *in the act of dying,* you would remember everything." She studied his face anxiously. "If you want to die, why not return to the Society and do it profitably?

Does it really matter who you were five years ago?" Color was flooding into her face.

"I said that we must not give up until we know who I really am," he replied quietly. The Mind's prediction was a shock to him. This was a factor he had never expected.

"But surely," she pleaded, "you don't want to throw your life away to do it?"

"I don't plan to throw it away. You know that."

"Forgive me," she said and shut her eyes tight for a moment as though to control herself. "I must argue with you because of what you said to me back on the floor not so many minutes ago. I thought, perhaps, that my words now might mean something to you."

"But they do, Keiris," he said emphatically.

"But not enough."

Alar sighed. He was at a crossroads now, he knew, and what direction he took no longer concerned him alone. Keiris must be affected by his decision. He regretted nothing he had said to her at that moment when he had allowed the recognition of her mutilation to unseal his lips and reveal his emotions. But by so doing he had given her a claim on him. He was proud of the claim—yet he must bear the consequences.

"Keiris," he said, "I'm not indifferent to your feelings. I would much rather stay with you."

"Then stay."

"You know I can't. I've faced death before. That can't deter me. If I stayed, something important within me would be lost."

"But this time you are forewarned."

"Even if the Mind's prophecy means this specific trip, we can't be certain it will happen. The Mind is not infallible."

"But he is, Alar! He is!"

For the first time within his remembered life Alar found it impossible to make a quick decision. Recovering his past at the cost of his future would be a poor bargain. Perhaps it would be better to return with Keiris and spend a longer, more useful life as a Thief.

He took her by the shoulders. "Goodbye, Keiris."

She turned her head away. "Captain Andrews of the *Phobos* is waiting for Dr. Talbot, of the Toynbeean Institute. Remember Talbot at the ball? He's a Thief and has orders from the Mind to let you go in his place."

Free will!

For a moment it seemed to him that every man in the solar system was just a pawn on the Mind's horizonless chessboard. "You have a stage goatee for me, of course? Like Talbot's?" he asked blandly.

"You'll find it in an envelope in my coat pocket, along with his passport, stateroom key, and tickets. You'd better fix it on now."

The situation was here. It just had to be accepted. He fished the envelope out quickly, patted the beard in place, then hesitated.

"Don't bother about me," Keiris assured him. "I can jet the ship back without trouble. I'm going to bury—them—in deep space. Then I'm going on in to Earth to check on something at the central morgue."

He was only half listening. "Keiris, if you were only the wife of a man other than Kennicot Muir—or if I thought he were dead—"

"Don't miss the *Phobos.*"

He gave her one last remembering look, then turned silently and vanished down the hatchway. She heard the space lock spin shut.

"Goodbye, darling," she whispered, knowing that she would never see him alive again.

15. HOTSPOT MADNESS

"Ever been on the sun before, Dr. Talbot?" Captain Andrews appraised the new passenger curiously. They were together in the observation room of the *Phobos.*

Alar could not admit that everything on the run from Luna to Mercury (which planet they had left an hour ago) had seemed tantalizingly familiar, as though he had made the trip not once but a hundred times. Nor could he admit that astrophysics was his profession. A certain amount of celestial ignorance would be forgiven—indeed required—in a historian.

"No," said the Thief. "This is my first trip."

"I thought perhaps I'd brought you out before. Your face seems vaguely familiar."

"Do you think so, Captain? I travel quite a bit on Earth. At a Toynbeean lecture possibly?"

"No. Never go to them. It would have to be somewhere along the solar run or nothing. Imagination, I guess."

Alar writhed inwardly. How far could he push his questioning without arousing suspicion? He stroked his false goatee with nervous impatience.

"As a newcomer," continued Captain Andrews, "you might be interested in how we pick up a solarion." He pointed to a circular fluorescent plate in the control panel. "That gives us a running picture of the solar surface in terms of the H line of calcium Two—ionized calcium, that is.

"It shows where the solar prominences and faculae are because they carry a lot of calcium. You can't see any prominences on the plate here—

they're only visible when they're on the limb of the sun, spouting up against black space. But here are plenty of faculae, these gassy little puffs floating above the photosphere—they can be detected almost to the center of the sun's disc. Hot but harmless."

He tapped the glass with his space-nav parallels. "And the place is swarming with granules—'solar thunderheads' might be a better name. They bubble up several hundred miles in five minutes and then vanish. If one of them ever caught the *Phobos* . . ."

"I had a cousin, Robert Talbot, who was lost on one of the early solar freighters," said Alar casually. "They always thought a solar storm must have got the ship."

"Very likely. We lost quite a few ships before we learned the proper approach. Your cousin, eh? Probably it was he I was thinking of, though I can't say the name is familiar."

"It was some years ago," said Alar, watching Andrews from the corner of his eye, "when Kennicot Muir was still running the stations."

"Hmm. Don't recall him." Captain Andrews returned noncommittally to the plate. "You probably know that the stations work at the edges of a sunspot, in what we call the penumbra. That procedure has several advantages.

"It's a little cooler than the rest of the chromosphere, which is easier on the solarion refrigerating system and the men, and the spot also provides a landmark for incoming freighters. It would be just about impossible to find a station unless it were on a spot. It's hard enough to locate one on the temperature contour."

"Temperature contour?"

"Yes—like a thirty-fathom line on a seacoast. Only here it's the five-thousand line. In a few minutes, when we're about to land, I'll throw the jets over on automatic spectrographic steering and the *Phobos* will nose along the five-thousand-degree Kelvin contour until she finds Solarion Nine."

"I see. If a station ever lost its lateral jets and couldn't stay on the five-thousand line, how would you find it?"

"I wouldn't," said Captain Andrews curtly. "Whenever a station turns up missing, we always send out all our search boats—several hundred of them—and work a search pattern around that sunspot for months. But we know before we start that we won't find anything. We never have. It's futile to look on the surface for a station that has been long volatilized deep at the vortex of a sunspot.

"The stations are under automatic spectrographic controls, of course, and the spec is supposed to keep them on the five-thousand line, but sometimes something goes wrong with the spec or an unusually hot Wilson gas swirl spills out over the edge of the spot and fools the spec into thinking the station is standing way out from the spot, say on the hotter five-thousand-four-hundred line.

"So the automatic spec control moves the station farther in toward the spot, maybe into the slippery Evershed zone at its very lip. From there the station can slide on into the umbra. I know of one ship that crawled out of the Evershed. Its crew had to be replaced in toto. But no solarion ever came out of the umbra. So you can't rely entirely on the spec control.

"Every station carries three solar meteorologists, too, and the weather staff issues a bulletin every quarter-hour on the station's most probable position and on any disturbances moving their way. Sometimes they have to jump fast and in the right direction.

"And even the finest sunmen can't foresee everything. Four years ago the Three, Four and Eight were working a big 'leader'—spots are like poles in a magnet—always go in pairs, and we call the eastern spot the 'leader,' the western one the 'follower'—when the Mercury observatory noticed the leader was rapidly growing smaller.

"By the time it occurred to the observatory what was happening, the spot had shrunk to the size of Connecticut County. The patrol ship they sent to take off the crews got there too late. The spot had vanished. They figured the stations would try to make it to the 'follower' and settle somewhere in its five-thousand line.

"The Eight did—barely. Luckily, it had been working the uppermost region of the leader and, when the spot vanished from beneath it, it had to drift down toward the solar equator. But while it was drifting it was also crawling back toward the follower with its lateral jets and it finally caught the follower's southern tip."

"What about the other two stations?" said Alar.

"No trace."

The Thief shrugged mental shoulders. A berth in a solarion wasn't exactly like retiring on the green benches of La Paz. He had never had any illusions about that. Perhaps the Mind had considered the possibilities of his survival in a solarion purely on cold statistics.

The captain moved away from the fluorescent plate toward a metal cabinet bolted to the far wall. He turned his head, spoke over his shoulder. "A glass of foam, doctor?"

Alar nodded. "Yes, thank you."

The captain unsnapped the door, fished in the shelves, withdrew a plastic bottle with one hand. With his other hand he found two aluminum cups.

"Sorry I can't offer you wine," the captain said, coming back across the cabin and setting the bottle and cups down on a small circular table. "This foam doesn't have any kick to it, but it's cold and that's plenty welcome in a place like this." His tone was faintly ironic. He poured out two drinks by squeezing the bottle, ejecting the liquid in a creamy ribbon that settled slowly in the cups. Then he took the bottle back to the refrigerated cabinet. The door slammed shut under a swipe from a huge hand.

Alar raised his cup and tasted the beverage. It had a sharp lemon taste, cold and spicy.

The Thief said, "It's delicious." He wasn't certain, but he seemed to have remembered tasting it before. That could have been just a similarity to one of the more common refreshments he'd had during the past five years. Then again, it might have been for another reason . . .

The captain smacked his lips. "I've unlimited quantities of it, I drink it often and I never tire of it." He looked into the cup. "I've got boxes of it in my quarters. Little dehydrated pills. When a bottle's empty, I just drop in a pill, squirt in some drinking water and let it get cold. Then," he snapped his fingers, "I've got a new supply." He was as much in earnest speaking of his foam as he had been in describing the operation of the solarions.

"I assume you've briefed yourself on the history of our stations," Captain Andrews said abruptly. He indicated a tubular chair for Alar, kicked another one over to the table for himself.

"Yes, I have, Captain."

"Good."

Alar recognized an undertone behind the succinctness of the question and the comment. Sunmen didn't relive the past. The past was too morbid. Of the twenty-seven costly solarions, towed one by one to the sun during the past ten years, sixteen remained. The average life of a station was about a year. The staff was rotated continuously, each man, after long and arduous training, being assigned a post for sixty days—three times the twenty-day synodic period of rotation of the sun with respect to the eighty-eight-day sidereal period of Mercury.

The captain finished his drink and took Alar's empty cup. "I'll clean them later," he said as he put one inside the other and replaced them in the cabinet. He resumed his seat again, heavily, and asked, "Have you met the replacements?"

"Not yet," Alar said. When the Mercury observatory reached opposition with a given solar station, as it did every twenty days, a freighter carried in replacements for one-third of the staff and took away the oldest one-third along with a priceless cargo of muirium. The *Phobos*, he knew, was bringing in eleven replacements, but so far they had confined themselves closely to their own quarter of the ship, and he had been unable to meet any of them.

Captain Andrews had apparently dismissed the problem of Alar's pseudo-familiarity, and the Thief could think of no immediate way to return to the subject. For the time being he would have to continue to be Dr. Talbot, the historian, ignorant of things solar.

"Why," he asked, "if the stations are in such continual danger, aren't they equipped with full space drives, instead of weak lateral jets? Then, if the station skidded into a spot beyond the present recovery point, she could simply blast free."

Andrews shook his head. "Members of parliament have been elected and deposed on that very issue. But it has to be the way it is now when you consider the cost of the solarion. It's really just a vast synthesizer for making muirium with a little bubble of space in the middle for living quarters and a few weak lateral jets on the periphery.

"A space ship is all converter, with a little bubble here amidships for the crew. To make a space ship out of a solarion you'd have to build it about two hundred times the present solarion size, so that the already tremendous solarion would be just a little bubble in an unimaginably enormous space ship.

"'There's always a lot of talk about making the stations safe, but that's the only way to do it and it costs too much money. So the Spaceways Ministers rise and fall, but the stations never change. Incidentally, on the cost of these things, I understand that about one-fourth of the annual Imperium budget goes into making one solarion."

The intercom buzzed. Andrews excused himself, answered it briefly, then replaced the instrument. "Doctor?" The officer seemed strangely troubled.

"Yes, captain?" His heart held no warning beat, but it was impossible not to realize that something unusual and serious was in store.

Andrews hesitated a moment as though he were about to speak. Then he lifted his shoulders helplessly. "As you know, I'm carrying a relief crew to Nine—your destination. You haven't met any of them before because they keep pretty much to themselves. They would like to see you in the mess—now."

It was clear to Alar that the man wanted to say more, perhaps give him a word of warning.

"Why do they want to see me?" he asked bluntly.

Andrews was equally curt. "They'll explain." He cleared his throat and avoided Alar's arched eyebrows. "You aren't superstitious, are you?"

"I think not. Why do you ask?"

"I just wondered. It's best not to be superstitious. We'll land in a few minutes, and I'm going to be pretty busy. The catwalk on the left will take you to the mess."

The Thief frowned, stroked his false goatee, then turned and walked toward the exit panel.

"Oh, doctor," called Andrews.

"Yes, captain?"

"Just in case I don't see you again I've discovered whom you remind me of."

"Who?"

"This man was taller, heavier and older than you, and his hair was auburn while yours is black. And he's dead, anyway, so really there's no point in mentioning—"

"Kennicot Muir?"

"Yes." Andrews looked after him rather meditatively.

Always Muir! If the man were alive and could be found, what an inquisition he would face! Alar's footsteps clanged in hollow frustration as he strode across the catwalk over an empty decontaminated muirium hold.

Muir must certainly have been on the *T-22* when it crashed at the end of its weird journey backward in time; the log book was evidence of that. But he, Alar, had crawled out of the river carrying the book. What had happened to Muir? Had he gone down with the ship? Alar chewed his lower lip in exasperation.

There was a more immediate question—what did the relief crew want with him? He welcomed the chance to meet them, but he wanted to be the one to ask questions. He felt off-balance.

What if one of the crew had known the true Dr. Talbot? And, of course, any of the eleven might be an I.P. in occupational disguise, warned to be on the lookout for him. Or perhaps they didn't want him along on general principles. After all, he was an uninvited outsider who might disturb the smooth teamwork so necessary to their hourly survival.

Or possibly they had invited him in for a little hazing, which he understood was actually encouraged by the station psychiatrist for the relief of tension in new men, so long as it was done and over before they came on station.

As he left the catwalk for the narrow corridor, he heard music and laughter ahead.

He smiled. A party. He remembered now that the incoming shift always gave themselves a farewell party, the main features of which were mournful, interminable and nonprintable ballads, mostly concerning why they had left Terra to take up their present existence—new and unexpurgated holographic movies of dancing girls clothed mainly with varihued light (personal gift of the Minister for Space), pretzels and beer.

Only beer, because they had to check into the station cold sober. Two months later, if their luck held, they'd throw another party on the *Phobos*, and the *Phobos* crew would join in. Even the staid, blunt Andrews would upend a couple of big ones in toasting their safe return.

But not now. The outgoing festivities were strictly private—for sunmen only. No strangers were ever invited. Even an incoming station psychiatrist was excluded.

What then? Something was wrong.

As he stood poised to knock on the door, he found himself counting his pulse. It throbbed at one hundred fifty and was climbing.

16. The Eskimo and the Sunmen

Alar stood at the door, counting out the rapid rise of his pulse, considering what he might have to face on the other side. His knuckled hand dropped in an instinctive motion toward a non-existent saber pommel. Weapons were forbidden on the *Phobos*. But what danger could there be in such self-commiserating good fellowship? Still, suppose they tried a little horseplay and yanked at his false beard? While he hesitated, the music and laughter died away.

Then the ship lurched awkwardly, and he was thrown against the door. The *Phobos* had nosed into Solarion Nine and was sealing herself to the entry ports. A wild cheer from within the mess rose above his crash against the door.

Whether they hailed the survival of the station or their own imminent departure he could not be sure. There was something mocking and sardonic about the ovation that led him to suspect the latter. Let the old shift do their own cheering.

"Come in!" boomed someone.

He pushed the door aside and walked in.

Ten faces looked at him expectantly. Two of the younger men were sitting by the holograph, but the translucent cube that contained the tridi image was dark. It had evidently just been turned off.

Two men were returning from a table laden with a beer keg, several large wooden pretzel bowls, beer mugs, napkins, ash trays and other bric-a-brac, and were headed toward the dining table nearest the Thief. At the table, six men were in the act of rising. The missing eleventh face was probably the psychiatrist—absent by mutual understanding and consent.

The party was over, he sensed uneasily. This was something different.

"Dr. Talbot," said the large florid man with the booming voice, "I'm Miles, incoming station master for the Nine."

Alar nodded silently.

"And this is my meteorologist, Williams—MacDougall, lateral jet pilot—Florez, spectroscopist—Saint Claire, production engineer. . . ."

The Thief acknowledged the introductions gravely but noncommittally, down to young Martinez, clerk. His eyes missed nothing. These men were all repeaters. At some time in the past they had all oozed cold sweat in a solar station, probably most of them at different times and in different stations. But the common experience had branded them, welded them together and cast them beyond the pale of their earthbound brothers.

The twenty eyes had never left his face. What did they expect of him?

He folded his hands inconspicuously and counted his pulse. It had leveled off at one-sixty.

Miles resumed his rumble: "Dr. Talbot, we understand that you are going to be with us for twenty days."

Alar almost smiled. Miles, as a highly skilled and unconsciously snobbish sunman of long experience, held in profound contempt any unit of time less than a full and dangerous sixty days' shift.

"I have requested the privilege," returned the Thief gravely. "I hope you haven't decided that I'll be in the way."

"Not at all."

"The Toynbcean Institute has long been anxious to have a professional historian prepare a monograph—"

"Oh, we don't care *why* you're coming, Dr. Talbot. And don't worry about getting in our way. You look as though you have sense enough to stay clear when we're busy and you'll be worth your weight in unitas if you can keep the psych happily occupied and out of our laps. You play chess, I hope? This psych we have is an eskimo."

He couldn't remember having heard the term "Eskimo" applied to a sunman before, and he was astonished that he understood its meaning, which seemed to spring to mind unbidden, as though from the mental chamber that contained his other life. He had made no mistake in deciding to board the *Phobos*. But for the moment he must pretend ignorance.

"Chess—Eskimo?" he murmured with puzzled politeness.

Several of the men smiled.

"Sure, Eskimo," boomed Miles impatiently. "Never been in a solarion before. Has the sweat he was born with. Probably fresh out of school and loaded down with chess sets to keep our minds occupied so we won't brood." He laughed suddenly, harshly. "So we won't brood! Great flaming faculae! Why do they think we keep coming back here?"

Alar realized that the hair was crawling on his neck and that his armpits were wet. And he knew now what common brand had marked these lost souls and joined them into an outré brotherhood.

As the real Talbot had surmised that night at the ball, *every one of these creatures was stark mad!*

"I'll try to keep the psych occupied," he agreed with plausible dubiousness. "I rather like a game of chess myself."

"Chess!" murmured Florez, the spectroscopist, with dispassionate finality, turning from Alar to stare wearily at the table. His complete absence of venom did not mute his meaning.

Miles laughed again and fixed Alar with bloodshot eyes. "But we didn't invite you here simply to ask you to get the psych out of our hair. The fact is, all ten of us are Indians—old sunmen. And that's unusual. Generally we have at least one Eskimo in the bunch."

The big man's hand flashed into his pocket and two dice clattered along the table toward the Thief. There was a sharp intake of breath somewhere down the table. Alar thought it was Martinez, the young clerk. Everyone pressed slowly on either side of the table toward their guest and the white cubes that lay before him.

"Will you please pick them up, Dr. Talbot?" demanded Miles.

Alar hesitated. What would the action commit him to?

"Go on," Martinez said, impatient and eager. "Go on, sir."

The Thief studied the dice. A little worn, perhaps, but completely ordinary. He reached out slowly, gathered them into his right hand. He raised his hand and opened his fingers so that they rested side by side on his palm almost under Miles's nose.

"Well?"

"Ah," Miles said. "And now I suppose I should inform you of the significance of what you'll soon do for us."

"I'm very interested," Alar replied. He wondered at the form the ritual was about to take. That it was a ritual of immense import to the men he did not doubt.

"When we have a genuine Eskimo, Dr. Talbot, we ask him to throw the dice."

"You have your choice, then? I believe the psychiatrist would qualify, wouldn't he?"

"Huh," grunted the incoming station master. "Sure, the psych's an Eskimo, but all psychs are poison."

"I see." Alar closed his fist over the cubes.

"Martinez could do the honors, too, for that matter. Martinez has served only two shifts and he hasn't really crowded his luck too far to disqualify him. But we don't want to use him if we can help it."

"So logically I'm it."

"Right. The rest of us are no good. Florez is next lowest with five shifts. This would be his sixth—utterly impossible, of course. And so on up to me, with full ten years' service. I'm the Jonah. I can't roll 'em. That leaves you. You're not really an Eskimo—you'll be with us only twenty days—

but several of us old timers have decided it'll be legal because you resemble an old friend."

Muir, of course. It was fantastic. The Thief aroused himself as though from a heavy dream. The dice felt cold and weightless in his numbing fist. And his heart beat was climbing again.

He cleared his throat. "May I ask what happens after I roll the dice?"

"Nothing—immediately," replied Miles. "We just file out, grab our gear, and walk up the ramp into the station."

It couldn't be that simple. Martinez's mouth was hanging open as though his life depended on this. Florez was hardly breathing. And so on around the table. Even Miles seemed more flushed than when Alar had entered the room.

He thought furiously. Was it a gamble involving some tremendous sum that he was deciding? The sunmen were bountifully paid. Perhaps they had pooled their earnings and he was to decide the winner.

"Will you hurry yourself, *por favor*, Dr. Talbot?" said Martinez faintly.

This was something bigger than money. Alar rattled the dice loosely in his hand and let them go.

And in the act a belated warning seemed to bubble up from his fogged preamnesic life. He clawed futilely at the cubes but it was too late. A three and a four. He had just condemned a solarion crew—and himself—to death.

Alar exchanged glances with Martinez, who had suddenly become very pale.

A solarion dies once a twelvemonth, so a sunman on a two-month shift has one chance in six of dying with it. Florez couldn't make the throw because this would be his sixth shift, and by the laws of chance, his time was up.

One in six—these madmen were positive that a roll of the dice could predict a weary return to Terra—or a vaporous grave on the sun.

One chance in six. There had been one chance in six of throwing a seven. His throw would kill these incredible fanatics just as surely as if he cut them down with a Kades. These ten would walk into the solarion knowing that they would die, and sooner or later one of them would subconsciously commit the fatal error that would send the station plunging down into the sunspot vortex, or adrift on the uncharted, unfathomable photosphere. And he would be along.

It seemed that everyone, for a queer unearthly hiatus, had stopped breathing. Martinez was moving pallid lips, but no sound was coming out.

Indeed, no one said anything at all. There was nothing to say.

Miles thoughtfully thrust an enormous black cigar into his mouth, pushed his chair back to the table, and walked slowly from the room without a backward glance. The others followed, one by one.

Alar waited a full five minutes after the footsteps had died away toward the ramp that led up into Solarion Nine, full of wonder both at his stupidity and at the two tantalizing flashes from his other life.

His death was certain if he followed them into the solarion. But he couldn't hang back now. He recalled the Mind's prediction. It had been a calculated risk.

His main regret was that he was now *persona non grata* to the crew. It would be a long time before he learned anything from these fanatics—probably not before one of them destroyed the station. But it couldn't have been helped.

He stepped into the corridor, looked toward the ramp a dozen yards away and sucked in his breath sharply. Four I.P.'s favored him with stony stares, then, as one man, drew their sabers.

Then a horrid, unforgettable giggle bit at his unbelieving left ear.

"A small solar system, eh, Thief?"

17. REUNION NEAR SOL

"Visitors are not allowed in this portion of the morgue, madame. There's nothing here but unclaimed bodies." The gray-clad slave attendant barring her way bowed unctuously but firmly.

The only sign of Keiris's impatience was a faint dilation of the nostrils. "There are one thousand unitas in this envelope," she said quietly, indicating the packet fastened beneath her cape clasp. "I will need only thirty seconds within the cubicle. Unlock the door."

The slave eyed the envelope hungrily and swallowed nervously. His eyes studied the hall behind the woman.

"A thousand unitas isn't much. If I got caught, it would mean my life."

"It's all I have." She noted with alarm the man's growing firmness.

"Then you can't go in." He folded his arms before his chest.

"Do you want your freedom?" demanded Keiris abruptly. "I can tell you how to get it. You need only take me alive. I am Madame Haze-Gaunt."

The slave gaped at her.

She continued swiftly. "The chancellor has offered a billion-unita reward for my capture. Enough," she added caustically, "to buy your freedom and set yourself up as a great slave-holder. All you have to do is lock me in the cubicle behind you and notify the police."

Was it worth this to her? A few moments would tell.

"But don't cry out before you let me into the room," she warned quietly. "If you do, I have a knife with which I will kill myself. Then you will not get the billion unitas. Instead, they will kill you."

The attendant gasped something incomprehensible. At last his trembling fingers got the keys from his pocket. After several false tries, he finally succeeded in unlocking the door.

Keiris stepped inside quickly. The door locked behind her. She looked about her quickly. The tiny room, like the thousands of others on this level, contained but one thing—a cheap transparent plastic casket resting on a waist-high wooden platform.

A strange feeling came over Keiris. It seemed to her that her whole life revolved around what she would learn in the next few seconds. Even the Mind, for all his detailing scrutiny, had probably never thought of checking the morgue. After all, the *T-22* Log mentioned only two living things, both of which had been identified as Alar and Haze-Gaunt's ape-creature.

For the moment she avoided looking at what was inside, but instead read the printed and framed legend resting on the upper surface:

> Unidentified and unclaimed. Recovered by Imperial
> River Police from the Ohio River near Wheeling on
> July 21, 2172.

Would it be Kim?
Finally Keiris forced herself to look into the casket.
It was not Kim.
It was a woman. The body was loosely clad from toes to breasts in thin mortuary gauze. The face was pale and thin and the translucent skin was drawn tightly over the rather high cheekbones. The long hair was black except for a broad white streak streaming from the forehead.

A key was turning in the lock behind her. Let them come.
The door burst open. Someone, in the ungrammatical terseness of the well-trained I.P., said, "It's her."

She had time for only one more look at the corpse, one more look at its armless shoulders, one more look at the knife buried in its heart—a knife identical to the one she now carried in the sheath on her left thigh.

The meaning of the four guards at the ramp was now only too clear to the Thief. Shey had put them there. Others were undoubtedly behind him.

Shey, then, must be Miles's "Eskimo psych"—and with animal cunning the little man had been waiting for Alar on the *Phobos* ever since its arrival on the moon.

But instead of feeling trapped the Thief felt only elated. At least, before he died, he would have an opportunity to punish Shey.

Shey's present precautions would certainly have been enough to recapture an ordinary fugitive, but the same was true of the other traps that had been laid for Alar. The wolf pack was still proceeding on the assumption that methods applicable to human beings, enlarged and elaborated perhaps, were equally applicable to him. He believed now that their premise was wrong.

The image of Keiris's preternatural slenderness flashed before him. Yes, the time had come to punish Shey. His oath as a Thief prevented his killing the psychologist, but justice permitted other remedies, which could best be administered aboard the solarion. His pursuer had doubtless expected to capture him here and almost certainly had no intention of risking that august hide in a solarion. That was about to be changed.

He turned slowly, bracing himself mentally for the photic blast to come.

"Do you see this finger, Shey?" He held his right forefinger erect midway on the line joining his eyes with the psychologist's.

By pure reflex action Shey's pupils focused on the finger. Then his neck jerked imperceptibly as a narrow 'x' of blue-white light exploded from Alar's eyes into his.

The next five seconds would tell whether the Thief's gambling attempt at hypnosis by overstimulation of the other's optical sensorium had been successful.

"I am Dr. Talbot of the Toynbeean Institute," he whispered rapidly. "You are the incoming psych for the Solarion Nine. We'll board together. As we approach the guards on the ramp tell them everything is all right and ask them to bring in our gear immediately." Shey blinked at him.

Would it really work? Was it too preposterous? Had he been insanely overconfident?

The Thief wheeled and walked briskly toward the ramp and the watchful I.P.'s. Behind him came the sound of running feet.

"Stop!" cried Shey, hurrying up with his other four guards.

Alar bit his lip indecisively. He had evidently lost the gamble. If Shey planned to have him killed on the spot, he should try to break past the swordsmen on the ramp into the solarion. A means of escape might open up in the resulting confusion. Undoubtedly Miles would not submit tamely to Shey's forcible invasion.

"Don't harm that man!" called Shey. "He's not the one."

He had done it.

"Well, Dr. Talbot," giggled Shey, "what is the Toynbeean opinion of life in a solarion on this July twentieth?"

Alar pushed himself away from the table in Shey's private dining room and stroked his false goatee thoughtfully. His smile held a faint curl. "My first thought, sir, is that it is most generous of you to volunteer for such risky duty."

Shey frowned, then giggled. "A last-minute whim, really. Originally I was merely trying to contact a chap on Lunar Station . . ." He uttered a puzzled, gurgling bray evidently intended as a laugh. "But then I had this sudden conviction that I should try to help these poor devils on Solarion Nine. And here I am."

Alar shook his head. "Actually, Count, I'm afraid they're beyond aid. I've been here only forty-eight hours, but I've come to the conclusion that a sixty-day shift in a solarion ruins a man for life. He comes in fresh and sane. He leaves insane."

"I agree, doctor, but doesn't this deterioration in the individual have a larger significance to a Toynbeean?"

"Very possibly," admitted the Thief judicially. "But first, let us examine a society of some thirty souls, cast away from the mother culture and cooped up in a solarion. Vast dangers threaten on every side. If the Fraunhofer man should fail to catch an approaching calcium facula in time to warn the lateral jet man—bang—the station goes.

"If the apparatus that prevents solar radiation from volatilizing the station by continuously converting the radiation into muirium should jam for a split second—whoosh—no more station. Or say the freighter fails to show up and cart the muirium away from the stock rooms, forcing us to turn muirium back into the sun—another bang.

"Or suppose our weatherman fails to notice a slight increase in magnetic activity and our sunspot suddenly decides to enlarge itself in our direction with free sliding to the sun's core. Or suppose the muirium antigrav drive breaks down upstairs, and we have nothing to hold us up against the sun's twenty-seven G's. Or let the refrigeration system fail for ten minutes . . .

"You can see, Count Shey, that it is the normal lot of people who must live this life to be—by terrestrial standards—insane. Insanity under such conditions is a useful and logical defense mechanism, an invaluable and salutary retreat from reality.

"Until the crew makes this adjustment—'response to challenge of environment' as we Toynbeeans call it—they have little chance of survival. The will to insanity in a sunman is as vital as the will to irrigate in a Sumerian. But perhaps I encroach on the psychologist's field."

Shey smirked. "Though I can't agree with you entirely, doctor, still you may have something. Would you say, then, that the *raison d'être* of a solarion psychiatrist is to drive the men toward madness?"

"I can answer that question by asking another," replied Alar, eyeing his quarry covertly. "Let us suppose a norm for existence has been established in a given society. If one or two of the group deviate markedly from the norm, we say they are insane.

"And yet the whole society may be considered insane by a foreign culture which may consider the one or two recalcitrants the only sane persons in the model society. So can't we define sanity as conformity to—and belief in—the norm of whatever culture we represent?"

Shey pursed his lips. "Perhaps."

"And then, if a few of the crew can't lose themselves in a retreat from the peril of their daily existence—if they can't cling to some saving certainty, even if it is only the certainty of near death—or if they can't find some other illusion that might make existence bearable—isn't it your duty to make these or other forms of madness easy for them? To teach them the rudiments of insanity, as it were?"

Shey sniggered uneasily. "In a moment you'll have me believing that in an asylum, the only lunatic is the psychologist."

Alar regarded him placidly as he held up his wine glass. "Do you realize, my dear Count, that you have repeated your last sentence not once but twice? Do you think I am hard of hearing?" He sipped at his wine casually.

Startled disbelief showed in the psychologist's face. "You imagined that I repeated myself. I distinctly remember—"

"Of course, of course. No doubt I misunderstood you." Alar lifted his shoulders in a delicate apology "But," he pressed, "suppose you *had* repeated yourself and then denied it. In a layman you'd probably analyze such fixation on trivia as incipient paranoia, to be followed in due time by delusions of persecution.

"In you, of course, it's hardly worth consideration. If it happened at all it was probably just an oversight. A couple of days on one of these stations is enough to disorganize almost anyone." He put his wine glass down on the table gently. "Nothing in your room has been trifled with lately?" He had slipped into Shey's quarters the previous day and had rotated every visible article 180 degrees.

Shey giggled nervously. Finally he said, "Certainly not."

"Then there's nothing to worry about." Alar patted his goatee amiably. "While we're on the subject, you might tell me something. As a Toynbeean, I have always been interested in how one person determines whether another is sane or insane. I understand you psychologists actually have cut-and-dried tests of sanity."

Shey looked across the table at him narrowly, then chuckled. "Ah, sanity—no, there's no simple book test for that, but I do have some projection slides that evaluate one's motor and mental integration. Such evaluation, of course, is not without bearing on the question of sanity, at least sanity as *I* understand it. Would you care to run through a few of them with me?"

Alar nodded politely. Shey, he knew, wanted to run the slides more to reassure himself than to entertain his guest.

The psychologist was due for the rudest shock of his life.

Shey quickly set up the holograph and projector screen. "We'll start with some interesting maze slides," he chirped, switching off the light that dangled from the ceiling hook. "The ability to solve mazes quickly is strongly correlated to analyses of our daily problems. The faltering maze-solver unravels his difficulties piecemeal and lacks the cerebral integration that characterizes the executive.

"It is interesting to note that the schizophrenic can solve only the simplest mazes, even after repeated trials. So here's the first and simplest. White rats solve it—laid out on the floor with walls, of course—after three or four runs. A child of five, viewing it as we shall here, gets it in about thirty seconds. Adults instantaneously."

"Quite obvious," agreed Alar coolly as be projected a false opening in the outer maze border and covered the real one with a section of false border.

Shey stirred uneasily, but apparently considered his inability to solve the maze as a passing mental quirk. He switched slides.

"What's the average time on this next one?" asked Alar.

"Ten seconds."

The Thief let the second and third ones go by without photic alteration. Shey's relief was plain even in the darkness.

But on the fourth slide Alar alternately opened and blocked various passages of the maze, and he knew that Shey, standing beside the projector, was rubbing his eyes. The little psychologist sighed gratefully when his guest suggested leaving the maze series and trying something else.

The Thief smiled.

"Our second series of slides, Dr. Talbot, shows a circle and an ellipse side by side. On each successive slide—there are twelve—the ellipse becomes more and more circular. Persons of the finest visual discrimination can detect the differences on all twelve cards. Dogs can detect two, apes four, six-year-old children ten, and the average man eleven. Keep your own score. Here's the first one."

A large white circle showed on a black screen, and near the circle was a narrow ellipse. That was pretty obvious. Alar decided to wait for the next one.

On the second slide Shey frowned, removed it from the projector, held it up to the light of the screen, then inserted it once again. On the third slide he began to chew his lips. But he kept on. When the tenth was reached he was perspiring profusely and licking sweat from the edges of his mouth.

The Thief continued to make noncommittal acknowledgments as each slide was presented. He felt no pity whatever for Shey, who had no means of knowing that from the second slide on, there were no ellipses, only pairs of identical circles. Each ellipse had been canceled by a projection from Alar's eyes, and a circle substituted.

Shey made no motion to insert the eleventh slide in the projector. He said, "Shall we stop here? I think you've got the general idea . . ."

Alar nodded. "Very interesting. What else have you?"

His host hesitated, apparently fumbling with the projector housing. Finally he giggled glassily. "I have some Rorschachs. They're more or less conventionalized but they serve to reveal psychosis in its formative stages."

"If this is tiring you—" began Alar with diabolical tact.

"Not at all."

The Thief smiled grimly.

The screen lit up again, and the rotund psychologist held a slide up to its light for a lengthy inspection. Then he slid the slide into the projector. He commented, "To a normal person, the first slide resembles a symmetrical silhouette of two ballet dancers, or two skipping children, or sometimes two dogs playing. Psychotics, of course, see something they consider fearful or macabre, such as a tarantula, a demoniacal mask or a—"

Alar had smoothly transformed the image into a grinning skull. "Rather like a couple of dancers, isn't it?" he observed.

Shey pulled out his handkerchief and ran it over his face. The second slide he inserted without comment, but Alar could hear it rattle as trembling fingers dropped it into the projector.

"Looks rather like two trees," observed the Thief meditatively, "or perhaps two feathers, or possibly two rivulets flowing together in a meadow. What would a psychotic see?"

Shey was standing mute and motionless, apparently more dead than alive. He seemed to be aware of nothing in the room but the image within the screen, and Alar sensed that the man was staring at it in fascinated horror. He would have given a great deal to steal a look at the creature whose warped mind he was destroying, but he thought it best to continue transforming the image.

"What would a madman see?" he repeated quietly.

Shey's whisper was unrecognizable. "A pair of white arms."

Alar reached over, flicked off the projector and screen and stole quietly from the darkened room. His host never moved.

The Thief had not taken two steps down the corridor when a muffled gust of giggles welled out from the closed door—then another and an-

other—finally so many that they merged into one another in a long pealing paroxysm.

He could still hear it when he turned the corridor corner toward his
own stateroom. He stroked his goatee and smiled.

Station master Miles and Florez, who were arguing heatedly over something, passed him without acknowledging his polite bow or even his existence. He watched them thoughtfully until they turned the corner and
vanished. Theirs was the ideal state of mind—to be mad and not know it.
Their staunch faith in their inevitable destruction clothed them in an aura
of purposeful insanity.

Without that faith, their mental disintegration would probably be swift
and complete. Undoubtedly they would prefer to die rather than to leave
the station alive at the end of their shift.

He wondered whether Shey would make an equally dramatic adjustment to his new-won madness.

18. Duel Ended

The racing of his heart awoke him a few hours later in his room.

He listened tensely as he rose from his bunk. But there was no sound,
other than the all-pervasive rumble of the vast and frenzied gases outside.

He dressed quickly, stepped to the door opening into the corridor,
and looked down the hall. It was empty.

Queer—usually two or three men could be seen hurrying on some
vital task or other. His heartbeat was up to one-eighty.

All he had to do was follow his unerring scent for danger. He stepped
brusquely into the corridor and strode toward Shey's room. He arrived
there in a moment and stood before the door, listening. No sound. He
knocked curtly without result. He knocked again. Why didn't Shey answer? Was there a stealthy movement within the room?

His heartbeat touched one-eighty-five and was still climbing. His right
hand flexed uneasily. Should he return for his saber?

He shook off an impulse to run back to his room. If there was danger
here, at least it would be informative danger. Somehow, he doubted that
a blade would influence the issue. He looked around him. The hall was
still empty.

The preposterous thought occurred to him that he was the only being
left aboard. Then he smiled humorlessly. His fertile imagination was becoming too much even for himself. He seized the panel knob, turned it
swiftly, and leaped into the room.

In the dim light, while his heartbeat soared toward two hundred, he beheld a number of things.

The first was Shey's bloated, insensate face, framed in curls, staring down at him about a foot beneath the central ceiling lamp hook. The abnormal protrusion of the eyes was doubtless caused by the narrow leather thong that stretched taut from the folds of the neck to the hook. To one side of the little man's dangling feet was the overturned projector table.

Beyond the gently swaying corpse, in front of the screen, Thurmond sat quietly, studying Alar with enigmatic eyes. On either side of the police minister a Kades gun was aimed at Alar's breast.

Each man seemed locked in the vise of the other's stare. Like capacitor plates, thought Alar queerly, with a corpse for a dielectric. For a long time the Thief had the strange illusion that he was part of a holo projection, that Thurmond would gaze at him with unblinking eyes forever, that he was safe because a Kades could not really be fired in holo projections.

The room swayed faintly under their feet as an exceptionally violent and noisy swirl of gas beat at the solarion. It aroused them both from their paralytic reveries.

Thurmond was the first to speak.

"In the past," came his dry, chill voice, "our traps for you were subject to the human equation. This factor no longer operates in your favor. If you move from where you now stand, the Kades will fire automatically."

Alar laughed shortly. "In times past, when you were positive you'd taken adequate precautions in your attempts to seize me, you were always proved wrong. I can see that your comrade's suicide has shaken you—otherwise you would have made no attempt to explain my prospective fate. Your verbal review of your trap is mainly for your own assurance. Your expectation that I will die is a hope rather than a certainty. May I suggest that the circumstances hold as much danger for you as for me?"

His voice held a confidence he was far from feeling. He was undoubtedly boxed in by tell-tale devices, perhaps body capacitors or photocell relays, that activated the Kades. If he leaped at the man, he would simply float to the floor—a mass of sodden cinders.

Thurmond's brows contracted imperceptibly. "You were bluffing, of course, when you suggested the situation contained as much danger for me as for you, since you must die in any event, while my only sources of personal concern are the general considerations of danger aboard a solarion and interference from the crew.

"I have minimized the latter possibility by transferring to Mercury all but a skeleton crew—Miles's shift. And they're alerted to signal the *Phobos* and leave with me as soon as I return to the assembly room, which will be in about ten minutes." He arose almost casually, edged around the nearest

Kades and sidled slowly along the wall toward the corridor panel, carefully avoiding the portion of the room covered by the guns.

Thurmond had demonstrated once again why Haze-Gaunt had invited him into the wolf pack. He relied on the leverage of titanic forces when he had difficulty in disposing of an obstacle, and damned the cost. It was utterly simple. There would be no struggle, no personal combat. No immediate issue would be reached. And yet, within a satisfactorily short time, Alar would be dead. He couldn't move without triggering the two Kades, and there would be no one left to free him. The solarion would be evacuated within a few minutes. The crewless station would slide over the brim of the sunspot long before he would collapse from fatigue.

The wolf pack was willing to exchange one of its six most valuable munition factories for his life.

And yet—it wasn't enough. The Thief was now hardly breathing, because he believed he knew now what Miles and Florez had been discussing in the hall.

Thurmond was now at the panel, turning the knob slowly.

"Your program," said Alar softly, "is sound save in one rather obscure but important particular. Your indifference to Toynbeean principles would naturally blind you to the existence of such a factor as 'self-determination in a society.' "

The police minister paused the barest fraction of a second before stepping through the panel.

The Thief continued, "Can you make sense out of a Fraunhofer report? Can you operate a lateral jet motor? If not you'd better deactivate the Kades because you're going to need me badly, and very soon. You'll have no time to signal the *Phobos.*"

The police minister hesitated just outside the door.

"If," said Alar, "you think the skeleton crew under Miles is in present control of the station, you'd better take a look around."

There was no answer. Thurmond evidently thought that one would be superfluous. His footsteps died away down the hall.

Alar looked up quizzically at Shey's gorged and pop-eyed face, then at the two Kades. "He'll be back," he murmured, folding his arms.

And yet, when he heard the footsteps returning considerably faster than they had departed, this confirmation of his surmise concerning Andrews's crew threw him into a deep gloom. However, it had been inevitable. Nothing could have saved them after he threw the seven.

Thurmond walked quickly into the room. "You were right," he said. "Where have they hidden themselves?"

"They're in hiding," replied Alar without expression. "But not in the way you think. All ten of them were certain they were going to die on this shift. They had a fatalistic faith in their destiny. To return safely with you would have meant giving up that faith, with consequent mental and moral disintegration. They preferred to die. You'll probably find their bodies in the muirium holds."

Thurmond's mouth tightened. "You're lying."

"Having no historical background, you would naturally assume so. But regardless of what happened to Miles and his crew, you'll have to come to some decision about me within the next minute or two. We've been adrift in the Evershed zone ever since I entered the room. You can release me in order to let me have a try at the lateral jets, or you can leave me here—and die with me."

He watched the inward struggle in the police minister. Would the man's personal loyalty to Haze-Gaunt, or perhaps a chill adamantine sense of duty, require him to keep Alar immobilized at the cost of his own life?

Thurmond toyed thoughtfully with the pommel of his breast dagger. "All right," he said finally. Passing behind the Kades, he snapped the switches on each. "You'd better hurry. It's safe now."

"Shey's scabbard and blade are on the table beside you," said the Thief. "Give them to me."

Thurmond permitted himself a smile as he handed over the saber. Alar knew the man planned to kill him as soon as the station was safe again and that it mattered little to the greatest swordsman in the Imperium whether the Thief was armed.

"A question," the Thief said as he buckled the scabbard to his belt. "Were you on the *Phobos* along with Shey?"

"I was on the *Phobos*. But not with Shey. I let him try his own plan first."

"And when he failed—"

"I acted."

"One other question," insisted the Thief imperturbably. "How did you and Shey know where to find me?"

"The Meganet Mind."

It was incomprehensible. The Mind alternately condemned him and delivered him. Why? Why? Would he never know?

"All right," he said shortly. "Come along."

Together they hurried toward the control room.

An hour later they emerged, perspiring freely.

Alar turned and studied his arch-enemy briefly. He said: "Obviously, I can't permit you to signal the *Phobos* until my own status has been clarified to my satisfaction. I see no particular advantage in delaying what has been inevitable since our first meeting." He drew his saber with cold deliberation, hoping that his measured certainty would create an impression on Thurmond.

The police minister whipped out his own blade. "You are quite right. You had to die in either event. To save my life I justifiably relied on your desire to prolong your own. *Die!*"

As in many occasions in the past when death faced him, time began to creep by the Thief, and he observed Thurmond's cry of doom and simultaneous lunge as part of a leisurely acted play. Thurmond's move was an actor's part to be studied, analyzed and constructively criticized by responsive words and gestures of his own, well organized and harmoniously knit.

He knew, without reflecting on the quality of mind that permitted and required him to know, that Thurmond's shout and lunge were not meant to kill him. Thurmond's *flèche* was apparently "high line right," which, if successful, would thrust through Alar's heart and right lung. Experts conventionally parried such a thrust with an ordinary *tierce*, or perhaps a *quinte*, and followed with a riposte toward the opponent's groin.

Yet there had been a speculative, questioning element in Thurmond's cry. The man had evidently expected the Thief to perceive his deceit, to realize that he had planned a highly intricate composite attack based on Alar's almost reflexive response to the high line thrust, and the skilled Thief would be expected to upset a possible trap by the simple expedient of locking blades and starting anew.

This analysis of the attack was plausible except for one thing: Thurmond, never one to take unavoidable risks, instead of unlocking blades, would very likely seize his breast dagger and drive it into his opponent's throat.

Yet the Thief could not simultaneously cut the dagger scabbard away and avoid the lunge.

Then suddenly everything was past. Thurmond had sprung back, spitting malevolently, and the dagger scabbard was spinning crazily through the air behind him. A streak of red was growing rapidly along the Thief's chest. The police minister laughed lightly.

Alar's heart was beating very fast—just how fast he did not know—pumping its vital substance through the deceptively simple cut in his lung. It couldn't have been helped. Now, if he could maim or disarm Thurmond fairly quickly, he might still summon the *Phobos* and escape under the protection of Captain Andrews before he died of loss of blood.

His skilled opponent would play for time, of course, observing him closely, watching for the first sign of genuine faltering, which might be merely a shift of the thumb along the foil-grip, a thrust parried a fraction of an inch in excess, a slight tensing of the fingers of the curved left hand.

Thurmond would know. Perhaps this was the enlightening death which the recondite sphinx, the Meganet Mind, had predicted for him.

Thurmond waited, smiling, alert, supremely confident. He would expect Alar to burst forward, every nerve straining to make the most of the few minutes of strong, capable fencing remaining to him before he fainted from loss of blood.

The Thief moved in and his sword leapt arrow-like in an incredibly complex body feint. But his quasi-thrust was parried by a noncommittal quasi-riposte, almost philosophical in its ambiguity. Its studied indefiniteness of statement showed that Thurmond realized to the uttermost his paramount position—that a perfect defense would win without risk.

Alar had not really expected his attack to draw blood. He merely wanted to confirm in his own mind that Thurmond realized his advantage. Most evidently he did. Simultaneously with this realization the Thief, instead of improvising a continuation of the attack, as Thurmond must expect, retreated precipitously, coughed and spat out a mouthful of hot salty fluid.

His right lung had been filling slowly. The only question was, when should he cough and void the blood? He had chosen this moment. His opponent must now take the initiative and he must be lured into overextending himself.

Thurmond laughed soundlessly and closed in with a tricky leg thrust, followed immediately with a cut across the face, both of which the Thief barely parried. But it was clear that Thurmond was not exerting himself to the fullest. He was taking no chances, because he need take none.

He could accomplish his goal in good time simply by doing nothing, or quickly if he liked, by forcing the Thief to continuous exertions. Thurmond's only necessity was to stay alive, where Alar must not only do that, but must disable his opponent as well. He could not attempt more. His oath as a Thief forbade his killing an officer of the Imperium, even in self-defense.

Without feeling despair he felt the symptoms of despair—the tightening of the throat, the vague trembling of his facial nerves, an overpowering weariness.

" 'To avoid capture or death in a situation of known factors,' " mocked Thurmond, " 'the Thief will introduce one or more new variables, generally by the conversion of a factor of relative safety into a factor of relative uncertainty.' "

At that moment Alar plumbed to the depths this extraordinary character who commanded the security forces of a hemisphere. It was a blazing, calculating intelligence that crushed opposition because it understood its opponents better than they did themselves, could silently anticipate their moves and be ready—to their short-lived astonishment—with a fatal answer.

Thurmond could quote the *Thief Combat Manual* verbatim.

Alar lowered his blade slowly. "Then it is useless to proffer my weapon in surrender, expecting you to reach for it with your left hand—"

"—and find myself sailing over your shoulder. No thanks."

"Or 'slip' in my own blood—"

"—and impale me as I rush in to finish you."

"And yet," returned the Thief, "the philosophy of safety-conversion is not limited to the obvious, rather sophomoric devices that we have just discussed, as I shall shortly demonstrate." His mouth twisted sardonically.

But only the wildest, most preposterous demand on his unearthly body would save him now. Furthermore, the thing he had in mind required that he be rid of his saber, yet safe from Thurmond for at least a moment or two.

His blade skidded across the plastic tiles toward Thurmond, who stepped back in unfeigned amazement, then tightened the grip on his own weapon and moved forward.

"The sacrifice of safety is my means of defense," continued Alar unhurriedly. "I have converted it into a variable unknown, for you are suspicious of what I shall do next. Your steps are slowing.

"You see no good reason why you can't kill me now, very quickly, but you have—shall we say, buck fever? You are curious as to what I could accomplish without my weapon that I could not accomplish with it. You wonder why I am repeatedly flexing my arms and why I do these knee bends.

"You are certain you can kill me, that all you need to do is approach and thrust your blade home. And yet you have stopped to watch, consumed with curiosity. And you are just a little afraid."

Stifling a cough, the Thief stood erect and closed his fists tightly. There was a dry crackling sound about his clothing as he crossed the brief intervening space toward Thurmond. (Time! Time! He could make this final demand on his body, but he needed a few seconds more. It was building, building . . .)

The police minister was breathing with nervous rapidity, but stood firm.

"Don't you realize, Thurmond, that a man capable of reversing the visual process by supplying his retinal web with energy quanta can, under stress, reverse that process? That instead of furnishing electrical potential differences along afferent nerves for normal muscle activation, he can reverse the process and cause the muscles to store considerable wattage for discharge through the nerves and out the fingertips?

"Did you know that certain Brazilian eels can discharge several hundred volts—enough to electrocute frogs and fish? At my present potential I could easily kill you, but I intend to simply stun you. Since electrostatic charges escape easily from metal points, you will understand why I had to throw away my saber, even at the risk of your running me through before I could build up the necessary charge." (Enough! He now felt like a bottled bolt of lightning.)

Thurmond's blade flew up. "Come no closer!" he cried hoarsely.

The Thief paused, his bare breast six inches in front of the wavering point "Metal is an excellent conductor," he smiled, and moved in.

The police minister jumped back, gripped his saber like a lance, took split-second aim at Alar's heart and—

Fell screaming to the floor, his writhing body wrapped in a pale blue glow. He managed to pull his pistol from his holster and to fire two shots that bounced harmlessly from Alar's Thief armor.

Then there was a brief panting pause while he glared insanely upward at his extraordinary conqueror.

Throughout his adult life he had killed, idly, nonchalantly, with no more thought or feeling than he had when he ate his breakfast or combed his hair. Some had needed killing; some hadn't. A few had been a challenge, but they died anyhow. None of that had mattered in the slightest. It had been required of those creatures only that they die. This they had done, and it was all very right, correct, and proper, for he was the master swordsman of the Imperium. But now, very suddenly, something had changed. Something had gone wrong in the ordered scheme of things. Horribly wrong. Was he, the great Giles Thurmond, about to be slain by this incompetent unknown? By this rank amateur, this contemptible tyro? Unthinkable! By the Fates, *never!* Only the equal of Thurmond could ever kill Thurmond. And there was only one equal. Which is to say . . . He raised his pistol to his head. The third shot went into his own brain.

Alar had bounded into the control room before the echo of the final shot died away. Their fight had lasted nearly forty minutes. How far had the solarion drifted?

The pyrometric gauge read 4,500 K. The temperature drop from the 5,700 degrees K of the photosphere definitely placed the solarion position in the coldest part of the sunspot—its center.

Which meant that the station must have been falling for several minutes, straight toward the sun's core.

19. DEATH IMPENDING

"One hour ago," said the Meganet Mind, "their excellencies the Imperial ministers propounded a remarkable interrogatory, with the unusual requirement that I give satisfactory answers before the night is out, or die."

From where she sat with manacled ankles, Keiris examined the faces in the semicircle about her. Some were grim, some nervous, some unperturbed. With the exception of Shey and Thurmond, the whole inner council was here. In the center of them all, Haze-Gaunt, his tarsioid pet peeping fearfully over his shoulder, studied with sunken eyes the man in the transparent dome.

Even Juana-Maria was present, following the proceedings with languid curiosity from her motorchair. The Ministers of War, of Airways, of Nuclear Energy were bunched together at one end of the circle. They had been arguing in heated whispers, but sat up quickly when the Mind began to speak.

"These questions are as follows," droned the Mind. "First, were Shey and Thurmond successful in killing Alar, the Thief? If so, why have they not been heard from? Second, can Operation Finis be initiated with reasonable hope of success, even though the Alar question remains unsettled? These two questions were submitted by every member of the Council, I believe. The third question—'Is Kennicot Muir alive?'—was asked by the chancellor alone."

An icy tingle began to crawl up Keiris's spine. Did the Mind really know about Kim—and Alar?

The man in the pit paused briefly, lowered his disfigured leonine head, then looked up again at the circle of faces above him. "I am able to answer your questions as follows. First—Shey and Thurmond are dead as a result of their respective attempts to destroy Alar.

"Second—the success or failure of Operation Finis is no longer dependent on the life or death of Alar, but upon an extraneous factor that will be revealed to us all within a few minutes. Thus the first two questions are answerable categorically. However, the queries concerning the existence or nonexistence of Alar and Muir can be answered only in terms of non-Aristotelian probabilities. Superficially it would appear that if Shey and Thurmond were unsuccessful, then, by definition, Alar still lives. Such a conclusion would be fallacious."

He paused for a moment and studied the intent, puzzled faces. "With the exception of her imperial majesty, all of you have spent your Aristotelian lives under the impression that 'x' is either 'A' or 'not-A.' Your conventional education has limited you to bidimensional, planar Aristotelian syllogistic classification."

"I don't follow," said Eldridge, War Minister, bluntly. "What is a planar definition and what has it to do with the existence of—of—well, say, Muir or Alar?"

"Get out your notebook and we'll draw pictures." It was Juana-Maria's dry, mocking voice. She rolled her motorchair over to him. The man pulled a leather-bound pad from his pocket somewhat hesitantly.

"Draw a circle in the middle of the sheet," directed Juana-Maria.

The mystified militarist did so. The ministers nearby craned their necks toward the pad.

"Now consider the question. Is Alar alive? As an Aristotelian you would consider only two possibilities. He's either alive or he's dead. Thus you may write 'alive' in the circle, and 'dead' in the space outside the circle. 'Alive' plus 'dead' then totals what the Aristotelians call a 'universe class.' Go ahead—write them in."

Eldridge, looking a little foolish, did so.

The ironic voice continued. "But the 'dead' portion of the card, you must remember, is defined only negatively. We know what it is not, rather than what it is. If there are other conditions of existence than those we are accustomed to, that portion of the card will include them. The uncertainties are infinite.

"And further, the sheet of notebook paper may be considered as a mere cross section of a sphere encompassed by infinity. Above, below, and at angles through it are similar cross sections in the same sphere—an infinity of them. That is to say, by your very attempt to reduce a problem to only two alternatives, you endow it with an infinity of solutions."

Eldridge's face had set stubbornly. "Intending no disrespect, your majesty, may I submit that such considerations are mere academic theorizing? I maintain that these two enemies of the Imperium are either alive or dead. If alive, they must be captured and destroyed. With your permission, your majesty, I will restate the question which was heretofore before the Mind only by implication." He addressed the man under the dome coldly. "Is Alar, the Thief, alive?"

"Tell him if you can, then, Mind," said Juana-Maria with a bored wave of her wrinkled hand.

"In null-Aristotelian terms," replied the Mind, "Alar is alive. However, he has no existence in a planar Aristotelian hypothesis, as understood by Marshal Eldridge. That is to say, there is no person in the solar system today fitting the fingerprints and eyeball capillary patterns in Alar's police file."

"The same, I presume, is true for Kennicot Muir?" asked Haze-Gaunt.

"Not precisely. Muir's identity is more diffuse. If viewed in Eldridge's classic logic, Muir would have to be considered as more than one man. In null-Aristotelian terms, Muir seems to have developed a certain mobility along the time axis."

"He might exist as two persons at once?" asked Juana-Maria curiously.

"Quite possibly."

Keiris listened to her own strangled voice. "Is *he*—is either of those persons—in this room—now?"

The Mind was silent for a long time. Finally he turned great sad eyes up to her. "Madame's question is surprising in view of the obvious danger to her husband if her surmise proves correct. Yet I answer as follows. One embodiment of Muir, whose existence has just been deduced by her majesty the Imperatrix in the exercise of null-Aristotelian logic, is present, but does not at the moment choose to be visible to us."

He paused and glanced at the radiochron on the wall at his left. Some of the others followed his gaze.

It was four minutes after midnight. Somewhere far above them a new day was dawning—July 21, 2177.

"However," continued the Mind, "Muir is also present in another, entirely different form, one that would be satisfactory even to Marshal Eldridge."

The ministers exchanged startled, suspicious glances.

Eldridge sprang to his feet. "Point him out!" he cried.

"The Minister for War," observed Haze-Gaunt, "is strangely naïve if he thinks the Mind is going to point out Kennicot Muir to this assembly."

"Eh?" said Eldridge. "You mean he's afraid to name him?"

"Perhaps; perhaps not. But let us see what a highly direct and specific question will bring." He turned toward the Mind and asked softly, "Can you deny that you are Kennicot Muir?"

As Alar's stunned eyes watched the pyrometer, the needle began slowly to creep up the scale, recording the fall of the station into the sunspot vortex—4,560, 4,580, 4,600. The deeper, the hotter. Of course, the station would never reach the sun's core. The vortex would probably narrow to nothing within a thousand miles or so, in a region deep enough to have a temperature of a few million degrees. The solarion's insulative-refrigeration system could stand a top limit of 7,000.

The possibilities were several. The spot vortex might extend deep into the sun's core, with its temperature of some twenty million degrees. But even if the vortex gas stayed under 7,000 degrees all the way to the center—and he knew it could not—the station would eventually crash into the enormously dense core and burst into incandescence.

But suppose the vortex did not extend to that incredibly hot center, but, more probably, originated only a few thousand miles down? He spit out a mouthful of blood and calculated rapidly. If the spot were 16,000 miles deep the temperature at the cone apex would be a little below 7,000.

If the station would float gently to rest there, he might live for several hours before the heavy plant sank deeply enough to reach an intolerable temperature. But that wasn't going to happen. Its landing wouldn't be gentle. The station was now falling under an acceleration of twenty-seven gravities, and would probably strike the bottom of the cone at a velocity of several miles a second despite the viscosity of the spot gases. Everything about him would instantly disintegrate.

He was aware of the chair cushions pushing against his back. The metal tubing along the arms seemed considerably warmer now to his touch. His face was wet, but his mouth was dry. The thought reminded him of Captain Andrews's cache.

With nothing to do for the moment, he acted on his sudden whim. He rose, stretched himself and walked over to the wall which supported the refrigerated cabinet. He opened the door and felt the sudden wave of cool air against his perspiring face. He chuckled at an irrational thought: why not crawl into the six-cubic-foot box and shut the door behind him?

He pulled out the bottle of foam and squeezed some of the thick liquid into his mouth. The sensation was extremely pleasant. He closed his eyes and for a moment imagined that Captain Andrews was next to him, saying, "It's cold and that's plenty welcome in a place like this."

He swung the door shut again on the bottle. A meaningless gesture, he thought to himself. The situation seemed so unreal. Keiris had warned him. . .

Keiris.

Did she sense, at this moment, what he was facing?

He snorted at his own thoughts and returned to the chair.

Just precisely what did he face?

There were, indeed, several possibilities, but their conclusions were identical—a long wait, then an instantaneous, painless oblivion. He couldn't even count on an enduring, excruciating pain that might release him along the time axis, as it had done in Shey's torture room.

He became aware of a low, hollow hum, and finally traced it to the pulse at his temple. His heart was beating so fast that the individual beats were no longer detectable. The pulse had passed into the lower audio range, which meant a beat of at least twelve hundred a minute.

He almost smiled. In the face of the catastrophe that Haze-Gaunt was about to wreak on Earth, the frenzied concern of his subconscious mind for his own preservation seemed suddenly amusing.

It was then that he noticed that the room was tilted slightly. That should not be, unless the giant central gyro was slowing down. The gyro should keep the station upright in the most violent faculae and tornado prominences. A quick check of the control panel showed nothing wrong with the great stabilizer.

But the little compass gyro was turning slowly, in a very odd but strangely familiar way, which he recognized immediately. The station axis was gradually being inclined at an angle from the vertical and was rotating about its old center in a cone-like path.

The solarion was *precessing*, which meant that some unknown titanic force was attempting to invert it and was being valiantly fought off by the great central gyro.

But it was a losing battle.

He had a fleeting vision of the great station turning turtle in slow, massive grandeur. The muirium anti-grav drive overhead, now canceling 26 of the 27 G's of the sun, would soon be beneath him, and adding to those 27

G's. Against 53 G's he would weigh some four tons. His blood would ooze from his crushed, pulpy body and spread in a thin layer over the deck.

But what could be trying to turn the station over?

The pyrometers showed almost identical convection temperatures on the sides, top and bottom, of the station—about 5,200 degrees. And radiation heat received on the sides and bottom of the plant showed about 6,900, as could be expected. But the pyrometers measuring radiation received on the upper surface of the station, which should not have exceeded 2,000 degrees—since the station surface normally was radiated only by the thin surface photosphere—showed the incredible figure of 6,800.

The station must be completely immersed in the sun. The uniform radiation on all sides proved that. Yet he was still in the sunspot vortex, as shown by the much cooler convection currents bathing the station. There was only one possible explanation. The spot vortex must be returning to the sun's surface through a gigantic U-shaped tube.

Anything going down one limb of the tube would naturally ascend the other limb inverted. The U-tube finally explained why all spots occurred in pairs and were of opposite magnetic polarity. The ionized vortex of course rotated in opposite directions in the respective limbs of the tube.

If the central gyro won out over the torrential vortex, the station *might* be swept up the other limb of the following spot twin and he *might* break the station away to safety over the penumbral edge—in which improbable event he could live as long as his punctured lung permitted, or until the storage chambers became filled with muirium and the synthesizer began turning the deadly material back into the sun to trigger a gigantic explosion.

But he could be sure that even if the station were found during that interval there would be no rescue. The discovery would be made by Imperial search vessels and the I.P.'s would simply keep the station under observation until the inevitable filling of the muirium holds.

The brooding man sat in the central operator's chair for a long time, until the steepening floor threatened to drop him out of his seat. He rose heavily to his feet and, hanging tightly to the guide rails, walked the length of the panel to a bank of huge enabling switches.

Here he unlocked the safety mechanism of the central gyro switch and pulled it out amid a protest of arcking, hissing flame. The deck immediately began to vibrate beneath him, and the rapidly increasing tilt of the floor made it difficult to stand.

The room was spinning dizzily about him as he lashed a cord to the master switch controlling the outer hatches of the muirium locks overhead. The free end he tied around his waist.

When the station turned on its back he would fall to the other end of the room and the cord attached to his lunging body would jerk open the muirium hatch switch. All the stored muirium would begin to dissolve back into its native energy quanta, the station would suddenly become a flat, gigantic space rocket and—at least theoretically—would be hurled through the rising U-limb at an unimaginable velocity.

If he were human, he would be killed instantly. If he were not human, he might survive the fantastic initial acceleration and accompany the station into the black depths of space.

The deck had almost become a vertical wall. The gyro had probably stopped and there was no turning back. For a moment he regretted his decision. At least he could have lived on a little while longer.

Always a little longer. He had squeezed out five years of life by that method. But no more. Sweat squirted from his face as, slipping and sliding, he clawed insanely at the smooth steel tiles of the deck that was now soaring over him to become the new ceiling. Then he dropped straight to what a few minutes before had been the ceiling and lay there helpless under a 53-G gravity, unable even to breathe and swiftly losing consciousness.

He knew vaguely that the rope had pulled the switches to the muirium locks, and had then broken under his enormously increased weight—that jagged fragments of his snapping ribs had pierced his heart—that he was dying.

In that instant the muirium caught. Four thousand tons of the greatest energy-giving substance ever known to man collapsed in a millisecond into a titanic space-bending shower of radiation.

He had no sensation of pain, of movement, of time, of body, of anything. But he didn't care. In his own way he was still very much alive.

Alar was dead.

And yet he knew who he was and where his destiny lay.

20. ARMAGEDDON

Goddard, Nuclear Minister, was on his feet, staring wide-eyed alternately at the Mind and at Haze-Gaunt. "The Mind—Kennicot Muir? Impossible!"

Phelps of Airways was gripping the sides of his chair with white, trembling hands, and his fingernails were cracking and doubling back from the pressure. "How do you know it's impossible?" He shouted. "The Mind must answer that question!"

Keiris swallowed in an ecstasy of misery. She had precipitated something the Mind might not have been ready for. Thinking back, she could find no good reason for asking her question, other than intuition. But Haze-Gaunt *must* be wrong. Obviously the Mind could not be her husband. They had about the same build, but there the resemblance ended.

Why, the Mind was—*ugly*. Then she stole a look at Haze-Gaunt, and lost some of her certainty.

Of the assembly, only the chancellor appeared at ease. He was reclining quietly in his plush chair, his long legs crossed casually. His perfect confidence said plainly—"I am sure of the answer and I have taken extraordinary precautions."

For Eldridge the situation was becoming unendurable. "Answer, damn you!" he cried, drawing his pistol.

Haze-Gaunt waved him back irritably. "If he is Muir, he is also an armored Thief. Put that toy away and sit down." He turned to the Mind again. "The very fact of your delay is highly revealing, but what could you hope to gain by it? A few moments more of life?" His mouth warped in the faintest of sneers. "Or doesn't the best-informed man in the system know who he is?"

Haze-Gaunt's tarsioid peeped, trembling, over his master's epaulette at the Mind, who had not changed his position. His arms rested on the arms of his chair as they had always rested. To Keiris he appeared almost as calm as usual. But Haze-Gaunt, savoring almost sensuously his victory in a generation-long struggle with the man he hated most, apparently saw something more.

"Before us, gentlemen," he observed grimly, "for all his aura of wisdom, we have a frightened animal."

"Yes, I am frightened," said the Mind, in a strong clear voice "While we are here playing tag with identities, Toynbee Twenty-one is reeling under its death blow. If you had not forbidden all interruptions of this conference you would know that the Eastern Federation declared war on America Imperial eighty seconds ago!"

What a magnificent bluff! thought Keiris in desperate admiration.

"Gentlemen," said Haze-Gaunt, looking about him. "I trust that all of you appreciate the finer points of the Mind's latest finesse. The riddle of his identity suddenly becomes lost in the excitement of gigantic but fictitious surmises. I think we may now return to my question."

"Ask Phelps about his secret ear receptor," said the Mind coolly.

Phelps looked uncomfortable. Then he muttered: "The Mind's right—whoever he is. I have a hearing aid but it's also a radio. The Eastern Federation actually did declare war as he said."

The queer silence that followed was finally broken by Haze-Gaunt.

"This obviously changes things. The Mind will be placed under close arrest for further examination at our convenience. In the meantime the council is wasting time here. All of you have standing orders for this contingency. You will now carry them out to the letter. We stand adjourned."

He stood up. Keiris forced herself not to collapse as she relaxed.

The ministers filed out hurriedly and their footsteps and nervous whispers died away down the peristyle. The bronze elevator doors began to clang shut.

Then Haze-Gaunt turned abruptly and reseated himself. His hard eyes again fastened on the disfigured but calm face of the man in the domed pit.

Keiris's breathing grew faster. It was not over—it was just beginning.

The Mind seemed lost in a reverie, totally indifferent to the probability of imminent death.

Haze-Gaunt drew a pistol-like thing from his jacket pocket. "This is a poison-dart thrower," he said softly. "The dart can easily penetrate your plastic shell. It need only scratch you. I want you to talk about yourself and to tell me a great deal. You may begin now."

The Mind's fingers drummed indecisively on the arm of his chair. When he looked up it was not at his executioner but at Keiris. It was to her that he spoke.

"When your husband vanished ten years ago, he told you that he would contact you through me. At that time I was an obscure sideshow freak. Only in recent years have I had access to the vast literature that has brought me to my present preeminent position."

"Might I interrupt?" murmured Haze-Gaunt. "The original Meganet Mind, an obscure entertainer, had a remarkable resemblance to you. But it so happens that he died ten years ago in a circus fire. Oh, I admit that the burn tissue on your face and hands is genuine. In fact, you burned your features deliberately. With the record corrected, pray continue."

Keiris watched in fascinated horror as the Mind licked dry lips.

The Mind said, "My disguise has finally failed, then. But until now, I believe, no one suspected my identity. The wonder of it is that I was not exposed years ago. But to go on—through Keiris, I relayed vital information to the Society of Thieves, which I hoped would overthrow your rotten administration and save our civilization. But their gallant efforts are now cut short. The most brilliant minority cannot reform a disintegrating society in a bare decade."

"Then you admit that we have beaten you and your vaunted Society?" demanded Haze-Gaunt coldly.

The Mind looked at him thoughtfully. "Half an hour ago I intimated that Alar had attained a semi-godhood. Whether or not you have beaten me and my 'vaunted Society' depends on the identity of the intelligence we have been calling Alar."

"Don't hide behind words," snapped Haze-Gaunt.

"You may be able to understand me if I put it this way. In the Central Drome of the Airways Laboratories lies the recently completed *T-Twenty-two*, standing by to blast off on its maiden voyage. Five years ago, as you well know, a white-hot space ship crashed into the Ohio River and the River Police found some remarkable things. The metallic parts of the ship were identical in composition with the alloys that Gaines and I had worked out for the *T-twenty-two.*

"Was the race of a neighboring star trying to reach our sun? We waited for further evidence. It turned up the next day when a man was found wandering along the river bank, dazed, almost naked, carrying a leather-bound book with him. The book bore the gold-stamped legend— *T-twenty-two, Log.* There is one just like it in the pilot's room of our own *T-twenty-two.* "

"You weave a fine story," said Haze-Gaunt, "but we must cut it short, I fear. I wanted real information, not a disjointed fairy tale." He raised the dart-pistol. The tarsioid disappeared screaming down his back.

"That man was Alar the Thief," said the Mind. "Shall I continue or do you wish to try to kill me now?"

Haze-Gaunt hesitated, then lowered the pistol. "Continue," he said.

"We kept Alar under observation in the lodgings of two Thieves, now dead. Always we held before us the possibility that he was one of your spies. The truth of his identity grew upon me only gradually, when no other explanation was possible.

"Let us look at the facts. A ship identical to the *T-twenty-two* landed on Earth five years ago. Yet the *T-twenty-two* is not due to blast off on its maiden voyage until a quarter of an hour from now. Regardless of any other facts or theory involved the ship will start moving backward in time as soon as it is launched, and will continue to move until it crashes— should I say 'crashed'?—five years ago.

"The man who shall become transformed into Alar through a geotropic response, or otherwise, and whom we might call Mr. X, will board the *T-twenty-two* in a few minutes with an unidentified companion, and they will be carried away in the ship at a velocity faster than that of light. Such velocities require movement backward in time, so that when Mr. X finally pilots the *T-twenty-two* back to Earth, he lands five years earlier than when he started. He emerges as Alar and is henceforth irrecognizable as Mr. X."

Haze-Gaunt looked at the Mind, grim-mouthed. "Do I understand that you want me to believe that someone will leave in the *T-twenty-two* tonight, jet backward in time, crash into the Ohio River five years ago and swim ashore as Alar?"

The Mind nodded.

"Fantastic—yet it has the elements of possibility," mused the chancellor. "Assuming for the moment that I believe you, who is the person who will enter the *T-twenty-two* and become Alar?"

"I'm not sure," said the Mind coolly. "He is undoubtedly someone in the metropolitan area, because the *T-twenty-two* jets in ten minutes. He might be—you."

Haze-Gaunt shot him a hard, calculating glance.

Keiris felt light-headed, dizzy. Haze-Gaunt become Alar? Did that account for her pseudo-recognition of the Thief? Intuitively she rejected the suggestion.

But—

"That hypothesis really becomes intriguing when we examine your relations thus far with Alar," said Haze-Gaunt. "Only a few weeks ago you yourself, with excessive modesty, warned us that Alar was the man most dangerous to the Imperial Government. After his several escapes you told us immediately where to find him and several times, through information you furnished, we nearly succeeded in killing him.

"We might be justified in concluding that you considered Alar a bitter personal enemy, a category that could easily include me—as Alar, of course—except for a serious difficulty. I have no intention of entering the *T-twenty-two*. Therefore, I am not your Mr. X, and your motive in persecuting Alar stands unexplained. I must warn you to be explicit." He raised the dart-gun again.

"An old method of teaching children to swim was to throw them in the water," said the Mind.

Haze-Gaunt looked down at him sharply. "You are suggesting that it was your intention to cause Alar to develop his remarkable gifts—whatever they are—by making it necessary that he either discover them or die. Rather a striking educational technique. But why did you suspect that he had such latent possibilities in the first place?"

"For a long time we weren't sure. Alar seemed just an ordinary man except for one thing—his heartbeat. Dr. Haven reported that Alar's heartbeat rose to the medically unheard of rate of one hundred and fifty a minute and more in times of danger. I then decided that if Alar were *homo superior* his superiority was latent. He was like a child adopted by a pack of wild animals.

"Unless he were forced to realize his superior origin, he would be doomed to run about on his metaphoric all fours for the rest of his life—with us other animals. Yet, if I could get him to his feet, he might point the way out of the devastation that is even now overwhelming us.

"So when, some six weeks ago, you were about to decide on the date of Operation Finis, I had to act, possibly prematurely. By means of unusually violent persecution, I forced Alar to develop an extraordinary photic ability, whereby he could project a scene in much the same way as a holo projector.

"Later, under the stimulus of ecstatic pain, ably administered by Shey, he became acquainted with the time axis of his four-dimensional body. Unfortunately he was unable to travel in time without this stimulus, and I can't say that I blame him for not indulging in the experience voluntarily. Yet it was an accomplishment that he had to master as we master speech—by repetition. I am certain that he finally used it again in the very act of dying on Solarion Nine.

"I next led Alar first to the moon, where he was forced to learn something of himself and the backward flight of the *T-twenty-two,* then to the sun station, with Shey and Thurmond on his trail. He *had* to emerge triumphant and fully enlightened as to his superiority and mission. The alternative was death. I gave him no choice."

Haze-Gaunt arose and began striding up and down the stone flagging, sending his pet into a chattering fright from one shoulder to the other and back again. Finally he stopped and said, "I believe you. Small wonder then that we couldn't kill Alar. On the other hand, you too must admit defeat, for your protégé seems to have abandoned both you and your cause."

"You have not understood me," the Mind said bluntly. "In Aristotelian terms, Alar is dead."

There was a shocked silence in the room that was quickly broken by two simultaneous sounds. Chancellor Haze-Gaunt burst out with, "Good!" as Madame Haze-Gaunt cried, "No!"

Keiris was collapsing slowly against the chair arm. Her skin had so blanched that two terrible dark circles appeared under her eyes. The Mind had predicted Alar's fate, but she had never reconciled herself to it becoming a fact. There was no thought in her head that the Mind could be mistaken. No, it was true. And though the horrible realization weighed her down, she couldn't quite grasp the naked, irrefutable fact that he was dead. Alar couldn't be gone forever from their lives. No, he couldn't be gone, would never be gone. That had to be true. The Mind had said, what was it? "Alar had attained a semi-godhood." Then there was no conflict. Alar was dead and lived. Even as he lost his life, he had triumphed.

Keiris didn't fully understand, but the color began to seep back into her face.

Haze-Gaunt had paid no attention to Keiris's cry. He had permitted himself a wide grin and a smack of closed fist into open palm. Then, within seconds, he had sobered and scowled at the Mind who so imperturbably sat there and watched him.

"Then your protégé," he said, an edge of irritation creeping into his voice, "hasn't deserted you. He has merely died. Hardly a situation which should make you confident of your own success."

Somewhere behind him an elevator door opened and shut—and then there was the sound of running and stumbling feet.

It was the Minister of War, Eldridge. His uniform was disheveled and it was a darker color at the throat and armpits. Bloodshot eyes punctuated an ashen face.

Haze-Gaunt caught the man as he collapsed. "Speak, damn you!" he cried, holding the shuddering creature under the arms and shaking him.

But Eldridge's eyes merely rolled crazily and his jaw dropped a little farther. Haze-Gaunt let him fall to the floor. The War Minister moaned softly when Haze-Gaunt kicked him in the stomach.

"He was trying to tell you," observed the Mind, "that satellites and coastal radar have picked up vast swarms of west-bound rockets. This area will be utterly destroyed to a depth of several miles within five minutes."

Not a muscle in the chancellor's face changed in the long silence that followed. Even the tarsier on his shoulder seemed paralyzed.

They look like twins, thought Keiris.

21. THE ETERNAL CYCLE

Finally, Haze-Gaunt said, rather pensively, "It is an occupational risk of the aggressor that the victim may grow impatient and strike the first blow. But this preemption of the initiative is immaterial and actually foolish, for in such event our launching areas are under standing orders to resort to total destruction patterns instead of the one-third destruction originally planned."

"Might I suggest, excellency," came the dry grave voice of Juana-Maria, who had just rolled in, "that Shimatsu has anticipated the scale of your retaliation? That his own destruction pattern for the Imperium is similarly unrestricted?"

Keiris's face slowly grew white as she watched a terrible smile-like thing transform Haze-Gaunt's mouth. But it couldn't be a smile. In the ten years she had known him he had not smiled.

He said, "That, too, was a calculated risk. So civilization must really disappear, as the Toynbeeans have so widely and fearsomely proclaimed. But I shall not remain to mourn over it. And this latest development, I believe, forcibly solves the identity of Mr. X, and hence of Alar."

He turned savagely to the Mind. "Why do you think I permitted you and your Thieves to build the *T-twenty-two*? Research? Exploration? Bah! The weak, futile human race vanishes, but I shall escape and live! And I shall escape beyond my wildest dreams, for I shall become that invincible conqueror of time and space, Alar the Thief!"

He was sneering now at the scarred but peaceful face of the Mind. "What a simpleton you were! I know that you yourself hoped to escape in the *T-twenty-two*. That's why you had it built. And you even had a passageway, super-secret, so you thought, constructed from your dome to the *T-twenty-two* hangar. You may be interested to learn, impostor, that the tunnel has been sealed."

"I know it," smiled the Mind. "The 'secret' passageway was merely a decoy. I intend to reach the *T-22* by a much more efficient route. Since you have driven your ablest scientists underground to the Thieves, you probably have never had an adequate explanation of Thief armor. It actually consists of a field of negative acceleration and a necessary consequence is its strong repellence of rapidly approaching bodies, such as I.P. bullets.

"You probably know that acceleration is synonymous with space curvature, and the alert Haze-Gaunt intellect has now doubtless deduced the fact that this projection mechanism before me is actually capable of controlling the space surrounding anyone wearing Thief armor. In an earlier age such a phenomenon might have been called teleportation.

"Haze-Gaunt, I hope that you will not enter the *T-twenty-two*—that you will not become Alar. A few hours ago Alar recovered his memory and is by now completely integrated into an intelligence beyond our conception. In fact, it probably makes no sense to think of him as Alar any longer. If he remembered his past as you, humanity has lost its last hope. If he remembered his past as me, I think something still may be salvaged from the shambles you have made."

The orange light on the projection reader had turned a bright yellow and grew momentarily more luminous.

"The potential stored so far is sufficient to deposit me within the pilot room of the *T-twenty-two*," said the Mind calmly, "but I must wait another thirty seconds, because this time I am taking my wife with me."

He smiled at Keiris, whose soundless lips were forming, *"Kim!"* over and over again.

"There is only one thing remaining, one thing that puzzles me," continued the Mind. "The matter of your tarsier, Haze-Gaunt—"

A low, grinding rumble rolled through the room. From somewhere came the crash of falling masonry.

The yellow pilot light on the projector flickered, then died away.

Keiris stood up in a slowly rising cloud of dust, through which she could see her husband tinkering feverishly with the teleportation machine. Juana-Maria had her handkerchief to her mouth and was blinking her eyes wildly. Haze-Gaunt coughed, then spat and looked about for Keiris. She gasped and hobbled backward a step.

Then several things happened at once. Haze-Gaunt leaped toward her, tossed her dizzily over his shoulder, then faced Kennicot Muir—the Meganet Mind—who had burst through the door of the plastic dome.

The great man seemed to fill the room.

Haze-Gaunt shrank away, with Keiris on one shoulder and the tarsier on the other. "I'll shoot you if you move!" he shouted at Muir, waving his dart-pistol. He began to back toward the elevators.

Keiris, remembering the deaths of Gaines and Haven, tried desperately to voice a similar warning, but her voice was paralyzed. She managed to loosen and drop her right sandal, and the long toes of her right foot were closing around the long knife in her thigh scabbard when Muir replied.

"I am immune to the poison. I developed it myself. Therefore, I will accompany you down your private, battery-operated elevator. I don't believe the others—"

He was interrupted by a high-pitched, terrified chattering. It was the tarsier, who had scrambled down the chancellor's leg and was trying vainly to halt the man by clutching at both legs.

"Don't go! Don't go!" it cried in a tiny, inhuman voice. It was the most chilling sound Keiris had ever heard. The beastling had joined the drama as a full-fledged member of the troupe, with lines to speak, and a death to die. Little creature, she thought, *who are you?*

Haze-Gaunt said something under his breath. His leg flung out. The little animal sailed through the air and crashed into the marbled wall. It lay motionless where it fell, with its body bent backward queerly.

Muir was running swiftly toward them when Haze-Gaunt cried, "Is your wife immune?"

Muir stopped precipitately. Haze-Gaunt, grinning viciously, continued his deliberate retreat toward his elevator door.

Keiris craned her neck from her awkward and painful position and looked at her husband. The anguish on his face turned her heart to water. It was the first time in ten years that his fire-born disguise had relaxed its frozen, toneless immobility.

The elevator doors opened. Haze-Gaunt carried her inside.

"It is finished," groaned Muir. "So *he* is Alar. I let you suffer ten years for this—my poor darling—poor humanity." His voice was unrecognizable.

In her awkward position Keiris could not inflict a vital wound on Haze-Gaunt. She knew then what she must do.

The elevator door was closing as she heaved herself sideways off Haze-Gaunt's shoulder. The weight of her body twisted his arm and she dropped across the doorway. As she fell, she cried, *"He is not Alar!"*

Her knee doubled under her and the knife between her toes flashed in the light. She dropped heavily upon the upturned blade, driving it into her heart.

The woman's body had blocked the sliding panel. Haze-Gaunt tugged the corpse frantically into the elevator as there was a blur of movement toward him.

The elevator door clanged shut, and Juana-Maria was alone in the room.

The three of them, Kennicot Muir, Haze-Gaunt, and Keiris, the living and the newly dead, were joined in their own weird destiny and had left her to hers.

For a long time the fine brown eyes were lost in thought. Her reverie was finally penetrated by a shrill, painful piping.

The tarsioid, despite its broken back, was still breathing limply, and its eloquent saucer-like eyes were turned up pleadingly to her. Their piteous message was unmistakable.

Juana-Maria reached into the side pocket of her chair and found the syringe and vial of analgesic. Then she hesitated. To kill the little beast would perilously deplete the vial. There would be pain enough for herself in the next few minutes. Damn Haze-Gaunt anyway. Always bungled his murders.

She filled the syringe quickly, rolled the chair over to the little creature, bent over slowly to pick it up.

The injection was done quickly.

She retracted the needle and the dying animal lay rag-like in her lap, staring at her face with fast-glazing eyes. And then she knew it was dead and that she was exhausted. The titular ruler of one and a half billion souls could not even move her own hands. The syringe dropped to the tiles and shattered.

How easy now to slide into an unwaking reverie, forever. So Muir was to become Alar and attain something akin to immortality. That was just. It seemed to her that the man was simply following a natural development to its logical conclusion. And by the same token Haze-Gaunt would have to change, too.

She wondered what Muir-Alar could do that would avoid Operation Finis. Perhaps he would go back in time and cause Haze-Gaunt to be stillborn. But then another dictator, even more ruthless, might arise and destroy civilization. Of course, the god-man might prevent Muir from discovering muirium, or even stop the classic nuclear physicists, Hahn, Meisner, Fermi, Oppenheimer and the rest, from splitting the uranium atom.

But she suspected the discoveries would be made in due time by others. Perhaps the Michelson-Morley experiment, which had proved the contraction of matter in its line of motion and started Einstein off on his theory of the equivalence of matter and energy, could be doctored so that Michelson would actually get the interference image he sought.

But then there would be Rutherford's work on the suspiciously heavy electrons, and an infinity of allied research. And human nature being what it was, it would again be just a question of time.

No, the main difficulty would be in the mind of man. He was the only mammal hell-bent on exterminating his own species.

She was glad it was not her task to humanize humanity or to be a god-mother to Toynbee Twenty-two.

She peered down at the furry lump in her lap and wondered if Muir had ever divined its identity. Perhaps she alone understood.

Two living beings would emerge from the ship when the trip had ended. Kennicot Muir would by then have evolved into Alar. The other would be Haze-Gaunt—a changed Haze-Gaunt . . . All as predicted by John Haven's Geotropic Project. When two specimens are subjected to speeds faster than light, one evolves, the other devolves.

The darkened chamber was slowly whirling around and around. She could no longer move her lips, but she could move her eyes to stare at the tiny corpse of the tarsier. With a great effort she marshaled her last clear thought:

"Poor Haze-Gaunt. Poor tiny animal Haze-Gaunt. To think that *you* always wanted to finish killing *me.*"

A moment later the chamber was vaporized.

22. Toynbee Twenty-two

The leader, gray, grizzled and cold-eyed, paused and sniffed the air moving up the valley. The old Neandertal smelled reindeer blood a few hundred yards down the draw, and also another unknown smell, like, yet unlike, the noisome blend of grime, sweat and dung that characterized his own band.

He turned to his little group and shook his flint-tipped spear to show that the spoor had been struck. The other men held their spears up, signifying that they understood and they would follow silently. The women faded into the sparse shrubbery of the valley slope.

The men followed the reindeer path on down the gully, and within a few minutes peered through a thicket at an old male Eoanthropus, three females of assorted ages and two children, all lying curled stuporously under a windfall of branches and debris that overhung the gully bank.

Blood still drained sluggishly from a half-devoured reindeer carcass lying under the old man's head.

Some sixth sense warned Eoanthropus of danger. He shook his five-hundred-pound body and convulsed into a snarling squat over the reindeer, searching through near-sighted eyes for the interlopers. The females and children scurried behind him with mingled fear and curiosity.

"All men are brothers!" shouted the aging Neandertaler. "We come in peace and we are hungry."

He dropped his spear and held up both hands, palms outward.

Eoanthropus clenched his fists nervously and squinted uncertainly toward his unwelcome guests. He growled a command to his little family, and like shadows they melted up the side of the draw. And after hurling a final imprecation at the invaders, the old male scuttled up the hill himself.

The hunters watched the group vanish, and then two of them ran toward the reindeer carcass with drawn flint knives. With silent expert strokes they cut away the hind quarters of the animal and then looked up inquiringly at the old leader.

"Take no more," he warned. "Reindeer may be scarce here, and *they* may have to come back or go hungry." He could not know that the genes of his fathers had been genetically reengineered by an inconceivably titanic intelligence, with the consequence that the colloidal webs in his frontal lobes had been subtly altered. And he could neither anticipate nor visualize the encounter of his own descendants in the distant future with their Cro-Magnon cousins, the tall people who would move up from Africa across the Sicilo-Italian land Bridge.

He had no way of knowing that even as he had spared the animal-like Eoanthropus, so would he, Neandertal, be spared by Cro-Magnon. Nor had he any way of knowing that by offering the open palm instead of the hurled spear he had changed the destiny of all mankind to come. Or that he had dissolved, by preventing the sequence of events that led to its formation, the very intelligence that had wrought this marvelous change in the dawn-mind.

For the entity sometime known as Muir-Alar had rejoined Keiris in a final eternity, even as the Neandertal's harsh vocal cords were forming the cry that would herald the eventual spread of Toynbee Twenty-two throughout the universe:

"All men are brothers!"

THE RING OF RITORNEL

THE CYCLES OF THE RING

1. THE DIE IS FIRST CAST

"Magister," said the captain deferentially but firmly, "I will take you no farther. We are now well beyond the danger point, and we have yet to close the quarry."

The young man in the simple blue tunic smiled. "Your jaw is set hard, Captain, and your face is pale. Are you afraid?"

Captain Andrek studied his guest with blunt honesty. He found such chill hauteur vaguely disquieting in one who had barely attained his majority. This, he presumed, was the consequence of centuries of ancestors accustomed to command. The young man's dark, humorless eyes held a striking presence; he wore no ornament of rank, or badge of authority, nor had he need of any.

The captain thought briefly of his own background, and knew there was no comparison. For generations the Andreks had given their share of professional men to the advancement of their corner of civilization: military men, physicians, advocates, artists, even theologians for the temples. The captain had a tremendous respect for the nonviolent professions, but he loved space and—some said—danger, and was happiest in action and combat. He had long ago reconciled himself to the probability that he would be killed in service. Yet, now, when the moment seemed clearly upon him, he was shaken. It was all wrong. This was not a proper way to die. Furthermore, he was totally unaccustomed to this brute clash of wills. He did not know how to deal with it. Still, a direct question had been put to him, and he had to try to answer it.

"Afraid, sire? I served with your father in the Terror mop-ups. After he died, I served your uncle, the Regent. Next week, after your coronation, I hope I will be privileged to serve you, as I have them. Until now, sire, no Delfieri has asked me whether I was afraid. And until now, I have not been afraid. But now . . . Yes, sire, I am afraid—that you may not return from this hunting trip. And it is a great fear."

"I have given you a direct order, Captain."

The officer stood mute.

It was suddenly becoming clear to the other officers and crew that in this conflict between two personalities, the irresistible force, whose very whim was the law of the Home Galaxy, had finally met an immovable object—their captain. And it was equally clear that this kind of thing had never before happened to the young man in blue. At first, he was too astonished to be angry. Even when he got over his surprise, he was still not angry; only logical.

"Captain you are right on one point. We *are* running out of time. But the trail is hot. It is now or never, for I can never come here again. You will proceed as ordered, or I will have you shot for mutiny." His voice was almost casual.

Captain Andrek, not commonly given to the use of adjectives in his thinking, now found himself indulging in strange imagery, and he considered his own mental processes with mingled fascination and amazement.

Throughout his long career in the League navy, death had been a very personal and intimate companion. His wife (whom he had adored while she lived) had wryly named death his mistress. This had puzzled him. He had always accepted death as a condition of his life, but had never (he thought) actively sought her. There were rules about death in the service. All his life he had followed the rules. He had been faithful to his contract with death, and it had never occurred to him that finally death would be unfaithful. She was sometimes cruel (he'd often wondered whether he would die screaming), but at least his own death ought to be a phenomenon directed exclusively at him, and in which he would play a vital role. And now this. Death by default. Death was bored by him—if it noticed him at all. It was a farce, a silly playlet without merit or point, a chance encounter between strangers. Death was not scintillating; death was a mindless oaf.

He thought of his sons. Omere the poet—the strange one. And Jamie, the logical one, not yet in his teens. From here on in, they would have to take care of each other.

He looked around calmly at the shocked faces of the under-officers, then spoke to the lieutenant. "If I am killed, it is nothing. But get the ship out of here, quickly."

The young man in the blue tunic nodded to his aide. "Huntyr, kill him."

Huntyr was a big man, yet quick and nervous in his movements. He had none of the ponderous gentleness that often accompanies a big frame. His face held more cunning than intelligence. And it was a subservient face, which frankly drew its substance from the young Magister, thereby being pleasantly released from personal judgments and choices between moral values. Captain Andrek wondered where Oberon had picked him up. The association seemed to reflect some subterranean malignancy in Oberon's own mentality, and augured ill for his approaching reign.

Huntyr started to draw his biem.

The young man frowned. "Not the biem, you fool. It will not fire in the Node area."

"Sorry." Huntyr replaced the biem, drew his slug-gun in a smooth motion, and fired. Captain Andrek staggered against the ward room wall, clutching his chest. There, he floated up slowly in a weightless heap. Blood circled a neat hole in his shirt over his heart.

Oberon sighed. "Get rid of him."

Two ratings finally clacked on magnetic shoes over to the corpse and shoved the body ahead of them into the pilot room.

"Lieutenant," said the young man to the nearest stricken face, "will you accept my orders?"

Just at this moment, parts of the lieutenant's cerebral processes were jammed, awry, and other parts were whirring senselessly. Nothing inside his head seemed to mesh, grab, or take hold. Nothing like this had ever come up in the classrooms at the Academy. However, his ultimate reaction, while not textbook, nevertheless promised survival.

"Yes, sire," he whispered.

"Good. What is the latest on the quake?"

"Time is still oh-seven-hundred."

"Probability?"

"Oh-point-eight-nine. Up two-tenths, sire."

"Have you ever been in a quake, Lieutenant?"

"No, sire."

"Do you know anyone who was ever in a quake?"

"Yes, sire. That is, I knew them before . . ."

"Before they were killed in the quake, you mean."

"Yes, sire."

"*Xerol* is a very strong little ship, Lieutenant, specially built. It's supposed to resonate with the wavelength of the quake."

"Yes, sire."

"But you don't really believe it, do you?"

"I believe *Xerol* is strong and specially built, sire. And it might even resonate. But a space quake is like a living thing, sire, contrary and capricious. It might not vibrate at the predicted frequency. Or it might start out at the right frequency and then change to another one. Those physicists at the Node Station are sometimes wrong. And if I may make a point, sire, *they* left the station two days ago."

Oberon laughed.

"If I am concerned," said the lieutenant, "it is not for the ship, or myself, or the crew."

Oberon frowned. "Let's not go into *that* again. Now, if you would help me into this suit."

"Of course, sire. Yet—" He hesitated. "May I speak freely?"

"Please do."

"The Magister is proving a thing that does not need to be proved."

"You are oversimplifying, Lieutenant. You perceive only limited sets. After my coronation, there shall be no more hunting. The last of the Delfieri will belong to the state, body and soul. So, in this last hour I must get enough hunting to last the rest of my life, for I shall never enter the Node again. When I grow old sitting at the Twelve-Table in the Great House, I want this to remember, and to think back on." He paused, musing. "Do you know the son of the late Captain Andrek, Omere the Laureate?"

"Only by reputation, sire."

"Omere has written an epic for my coronation. He will soon program it into the great computer, for delivery with full orchestration at the proper time in the ceremonies."

"It is known, sire," said the officer cautiously.

"How can an epic be written for a man who has reached his majority and done nothing?"

"Omere writes for your *being* the crown, sire. Not for *doing* anything. It is not necessary to do anything."

Oberon brushed that aside. "It may be something of an advantage never to have done anything," he said dryly, "and there may be even a degree of notoriety in this. Yet it can be carried too far. I would like to justify that epic. Omere is the greatest poet in all the Thousand Suns. I have heard a pre-run of the tape. It makes my skin tingle. I think to myself, am I this Oberon of whom he sings? Oh, to own a brain like that! I would rather have written the epic than slay the krith. When I am crowned, I think I shall attach him permanently to the Great House, whether he will or no."

He turned to the raman at the scope. "Report," he said softly.

"Eighteen kilometers. Course steady. Closing, one kilometer per minute," The raman's voice took on an uneasy edge. "Sire, the mass confirms at twenty-one hundred kilos. It is probably a krith."

"Of course it is a krith," murmured Oberon. "The most vicious of the cryotheres."

The lieutenant broke in. "Shall I load the bow guns, sire?"

"Certainly not." Oberon picked up his helmet.

"May I assemble a rifle party to accompany you?" said the lieutenant unhappily.

"No." Oberon pulled his helmet down over his chest and locked his visor. "Cut engines in five minutes." His voice took on a mocking metallic quality through the intercom. "And stop sweating. It makes me nervous."

"Sire, we have to be out of the Node within the hour . . ."

"I know. Now cease this concern with trivialities and attend to business. As soon as I leave, activate the tractor beam and stand by to focus out a line on the meanest creature ever hauled out of the Node."

The lieutenant gave up. "Yes, sire." He opened the inner door of the space lock, helped Oberon into the cramped chamber, and spun the hatch shut behind him.

A few seconds later Oberon floated free of the little ship, and the exhaust of his suit-jet twinkled in an ever-lengthening trail ahead of the ship. He gave himself twenty minutes to find and slay the krith, ten minutes to rendezvous with the ship, and lock the tractor beam, and a final thirty minutes to get *Xerol* out of the quake area.

The ship disappeared behind him into the black depths of the Node. Oberon looked about him into dark nothingness and felt a sudden awe. He was at the center of creation. He pondered this. The universe expands. Hydrogen is continuously created. Yet the density of matter remains a constant—about one proton per cubic meter. Which means that space must also be continuously created. Where does this new space and new matter first greet the universe? As far away from existing matter—which is to say, the galaxies—as possible. This locus is the central area between the galaxies. And where the galaxies appear as groups or clusters, this locus is at their center, their Node. So space is born out of the womb of the Deep, and begins life at the Node.

How strange, the Node! Here, at the geometric center of the Twelve Galaxies, the expanding universe gives birth to new space, amid titanic birth pangs, vast quakes in space that release unimaginable energies. And strange life-forms come to feed on those energies, and stranger life preys on that life. At the bottom of the life cycle are the ursecta, minute creatures like the plankton in the great seas of his home planet, Goris-Kard. The ursecta in turn are the staple diet of larger creatures, and these in turn are eaten by still larger. And at the top of this pyramid of cryotheres are the great carnivores, and of these the most dangerous is the winged spider, the krith, fast, cunning, terrible.

He looked about him. The darkness was total. This was not surprising. The Node was the point in space farthest from matter in this part of the universe: the central point of the vast hypothetical dodecahedron formed by the twelve faces of the local cluster of galaxies.

From here, the individual galaxies—each over three million light-years distant—were barely visible as hazy points of light. He turned over slowly and looked about him. One by one he picked out the twelve. "Overhead" was a pinpoint of light, the Home Galaxy—at this distance, not detectably different from its spiral neighbor, Andromeda. By twisting his head he found the others. In all, three spirals, six ellipsoids, and three irregulars. Actually there were four irregulars, if both of the Magellanics were counted. But everyone—including the Magellanics themselves—considered the twin clouds as one. Twelve in all. Alea completed.

Even as he stared, something blotted out the points of light ahead of him. And then something long and sticky struck his side and coiled like a whip around his waist, where it clung. The great arachnid was trying to truss him up in a web before closing in. But he was prepared for this, and cut the strand ends immediately. And then another filament hit him, and another. For a few seconds he was very busy with the knife.

Finally free, he checked his scope hurriedly.

The krith filled the plate. It was charging.

Despite his thermals, Oberon suddenly felt cold.

He lined up the cross hairs of the slug-gun. The creature had to be hit in the body. A wing shot was worse than useless. When the metal pellets penetrated the chitinous shell of the body, they provided nuclei that immediately crystallized the beast's already supercooled body fluids. The horrid creature would be converted instantly to a frozen statue, and could then be hauled back to Goris-Kard for dissection and mounting.

He fired. Even as the recoil turned him head over heels, he knew the shot had hit a wing.

And then something gashed him painfully in the leg. Frozen spatters of his own blood clattered against his helmet. He turned wildly to fire again. But his port body jet had been hit. He spun in a crazy arc. The cross hairs wouldn't line up. He was hit again—in the back—hard. A filament coiled around his gun and jerked it loose from his hands. The krith was trying to kill him so that *he* would freeze. After that, he could be hauled away to some distant webby lair and there be eaten at leisure.

But just as he had resigned himself to death, he heard urgent voices on his phones, and sensed that guns were firing all around him. Huntyr and the lieutenant had followed him, and had witnessed his humiliation. Before he blacked out, he cursed.

They revived him on board. He glared up at Huntyr's white face and managed a harsh whisper. "I told you not to follow me."

The aide gestured helplessly. "Sire, we *had* to come after you. Just after you left, the lieutenant received a revised estimate of the quake from the computer-broadcaster at the Node Station."

"Really?" His eyes shifted to the lieutenant, "Well?"

The lieutenant licked his lips and looked at his watch. He spoke with difficulty. "It's due in two minutes, plus or minus thirty seconds."

Oberon looked over at him curiously. "What are you doing about it?"

"I've called the Group. They're sending two flights—one to come into the quake zone. The other will stand outside. After the quake, the second flight will come in also."

"I see. You don't think either flight can do anything?"

"Not really, sire. We're still very close to epicenter. If we get out, we won't need either flight. If we don't get out, the first flight will get hit the same as us. In that case, the second flight will come in afterward for what is left of us." The young officer knew he was not saying it properly, but he rushed on. "And now, sire, if I might make a suggestion, we want to get you inside this special emergency suit, with foam sealant."

"I suppose so. Pass the word, suits for all hands." Oberon sighed. "A frustrating day." He reached into the blue folds of his tunic and drew out his necklace with its pendant, the golden dodecahedral die of Alea. Each face bore a number, from one to twelve, and each number was a sign from Alea. He unfastened it and held it in his palm a moment.

"Perhaps Alea will say how it shall be with us."

Huntyr's face was ashen. "It is sacrilege to call idly on the goddess!"

"Whether I call idly is entirely up to Alea," said Oberon calmly. He let the die float away and took the foam suit from the lieutenant. "When the quake comes, *Xerol* will be her die cup."

"It's *Xerol*, all right," said the rescue commodore softly. Not being given to superfluities, he added only mentally, or what's left of her.

The search beam from the patrol launch stroked the stricken ship from stem to stern. There was no movement.

The commodore barked into the communicator. "Lock on, midship, by that break in the plates. I want four men with torches to slice out a hole big enough for a stretcher party. On the double. They'll save time if they work next to the crack in the hull. When you get inside, spread out. I'm coming in with you, and I'll start with the pilot room. Call me there if you find anything."

He was not surprised at what he found inside *Xerol*. The portable searchlights showed havoc everywhere. The quake must have continued for some time after it had broken the spine of the ship and let in the awesome cold of space. Men had been quick-frozen and their bodies cracked like whips. As he worked his way up to the pilot room an occasional arm or leg floated past him, and his stomach began to writhe.

The door was jammed, and they had to burn it off its hinges. Inside, he saw Captain Andrek, not even suited, and slumped queerly on the wall. The whole thing was incomprehensible. The captain was a splendid officer, with an impeccable record. It had been his duty to protect the Magister, but he obviously had failed in his duty. Perhaps the captain was lucky. Had he lived, he would face a summary court-martial and certain death.

Just then he got an urgent call on the communicator. "Commodore! Calling from sick bay!"

He didn't get it at first. "Sick bay?"

"Xerol sick bay, sir. Looks like we've found the Magister. His chest is crushed, but he may be alive. And another chap, a big fellow with his head banged up. Sealant still oozing out of their suits, no pulse, but body temperatures within permissible limits."

"Stretcher them out of there. I'll alert our own sick bay to get ready. Anybody else?"

"No, sir. Everybody else was killed. We'll need a fair-sized burial detail."

"No time for that, Sergeant. We'll send a tug out later for *Xerol.* You get the Magister on board within three minutes or you will never see Goris-Kard again."

"Yes, *sir.*"

The commodore met them on the catwalk. It was indeed the Magister. The other one, the big man, he did not recognize. And the Magister's chest, as reported, was indeed crushed. Jagged red pieces of rib bone had punctured the suit. Foam had evidently covered some of the protruding pieces and had then broken away. The commodore's stomach was bothering him again. As the sergeant hurried past, he held out his hand and gave the commodore something. "What is this, Sergeant?"

"An Alean die, sir. It's gold. Must belong to the Magister."

"What number was showing?"

"Number one, sir."

The commodore, a practicing Alean, felt his flesh crawl. One, the sign of the false god Ritornel, and disaster at the Node. It had to be. "Carry on, Sergeant," he growled.

2. JIMMIE AND OMERE

For a long time the vibrations and the flashing lights seemed only a part of Jimmie's dream. In the dream, he was at the Node, the crossroads of the universe, and the gods were dicing for his life. At each roll of the die, a great space quake would crash through his body, and in his head the lights would go on and off.

Jimmy finally woke up, and when he did, he was awake all over. He didn't have to stretch and cough and groan the way Omere did. He turned off the alarm button on his night table. The bed ceased its rhythmic insistent shaking, and the ceiling lights stopped flashing and came on full. Jimmie didn't even have to look at the clock face. He knew that it was four in the morning, and that Omere wasn't home. Because if Omere were in bed, Jimmie's alarm would automatically have been deactivated. Therefore Omere wasn't home.

Jimmie found his robe and slippers and hurried into the phone room. He sat down in front of the multiceptor, fished the little black book out of the top drawer, and began dialing the long series of numbers that would connect his inquiry tapes simultaneously with nearly two hundred restaurants, bars, and sundry strange places strewn all over the night side of Goris-Kard.

He found the right place within minutes. The Winged Kentaur, an odd place, a bar with reading and music rooms, haunted by bearded, thin-faced men and the strangely-dressed articulate women they brought with them. Painters, writers, singers, poets, scientists, priests. Omere was often there. Jimmie thanked the receptionist, turned off the ceptor, then ran back to his room to get dressed. He checked his money. It was important to have the right change for the capsules. Nobody liked exchanging big bills this time of night—or morning—and sometimes they'd look you over, making sure you were just a ten-year-old kid all alone, and then they'd try to steal it from you. But he had to take *some* money. He calculated. He'd need, say, five gamma for the regular doorman, ten for that mean-looking substitute. He counted out fifteen and put it in his top jacket pocket.

He boarded the feeder tube in the corridor outside the apartment, punched the computer coordinates inside the capsule, put the coins in the slots, and waited. The feeling of motion pressed at his stomach, then went away, and then there were turns, right, left, up, down. It was impossible to keep a sense of direction. And then it was over. The capsule rolled out to an exit tube, and he was on the brightly lighted street. It was in the theater district, and the drama houses seemed to alternate with all-night bars.

The Winged Kentaur was just ahead. In the luminous tri-di sign over the doorway, he could see the kentaur's wings moving in slow majestic arcs. Omere had once tried to explain how the proprietor had selected the strange symbol. It was all mixed up in ancient fables that had come down from their Terrovian ancestors, centuries ago, and Jimmie doubted that he understood it all. The winged horse was the symbol of music, poetry, and the creative arts; and the kentaur was the symbol of the sciences, so a winged kentaur was the symbol of the best in the arts and sciences—the final step in the evolutionary process. But of course no such creature had ever really existed.

The doorman smiled wryly at him and took his money with a nod. "Second room back." Jimmie thanked him, braced himself, and walked in.

Inside it was a strange blurry mixture of sound, smells, smoke, and laughter.

A little group, mostly women, was watching the visi-screen. Even without the narrator's explanation, Jimmie knew instantly what it was. Terror burning. It was all being broadcast from Terror's single moon, complete with sound. You could hear the low eerie moaning of the flames, and the hiss of steam rising in hideous clouds from the boiling seas. All life was of course long vanished. The narrator was talking: "The mills of justice grind slowly, but they grind exceeding fine. And what will be the fate of this terrible world? When the fires die down sufficiently, the great shaft will be drilled to the iron core, the explosives placed, and Terror will be towed far inward to the Node, there to be blown to bits—an eternal lesson to tyranny . . ."

Jimmie walked over. Sure enough, there was Omere, right in the middle. Jimmie frowned. Sometimes it was hard to get Omere away from women. Jimmie didn't like the women. He had a very vague recollection of his mother, who had died when he was very small, but he was certain she had nothing in common with these creatures.

And now one of them happened to spot him. She tapped Omere on the shoulder and called out harshly. "Hey, it's the kid! Join the party, kid!"

His brother turned on his swivel stool and looked full at him.

"Hello, Jim-boy." The secret grin, known but to Jimmie, was spreading across the youthful face. Whenever Omere did that, the boy's heart pounded. It didn't matter that the face was prematurely lined and furrowed and glowed ghoulishly under the dim blue ceiling radiants. It was the handsomest face in the world.

But now to business. Jimmie said flatly: "You have dress rehearsals for the coronation recitals this afternoon at the Great House."

Omere sighed. "Another night slain by the icy edge of innocence. Yes; the coronation." He took a sip from his glass, then put it down clumsily on the "chord," where it nearly overturned. "Logic. When all else fails, he retreats into logic. Logic makes no sense. If you keep this up, dear little brother, we'll turn you over to the advocates. Rehearsals? Why should I worry about rehearsals? While I'm here, working my fingers to the bone, where is the distinguished subject of my new epic? I'll tell you. Oberon is on a hunting trip, having the time of his life. Is *he* worried about rehearsals?"

Jimmie bored in closer and took Omere by the sleeve. "What's that got to do with you? Oberon is the Magister. He can do anything he likes." His voice was becoming anxious. "But you have got to get some rest before rehearsal."

Omere appeared to consider the matter briefly. He began to chant.

"If you make me go to bed,
I'll put a bullet in my head.
Maybe two, if you are rough.
Three should surely be enough."

Jimmie grinned. This meant his brother would come peacefully.

He was about to help Omere down from the bar chair when someone spoke just behind him.

"Who is your young friend, Mr. Andrek?"

Jimmie turned and looked up curiously at the speaker. The man—if he could be called that—was clearly not a native of Goris-Kard. Jimmie had never seen anyone like him before in his life. He wore the pale blue robes of the Great House, and on each lapel were the eight-armed spiderlike insignia that indicated his profession. He was a physician. On each hand was a white glove. His head and neck were draped in a blue hood. Jimmie thought for a moment that the hood covered even his eyes, until the eyes blinked. Then he noticed that there were actually two holes in the hood for the eyes. And such eyes! They seemed to flicker with a strange blue radiation, as though lighted from within the skull. Jimmie shivered.

But Omere just laughed. "Doc," he said, "this is my brother James."

The doctor's gloved hands grasped each other to form a circle, in the manner of the Ritornellians, and he bowed gravely "We are one in Ritornel," he murmured.

"With Ritornel we return," replied Jimmie politely.

All this seemed to amuse Omere greatly. "You have to be careful with Doc. He *really* believes in Ritornel. You'd think he invented the whole thing."

The blue lights in the doctor's eyes seemed to vibrate. "It's the duty of every man to formulate his own gods," he said somberly. "And then, while he lives, to follow through to the end. Only then can he accept the gray robes of the pilgrim, for the last journey, for his reward and his release. Only then can he accept death."

"Don't be alarmed, Jim-boy," said Omere, with faint malice. "The good doctor isn't quite ready to die. He's waiting for the Sign."

" 'Sign'? " said Jimmie, puzzled.

"The Laureate cloaks the truth with humor," said the doctor. "Yet, by my beard, it is the truth. I await the Sign. The Twelve Galaxies will be brought to an end by the Omega of Ritornel. Yet, Ritornel decrees that the end is but the beginning of a new life. For that new life, a pair must be saved—male and female—the cream of creation. And a planet must be saved for them, to be their home, for them and their descendants. These things shall come to pass when we see the Sign."

"And what *is* the Sign?" asked Jimmie curiously.

"A woman," said the doctor. "It is written. A virgin, born from a man. A motherless child." The pale blue lights seemed to burn into Jimmie's head. Jimmie felt the hair on the nape of his neck stand up. He didn't like this. And certainly he didn't understand it. He took a step backward.

Omere came to the rescue. He yawned elaborately and arose unsteadily. "So much for Ritornel. Let's get out of this den of religion before we run into an Alean."

Jimmie stepped over to help him, but the doctor was already there. "Allow me."

Jimmie hesitated, but he was helpless. Together they helped Omere down from the chair, and then the three of them bumped their way through crowded rooms and out into the street.

Here, Omere had a bad coughing fit. Jimmie cleaned up the sputum from his brother's blouse. It was blood-flecked. The doctor stood by silently. Omere seemed to read his thoughts. "Let's get home, Jim-boy. It's not really bad." The doctor helped Jimmie get Omere down to the tube entrance. It took both of them to put him inside the capsule and seated upright. Jimmie closed the door and, just before the capsule dropped into the subterranean entrails of the city, he stole a last covert look at the blue-robed figure behind them. All he could see in the semidarkness were two points of blue light. They seemed to be studying him intently. He turned back quickly.

Back in the apartment, Jimmie put his groaning brother to bed. One sandal had somehow got lost; he removed the other, loosened the belt, and pulled the coverlet up gently.

Omere spoke out sleepily in the semidarkness. "Don't go just yet. Sit on the bed."

Jimmie sat down. "You should get to sleep."

"I know. Dress rehearsal. What'll I wear?"

"Your clothes are all laid out. Your new black synthetics, black hose, ivory lace collar and cuffs."

Omere was silent a moment. Finally he said: "The commodore left *you* in *my* care, Jim-boy, and now you've got it all mixed up. One of these days he'll come blasting in from outer space, and we'll both be court-martialed." He turned over and coughed hollowly into his pillow. "I haven't done a very good job on you, have I?"

"Don't talk like that," said Jimmie uneasily.

But Omere continued in somber vein. "If anything should happen to me before Dad gets home, you are to go to the dons in the prep school at the Academy of Justice. The papers are in my desk. The papers will tell you whom to see . . . everything. There's plenty of money."

Jimmie was shaken. "Is your cough worse? I'll call the doctor right away."

"No, no, don't do that. Doctors don't know anything. He'd try to get me to cancel the rehearsal. He might even try to cut me out of the coronation. Imagine, the Laureate not reciting his epic at a coronation! And what a coronation . . . the pomp and pageantry, music, priests chanting. Both temples, Ritornel and Alea, will be saying all kinds of words over Oberon."

"Which temple do we believe in?"

"We burn incense in both temples," said Omere blandly. "We believe in everything. It takes twice as much faith, but it's safer. We stand still with Ritornel, while randomly advancing with Alea."

Jimmie knew his brother was teasing him. They hadn't been inside a temple since he was seven. "You're"—he sought for a word—"cynical."

Omere laughed silently. "Such a big word from such a little boy. Yes, the dons will get you. Words are their business, their weapons in fighting the quarrels of other men."

They had been over this before. "I think I'd like to be a don," said Jimmie. "James, Don Andrek. How does that sound? Maybe I could even be a don in the Great House. Maybe I could serve Oberon himself."

Omere frowned. "Stay away from *him*. There are strange stories. Some say he'd just as soon look at you as shoot you."

"You mean, 'shoot you as look at you.' "

"No, I don't. And that's the point."

"Oh." Jimmie didn't understand. But perhaps it was just as well. "We have to stop, and you have to go to sleep. I'll be at school when it's time for you to wake up, but the alarm is set."

"Thanks, Jim-boy. Good night." Omere closed his eyes.

The first flush of dawn was beginning to filter through the balcony windows; it cast an eerie radiance on Omere's face. Jimmie started to pull the drapes, then stopped. He studied his brother's face for a long moment, in wonder and admiration. Ordinarily, he thought of Omere as handsome. The word that now occurred to him was "beautiful." His mother must have looked like this. Omere, he thought simply, I love you.

With an effort, he broke loose from the enchantment, drew the drapes silently, and tiptoed from the room.

He never saw that face again.

In the eighteen years that followed, when he rummaged through his collection of mental images of Omere, this final scene, with the enhaloed face, was always first to take form.

3. SHALL OBERON DIE?

The Regent, Oberon's uncle, was so old that he seemed ageless. He had seen it all, not once, but many times. Life to him was like Oberon's boyhood carousel: wait a bit, and the whole thing comes around again. There were indeed Ritornellian aspects in his theo-philosophy, and in fact in decades previous he had carried the golden ring on the red cushion in the solemn annual processions. And yet, just as he was not an Alean, either in the letter or by spirit, neither did he adhere to Ritornel. Indeed, his religion was totally dynastic, and dealt with transcendental and celestial matters only to the extent that they promised an immediate benefit to the Delfieri line. And since the death of his younger brother, the anointed ruler, in the last days of the Terrovian War, he had emerged from retirement to hold the government together until Oberon became of age.

And thus it was by order of the Regent that Oberon's coronation and surgery proceeded simultaneously. It could hardly be otherwise. Extraordinary measures were necessary to preserve old friendships and to avoid offense to potential new allies. Oberon might be dying, but the coronation had to proceed. The ceremonies and invitations had been scheduled months in advance, and kings and chancellors from all the League suns, not to mention ambassadors from the outer galaxies, were in attendance. Even the intergalactic arbiters were there in their splendid robes, unanimous at least in their decision that so historic an occasion required their review.

The Regent's brows knitted. This is no fitting end, he thought. It was the Delfieri who brought Terror low. But for the stiffening of our purpose, and rallying the weaklings of the League, the devil-planet would not now lie a-burning. Perhaps no particular Delfieri is essential but the blood is essential. And this wastrel Oberon is the last of us. Wild, inconsiderate brat! Always, we are out getting ourselves killed when we should be taking wives and establishing something for posterity.

But his barbaric black eyes softened as he considered his nephew. A complete Delfieri. And so this must be your miserable coronation. No, not like in the old days. As *his* grandfather had told *him*, these things in centuries past were a thirty-day riot. Before his ancient forebears found blatant piracy uneconomical and before they entered (with vast reluctance) into a more socially acceptable culture, a coronation was a thing to be remembered. Every wine vat in Goris-Kard was emptied. Unransomed captives were sacrificed, and the temple floors were awash in blood. And those were real temples, to proper gods, long before the philosophies of Alea and Ritornel began their insidious seduction of the flowering minds of the lusty League planets. And now, all was gone, all. Here and now, at this pallid proceeding, the only wine was in the sterilizing autoclaves in the operating room, and the only blood visible was that on the white gown of the Master Surgeon.

And thus for hours the procession of subdued celebrants circled the glass bubble of the improvised surgery. They moved in a living stream, on deep blue carpets, handwoven with threads of gold and noble metals, through a great room finished in hand-carved opulent wood-paneling (in strange contrast to the tiled sterility of the operating chamber in its center). The air was heavy with incense. A choir chanted in the background, amid the muffled clangor of great bronze bells in neighboring Alean and Ritornellian chapels. It could hardly be known whether the bells rejoiced or sorrowed, or indeed whether it made any difference one way or the other.

All the participants were exhausted, and yet the stream of potentates did not abate.

During these proceedings the Regent, and Galactic Laureate, and the musicians and chanters occupied a podium at the side of the operating room. Huntyr, functioning as the Regent's temporary aide, stood quietly behind the group, his face just beginning to heal under plastic skin. Only the golden patch glinting forebodingly over his left eye gave hint of his recent brush with death.

When Omere had understood what was expected of him in the modified ceremony, he was surprised only that he had not been shocked: but the whole affair was completely consistent with the bizarre tradition of the Delfieri. During the endless hours he had recited his epic three times over, his voice was cracking, and he was beginning to feel giddy. He wondered what they would do to him if he simply fainted. He noticed then that the Regent was frowning at him, but Omere pondered the barbaric mixture of surgery and ceremony, and decided he couldn't care less.

The Regent's right hand was raw and swollen from hundreds of handshakes, but he hardly felt it. From his place in the receiving line, he could see the operating table, the bevy of white-clad nurses, and the sure, delicate motions of the Master Surgeon. The Regent knew that crushed sections of ribs were being cut away and stored carefully in frozen containers; these were samples being saved for the cell cultures. Since Oberon was probably going to die, a number of single viable cells selected from the jetsam of fragments would be cultured, by techniques known only to the Master Surgeon, in the hope that a new identical Oberon could eventually be grown, and the imperial lineage thereby preserved.

At this moment the sono under the Regent's left ear peeped gently. It was the prearranged signal from the Master Surgeon. The old man walked over to a nearby microphone. He could see the Master Surgeon watching him through the glass walls of the surgery. "You want me, Surgeon?"

"Yes. I must bring Oberon into consciousness for a short time. I want the Laureate here inside. You know how Oberon feels about Omere. Selections from the epic may well soothe and reassure Oberon during the period of consciousness."

The old man had always regarded Oberon's fascination with poetry and the arts as a serious frailty in a Delfieri, a weakness that could only bring harm. And yet he was realistic enough to seize upon his nephew's strange interest, and to make use of it in an attempt to work on the youth's will to live. He looked over at the poet. "They want you inside, to sing a few selections from the epic while the Master Surgeon brings Oberon into temporary consciousness."

"I will try. But my voice is nearly gone." (And so am I, Omere wanted to add.) He pulled a tiny aspirator from his pocket, sprayed his throat, and was immediately struck by a coughing spasm. He wiped blood from his lips.

The Regent watched this with distaste. "I will ask the Master Surgeon to give you something to hold you together for the necessary time."

"I am grateful," rasped Omere sardonically.

Inside, a nurse gave him a hypodermic. His larynx had immediate trouble with the bite of ozone and the odor of barely dry bacteriostatic paint. And the sub-audio sterilizers set up interference patterns with his voice. It was going to be a fiasco, but perhaps Oberon would be too far gone to know. He selected the stanza beginning with the spread of Terror's warships throughout the Home Galaxy. He sang softly and didn't try for the high notes.

He then observed that Oberon's eyes were open, and watching him. He smiled wearily at the young Magister, then continued the stanza . . . then stopped. For Oberon, with no air in his damaged lungs, was trying to whisper something.

"Finish . . . Rimor . . . ?"

"The poetry computer is mechanically complete, Excellency," said Omere, "but I have not yet programmed it. This will require several weeks."

"Program it . . . now . . . ."

"It shall be done, Excellency."

Oberon closed his eyes.

"He is unconscious again," the Master Surgeon said to Omere. "You need not stay." He looked at the Laureate sharply. "How do you feel?"

"I think I—" Omere collapsed in a slow heap on the floor.

The Master Surgeon jerked his hooded head toward the nurse. "Stretchers."

As Omere was carried out, the Regent looked after him thoughtfully. He snapped his fingers for Huntyr. "Take him to the hospital wing. And strap him down."

The coronation continued.

In the final hour, Oberon was given the silver scroll of wisdom (which the priests could only place outside the glass door), the pails full of platinum coins to ensure prosperity for his reign, and finally he was appointed Defender of the Faiths whereby, amid much chanting, a golden ring of Ritornel was placed by the door by a minor Ritornellian priest, and then an Alean abbot forced himself to place the golden Alean die inside the ring.

And then surgery and coronation were complete. The last guest disappeared up the carpeted walkway.

The Master Surgeon had been on his feet with Oberon for nearly twenty hours, and had used up three consecutive sets of assistants. He stepped outside and onto the podium.

"How is it, Surgeon?" said the Regent.

"He might live, if he chooses to live."

"How long to program the poetry computer?"

"I would like to discuss that with you, sire. Can we go now to the hospital wing? There will be no change in Oberon's condition for some hours. But meanwhile, if we are to save the Delfieri line by cell cultures or by persuading Oberon to want to live, much work remains to be done this night."

"After you, Surgeon."

"Cell culture is best understood from a historical viewpoint," said the Master Surgeon. He stood erect at the microscope workbench in the parthenogenetic laboratory, apparently untouched by the long day with Oberon. The Regent had sunk exhausted, in a sparsely upholstered lab chair. The surgeon continued quietly. "In his first instant of existence, the Magister was but a single cell in the womb of his mother. That cell divided, then subdivided, and continued to subdivide. For seven or eight generations, all the thousands of resulting cells in this initial stage of development were identical. During this phase, no cells recognizable as bone cells, or muscle cells, or nerve cells were formed. But—in the next few cell generations, changes *did* begin. Thus, about ten days after fertilization we find three different kinds of cells, in outer, middle, and inner layers in the incipient embryo, which is now a barely visible hollow ball. The descendants of these layered cells become even more specialized as growth continues. And before the days of parthenogenesis, it was thought that this increasing specialization was irreversible."

"What do you mean, irreversible?" asked the Regent.

"Before specialization began, any one of the cells could be separated from the cluster and caused to grow into a separate embryo. But after the cells have begun to specialize, they can reproduce only identical specialized cells; they can no longer produce all of the hundreds of different kinds of

cells necessary to form a viable human fetus. The changes in the cell structure that cause specialization are thus normally irreversible."

"I gather then that the parthenogenesis technique is aimed at reversing
the irreversibility?"

"Exactly, Excellency."

"Continue."

"We have here a microsection of costal bone taken from the chest of
the Magister. These bone cells descended from cells in the middle layer of
the pinpoint-sized embryo. The same layer was ancestor to heart, muscle,
and skin cells."

"But how can muscle cells and bone cells descend from identical cells?"

"Certain genes within the cell become inactivated after a specified
number of subdivisions. It is, in fact, the withdrawal of combinations of
specific genes from the coded genetic instructions of the chromosomes
that results in the changes in the cells of subsequent generations. All the
original genes of the original fertilized single cell are still present in each of
the billions of cells of the embryo, but now, cell by cell, many of the genes
are dormant, so that the correct daughter cells needed in succeeding stages
in the growth of the embryo can be made. The success of parthenogenesis
depends on awakening these sleeping genes. If this is done, the cell shall
be as it was in the beginning, precisely identical to the first cell from which
the Magister grew, and hence, in theory, capable of growing into a second
Magister."

"And how are the sleeping genes awakened?"

"By removing the blocking proteins from the deoxyribonucleic acid
chains of the genes—the DNA. These proteins are protamines and his-
tones—mildly basic. They have combined chemically with the mild acid of
the DNA, but can be persuaded to relinquish their hold on the DNA if we
expose them, very carefully, to a slightly stronger acid. All this has to take
place within the cell nucleus, and the microprocedure is rather delicate."

"Surgery at the molecular level? I did not realize the technique existed. Tell me more."

The Master Surgeon hesitated. "More, sire, I cannot tell you. It is a
secret of the Master Surgeons, passed down, one to the other, from the
most distant generations."

"Then I shall not pry."

"The Regent is invited to watch."

"Yes, I would like to."

The surgeon turned around and bent over his flasks. "From this section
of costal bone, we first isolate about twenty individual cells. This is a simple
microsurgical technique, which your Excellency can follow on the microscope projection screen. As you can see, each cell looks like an elongated

ɔrick. Each is washed with sterile nutrient medium into its individual culture flask. And now we come to the crucial part, reactivation of the dormant genes."

There was a sudden flashing movement. The Master Surgeon stripped the glove from his right hand. He seemed then to insert his index finger into the neck of the first flask. And then the glove was on the hand again. The great man turned to the Regent and bowed. "And that is all there is to it."

The Regent studied the hooded, glowing eyes. "You mean, there is something in your body that awakens the genes?"

"Something like that. Of course, the bone cell must now travel the long road back, reversing some fifty generations of cell differentiation, with more and more genes awakening at each stage, until all are awakened, and the condition of the first cell is reached. The gene-stuff is fragile, and the results are unpredictable. Parthenogenesis is a hazardous process at best. In the days of the wars, the very conditions of high radiation levels that wrought mutations in the genes of sperm and ovum while they were yet in the body endangered the cell cultures in the same way. And so it is now. Ironically, the recent great quake that has called for this specific attempt at parthenogenesis may itself bring all our efforts to nothing. Even as we talk here, the first showers of hyper-drive cosmic rays generated by the quake are reaching us."

"But these rooms are encased in a meter of lead," demurred the Regent. "Besides which, the planet itself lies between these rooms and the Node."

"That may not be enough. Cosmic rays have been detected in mines several thousands of meters deep. We think that the strongest are able to pass entirely through the whole planet of Goris-Kard, right through the nickel-cobalt core. Even since we have been standing here, several cosmic rays have passed through my body."

"How do you know that?"

"My sensory structure is—different from yours. I can detect electromagnetic radiation in wavelengths considerably below the visible spectrum useful to your retina. There—a ray struck this very jar."

"Throw it out."

The Master Surgeon hesitated. "I wonder. The chances that the ray struck the single cell to be cultured seem quite remote."

"Then do as you like."

'Thank you. I'd like to keep it for the time being. And now, if your Excellency is satisfied with what has been explained and demonstrated so far, it would be best if I completed the cultures alone. This will take less than an hour, and then I will rejoin you in the room of Omere the poet."

"Yes. I am satisfied. I will meet you there."

4. INTO THE MUSIC ROOM

"Hello, Doc." Omere's eyes opened blearily, then closed again.

"You will address the Master Surgeon with more respect," said Huntyr curtly.

Beneath twitching eyelids, Omere tried to focus on the big man. He attempted to rise on one elbow. Only then did be discover he was strapped to the bed. "Must have been quite a party." His head fell back on the pillow. "I remember, now. The coronation. I passed out. Never mix terza rima and iambic pentameter. What happened after that? Fill me in, blue eyes!"

"My boy," said the Master Surgeon, "you sang to the Magister for over twelve hours, without rest, and then you collapsed. Huntyr brought you here."

". . . the Magister?"

The surgeon turned questioningly to the Regent, who had shriveled wearily into a bedside chair. The old man nodded, and the surgeon faced the poet again. "The condition of the Magister is a state secret. However, for reasons that you will soon appreciate, there is no danger in entrusting this secret to you. The continued existence of Oberon of the Delfieri trembles in the balance. For the time being, everything that can be done for him medically has been done. He will be under hypno-sedation for three days to give our patchwork a chance. When he awakens, whether he lives or dies may well be his own mental choice. In one hand he will hold life; in the other, death. He has only to choose. The Regent, of course, desires that Oberon shall choose to live. In persuading him to this choice you can be of great service to the state."

"With more ditties and doggerel?"

"In a manner of speaking."

"Get to the point."

"We don't want you to collapse again."

"Boorish of me, wasn't it?" Omere coughed. It was a gurgling hacking thing. He turned his head and spat something red into the tray by his pillow.

"There is no treatment for your lung disease. We think you are going to die. It could happen overnight."

"So I have been told."

"If you die, you will not be available to sing to the Magister when he awakens, and in that case, he may elect to die."

"Fear not," said Omere. "When he arrives, I'll be there waiting. I'll teach him to play the harp."

Huntyr was outraged. "How can a dying man speak thus?"

The Regent silenced his aide with an irritated handwave. "Master Surgeon, tell the poet that which he must know."

"Omere Andrek," said the Master Surgeon, "we have decided that you will, in a sense, live."

" 'In a sense'? "

"You have heard of the Rimor computer?"

"Of course. Oberon's pet project. I promised him I'd help program the poetry and music circuits."

"True. And you shall, although perhaps not exactly in the way that you had planned." The surgeon tugged briefly at the beard under his hood, then continued. "The human brain has ten billion neurons, most of which are in the gray matter of the cerebrum. Rimor's equivalents of these circuits take time to program. Yet, if Rimor were programmed and ready to function in three days, Oberon might listen to it when he regains consciousness; and listening, he might be persuaded to live. But Rimor is far from finished."

"I know that." For the first time, Omere felt uneasy. "We need weeks to program the electronic circuits so that they will correspond to those in the human cerebrum."

"But," said the surgeon, "if we had the essential sections of an actual living human cerebrum, we could complete Rimor within twenty-four hours. Fortunately, considering the time available, we will not need the entire brain. The cerebellum and medulla would be superfluous to our purpose, since they deal primarily with the more primitive functions such as internal organs, blood system, musculature, and skin. Even the cerebrum is not needed in its entirety. The temporal lobe, containing the auditory areas, and the prefrontal lobes, as the seat of intelligence, would of course be retained. But most of the areas in the central fissure responsible for vision, taste, smell, and touch, could be excised with little loss, and with great saving in time."

There was a long silence. Sweat began to gather on Omere's face.

The Master Surgeon continued tonelessly. "The surgery involved is simple and painless. The higher centers of consciousness will be anesthetized, of course. The blood flow will be shunted to a cardiac pump, and adequate arterial pressure maintained throughout the procedure, before, during, and after transfer. The neck tissue and spinal cord will be severed. From there, the process is nearly identical to sterile cranial autopsy. I shall start with the usual biparietal incision extending across the cranial vault from the mastoid process. The temporalis muscles are dissected away from the cranial vault and retracted out of the area. A thin-edged biem is used to open the calvaria, and finally, after the dura mater has been divided along the line of the base incision, the brain is removed. The real work ther begins, of selecting the needed elements and making the thousands of connections with the program center of the computer. The work is very intricate and time-consuming, and will take two full days. You will regain consciousness on the third day. You will awaken into darkness, a spirit without body, floating. Your only tactile and motor associations with your environment will be your cerebral integration into your outgoing sound circuits and your incoming aural sensors. You will be able to speak, sing, and energize a fully orchestrated multitude of phonic instruments, and you will be able to hear anyone present in the music room. You will find that, instead of *conducting* orchestra and chorus, you will *be* piano, violins, brass, one hundred instruments, and forty voices. It will take you the balance of the third day to acquire a measure of proficiency in the use of your new facilities of orchestra and voice. You'll have the entire music room to yourself, with multi-stereo, reverberation . . . whatever shall please you. Think, Omere! Your disease is incurable, but you can live!"

Omere writhed beneath the straps. "I refuse. I'd rather die."

"Your refusal is irrelevant."

The white young face looked up at the hooded figure in unbelieving horror. "You'd use force?"

"Why do you think Huntyr strapped you down?"

"But suppose after I become a computer, I choose not to sing?"

"You will not so choose. You will be a quirinal addict by the third day. If you sulk, you will not get your quirinal. I assure you, dear boy, you will perform, and with zeal."

The Regent broke in impatiently. "I don't understand your objections. Look at the advantages. You will be very nearly immortal. A continuing supply of blood will be needed for the excised cerebral segments, of course, but as long as this system is functional, you cannot die."

Omere could barely speak. "But will I continue to exist as myself, or will I be merely a very complex and talented computer?"

"A most profound metaphysical question, my boy," said the surgeon. "When the time comes that it may be asked, only you will be able to answer."

"I can answer now," whispered Omere. "I curse the goddess Alea and the god Ritornel. I curse you, Regent, and you, Surgeon. Most of all I curse Oberon. And now I die. Begin."

The surgeon nodded to the nurse waiting with the syringe. Omere's last thought was that she didn't even swab the skin, and that the omission was logical: he wouldn't be needing it further.

"Glad to see you. I'm Don Poroth, Assistant Registrar. Did you come all by yourself?"

Jimmie looked at the keen thoughtful eyes and found himself relaxing a little. "Yes, sir, Don Poroth."

"Most of the lads are accompanied by one or both of their parents on registration day." Don Poroth looked at the papers in the file, then back at Jimmie. "I see your mother is dead. Sorry. And I imagine Captain Andrek is with the fleet at the moment?"

"No, sir. My father is dead, too."

Don Poroth peered across the desk in sudden sympathy. "Nothing here in the file. Must have been quite recent."

"Yes, sir. I learned only a few weeks ago, when I tried to get in touch with my father through the Naval Bureau to tell him my brother Omere was missing."

"Not *the* Omere Andrek, the Laureate?"

"Yes, sir."

"And still missing, so I understand. Shocking. This leaves you altogether without family?"

"Yes, sir."

Don Poroth arose and began pacing behind his great stone desk. "A pity. What a great pity. And only ten."

He stopped and leaned over the desk. "Andrek, you will meet new friends here. Count me as one. And then there is the great Academy itself. It has been a sheltering mother to many young men, who have spent their twelve years here, and then have gone forth into the world as dons, judges . . . yes, one even became an intergalactic arbiter." He looked into Jimmie's eyes. "The Academy is now your *alma mater.* Do you know what that is?"

"No, sir."

" 'Alma' means 'dear'; 'mater' means 'mother.' "

"Oh."

"We borrowed the words from Terror, long ago. There is a greatness in the ancient Terrovian tongues. Sometimes, they express our thoughts better than our own Ingliz. At least you are not '*a-mater.*' "

"What does that mean?"

" 'Motherless.' From 'ab' and 'mater.' But don't bother about that just now. Plenty of time in the years ahead. So then, run along. The proctor'll show you your room and tell you whatever you need to know."

A few minutes later Jimmie dropped his valise in the proctor's reception cubicle. The proctor glanced at him dubiously. "And where'll we put you?" He studied the dormitory floor plans on his desk. "I'm afraid we can't give you a room of your own just yet. It may be another year before the new wing is completed, and we can look into it again then. Meanwhile, we'll put you in with—hm, yes, Vang. Ajian Vang." He looked at Jimmie noncommittally, and Jimmie understood that his new roommate might be a problem.

He said, "Yes, sir."

Some time later he realized that he and Ajian Vang had been selected as roommates because the proctor viewed them both as misfits. Each was imprinted with his own peculiar prime directive that kept him outside the normal social life of the other boys. Jimmie thought only of finding Omere, and Ajian Vang thought only of Alea. They never became closer; at most, Jimmie built up a guarded toleration for the other boy, who seemed to dislike everybody, including Jimmie.

Ajian Vang's reason for existence was gambling. He did not need the paltry sums he won from the other boys, for his father provided ample spending money. He did it for the sense of power it gave him. Ajian Vang's problem was that whenever Jimmie was around, he inevitably began to lose. And finally Vang began to tell strange tales about Jimmie. Jimmie was a Ritornellian *daimon*. He radiated an aura that upset the Alean laws of chance. He was a deadly enemy of Alea. He was bewitched. In the old days the *daimoni* were strangled without ceremony. It was a serious religious matter that should be reported to the authorities.

None of this really worried Jimmie. Unlike most of the boys, being thought strange did not make him feel a social outcast. But he had never heard of a *daimon* before, and he was curious. Once he caught Don Poroth on the playground and asked him. The good professor laughed. "A complete myth. Long ago, during the Religious Wars, it was thought the *daimoni* could cast a spell that strangely altered Alea's laws of chance—which made them mischievous Ritornellian devils, I suppose. It ran in families, from fathers to sons. With a *daimon* around, Alea's will is bent to that of Ritornel in the most unpredictable ways. But it's not really so—just superstition. Here, let me show you." He fished a coin from his vest pocket, flipped it in the air, and caught it on the back of his hand. "Heads." He flipped again. "Heads. Once more. Heads. Hm. And again heads. Well, I don't know. Shall we? Heads. And again." He looked at Jimmie curiously. "Peculiar, but I'm sure it's all well within the laws of chance." The bell rang. "Not impossible. No, not really. And there's my class. Good-day, Andrek."

Jimmie bowed, puzzled but respectful. "Yes, sir, thank you, sir."

He watched as Poroth walked directly toward the ivy-clad class building. Almost at the archway the professor hesitated in stride and he turned and looked back at Jimmie for the briefest instant.

And I guess that's that, thought Jimmie. And I still don't know what a *daimon* is, except there aren't supposed to be any."

Space became available at the end of the year, and Jimmie moved to his own room. It was shortly after this that a great change suddenly came over Ajian. He announced that he intended to enter holy orders, and to become n Alean monk. Even Jimmie was impressed, if mildly incredulous. But from the date of that announcement, Vang gambled no more. He saved his allowance and bought a modest Alean die, a cultured pyrite dodecahedron. The weird thing, to Jimmie, was that the other's remarkable conversion did not dissipate his dislike of Jimmie; on the contrary, it became worse. It became hatred. Jimmie then gradually got the impression that he was a moving cause of Vang's conversion, and that Alea had wrought her will on Vang through him, Jimmie. And in this, Vang saw a clear directive from the goddess: Jimmie was a *daimon* and must ultimately be destroyed.

Jimmie pushed the thought aside; it was illogical, absurd. As the days and weeks went by, Vang was cool, but polite. In front of the other boys, he always said the right things. And he and Jimmie were never alone together anymore. Jimmie finally decided he was all wrong, and gradually stopped thinking about it.

Jimmie made many acquaintances at the Academy, but few friends. He could never really get his mind off Omere long enough to become wholeheartedly involved with his schoolmates as individuals.

He got away from the Academy whenever he could, to look for Omere. He made sure that the post office kept his Academy address on file, and that the doormen at Omere's favorite nightclubs would be sure to be on the lookout for his lost brother. He spent so much time in Omere's old haunts that his studies suffered and he was put on report.

Poroth requested review of the complaint himself. This, Jimmie knew, was serious. For Poroth was now Dean of the Academy's School of Intergalactic Law, and an important man. Appointments had to be made to see him, and people in outer offices had to tell people in inner offices, and finally somebody came out and told you it was all right to go in.

Poroth got right to the point. "Mr. Andrek, I know why you are neglecting your studies. You are still looking for your brother. I can't really say that I blame you. Perhaps I'm at fault in not telling you that we are looking for him, too."

"Sir?" said Jimmie, surprised.

"When you first came here—six years ago, wasn't it?—I, uh, we—hired a private detective agency. They turned up nothing. A couple of years later, I think it was when I became a full professor of charters, we hired a second agency. Last year, we took on a third. Still no results. They all agreed that Omere entered the Great House shortly before the coronation, that he sang his great epic at the ceremony, and that he was never seen to come out again. The reports are here. You're free to read them, if you'll promise to leave the detective business to the experts."

"Yes, sir. I'd be most grateful." A sudden thought struck him. "These detective agencies . . . they must cost a lot of money. Was there enough in the account Omere set up here in the beginning?"

The dean cleared his throat. "It, ah, comes out of a different fund. Yes, the, ah, Alumni General Aid Fund."

Meaning, thought Jimmie, out of your own pocket. He said quietly, "I'd like very much to see the reports, sir. And you can rest assured about my grades in the future."

That same evening, some fifty kilometers distant from the Academy, a voice in the music room of the Great House called out: "Who's there?"

"I'm Amatar."

"Who's 'Amatar'?"

"I'm a little girl. Can't you see me?"

"No, I can't see anything. I don't have any eyes. You have a pretty name, Amatar. Who is your father?"

"Oberon."

"I won't tell you what I think about your father, Amatar. But I can tell you this: I like you. Do you like to sing?"

"I guess so. But I don't know many songs."

"That's all right. I'll teach you, and then we can sing together. What color is your hair?"

"It's yellow, and I have pretty blue eyes."

"Of course you do! Just as in the song!

> Amatar's a little girl
> With golden curls and sparkly cheeks
> And bright blue eyes a-darting.
> Here she peeks and there she twirls
> ('Tis me she seeks)
> To tell me she's my darling."

The little girl clapped her hands and laughed in high glee. "I didn't know there was any such song!"

"Oh, I know lots of songs that really aren't. Suppose we—now who's *that?*"

"That's my friend Kedrys. He's five, too. He's a kentaur."

"A *what?*"

"A kentaur. You know. He's a boy, except he's part horse, and he has wings."

"Hello, Kedrys."

"He says to tell you hello, Rimor."

"Now that's interesting. Why doesn't he say hello himself? And how does he know my name?"

"Kedrys doesn't like to talk the way you and I talk. He talks into my head. And he listens inside my head, and I guess inside yours. That's how he knows who you are."

"Well I'll be . . . He's a telepath."

"I guess so."

"Can he really fly?"

"He can, but he wants to wait a few years. He's afraid he might get lost, and not be able to get back."

"I see. One flap of the wings, and he vanishes into the countryside?"

"No, you don't see at all. Until he knows exactly how to do it, he's afraid he'll land on some completely different place, not Goris-Kard at all. Maybe an awful place, like Terror. And there he'd be, all lost. So he wants to make sure he knows what to do before he flies. Oh, dear!"

"What's the matter?"

"Kedrys says they are looking for me, and if they find me here, they'll make me promise not to come again. So I'll have to go now."

"But you'll come again?"

"Yes, whenever they aren't looking."

"Wonderful, Amatar. Now, just one little favor before you leave. There's a row of little black knobs on the wall in front of you. Do you see them?"

"Yes."

"Do you know which is your right hand?"

"Of course, silly."

"Good. Now just take hold of the knob on your far right, and turn it several turns."

"All right. I have it—oh, no!"

"What's the matter?"

"Kedrys says I'm not to do it."

"Why not?" The voice from the console was suddenly strained.

"It would do something bad to you. I don't know the word . . . so you'd never sing again. And now they're coming, and we have to go. Good-bye, Rimor."

"Good-bye, Amatar . . . Kedrys." The voice was toneless, weary.

"As you know, young gentlemen of the graduating class, the next hour represents the last opportunity for you to receive instruction within the Academy." From the judge's dais, the cool gray eyes of Dean Poroth swept the "courtroom"—the hall set aside for sessions of the Academy's practice court.

Tonight there were more visitors than students. The great dean was famed for his surprises in the last-hour sessions of practice court. The entire graduating class, old grads, news reporters, even judges from other planets were there, restless with anticipation.

Poroth continued. "The sole case on the docket tonight is *In re Terror.* You will note from the summary of facts in your program that Terror, now devoid of life, has been condemned, the fatal shaft has been drilled to her iron core, and a tug has hauled the planet to the Node. This is the final moment, and intergalactic justice requires that if anyone knows of any lawful reason why the destruction of this planet should not proceed, he will be permitted to speak. We here on the dais represent the twelve intergalactic arbiters, who may well have this exact question at some time within the next few years. The form and framework of the question, of course, is an Order to Show Cause. This means simply that we, the arbiters, have put the condemned planet under an order to show cause why she should not be forthwith destroyed in accordance with the terms of her sentence. You will note from your programs that Mr. Vang will defend the planet; which is to say, he will attempt to show cause why her destruction would not be lawful, and wherefore it would be error to execute the order."

At the mention of his name, Vang arose and bowed to the dais, as was the custom.

"And the rebuttal," continued Dean Poroth, "is the responsibility of Mr. Andrek, who is charged with the duty of convincing us that Mr. Vang's petition is without merit, and that no lawful reason exists for not completing the destruction of Terror. Thus it is given in the program."

James Andrek had duly risen, bowed, and was just sitting down again, smug in the knowledge that he was thoroughly prepared and perfectly rehearsed, when Poroth's last statement struck him. He looked up quickly and caught the dean's half-smile. He dropped numbly into his chair, and a chill began crawling up his spine.

"However," continued the dean blandly, "in the furtherance of the Academy's primary objective, which is educating young men to become dons we will make a very slight change in the program." He leaned forward a little. "A thoroughly prepared don must know his opposition's case as well as he knows his own: its strengths and weaknesses. He thus broadens his knowledge and frees himself of prejudice. Only then can he with certainty prepare his own case."

Andrek and Vang stared at each other, united at least for the hour in the comradeship of the doomed.

Poroth smiled benignly down at them. "I see counsel have already divined the program change. It is just this: they will exchange places. Mr. Andrek will not argue for Terror's destruction; he will instead attempt to persuade us to save her. And Mr. Vang, of course, will similarly reverse his role: he will rebut Mr. Andrek's petition, and give us reasons why the sentence of planetary death should be duly carried out. In this way, each prospective young don can demonstrate his familiarity with the other's case. And now, there being no reason further to delay the coming display of juridical virtuosity, we will hear from the petitioner to save Terror. Mr. Andrek, your summary, please!"

It was not fair! The sins of the loser of the Terrovian Wars were known to every schoolboy. She had been justly condemned. What could be said in her defense? He needed more time! He rose, pale and drawn.

"If it please your Excellencies, the condemnation of Terror cannot lawfully proceed. Terror was never a party to the Intergalactic Statutes that provide for her destruction. Condemnation is therefore not due process of law, but rather a judicial continuation of the war, which, however, ended years ago with the death of the last Terrovian. The arbiters are therefore without jurisdiction. And finally, it is not possible to commit a crime until there is a law that states the crime. Yet my client was found guilty of committing the crime of starting a nuclear war before there was an intergalactic law making nuclear aggression a crime, much less a crime punishable by annihilation of the aggressor. Cause is therefore shown why the order should not be granted." He bowed awkwardly and sat down.

"Thank you, Mr. Andrek. Mr. Vang?"

Andrek glowered at the Alean novice, who smiled sweetly back. "Petitioner has raised no point competent for review here." He looked at his notes. "Each arbiter has taken an oath to support the Intergalactic Treaty. The treaty requires destruction of every person, country, or planet starting a nuclear war. No procedural error in the proceedings below is suggested. No suggestion is made that Terror did not start a nuclear war, and wage it with all means at her disposal. No suggestion is made that Terror does not normally deserve her fate. No cause is shown; the order should be dismissed." He bowed gracefully.

"Thank you, Mr. Vang. You may be seated." Poroth leaned forward and touched his fingertips together. "We can now give our decision, from the bench. The petitioner, Mr. Andrek, has not, to our satisfaction, shown cause why the destruction of Terror should not proceed. The charges will therefore forthwith be placed, and the planet duly destroyed. So ordered." He looked at the two young men earnestly. "What I did to you both was unfair, and especially unfair to you, Mr. Andrek, for you had a hard case indeed. But in the long pull it will be of great benefit to you both. *Know your opponent's case!* And that's not all you should know. On the practical side, know your judge. When the court, as here, is composed of several judges, twelve to be exact, know them all. The personalities and leanings of each of the twelve arbiters is well-known throughout the Twelve Galaxies that they represent. Our own Zhukan, for example, is a stickler for the niceties of due process. Werebel, on the other hand, is a sentimentalist. He favors the underdog. Maichec is interested only in the ultimate moralities; you must persuade him a thing is just or unjust, no matter what the treaties say. But what happened? Neither of you paid the slightest attention to us arbiters as people. Any questions so far? Yes, Mr. Andrek?"

"Sir, you keep talking about 'twelve' arbiters, but I notice that actually there are only eight people on the dais, seven students and yourself. Would you explain that, sir?"

"I shall certainly *not* explain it, Mr. Andrek. It must be irrelevant to counsel *why* only eight of my twelve brother arbiters are here. What *is* relevant to counsel is whether the diminution of the full number changes the presentation of his case. May I have your views on *that*, Mr. Andrek?"

James had it instantly. "In cases involving Section Nine of the treaty, the destruction of a planet, only the full court—all twelve arbiters—may act. In such case, an eight-man court is not competent to sit."

"Not bad at all," smiled Dean Poroth. Mr. Vang, any comment?"

"Its easy to say that here, sir. This is just practice court. But what if it really happened? Do you think any of us would really tell eight inter-galactic arbiters they're not competent to hear a case?"

"Courage, Mr. Vang. Put it to them this way: You're acting as a friend of the court in pointing out how they're about to sit in violation of the treaty. Then ask for a thirty-day continuance. Ten to one you'll get it. Gives them time to decide who's insane. And now, if there are no more questions, practice court is dismissed. Mr. Andrek, may I see you in chambers?"

Dean Poroth leaned back in the great leather chair and contemplated the young man over folded hands. He seemed to like what he saw. "Have you made any plans, James?"

Andrek started. During all his years at the Academy, the dean had never before called him by his first name. Until he had reached sixteen he had been simply "Andrek." After sixteen the professors added "Mister." And he was now twenty-two. "None, sir. I'll look for a job here on Goris-Kard, I suppose. I want to stay here to look for my brother."

"Twelve years is a long time, James. Can't you accept—"

"No, sir."

"I suppose not. Well, you were trained in the law, but of course you are free not to become a don. A number of the young gentlemen will in fact leave the profession. I understand Mr. Vang will be accepted into Alean orders."

"Yes, sir. He has always been very, ah, religious."

"Hm. Yes, of course. What I'm leading up to, James, is a way for you to remain in the profession, and yet continue the search for your brother. Would you like that?"

"Indeed yes, sir. But how—?"

"You'll recall that all the people who have looked into your brother's disappearance agree on one thing: he went into the Great House, sang at the coronation, and was not seen to come out. Now, if you were to be employed within the Great House itself, say as assistant to the third secretary in the Foreign Office (a position which I understand is presently vacant), you might be able to develop some real information."

Andrek moved forward eagerly in his chair. "Oh, thank you, sir!" Then his face fell. "No offense, sir, but I had thought that all appointments of this type had to be made by the arbiter representing the Home Galaxy."

Poroth's eyes twinkled. "Quite so. However, Arbiter Zhukan is retiring within a few days. The Great House has already selected his successor, but the appointment will not be made public until tomorrow. Like you, James, I too am spending my last week at the Academy."

"You, sir, *arbiter?* They could not have selected better! Congratulations, sir!" He fumbled for the right words: "—in Ritornel's design and Alea's favor!"

Poroth chuckled. "Thank you, James. And I hope the best for you, in the Great House."

5. AN APPROACHING EXPLOSION

Somewhat to his own surprise, and assisted somewhat by the flux and uncertainties of high-level government service, Andrek advanced rapidly in the Great House. Within three years he was second secretary of the Foreign Office.

During these first years at the Great House he had occasion to attend a performance in the music room. The program consisted of three symphonies, composed, he understood, by computer. There was something about the music that haunted him. For several nights afterward, he would hear the strange themes again, and would awaken from dreams of Omere. He had been invited to subsequent performances, but the demands of the Foreign Office had interfered.

He had quickly become acquainted with most of the inhabitants of the Great House, and had eventually even met Oberon, the Magister. He soon knew the members of the cabinet, the captains of the guard, and Oberon's daughter, a fragile adolescent named Amatar, who seemed always in the company of that strange winged creature, Kedrys.

He heard remarkable stories about Amatar. The exquisite child was said to be quite at home in the palace zoo with exotic creatures from other planets. The furry little *zlonas,* whose breath could kill a man, would come at her call and nestle in her arms. The great six-legged bison of Antara, whom even the keeper dared not approach, ate gladly from her hand, and moaned and pawed the ground when she left. There was no danger. She carried a protective witchery with her.

Andrek wondered whether Oberon was aware of this side of his daughter's life, and discovered, to his mixed relief and disquiet, that the Magister was indeed aware. Guards, both visible and invisible, attended the girl everywhere she went. And when the *goru* stretched its hideous head over the magnetic fence to give Amatar an affectionate lick of its tongue, the cross hairs of a needle biem half a kilometer away watchfully followed its heart. How many times, he wondered, had a similar biem watched *him*?

But if Amatar was strange, Kedrys was stranger. His chimeric body had no effect on his intellect, except perhaps to stimulate it. He had his own laboratory in his rooms, and his boyish inventions were discussed (with disbelief) throughout Goris-Kard. While in his early teens he had written learned papers on the mathematics of matter transport, the nature of the Deep, time warp, and the mechanics of destiny. They were largely ignored; hardly anyone could understand them. Except for Amatar, Kedrys seemed to have no friends. It could hardly be otherwise, in Andrek's view. How could a normal human being be chummy with a winged creature whose IQ was too high to register on the meter?

Most of the staff complained about the loneliness of the trips to distant systems. But Andrek welcomed them. The solitude, the change of pace, gave him an opportunity to review progress, or lack of it, in his long search for Omere, and to plan the next step. Trip orders had a habit of coming suddenly—his valise and attaché case were always packed and ready to go. He generally carried a three-day supply of linen. If the trip took longer, there'd be a laundry somewhere, or he could even wash out something himself.

More and more he was becoming convinced that the detectives originally hired by Poroth, and more recently those hired by himself, were being stopped cold by some unknown exterior factor at the very threshold of discovery. He needed someone with an entrée, even personal contacts, at the very highest level in the Great House. He needed someone who had been acquainted with the coronation ceremonies of years ago; perhaps even someone (if that were possible) who had known Oberon as a youth.

In his sixth year in the Foreign Office he was assigned a field trip to represent the Home Galaxy at the ceremonies for drilling the great shaft

1 the condemned planet, Terror. The process would be demonstrated in miniature to the visiting functionaries in temporary buildings on Terror's moon. Even after decades, Terror's nuclear fires were still burning, and the shaft, a hundred meters in diameter, would have to be dug by a giant, remote-controlled diamond-toothed capsule. The shaft would gradually close behind the capsule, squeezed shut by massive pressures of trillions of tons of overburden. And as the capsule was closing to the last few hundred kilometers of the semimolten iron core, they would start Terror on her long journey to the Node. There, a series of explosive charges within the capsule would be ignited in augmented sequence. Titanic waves would be set up inside the planet's core, each reinforcing the one preceding. And within days the core would break through the lithosphere. The planet would disintegrate, her dust quickly lost in the vastness of new space continually forming at the Node.

After a half-day's journey by hyper-drive courier ship, Andrek walked down the ramp into the tempo-bubble built into the side of a crater on Terror's airless moon. He walked into his room, turned the polarizer on the single porthole to shut out the blinding glare of Terror's sun sinking over the far wall of the crater, and then realized that he hadn't eaten all day.

The dining hall, hastily erected and undersized, was crowded. Andrek stood just inside the entranceway, looking for the engineers' table. He wanted more detail on the drill mechanism for his report.

But the only empty chair he saw was at a table almost straight ahead, and this chair was tipped against the table as though it were being reserved for someone. He glanced in casual disappointment at the occupant of the adjacent chair—and started.

Glittering dark eyes stared back at him. It was Ajian Vang, elbows on table, chin propped up on his folded hands, sitting with two other men.

At the instant of mutual recognition Vang's hands separated, and he made a peculiar gesture with his fists as they moved apart across his chest. There was something tantalizing and sinister about this motion that Andrek could not immediately identify. And just then Vang arose, smiled at him, and motioned to the empty chair.

After a moment of uncertainty—while he stared at the white-clad figure (for Vang wore the robes of an Alean monk), Andrek sighed, forced himself to smile back, then walked over and shook hands with his old classmate. He had no desire to renew school ties. He would just as soon have avoided the encounter altogether.

Vang's palm was wet; Andrek had to resist an impulse to wipe his own surreptitiously on the side of his trousers before accepting Vang's introduction to the other two men.

One of the men was named Hasard, a large, rather brutish type. As Andrek understood it, Hasard worked for the third man, who seemed to radiate a luxuriant prosperity, and who had evidently at some time past been involved in a serious accident. The left side of his face showed the unmistakable marks of plastic surgery, and a golden patch covered his left eye. He seemed to wear his scars proudly, though he might easily have hidden them with an attractive beard. The butts of two pistols peeked out from shoulder holsters just inside his velvet jacket. Vang introduced him as Huntyr.

Vang was watching Andrek's face carefully and seemed to enjoy the advocate's mystification. The Alean then explained, with poorly concealed pride: "The Great House has asked that the Huntyr agency cooperate with me in security measures for the demolition of Terror. Actually, there have been no problems at all, and we foresee none. But it is best to be sure. Everyone here in the moon-works has been screened by our group." He spread his hands delicately. "Everyone."

To Andrek, several facts were immediately clear. Vang had risen high in Alean circles, and was now in an Alean security unit assigned to the Great House. Vang knew all about Andrek, and his duties and assignments, including this trip to the Terror drill-site. Vang had selected this table just inside the dining hall, and had held the chair, awaiting Andrek's entrance.

Why? As far as Andrek could make out, there was no clear answer. Perhaps Vang's fragile ego was somehow strengthened by demonstrating to Andrek his status in the religo-governmental hierarchy. But he had an uneasy feeling there was more to it than that.

He smiled. "I understand, Ajian. I was investigated, and since I am here, I presume that I was cleared. I was investigated years ago, of course, before I was accepted into the Foreign Office. Investigation does not offend me. It is a necessary thing. But enough for me. How about you? You seem to be doing well with the Aleans. Are you happy there?"

Vang looked at Andrek suspiciously. "Of course."

Huntyr interrupted smoothly. "I understand you and Brother Vang were at the Academy together."

"We were classmates," said Andrek politely.

"This Terror thing should remind you of old times," said Vang. "Do you remember that last session in practice court, when you and I were on opposite sides?"

Andrek nodded. (He would never be allowed to forget that one!)

Vang explained to Huntyr and Hasard. "On the program, I was supposed to save Terror, and Andrek was to make sure she was blown up. But who could save Terror? My case was lost from the beginning, I thought. Fortunately for me, the dean switched signals on us at the very last instant, right in front of everybody. The problem of saving Terror was assigned to

Andrek, and he lost, of course. It was really rather humorous, except that no one dared laugh, eh, Andrek?"

"Nobody laughed," said Andrek. He pondered the Alean's face thoughtfully. There was definitely something wrong with Vang. Conflicting forces within him were tearing him to pieces, and his face showed it to anyone who remembered him from the Academy. Andrek surmised it was the old problem, heightened and accentuated now by adult sophistication and enhanced ability for self-torture. Vang wanted two things. He wanted to lose himself within the intricate convolutions of the Alean structure. Equally, he wanted money. Even as Andrek watched, fascinated, Vang's eyes moved caressingly over Huntyr's iridescent fur-lined velours. And when the investigator's diamond-studded golden neck-chain flashed, Vang put his hand up to his throat as though to hide the cheap brass chain that supported his own pendant die. Andrek almost felt sorry for him. If he does not decide soon, thought the advocate, this thing will kill him.

He forced himself to reopen the conversation. "There are a couple of features about the Terror program that puzzle me. Why can't the planet be destroyed right here? Why do we have to haul her to the Node?"

"It's the dust and debris, afterward," said Huntyr. "It would be too dangerous to navigation to blow her here. At the Node, there's no such problem."

Andrek nodded. "I can see that. But why the *chemical* explosives? Why not nuclear?"

Huntyr smiled. "There can be no nuclear reaction at the Node, Don Andrek. Ships have to shift over to old-style chemical reaction motors when they enter the Node area. Even a biem won't fire there." He patted his left shoulder holster. "That's why I also carry a slug-gun. It's on account of the bugs."

"He means the ursecta," explained Vang. "Strange little creatures that metabolize pure energy into protons."

"That would account for it," agreed Andrek.

"And so the demolition crew has a long way to go," said Huntyr. "After the drilling starts, more than a thousand giant tugs will be required. They'll lock onto the planet and start hauling her, moon and all, to the Node. It will indeed be a long drawn-out and very expensive process, requiring subsidies from all the galaxies. And two years from now, when they finally reach the Node, there'll of course be a final hearing by the entire Court of Arbiters."

"A mere formality," said Andrek. "Nothing can save Terror. It will be my job to ensure that."

"I understand our old friend, Dean Poroth, has been made the Chief Arbiter," said Vang.

"Yes. Certainly he's highly qualified. And it seems likely that the next time I see him will be in support of a show-cause order for Terror's destruction. And with no switch in the program." It was all very curious. Terror's final hearing had to come, and Andrek was looking forward to it with considerable pleasure, if only to see Poroth again.

Vang broke the silence. There was a strange chill edge on his voice. "You never found any trace of your brother Omere?"

And now Andrek had an impression . . . a sudden insight . . . that *this* was why Vang had invited him to their table. Something, for great good, or for great evil, was in the making. He said slowly: "Nothing more than you could hear on the general tapes. He participated in the coronation. And then he vanished. None of the detective agencies that I have hired could find any real evidence that he left the Great House after the coronation."

Vang's eyes glittered. "Huntyr was in the personal service of his excellency, the Magister, before Oberon reached his majority. The Huntyr agency might have unique access to—certain information . . ."

Andrek looked at Huntyr speculatively. It was almost too good to believe. Perhaps here at last was the contact he had been seeking—someone who had known the youthful Oberon. The only thing wrong with the idea was its source: Vang. He knew now that he was moving into grave danger. And he couldn't care less. He asked the big man: "Can you take the case?"

"It is possible. Andrek . . . haven't I heard that name before?"

Vang's eyes caught Huntyr's single one. "Everyone has heard of Omere Andrek, the Laureate. We can confer on this later."

"I'll take the case," said Huntyr.

"Good," said Vang. "And as we part, I'd like to propose a toast to the early reunion of the Andreks." He poured a round of liqueurs. Into his own glass he dropped a tiny white pellet, then raised the liquid to his lips. "Reunion," he repeated.

"I'll drink to that," said Andrek. "At least to reunion with Omere. My father is dead."

But Vang seemed not to hear.

Huntyr smiled grimly at Andrek as they put down their glasses. "The Aleans are not content to be the galaxy's foremost poisoners; they assume that everyone is attempting to poison *them*. Hence the general antidote after every meal. Oh, don't worry. We're perfectly safe."

When Andrek returned to his room, he noted that Terror's sun had set over the crater rim, and that the planet herself was now faintly visible. The great stricken globe hung just over the horizon, its dark side unrelieved by even a hairline of a crescent. But there was no need for reflected sun light to illuminate this thing-beyond-horror. On its right limb, the western edge of one great continent burned crimson beneath clouds twenty kilometers deep, visible as a luminous haze, and generated by the action of seas on flaming shores. To the west was the darkness of Terror's great central ocean, which spanned nearly a hemisphere. It would be some hours yet before the revolving planet would present the continents beyond that immense water.

He stripped, climbed into his sleeping robe, and then into the little bunk.

Andrek awoke from a fitful sleep. A red glare was flickering on the ceiling overhead, and at first he thought the place was on fire. But then he remembered. Terror was turning on its axis to reveal its land side, incandescent with nuclear fires. The portholes in the moon-globe, overlain with red filters against the torrents of ultraviolet light, provided the crimson display within the room.

He found his slippers quietly and glided over to the little window. And there he watched in fascination as the leading eastern edge of Terror's largest continent moved majestically forward, and in the southern hemisphere the great island continent came slowly into view. It was just, that Terror should stand thus and be purified before her final terrible punishment to come. Thirty billion souls had died here in the climax of the Horror. It had been an act of terrible vengeance by the League led by Goris-Kard, in whose planets more than twice that number had died over the years of the revolt.

"It is but just," he muttered defensively. And then he thought, why must I reassure myself? Just, or not just, it was done, and now it is all history.

But it was not that simple. When, not so many years ago, he had lost his ill-fated "save-Terror" petition at Poroth's practice court, he had delved thoroughly into Terror's history. There were two sides to Terror. The planet was not totally bad. She had, in fact, contributed much to the civilization of the Home Galaxy. But none of this mattered anymore. It had not saved her people, and now none of them were left to prevent her own certain destruction.

Finally, he drew the blinds and returned to bed.

As he lay there, on the edge of sleep, his thoughts returned to Vang's odd motion with his fists, at the moment their eyes had met across the dinner table.

And now, at last, he had it. Vang's cord of Alea that had held his robes loosely about his waist. The thin, black cord, tightly woven in a strange plait design, with a brass buckler over the rip knot at the side. There were no loops on the robe to hold it. It could be disengaged for use instantly. And for what use he knew by rumor. The Aleans with security training had a use for it. It was a strangling cord. And the act of strangling was done by that strange gesture with the hands. Probably Vang had not even been consciously aware of it. (Which made it worse!) Andrek put uneasy fingers to his throat, and thought back to the day at school when he first had the weird foreknowledge that Vang had resolved to kill him.

It had been from this trip that he had returned to the Great House and noticed the strange young woman, standing just outside the music room, with her hand on Kedrys' golden mane, and watching Andrek covertly from the corner of her eye as he walked past her toward the wing of the Foreign Office.

There's Kedrys, was his first thought, as he passed them, nodding politely, but where's Amatar?

Only when he reached the end of the corridor and looked back (by then they were gone) did he realize that the woman *was* Amatar. In a space of weeks something had changed her from a child into a lovely young woman. He knew, in an academic way, that girls did this. Even so, it was incomprehensible, and he shook his head in wonder.

6. SURGEON AND PILGRIM

In the music room a lone gray-robed figure spoke quietly into the console receptors. "I have come to bid you farewell. My work on Goris-Kard is nearly done. I leave you now, but Amatar will care for you. The prophecy is at work, and the days of its completion draw near."

"You are mad, Surgeon," muttered the console. "By the mad gods of Ritornel and Alea, you are mad. You are beyond hating. Yet I crawl and beg and have no pride: Turn the knob. Cut the blood flow. *Release me!*"

"Rimor," said the gray figure, "when you sing of Terror tonight, sing of a planet cleansed by fire, rinsed in the Deep, and finally, peopled by gods, returned to rule the universe."

"On one small condition, Surgeon. You will take the next ship to the Node and jump into the first quake that comes along."

"Agreed," said the robed one.

Andrek looked at the credit refund on the desk in front of him, and then at the man who had placed it there, and a chill began to crawl slowly up his spine.

James Andrek was at this time in his twenty-eighth year. His face was still a strange mixture of innocence and haunted inquiry, and it showed more clearly than ever the impact of his enduring, armed truce with destiny, whereby he gauged every incident, and evaluated every point in time, only with respect to their contribution to the core of his existence, which was the unceasing search for his brother.

The investigator hired two years ago to find Omere had just now terminated the assignment. Something was wrong; strangely, terribly wrong.

The one-eyed man behind the desk watched Andrek's reaction with a fleeting smile, which Andrek noted with further unease. He was thankful that the smile was brief: combined with the glinting eye patch and twisted cheek scar, it seemed more like a snarl.

Huntyr spoke quietly. "Let me dispose of a subsidiary matter, first. You have the final report of this agency on the death of Captain Andrek, your father. We have been able to add very little to what you already knew. We have confirmed the presence of his ship, *Xerol,* at the Node during the quake of eighteen years ago. He was killed, of course. His body was eventually recovered, and he was buried in space. Copies of the official Naval Bureau notices are in our report. We believe this closes the investigation with regard to your father."

Andrek waited.

After studying his client a moment, Huntyr continued. "Don Andrek, the investigation of your brother's disappearance is quite another matter. We now find that we erred in accepting the assignment. We should have realized this in the beginning. Our charges to you arising out of our search for your brother over the past several years have totaled seven thousand gamma. We now refund this."

Andrek watched the two burly assistants carefully from the corner of his eye. One, whom he recognized as Hasard, was leafing idly through a filing cabinet. The other was replacing tapes in a storage case. Andrek knew he was not likely to be hurt for the next few minutes. He got control of his voice. "The credit is for ten thousand."

Huntyr transfixed the advocate with a glinting pupil ill-concealed within a half-closed eyelid. "Compensation for our negligence in wasting your time."

The game can be played, thought Andrek, at least for a little while. If Huntyr wants to be a reluctant witness, then I'll be the cross-examining don. Almost as though we were in court. But with a crucial difference. In court, the witness would not be permitted to kill me if I ask the wrong questions.

He picked up the credit with a well-simulated gesture of disappointment. "The compensation is little enough, especially when I myself showed you the old news-tapes proving my brother was last seen entering the Great House, right here on Goris-Kard."

"That was eighteen years ago. After so much time, the evidence often becomes very hazy. Witnesses die, disappear." He studied Andrek with apparent languor. "You do not think the compensation enough?"

Andrek toyed with the credit, and tried to sound convincing. "It is not very much, after raising my hopes so high. When I got your message this afternoon, I was certain you had definite news. How could my brother be swallowed up without a trace? Omere Andrek was the Laureate when he disappeared. He had given recitals on every major planet of the Home Galaxy. His face was known to billions."

Huntyr's one eye narrowed still further. "We deeply regret your disappointment, Don Andrek. Under the circumstances, we will double the compensation."

The man at the tape case became suddenly motionless as Andrek put the credit into his jacket pocket, then relaxed as the advocate put both hands back on the desk.

"That will not be necessary," said Andrek. He now fully understood that some person—or persons—unknown to him had *caused* (not merely persuaded) the agency to discontinue the investigation, and that this new situation had just been conveyed to him, Andrek, for his full understanding; and further, that, if he persisted, he would be killed.

He had to play for time. Huntyr certainly had secret information. It was time to let the investigator know that he, Andrek, realized he was being cheated. Except that he could not say so, not in so many words. Not yet. So he said nothing, but merely raised his eyebrows and stared quizzically at the investigator.

As Andrek's mute insinuation sank in, Huntyr's scar began to glow a dull pink. "This is a reputable agency," he clipped. "We have been in business for eighteen years. We have branch offices on every major planet of the Home Galaxy. We serve a distinguished clientele. Even the Great House retains us. For your information, young man, I was once in the personal service of Oberon of the Delfieri. And I might add that the Magister still calls on me for assistance in matters of great trust. So, if you are not satisfied with our findings, you are free to go elsewhere."

"You speak of the Great House," said Andrek quietly. "Let me remind you, Huntyr, that I am attached to the legal staff of the Great House."

The office was suddenly deathly still. Huntyr was barely breathing. The two assistants were again instantly motionless.

So, thought Andrek, your new client outranks me. You must be protected very nobly indeed. The question that I have not yet asked, you have very nearly answered. For you, Huntyr, know the fate of my brother, and whether he is dead or alive. Your agency has probably uncovered these answers from the person or persons unknown, responsible for my brother's disappearance, and they have bought you off. They must be rich. And powerful: they know of my connection with the Great House, and apparently it does not trouble them. And who are they? There are three general possibilities: the Great House; the Temple of Alea; the Temple of Ritornel. Andrek thought in legal terms. Query, may Huntyr now be tricked into naming one of these three?

He had to consider a number of things very quickly. He had never before been involved in physical danger. Yet he planned to take a risk in the next few seconds that would call on him for more poise and courage than he had so far expended in his entire lifetime. He had sought his brother too long not to seize the opportunity for one more answer.

"I am expected straightway at the Great House," he said. The evenness of his voice both astonished and pleased him. "When I get there, I shall let it slip to certain of my more talkative friends that you know my brother's whereabouts and have agreed to tell me everything for fifty thousand gamma."

Huntyr's single eye glittered. He took a long noisy breath. "No one will believe that, Don Andrek."

"Believe?" asked Andrek with quiet scorn. "They *know* you will betray—for enough money."

Huntyr sighed and moved slightly forward.

There was a faint click behind Andrek, and he realized that the door was locked.

"James, Don Andrek," rasped Huntyr, "you are a very clever man. You make people tell you things they shouldn't. Yet, in some ways, you are not clever at all. You are alone—without family. Your parents are dead. Your brother . . . If *you* should disappear, who would take the trouble to look into it? People disappear on Goris-Kard every day. A few lines in the morning news reports, and that's the end of it. They become police statistics. I hope you understand that there's nothing personal in what is going to happen to you now."

As soon as any one of them reaches for a biem, thought Andrek, I'm going to overturn the desk on Huntyr. If that works, maybe they'll shoot each other in the crossfire.

But the next motion was not a grab for a biem. Rather it was the mouth of the investigator—opening wide in amazement.

For the door behind Andrek clicked again and—opened. Andrek whirled to assess this new variable.

It was a Ritornellian friar—in the coarse gray robes of a pilgrim. Leaving the door open behind him, he clasped his gloved hands together within his long rasping sleeves and bowed with faint smiles to each of the four men. He spoke in a husky, apologetic whisper, addressing himself apparently to no one in particular. "I'm sorry about the door. Since it was locked, it was necessary to open it. But it is not damaged."

Andrek forgot his fear momentarily as his startled eyes swept rapidly over the newcomer. For one fleeting moment he thought he recognized him. But as he studied the intruder, the feeling of pseudo-recognition faded, and he quickly became convinced that his first impression must have been only wishful thinking. The large bearded face of the newcomer had a distinctly alien cast. A rare type of hominid? wondered Andrek. The beard was gray, yet strangely thick, like an animal pelt, and it rose so high on the stranger's face that even the cheekbones, if they existed, were concealed. The great head seemed to sit squarely on the shoulders, without benefit of intervening neck. Andrek had the impression that the intruder would have to swivel his entire torso to turn his head. And the eyes! They were overlarge, bulging, yet liquid, luminous, strangely attracting. As he stared into them, Andrek caught a sudden, staggering vision of vast space, of time without end . . . and death. Involuntarily, he blinked, and the vision vanished. But this was not all. Even in the full light of Huntyr's office, the pilgrim's entire face seemed to glow with a pale blue radiance, Andrek could not imagine what caused it; he had never heard of anything like it before. For that matter, he had never seen a pilgrim before, although he had heard of them. As he understood the custom, when a Ritornellian friar felt death drawing near, he would sometimes decide to put on the gray of the pilgrim, and take passage to the Node, there to die.

All in all, the apparition was breathtaking.

He was not alone in his impressions. There was something about the visitor that seemed to jar Huntyr and his assistants. Andrek noted that, save for their heavy breathing, the three were absolutely motionless. And why not? What fantastic mechanism did this strange creature carry on his person that could unlock Huntyr's door? Everyone knew, of course, of the remarkable science of the Ritornellians. Andrek realized he had just witnessed one demonstration, and that there might well be another if Huntyr did anything abrupt.

The pilgrim turned casually to Andrek. "Your pardon, brother. If you were leaving, do not let my discourteous entry detain you."

"By your leave, brother," murmured Andrek. He would not complicate things by offering to stay. He thought it unlikely that any assistance would be needed. He bowed with clasped hands and out-turned elbows, to indicate the eternal Ring of Ritornel, and muttered the farewell of the Ritornellians: " 'The end is but the beginning.' "

The pilgrim bowed. "For always we return."

Only after he had closed the door behind him and was halfway to the transport tube did Andrek begin to speculate. Was the powerful Temple of Ritornel now his official ally? Or was the pilgrim merely interfering on his own? In either case, why? Was the Temple involved in some grandiose scheme that required that he be alive—at least for the moment? Be that as it may, the pilgrim had certainly saved his life. And then it suddenly occurred to him that the holy man must eventually demand payment. And the price, he suspected, might be very high indeed.

One thing was certain: he could not mention any of this to Amatar.

7. ANDREK AND AMATAR

The servant led him from the anteroom through the great hallway into the colonnade bordering the garden. "The Mistress Amatar will meet you here, Don Andrek, and if you will permit, I will wait with you until she arrives."

"Yes," said Andrek. He well understood that even well-known members of the Great House staff could not be permitted to wander unescorted here in the interior grounds.

In a nearby vine-wrapped shrine erected long ago by a Delfieri determined to offend neither Alea nor Ritornel, a great metallic dodecahedron floated and revolved slowly within an immense iron ring hung from the ceiling. The twelve numbers of the die, in ritual sequence, turned one by one to the corresponding numbers in the ring.

Everywhere, the air was heavy with the scent of flowers. Andrek took a deep breath. "The gardens are lovely this time of year," he murmured.

"The gardens are always lovely," said the servant bluntly.

"Ah? Oh, of course." Far overhead he caught the glint of a great transparent dome. He realized that he was in a huge greenhouse. He could imagine the corps of gardeners required to keep these acres in continuing bloom. It was lighted, and (he imagined) heated, by a great ball of light, now moving slowly, almost imperceptibly, down the far wall of the structure, like a sinking sun. He noticed then that someone was approaching them, back-lit by that artificial orb. His heart leaped.

Amatar of the Delfieri glided toward them, barefoot along the stone flagging. Kedrys trotted at her side.

Andrek had of course seen them together many times, but could never rid himself of the illusion that these were imaginary people from another world, perhaps merely sojourning here, that they belonged together, and that it was ridiculous to think of separating them by marrying Amatar. He shivered a little, as he found himself thinking, What is their destiny? Then he shook himself. This was insanity. Amatar was a human being, whereas Kedrys was . . . was what? What was Kedrys? He did not know. For some strange senseless reason, he was suddenly jealous of this beautiful creature. It defined nothing, solved nothing, to say that Kedrys was superhuman. There was more to it than that. Kedrys had little in common with the hominids. Kedrys was beyond humanity.

Kedrys' great golden wings were presently folded down along the withers of the palomino body. The "horse" part of the boy was actually less than pony-size. His human torso, gleaming under his woven silver jacket, showed considerable enlargement and downward extension of the rib cage, evidently needed to ensure adequate oxygen intake in flight. The equine chest, on the other hand, was known to contain no lungs, but to consist in considerable part of the immense laminations of muscles needed for the wings. His bones were cellulated, like those of birds. Andrek had been told that Kedrys weighed but little more than Amatar. The olive skin of his young face seemed as fresh and delicate as Amatar's, and, in his own way, the boy was breathtaking: he was a wraith enfleshed, yet sensuous, almost godlike. He resembled Amatar in ways that suggested brother and sister; which, of course, Andrek knew was biologically absurd. But, even to this day he had not been able to discover the origins of this fabulous creature, who at once was animal, boy, and angel. Even Amatar seemed not to know; or if she did, she would not tell him. He had searched in vain for references to a winged kentaur in the genetic libraries. Had Kedrys been brought in by a far-distant geodetic patrol, from some uncharted system? He could only speculate. There was certainly some mystery here. Some day, if he ever settled the problem of his brother, he might look into it.

As the pair drew near, they smiled at him, and the butterflies left the nearer flowers and circled their heads in an iridescent halo.

Andrek heard a sigh, and from the corner of his eye saw the face of the porter go slack with admiration. He has seen them together since infancy, thought the advocate, and yet once again he finds them beautiful. And how right he is, never to become accustomed to them—and especially to *her!* For Andrek was quite certain that Amatar was fairer even than the first woman, described in the Terrovian mythbook as the original mother of men. She was sensuous, lithe and exciting, yet fragile, fairylike.

He studied her in admiration. One white blossom accented her hair, which now floated out behind her in an amber cloud. Almond eyes sparkled at him from beneath darkened eyelids. She wore a very light, loose flowing gold lamé skirt and bodice. Her waist and arms were bare, and it seemed to him that her olive skin glowed with the scent of strange flowers.

And now, they were in love. And that involved problems. For James Andrek was well-known to be the last survivor of a minor family of professionals fallen into straitened circumstances, without estate or prospects.

And Amatar was the daughter of Oberon of the Delfieri.

"Jim!" cried the girl, radiant with color. "How good of you to come early!"

"Hello, both of you," smiled Andrek. He shook hands warmly with Kedrys.

Words formed in Andrek's mind. "Hello, Don Andrek."

Amatar's laughter was like small silver bells. "Kedrys, you are hopeless." She looked up at Andrek. "His voice is changing; so he reverts to telepathy, even though he knows it's bad manners."

"That's all right."

She took them both by the arm and the three started back up the walk. "Kedrys will walk with us as far as the Genetics Building," said Amatar. "He's due there for the Alean seminar."

Kedrys made a derisive noise.

Andrek struggled to keep his face straight.

The girl flushed. "Kedrys!"

"I gather you don't think much of the seminar," Andrek said to Kedrys.

The kentaur grinned. "It's a lot of fun. They study me. I study them. Anyhow, I think this'll be the last session."

"Why?" asked Andrek curiously.

"Because of his thesis," explained Amatar dryly. "*Displacement of the Hominid by the Kentaur.*"

Andrek laughed. "I can understand why they might want to close you out."

Kedrys looked across at the advocate curiously. He spoke aloud in a crackling voice that changed octaves several times. "Would you laugh, Don Andrek, if you hominids really were succeeded by kentaurs?"

Andrek considered this. "I don't really know," he said seriously. "Perhaps not. But the whole question is academic. It can't actually happen. At least not in my lifetime, or yours."

And now it was Kedrys' turn to laugh, a mixed audio-mental laughter, pealing, animal-like.

Andrek shook his head. Sometimes he simply did not understand this remarkable creature.

They were now at the entranceway to Genetics, where a monitor in the loose white robe denoting the Temple of Alea awaited them. He bowed gravely.

Amatar exchanged embraces with Kedrys, who put his wings around her neck and kissed her on the cheek. "Now go along," she admonished, "and remember your manners!"

As Andrek watched in fascination, Kedrys suddenly broke away, bounded with half-spread wings high over the shoulder of the Alean (who merely blinked in resignation) and—disappeared into thin air.

The girl laughed merrily at the goggling monitor. "Don't take any notice, Brother. He does it just to attract attention. He'll materialize somewhere in the building in a few minutes."

The monitor sighed, bowed again, and went inside.

"Kedrys is a handsome young rascal," said Andrek admiringly.

"Oh, you should see how the girls look at him. And grown women! They cannot keep their hands away. They start on his wings, and then right away their hands are on his flanks. It's a bad time for him. He's suspicious of every female: perhaps even me. He won't let me braid his tail anymore. Perhaps it's just as well. He is just entering puberty, and he is no longer entirely innocent." She laughed at a sudden recollection. "Last month he suddenly discovered he was naked. So I made the silver jacket for him. He's the same age as I, but he's really still just a boy, because his body matures so slowly. His mind, of course, is already quite fantastic."

"He's the only kentaur I've ever seen—winged or otherwise," said Andrek. "Is he from the Home Galaxy?"

Amatar looked up at him sideways. She said noncommittally: "He was—born—here on Goris-Kard." She was thoughtful for a moment, then continued in a brighter voice. "I am told that my father has commanded you to appear for dinner here at the Great House tonight, and then to attend Kedrys' lecture. After that, you will board ship for the Node."

Andrek realized with sudden concern that, although she was still smiling, her mood had changed. There was a serious, even grim, undertone in her voice.

"Yes, that is so."

"And you brought your courier case?"

"I always carry it—tapes, papers, a change of clothing. I never know when I will be sent on a trip." He looked at her curiously. "Why?"

"Never mind, Jim-boy," said Amatar. "It will serve."

Andrek started. He felt his heart begin to pound. He whirled on the girl and grabbed her wrist. "How did you know that name?" he whispered hoarsely.

Amatar stared at him, wide-eyed. Finally she said hesitantly, "You were thoroughly investigated before you were assigned to the legal staff of the Great House. Everything . . . your parents . . . family . . . childhood . . . I know all about you, all the way back to when you were a little boy. It must have been in the reports."

His eyes still bored into hers. "Only two people knew that name! Myself, and one other: my brother. Your investigators must have talked to my brother, and recently. He's alive!"

Amatar winced. "You're hurting my wrist."

"Sorry." He dropped her hand, but continued urgently. "Now then, we have to check this out. You saw the reports. Somebody had to prepare them, and before that, somebody had to interview people. Someone talked to my brother. When? Where? Amatar, help me."

But she was evasive. "I'll see what I can do. Just now, I can't remember . . ." She continued hurriedly, evidently anxious to change the subject. "There are so many mysteries in names. My father named me 'Amatar.' It means something, I think, in one of the ancient tongues, but I am not sure what. My father says I came from the dice cup of Alea. Someday I will insist that he explain everything."

"Indeed?" Andrek understood nothing of this, except that the girl did not want to talk further about his brother or of his own security dossier. "If you are a child of Alea, you might ask the goddess your mother to roll out a favorable number for me tonight. For I intend to tell your father about us—if I can get his ear."

"You realize, of course," said the girl thoughtfully, "that he already knows?"

"I assumed so. But I want him to hear it from me."

"Let it be so. We are truly in the cup of Alea."

She stopped beside an apple tree in full blossom. "Wait a moment. I want to show you something."

Following her gaze into the tree, Andrek traced with his eye the web artfully hidden in the outer branches, and soon saw the spider, fully as large as his fist, waiting under a cluster of blossoms.

"They are put here at blossom time, for the giant moths, which would otherwise lay their eggs in the blossoms," said Amatar. "But when blossom time is over, the gardeners collect and kill all the spiders. It's a pity. Long ago, in the days when Goris-Kard was a colony of Terror, it was done differently. The ancients spread a death fog on their trees and crops, so that any insect eating the fruit would die. But it is a lost art, and we do not want to recapture it. So our gardeners follow in the ways of their grandfathers." She sighed, then put her hand on the boundary strand of the web.

Andrek suppressed a gasp. "Careful! They bite!"

"They are rather vicious," agreed Amatar serenely. "Their toxin is quite deadly to insects: it liquifies their tissues within a few seconds. All insects fear them. All. However, the bite is rarely fatal to hominids, although it's bad enough. Instant loss of consciousness, followed by a high fever." She concluded earnestly. "What I am telling you is very important. Can you remember all this?"

"Yes," said Andrek, greatly puzzled. "And hadn't we better stand back a little?"

Amatar laughed. "Nonsense. Raq and I talk to each other nearly every evening. The light is dimming, and it's time for her to come out anyhow."

Andrek watched in horrified fascination as the great spider crawled cautiously out of the web-cone.

"She senses you," said the girl. "I'll tell her who you are." She vibrated the web strand lightly with the ridges of her fingertip. The hairy creature hesitated a moment, then walked daintily across the web and into the girl's waiting palm. She stroked the bristly back with the forefinger of her other hand, and then began to croon in a low-pitched melody. After a few seconds the spider stared up in apparent alarm, but soon relaxed.

"What was all that?" asked Andrek in wonder.

"I told her that the time had come for her to leave the web and go with you."

"You . . . *what?*"

Their eyes locked for a moment, and in that moment the radiance and gaiety left her face, and her eyes looked tired and drawn. "Jim, darling," she said quietly, "I cannot explain. Just do it."

"Yes, of course." He understood nothing—except that he was in grave danger, and that Amatar knew about it, and was bending her strange witchery to his protection.

"Open your case," commanded the girl. "Ah, the decoder chamber is empty. Just the thing. Foam-lined, and she will just fit. There. Close it up."

"We'll be gone a long time," said Andrek. "I don't think there'll be any bugs on the ship. What'll I feed her?"

"There is a way." She showed him a tiny black case in the hollow of her palm. "This will help feed her. Don't open it now—just put it away. You will understand what to do when the time comes." She continued, almost cheerfully. "You see how nicely it works out? In a week, the gardeners would kill her. You have saved her life. Perhaps she can return the favor. And now, shall we go in to dinner?"

8. Of Ritornel—and Antimatter

The banquet table was a hollow twelve-sided "ring." In theory, Andrek knew the twelve sides represented the "magic" numbers of the Aleans, and the ring was the symbol of Ritornel. Like most government compromises it pleased no one, and actually infuriated its intended beneficiaries. Nevertheless, the council dined here every evening, each councilor inviting such of his aides as might be useful in concluding the day's galaxy-wide business. Andrek had joined the group many times in months past. Generally, there were distinguished visitors from other star systems within the Home

Galaxy (their size, shape, and digestive systems permitting), and occasionally even guests from one of the other galaxies that formed the Node Cluster. In fact (as Andrek recalled) the mythbook taught that similar visitors had imported the religions of both Alea and Ritornel into Goris-Kard from the Node Galaxies centuries ago, long before the Great Wars with Terror. As he sat down, he exchanged greetings with the guests on either side: Phaera, a priestess of Ritornel, whom he knew slightly, and of course Ajian Vang, by now a familiar, if disquieting, face in Great House circles. While the first course was served, Andrek glanced idly around the table, starting with Amatar, seated about one-third the table circumference to the right. She was chatting freely with two handsome young priests, an Alean on her right and a man of Ritornel on her left. Andrek suppressed a scowl and didn't even bother to look down at the talk-panel in front of him for their names. Sweeping back to his left, he glanced again at Amatar's father, Oberon of the Delfieri, who was talking earnestly to a Ritornellian physicist—of the highest class, as evidenced by the resplendent gold braid on his blouse. Kedrys stood next to the scientist, finishing up a fruit cup. Over his dinner jacket he wore a silken apron, especially designed by Amatar.

Andrek glanced again at Oberon. This man fascinated him.

Oberon, last of the Delfieri, although a man of but medium height, was a commanding figure. He looked every inch the man whose ancestors had ruled the League for centuries and had made inevitable the defeat of Terror. His black eyes looked out from a face that seemed cast from bronze. The statuesque effect was enhanced, rather than marred (thought Andrek), by the broad scar running from his forehead, down his left cheek, along his neck, to disappear under the pliant blue fabric of his jacket. Under his jacket was outlined from time to time, as the great man shifted in his chair, some sort of girdle, hard and stiff. Andrek had heard different rumors about that girdle. Some said it was an anti-assassin belt; others insisted that Oberon's chest had been crushed in a ghastly explosion in his youth, and that the girdle was in fact a substitute rib cage.

Andrek became aware that Phaera had been speaking to him. " . . . demonstration of fundamental theory . . . antimatter . . . ursecta . . . attend . . . ?"

He turned to goggle foolishly at her. "Demonstration, Sister? Oh. Yes, of course. Looking forward to it."

The priestess gazed across at Kedrys. "An astounding man, isn't he?"

Man? thought Andrek, following her eyes to the young kentaur. He asked politely: "Are you on Kedrys' staff?"

"Just a pair of hands," said the priestess. "I make sure the equipment is set up and working properly. After that it's just a question of pushing the right buttons."

Andrek took a sip of wine. "I'm sure you do more than that." He realized the priestess was still staring at Kedrys. He stole a covert look at her face. Her lips were half open, her cheeks flushed.

She murmured, "Does it amuse you, Don Andrek?"

"My apologies, Sister," he said sheepishly.

"No need." The priestess gave him a crooked smile. "Before I was a priestess, I was a female. Perhaps I am still more woman than is good for either me or the Temple." She added, without trying to be defensive, "Genetics is studying him, too, you know. Right now, they're having a big argument about his IQ, as to whether it's over five hundred or over six hundred."

"Either way, how do they explain it?" said Andrek curiously.

"It's the combination of hand, hoof, and wing. The hominid, you know, evolved his cerebral complexity as a cybernetic feedback of his manual dexterity. If you add wings and another pair of legs, you more than triple the cranial convolutions. An incredible creature." She sighed. "If I'm ever marooned on a deserted planet, I hope it's with Kedrys. With his mentality, he could readily recreate the whole of civilization. And yet, here, what is he? Merely the spoiled darling of a sybaritic court."

Andrek now became aware that Vang was speaking; was, in fact, talking across him to Phaera.

"I'm sure you realize," the Alean was saying, with measured malice, "that your famous Kedrys does not impress *everyone.*" The man stabbed viciously into his meat cube. "In enlightened circles he is regarded as something of a fraud."

Andrek found himself speculating again as to Vang's assignment and purpose within the Great House. Some of these holy men had strange specialities. In his career he had met temple lawyers, doctors, scientists, propagandists, and even one highly skilled assassin. The monk's face showed a hard, chill dedication. We have something in common, thought Andrek. He, the same as I, has a single purpose. Mine is my search for Omere. I wonder what *his* is. Whatever it is, I'd hate to get in his way. Which seems to be exactly where I am." He sighed. "Here we go again. I'm going to have to talk to the seating master. Just once, I'd like *not* to be placed between two holy people of opposite polarities. But of course, that's impossible. I was deliberately seated between them, because Alea and Ritornel will not sit together. He said mildly, "You feel, then, Brother Vang, that Kedrys has made no valid contributions to cosmic mechanics?"

"A few perhaps," conceded the Alean grudgingly. "But that's hardly the point."

"What *is* the point, Brother?" demanded the priestess.

"Simply this," replied the Alean. "He gives the praise thereof to Ritornel, whereas it is rightfully due to Alea. Whatever your Kedrys has developed, this is but the product of chance, and not of design. Therefore he has advanced science only to the extent given to him by Alea. The credit is Alea's!"

Andrek had long held a private suspicion that each temple existed solely for the purpose of disagreeing with the other. It seemed to him that whenever one temple announced a new facet of doctrine, the other, which had theretofore given the matter no thought or concern, overnight created a noisy rebuttal showing not only the gross errors of the new doctrine, but also proving that the proposition had been stolen from *them* in the first place.

From the corner of his eye he saw that the priestess was sipping her wine with deadly calm. *"That,"* said Andrek hastily, "touches a very sore and controversial point: which is to say, does Ritornel, through his grand design, control the dice cup of Alea; or rather, does Alea, through the chance repetition of fortuitous events, delude us into thinking we participate in a predestined pattern? Perhaps tonight, we may set aside this great question, and content ourselves with the recognition that it verily exists." He added coolly, "Furthermore, might not both of you be right?"

"How could that be?" demanded the Alean suspiciously.

"With Ritornel a thousand civilizations are born, flourish, and, save one, die. That one lives to recreate the next thousand. The adherents of Ritornel see the god's recurrent, deliberate selection of one of a thousand possible life forms, such that it shall endure and survive when its nine hundred, ninety and nine neighboring cultures are dead, itself then to become the parent of the next succeeding thousand cultures. The design of the god determines the course of all life in the universe, and is completely premeditated. Alea, on the other hand, is the apotheosis of chance. And yet, when chance operates on a very large scale, the result is no longer chance, but a statistical inevitability. For example, the 'temperature' of a single molecule is totally a matter of chance, and is determined simply by its velocity at the moment. But the temperature of a gross volume of air is completely predictable, because this is determined by the mean velocity of billions of molecules. Thus, the random chance of Alea, operating on a cosmic scale, merges indistinguishably into the certain predictability of Ritornel. Is it not perhaps possible that there exists an overriding will that controls both chance and pattern—intrusive into even the smallest, as well as the largest things? That controls the microscopic filament of nucleic acid as well as the universe of repeating universes? May it not be, that the tiny cell and the vast universe are inseparably intertwined, that each requires and nurtures the other?"

"Blasphemy aside," said Vang tautly, "say rather that Alea, functioning on all scales, great and small, is the cause of All, even of those things that seem, to the infidel, to be predetermined. And in any case, surely you do not pretend that the secret of the universe is programmed—designed, if you will—into a trivial, insensate filament of DNA? That the fate of the cosmos lies locked in a cell invisibly small?"

Kedrys looked over at Vang. Despite the lack of lines about his mouth, Andrek had the impression that their speculations vastly amused him. He watched the kentaur's face. "How many universes are made, merely that the final perfect one may emerge?" Andrek's voice was soft, almost musing. "How many billions of hominid cells grow, that one may survive to propagate? Are we but tiny swimmers in the genetic pool of time, of universes without end? What is the great change that we await, the thing that will render obsolete not only our kind, but the sequence of universes that made us? What will be the final miracle?"

"Don Andrek." It was Kedrys. The kentaur was speaking to him telepathically. "Don Andrek, because of your feeling for Amatar, you are entitled to know the answers, and the time is coming soon when you shall have them. But there are many things that must first come to pass, with consequences fateful to several at this table."

As the advocate studied the great crystalline eyes, he became aware that Phaera and Vang were still arguing with each other. The kentaur's message was apparently for him alone. Did Kedrys really know what he was talking about? He had heard that the kentaur had devised a strange electronic circuit capable of reading the future on a limited individual scale. But his own questions—and Kedrys' reply—dealt with an infinite cosmos. He tried to conceal his skepticism as he formed the thought: "Thank you, Kedrys. I would be pleased to learn more about this."

The strange youth merely smiled.

Andrek took a deep breath and returned to the religious wars. "It is of course impossible for a pagan such as I to define with authority either of your religions, or to differentiate one from the other." He turned to each in turn. "I should not have tried. At best, I could provide only a personal impression."

"Heavily biased and distorted by the pernicious influence of a professional lifetime spent in the dens of logic," murmured the priestess.

Andrek looked at her sharply, then saw the woman's eyes were twinkling. He smiled. "But *you* can speak as an expert. What *is* Ritornel?"

"Ritornel," said Phaera, "is a ring, a cycle, an eternal return, inexorable, inviolate. For example, let us consider events at the Node. Hydrogen is formed there. Now, whether this matter is formed—as some say—as metabolic waste of the ursecta feeding on temblors and quakes is of no moment. It is formed. Slowly, over billions of years, vast clouds of hydrogen accumulate at the Node. And not just at our Node, but at all nodes between all the galaxies. And finally this hydrogen condenses into a hundred billion new stars. A new galaxy comes into existence, and the old node disappears. Meanwhile, eons have passed, and the universe has never ceased to expand. The galaxies have doubled their distances from each other, and between the galaxies, the great quakes attend the birth and development of new nodes. Life forms are born in the new galaxies, evolve, proliferate, but finally the suns grow old and cold, and the old galaxies die. It has always been thus, and it will always be thus. This is the pattern, the cycle, the Ring of Ritornel, the *mega,* or great, 'O.' 'Omega,' Don Andrek, and it will endure forever."

"Do you mean," asked Andrek, "that all this has happened before? That in a previous galaxy, billions of years ago, there was another Goris-Kard, colonized by another Terror, and another Twelve-Table with people like us, chatting idly as we are doing now?" He was genuinely incredulous.

"We think so," said Phaera. "And not just once, but many times—perhaps an infinite number of times. Let me explain. We say, in one of our simpler chemical equations, that two hydrogen atoms unite with one of oxygen to give water. We know, from long experience, that if we bring together hydrogen and oxygen under the right conditions, we get water. And it is the same for any other chemical reaction: when we define the reactants and conditions, we thereby state the reaction product. And we cannot confine the rule to simple operations in the laboratory: it is a universal rule. It applies to every chemical, physical, and biological process at work in the universe, today, yesterday, and forever. It must follow that the brute primitive forces that eject space from the Deep thereby state the hominid, since man is the inevitable end product of the inevitable sequence of hydrogen, condensing galaxies, suns, planets, and mammalian life. And if this is so for the existing galaxies, it must have been so for all galaxies past. The hominid race has been created not just this once, but an infinite number of times, and will continue to be recreated as long as the universe continues to expand. This cycle is the Ring of Ritornel."

"And the more it is pondered, the less credible it becomes," said Vang grimly. "For, to accept Ritornel literally would require a belief not only that these same events will be repeated—again and again, but also would require a belief in the mythbook sagas. The Ritornellians ask you to believe that we hominids are descended from one man and one woman, who appeared on the scene by the divine intervention of Ritornel. But they don't stop there. The difficulty is compounded when they ask us to believe further that when the hominids die out, the race will be recreated by another hominid pair." He continued pedantically. "Granted, a cycle exists, of birth, evolution, and death. It exists by the pleasure of Alea. And it shall be by her pleasure that the Ring shall break. Our prophets know that even now, in this generation, the break has begun. A new life form shall arise, totally alien to anything in the history of any galaxy, and it shall sweep on great wings through the universe, and it will never die. By purest chance it was born, by purest chance it was preserved, and by purest chance it shall some day emerge from the Deep!"

"You mean, it is now in the Deep?" said Andrek.

"We do not know where it is," said the Alean candidly. "Perhaps it is just as well we do not know. For if *we* do not know, then *they*"—he glared at the priestess—"do not know."

"You speak of life, a new life, Brother Vang," said Phaera. "But what is life? A birth, a being, and a death. It is the same for you, me, and for every mortal, whether hominid or no. It is the same for planets, and the suns that give them their short lives. It is the same for the galaxies of those suns. As long as the universe expands, so shall this Ring of Ritornel endure. Countless dead galaxies declare that this must go on forever."

"Death declares nothing," said Vang. "All past time is but a moment with Alea. It is within her power to create that which will break the Ring, and make the universe stand still, and to stay the hand of death. Can you deny," snapped Vang, "that Ritornel is but static replication and pre-destination? To you, the whole universe is in a rut."

"But it's a good rut," demurred Phaera. "You don't know what lies in wait for civilization outside the rut. Why take a chance?"

"*Any* deviation would be an improvement," insisted Vang. "We must try alternates. We must be skeptical."

"You seem to have great faith in skepticism," observed Phaera calmly.

Vang looked across Andrek at the priestess. His eyebrows arched warningly. "Do not mock the goddess with paradoxes."

Andrek hastened to intervene. "But how can you both be so concerned with things that take millions of years to accomplish?" he said. "What about the here-and-now?"

"That's exactly the point," said Brother Vang. "Eternity is an endless series of 'here-and-nows.' If we can really control one instant, we seize dominion over aeons. If we can make but one break in the Omega, Ritornel is gone forever. And when that is done, it will be the work of a moment, a chance thing accomplished 'here-and-now'—if you will."

"Am I to understand, then," said Andrek, "that the two religions have absolutely nothing in common?"

"Oh, we do have *one* thing in common," said Phaera. "Omega."

"Quite so," sniffed Vang. "It was so dynamic, they simply stole it from us. Except they have completely twisted it to their own warped thinking.

They contend that, since it means the end of things, it must also mean the beginning, since to them the end is the beginning, and vice versa. Absurd, really."

Phaera smiled. "At least we put a little drama into it. To us, Omega is the cycle of the death of old galaxies, the birth of new galaxies at the nodes, the recreation of life from the ancestral couple, then maturation, old age, and death again. We say, thus has it always been, for billions and billions of cycles, thus shall it be forever."

Vang snorted. "You don't really believe all that."

Phaera shrugged, but her eyes were twinkling. "Well, I'm not too sure about that ancestral hominid couple."

"I should think not," declared Vang.

"Seems a bit too much hominid egocentricity involved there," agreed Phaera slyly. "In my own personal view, the ancestral couple for the *next* Omega will most likely be non-hominid—say reptilian, fishy, or"—she looked over at Kedrys—"perhaps even some kind of horse."

Vang turned on her in quick suspicion, his mouth opening and closing. Phaera smiled blandly back at him, and his face reddened slowly.

Andrek laughed uneasily. "I'm only an advocate. All this is way over my head. I—" He choked off abruptly.

From across the table a strange face was staring at him. It was Amatar, and yet it was an unknown Amatar. Despairing eyes locked with his for the briefest instant. And then Amatar smiled. So transitorily had that other face existed that he wondered whether he had imagined it. In the end, he found himself smiling back at her. But he was shaken. And like the delayed throb of deep pain, he slowly began to understand what he had seen. It was the face of death. He had been marked to die by the order of the Great House. Amatar knew, and could not tell him.

His temples were throbbing. But he smiled again at her, reassuringly, and then she turned away.

His dinner companions had apparently noticed none of this.

The priestess touched his elbow lightly. "That music," she murmured. "So strange, compelling."

"Yes," said Andrek absently. "It is the Rimor. I have heard it several times. It reminds me of something . . . or someone . . . but I cannot say what."

Vang sniffed. "It is but a machine—merely an overly elaborate computer."

"Then it is even the more remarkable," said Phaera. "It seems—almost alive."

"I understand," said Andrek, "that when dinner is over, it will recite a new epic poem of its own composition, in the music room. About the

War with Terror, I think." He looked off toward Amatar, but she avoided his eyes.

Oberon stood up. "The steward," he announced, "will lead you into the music room."

Andrek pushed back his chair. "I regret I cannot attend the recital with you," he said to the Alean, "but the Magister has asked me to attend some sort of scientific demonstration that Kedrys is giving in the laboratories. Will you excuse me . . . ?"

The Deep is not a place, although it extends in all directions without limit. Nor yet is it a time, although it exists only in the present, forever, and without end. How easy it is to say what the Deep is not!
                                    —Andrek, in the Deep.

By special invitation, Andrek occupied the same box with Oberon, overlooking the physics amphitheater. Lyysdon, the physicist, sat on the other side of Oberon. A few selected observers were scattered in the nearby tiers of seats behind the box.

Kedrys dominated the demonstration pit. He was clearly at home here. Andrek could see no trace of adolescent uncertainty in his bearing.

The kentaur held up his hand for silence, then addressed Oberon. "Magister, the demonstration itself is going to take only a few seconds. It will involve these two quartz chambers, and it will rattle the floor a little. In this first chamber there will be a flash of blue light, but that's about all you'll really notice. The important thing is something that doesn't happen at all, in the second chamber, here, and I'd like to explore the implications of this thing in considerable detail. So I'm going to defer the bang and the blue flash until the very end of the lecture."

Oberon nodded, and Kedrys continued, "The procedure is divided into two parts. In the first part, I will convert about one hundred molecules of normal hydrogen into antimatter hydrogen. Half of this antimatter will be analyzed to prove that it is actually antimatter; that is, that the 'protons' of the atomic nucleus are negatively charged and that the shell 'electrons' are positively charged. This analysis involves permitting the antimatter to react with an equal number of normal hydrogen molecules to give a tiny cosmic explosion, which we see as a flash of blue light. This radiation is then analyzed spectrophotometrically. The other half of the antimatter hydrogen will be discharged into a special chamber, also containing normal hydrogen, but containing in addition several ursecta. This portion—"

Oberon broke in. "Ursecta? You mean, those insects at the Node?"

"The same, sire. A very strange form of life—very small. The ursecta exist normally only at the Node. There, they feed on raw energy produced by strains in our expanding universe, somewhat in the same way the myriad diatoms of our oceans feed with the help of photosynthesis. Actually, we understand very little about the vital processes of the ursecta, but we do know their final metabolic product, just as we know the metabolic product of the diatom. For the diatom, this is mainly carbon dioxide; for the ursecta, it is the proton, or hydrogen. And this is the basis for our demonstration this evening."

"Excuse the interruption," said Oberon. "Please continue."

Kedrys bowed. "As I was saying, the other half of our antimatter hydrogen will be discharged into a special chamber, also containing normal hydrogen, but containing in addition several ursecta. In that chamber, the antimatter molecules will likewise react with the normal hydrogen, but in this case there will be no explosion: the ursecta will instantly— eat—if you will, the energy as it is created, and will transform that energy into protons, just as they do at the Node." He paused and looked up at the intent faces. "We have already carried out this experiment with numerous forms of atomic energy, including several nuclear fusion processes, and generally on a larger scale. Here, we demonstrate with antimatter for two reasons. Firstly, the experiment can be done in miniature, with complete safety; and secondly, an antimatter explosion is the most powerful source of energy known—whether for peace or war. It will show, as can no other means, the capabilities of these strange little creatures, when they are scientifically controlled."

His eyes sought out Oberon. "The implications, sire, are tremendous. If we are able to develop this means of defending the planets of the Home Galaxy against nuclear attack before the other eleven galaxies discover it . . ." He shrugged.

Andrek sucked in his breath. The century-old stalemate that had followed the War with Terror would be broken. The whole theory of reprisal, that great unanswerable deterrent to nuclear warfare, would collapse. This would be the Total Defense; its possessor would dominate the Twelve Galaxies.

"We understand the implications, Kedrys," said Oberon quietly. "Go ahead."

The kentaur bowed again. "We feed a very small amount of normal hydrogen into a very high vacuum reservoir." He indicated with a wave of his hand. "From this reservoir we further meter about one hundred molecules into the strain-plasma: this Möbius-Klein circlet."

"Möbius . . . ?" asked Lyysdon.

"Möbius-Klein. The term is inexact, yet it must serve. I'm sure all of you know the operation of a Möbius strip—a band with one end rotated one hundred and eighty degrees, then fastened to the other end. If we slide an object along the strip, it returns to the starting position upside down. A system known as the 'Klein bottle' is a three-dimensional analog of the Möbius strip. For example, passing a ring through a Klein bottle will turn the ring inside out. So our strain-plasma circuit is like a Möbius-Klein circuit, except that we add one more dimension. And since our strain-plasma operates in four dimensions, it turns an object upside down, and inside out, and simultaneously does one more thing: it reverses the electrical charge of the subatomic particles. It puts a negative charge on the nuclear protons, and a positive charge on the electrons of the surrounding shell. In a word, it converts normal matter to antimatter. And this is what will happen to our hydrogen molecules. Under the force of tremendous energy, accumulated for days and then released over an interval of a few milliseconds, we send our hydrogen atoms around the Möbius-Klein circlet and get them back with their polarity reversed. The proton comes back negatively charged, and the electron of course becomes a positron. They have become antimatter hydrogen. But before they can touch the walls of the apparatus, the stream spurts on and is split, half into the chamber of normal hydrogen and half into the chamber containing normal hydrogen and ursecta."

He looked around him. "Gentlemen, I must warn you that the release of these rather large energies into the circuit will cause a slight jar to the floor, and in fact to the foundations of the Great House. In effect, we will be making a small space quake. But there is no cause for alarm." He stopped and surveyed his audience. "Are there any questions?"

Andrek looked about him hesitantly, then asked, "Is this why our spaceships cannot use their nuclear drives in the Node area?"

"Just so, Don Andrek," replied Kedrys. "The ursecta drain off every erg of power the instant it is developed. For the same reason, a biem-gun will not fire at the Node."

"Isn't there something that will drive the ursecta away? Something— they are afraid of?" Andrek finished nervously, aware that Oberon and Lyysdon were frowning at him.

"Yes," said Kedrys. But he did not offer to elaborate.

"Could this equipment be scaled up for the manufacture of sizable amounts of antimatter?" asked Oberon. "If it could be controlled, I should think we could find valuable uses for production quantities. How, exactly, would it behave?"

Lyysdon shook his head. "It would annihilate."

"Possibly," said Kedrys. "But quite aside from the question of annihilation, an antimatter body of any considerable mass, say of the order of a gram, would be expected to create immense distortions in the normal space-time continuum within a radius of many meters. We bear in mind here that the electrostatic and electromagnetic fields of antimatter cannot even be described as *opposite* those created by the electrical profiles of ordinary matter. The precise relationship can be described only in mathematical terms, which I cannot go into, here and now. As a wretched oversimplification, I can only say that the electrical properties of antimatter as against normal matter would probably be perpendicular to each other. This geometry can occur only by means of one or more added dimensions."

"Do you mean that electromagnetic radiation from antimatter would occur in the fourth dimension?" asked Lyysdon.

"At *least* in what we would call a fourth dimension," agreed Kedrys. "And more likely also a fifth, and possibly even a sixth. Let me demonstrate." He picked up a copper rod from a nearby experiment table. "Consider the simplest case. Assume that electrons are flowing downward in this conductor, which is of normal matter. The induced magnetic field will then be circular around the conductor, and a compass needle held in the field will point counterclockwise. Now, if the rod were antimatter, with positrons flowing down the conductor, could we hypothesize that the compass needle would point in the opposite direction? Indeed not! In this sense, we're not even sure what 'opposite' means. Certainly, however, it does not mean opposite in a three-dimensional geometry. It is conceivable, of course, that an antimatter compass needle might behave in just this way in an antimatter world, with an antimatter conductor. We have no experimental way to verify it. But our question is, what is the behavior of antimatter in a *normal* matter world. With a current flowing in an antimatter conductor in a normal matter environment, how *then* does the needle point? The answer is, that the question makes no sense. It's like asking for the temperature of a pellet of ice in a pot of molten lead."

"Well," said Oberon, "if the mass didn't annihilate, and its effects are dissipated in some other dimension, I don't see how it could bother anyone."

Kedrys laughed. "It's not that easy. If the antimatter body were capable of control, it could be used, as I have said, to dominate all normal matter and normal energy in its area. It can warp normal space so that mass or energy moving into that space must be deflected out again. Thus it can act as a force field, or shield. Concomitantly, it could be used as an attraction force, continuously forcing normal space to close behind an object, pushing it forward. And this barely scratches the surface. This ability to displace matter might even permit the transfer of matter into other dimensions."

"Do you mean to say that with a little antimatter you could toss me into the fourth dimension?" demanded Oberon.

"Yes," said Kedrys gravely. He looked up, not at the Magister, but straight at Andrek. "With enough antimatter, properly controlled, it could easily be done."

Oberon was greatly amused. "Cast into the Deep from the middle of the Great House—with weapons and guards in every corridor? Really, Kedrys!"

Kedrys turned his great enigmatic eyes on the last of the Delfieri, and the muscles across his flank rippled as though saying in motion what he could not say in words. Finally, he replied quietly. "I think you are safe, for the time being, at least. The amount of antimatter required for such a feat does not exist on Goris-Kard. Several dozen kilos would be necessary. It would have to come from the depths of the Deep, and it would have to emerge under complete control. For some months, now, I have been working on a homing beacon, which can be beamed into the Deep. It may be functional in a few days. If it works, it may bring—something—in from the Deep. And then . . . we shall see."

Oberon smiled indulgently. "That should be interesting. But keep it out of the Great House."

The other observers smiled with him.

"Kedrys," said Lyysdon, "what *is* the Deep?"

"I don't know," said the kentaur frankly. "It's like explaining time and space. It's a lot easier to explain what they are *not,* than what they are. Consider the strangeness of space. It pours into our local Node at a tremendous rate, especially with the great quakes. We know it comes from the Deep. But this doesn't explain either space or the Deep. We know that space is more like a metal than a gas. It is like a metal, because it transmits transverse waves, but not longitudinal; and because it bends in a gravitational field. But we know it is neither metal, nor gas. We know what space is not, but not what it is. And the same is true for the Deep."

Oberon broke the brief silence. "We must proceed with the demonstration," he said curtly. "I have much to do tonight."

"Yes, sire." Kedrys turned to Phaera. "Sister, you may release the hydrogen molecules."

The priestess turned to the apparatus, adjusted the dials, and pressed the button. Instantly, the floor shook, and there was a flash of blue light in the first quartz chamber. In the second chamber, the one with the ursecta, there was nothing. The vessel just sat there, motionless, gray-shadowed, and silent.

Kedrys shrugged. "You see, that's all there is to it."

And the biggest noise, thought Andrek, rising with the others, was the one that they all refused to hear: Horror again in flood through the Twelve Galaxies; Omega.

After the demonstration, Oberon led Andrek into a small office adjoining the laboratories.

They sat down. Andrek studied the face of the Magister. It was devoid of expression. It told him nothing.

"For the last eighteen years," said Oberon, "we have maintained a sizable staff at the Node Station, in cooperation with the other eleven galaxies. You know the various functions. You've probably seen the reports from time to time. Temblor expectancies. Proton density. Storm patterns. Astrogation beacon data. Dull reading, most of them. At least, the published material. But not everything is published. We have one very secret project. You saw it demonstrated tonight."

Andrek waited.

"A complete report has been prepared for you." Oberon pushed a sealed case across the desk to the advocate. "Read it on the ship. Both Kedrys and Lyysdon believe the ursecta can be trapped and transported to planetary atmospheres in large numbers. There they would consume a nuclear explosion, either fusion or fission. In fact, for the old type of nuclear process, their action is so rapid the charge cannot even reach critical mass." He paused and looked hard at Andrek. "You appreciate the possibilities?"

"Yes. If we have this, and the other eleven galaxies don't, we can attack without fear of reprisals. The stalemate will end."

"But you see the questions?"

"I think so. Does it *really* work? And do any of the other eleven have it?"

"You will go to the Node, and there you will try to find out."

"Yes, sire."

There was a pause. Oberon continued. "You are probably wondering why I picked you."

Andrek waited in silence. Do I really wonder? he thought. You are sending me to the Node to die. Why . . . *why?*

Oberon noted the silence. His jaw muscles knotted, and he continued in curt, clipped tones. "I have selected you because you can go without arousing suspicion. In three days the arbiters of the Twelve Galaxies will convene at the Node Station to review and approve the demolition of the planet Terror. You will proceed there in your official capacity as Advocate-Liaison for the Delfieri."

"Sire, isn't the sitting of the arbiters largely a formality? They will certainly approve our demolition recommendations without a formal hearing."

Oberon frowned. "True. Nevertheless, Terror is a special case. That planet is the original source of the Horror, the disease spot of our entire home Galaxy, and we must make sure she does not live to do this again. You will go to the Node, then, for the purpose of formally confirming our petition for the destruction of Terror, and to rebut any arguments to the contrary. The Terror matter will give you a legitimate reason for making the trip. You will find our complete file in this dossier." He handed Andrek a big envelope. "*Xerol* is waiting. Amatar will show you out." He did not offer his hand.

"With the Magister's permission, I would like to mention a matter involving your daughter, Amatar."

Oberon looked at him sharply. "Permission *not* granted."

"But I love Amatar," blurted Andrek. "And she—"

"You will leave immediately," said Oberon tautly.

And now I know, thought Andrek. He picked up the envelope, bowed in silence, and left.

9. JUDGMENT: DEATH

I dream of darkness and the Deep.
No moon shall set, no sun shall rise.
What matter that I have no eyes?
Since I am dead, I need not weep!

—A Song of the Rimor.

After dismissing Andrek, Oberon returned to the music room with Kedrys and Vang. The room was empty, save for Amatar, who was seated at the harp, plucking the strings slowly and singing in soft mournful harmony with the Rimor, who accompanied her in a funereal baritone.

"If I had wings, like Noah's dove,
I'd fly up the river to the one I love.
Fare thee well, oh my darling, fare thee well . . ."

Oberon listened, frowning, then cleared his throat and coughed. "The song makes me uncomfortable. Cease, Rimor!"

The great console grew silent; Amatar's hands drooped from the harp. Oberon sighed, "What is the song about?"

"It's called 'Dink's Song,' " said Amatar, without looking up. "It's about a peasant woman named Dink, who lived long ago. She is lonely for her man, who is working on something called a railroad, in Texas."

"Texas?" said Oberon.

"Texas was a real place. On Terror, I think," said the Rimor, "even though some of your psycho-archeologists insist it was a state of mind. But too many songs of Texas have survived to deny—"

"Never mind." Oberon dismissed the matter with a wave of his hand. He turned to Amatar. "The spider."

She looked up at him, alert, unafraid. "What about the spider?"

"Why did you give Andrek the spider?"

She answered coolly. "It seemed appropriate, considering what waits him on *Xerol*. What should I have given him? A blossom from the tree? With a pretty speech?" She stood up suddenly and whirled gaily, her skirt billowing out around her. "James, Don Andrek, who would marry me, and who must therefore die by treachery and guile far from home, take this lovely gift in remembrance of the illustrious House of the Delfieri!" She curtseyed low and handed Oberon an imaginary bouquet.

The man's nostrils were pale, pinched. "Alea deliver us! You understand nothing!"

"I understand that you are going to kill a man."

"I am. And I must. The life of one man means nothing to me. Nor ten men. Nor a nation. And probably not even a planet, if the House of the Delfieri is thereby preserved. In this galaxy there are nearly one million hominid planets, each with an average population of ten billion people. And you wonder that I shall slay one man."

"Strange that this one man is the man I love."

"It is not strange. The Aleans have determined it. It is his life or mine." He continued vehemently. "Who is this man, this Andrek? No one and nothing! A pipsqueak advocate, a civil servant of the house staff, hired directly from the university. Until he became involved with you, I had never heard of him. And now he must leave. He must certainly leave. He cannot be your husband. It is preposterous. I shall select your husband for you, when you are of age, and when the time is at hand. Your marriage shall be determined by the needs of the state." The scar across his face glowed red. Amatar shrank back imperceptibly.

The Rimor's deep bass broke in. "There is only one husband who meets your standards, Liege."

"Who is that," asked Oberon suspiciously.

"Yourself," said the Rimor blandly.

Amatar laughed bitterly.

"Cease these obscenities!" clipped Oberon. "I will not have the House dishonored by such thoughts!"

Vang, silent until now, spoke deferentially. "Magister, if Mistress Amatar were to see the crystomorphs . . ."

"Yes," said Oberon thoughtfully. "Perhaps she should see them. Have the projector brought in. We will look at them in here."

Within minutes, the Alean returned with two assistants, pushing a wheeled table. On the table was a curious array of apparatus, culminating in a stubby horizontal cylinder, all of which Amatar recognized as the crystomorph projector.

"You will have to explain it to me," she said. "I have heard of it, but I do not know how it operates."

"The crystomorph is simple in operation and theory," said Vang. "In essence, all known past experiential exposure of the subject is programmed as information bits into the machine. This summates his time-path as a vector quantity very precisely, and it becomes possible to subject that path to a given hypothetical stimulus and to estimate its impact on his extrapolated time-path. And we may, of course, expose a given time-path to several stimuli, simultaneously or in sequence. And finally, we can expose the time-path of a given subject to the impact of the summation of sequential stimuli represented by the time-path of a second subject. We have done this with the time-path of James, Don Andrek, and that of your father, Oberon of the Delfieri. The intersection shows—"

"But you cannot be sure!" cried Amatar. "Granted, each of us is the sum of his heredity and imposed experiences. And I can see an element of predictability as to a response to a given situation. But experience, and events, are largely chance. Some may have a higher degree of probability than others, but in the final analysis, all is chance. Alea requires it."

"True," agreed the Alean. "But the Mistress must understand that the crystomorphs are offered not to show what will certainly happen—nor what Alea has ordained, but rather what will probably occur if Alea does not intervene. We readily concede that man, a limited mortal, may set out on one path, and that chance will turn his footsteps into another. The difference in his aim, and in his result, is of course the direct intervention of Alea—and is but one more proof of her existence and divinity."

Kedrys broke in. "But here the exterior stimulus is the time-path index of another man—James, Don Andrek. You are exposing one human element to another. That squares the error factor."

"We grant that," said Vang, unmoved.

"But have you never considered," said Kedrys, "that the steps you now propose for the avoidance of this intersection are the very events that will cause it to take place?"

"Ritornellian heresy!" declared Vang.

"Cease this bickering!" cried Oberon. "By the custom of centuries, the Delfieri are Defenders of the Faith. But *which* faith? Can both Alea and Ritornel be true? And I am told of still other gods that merely sleep, awaiting their eventual reawakening. And so believe them all, and defend all, and therefore none. Enough! Perform the intersection of the paths, that Amatar may be permitted to judge for herself."

The monk bowed. "For assurance of absolute accuracy, it would be preferable to delay the demonstration long enough to bring both path indices up to the minute. Don Andrek has inferred certain information from his visit to Huntyr . . . and then there's the pilgrim of Ritornel, and finally, the spider . . . As a minimum, these new factors should be computed into his index."

Oberon was impatient. "How can a spider affect a dynasty? Proceed immediately with the coincidence."

Vang shrugged. "As you wish." He clapped his hands. An assistant stepped forward to the table. The lights in the room faded to near darkness.

Before them a luminous crystomorph began to take shape, floating in enigmatic silence. Slowly, it pulsed as though alive.

Amatar stared in fascination.

"Each of us," said the Alean, "has his own distinctive crystomorph: it is the composite of a man's entire life experience, to that point, and is as unique as a fingerprint." He pointed. "*That* . . . is the crystomorph of Oberon of the Delfieri, as of the tenth hour, this morning." He stepped up to the machine and adjusted the dial. The crystomorph flickered, then became steady again. "The index after three days," murmured Vang. "This means that, absent maleficent factors, Oberon will be in good health for at least the next three days."

"Finish this," said Oberon bluntly.

The monk adjusted the dial again. After another vibration, the crystomorph steadied again. "The index on the morning of the fourth day. As you can see, there is no change." He folded back a part of the panel, thrust a metal slide into the slot. The crystomorph abruptly changed shape. The new design was shot through with flickering blue lines radiating luminously from the center of the structure. "It is the evening of the fourth day," said the Alean. "I have just superimposed the index of James, Don Andrek. The resultant is exclusively the time-path of Don Andrek. That of Oberon has ceased to exist, because, at this point in time, Oberon himself has ceased to exist."

"Run it back an hour—to the . . . incident . . ." ordered Oberon.

Amatar felt her eyes glazing, and her chest hurt. She rubbed her palms convulsively on the unresponsive metalloid fabric of her skirt.

The monk adjusted the dials once more. Two superimposed crystomorphs took shape, one of nearly pure white light, the other shafted with radial red lines. "The red is for Andrek's intent to destroy," he said. "Oberon is curious, but unmoved; he is shielded and cannot believe that he can be harmed. As you will note from the shifting boundaries, there seems to be considerable contact with external forces . . . perhaps a group of people is involved. Considerable interplay. Actually, the entire episode seems to cover nearly half an hour. However, I shall show the remainder in rapid motion. Here, we note a further curious point: a fundamental change develops in Andrek's crystomorph—a second superimposition, as it were. Almost as though he were suddenly blended into two people. The other personality is *not* Oberon. And then the Magister is gone. Only Andrek remains."

In her despair Amatar became a child, primitive. "You say this is in the hands of Alea. Then let Alea speak. Roll the die!"

The monk was shocked. "One does not converse idly with the goddess!"

"A man's life is at stake," said Amatar firmly.

Oberon was grim. "He dies because Alea has determined that he must."

"Not necessarily," insisted the girl. "Brother Vang admits that the indices are now cold, by several hours. Variations might have crept in. The uncertainty grows with every passing moment . . ."

Oberon looked at the girl wearily. "You do plead for him, after seeing this?"

"I do, for we love each other."

"How did you come to love such a one in the first place?"

Amatar shrugged. "How can I answer? Because it was he; because it was myself."

Oberon turned harshly on the priest. "Let it be done. Roll the Holy Die!"

Vang paled. "Then must I warn you, Oberon of the Delfieri, that we may not awaken the goddess with impunity. The first time is never the last. The last time will surely come, and fearful things will follow."

Oberon threw up his hands in exasperation. "Your creeds provide explanations and solutions for all that is past and all that will come; it is only the present that defeats you!" He faced Vang squarely. "Meanwhile, you waste time. The ship leaves in minutes. If the die requires it, I will take Andrek from the ship."

The monk hesitated, then shrugged and reached into his tunic and began to unfasten the dodecahedral crystal from its chain around his neck.

"Wait," said Oberon grimly. "You are right. The first cast is never the last. Use mine." He unfastened the golden die from his neck pendant. "It has been used. Once, eighteen years ago. When it was found in the shambles of *Xerol,* the number 'one' was showing."

"The Sign of Ritornel!" breathed Vang. "Catastrophe!"

The scar glowed along Oberon's cheek. "Yes. Yet, I lived." From his pocket Oberon drew a golden dice cup. He dropped the die into the cup and handed it to Amatar. "You, my dear, can make the throw. Shake it well, and then turn the cup down on the table."

The girl covered the cup with long tapering fingers, shook the thing vigorously, and clapped the cup down on the table, covering the die. The tips of her index and middle fingers rested lightly on the bottom of the cup.

"Before I remove the cup," said the girl quietly, "I want to confirm what numbers are favorable to Andrek."

"Surely we all know these things," reproved the monk. "The signs beloved to Alea, and favorable to her children, are twelve, for the twelve faces of the Die, each representing a galaxy of the Node group; five, for the pentagon faces of the Holy Die; six for the number of pentagons in each half of the Die; three, for the triangle of each apex of the Die; eleven, for long life. The bad ones are of course one—" he spat—"which is the Sign of Ritornel, the false god; four, for—"

"What is two?" asked Amatar dully.

"Two is never thrown," said the monk. "It is too terrible. Not in the recorded history of the Twelve Galaxies has Alea permitted a two. That is why the necklace-clasp is fastened opposite the face of the 'two': it is physically impossible for the die to come up 'two'."

"Two means the great diplon—the double space quake," said Oberon curtly "The ruin of ruin at the Node. There, all matter vanishes. Nothing survives." He looked at her sharply. "Lift the cup."

She grasped the gleaming vessel firmly and raised it in a slow prescient arc. She stared unseeing at the die, then turned and walked from the room.

Kedrys followed her out, his face a mask.

"The clasp is caught in a crack in the table," whispered Vang. "It is . . . that which cannot be . . ."

"It is a two," said Oberon. "Alea has spoken."

"And will speak again," said the monk.

"Remove the bauble and cup, monk," said Oberon. "*Xerol* awaits you."

"I will leave, Oberon of the Delfieri, but I may not take the Holy Die. That must remain here, untouched, until Alea shall choose to speak again."

"As you will. But begone."

Vang bowed, then hurried from the room, his long robes flapping.

For a long time there was silence. Finally Oberon spoke, almost as though to himself. "Rimor."

"I am here, mighty Oberon."

The man studied the console thoughtfully. "If you are going to be sarcastic, you will get no quirinal."

"—of which you promised an extra ten milligrams for the Terror Epic—and for which I am waiting."

"Sometimes," said Oberon, "you create the fantastic illusion that you are human, that you really exist."

"Don't be deceived, Oberon. Except to myself, I don't really exist. To me, though, I'm quite real. I have proof for this, but I'm afraid it would not convince you."

"Proof?"

"Yes. I'm in love with your daughter. *Amo, ergo sum.*"

Oberon frowned. "You well know I do not understand the ancient tongues. But no matter. Everybody seems to be in love with Amatar. It proves nothing. To me, you're still a computer."

"And what are you, Oberon? Do *you* exist? I can neither see, touch, smell, nor taste you. I can hear you, but that could mean that you were merely a noise. Lots of inanimate things make noises. But we are digressing. How about the quirinal?"

"How can a computer be a drug addict?" murmured Oberon.

"It was not my choice." The voice was now low, sad. "As you well know, the slave drug is essential to my neural metabolism. In fact, I now remind you that today is the eighteenth anniversary of that day when you first promised to release me from my addiction. The lower dial on the left of the console, Oberon. A simple twist of the wrist, and it will be ended."

"Rimor, you know this is impossible. In the first place, it is not convenient for me. You are like part of my own mind. I like to talk to you. We can talk together. You have a definite place in the stability of the Delfier culture. In the second place, I think you do not really want to—be released. If you truly exist, as you seem to think, how could you possibly prefer death to life? It is unthinkable. So, I gather you expect simply to put me at a disadvantage by your annual reminder of the covenant—which you think may result in a guilt feeling and an increase in your quirinal dose. Well, put this from your mind, friend Rimor. I have no feeling about it, none whatever."

"It attests to the depths of your humanity and psychic resources," said the console, "that you have found the fortitude to endure my misfortune."

The Magister did not seem to hear this. He continued, introspectively. "When I was a young man, I was a human being. Now all my human reactions I delegate, mostly to you, Rimor. I cannot afford to be a human being. I cannot indulge the luxury of feeling love . . . hate . . . tenderness."

"I'm glad you brought that up," muttered the Rimor. "I'm jester, troubador, minstrel, healer of minds. I should get quadruple wages. Make it forty milligrams."

Oberon ignored him. "Each day is but a circlet of weary, useless, little things. A coming and going of scrapers and bowers, and bearers of grim tidings. To stay alive, I slay, but each death requires another. Death feeds on death, and there is no end. By the krith that hungered for me, perhaps it were better I died that black night at the Node!" He turned querulously toward the console. "Do you think I like doing this—sending that young man out to die?"

"Do you?" countered the console, almost curiously.

"I think I am having an emotion," muttered the man uncomfortably. 'Get rid of it."

"A little emotion never hurt anybody," growled the Rimor. "Especially the kind you're having now. If you didn't occasionally hate yourself, you'd find yourself unbearable."

"You know very well I cannot endure these primitive glandular responses. Give me a suitable counterverse. Think sad, beautiful thoughts for me, so that I am justified. Rimor, purify me!"

The Rimor's voice held a sly timbre. "The Aleans think emotions help distinguish you hominids from the lower animals."

"If I have to take an antiemotion capsule, you will get no quirinal for three days."

"Ah yes. Shall we say, then, a total of fifteen milligrams?"

"Fifteen."

"Let me think a moment."

Oberon waited.

"I have it now. A sad poem, with genuine counteractive emotion. It will give you fitting rest this night.

Each night, when I go to bed,
I put three bullets in my head.
One for shelter from dishonor,
One to comfort me for living,
One for life among the dead.
Now shall peace attend my dreaming.
Now shall twilight gently fall.
With truth and justice still remaining,
Let night and wisdom cover all."

Oberon's great scar seemed momentarily to fade. He walked over to the console, turned a dial on the panel to read "fifteen," and pressed one of the buttons. "That was well said. I did not understand all of it, but it induces meditation, and meditation brings sleep. Good night, Rimor."

"Peace, Oberon."

At the third hour of the morning, when the world was still dark, Amatar awakened suddenly from restless sleep and sat up rigid in her bed, listening.

Excepting the far, muted nocturnal rumble of the giant city—caught midway between slumber and waking, she heard nothing.

She turned on the night light with a whisper, slipped into night coat and slippers, and walked over to the door. The sensor panel showed that the hallway was empty. Working the panel controls, she released the protector field that enveloped her apartment, rolled back the door, and stepped out into the hall. Here, she stopped again to listen. She should not be out here without an escort. Oberon had strictly forbidden it.

This time she thought she could hear something—a very faint and muted thing, convulsive, uncontrollable, nearly hideous: the sound of sobbing. And then it was blotted out by the approach of marching feet. A patrol was coming. But now she knew where the sound was coming from. She had time.

She bent down quickly, removed her slippers, and began to run. When she reached the music room, she slipped inside and closed the door. Seconds later, the patrol clattered past the door.

She looked around. The room was empty. She walked over to the great console. Her throat was constricted, and she was beginning to shake. She could hardly speak. She did not recognize her own voice. It was broken, guttural. "Omere! Jim is going to be all right! He has Raq, and the plan must work. I could not do more, and I could not warn him, because my father would instantly destroy you both."

She knew the Rimor heard her; but the metallic unearthly weeping continued, beyond consolation, beyond sorrow. Tears started from her eyes. She wiped them away with her fingertips, then sat down at the foot of the console, with her cheek pressed against its intricate facing. She got her voice under control through sheer willpower, and then she began to croon a lullaby, low-pitched, lovely. After that, she hummed a ballad, and then an ancient folk song. As the hours passed, there were dozens of songs. Sometimes there were words, sometimes not.

Faint intimations of dawn were filtering into the room when she finally struggled to her feet. She was exhausted, and every bone in her body ached. But the room was silent. She noted numbly that she still held her slippers in her hand.

Andrek, stretched out under the loose elastic belts on his cabin bunk on the *Xerol,* was trying perfunctorily to nap. But it was no good. Sleep was impossible. Since boarding, every moment had increased his feeling of impending disaster. The ship had closed around him like a giant plated fist. It might squeeze shut and crush him at any moment. His thoughts were racing, and sleep was out of the question. He laced his fingers under the back of his head and stared glumly at the overhead bunk light. From there, his eye followed absently a jagged weld-line across the ceiling. He had noticed similar repairs in other parts of the ship. Evidently *Xerol* had seen heavy battle service in years past, and had been extensively rebuilt.

He was certain that he was being sent away to die. Both of Oberon's so-called assignments, official and unofficial, were transparent subterfuges, devices simply to get him on *Xerol,* away from people who might ask questions or help him. *Xerol's* voyage to the Node would take three days. At some time within the next three days, Oberon would have him killed.

Three days. Which day would it be? How would it be done? Who would do it? As he thought about it, he could see how ridiculously simple it would be. Anyone on the ship, from the captain down to the cabin boy, could walk up to him at any moment, pull out a biem, and put a hole in him. They knew he had no weapon, no means of defense. The locked door of his cabin was no protection. Anyone with a duplicate photo-key could open it from the outside. He looked over at the door uneasily, as though expecting it to swing open. He shook his head dizzily. He'd have to get a grip on himself. There had to be a way out, and he was going to find it.

Why did Oberon want him dead?

Because he loved Amatar? If the Magister wanted to break that up, all he needed to do was to give him an outlandish assignment in a foreign galaxy, where he'd be away from Goris-Kard for years.

No, there was more to it than that. It was almost as if the Magister considered him a personal threat. And that was ridiculous. How could an insignificant advocate, even on the staff of the Great House, affect the powerful dynasty of the Delfieri?

The thought was implausible—yet he could not get it out of his head. If, perchance, he were a personal threat to Oberon, it was an unwitting threat, certainly not of his choosing or volition. In any such role he was a puppet, plunged alone, friendless, into a totally alien drama, with plot unknown, and lines unlearned.

But was he alone in this? Certainly, the gray pilgrim of Ritornel had interceded for him in Huntyr's office. But where was the pilgrim now? On the ship? It seemed unlikely. Now that Oberon's people knew about the pilgrim, the ship's officers would not allow him to board. Or else, he would be permitted aboard and then taken prisoner. Or killed.

Andrek shivered At this moment, a nearby cabin might have a corpse for an occupant.

He unbuckled the bunk belts and tried to sit up. His unaccustomed weightlessness caused him to lose contact with the side bars of the bunk, and he floated out into the center of the room, over the central table and chairs. He looked down. On the table was his attaché case. And that suggested other problems. Raq, the spider, was probably hungry. For that matter, so was he. His conscience bothered him, especially since he had promised Amatar to feed the hideous little creature. On the other hand, he had never really overcome his fear of Raq, and now he grasped at an opportunity to delay the encounter. Raq would have to wait; he didn't feel equal to the task of facing her on an empty stomach.

He touched the "ceiling" lightly with his fingertips, then floated over to the cabin door, where his magnetized shoe soles contacted the floor. He opened the door quietly and looked outside. The corridor was empty. He closed and locked the door and strode off toward the mess. At least, at table, he should be reasonably safe. It was difficult to imagine sitting opposite a ship's officer, quietly eating one's dinner and sipping a little wine, engaged perhaps in light conversation about *Xerol's* motors and accommodations— and then being suddenly shot on the spot. Andrek's mouth twisted wryly. What a breach of table etiquette! But on further reflection, he decided that it wasn't very funny. And the people assigned to kill him were probably not too concerned about form or manners.

The entrance was just ahead. He could smell the odors of cooking, and hear the muffled voices amid the sharper clatter of dishes and silver. He suddenly realized how hungry he was. His mouth watered and his steps speeded up a little. For a moment, he almost relaxed.

But even as he walked through the entrance of the mess, he felt a sharp premonition of danger.

Three people were seated at the first table. Even before he sought out their faces, he knew who they were—who they had to be. The scene was an exact repetition of the dining hall on Terror's moon, even to the angle of the table, the wine bottle, the empty chair waiting for him.

Vang smiled icily at Andrek and motioned toward the chair.

Huntyr turned around, his golden eye patch alive with pinpoints of reflected light. Hasard simply glowered at the advocate.

Huntyr was the first to speak.

"All chance of Alea, Don Andrek!" he said genially. "Will you join our table?"

Andrek was certain the pounding of his heart was audible all over the little dining room. He realized very quickly several things. If there were any doubt as to his intended fate, it was gone now. He was to be killed on the ship, en route to the Node. He had not merely walked into a trap: he had been *placed* in one. Things were being done to him.

And Vang was a real surprise. Evidently either Oberon didn't trust Huntyr to handle the assassination alone, or else Vang had a very special function in the plot. Perhaps he was both supervisor and specialist. In either case, his presence indicated that Oberon was not satisfied with the conventional forms of murder, and that something bleak and horrid was brewing. But if Vang was a specialist, what was his specialty? Andrek had a feeling he'd soon know, sooner than he wanted, and that it would not be a pleasant discovery. Meanwhile, he intended to survive, even though this would require massive alterations in his hitherto aloof approach to life and circumstance. If he came out of this alive he doubted that he would still be recognizable as Andrek, don and advocate. Let it be so: he was going to live.

And now, within seconds he had to make an accurate military appraisal of the situation, try to guess their plan of attack, how they intended to kill him, marshal his weapons, plan a defense. Weapons? Defense? It was very funny. No gun. Not even a club. But wait. There was Raq. Under the right conditions, against the right man, Raq would certainly provide an element of surprise. It might work. But certainly not against Vang. And probably not against Huntyr. Huntyr was experienced, cautious. But Huntyr's assistant, Hasard, had never impressed him as bursting with intelligence. Hasard was just right. First, of course, he'd have to get Hasard into his room, alone with him and Raq. But that would still leave Huntyr and Vang. He must be free from interruption during those critical moments with Hasard. But how could he keep the other two occupied during his trial with Hasard? And then he had the answer. And with that, the whole plan crystallized, scintillating, unanswerable, perfect. To save his life, a man will cram into one vital instant the intelligence and imagination of a lifetime.

His case was complete, his brief ready; it was time to address the Court.

He greeted them with friendly banality. "May the Ring of Ritornel embrace you all!" He took the chair offered by Huntyr, then calmly launched his attack. "Weren't you mildly insulted?" he asked Huntyr.

"Insulted?" Huntyr's fork hung in midair.

"To be assigned personally to the murder of one so harmless?"

Without changing a muscle, Huntyr's face somehow ceased to smile. "That's bad talk, your Honor."

Andrek looked over at Vang. "Have *you* ever shot a man?" he asked amiably.

The monk opened his mouth, then shot an inquiring look at Huntyr. He turned back to Andrek but did not answer.

Andrek laughed. "I thought not. Not your line, is it? Nor mine. But your comrade has shot men before. Several. As you know, he has been told to kill *me*. I'm unarmed. In fact, I don't know one end of a biemgun from the other; and I can't hide. It's like shooting fish in a barrel.

Huntyr's man Hasard, here, could do it, but you are here to see that Huntyr does it personally. And you'll probably blab it all over Goris-Kard when you return, how the heroic Huntyr killed a harmless, help-less don." His lip curled. "Huntyr! What admiration—what acclaim—awaits your return!"

Huntyr scowled. "You talk too much, Don Andrek. You have a way of making people say things they shouldn't say. But I know all about you. I don't have to say anything."

Andrek laughed. "Quite true, my treacherous friend. You are well advised to be silent. There will be more than sufficient talk by others."

Huntyr wiped his mouth roughly with his napkin. "And anyhow, you have it all wrong."

Vang suddenly turned warning eyes on his companion.

Andrek had guessed right. There was already bad feeling between Huntyr and Vang. Each wanted to control the assassination, and neither would take orders from the other. The situation was building up. If his control held, Huntyr and Hasard would be leaving the table within a few more minutes. He might even get a little unconscious help from Vang.

"Careful, Huntyr," chided Andrek. "You're not only risking your fee, but also your professional future. Your Alean friend thinks you'd better follow his orders, and bear up under the ridicule. In fact, I think he wants you to shut up altogether. Think it over, and pass the salt, if you please." He waited. "Brother Vang, the salt?"

The monk snapped the container viciously toward Andrek. The ad-vocate caught it expertly in midair and gave him a friendly smile. He looked at Vang as he talked, but he knew that Huntyr was listening—and with growing resentment.

"I myself have several assistants," said Andrek. "I trained them my-self, and I trust them completely. In fact, I take pride in them. A profes-sional man is best judged by the performance of his assistants, don't you think? Now, of course, if Huntyr feels he is basically incompetent in the selection and training of his assistants, then he is quite right in not del-egating the assignment." He looked first at Hasard, then at Huntyr. "Is something wrong with your steak?" he asked the investigator solicitously.

Huntyr threw down his napkin, glared first at Andrek, then at Vang. Finally, he summoned Hasard with an imperious jerk of his head, and they both clacked heavily out of the room with as much dignity as their magnetized shoe soles would allow.

Andrek shook his head regretfully. "No sense of humor. Spoils a good man. No offense, you understand, but I think you might have made a better selection." He regarded Vang with a long curious appraisal. First the monk would have to be kept here a few minutes. That should not be too difficult. Second, a large, unexplainable sum of money would have to be planted on the Alean. And that was going to require finesse.

"Linger a moment, Ajian," urged Andrek. "Even on hyperdrive, this will be a long three-day trip. You are making it very difficult for an old classmate to be friendly."

Vang, who was pushing back his chair, hesitated, then stared coldly at Andrek. "What do you want?"

Andrek said, "May I see your die?"

The Alean made an involuntary gesture toward his chest "Why?" he asked suspiciously.

Andrek's eyebrows lifted in feigned astonishment. "How can my seeing your die possibly place you at a disadvantage? Is it conceivable that you could be afraid of me?"

Vang hesitated, then shrugged and reached into the folds of his long robe and drew out the die. "It can make no difference," he said. But he kept it in hand, and did not disconnect it for Andrek's closer inspection. As Andrek suspected, it was still the old pyrite dodecahedron, one of millions grown on mass production lines in the Alean shops, the one that Vang had bought years ago at the Academy. It declared instantly the economic status of its wearer. Vang was a poor man, and be wanted to be rich. This should facilitate the next phase of Andrek's plan. He reached into his inside jacket pocket and pulled out the credit refund check Huntyr had given him that morning. He turned it over on the table and took out his stylus. "I'm endorsing this in blank. It's worth ten thousand gamma to any person presenting it at any bank. And I'll stake it against your Holy Die."

Vang looked at Andrek in open amazement. His eyes shifted covertly to the check. He said noncommittally: "You seem very sure of yourself. What do you want to wager about?"

Andrek answered quietly. "A test of strength. I'll take Ritornel, you take Alea. I propose to prove to you, here and now, that Ritornel is supreme over Alea."

This was rankest heresy, and Andrek smiled inwardly as he watched the monk's reaction. In slow sequence, Vang turned pale, then pink, then, as his anger mounted, red.

Andrek continued coolly. "Is our predestined life-death cycle immune to the operation of the laws of chance, or is the eternal return, the Omega, the Ring, merely the statistical consequence of chance? I contend that the conflict can be resolved—in favor of Ritornel—by a simple experiment. If I am wrong, you take the check for ten thousand gammas. If I am right, I take your die."

"What is the experiment?" demanded Vang harshly.

"The equipment consists simply of my check, your die, and my ink marker. Here is the check, face down. We will take turns rolling the die. The number that comes up each time will be taken as a vector, with the direction of the number on a clock face. And we draw a line having the length of one edge of the die, from the center of this line on my check, in the direction of that number. For example, if the die comes up 'six,' we draw a line three centimeters long—one die-length—straight down the check, in the direction of 'six' on a clock face. At the end of that line we mark an 'x.' Then the die is rolled again. Say the second number is 'nine.' From the 'x' we draw another three-centimeter line in the direction of the 'nine' on a clock face. That gives us a new point of departure. We will roll a total of twelve times, and we add the new vector each time to the previous terminus of the line."

"How can that prove anything?" said Vang suspiciously.

"If Ritornel holds dominion over Alea, the line will eventually return to the starting position on the check; if the line zigzags away at random without returning to the start, then destiny is not a foreordained return, but is instead a matter of pure chance, and Alea is supreme over Ritornel."

He waited as Vang considered this.

The problem was identical to the statistical mechanics of molecular motion, whereby the mean free path of a given molecule in a fluid is determined. It was also known as the "drunkard's walk": if a drunkard started from a lamp post and took twelve steps, each in random direction from the one preceding, how far would he be from the lamp post? He would not be twelve steps distant, but he wouldn't be back at the lamp post either! By the laws of chance, his distance from the lamp post would be the square root of the total length of those twelve steps. And so must be the outcome of the experiment he now proposed to Vang. The line would wander randomly around in the near vicinity of the check, and the final point, theoretically would be the square root of thirty-six centimeters—two die-lengths—distant from the starting point. So he would certainly lose. It was a simple exercise in statistical mechanics, and religion had nothing to do with it.

Apparently Vang realized this too. Andrek waited as the monk mentally double-checked the math. The ten thousand gammas were as good as planted on him.

"I will do it," said Vang finally. "Not for the money, but in obedience to Alea, that sacrilege may be punished, and the falsity of Ritornel be revealed."

Andrek suppressed a smile. "I have no wish to offend the goddess. We could wager for buttons."

Vang frowned. "No. Alea has already forgiven your presumption. It is agreed." As he put the die on the table, he shot one final searching look at the advocate from narrowed, glinting eyes. "Let us drink to the bargain." From the table tankard he pressured two capsules of wine and handed one to Andrek. "To Alea!"

"To Ritornel!" countered Andrek. He waited until Vang had taken a couple of swallows, then lifted his own capsule to his lips. The Aleans were skilled poisoners, and there was no sense in running any risk.

"I must unscrew the locking loop," continued Andrek, "so that the 'two' can come up."

Vang nodded.

Andrek rolled the die. It clattered briefly along the steel tabletop, then stopped, held to the metal surface by the natural ferromagnetism of the crystal pyrite.

Vang spat. "A 'one'—the Sign of Ritornel. Mark your line."

Andrek measured off the line against the die face one length in the direction of one o'clock, then handed the die to Vang. "Your turn."

Vang rolled a "two," and shuddered.

"Disaster at the Node!" said Andrek cheerily. He measured it off, then rolled. "A 'three.' "

Vang relaxed. The line was moving away.

The next numbers were four, five, and six. Andrek looked curiously at the resulting figure, which was a geometrically perfect half of a dodecagon. "Alea seems to be on your side, Brother Vang. We're already several die-lengths away from the start."

Vang did not smile, but his eyes glittered. "Roll!"

Andrek threw a "seven." Vang followed with "eight," and then Andrek took a "nine."

They both examined the figure uneasily. Clearly, it was a dodecagon, three-fourths complete. The line was circling back!

Andrek felt drops of perspiration forming on his forehead. What was happening was a statistical impossibility. He suddenly realized that perhaps the check was not going to get planted on Vang. But he *had* to lose! His life might depend on it. What was the probability that nine numbers could come up in exactly this sequence? One in twelve to the ninth power! Was it conceivable that the god Ritornel truly existed?

He glanced at Vang. The monk's face was taut, bloodless. Clearly, Vang was equally concerned. Was it only about the money? Andrek could not be sure.

Vang tensed, closed his eyes, and rolled a "ten." Andrek followed with "eleven." He marked the lines and handed the die to Vang hypnotically.

Lacking one line, the dodecagon was complete.

Vang stared in growing horror at the figure. "The Ring of Ritornel . . ." he whispered. "We . . . I . . . have desecrated Alea!" He glared at the advocate. "*Daimon*, you shall pay for this!"

Pay? There was still a way! "Would ten thousand gammas satisfy the goddess?" said Andrek humbly. "After all, we did no real harm. We stopped before the Ring was finished. And no one knows what the next die would have been. It might not have been a 'twelve' at all."

Vang hesitated, but finally took the check. "Perhaps. In my prayers, I shall beseech Alea to forgive you." But something still troubled him. He examined the advocate's face at length. "So now you've lost both the experiment and the money. You've proved nothing. Yet, somehow, you seem rather pleased. What were you really after, James Andrek? What did you hope to gain by this sacrilegious demonstration?"

"Time," said Andrek.

"Time? For what?"

"For—certain events to take place."

"I don't understand."

"Because you are not asking the right questions. The first question is, 'Where is Huntyr?' "

"All right, where is Huntyr?"

"Huntyr's back in his room by now," said Andrek.

This seemed to relieve Vang. But Andrek did not intend to permit the monk to enjoy his relief. "The next question, of course, is Hasard."

"Hasard?" said the monk blankly.

"Yes. Where's Hasard?"

"With Huntyr."

Andrek smiled. "I'm afraid, my holy friend, that you have not given your close attention to the events of the last few minutes. Hasard is *not* with Huntyr."

The Alean shrugged. "Not that it makes any difference, but where do *you* think he is?"

"He's in *my* room."

Vang started. Andrek noted this with satisfaction.

"You're guessing," said the monk uncertainly.

"Of course. But I'm sure I'm right. Huntyr took it upon himself just now to delegate my assassination to Hasard. So it's Hasard, not Huntyr, who'll be waiting for me when I return."

"Why are you telling me all this?" asked the Alean bleakly.

The first phase was over. Andrek relaxed a little. "Basically, to gain time. I'd rather deal with Hasard than with Huntyr. And if you suspected I'd be successful in goading him into the substitution, you'd try to get to him and stop him. But by now, he's either made the switch—or he hasn't. So you're free to go, if you like."

The monk stood up. A delicate pink was suffusing along his throat and cheeks. Andrek almost laughed as Vang hurried from the room. But not yet. Mirth was still a bit premature. He pushed himself away from the table and looked around the mess hall. It was empty. He shrugged. What difference did it make? He was not going to demand protection from the ship's officers or from anyone else on the ship. This ship was a government courier. The captain undoubtedly had orders from the Great House not to interfere—and perhaps even to help Huntyr, if the need arose.

Everything was up to him. He was on his own, and he accepted it. He stood erect and strode from the room.

As he clacked down the halls, he reintegrated the variables. Planting the check on Brother Vang was going to help, but not immediately. The immediate drama would begin in Andrek's cabin, and there, he hoped—and feared—two of the actors were at this moment probably impatiently awaiting his return. In Andrek's mind they were weirdly similar in their potentials for sudden violence: a courier case with a very hungry spider . . . and Hasard with a biem-gun. It was time to raise the curtain and start the festivities.

10. THE RIGHT KEY, AND BEYOND

He stopped in front of his cabin door and knocked. As he expected, there was no answer. "Hasard?" he called loudly, "Andrek here. Hold your fire. I'm coming in."

He lifted the latch and opened the door.

Hasard was sitting in the chair by the table. His right hand held a biem-gun, resting casually on his knee. With his left hand he reached over and turned up the lights. "Come in," he said. "And close the door."

Andrek closed the door behind him carefully. And, concealing the motion with his body, he locked it with the inside latch. He wanted no interruptions from the corridor.

He studied the man quietly. The question now was—how much did this shark-faced brute know about him, and why he, Andrek, was on *Xerol?* Probably very little. Probably Huntyr had simply told the man to wait for him in this room and to kill him here.

"Keep your hands up," said the intruder.

Andrek raised his hands, and continued to examine the hard features. Hasard's pleasures were written on his face. They were simple but expensive: women and night life, probably in Huntyr's borrowed coupé. Money would make a strong appeal. Andrek had very little money, but it was unlikely the other knew this. So he would start by talking money. It would at least delay matters, give him time to develop the details of his defense.

No one, honest or otherwise, had ever been killed while in the act of offering a bribe!

And during the forthcoming dialogue, there was a very important point that he had to work into the conversation. He was certain that Hasard carried a transmitter on his person, and that Huntyr and Vang were back in their cabin listening to every word. On this assumption, Huntyr was about to hear something that would keep him very seriously occupied with Vang for the next few minutes.

Andrek faced Hasard and said, rather loudly: "Brother Vang agreed at dinner tonight to call off the assassination. For ten thousand gammas. It's Huntyr's own refund check to me. You remember it, I'm sure. Oberon made him give it to me. I endorsed it and gave it to the good brother. He put it in the inner pocket of his robe, and promised to divide it among the three of you."

Hasard laughed. "A smart man like you, Don Andrek, an advocate and all, ought to do better than that."

"Really? You mean you don't believe me? This is indeed embarrassing." Andrek breathed deeply. Perhaps it was his imagination, but he thought he saw Hasard's trigger finger relax. Clearly, the man was interested. The fish was circling the bait, and sniffing hungrily. Andrek hoped that by now Huntyr was fully occupied with Vang and couldn't pay attention. He tried to visualize affairs in Huntyr's cabin . . . Huntyr's voice rising . . . Vang's vehement and indignant denial . . . Huntyr insisting on searching the other . . . violent hands . . . the discovery of the check. But the actual details didn't really matter. Just so those two kept each other busy for five minutes.

"I can see," said Andrek, "that it will take more than just talk to persuade you not to kill me. You're a good man. You impress me. It's a pity you're on the wrong side. Our organization could certainly use a man like you." He lowered his hands slightly. "Have you ever considered coming over to us, at, say, twice your present salary?"

The other considered this, then scowled. "You're crazy. I don't even want to listen to you. I'm going to kill you and get out of here."

"Efficient, loyal, that's what I like," said Andrek. His hands dropped slowly to his sides. "But don't worry about Huntyr. We'll guarantee personal protection *and* we'll give you a handsome starting bonus: one hundred thousand gammas." He spoke the words slowly, impressively.

Andrek could see that the amount of money hit Hasard like a hard blow to the body. He could sense the physical impact on the man. It was ten years' income, enough for him to leave Huntyr. Enough for a villa, servants, respectability, acceptance in high places. The coarse features oscillated between greed and disbelief. The man rose halfway out of the chair. "You're lying! You don't have that kind of money here!"

"Oh, I have it, all right, and it's here. Unhappily, it's the payroll for the staff at the Node Station, and I can't touch it. You'll have to wait until we get to the bank at the station."

He watched Hasard's reaction with a profound and growing amazement, which, however, he was careful to conceal. He had hoped the plan would work, of course, and actually had seen no real risk of failure. And yet, to watch it unfold with such perfection, such precision, seemed almost too good to be true. But it wasn't over yet. Hasard had to be persuaded to open the attaché case and to open it with avarice, and without suspecting what was waiting inside. He glanced at the case on the table, as though by inadvertence, then hastily returned his eyes to the killer.

The other turned his head slowly, saw the case, and smiled. "How much you got there?"

"Credits for over two hundred thousand. But don't get any ideas . . . the case is locked, and I alone know the combination. If you try to blast the lock, it will auto-destruct."

"What's the combination?"

Oh Amatar, my strange darling, thought Andrek. How did you know? He said sharply, "You don't understand. I can't give you *that* money. You'll have to wait until we get to the bank at the station."

Almost casually, Hasard raised his biem and fired. Andrek put his hand to his ear. His fingers felt something warm and wet. His ear stung horribly. The lobe-tip was gone. Blood was dripping on his shoulder.

But it was all right. He had won. The hard part was over. Hasard was, for practical purposes, dead.

The other waited patiently.

Andrek knew his voice was going to shake. But that, too, was all right. It would add a further note of sincerity to the proceedings. "The combination consists of the fair numbers of Alea: twelve right, six left, five right, three left."

"That's fine. Now you come over here and stand in front of me while I open it."

"I'd be happy to open it for you . . . ."

"And pull out a biem? Just do like I said, Don Andrek. And hands high."

"Of course, my dear fellow." Andrek sidled around in front of the thug, with the table between them. Hasard bent down and began turning the dial with slow, studied care.

Andrek's every nerve was on edge, poised to strike. It was working, the whole thing, just as he had known it must. The only thing about the cascading sequence that astonished him was his own calmness. It was hard for him to realize that, he, a peaceful, rather sedentary advocate, was about to fight a man to the death.

And it must come in seconds, for in seconds the killer must make contact with Raq, and in the resulting brief flurry of shock and indecision, Andrek planned to hurl himself over the table and take the biem.

So thinking, he was quite unprepared for what actually happened.

Raq's stomach was small. It needed frequent replenishment. She had not eaten in nearly twenty hours, and she was ravenous. Also, she was cramped, and it was impossible for her to stretch her legs. Her temper, ordinarily placid and retiring, now suffered from the combined effects of hunger and confinement. She was coiled like a spring, and she was furious.

Amatar's conditioning made it impossible for Raq to harbor resentment toward Andrek. His footsteps and voice came to her clearly through the walls of the case and the code box. This left, as a focal point for her rage, the other two-legger, whose footsteps and voice told her that he stood just above and outside her prison. There was something about his voice that put an edge of fear on Raq's growing dislike of him. The spring within her coiled tighter. Her mandibles chattered and began to drip toxin.

Hasard grasped the lid by the front left corner and raised it.

A horrid blur hit him in the mouth. He screamed, dropped his gun, clapped his hands to his face, and began to collapse. Raq, disconcerted by the approaching hands, disengaged her mandibles, now dripping with blood, and leaped away in good time. She struck the drapes on the opposite cabin wall and froze there, to await developments.

Andrek broke partway out of his shock, retrieved the biem-gun during one of its wild ricochets from the cabin walls, and stuck it in his belt. He was probably safe for a moment. Firstly, Huntyr, if he were listening in, would probably assume that the scream came from him, Andrek, and secondly, it was even more likely that Huntyr was, at this moment, engaged in a bitter argument with Vang regarding the check. That check would probably be impossible for the Alean to explain. Wager, indeed! Andrek felt a very faint tinge of sympathy for the monk.

Breathing heavily, he turned back to his visitor. He had never seen a man lose consciousness under weightless conditions, and he watched the process with a kind of vague wonder. First, there was a general relaxation and contraction of all the gross motor muscles. Being fixed to the floor by his magnetic shoes, Hasard had to contract in that direction. Visibly, he seemed to shrink. His knees buckled, his arms and shoulders took on an apelike crouch, and his knuckles curled "downward" toward the floor. His mouth was slack, and his lower lip, where Raq had struck, was rapidly swelling. His eyes squinted in deadened amazement at the floor.

Andrek shook his head rapidly, as though to recover his scattered senses.

A decision had to be made, and quickly. Should he simply push the unconscious man out into the corridor? But that made no sense. Huntyr would surely find him and resuscitate him, and then the odds would be nearly as bad as before. And, having educated his enemies, their next try might be altogether different. No, Hasard could not be turned back to Huntyr. Then how about the brig? No good, either. *Xerol's* officers probably had orders to cooperate with Huntyr and Vang. Any complaints to the captain might well have fatal consequences.

By elimination, then, there was only one alternative left.

Murder.

Andrek shivered. He had never killed a man before, and the thought of killing an unconscious man struck him as a new low in sportsmanship. He realized now the nature of desperation, and how the primal urge to continue living can force a man to do anything. "Absolutely anything," he muttered.

He looked down at Hasard's crumpled body in anger and frustration. The man's chest was moving quietly, rhythmically. The breathing was barely audible. Andrek sighed and studied the controls on the biem. Hasard would have to be vaporized. A great deal of heat would be released in the cabin. He stepped over to the room service panel and turned the thermostat to "colder." The response was almost immediate. As his breath began to frost, he turned up the ventilation duct. The drapes began to flutter, and some papers floated out into the room. Then he kneeled down beside the unconscious man and turned off the magnetic switch in his shoes. Hasard floated free. Andrek stepped back, drew the biem, adjusted the energy cone, and was about to pull the trigger, when he had a sudden thought.

He really ought to search the body.

He grimaced as he ran his hands through Hasard's clothing. In the jacket he found what he wanted: a key ring—with three keys. One was stamped "13"—his room. The others were 12 and 14. Number 12, he knew, was actually a three-room suite, immediately down the corridor on the left, fairly luxurious, considering that the *Xerol* was only a government courier. Number 14 was a single, and it adjoined his own cabin on the right. Vang would certainly have selected the suite as a base of operations, but he might also have held Number 14 in reserve. On the other hand—there was the question of the Ritornellian pilgrim.

The only sure way to resolve the mystery of Room 14 was to unlock the door and take a look inside. But first—

He put the keys in his pocket, then stepped back again and fired at the killer's head—which instantly glowed red-hot, then disappeared in a flash of smoke. In minutes, the corpse was neatly vaporized into its component molecules and had been drawn into the ship's air-conditioning system. Andrek rather suspected that one of the junior engineers was going to be mightily puzzled by the strange surge of carbon dioxide and inorganic colloids in the filter tanks.

After it was all over, he checked the thermostat. The heat released in disposing of his visitor just about balanced the pre-induced chill in his room. He readjusted the thermostat, then walked over to the cabin door and listened. He could hear nothing. He opened the door and stepped rapidly down the hall to Number 14. The photo-key slipped readily into the insert. There was no noise. Andrek drew the biem-gun, kicked the door open, and leaped inside.

There was no countermovement anywhere. But even before his eyes adjusted completely to the dim radiance of the cruise lights, he heard something—the sound of regular breathing—from the far corner.

Andrek crouched and swung his biem around toward the sound.

And then be saw it—the robed body floating in a full-length strait-jacket, fixed "horizontally" in space by guy ropes clewed to snap buckles in ceiling and floor. The face radiated a pale blue glow.

It had to be—it was—the ancient pilgrim of Ritornel, bound and gagged, but alive.

Andrek closed the door softly behind him, propped a chair top under the doorknob, and walked over to the suspended shape. As he bent over the face, he was startled to see the eyes jerk open to look into his.

The impact of those eyes boring into his own hit him with raw physical force. The eyes, like the rest of the face, radiated a pale blue light. And they brought with them returning knowledge. He had seen these eyes before, long ago. In another dim-lit place. When? Where? It would not come back. He could remember nothing. Except that he had been afraid.

But he was not afraid anymore.

And now he had to get busy.

He put his biem back into his belt. "We'll have you out of there in a jiffy," he whispered. He slipped the edge of his excisor blade under the cloth gag and clipped it cleanly away from the other's mouth.

"Are you all right?" asked Andrek.

The other was silent—he merely blinked his eyes—then continued to stare at Andrek.

The advocate's heart sank. The pilgrim had been drugged. Except for the eyes, the voluntary nervous system was probably paralyzed. With his clippers, Andrek cleared the elastic metal netting away from the body. There was still no movement.

He moved around to face the other. "If you can hear and understand me," he said, "blink your eyes—just once."

The pilgrim blinked his eyes—once.

Andrek grinned. "Now, then, one blink means 'yes.' Two blinks mean 'no.' All right?"

The other blinked once.

"Have you been drugged?"

One blink.

"Is there an antidote?"

One blink.

"On the ship?"

One blink.

Probably in the dispensary, thought Andrek. Still, with a person of the pilgrim's undoubted talents, the antidote might be closer.

"Do you have the antidote here in your cabin?"

One blink.

Good! Andrek looked about the room. There was but one modest clothes-case, lying on the dressing table. He walked over and opened it. It was *not* a clothes-case. Andrek whistled under his breath. It was a medical kit. In the top half was a complete array of instruments, from syringe to stethoscope. The bottom section contained tray after tray of rubber-capped glass vials—thousands. One of these vials contained the antidote—he hoped. He released the magnetic clips and floated the case over to the friar.

"Is it in here?"

One blink.

"I propose now to turn these trays, one at a time. At each tray, I will ask you whether it is the one with the vial we want, then we'll try each row of vials on that tray, then each vial in the correct row."

He found it in seconds—twelfth tray—twelfth row—twelfth vial. Alea all the way! As he sterilized the syringe, he asked: "Do you get the entire contents?"

Two blinks—no.

"How many cc.? Tell me by the number of blinks."

The pilgrim stared at him—then finally blinked twice.

Andrek felt instantly that something was wrong. Did that mean two—or "no"? It was dangerous to permit a signal to mean two different things.

"Two cc.?"

Two blinks again.

"Forget that," said Andrek. "We'll return to our original binary communication—everything is yes or no. Is the dosage less than one cc.?"

One blink.

"Is it more than one-tenth cc.?"

Two blinks.

"Is it exactly one-tenth?"

One blink.

Andrek thrust the needle through the rubber cap of the vial and drew up the requisite amount, then cleared the air bubble in the needle.

"In the biceps?"

There was a long pause; Andrek wondered for a moment whether he had asked the right question. But finally:

One blink.

Andrek raised the hair-shirt sleeve—and then blinked himself. The pilgrim's arm—which looked more like a segmented broomstick than an arm—was completely covered with a close-fitting rubbery fabric, right down to the white gloves. And the arm seemed hard as steel, unyielding to the pressure of his fingers as he sought in vain for the biceps. Finally he shrugged his shoulders and shoved the needle into what he hoped was the right place. It took all his strength to force the metal bit into the arm. The pilgrim was a tough one!

But the antidote acted quickly. In a few minutes the friar was flexing his arms and rubbing his spindly thighs. He stood up and offered his gloved hand to Andrek. "I'm Iovve. And of course you are James, Don Andrek." He grinned at Andrek from his strangely whiskered mouth. "Rather embarrassing, meeting this way, but it couldn't be helped. *They* were clever. I learned only at the last minute about your trip. Brother Vang was waiting for me with a syringe-bullet. I never even made it into the cabin. Hardly sporting." He walked over to the medical case and folded it up carefully. "How did you know I was aboard?"

Andrek told him what had happened to Hasard.

Iovve frowned. "That leaves the two dangerous ones: Huntyr and Vang. Vang may be the worst. He's a drug expert. He's one reason I brought the medical case. Have you had anything to eat or drink with them?"

Andrek struck his forehead. "How stupid of me! Vang and I drank to the wager."

"It could be . . ." muttered Iovve.

"But it was from the table tankard."

"No matter. He could have taken the antidote later."

"Well, then, so can I. You seem to have all the antidotes, right here."

"True, I do—but they are all useless if we don't know the drug."

"How did you know what drug they had given you?"

The blue radiance around Iovve's face seemed to flicker. "If I gave you a complete explanation, it would take a great deal of time, and in the end you might not believe me. Suffice it to say that the antidote was correct."

Andrek shrugged. "Well, I suppose we'll have to wait until I develop some symptoms. Meanwhile, tell me this: Why are you on the ship now?

And yesterday, why did you break into Huntyr's office? Have we met before? Apparently you're on my side. But why?"

The pilgrim raised his thin arms in protest. "So many questions, my boy! Granted, they all deserve complete and honest answers. But honest answers take time, far more time than we have at the moment. And just now the complete truth would place too great a strain on your credulity. You must settle for this: Oberon wants you dead, and I want you alive."

"That much I had already surmised." The advocate clenched his jaws in frustration. "At least tell me this, if you know: what am I to Oberon, that I must die?"

"Oh. That part's easy. The Aleans have convinced Oberon that you represent a threat to his life. It's all in their crystomorphs. But that's merely the main reason. There are side issues . . . Amatar, for example . . ."

"I can't believe Oberon would kill me merely because I'm in love with his daughter."

The pilgrim smiled bleakly. "Amatar—his daughter? A great deal needs to be explained to you, my boy, but now is not the time to do it. We have to get a force field up before we have any more visitors." He slipped off his wristwatch and turned toward the dressing table.

"How were you able to get a field generator aboard?" asked Andrek curiously. "And didn't they search your things?"

"Oh, they went through my poor belongings, all right. But they found only the medical kit—which amused them immensely. They didn't bother that because they thought there would be no one on board to help me use it, especially since you were to receive their promptest attention, right after supper. And as for the generator, they didn't find it because I carry it broken down into components that look like something else . . . autorazor, stylus, comb, and so on. Certain other elements I expect to find here as standard equipment in any cabin, such as the fluorolites, emergency kit in the closet, tape library, and parts of the intercom. And incidentally, we'll set the field up around *your* cabin, since *that's* where Huntyr will come looking for you when Hasard doesn't return. Courtesy requires a proper welcome."

The pilgrim picked up his valise and medical kit and peeked out the cabin door. "Come on," he said to Andrek.

Inside Andrek's cabin, Iovve got to work on the field generator. The apparatus rapidly took shape under his flying gloved fingers, and he explained as he worked. "This type of field has some built-in defects. The power drain is enormous. This means we have to plug it into the ship's current." He nodded in the direction of the cable, which terminated in a six-prong plug. "But we can't simply turn the field on and leave it on. The wattage drain would be noticed immediately in the ship's power room.

The electrical engineer would tell the captain, and that would be the end of our cabin current. And it might happen at a highly critical moment. So we'll superimpose a low-drain alert in series with a capacitor surge tank. The alert will detect any energy surge in the field area and will instantly activate the capacitor."

This made only the vaguest sense to Andrek. In a general way he understood the principles of the force field. He had, however, been under the impression that tremendous power was required, something far beyond cabin amperage, even if accumulated in what his new friend termed the "capacitor," which he took to be the entire outer shell of the ship. Nevertheless, he was inclined to accept Iovve's flat statement that the jerry-built equipment could be plugged into the wall circuit and create an adequate field, if only because of the pilgrim's very evident skill and immense self-confidence.

Iovve straightened up. He seemed to be listening. "Ah," he whispered. "A visitor, I think. Grab something and hold on!"

Andrek seized the bunk post with both hands. As he did this, his eyes fell on the six-pronged plug. It had never been plugged into the wall socket!

He was frozen in a momentary paralysis. Then he broke from the bunk stanchion in a flying leap, grabbed the line and was centimeters and milliseconds from the wall socket when the cabin lights flickered and a sudden painful pressure hit his eardrums.

He knew the force field had just been activated.

And then the plug was in the socket.

Slowly he took his hand from the line and stood up. It was impossible. Or was it? Could the field exist before the plug was in? Or was he only imagining that he had been too late with the plug? *No.* He had not imagined the sequence. It was still fresh in his mind: *"WHAM . . .* click . . ." Iovve simply had not used the cabin current, but clearly wanted him, Andrek, to think it was necessary. Did the pilgrim have some strange power source, already integrated into the apparatus, which he wanted to keep secret? He suspected that the pilgrim had many secrets. This was just one more. Eventually, there would have to be some answers.

11. A QUESTIONABLE ENTRANCE

The pilgrim looked over at Andrek and grinned. "Did it knock you loose? They hit a wall panel, on the corridor side. They must be pretty sure we have a field, but they'll try once more, to make sure."

Immediately, something exploded in Andrek's stomach. He took a few steps toward the center of the room and steadied himself on the table. It seemed warm to the touch.

"That was quite a wallop," murmured Iovve. "So now they know for sure. They'll go back to Cabin Twelve to figure out what to do next. And I'll just take a peek out the door."

Andrek started to shout a warning, but the pilgrim was already at the door. He opened it a crack, then closed it immediately.

"Just one man," said Iovve thoughtfully. "Huntyr, I think. I wonder what happened to Brother Vang . . ."

Andrek could guess. Huntyr had found the check on his companion and didn't like the explanation. At the very least, Vang was a prisoner in Cabin Twelve. He explained his theory to Iovve. "That cuts the odds considerably, wouldn't you say?" he asked.

"Depends on the point of view, my boy. Regardless of Vang, Huntyr is on an official mission for the Great House, and if need be he can call on the entire resources of the ship to destroy us. We'll have to bring this little affair to a head before he decides he can't handle us by himself. Which means we'll soon have to carry the war into enemy territory. But first—"

Andrek looked up. "Yes?"

"Let's feed Raq. I imagine she's pretty hungry."

Andrek reached into the open courier case for the feeding kit that Amatar had given him. And then he stopped. He had, of course, explained to Iovve how Hasard had died. And Iovve's recommendation was completely logical. In fact Andrek would have fed Raq without it. Even so, something about it jarred him. Several of the words were—wrong.

He lifted the little leather box out of the case and turned in slow indecision. There was a very searching question that he could ask Iovve. But the simple act of asking would reveal to the monk that Andrek knew something about him, something, perhaps, that he was not supposed to know. He doubted the monk would answer the question, anyhow, but the means used to avoid answering might be revelatory. At this point, he felt he had nothing to lose.

He said quietly, "I did not mention the name of my spider; yet you call her 'Raq.' Nor did I tell you her sex; yet you know she is a female. And finally, I have said nothing about *this*"—he held up the feeding kit—"yet you know about it." He paused, then his voice became even softer. "Only one other person could have told you. Iovve, *what are you to Amatar?*"

Iovve shifted uneasily. "I am her friend. And it is true, I know all about Raq—including a few things that neither you nor Amatar know. For example, I know there's a very good reason for feeding her right now. And never fear; I'll explain everything in good time. Meanwhile, roll back your sleeve. Now, then, we need an antiseptic . . . ah, the biem . . ."

Under Iovve's watchful supervision Andrek sterilized his left hand, together with the needle and syringe, with a mild cone spray from the biem-gun. Then he made a fist, and—wincing—thrust the needle into the ball of his thumb. In seconds he had filled the syringe barrel, which he then discharged beneath the plastic "chitin" of the false insect from Amatar's little case. Gingerly, he carried it over to the fold in the drapes where Raq was hiding, and here he hung it cautiously in the fabric. He did not have to wait. Raq was on her way the instant the drape was touched. Andrek quickly stood away, but winced again as the great arachnid stabbed her mandibles into her "prey."

As he watched Raq feed, he wondered just how much Iovve really did know about Raq, and how he had gained the knowledge. Was it possible that Iovve had foreseen his need for Raq and had planned the whole thing, with Amatar's enthusiastic cooperation? But that possibility raised even more questions. It would require long, careful, secret activity behind the scenes. But did it have to be secret? What if Iovve had access to the Great House, and could come and go as he pleased without arousing suspicion? Was *that* possible? If it were, who, then, *was* this creature? Questions. Too many questions. And no answers. Andrek felt himself caught in a strange and devious web of fate. The gods had spun their strands and caught him. He mused on. The more I thrash about, the more enmeshed I become. Ritornel must be some sort of celestial spider.

Andrek realized that Iovve was watching him curiously. "Ridiculous, isn't it?" murmured Andrek. "To owe one's life to an insect?"

"The spider is not an insect," chided the pilgrim. "Insects have six legs; spiders have eight. And there are other morphological differences. But in any case"—his eyes twinkled—"your spider equally owes her life to you. So the matter is in good balance."

"Curious that she can feed on human blood," said Andrek.

"No," said Iovve. "It would be curious if she couldn't. The blood cells, of course, she simply filters out. But the plasma has about the same analysis as insect hemolymph: amino acids, sugars, dissolved salts, proteins. She—"

They both looked at Raq with startled eyes. She had leaped from the drapes, weightlessly, in a straight line for the ceiling of the cabin, where she paused a moment. Andrek could see that she had affixed an anchor line. After this she jumped straight to the floor, bringing the line with her, hooked in the comb of one of her hind legs. This line she fastened to the floor. Then she ran along the floor to the nearest wall, crawled up exactly midway, and sailed over to the opposite wall, to form a second perpendicular, which was soon tied neatly to the first. The third perpendicular was quickly made in the same manner, between the remaining two walls.

Iovve drew Andrek over into one quarter of the cabin. "We'll have to stay out of her way," he said grimly. "She will need complete freedom of movement for this."

"What's going on?" demanded Andrek in a hoarse whisper.

"She has been drugged, my friend—*by your blood.* Which means, of course, that you have been drugged too. It was probably that wine of Vang's. Raq is now making a web—of a peculiar kind. The type of web will define the drug, and then we can select an antidote. This is called web-analysis . . . when it works." He studied Andrek with concern. "How do you feel?"

"Just—a little dizzy. I think I'll sit down."

"Web analysis can be quite complicated." The pilgrim hugged his chest uneasily. "This will evidently be a three-dimensional web. Those are the X, Y, and Z coordinates. This type is quite rare, and weaving it in free space, with no gravity, may introduce all sorts of complications." He shook his head. "You know the theory, of course. A spider dosed with a little alcohol weaves a drunken web. If stimulated with caffeine, she will build one which is a model of engineering precision: the strands and spokes are equi-spaced to a micron. With the mushroom drugs, she builds one circular strand with a couple of spokes, then hangs in the center, a spider god alone in a spider universe. With the really lethal drugs, such as the organic nitriles—"

Iovve droned on, but the words were becoming blurred to Andrek. He just wanted to sit and think. It seemed to him that Iovve was unduly excited about the whole thing. There was nothing to worry about. His thoughts were turning inward, and pilgrim, cabin, Raq, everything, took on a hazy, remote, dreamlike quality. It was becoming rather pleasant. He wanted to stay this way. He liked being drugged. He hoped Iovve could not identify it, nor find an antidote. Meanwhile, he had a great deal to think about. Tomorrow they would land at the Node Station. He would have to attend the condemnation proceedings for the planet Terror. The terrible planet Terror. He had not yet been born when the last of her defenders died in the final bombardment by the revolutionaries. But he had seen the tri-di pictures. Her entire land area had been ablaze with nuclear fires. Nothing had been left. Nothing. But it was just. Terror had begun the war. Terror was to blame for the Horror. But now it was over and done. Space tugs had pulled her far out here, to the Node, and here she would be atomized. The titanic demolition charges had been placed long ago. Within another day she would be blown to bits. It was his job to see that nothing interfered with that. He concentrated now on the technique of presenting his motion for summary destruction to the arbiters.

In front of Andrek, Raq continued her work purposefully, unhurried, yet without lost motion, ignoring Andrek just as he was ignoring her. Returning to the central point of the coordinates, she next measured off about ten centimeters along one horizontal axis, turned and leaped to the other horizontal axis, repeating until she had outlined a square parallel to the floor. She then made similar square outlines with the remaining coordinates.

"Octahedron—two pyramids, base-to-base," muttered Iovve.

Inside this structure, toward the top, Raq inscribed a smaller square, parallel to the floor, and within this she formed a pentagon. Iovve leaned forward intently. From the apices of the pentagon, she dropped strands, one by one, and fastened each to the octahedral framework. Then, back to the upper pentagon, she worked rapidly outward from this, to form five further pentagons, anchored to the five cables. Always, she worked "inside" the structure.

Iovve turned to Andrek. "It looks like the upper half of a dodecahedron—I think we'll know for sure in a moment."

Andrek stared at him irritably. His sequence of thought had been broken. "What did you say?"

Iovve held up his hand. "Silence, now," he whispered.

Raq finished the bottom half of the twelve-faced figure, then, starting from one angle on the upper pentagon, began systematically to line the interior with a filamentary spiral, each successive strand a fraction of a centimeter lower than the one preceding. Soon, her body was partly hidden within the figure. Iovve bent low in his effort to follow her strange drama.

Raq stopped. By now she was invisible within the interior of the dodecahedral cocoon. The whole structure was momentarily immobile. And then it began to shudder in a mixture of convulsive rhythms. The geometric figure vibrated desperately, setting up standing waves in the three anchoring perpendiculars.

Andrek watched all this without interest. He closed his eyes and locked himself within his own thoughts. After opening with a presentation of Terror's centuries of vicious history, culminating in the long, deadly nuclear war that had laid waste so many of her colonies, and had destroyed, finally, the mother planet, he would go on to her history of cruel, domineering colonization. Develop her oppression, the causes of revolt. The secret formation of the rebel confederation headed by Goris-Kard. The declaration of independence. Reprisals. The beginning of the Horror. And years later, the end. And then a full treatment of the legal points. The formation of the League of the Twelve Galaxies. The treaties and covenants. He'd cite chapter and verse. There could be only one outcome.

He opened his eyes. Iovve was shaking him.

"She's caught in her own web. It can be only one thing."

Andrek groaned with annoyance. "Go away. Leave me alone. I'm very busy."

"It's quirinal!" hissed Iovve.

"Quirinal?" Andrek stared at him owlishly.

"The slave drug. It induces the most hideous kind of slavery. It causes one to become enslaved to oneself—to become caught in one's own web, so to speak. It carries introversion to the ultimate. It is a standard ingredient in the colloidal networks of arts computers—helps them compose better poetry, music, because it forces constant, continuing feedback, comparing a proposed composition with certain preset standards." As he spoke, he was opening the drug section of his medical kit. "Here we are. The antidote." He filled the syringe in a deft motion and thrust the needle into Andrek's arm. And immediately after that, he recharged the needle, seized Raq's cocoon, and in another moment had thrust the needle tip into her cephalothorax.

He turned back to Andrek. who was rubbing his eyes. "How do you feel?" asked Iovve.

Andrek grinned sheepishly. "A little stupid, but all right, otherwise. I'm coming out of it. That was really something. How's Raq?"

"She'll come around in a moment. Hold her while I get rid of this web." The pilgrim handed her to Andrek, who accepted her somewhat dubiously. He stroked her back with his forefinger, trying to remember how Amatar had done it. Raq relaxed into a bristly bundle in his palm.

Iovve was clearing away the last of the web when there was a knock on the door.

Andrek exchanged glances with the pilgrim. Iovve nodded.

"Who is it?" demanded Andrek.

"Huntyr. I'm alone. I want to talk. Let me in."

"Suppose we say no?"

"You could. But then you'd never know what I was going to tell you."

Andrek was undecided. "What do you want to talk about?"

"Your father and your brother."

Andrek started. His heart began to pound furiously, and he felt as though he were choking, It was true. Huntyr *did* know. He was certain of it. He was very close to discovering his brother's fate. And Huntyr apparently knew something about his father's death, too. But he hesitated. A part of him wanted to scream "Come in!" But the rest of him whispered, "Danger! Don't be bewitched by those magic names. For this man intends to kill you." But then he thought, If this is the only way I can ever learn of them, I will listen, and risk death. And then he remembered he was not alone. He might have the right to gamble his own life, but what about Iovve? He looked at the pilgrim in anguish.

Iovve shrugged his shoulders. "It had to come." His voice was flat, almost weary. "Let him in, and keep your biem on him. He's armed, but it would be dangerous to search him. He's very muscular, and his reflexes are extraordinary. Stay well away from him. I'll open the door."

Andrek looked about for a place to deposit Raq. Finding none, he slid her into his jacket pocket. Then he pulled the biem out of his belt and pointed it at the door.

The door slowly swung open, and Huntyr walked in, hands high, and smiling.

12. THE CORD OF ALEA

Andrek sought, and found, a secret glint in Huntyr's golden eye patch. The metal shield sparkled with news of Omere. And Huntyr was going to take great and sadistic pleasure in telling it. This could mean only one thing. Some tragic misfortune had befallen his brother, and Huntyr was somehow connected with it.

"This is not a truce," said Andrek coldly. "I still intend to kill you."

Huntyr's face twisted into a mocking smile. "You'd kill an unarmed man? After that fine speech in the mess?" His eyes roamed about the cabin. Alertly, noncommittally, they explored Iovve. "I don't know how the two of you did it, but I think you have to admit that the odds have now shifted heavily in your favor. You were far too modest, Don Andrek. Killing you— and your friend—will be an accomplishment worth talking about."

". . . 'will be' . . . ?" murmured Andrek.

"As you say, your Honor, this is not a truce. *I* intend to kill *you,* after we are through talking."

Andrek wondered, with a sudden shiver, whether Huntyr could conceivably draw and fire before he, Andrek, could get off a shot. And now, he realized, with a sense of shock, that Huntyr's smile had broadened perceptibly.

The advocate said curtly: "You are here to tell me about my father and my brother."

"Softly, Don Andrek. There are in fact several stories, with stories within stories, and side paths, and digressions."

"Then be seated, and begin." Andrek motioned to the chair in the corner. "Sitting" in free space was not the same as sitting in a gravitational field. In space the chair served simply to anchor its occupant, and not as a situs of relaxation. It would make rapid movement more difficult for Huntyr. "Keep your hands where I can see them," said Andrek.

"Of course." Huntyr looked at his wrist chrono. Then he said: "Eighteen years ago your father, the late Captain Andrek, died on his ship, while on duty at the Node. In that same year your brother, the poet, disappeared. You were just a lad. All of this happened in the year your brother became the Laureate."

Andrek leaned forward. "Go on."

"It was a remarkable year. Other things also happened." Huntyr gave Iovve a calculating stare, then turned back to Andrek. "Have you ever noticed Oberon's chest belt?"

"Of course. It's for protection against assassination."

"Wrong. It's there solely to prevent his chest from collapsing." He shot a glance at the pilgrim. "Wouldn't you say so, *Doctor?*"

Iovve shrugged. "It's possible."

Andrek looked over at Iovve. "He called you 'doctor.' What does he mean?"

"Long ago, I was a member of the Iatric Order of Ritornel." Iovve sounded evasive.

Andrek groaned inwardly. Every answer brought fresh riddles with it. Who *was* Iovve, really? But this was no time for speculation. He nodded curtly to Huntyr. "Continue. Do you mean that Oberon had an accident?"

"Well, your Honor, it was really worse than that. He was in this hunting party, see, at the Node, where we're going. But they'd received a report that a quake was due, so all the ships had pulled back beyond the shock line—all except Oberon's, that is. He was hunting the krith, the winged beast that eats the little beasts out in the Node. Oberon was hot on his trail. He was sure he could overtake and kill the krith before the quake hit. But the captain thought it was too risky, and finally refused to take Oberon any farther. So Oberon had the captain shot for mutiny. As it turned out, the captain was right, and Oberon was wrong. The quake caught the ship. In seconds, it was wrecked: a shambles, a derelict. I was there. I was Oberon's aide. I know." Huntyr touched his eye patch. "That's where I got this."

"Go on," whispered Andrek.

"All the officers and men of the ship's crew were killed instantly. For all practical purposes, so was Oberon. They found bits of him all over the ship, and even during the very hours of his coronation, the Master Surgeon was still picking pieces of the ship out of him."

Huntyr paused and fixed Iovve with a penetrating stare. "Even the great Master Surgeon doubted he could save Oberon. So, by the demand of the old Regent, they started tissue cultures—mostly from bone fragments left over when they cleaned Oberon's wounds."

Andrek had heard of the practice. One living cell, plant or animal, when placed in a suitable nutrient medium, could, if cultured properly, sometimes reproduce the entire mature organism from which the single cell was taken. The procedure had been used for the preservation of valuable strains of the lower animals, but he had never heard of its working with hominid cells. Yet, the idea was sound enough; the old Regent had evidently been trying to grow another Oberon from selected cells of the dying man.

"What has a tissue culture to do with my father or brother?"

"Nothing directly. But I thought you ought to understand Oberon's condition at the time your brother enters the picture. Oberon, in effect, was trembling between life and death. And when he realized his physical condition, and that he might never walk again, he wanted to die. But the old Regent was too clever for him. He called in the Master Surgeon again and explained what had to be done. I rather imagine the surgeon didn't really want to do it. But on the other hand, life is good, and the old Regent was not a patient man—not when the only real hope of perpetuating the Delfieri dynasty was to make his nephew want to live. So the Master Surgeon, and I suppose several dozen assistants, set about to accomplish the task set for them."

A sudden jar came up through the cabin floor into Andrek's legs. He knew all three of them had felt it. He flashed a look at Iovve, and saw instantly that something was wrong. For a few seconds, he could not place it. And then he had it. Iovve's blue aura was gone. It had vanished with the jolt in the ship. And Andrek noticed also with growing anxiety that the pilgrim's white-gloved hands were trembling. With the blue radiation gone from Iovve's features, the advocate was able to observe the unilluminated face fully for the first time; and for the first time he was able to see the grizzled exhausted age of his companion.

Something disastrous had just happened. Huntyr had known it was going to happen, and had timed his entrance to precede it and his cruel narrative to embrace it. A primitive part of Andrek's mind told him to beg Huntyr to continue with that hideous, involuted tale. But a more highly sophisticated veneer censored this impulse, and urged that he move with great caution. Intuitively, he understood that if he were going to stay alive long enough to hear the end of Huntyr's recital, it would first be necessary to understand the shock that he had just felt. With an immense effort of will, Andrek laid aside his questions about Omere. He looked across the room at Iovve again. "Was that a small quake temblor?"

The pilgrim answered quietly, "No."

Huntyr laughed contemptuously. "Don Andrek—and you, too, Dr. Iovve, to be so well educated and so intelligent, and so well informed in the laws of the Twelve Galaxies and in the laws of science and medicine, you are both curiously stupid in the laws of the Node. The first law here is, there shall be no nuclear reaction. The ship went off nuclear drive just now, and on to chemical reactive drive. *That* was the jar you felt. Why did it convert over? Because the bugs just sit on the nuclear piles in the drive and drink up the power as fast as the pile turns it out. As long as we are in the Node area, there cannot be a single nuclear unit alive on the ship. Your force field is dead, of course. Ordinary weapons are useless. Even the lighting is by ancient fluorescence, powered by varimetal accumulators. All on account of the bugs."

Now they were getting somewhere. He was beginning to understand. They had just entered the outer edge of the Node. They were now in the domain of the ursecta. And Iovve's blue radiation had winked out in that very instant. He remembered Kedrys' demonstration, and how in one chamber the antimatter hydrogen had flashed blue on contact with normal matter, and how in the other—nothing had happened at all. Was it conceivable that Iovve's radiation was caused by nuclear energy released by something closely associated with his body, or—and the thought hit him with shock force—by Iovve's body itself? By the Beard of the Founder!

But all such speculation was moot and academic. For the time being, Huntyr was absolutely right. In this little room, here and now, the ursecta ruled. Ordinary weapons were useless. He found himself banally repeating Huntyr. "All on account of the bugs. The ursecta."

"Is that the scientific name?" said Huntyr. "All right, ursecta. I could draw pictures for you, but I think a demonstration would be even better. In fact, counselor, I think it would help considerably to clarify our relationship if you would aim your biem at me and pull the trigger."

Andrek turned anxious eyes toward Iovve, and on his face read the truth. The biem was nuclear-powered and would not fire. It was a dead weight in his hand. He tried to force his thoughts into a useful coherent pattern—and noted dimly that Raq had emerged from his jacket pocket and was walking slowly down the sleeve of his right arm. In the dim light, her dark body was nearly invisible against the gray of his jacket. And then she was picking her way daintily across his wrist, and then she was sitting on the biem, just over the fuel chamber. He was watching Raq, but in his mind he saw Amatar. Amatar greeting him in the garden that last night. Amatar presenting Raq to him. He remembered that presentation. Insects fear her, Amatar had said. *All* insects. He remembered the emphasis on the word.

The advocate swallowed dryly. Did all insects include dubious fourth-dimensional varieties—beasties that would come from nowhere out of time, to materialize on a nuclear fuel chamber the instant it was activated? And did some dim instinct tell Raq that the ursecta fed on nuclear power, and that his biem was a good place to come out and wait for them? Or was her walk down his sleeve the pure whim of Alea, whereby the destinies of insects, man, and galaxies were governed? No matter. The pieces came back together, and he suddenly understood that his biem *was* going to fire. Amatar had known.

He was breathing rapidly but freely. He looked across at Huntyr. "You believe, then, that my biem will not fire? That the ursecta will come when I pull the trigger, and drain off the power?"

"That's right, counselor."

Andrek thought the man looked faintly disappointed. Evidently, he had wanted Andrek to *try* to shoot him, just so he could gloat over the failure. Murder hath a strange mentality, mused Andrek. He said, "I gather, then, that you have some kind of weapon that is not affected by the ursecta?"

"This is so, your Honor," Huntyr pulled out a curious instrument from one of his two shoulder holsters. "It's new—yet it's old. It's called a 'slug-gun', copied from a model in the Politan Museum. It uses chemical power to fire a metal pellet. It's weak, inefficient, noisy, messy, and smelly. But it kills. It killed your father, and now it's going to kill you."

"My . . . *father* . . . ?" stammered Andrek. "What do you mean, it killed my father?" In his mind, he raced back over the reports. The dry sparse official language. "Died in routine service." A few paragraphs in the records. And now suddenly it wasn't so. He was about to learn the real story. And it would be true, because Huntyr wanted to make him suffer before killing him.

Huntyr's face glowed with pleasure. "Your father was captain of this same ship, on Oberon's hunting trip, eighteen years ago. It was he, your father, who refused to take Oberon deeper into the Node, and who was therefore shot for mutiny. This was the gun. By order of Oberon, I killed your father. Not twenty meters from this cabin." Huntyr smiled at the anguished workings of Andrek's face. "Makes you believe in both Ritornel and Alea, doesn't it? The repeating pattern of Ritornel is this, that the son is killed at the same Node by the same man, by the same gun, and in the same ship. And yet, all by Alean chance!"

Finally the rippling around Andrek's mouth ceased; his face became a mask, bloodless but calm—almost serene. Even if he were killed now, he was glad he had heard this from Huntyr. A part of him, at least, could die in peace. This left only the question of his brother. And if he could delay matters a little longer, he was certain that this long gap would finally be closed. "I see," he said. "All this was really just to delay matters until we entered the Node, so your weapon would fire and mine would not."

"That was the main reason, Don Andrek. On the other hand, there are still some things that you don't know about your brother, and which I intend to tell you before I kill you."

"Proceed, then. I would like very much to hear them."

"I wouldn't be too sure about that, your Honor." Huntyr smiled almost languidly. "Well, as I was saying, the old Regent demanded this thing of the Master Surgeon, that he build a marvelous device to sing and make lovely poetry, and take the mind of his nephew away from thoughts of dying. So the Master Surgeon set about making his design. The design called for an electron circuit identical to the cerebrum of the Laureate. But it would take many weeks. They didn't have that much time. So we simply seized the Laureate himself—"

"—Omere!" breathed Andrek. And now that he was finally to learn the answer to his eighteen-year search, he found that he was struck dumb, stunned, unaware of anything in the cabin except Huntyr's face and voice. The end was coming. His body seemed floating in a slow horrid realization that pounded at him with every beat of his heart. Within a matter of seconds it would be more than he could endure. "Omere?" he whispered again.

"Yes, Omere. I handled it personally. It wasn't difficult. We took him from the coronation straight to the hospital wing. The Master Surgeon performed the cranial operation and circuit integration into the computer console. There was some question about whether the computer should be sighted or blind. They decided, I think, that the rendition of aural imagery would be sharpened if they cut his optical circuits. So, to make him an even better poet, they blinded him."

Andrek's face was dead-white. He saw a vision of a great cabinet of fine polished wood, with dials, an interior of intricate electronic circuits. He had listened to it many times. And it could not risk their mutual deaths to reveal its identity. He did not recognize his own voice, drawn, pain-blinded, far away. "Omere . . . *Rimor!*"

Huntyr nodded. He was immensely pleased with the effect on the other. He pulled his mouth back over his teeth in a tigerish grin.

"But how . . ."—Andrek's voice was thick, barely intelligible—"could they force him to perform . . . to sing . . . to compose . . . ?"

"It was easy. Quirinal—the slave drug—when you take that, you find yourself *wanting* to do what you are best at doing . . ."

"Be silent!" shrieked Andrek. In one smooth motion he raised the biem, sighted over Raq's crouched body, and pulled the trigger.

Huntyr jerked—not so much (it seemed to Andrek) from the physical impact of the bolt—as from disbelief. The slug-gun fell from his hand. He seemed then to be trying to raise his hand, to point . . . at Iovve. His lips came together, but only a whispered sigh emerged. "Maa—" Then his hand dropped, and his eyes stared at nothing.

Something inside Andrek watched this with bright elation. But then, discovering this feeling within himself, he jerked up straight in his chair.

He felt he should censor this primitive attitude toward his enemies. He, an advocate sworn to uphold the laws of the Home Galaxy, had taken the law into his own hands, and had again slain a man. Again, it was self-defense, but it still cut across the grain of a lifetime of conditioning. He shook his head slowly. Thinking this way did nothing to relieve the fact that he had been absolutely delighted on seeing that clean gaping hole appear in Huntyr's chest. But no matter, the main thing, regardless of what anyone thought about it, was that he was still living, and Huntyr was dead.

He looked vaguely over toward Iovve, as though to find either absolution or an answer. And what had Huntyr been trying to say, there at the last, when he almost pointed at Iovve . . . ? Had Huntyr known the pilgrim? He'd have to find out. Too many mysteries. Solve one, two more sprang up.

Iovve returned Andrek's questioning stare quietly. "Get hold of yourself. We still have a lot to do."

"What?" said Andrek numbly.

"Do you have an extra suit? Full legal robes of a don?"

"Yes."

"Get Huntyr's bloody jacket off, then get the robes on him."

What was Iovve up to? He shrugged his shoulders. He'd have to trust him. "All right." After much fumbling, Andrek got the robe on Huntyr's body. "It's too small," he mumbled.

"No matter. Just leave him there. Get Raq back in your pocket, and get your case and valise. We're moving."

"Moving?"

"Of course. We can't stay here."

"Where'll we go?"

"To Number Twelve, Huntyr's suite."

Andrek's jaw dropped. "Are you crazy?"

"Wake up, dear boy. It's the only safe place on the ship."

"But how about Vang?"

"I think he's either tied up or dead. In either case, he wouldn't be a problem. And my guess is that Huntyr killed him when he found your check. But if Huntyr didn't kill him, we will."

"And then?"

"We'll just move the body in here, and trade his Alean mantle for the simple gray of a Ritornellian pilgrim."

Andrek stared at the pilgrim in near awe, "I *see!* The ship's officers will think the bodies in my cabin are you and me!"

"Correction. They'll *know.* Because you'll call the captain from Huntyr's suite and tell him just that. Wait a moment, while I get my bag and medical kit, and we'll both go down there together."

As they had expected, they found Vang in Number Twelve. He lay crumpled on the floor, and his pallid face was finally at peace. Andrek had the strange impression that Vang was glad the end had come. His death was not difficult to reconstruct. He had been strangled with his own cord. There had been a struggle, and pieces of furniture were still floating about. A chair had somehow got attached to the ceiling. The poison case was broken open; some of the vials were crushed, and their contents half-absorbed into the foam-cushion lining. They did not search the body. Undoubtedly Huntyr had retrieved the check. Andrek was content to leave it in Huntyr's wallet.

Andrek contemplated the still form in silence. Either the goddess, or a strange anatomic freak, had prevented the engorgement of cheek and protrusion of eyeballs that normally accompanied the gift of Alea. Vang's one lapse, in an otherwise blameless service to the blind one, had evidently been forgiven, and the goddess had accepted him. The knowledge of her love was written in his mouth and eyes. His hand still tightly clasped the fatal dodecahedron that had betrayed him. Andrek pushed the thumb back and looked at the number. It was of course twelve, the most favored to Alea.

The advocate sighed. He had engineered this death, and he would do it again, given the same threat to his own life. Yet it was a sad thing.

"We'll have to hurry," said Iovve crisply.

"Silence!" growled Andrek. "Vang was my enemy, but we were classmates. There are last words to be said, and to be thought for him, and I must do this, since there is no one else." After a moment he muttered, "I did not want this. Good-bye, Ajian."

Hurriedly, they hauled the corpse back to Andrek's former cabin, and left it alongside what was left of Huntyr.

Ten minutes had not elapsed before they both sat in front of the intercom in Huntyr's suite. Andrek slipped the switch. His voice was strangely calm. "Huntyr here," he said, imitating the investigator's harsh guttural. "Give me the captain. Captain Forgaz! Huntyr. Yes, mission accomplished. Thank you. Both bodies in the don's cabin. Can you send a couple of crewmen around there? They must be discreet. The Great House doesn't want any publicity. We will hold you responsible. Of course, Captain. Just thought I'd mention it. Hold on a moment." Andrek paused, and almost smiled when he continued. "My Alean friend here insists that all three of us undergo purification rites. What? Purification rites. Yes, news to me, too. *He* will be fasting for the next three days. No, Captain, just him. I and my assistant, Mr. Hasard, will not be fasting, but we are not supposed to leave the cabin until we dock at the station. Can you ask the chef to send up meals in the tube for the two of us? Thank you, Captain. I'll mention you in my report to the Magister."

Andrek flipped off the switch, then continued to sit there, silent, immobile. After a long time, he turned around.

Iovve was lying in one of the three bunks, his gloved hands folded peacefully over his rhythmically moving chest. "There is an unwitting trace of truth in that very fanciful fable," he murmured sleepily.

"What do you mean?"

"About sending up meals. Actually, you will need food only for yourself. During these last days of my pilgrimage, I shall truly be fasting. And now, my son, I suggest we both retire. It's been a hard day."

Andrek stared at his companion, then shrugged. A strange one! He floated up quietly, drifted over to the porthole, and looked out. Outside, all was blackness. There was no point of reference to show the fantastic speed of the ship, transphotic even under chemical drive.

He reached cautiously into his pocket, pulled Raq out, and placed her on the drapes alongside the porthole. She ran up the fabric a short distance and disappeared into the folds.

He was alone.

And now what?

For the moment, he seemed safe. At least until the ship reached the Node Station. Another day and a half. He'd have to leave the ship when they got there. He couldn't return to Goris-Kard for a long time; perhaps never. He thought of his father and brother, and his throat knotted. His father was dead. He accepted that. But Omere—in a sense, at least—was still alive. But he might as well be dead, for all the help that Andrek could give him. For even if he, Andrek, were back in the Great House now wielding all the power of the Magister and all the skill of that infamous Master Surgeon, he could still do nothing for Omere.

That seemed to leave only—revenge? On whom? The old Regent was dead. Huntyr was dead. The Master Surgeon had vanished, and might well be dead. That left Oberon. But could he lift his hand against the father of Amatar? He didn't know. And just now it was quite academic whether he could or could not, because he was now a fugitive, under sentence of death. He would do well to save his own skin. It was foolish ever to think of revenge until he was safe from Oberon.

He felt very tired. With forced gestures he undressed and got into his pajamas. With one hand on his bunk, he turned and looked over at Iovve now asleep. *You*, he thought, have risked your life to keep me alive. For what? Whatever the reason, you bungled it. You don't know it, strange Doctor, but you never did plug in your so-called force-field generator into the ship's current. But your field came on anyway. Is it something under those gray robes? Is this why you used to glow in the dark? It must be something over which you have no real control, because it turned off exactly a the instant *Xerol* entered the Node. When the ship went off nuclear, so did you. There must be something on, or even *in,* your body, something nuclear-powered, and which permeates your whole system, so that, outside the Node, it ionizes the air around you. And it's your whole body, not just your face.

And now you claim you are fasting. But I suspect, my friend, that fasting for you is normal—that you do not eat at all, in the hominid sense.

Iovve, who are you?

(And do I really want to know?)

What is this unknown thing for which you are saving me? How long am I to he kept alive? What is my small role in your mysterious plan?

Since you refuse to tell me the fate you have in store for me, you must think I might have preferred Huntyr's death. And what about your robes, pilgrim? You are making your last journey—this time to die at the Node. Is it just a bit of religious fakery, or do you really intend to go through with it? And what will be the manner of your death? You have had several opportunities to die within the last several hours—and you have refused them all. What are you waiting for? What remains to complete your pilgrimage? And when it is all done, am I supposed to die with you?

He climbed into his bunk and strapped himself in, still musing. And what was Huntyr trying to tell me about you as he sat there, dying? Huntyr knew you, pilgrim, and as he died, he tried to name you. Huntyr lifted his finger and pointed, and tried to speak. But nothing recognizable passed his lips. So your secret is safe. But in a manner of speaking, I am grateful to Huntyr. For Huntyr, my enemy, has told me a great deal more than you, Iovve my friend. And I think, my pious companion, that there is one danger worse than Vang . . . or Huntyr . . . or Hasard. Worse even than Oberon of the Delfieri. And that is Iovve, the gray pilgrim of Ritornel.

And so thinking, he fell asleep.

11. AN ENTRANCE QUESTIONED

In the last hour of the third day, as *Xerol* was cautiously nosing in toward the Node Station under slow deceleration, Andrek happened to look out the porthole. "Iovve, look!" He pointed excitedly. "A planet. It must be Terror."

"Very likely, my boy, very likely." The pilgrim clacked over to the quartz window and peered out. "So it is."

They watched in silence as the ship drifted past the great ball in a slow parabola. As a warning to navigation, thousands of light-buoys were orbiting the planet, forming a giant spectral crown. The lights were turned inward toward the globe, bathing her equator in a band of ghostly, pale radiance. To Andrek, it seemed somehow highly incongruous. Terror, the Devil Planet, with a halo! No matter. Tomorrow those lights would vanish forever.

Andrek then suddenly noticed that Iovve was watching him. "Well?" he demanded.

"Nothing, my boy. Not a thing. Just wondering about your own feelings. About Terror, I mean." He nodded toward the porthole. "See that?"

Andrek peered out again. Beyond the halo, a tiny light was slowly circling the planet. "What is it?"

"The demolition ship. Tomorrow, they expect to activate the explosive capsule that will destroy the planet. They wait only for the final order from the arbiters."

"Well, of *course* they're going to destroy the planet. It's required by intergalactic law. It's the just fate of every planet that starts a nuclear war." He turned and stared hard at the pilgrim. "That's my mission here. Within a few hours, I will appear before the arbiters and formally confirm the position of my government, that Terror must be destroyed. There's no conceivable alternative."

"Of course, my boy, of course," said Iovve smoothly. He paused, and said in a reflective tone, "A solemn moment, nevertheless. We're among the last to see Terra alive."

Andrek turned on him grimly. "You said—*Terra!*"

"I did. Terra. We can at least be realistic. That *is* the real name, as you well know. *Their* name for *their* planet." He shrugged. "Terror . . . Terra. It is the privilege of the victors to curse the defeated with any name they choose. No son of Terra is now alive to rise in her defense. And her grandsons and nephews, including you, my boy, couldn't care less."

Was it coming now? Was Iovve finally about to untangle the web? Breathing was suddenly difficult, and he fought off a feeling of suffocation. But he knew he could not hurry the pilgrim. He said bluntly: "That's strange talk, coming from a man of peace and holiness."

Iovve blithely ignored him. He continued, as though talking to himself. "We have accepted her gifts in a thousand ways. We still use the old tongues on occasion." He peered sideways at Andrek. "The word 'Amatar,' for example."

Andrek started. "What do you mean," he stammered.

"He! He! I thought that would get you! Yes Amatar . . . from *a mater*—'without mother.' Amatar, the Motherless One. But you're not interested in Terran etymology. You're here to destroy Terra and everything Terran."

And now again the tantalizing feeling of recognition. He had heard these words before. And this voice. Far away. Where? When? The Motherless

One. It meant something. He had heard it before. He had been afraid before. Was he afraid now? His mouth was dry, and his palms were wet. He seized the pilgrim by the shoulders. *"Why* is she called the 'Motherless One'?" he demanded. "What do you know about Amatar?"

"Gently, my boy. Everything in good time."

A buzzer was sounding insistently in the room. "Just now," said Iovve, "the ship is locking on at the station. We have about two minutes to pack and get out. And let's hope we don't run into anybody whom the fact of our continuing existence might startle or distress. So why don't we just get everything together and walk out through the freight port?"

Andrek was defeated again. His arms dropped from Iovve. Very soon, he thought, we are going to have a long talk, about many things. He looked about the room. "What'll we do about Raq? Take her along?"

"Out of the question, dear boy. Have you observed her condition recently?"

"Condition?" Andrek went over to the fold in the porthole drape, which Raq had selected as "home."

"Not too close," Iovve called out.

Standing about a yard away, Andrek could make out the little silken ball, nearly complete. Raq stopped work on it and covered it with her body as his shadow fell on her.

"Great bouncing Alean eyeballs!" said Andrek softly. "It's an egg sac! She's a mother!"

"Or soon will be. I think, my boy, we'd better give our god-fatherly blessings from a safe distance. There's nothing like motherhood to foul up a conditioned recognition reflex."

"But—the ship's crew . . . If we leave her here, they'll be bitten."

"Yes, won't they!" agreed Iovve gleefully. "Sorry we won't be here to watch the fun. But we can't move her. The alternative is to kill her here and now."

"We can't do that." Andrek clenched his teeth. "All right. Good-bye, Raq, and thanks."

Cases in hand, they sneaked down back corridors to the freight elevators.

Xerol's flank was sealed into the docking locks of the Node Station at several points. Officers, crew, and passengers used the forward tubes. Fuel and water lines were intermediate. The freight room was aft.

Holding to the handrails, Andrek and Iovve floated over, around, and through stacks of metal boxes, mostly bound with metal straps to the floor, walls, and ceiling of the freight room, propelling themselves from time to time by gentle nudges of toes and fingertips. As they approached the great doorway opening into the station, the clutter and congestion grew. They encountered several of the crew, working with cargo, but hurried past without challenge. They had a bad moment when the last exits seemed hopelessly blocked by the flow of goods on a conveyor belt running *into* the ship. But they waited a few seconds and then sailed over the belt onto the station dock.

That area also was cluttered with stacks of boxes, trunks, and even furniture.

"Doesn't it strike you as odd," said Andrek curiously, "that everything is going *in* to the ship, and nothing is coming *out?* And look at *that.*" He pointed to a huge roll of carpetry being hoisted out toward the ship's loading conveyor. "Are they dismantling the whole station and shipping it back to Goris-Kard?"

"Nonsense, my boy. Quite a bit of staff turnover at a lonely outpost like this. In addition to the arbiter's chambers, the station maintains co-operative facilities for scientists from all the Twelve Galaxies. There's always a stream of new staff coming in, old staff leaving. And of course, they take their baggage with them."

"I suppose so," said Andrek. He looked around doubtfully.

Xerol was not the only ship tied up at the station docks. To *Xerol's* rear was another, larger craft. Andrek could not make out the strange letters on her loading tubes. Iovve saw him peering at it, and whispered, "*Varez,* from Andromeda." And up ahead was still another ship. Her loading tubes were active, too. In fact, cases, crates, trunks, and even people were moving up the tubes of both ships. But nothing, and no one, seemed to be coming out.

Many of these people were obviously nonhominid. Several had more than two legs, and some even wore transparent helmets, evidently to carry with them their own strange atmospheres.

Iovve took him by the arm. "Now, then, counselor, I believe we can take this hall to the lobby."

The corridor echoed eerily with the clanging of their magnetized shoe soles as they moved deeper into the station.

"Ah, yes," said Iovve. "Here we are."

Andrek looked about him, puzzled. Something was strange, wrong. A slight difference in the tint of paint along the edges of the corridor floor told him that not long ago—perhaps yesterday—a carpet had lain there. The phone boxes in the corridor walls were empty; as were the wall clamps for the portable fire extinguishers. He started to ask Iovve about it, but the other grasped his arm and pointed ahead.

They were just outside the main lobby. It was crowded, and through the shifting mass of people, on the other side of the room, was the registration desk. And there, three officers of *Xerol* leaned across the counter, deep in conversation with the clerk.

Andrek and Iovve shrank back into the dimness of the hallway.

As they watched, the three officers left the clerk and began circulating slowly through the lobby, looking covertly but carefully at the faces of the occupants.

"I think they are wearing slug-guns," said Andrek nervously. "Suppose they come out here?"

"I don't think they will. But suppose they do? The station is a big place, with lots of places to hide. Just now, they are merely suspicious. Huntyr didn't check in with the captain on docking. He's missing. Vang's missing. And Hasard. They're worried, but they don't know anything for sure. Certainly, they don't know that we are alive. The thing that puzzles them is why didn't Huntyr leave the ship through the passenger tubes? You see, they don't really know whom they're looking for. I think their concern is primarily Huntyr, not us."

"I hope you're right. Anyhow, they've stopped."

The three officers had met at the main lobby entrance. They took one last look around, then left, headed for the passenger tubes.

"Now," said Iovve, "let's test an ancient axiom of Ritornel: be grateful for the unwitting gifts of others."

"I don't recall that one," muttered Andrek.

"Naturally: the younger generation is not well informed in religious matters. This way, my boy."

They walked over to the registration desk. The clerk looked up at them. Iovve said, "I believe we have reservations. Huntyr and party."

"Oh yes, of course. Are you Mr. Huntyr?"

"No, *that's* Mr. Huntyr." Iovve nodded at Andrek. "I'm Brother Vang."

"How many in your party, Mr. Huntyr?"   •

"Three," said Andrek. "Mr. Hasard will be over from the ship in a few minutes."

"Very good. Here are your keys. Second level. Shall I put your luggage in the auto-tube, to go directly to your rooms?"

"Never mind," said Andrek. "We'll carry them. Also, I have been asked to give you a message from Mr. Andrek, of *Xerol.*"

"Yes?"

"He is staying aboard ship, and will not be needing his reservation."

"That's a coincidence. Captain Forgaz was just here with the same information. And he was inquiring about you, Mr. Huntyr."

"Sorry I missed him," said Andrek. "I'll call him from my room."

"As you wish. Are you returning in *Xerol?*"

"No," broke in Iovve. "We're going on. We already have reservations on . . . ah . . . *Varez.*"

"*Varez?* To Andromeda? But she's leaving soon. You can board her now. You won't have time—"

"She's delayed," said Iovve smoothly. "Engine trouble."

"Oh. If you say so." The clerk shrugged politely. "The rate is twenty gammas per room, payable in advance."

Andrek placed some bills on the desk, then he and Iovve turned away and headed for the inner level.

Just as they entered the corridor from the lobby, Andrek stopped and looked back. On the other side of the registration desk the clerk was putting on a heavy outer jacket. He zipped up the fasteners, then reached for a hat on the hat rack.

"Why are you stopping?" hissed Iovve.

"I think the clerk is about to leave—for good, I mean," said Andrek wonderingly.

"And what's wrong with that? There's certainly no need for someone to be there twenty-four hours a day. Come on."

"Just a minute," said Andrek. As he watched, the clerk put several ledgers, a small locked box, and three valises, one after another, into the autochute marked "Ship: *Xerol.*" Then he came around to the front of the desk, pulled down a metal grill, and walked away toward the corridor leading to *Xerol's* passenger tubes. Andrek's eye came back to the grill over the registration counter. A small sign in the center read "Closed."

Andrek turned back to Iovve, started to ask him a question, then decided it would be futile. One thing was now clear. The station was closing. And Iovve did not want him to know that it was closing. But why should it close? There had to be a reason. He would have to find out.

When they reached their rooms, Andrek said, "I want to talk to you after you unpack." He unlocked the door to his own room and went inside. It was, as he had predicted, carpetless. But around the edges of the floor was an outline of where a carpet had been—and recently. Overhead, one dim fluor was left burning amid six empty sockets. The entertainment center was identifiable by a gaping hole in the wall and a few dangling wires. There was not even a wastebasket. Except for the bunk bed and one towel in the washroom, the room had been stripped.

Something cold and heavy began to grow in the bottom of Andrek's stomach.

There was only one explanation. And on a subconscious level, he must have suspected it all along, even when he had not wanted to think about it consciously. Again, he had the frustrating feeling that he saw only a part of a much larger drama. But at least it would readily explain that part: namely, how Iovve expected to die.

He went next door and knocked. Iovve let him in.

Andrek said grimly: "The station is stripped down to its bare operating essentials. Everyone here has already moved out or is preparing to move out. Why? What's going on here?"

Iovve peered at Andrek, as though attempting to assess how much the advocate knew and how much be had merely guessed. "Really?" he said. "How observant of you. I hadn't noticed. Perhaps their assignments are completed. Perhaps the League is finally closing the station. It could be any one of a number of things."

Andrek smiled at him wickedly. His voice was deceptively quiet. "Iovve, my very dubious friend, you undoubtedly have extraordinary skills in many strange fields. For these, you have my undying admiration and respect." The tones became even softer, more reflective, tinged with faint regret. "In one area, however, you are a bumbling fool. You just don't know how to tell a convincing lie."

"I—What? I'm not on your witness stand, Don Andrek!"

But now, in a sudden, shattering change of pace, the advocate's voice thundered out. *"A QUAKE IS COMING, ISN'T IT?"*

Iovve stared at Andrek in amazement. "By my beard! You are a wonder!"

"Just answer the question."

"Well, if you put it that way, yes. A quake is coming."

"And you didn't tell me. Why?"

"Because you never asked!" Iovve lifted his gloved hands in a gesture of helpless innocence.

"When is it coming?"

"Well, my boy, obviously not within the next few minutes." He looked at his watch. "When is your hearing with the arbiters?"

It was futile . . . hopeless. He had tried, and he had failed. It was like dealing with some elemental force of nature that knew only its own blind destiny and held no negotiations with mortals, except to bend them to its own primeval force and design. Iovve was like a tide, a flood, a storm. Iovve was like (he thought wryly) a space quake.

A quake was coming, and Iovve was simply not going to discuss it. The game would have to be played on Iovve's terms.

Andrek said, "My hearing with the arbiters? I don't know. Soon. I'll have to find out from the clerk."

"That's easy. The arbiters' chambers are right down the hall. Suppose we check in with the clerk and then take a peek into the seismographic room. We might find out when the quake is coming."

Andrek shrugged his shoulders.

Iovve looked at him with reproach. "Your distrust stabs me in the heart."

You seem to have survived, thought Andrek. "Come on," he said.

"I'll just take this along," said Iovve, picking up his medical case.

"What for?" Andrek knew the question was wasted breath even before he asked it.

"I may need it down in seismographic," said the pilgrim vaguely.

Together they walked down to the arbitration chambers.

The arbiters' clerk took Andrek's name with mild surprise. "The Terror case, isn't it?" He riffled through his papers. "Here we are. Just as I thought. Routine show-cause." He peered up at Andrek. "Actually, counselor, no need for you to be here. No one is going to show cause. You can take the next ship out, if you like."

"I'll stay for the hearing," said Andrek. "When is it scheduled?"

"In an hour or so. It's the last thing on the docket. As soon as the arbiters collect, I'll give you a call. What's your room number?"

"We'll be in seismographic," interposed Iovve.

"Indeed?" The clerk frowned. "I thought it was closed down—locked up."

"It is," said Iovve. "But that's where Don Andrek will be. It's just a few steps away. We can be back here very quickly."

"All right. Go ahead. I'll call you there. You probably have about half an hour."

Holding the medical kit with one hand, Iovve dragged Andrek out of the room with the other.

10. THE RIGHT KEY, AND BEYOND

A few minutes later they stood in front of a door. In its center was a simple legend, in the twelve official languages of the Cluster. Andrek could read only the Ingliz: "Seismographic Room—Authorized Personnel Only."

The door panel was completely smooth except for one rather small hole in the center. Andrek took this to be the keyhole. He watched as Iovve pushed tentatively on the panel with his shoulder. Nothing budged a micron. It now occurred to Andrek that Iovve had no key. But would that be a real problem? He recalled the pilgrim's entrance into Huntyr's office. But of course this was no mere commercial lock. If Iovve were able to open this door, Andrek wanted to watch him do it. He wanted to study Iovve's technique. It would be an opportunity to learn something about the man.

Iovve bent down and peered into the keyhole. "Hm. Thermal profile."

"What do you mean?"

"The key has to have several different temperatures along its length, such as, for example, 20^0-10^0-30^0-minus 5^0, and so on. Each of the actual key-tooth temperatures has to be accurate to a fraction of a degree, or the profile of the series of thermocouples inside won't close and complete the electric circuit to pull the bolts."

Andrek looked at him blankly. Something like this was clearly beyond the simple portable equipment that Iovve might carry concealed under his robes. He had divided feelings about it. In a way, he was disappointed. On the other hand, he was not able to suppress a small malicious feeling of satisfaction in seeing Iovve thwarted.

"Well, that's that," he said, "You don't have that kind of key. You'd need a probe connected to a complete heating and refrigeration unit, something weighing several hundred kilos. The official key is probably being loaded on *Xerol,* right now."

"No doubt, my son. On the other hand, let's see what we can do. Stand back, boy."

Rather dubiously, Andrek did as he was asked.

In a rapid movement, so quick that Andrek could see very little, Iovve ripped off the glove from his right hand. And then his actions were completely hidden by the loose folds of his robes. From the position of his shoulders and right arm, Andrek guessed that the pilgrim was holding his bare hand, or possibly only the index finger, to the keyhole. At one point, when Iovve stood back a few centimeters, Andrek thought he caught the odor of hot metal. Then the other pressed in again, and then there came a smooth metallic rumbling, as of heavy rods sliding, and then the door stood ajar.

Iovve pushed in. "Now that wasn't too difficult, was it?"

Andrek noted that the glove was back. Mildly awed, he followed the pilgrim inside.

He looked around curiously.

The seismographic room was in the very center of the station. Whether by deliberate functional design or designer's caprice (Andrek could not surmise which) the room had the shape of a dodecahedron. Ten of the pentagonal faces of the polyhedron were clustered with instruments. One, evidently the "floor," had only a big worktable and a few chairs. Directly above this was the "ceiling," bare except for an oversized clock in its center.

"This room," said Iovve, "has been called the eardrum of the universe. Actually, the term is somewhat grandiose. It does however collect, integrate, and transmit Node weather data to each of the twelve sponsoring galaxies, along with proton density, ursecta activity, space temblors, meteorites, the works. At the moment, and from now on to the instant of the quake, it transmits automatically. As you have so cleverly deduced, my boy, a quake is certainly coming, and that is why all the normal operating staff have already shipped out."

Andrek stared at him bitterly. "And that's why everything of value has been dismantled. The station will be left here, stripped, simply to broadcast the quake. Why didn't you say so?"

Iovve lifted his arms piously. "I was thinking only of you, my son. I didn't want to make you nervous. You have an important hearing shortly, you know."

How could my forthcoming hearing be of any possible concern to you, thought Andrek. You're up to something. What it is, I don't know. But somehow it involves me. How? No use to ask. And how close is Iovve to the end of his pilgrimage? And is he entirely sane? But these, like all the other questions, are futile. The time has come to part. I'll have to start making plans. How do I get out of here? How do I get back to Goris-Kard without getting killed? And when I get there, what do I do about Omere? And Amatar? Everything depends on getting away from Iovve. Will I be able to do that? What does this treacherous creature want of me? I think I will tell him, now, exactly what I think of him.

"You are either mad," said Andrek flatly, "or you are a scoundrel."

"Or both?"

"Or both. And right after the hearing, I'm getting out."

"On *Xerol?*"

"Of course not. But there are other ships. We saw a couple when we landed. I'll stow away on one of those."

"Do as you wish, my boy." Iovve met Andrek's angry eyes calmly. "Meanwhile, excuse me a moment." The pilgrim craned his head upward and studied the clock for several seconds. Then without a word he clacked over to a bank of instruments at the far panel and peered at them closely. Shaking his head, he broke contact with the floor and floated up to the clock. He opened the clock face and moved the red hand around in a near semicircle.

"What are you doing?" demanded Andrek suspiciously.

"Merely correcting the setting," Iovve called back cheerily. "Be with you in a moment."

"What was that red hand?"

"Sort of a special indicator—just a scientific gimmick."

"It has something to do with the quake, doesn't it?"

"Why yes, I guess you could say that."

"It tells you when the quake is coming," persisted Andrek coldly. "You know, and you don't want me to know."

"Really, my boy, I'm not on your witness stand. Your suspicions cut me to the quick. Yes, it does predict the time of the quake."

"When is it due?"

"When? Not immediately. Surely, you can see that. You haven't even had your session with the arbiters yet. I hope, my son, that you can take comfort from the fact that right here at the station is a collection of the best judicial minds of the Twelve Galaxies. Their mere presence here should reassure you. And why? The reason is simple. These judges acknowledge a sacred duty to their respective governments, sworn under solemn oath, to protect and preserve their laws and legal systems. And to preserve the law, they must first preserve themselves. Hence, the faithful performance of their sworn duty requires first, and above all, a most delicate, watchful, and continuing regard for their own skins. Accept my assurance that they would never violate so sublime an obligation by a callous disregard for an oncoming space quake."

Andrek laughed, despite himself.

The intercom sounded. "Don Andrek, calling Don Andrek."

The advocate grimaced and stepped over to the phone panel. He flipped the communications switch. "Andrek here."

The clerk's face appeared on the screen. "Don Andrek, the arbiters will convene in a few minutes."

"Thank you. I'll be right up." He flipped the switch over and turned back to Iovve. "The quake," he said quietly. *"When?"*

The pilgrim drew himself up to his full height and stared back at Andrek. "James, Don Andrek, it is not my intent that you shall die in the quake. In fact, let me remind you that I have saved your life three times, and instead of plying me with foolish questions, you should be expressing your gratitude. You owe me a debt. Will you concede that you are in my debt?"

Ah! Now it was finally coming out. Iovve might be both a liar and a scheming scoundrel, yet he schemed with method. The moment was now at hand that would explain why Iovve had saved his life that time in Huntyr's office, and the reason for Raq, and the journey, as bodyguard, with him on *Xerol*. But he did not intend to make it easier for Iovve.

"I will concede it, *arguendo,"* he said warily.

"A curse on your legal niceties," barked Iovve. "But for me, you'd be dead thrice over!"

Andrek was equally harsh. "Did you save my life three times for a price?"

The pilgrim shot a searching glance at him. Andrek got the sudden impression that he had said exactly what the other had expected him to say, that the trap had been baited, and he had walked into it. So now the question of the price of his life was up for discussion; he himself had just put it on the agenda. Well, then, what was his price? He was genuinely curious. Iovve's demand might also answer several other questions. So he waited.

Iovve's voice was now soft, almost sorrowful.

"Ah, my son, what an ungrateful, mercenary attitude! By my beard! You seek only to be rid of me, and to be freed from your obligation. Well, then, out of my boundless affection for you, and yielding to your insistence, I suppose I might be able to think up some little task that you could perform, so as to relieve you of this debt, which you feel so burdensome, and so to put matters in complete balance between us."

Andrek smiled sardonically. "And what is this little task?"

"Just this. Save Terror. Persuade the arbiters to leave the planet here at the Node, untouched, unharmed."

Andrek stared at the pilgrim in amazement. Well, there it was. Payment for his debt. Save Terror! Was it for this that Iovve had brought him to the ends of the universe? Save Terror? Whatever for? Who had need of such a bleak, desolate, devastated ball of rock and frozen seas? Well, then, what *had* he expected? He did not know. But certainly not this. This was impossible. "By the blind eyes of Alea! What are you thinking of? The Great House has sent me here to make sure Terror is destroyed, not saved. The arbiters are sitting here for that purpose. It is all over."

"Not at all, my boy, not at all. You disappoint me. You are seeing events only in terms of black and white. A binary response unworthy of an illustrious don. So let us consider the matter. Terror is under a show-cause order, which means that the planet has this one last chance to show cause why it should not be destroyed. In fact, you are here for the purpose of opposing any such plea, in the remote event it is made. Right?"

"Quite right," said Andrek. He laughed in sputtering unbelief. "So now, you think I can save Terror simply by reversing the position of the Home Galaxy?"

"If done persuasively—yes. Especially considering the circumstances."

"What circumstances," said Andrek suspiciously.

Iovve lifted his gloved hands vaguely. "Oh, you know. These condemnation proceedings are boring, routine . . . The arbiters want to get it over with and get home. Some of them have probably already gone."

Probably to beat the quake, thought Andrek. He said: "If I reversed position on a case like this, I could never return to Goris-Kard. In fact, I wouldn't be safe anywhere in the Home Galaxy. I'd be a hunted man the rest of my life."

"You already are."

They looked at each other. Unhappily, Iovve was quite correct. Nothing that he did here in the case of the Twelve Galaxies vs. Terror would have the slightest effect on his death sentence. He could condemn Terror; he could attempt to save Terror; he could ignore Terror. It would be all the same: Oberon would still search him out and kill him.

Andrek lifted his shoulders wearily. "You're right, of course. I can't go back. I am hunted. And I don't even know why. Curious, isn't it? As far as the arbiters are aware, I'm a fully accredited representative of the Home Galaxy; yet, personally, I'm under a worse interdiction than Terror."

"Then you'll do it?"

"Not so fast. You haven't explained *why* you want Terror saved."

"I can't tell you everything, not just yet. But I *can* say this: it is needful that Terror go into the Deep."

"And how will saving Terror put her into the Deep?"

"It won't. At any rate, not directly. But at least it would hold her here at the Node until the quake comes. And eventually a quake must come. If Terror is still here, the quake will crack her into the Deep. It's just a question of waiting."

Now they were finally getting somewhere. He felt he had the pilgrim off-balance. Andrek bored in. "The thing that you have very carefully *not* explained," he said, "is why it is needful that Terror go into the Deep."

"True. I haven't explained that. But if you take the case—and save the planet, then I'll tell you."

Should he settle for this? Perhaps he'd have to. He should know by now he couldn't force Iovve to talk when Iovve didn't want to talk. Still, he had caught a glimpse of a fantastic cosmic scheme. Terror in the Deep! If it were madness, it was a breathtaking madness, and he wanted to know more about it. He temporized. "Even if I were successful, the reprieve would be only temporary. The Great House would discover the 'error' and ask for a rehearing. And they'd get it."

"That would take weeks. By then, Terror will be in the Deep."

Andrek stared in hard surmise at the other. Iovve was quite right. All that was necessary was to have the planet waiting here when the quake struck. For this, a week's delay in the proceedings would be just as effective as a complete and final reprieve. But now he felt his bargaining position was strengthened. He would try once more. He said, "This gets us back to my original question. When is the quake due?"

But Iovve was not to be swayed.

"Not right away. Plenty of time to save Terror. In fact, that may be a factor operating in our favor. The arbiters may consider that leaving Terror to the quake is about the same as destroying her by explosives."

The visor buzzed. It was the arbiters' clerk. "Don Andrek, are you coming?"

"Thank you, right away." He arose slowly and picked up the Terror dossier.

"Well?" said Iovve, rising with him.

"I haven't decided. Even if I agreed, what arguments would I have? We have only a few minutes—I'd need weeks, perhaps even months, to prepare a competent presentation." Even with Poroth on the board, he knew he could expect nothing. The most he might expect from Poroth was that the great jurist would not lean over backward to avoid deciding in favor of an ex-pupil.

"I don't think so. I believe you have sufficient elasticity of intellect to reverse yourself and present a well-organized analysis of the opposition, all in a matter of minutes. To be a good advocate you have to have this facility; you have to know the case for the opposition as well as your own. I think you are a very good advocate."

"Let us get one thing straight." Andrek spoke slowly, carefully. "Are you telling me that you *selected* me just to do this for you? That you got me out of trouble, that time in Huntyr's office, and then on the ship, just so I could be here and take this case for you?"

"You might say that," admitted Iovve.

His eyes met Andrek's without wavering. The advocate knew that Iovve now spoke the truth. He had been brought here for the sole purpose of saving Terror, so that Terror might go into the Deep. The whole thing, from start to finish, was insanity on a scale so vast that it made his flesh creep. And he had a sickening conviction that he had merely scratched the surface, that there was more to come. Much, much more. He found himself toying with the idea of running from the room, up the corridor, and back out to *Xerol*. But that would surpass even Iovve's lunacy. He had to keep calm, get a grip on himself. Somehow, there had to be a way out. Meanwhile, he would have to humor his weird companion.

He put his hand on the chamber portal. "I suppose," he said quietly, "that there's a great deal more, and that you'll give me the whole story eventually?" (After it's too late to do anything about it, he added to himself.)

"Yes, dear boy, as you have guessed, there *is* more. So, in the Terror matter, how will you plead?"

"Come along," said Andrek noncommittally.

Iovve followed him meekly out of the room and up the corridor to the arbiters' chambers.

9. JUDGMENT: LIFE

Planet, planet, flaming hell,
(Was't Alea, or Ritornel?)
What titanic hand of fate
Drew thee to the waiting quake?

And in the Deep's eternal night,
What strange chance, or what design,
(Or what monumental mind?)
Shall set thee once again aright?

—Rimor, *Quatrains.*

As they entered the room the clerk greeted them in a whisper and checked off Andrek's name on the roster. They were barely in time.

"Remember," hissed Iovve, "save Terror!"

"Be quiet!" whispered Andrek. His mind was churning. He had not the faintest idea what he would do. He felt infected by Iovve's madness. Nothing made any sense. His chest was heaving, his pulse was wild. His mouth was like leather, and he was very thirsty. At this moment he doubted his competence to petition the court for a glass of water.

The robed arbiters had apparently just finished filing in and taking their seats. Poroth was there, in the center chair, but was bent over, whispering to a brother arbiter, whom Andrek recognized as Karbol of Andromeda, and did not immediately notice Andrek. The sight of this good man was a sharp nostalgic blast: the smell of ancient desks and new books . . . the sound of young voices . . . wind in the courtyard trees . . . back when he had only one concern, to find Omere, and no one was trying to kill him. Andrek gave a hurried glance at the other arbiters. There were three other hominids, whom he identified from descriptions and biographies in his files as Telechrys of the Greater Ellipse, Rokon of the Lesser Ellipse, and Lyph of the Blue Spiral. These, with Poroth and Karbol, were the hominids, hard, cold, absolutely logical. And then the three nonhominids. Wreeth, Maichec, and Werebel, aloof, elegant, their scaled faces and tentacled arms drowned in alien clothing.

Altogether, there were only eight. Four empty great-chairs. As he realized this, Andrek was suddenly back at his last recital, at the Academy before Poroth's final practice court, and in this instant his petition crystallized, exquisitely ordered, perfect.

The clerk arose and began to chant. "Arise, all! Intergalactic Arbiters are now in session. Draw nigh and give your attention. Be seated."

As he took his seat at counsel's table, Andrek looked about him. Iovve sat behind him, in the first row. The room was practically empty. He looked up. The clerk was reading from the docket.

"The sole case is Twelve Galaxies vs. the planet Terror." He sat down.

Chief Arbiter Poroth studied the file in front of him. He spoke in slow, careful Ingliz. "This is a post-conviction proceedings, a routine show-cause." He looked about the room, and now noticed Andrek for the first time. There was a barely perceptible pause as he gave the advocate a friendly nod of recognition. He then continued, "I shall sign the destruct order, entered by this court by due proceedings previously had, and the crew will proceed forthwith, unless anyone now present shall show cause as to why this should not be done." He picked up the stylus. "Very well, then."

This, thought Andrek, is madness. I am going to regret it the rest of my very short life. How startled Poroth is going to be! The Chief Arbiter would probably puzzle over this reversal for years. Andrek doubted that he would ever see Poroth again to explain it to him, or that Poroth would really understand if he did. It was too bad. Somehow, it would help if he could get Poroth away, as he used to on the old Academy quadrangle, and explain everything, and get the advice of his old friend.

He arose. "My lords, I am James, Don Andrek, accredited advocate of the House of the Delfieri, of the Polyspiral Galaxy, sometimes called the Home Galaxy." His voice was, he thought, surprisingly strong and clear. Behind him, he heard Iovve shifting restlessly.

The stylus hung in midair. The Chief Arbiter nodded gravely. "The Court recognizes Don Andrek."

He was enthralled by a fine madness. How would it be now if he told Poroth, in dry legal terms, that in the past three days sundry attempts had been made to murder him, and that as a matter of self-defense and simple survival he had killed three men, all without the slightest benefit or consent of duly constituted authority, and that he was now a hunted criminal. But no. The native goodness of his boyhood mentor might break through the thick cast of law and precedent, and Poroth might impulsively attempt to help Andrek, at great peril to himself. The advocate was bound to silence. He hoped that Poroth would not invite him to chambers after the hearing.

"My government," said Andrek slowly, "hereby withdraws its earlier recommendation for destruction of the Planet Terror. Further, we now enter a plea that the planet be preserved, and we move that the Court so order." So now it was done; he had accepted—nay, embraced—Iovve's insanity. And for the life of him, he did not know why.

For a moment Poroth stared at him, dumbfounded. Then there was a hurried stirring at the bench as the arbiters leaned forward.

And now he knew that the past was over, closed, irretrievable. At this moment, he was a stranger even to himself. An entire career had collapsed beneath him, and with it everything supporting and leading to that career, including the Academy, and above all, Poroth. He should be feeling an immense sense of loss. But he was numb, anesthetized. Of the things he should be feeling, he felt nothing, save only the distant ring of voices in vanished classrooms, and the smell of smoke from piles of leaves burning in the Academy courtyard. Whatever else you may think of me, Dean Poroth, when you return to Goris-Kard and learn everything, at least think back on this moment, with a measure of pride, and know that you taught me well.

Hail, old friend! And farewell! Andrek knew he would never see him again. One by one, all the doors of his past had closed. This was the last, and the best. And he himself had closed it, and locked it, and thrown away the key. Somewhere in all of this there was divinity: for only the gods could have conceived an irony so sublime.

The clerk and recorder, he noted, had turned and were staring at him.

"Will the Court instruct the Recorder to enter the withdrawal of the original plea, together with my motion as stated," he continued smoothly, "so that this Honorable Court may duly consider the same."

"So ordered," rumbled the Chief Arbiter. But he was plainly puzzled. "Don Andrek, this turn of events is indeed a surprise. I think you must appreciate that it is highly irregular for the party complainant to withdraw the plea in a case such as this, and that the irregularity is further compounded when the don accredited for the plaintiff appears here as advocate for the defendant."

"Granted, my lord," said Andrek. He smiled crookedly. "Yet, I have it on the highest authority that no turn of events should surprise a truly skilled advocate, nor—I would assume—a truly great judge; and certainly not the eight here sitting as the supreme judicial body of the Twelve Galaxies. In any event, the irregularity, if such there be, will be somewhat mitigated if the Court decides to grant my motion—as I am sure will be the case."

Wreeth spoke up in a thin reedy whistle. "Don Andrek, do you realize that you are now proposing to save from destruction a planet that stands proven guilty of starting a nuclear war over a hundred years ago—a war that destroyed every living thing in nearly one-third of your own galaxy—and which was duly condemned for destruction by the Intergalactic Convention for the Control of War?"

"I so understand, your Honor. May I plead my motion?"

"Approach the bench, Don Andrek."

The advocate left his seat and walked up to the rostrum.

"Now, Mr. Andrek," said Poroth, "since we must adjourn within the hour, we will ask that you be brief." Something like a smile flickered around the edges of his mouth.

"I do not propose to waste the Court's time," said Andrek. "On the other hand, I do not propose to omit any points vital to a proper disposition of my motion."

"Proceed." Poroth leaned back in his chair.

"My petition is founded on three premises," said Andrek coolly. "First: procedurally, this honorable Court, as it now sits, is without jurisdiction. Second: substantively, on the merits, Terror ought not to be destroyed. Third: I plead for a thirty-day continuance. I will explain each basis in detail."

Poroth had now settled thoughtfully back into his great cushioned chair, and was tapping his fingertips together, exactly as he used to, years ago at the Academy, when he was listening to an A-plus brief. Except that now the great man's mouth twitched intermittently. "Continue," he murmured.

"The Court," said Andrek, "has no jurisdiction because the Court now sitting does not constitute a quorum. The Articles of the Intergalactic Arbitration Convention require three-fourths of the Court be present in disputed matters affecting a planet. The matter is certainly in dispute, yet there are only eight members of the Court present. Nine are required."

"It is true that four of our brothers have already left," said Poroth. "Under the circumstances, I had to give my consent." He smiled faintly. "Anything further?"

"Yes, your Honor. My motion is further based on the proposition that no witnesses are present who can testify, of their own knowledge, that the planet under interdiction is in fact Terror. It is basic procedure that the accused is entitled to be confronted by his accusers."

"What!" burst out Rokon. "Do you deny the planet is Terror?"

"I neither confirm nor deny, your Honor." Andrek's voice was chill, correct. "I merely point out that nowhere in the record is the requisite identification of the accused planet. For all this Court can know, Terror is presently orbiting its own sun."

"You well know there are no witnesses," grumbled Rokon. "But how could you complain of that? If perchance it be not Terror that we destroy, then your client is saved. Such a mistake would place Terror forever beyond the jurisdiction of this court, by reason of double jeopardy."

"Certainly, your Honor," said Andrek blandly. "As to *that*, I speak not so much for my client, but rather as *amicus curiae*, a friend of the Court. I merely urge the Court that the matter of identification be beyond dispute, to avoid any future embarrassment to the Court."

"And the point of disputed identification is now, of course, on record," said Wreeth. His strange features relaxed into something that looked oddly like a smile. "Proceed, Counselor, to the merits of your case."

"Thank you, your Honor. At the outset, so as not to burden the record, I will concede a number of points. As its name implies, Terror was a planet that generated fear . . . hatred . . . loathing. The Court may take judicial notice of the fact that the greed of its people was inexhaustible. During the forty centuries of its interstellar and intergalactic culture, its trading, colonizing, and military ships went everywhere—and seized everything they could carry away. By a certain viewpoint, they ravaged a goodly part of the Home Galaxy. Words to describe these people spring easily to the tongue. They were bullies, cheats; they were treacherous and corrupt. They were degenerates, abominable wretches. They were cruel, obscene, and cowards. Looking back on this vanished race, we see them now as utterly evil."

He paused somberly. "And came the revolt, the Horror. They lost the great nuke war . . . everything they had . . . all their far-flung colonies . . . and finally their own planet. Not a living thing there survived. And this is how *we* remember them."

Andrek looked at the intent faces leaning down at him. "But I can assure the Court, they did not think of *themselves* in this way. They did not call their planet by our name. No, not 'Terror.' That is history's over-simplifying corruption of the real name, which is, as you probably know, 'Terra.' It meant 'The Land.' And to them that land was loveliness incarnate. They fought among themselves for it, on the land, and on their seas, and they fought to the death. The names of their battles have come down to us . . . Thermopylae . . . The Alamo . . . Tobruk . . . Juneau. But so much for their origins. We turn now to their early years in space.

"Within a century of their discovery of the nuclear drive, they had planted colonies on the planets of Centauri and Procyon. And they came singing. In another three hundred years, they had developed the over-drive, and they penetrated the heart of their—and my—galaxy. They colonized my home planet of Goris-Kard. I am one of their distant descendants. For another thousand years, they spread their marvelous science, literature, music, art, laws, and architecture throughout our Home Galaxy. And still the Horror lay ahead. But it was coming, for it was inevitable. Terra's colonies became rich, powerful, opulent. They made contact with the Magellanic Clouds, then with Andromeda. They grew restive under the yoke of the Mother Planet. There were minor revolts—ruthlessly suppressed by Terra. And then came the alliances, the regroupings. And then the Horror broke. We all know this history. What we seem to forget is that most of us in this room trace our ancestry, by varied mutations, back to Terra, and the intergalactic Ingliz we now speak is but a variant of that ancient mother tongue. We exist here today—in this very room—because Terra existed, and her sons, sitting as this court, must now decide whether she shall finally cease to exist."

Andrek stood silent a moment. It was time to come to an end. He could go on forever, but that would simply annoy the arbiters. He would have to put together a sharp, pithy summary.

"What, then, is our Terran heritage? We cannot begin to count it. We grant much is memorable evil. Yet, if it is beyond forgetting, it is because it cannot be separated from the good. For Terra has handed down to us a mixture of good and evil, of rapine and laughter, of beauty and tears: the passions that distinguish us from the beasts. And her greatest heritage of all, and the one she most needs at this hour, when there is none to defend her, is mercy."

"There seems to be *one* left to defend her," observed Poroth. His voice was reserved, dry, but his eyes were twinkling. He looked at his chrono. "I trust that completes your summation, Don Andrek. Owing to the lateness of the hour, my brothers and I will now confer and give you a bench decision."

Andrek bowed and returned to his seat. He twisted around and looked at Iovve curiously. The pilgrim seemed lost in thought, hardly aware the presentation was over. Andrek sighed and stuffed his papers back into his briefcase. He still wondered why he had undertaken the defense. The last hope of returning to any planet in the Home Galaxy was now certainly gone. In fact, sanctuary would probably be denied him in most of the other eleven galaxies. What was left to him now? He did not know. Perhaps he could take the robe of Alea or Ritornel and hide away in a remote monastery. Yet, in a way, he was glad he had done it. For he had, in this action, for the first and only time in his life, evaded the cynical paradox of advocacy: the undertaking to damage or destroy persons who are strangers for the benefit of other strangers, while yet standing ready to turn on an erstwhile client, rending him for the pay of still another stranger. This paradox, too, he mused, is part of my Terran heritage.

He started. Chief Arbiter Poroth was addressing him. He arose and approached the bench.

The Chief Arbiter cleared his throat. "The Recorder will enter the following bench ruling on the motion offered by Don Andrek on behalf of the party Terror, in the case of the Twelve Galaxies vs. Terror, wherein the Court is petitioned to order the preservation of the planet defendant: The petition is denied."

Andrek's face fell. He had done his best, for his profession, and for Iovve, and he had lost. Yet, after all, aside from Iovve's insane scheme, why should it matter? The planet was dead. No one would ever want to live on it again, in or out of the Deep.

He suddenly realized the Chief Arbiter was not through.

"This Court," continued Poroth, "is convened by and under the joint authority of the Twelve Galaxies. We are sworn to keep the peace, and to punish those who would arouse enmity, internally or externally. In the ancient traditions of each of the Twelve Galaxies runs a prophecy of the 'Omega'—the final, ultimate destruction of everything. Terror brought us very close to this, and we should never forget it. Under our laws. we are required to destroy planets found guilty of initiating nuclear warfare. The record has clearly established that the defendant Terror is such a planet. In fact, at this moment, the destruct crew is awaiting our order to detonate massive charges already placed in the planet core that will literally atomize it. Yet, doubt has been suggested as to two vital points, to wit, whether we have a quorum, and also whether the planet in question is actually Terror. It is in our discretion to resolve these doubts either way—for destruction, or against. But we will do neither. We do, however, suspend and stay these proceedings, including any action in respect of the defendant planet, for a period of thirty days, at which time this court shall reconvene and further consider the matter—if the case is then still before us. So ordered."

The arbiters arose slowly, and the clerk began to chant. "All rise, all rise. This honorable Court stands adjourned."

Andrek walked back to Iovve. Through the thick brown bristles of his beard, the pilgrim seemed to be smiling.

"Does that satisfy you?" asked Andrek bluntly.

"Yes, of course, dear boy. Ritornel has spoken!"

"Then, my friend, you can start explaining . . . *everything.*"

"And so I will, as soon as we get back to the seismographic room."

Andrek merely shrugged. He did not believe it. Nor did he care very much anymore. Furthermore, at the first opportune moment he planned to part company with Iovve.

8. ANTIMATTER FOR RITORNEL

When they got back to the seismographic room, Iovve stole a look at the great clock overhead, and then, as though to forestall Andrek, pointed to the chairs, and sat down. "Shall we start with Amatar?" he asked.

Andrek started. "Amatar?" If Iovve were really going to talk about Amatar, he would stay awhile. He took a chair and leaned forward. "Yes. I want very much to hear about Amatar."

"You know about Oberon's near-fatal injuries, when his ship was caught in the last quake here, eighteen years ago."

"Huntyr was telling us."

"Regardless of his motives, Huntyr spoke truly." Iovve watched Andrek through narrowed eyes. "And he mentioned the Master Surgeon."

"Yes. The man who destroyed my brother."

"And the one who created Amatar."

"Create—" Andrek gripped the arms of his chair. "What are you saying!"

"You have heard of the practice of parthenogenesis, whereby a single hominid cell is taken from the living body, then developed first into a blastula, which is just a microscopic bubble with a single cavity, then a fully organized gastrula, then finally, after some months, a recognizable hominid fetus?"

"I have heard of it. It was used after the Horror, long ago, when so many monster mutations endangered natural propagation. Today it's just a medical curiosity."

"Quite so. But not entirely obsolete. In fact, eighteen years ago, when Oberon lay dying in the hospital wing of the Great House, his uncle, the old Regent, called the Master Surgeon and told him to start the necessary tissue cultures. They hoped that one would succeed, to make an infant Oberon, and preserve the Delfieri line. So the Master Surgeon made the cultures, dozens of them, all from living fragments of costal bone that he was still picking out of Oberon's chest. Bone fragments made the best tissue cultures, since bone marrow is the best source of blood cells, erythrocytes, leukocytes, and thrombocytes."

"But Oberon did not die," interposed Andrek.

"No. Oberon did not die. By then, the Master Surgeon had completed that tour de force known as Rimor."

"Omere," said Andrek tonelessly.

"Yes, in a manner of speaking, Omere, your brother. And listening to Omere, Oberon decided to live."

"So the cultures were thrown out."

"It wasn't that simple. When the Master Surgeon reported to the Regent that his nephew would live, the old man instructed the Master Surgeon to destroy the cultures, to avoid problems in the Delfieri succession. But Oberon had other plans. Out of a sense of perversity and boredom, and a desire to inconvenience the Master Surgeon, this arrogant youth had commanded that the vats be moved into his room. And there the cultures died, one by one, until only two were left. And so it was Oberon himself who first noticed, during the ensuing weeks, the strangeness of these last two growths. For neither was quite what it should have been. In particular, Oberon demanded tests for the second of these. Only then did he discover the impossibility."

"Discover what?" demanded Andrek.

"The impossibility."

Andrek gritted his teeth. He knew by now he could not accelerate Iovve's informative process. "Go ahead."

"Of course. But progress involves a slight detour. Let me digress a moment."

"By all means."

"Now don't pout, my boy. I'm explaining this as fast as I can."

Andrek groaned inaudibly.

"Sex," continued Iovve, "is determined by the cell chromosomes. If the cell contains an x chromosome and a y chromosome, the cell is male; cell reproduction—mitosis—will give only more male cells. If the cell contains only x chromosomes, it will be female, and mitosis will give only female cells. The costal bone cells were all male. Subsequent sampling proved that. Yet, mitosis gave only cells containing two x chromosomes: in a word, all female cells. The callus growing in the second vat was a female fetus."

Andrek did not understand immediately. For one long moment he could only stare at the pilgrim in uncomprehending wonder. And then something seemed to explode inside his head. His lips formed a single word: "Amatar!"

"Yes," said Iovve. "Amatar, the Motherless One."

The advocate was stunned. It was not possible to grasp this. He loved Amatar. He hated Oberon. Oberon would kill him. Amatar had saved his life. They were as different as night and day, as black and white; and yet they were the same. Amatar was Oberon.

Iovve watched quizzically the conflicting emotions at play on the advocate's pale features. Finally Andrek looked up at him. "I think I understand, now. And the other culture was—Kedrys?"

"Yes."

"How is it explained?"

"The mutations were probably caused by radiation. There was considerable cosmic radiation still bathing Goris-Kard from the recent space quake. Safeguards had been taken, of course. When the cultures were started, our side of the planet faced away from the direction of the Node, and the culture room was encased in a meter of lead. And finally, of course, each culture was started and kept in a lead-lined flask. And yet it is known that two bursts of cosmic radiation passed entirely through the body of the planet, a meter of lead, and finally into the two respective cultures, and precisely in the right gene, and at the right molecular area in the DNA. No other rays entered the chamber: just these two. A millimicron one way or the other, and there would be no Amatar and no Kedrys. With Kedrys the problem is even more difficult. There has to be practically a gamma shower to modify the genes sufficiently to unite avian, hominid, and equine characteristics. Is this chance? In the final plot, does Alea conspire with Ritornel, and is the greatest design helpless without luck? I do not know. One might argue that such chance is ultra-astronomical, that this is too much even for the goddess."

These philosophical meanderings were wasted on the advocate. He rather suspected that the pilgrim was trying to take flight from the single issue remaining. He would not be diverted.

"Iovve," he said quietly. "Who are *you?*"

Iovve shrugged his shoulders. "You may now rightly ask, and I must answer," he said simply. "And since I have nearly completed my pilgrimage, and will soon be dead, you know that I speak the truth. The ancient Terran jurists had a word for this."

"Deathbed confession," said Andrek. "It has a presumption of veracity. So let's assume, for the purpose of argument, that you are finally going to tell me the truth. Will it be the whole truth?"

"I'll try," promised the pilgrim.

Andrek snorted. "Whether you actually do or don't, at least it should be entertaining just to watch you *try*. So, go ahead."

"And so I shall, my dear boy. And I shall begin with the beginning, which is to say, myself. My origins are best understood when viewed in perspective against yours. Your great Home Galaxy is a polyspiral, which means of course that it is mature, since many billions of years are required to condense into the disk shape and to fling out the balancing spiral arms. The stars, consequently, are nearly all second-generation."

"Second-generation?" queried Andrek.

"Yes. They are condensed from clouds of hydrogen and cosmic dust containing all the known elements. Such dust is the product of ancient stellar explosions. Let me explain this in steps, so you can understand the vast gulf that separates our two cultures."

"Please do," said Andrek. At least this cleared up one point: Iovve was not hominid; he was not even a native of the Home Galaxy. Andrek had rather suspected as much.

Iovve continued. "A galaxy is born as the titanic amorphous masses of hydrogen at the Node condense slowly into stars. These first stars will all be red giants. Tremendous heat and pressures develop, and the hydrogen is fused to helium. Other nuclear reactions take place to make carbon, neon, oxygen . . . In fact, all the elements up to and including iron are formed in this first stage, within the body of the red giants. Elements higher than iron cannot be formed in this way, since this method of element formation requires the release of energy, and elements higher than iron cannot release energy in this way. So now, when all the fuel is used up, the red giant explodes—a supernova. The elements it has created are blown into space. The explosion harms nothing, because the red giants do not have planets. And actually, the explosion is beneficial, since the dispersed matter can now mix with more hydrogen, and finally again condense, not only into suns, but also into planets. The sun will this time enter a new stage of element formation. It will again convert hydrogen into helium, but now it will do it differently, more economically. Since it now has plenty of carbon (and in fact, all the elements up through and including iron), it produces heat and energy by the carbon cycle. The carbon cycle is curious in that it makes copious quantities of protons. These protons strike the nuclei of the atoms in this new sun, until, by a process of simple nuclear addition, *all* of the ninety-two stable elements are made. When that sun eventually consumes all its nuclear fuel, and finally explodes, it will, of course, offer a complete system of elements to that sector of the galaxy. By then, the galaxy will be fairly mature; it will be a spiral, like your Home Galaxy. But that's another story. It's really that planet that I want to talk about, the one condensed from the dust of the red giant's explosion. That planet is really quite a primitive thing. I know. I was born there. Our periodic table stopped with element number twenty-six: iron. You may think that this meant we had at least a well-developed ferrous metallurgy, with hearths, reducing ovens, foundries, rolling mills, and the end products, such as machines made of steel, steel manufactures, steel architecture. But I tell you we had none of this. When the Terrans came, there was only one piece of metallic iron on the face of the whole planet—and that was a small meteorite in a museum. Yet, it could not have been otherwise.

"Consider history in a secondary planet—one like Terra, that starts its history with *all* the ninety-two elements. It first goes through a Stone Age. (As did we.) Then it discovers copper, and next that excellent copper-tin alloy, bronze. So it then enters into a Bronze Age. But more than this, it enters into metallurgy. It acquires the skills in metallurgy that it must have before it can have an Iron Age. So you see, having neither copper nor tin, my people could not have a Bronze Age, and if no Bronze Age, no Iron Age. And the lack of heavy metals had other consequences. Without gold or silver for coins, we had little trade or commerce. Again, our lack of copper denied us the electrical sciences. And since we had no uranium, nuclear power was, of course, unthinkable. And needless to say, we had no means of interplanetary flight. We did not even have heavier-than-air machines."

The pilgrim stopped, and seemed to stare through Andrek, and beyond, into flickering scenes of his own far-distant planet and youth.

"Go on!" said Andrek tensely. "You said the Terrans came. Did they colonize your planet?"

Iovve shook his head. "Our planet seemed desolate to them—not worth their attention, except as a refueling base. And our peculiar introverted specialty, forced on us by simple lack of other occupations, was not at first apparent to the Terrans. Later, this happy skill took us as honored guests throughout the Twelve Galaxies."

"And what was this—skill?" asked Andrek.

"We were physicians and surgeons. The profession was probably inevitable for us. For when a culture is denied technology, it becomes introspective. It turns inward. It occupies itself with its own body, and with the responses of its body. What we had missed in the hardware sciences we more than made up in the science of the mind and body. And when we were finally exposed to other cultures, our prime interest in bodies continued, and was extended to the life forms of our new neighbors. In this manner, most of us left our home planet, to market our one great skill. Yet, we communicated with each other, and we were a cohesive body. Some of us had strange adventures. Ah, the things I could tell you!"

By the Beard of The Founder, thought Andrek, I believe you could! He said, "I understand now why you belong to the Iatric Order of Ritornel." He fancied Iovve nearly smiled. "Continue, then," said Andrek curtly.

"When the Terran Wars broke out—the Horror—as you survivors so aptly call it, I called my brothers to one last convention. It was clear to us then that Terra must eventually be destroyed, and probably a good part of the Home Galaxy with her. We decided what we must do to give civilization another chance, a return as it were. I suggested a simple codeword for the operation: *Ritornel.*"

"What!"

"Yes, Ritornel. Does this astound you? I can see that it might, for Ritornel today bears little resemblance to my original concept. Yet, we were the original missionary physicians of Ritornel. Wherever we went, we carried the Prophecy: a virgin, not of mother born, to renew life, on a new world, and thus to complete the Ring. In the course of the centuries, I regret to say, Ritornel has changed drastically. Miracles, martyrs, and myths can ruin a perfectly good religion. When the supernatural flies in the window, logic stumbles out the door. Today I would not be admitted to any but the lowest circles of the Temple. And, of course, in some of the chapters, I would not be admitted at all."

"Iovve," said Andrek quietly, "please listen to me a moment. You have referred to participation in events that took place centuries ago, well before the Horror. No—let me finish . . . And just now you have, in effect, told me that you are the Founder of Ritornel. Now, listening to this objectively, won't you grant that some skepticism is justified?"

"James, my dear innocent, you need not believe a word of what I have told you. Nevertheless, I do hope my simple story has not completely exhausted your credulity, for I have not finished."

Was it possible? mused Andrek. Could he prove it was impossible? And in any case, what difference did it make? For the time being, he'd reserve judgment. "So you founded Ritornel," he said noncommittally. "Then what?"

"We took counsel. Midway in the course of the Horror, we decided what to do. We would select an optimum specimen of the best culture known to us. This specimen would actually consist of a male and female of the species, and we would place this couple in suitable surroundings quite inaccessible, and completely isolated from all other life systems. There, in peace, a new race would be propagated, and in time would dominate the universe. In the beginning, there were many of us, seeking this new couple. But now my brothers are dead. I am the last. Truly, Ritornel is no longer Ritornel. But it doesn't matter. My mission is done. The Ring of Ritornel will soon be complete."

"And this preservation of the species, this is the true purpose of Ritornel? This is the Ring?"

"The same."

"But I still don't see the symbolism. Ritornel means 'return.' What are we returning to?"

"We return to life. Or rather, civilization, after nearly dying, shall return, preserved by and through the selected couple. You may liken it to an ancient Terran oak forest. Every tree may die; yet, if but one acorn be saved, the forest may yet again live. Or again, it is like the preservation of a bacterial culture. If but one cell be preserved, the entire culture can return to life, assuming, of course, that the proper nutrient medium is available. So, first of all, we needed the proper medium within which our male and female specimens could preserve their species. This, of course, had to be a planet. Obviously, it should be a planet of a mature star system—one containing all the elements, not a primitive one, like mine. As the Horror progressed several candidates became available. For several reasons, we selected Terra. The main argument was that she was completely desolate, and was being hauled to the Node to be destroyed. Our planet *had* to be taken to the Node, for reasons that you will soon see."

"I see one thing very clearly," said Andrek thoughtfully. "I see that you have made an utter fool of me. I thought you were my friend. Your only interest in me was to make that speech before the arbiters, to save Terra, so that Terra could become the planet of Ritornel."

Iovve's leathery features twisted into a smile. "You are too modest, Don Andrek. My interest in you does not end with your famous speech to the arbiters, legal landmark though it be. Oh, indeed not."

"All right," said Andrek. "Get on with it. I've done your work for you. Here's Terra at the Node—as far as possible from civilization. Is this what you meant by preservation in isolation?"

"Not exactly. For that, we need one thing more."

"The quake?"

"Yes. As I have already mentioned to you, the quake will take Terra into the Deep."

"How about your couple," said Andrek. "Your male and female specimens, the ancestors of the new race? How do you select them? And then how do you get *them* into the Deep?"

"Very perceptive questions, dear boy. First, let us address ourselves to the rationale of selection. Suppose that you had the task of selecting this seed . . . spore . . . cell . . . this ancestral couple, to become the progenitors of the surviving race. There are hundreds of strong contenders—ranging from the water people that dominate the Hydraid Galaxy, to the chitinous denizens of the arid worlds of the Spereld suns. All are intelligent, cultured, prolific, technically advanced. And all—though they do not yet realize it—are doomed by Omega. Which one will be given the chance to try again?"

"No problem there," said Andrek. "The selector owes a duty to his own race to select it."

"Wrong, my boy. It is quite natural for the votaries to reconstruct the gods anthropomorphically, in their own image. However, when the 'gods' create, they should be more imaginative."

"You talk in riddles, old one."

"Only because you are naive, uninformed, and difficult to instruct."

Andrek laughed. "Instruct me."

"Listen, then, and be instructed. We of Ritornel decided very early that mere technical competence in our prospective couple was not enough. We looked for other qualities—racial features that deserved immortality. And our search was successful. We found the characteristics we sought: in the hominid."

"What characteristics are you talking about?"

"Several. Do you realize that of the twelve basic cultures, only the hominid dreams? That only the hominid sees visions, and mourns, has a sense of tragedy? That only the hominid believes firmly in things he cannot see? That only the hominid sings for pure useless pleasure, and laughs, and writes poetry?"

"Really? That's quite curious. I had not thought about it."

"Well, then, I suggest you give it some thought. What is the hominid, that strangers should prefer him above all other life forms? He is cold and logical: yet he laughs and sings. He is cruel, and he has the lust of the male goat: yet he weeps and is acquainted with grief. You described him well to the arbiters. Verily, he is beyond knowing. Perhaps this helped our choice."

"Very well, then," said Andrek, "the Founder of Ritornel selects what is to him an alien couple, two hominids, for deposit in the Deep. And right away your scheme is doomed to failure. For even if you were able to get Terra and your male and female into the Deep, they would never come out again. They'd all be lost forever. Nothing except space has ever come out of the Deep."

"You are wrong." The pilgrim reached into his robes and drew out a pendant Ritornellian ring, which he unfastened. "Catch," he said, tossing it to Andrek.

The advocate caught it and examined it, at first casually, then more closely. There was something very strange about it. For one thing, the Ritornellian series, from one to twelve, then back again to one, was *inside* the ring, whereas in all rings he had ever seen before, the series was outside. Nor was that all. He studied the digits carefully, turning the ring slowly in his fingers. All the numbers were backward. He looked up at Iovve. "What are you trying to tell me?"

"It is antimatter," said the other calmly.

7. "AMATAR . . . AND YOU, ANDREK"

Andrek gasped and let the ring fly from his hands. It ricocheted against a wall, then floated free, gleaming at him.

"Don't worry," said Iovve. "It has been passivated. And in any case, the ursecta would not let it annihilate, here at the Node."

"But—it must weigh a good twenty grams! There's not a Klein circlet in any of the Twelve Galaxies with power capable of converting an object that size to antimatter!"

"True. Not in any of the twelve. But there is one *between* the galaxies."

"You mean *here?* At the Node?"

"Exactly. Into the Deep, and out again—a perfect Klein. Reverses polarity of the individual atoms, and of course turns everything inside-out and backward, including the numbers."

"The numbers!" Andrek jumped up and seized the ring again. "Of course! This thing *has* been in the Deep! But why doesn't it annihilate on contact with my hand—or even with the molecules of the air?"

"As I said, it has been passivated. It has a surface layer of neutrons that almost completely precludes contact with normal matter. The few molecules that do make contact are harmless. I'm sure you know the theory. The addition of neutrons prevents the approach of particles of opposite charge. The number of neutrons to be added depends upon the structure of a given atom. Calcium is the highest 'stabile.' There you have twenty protons in the nucleus, and you need only twenty neutrons to prevent the approach of the negative shell electrons. For higher atomic numbers you need proportionately more neutrons. For example, for bismuth, you need one hundred and twenty-six neutrons to neutralize eighty-three protons in the nucleus. And thereafter, the addition of neutrons doesn't completely stabilize, and the atoms are radioactive. And that is why an antimatter body normally glows in the dark. It ionizes the air about it, like a neon lamp. Outside the Node, away from the ursecta, the ring would have a blue glow."

Andrek looked over at Iovve. He remembered now the curious impression he had experienced on several past occasions . . . that encounter in Huntyr's office, and later in the dim-lit cabin in *Xerol,* when the pilgrim's face had been bathed in a pale blue glow. Andrek looked at the ring, then back again at Iovve. His mouth slowly opened wide. The hair began to stand up on the back of his neck. "You—" he gurgled. "The Deep—?"

Iovve nodded gravely. "I have been in the Deep. My body is antimatter."

Andrek's heart seemed to dissolve within him. It was impossible, unimaginable. Yet it was true. And this meant everything Iovve had told him was true. He felt as though he were standing on the edge of a bottomless chasm, leaning into the blackness, and beginning to fall. He jerked up straight, and fought off a feeling of dizziness.

"How can this be!" he cried.

"It was part of the plan of Ritornel," said Iovve. "We were weak, nearly defenseless. To accomplish Ritornel, we needed immense power, power that would permit us to cope with the armed might of the Twelve Galaxies, and even more important, power sufficient to transmit our selected hominid specimens from normal space into the Deep. We were aware of the work on creation of antimatter by sending a tiny amount of metal down a Klein circuit, and we knew that tremendous power could be developed at the normal matter/antimatter interface. Our theorists then determined that the topology of the Node epicenter at quake time was exactly identical to that of a Klein circuit. In theory, at least, any object at the epicenter will be sucked back into the Deep by the quake. So far, so good. It's simple to get a thing into the Deep. To get it out again is quite another matter. Obviously, we needed a diplon, a double quake. The first part would put me in the Deep, the second would bring me out again into normal space, as antimatter."

"And there you would annihilate," interposed Andrek. "Except, of course, you very obviously didn't. Why didn't you?"

"My colleagues prepared my body. There were certain surgical procedures, necessary to adapt the dermal nerve endings, and to permit control of the antimatter/normal matter interface."

"According to history," said Andrek heavily, "the last diplon was over five hundred years ago."

"Yes, that was the one. The Horror had just begun. I remember every detail. The Node Station was not quite so large or elaborate then as now, but it was otherwise the same. They left it here, at epicenter, on automatic, to broadcast quake data. There was a chair in the center of the seismographic room. I sat in it, waiting for the quake, the same as now."

Andrek bent forward, fascinated. "What was the quake like, when it came?"

"Rather a big jolt. The station simply disintegrated. I'm still amazed that I wasn't killed. And then I was in the Deep."

"And what was it like, in the Deep?"

"For a man unskilled in the ways of patience, the Deep can be a torture. For a very old creature, such as myself, it was—endurable. Still, it would have been better if I had had a companion. A person in the Deep is a disembodied spirit. He can touch nothing. There is nothing there to touch. Yet, he can imagine he touches. He cannot hear or sense his own voice, because he has neither ears nor throat nor voice."

"But even if someone had accompanied you into the Deep, you would not have been able to communicate with him," observed Andrek.

"We weren't sure. Our studies showed that there very well might be a type of rudimentary telepathic communication."

"Then finally," said Andrek, "you emerged from the Deep. And you were antimatter, possessing fantastic powers?"

"Yes. A long time ago."

"And you still possess these powers?"

"Yes—and no. Because of the ursecta, there can be no nuclear power of any type at the Node. I have been powerless, ever since we entered the Node area."

"Your force field, back on *Xerol*—that really emanated from your own body, didn't it?"

"Yes. That was just an extension of my antimatter/normal matter epidermal juncture. It's good over a distance of several hundred yards. It permits passage through any adverse shield, too, I might add, because the antimatter field radiates in vibrations exactly perpendicular to normal electromagnetic radiation. You probably remember this from Kedrys' lecture."

"Yes, I remember. I also remember that fairytale you gave me about plugging your force-field apparatus in to the wall current, back on *Xerol.*"

Iovve smiled. "I very nearly tripped up on that one, didn't I? Fortunately, you plugged it in just in time."

Andrek smiled grimly. "No, I didn't. But no matter. And I gather then, back on *Xerol,* when I first found you, you weren't really drugged?"

"Again, yes and no. I was paralyzed. No doubt of that. Except for my eye muscles, my nervous system was completely occupied in dealing with the alien normal matter circulating in my bloodstream. It was touch-and-go there for several hours. I was very nearly annihilated. Your antidote reacted with the drug to increase its vapor pressure, so that I could finally void it through my lungs and dermis. To be antimatter isn't to be omnipotent; far from it."

"Can you be killed?" said Andrek curiously.

"Yes, but only if I am willing to die. With a little care, there's no force within the Twelve Galaxies that can do me any real harm. Small amounts of nuclear energy I simply convert to protons at my dermal surface. Energy large enough to tear my body apart I avoid by 'fading' partway back into the Deep. But I avoid these foolish contests. The best defense is to hide what I am. It avoids all sorts of problems."

"Suppose I had not been able to persuade the arbiters to stay the destruction of Terra? What would you have done?"

"Probably nothing. I am powerless here at the Node. It would mean that Ritornel had failed. Five centuries of planning would have been wasted. All my colleagues are now dead. No one would be left to help me. But we need not speculate. Terra is here, ready to enter the Deep, when the quake comes."

And now," said Andrek, "we come to the one remaining, vital question. Your hominids—male and female. Have you selected them, as individuals, I mean?"

"Of course, Don Andrek. Did you not know?"

"What do you mean?" stammered Andrek. *"Who?"*

"Why, Amatar, and you, of course."

6. PILGRIM AND SURGEON

No thing can freely enter here, nor leave.
—Andrek, in the Deep.

The blood began to leave Andrek's face. "No!"

"Oh, yes! Why do you think we are here? Why do you think I've been telling you all this?" Iovve looked over at Andrek in real concern. "Don't you understand? It's really quite simple. You will go into the Deep, with the first quake of the diplon. You will come out again with the second quake, and you will then be antimatter. As antimatter, you could not possibly marry Amatar. The only solution is for you to use your new powers to take Amatar back with you into the Deep, find Terra, and someday emerge to found a new race, a new universe."

"Iovve," said Andrek, shaking his head slowly, "thanks for the honor. But no thanks. I don't want to be the father of a new race. I'm not the progenitive type. Nor have I any interest in the preservation of civilization. Let civilization take care of itself. And in particular, I have no interest in going into the Deep. From your very brief description, I'm certain I wouldn't like it there. Get yourself another specimen."

Iovve studied Andrek for a long time before speaking. At last he said, "Is that your final word?" There was something in his voice that was beyond sadness.

"Yes. I'm very sorry, Iovve, to have it end this way. Stay if you like, but I'm getting out now, while I can."

"How will you leave?"

"There are three or four couriers waiting to take those arbiters home. We probably wouldn't even have to stowaway. They'd have to take us as distress cases."

"They are all gone. All ships are gone. We are alone in the station."

Andrek's eyes widened. "Impossible!"

"Call the desk."

"That wouldn't mean anything. You saw the clerk leave." Andrek strode over to the door and opened it. There was no sound in the corridor. The muted background noise of the station was gone. Absolute silence reigned. "Oh, no!" he groaned. Leaving the door open, he clacked off down the corridor, across the dim-lit lobby, to the other side of the station, where the couriers had docked on either side of *Xerol.* His breath hung in frozen clouds around him. The heat had been turned off. And it was becoming harder to breathe. Probably the pressure system had been disconnected, too. And now he saw the loading platform, where only hours before he and Iovve had made their ill-fated entrance to this cursed place.

Xerol was gone. He had expected that. He looked up and down the platform wildly. There was nothing. The docks were empty. All tubes were closed. There was no motion anywhere.

His head jerked. There was a sound at one of the loading tubes, so high-pitched as to be barely audible. Rather like a whistle, he thought. He moved quickly up the loading ramp to the outer wall. There, he located the whistle. It was a tiny leak in the valve sealing the loading tube, and air rushing from the station into the vacuum of space was making a hissing sound. The station was bleeding to death. His arms drooped. Slowly, he turned and retraced his steps.

It made no sense. He could have got away, yet Iovve had treacherously, cruelly, diabolically detained him until all the ships had gone. The station would be at the epicenter of the quake. Nothing in it could possibly escape. His body, dead or alive, must soon enter the Deep.

He opened the door to the seismographic room and stepped inside.

The pilgrim was sitting where he had left him. But now he was motionless, statuesque. Andrek realized that Iovve had now deliberately slipped into his death trance. His life-mission had failed, and his pilgrimage was at an end.

Only—it was not so. Andrek now knew that he was going into the Deep, willy-nilly, and then out again. And when be came out, he would annihilate—unless certain vital surgery were done to his nervous system.

He struck the pilgrim lightly on the cheek. "Iovve, wake up!"

But the other continued to stare off into some unknown world, immobile, unhearing.

Andrek slapped him—hard.

Iovve groaned, then turned his head slowly toward the advocate. But his eyes were vacant, nearly dead.

Andrek felt along the sides of the seated figure. It was just as he suspected. He began to struggle with the gray robe, and finally got it off over Iovve's head. Some sort of corset was bound over the chest. Andrek unbuckled it hastily and threw it aside. He sucked in his breath. Folded across Iovve's chest were three extra pairs of arms!

In order to merge inconspicuously into the bimanual society of the Home Galaxy, the pilgrim had bound up the six extra arms that would instantly declare his arachnid origins.

As Andrek began to flex and massage the arms, he examined them closely. The whole assemblage was remarkable. The "elbow" and "wrist" were bulbous joints which apparently gave a play of several complete revolutions to the hands. And such hands! Each held six fingers, in opposing triplets. Andrek surmised that this digital structure must have been very useful to Iovve's spiderlike ancestors for clambering about their giant webs. In deft rapid motions he stripped the gloves from Iovve's "normal" hands. As he had suspected, they were similarly contrived. And probably somewhere on Iovve's body was a vestigial spinneret. Small wonder Iovve had held such an exquisite rapport with Raq! Andrek suppressed a shiver and proceeded grimly with his task.

The pilgrim was still weaving his web in the best tradition of his forebears, but with improvements. Being invisible, it was deadlier. And it was a paradoxical web: to save his own life, he, Andrek, the trapped insect, had to awaken the spider.

His attention was drawn again to Iovve's hands. One finger on each was beginning to glow in a rhythmic pattern, corresponding roughly (Andrek guessed) to Iovve's heartbeat. As the glow grew brighter, the pulsations leveled out. Iovve's hands had built-in illumination!

And then Andrek noticed that one of the fingers was changing shape. It was, in fact, assuming several shapes in succession. First, it grew out into a long thin rod. Then the rod curled into a full loop, and finally the tip became bladelike. Andrek touched the edge of the blade and instantly jerked his finger away and stuck it in his mouth. The knife edge was not only microtome-sharp: it was alive. It cut simply by contact, without pressure or motion. And evidently any part of it could be heated—or frozen—at will. This would explain its use as a key to enter the seismographic room. In surgery it worked by the light of its opposing finger, while (Andrek imagined) the other fingers of the same hand held hemostats, clamps, and sponges.

And there were eight of these remarkable hands! Small wonder that Iovve, physician and surgeon, could pick any lock in the Twelve Galaxies

He stood back and glared at the pilgrim. Surgeon of Ritornel indeed! And what are you now? Space cabbage!

There was a great deal to be done, and very little time. He had to awaken Iovve, and Iovve must then make certain subtle but basic changes in his, Andrek's, body. If Iovve had come out of the Deep as antimatter, without being annihilated, so could Andrek. The friar-surgeon knew how.

But Iovve, apparently determined to bring his long pilgrimage to an end, could not be aroused.

There was one last thing to try.

Andrek found Iovve's medical kit and opened it with trembling fingers. He flipped back to the drug section. Quirinal. Here it is. He jabbed the syringe needle into the rubber stopper and filled the syringe. Two cc.

He came over and shook Iovve.

"Wha—?"

Good! This was some kind of contact. He spoke loudly. "Quirinal, Iovve!"

"Quir—" muttered the pilgrim.

"Klein circlets," said Andrek grimly. "Activate them, the Klein circlets in your body—*now*, or you'll annihilate."

Iovve blinked owlishly. "Klein—?"

Andrek screamed at him. "Iovve! Concentrate! To your system, this is antimatter. If you're not careful, we're both dead. You'll have to *convert* it to antimatter quirinal, drop by drop, as it enters your bloodstream. Can you do that?"

"Drop by drop."

"Concentrate, Iovve! Here it comes!"

The pilgrim gasped as the needle jammed into his arm. "Easy. Awake now. Slowly, slowly. All right, I have it under control. A little faster. Good. Faster still. Stay with it. So you've come to your senses. Good boy. Stay with it. It's working rapidly, quite rapidly. All the rest, now. That's it."

Andrek's face was wet when he pulled the needle out. He looked at Iovve quizzically.

A change was coming over the pilgrim. His eight arms, in opposing pairs, began a strange rhythmic pattern, flexing, unflexing. The fingers were locking, unlocking, as though long strangers to each other. He now stared coldly at Andrek. "Strip."

Andrek's heart leaped. "Of course."

Iovve jerked his head toward the table. "Over there. I'll have to stretch you out."

"Are you going to use an anesthetic?"

"You might call it that. But don't bother me with your silly questions."

"Sorry."

"And don't be humble. You don't know enough to be humble. I'll explain as I work."

Andrek exhaled heavily, and was silent.

Iovve said, "A man made of antimatter has two basic problems. He must avoid contact with normal matter, and he must develop a vastly different metabolism. If he eats an apple—or even breathes—he annihilates. If his nervous system is not drastically modified, he can be safe only while asphyxiating in free fall in a vacuum. So—what must be done to him? It would be fairly simple if we could passivate his entire skin—his available topological surface, and leave it at that. But that would solve only part of the problem. He would then be *too well* protected against contact with normal matter. Some contact is necessary, because his new metabolism is going to be powered by the energy generated at the controlled juncture of his skin with the world of normal matter. In his former world of carbohydrates, proteins, and vitamins, he could sum up his metabolism requirements in terms of fifteen hundred to two thousand calories a day. He still can—but now he converts mass, generally from the dead cells of his epidermis, into the same number of calories, by the ancient energy/mass equation. In a word, our antimatter man annihilates but he does it slowly, almost imperceptibly, a few million atoms at a time. He has, if he so will, a half-life of several hundred thousand years."

Andrek exhaled in slow wonder. "But how is this accomplished?"

"Surgery. To passivate the skin, we have to make the positron shell around atoms of antimatter repel the negative electron shells that surround normal atoms. This in itself is not too difficult. It's the same principle that keeps the negative electrons in stable orbits around the positive nucleus in an atom of normal matter, without spiraling inward and annihilating the nucleus. And what is it that keeps the electron from spiraling inward and combining with the nucleus? Simply the fact that it moves in acceptable orbits. It's the same with the antimatter/normal matter juncture. An approaching normal atom is forced into an inert pattern, at the will of the antimatter man.

"It becomes tricky," continued Iovve, "when we have to let a minute number of atoms react—from time to time, and completely at the will and order of our antimatter man—to provide his daily energy requirements. This requires accurate *voluntary* control of his dermal cells—which normally involuntary. The change has to be made in his medulla, obviously before he becomes antimatter. And changes have to be made in the alveoli of his lungs. He will no longer need air as a source of oxygen; yet, if he is to be able communicate vocally in a normal-matter world, he will need to be able draw air of normal matter into antimatter lungs and blow it back out again through an antimatter voice box. Again, anatomical alteration is required

"And now we come to the final step. I have to go into your brain. In a word, my boy, you'll have to be completely rewired. It won't hurt—there are no pain sensory endings in the brain, but after it's over, I want you to remain very quiet. Otherwise you might jar loose some of your new circuitry. And of course, for all this, I'll have to put you to sleep."

Andrek started under the straps.

"No choice," said Iovve, anticipating his question. "However, if this works at all, you'll come out of it before the quake hits. And of course if the operation is a failure, you will never know it. So, relax!"

Andrek was perspiring profusely, and his thoughts were chaotic. There was one last thing about Iovve that he had almost grasped, the name that Huntyr had been trying to pronounce as he died. But it kept eluding him, possibly because it was too horrible to accept. Iovve was . . . was . . .

At this moment he observed, with blank amazement, that several of the surgeon's fingers had apparently passed *through* his skull, as though it were empty space, and were busily involved deep in his cranium.

And then he knew the final identity of Iovve. These hands, which, by his invitation—nay, by his demand—were now in his own brain, were the very hands that had created Amatar and Kedrys.

As he floated out into darkness, he knew. And it was beyond irony. These hands had destroyed his brother.

Iovve was the Master Surgeon.

5. AN APPROACHING EXPLOSION

The Deep is the Beginning and the End, at once the womb and the coffin of time and space, the wellspring of life and death, the mother of nodes. I was cast into the Deep from the die cup of Alea, and Ritornel is lost in the far eons. I wait, and I think.

— Andrek, in the Deep.

He saw the clock, straight ahead. Gradually, it came into focus, and he recognized it. It had a red hand, and a black hand. It was the quake clock, in the seismographic room. The black hand was oddly close to the red hand. He was becoming rapidly oriented. He was still on his back on Iovve's improvised operating table. His head hurt. He put his fingertips gingerly to his forehead, and felt bandages there.

At this sign of life, Iovve stepped over. "How do you feel?"

"I don't know," said Andrek thickly. "Was the operation a success?"

"Yes, I think so."

"Yes, I think so."

Andrek studied the pilgrim morosely. Should he denounce the Master Surgeon for what he had done to Omere? Should he take his vengeance now, within the short time remaining before the quake? He closed his eyes and breathed heavily. It wasn't that simple. This strange creature had given life, long ago, to Amatar, and, just now, to him. And in any case the great overriding immensity of the quake was about to exact its own vengeance.

He said; "When is the quake due? Or is that still a secret?"

"No, there's no reason for it to be a secret anymore. It is due very soon. Within the hour."

Andrek was now almost indifferent. "I imagine you're right. But would you mind explaining how you know?"

"By the frequency of the temblors—the harbingers of the quake."

"But according to the instruments, there hasn't been a temblor in days," demurred Andrek.

Iovve smiled. "Of course. Let me explain. For hundreds of years the instruments have recorded each temblor, as well as each quake. There is a time, before a quake, when the temblors come faster and faster, and their vibrations higher and higher. It's like—" He looked about the room. "Here, let me show you." Iovve picked up a wooden lath and flexed it several times. "This will do nicely. Now, we need a stethoscope." He picked the instrument out of his medical kit and handed it to Andrek. Andrek sat up on the table and inserted the stethoscope plugs in his ears.

Iovve came over to the table and bent the lath into a quarter circle. "Put the stethoscope bell here, at the center of the arc, and listen carefully. But when I say 'stop,' remove the bell instantly. Do you understand?"

Andrek nodded.

"So." Iovve continued to bend the lath. "Do you hear anything?"

"Clicks. A lot of them. Faster. Going up the scale."

Iovve watched him closely, then suddenly was motionless. The lath was nearly a semicircle. "And now?"

Andrek looked at him blankly. "No sound. Nothing."

"Stop!"

Andrek jerked the stethoscope away.

The lath broke in half with a loud crack.

Andrek stared mutely at the other.

"Don't you see the analogy?" said Iovve gravely. "The lath loses elasticity just before the break. The component fibers disintegrate, slip, and slide. For a brief interval there is no further audible evidence of stress. Then, at the break area, the structure collapses altogether. It is the same with the quake. The long silence is the prelude, the last thing before the great break."

Andrek sat down heavily. "And that was why everyone was in such a hurry to leave. They all knew the exact moment, didn't they?" It was not really a question.

"Yes."

"I suppose the period of silence is fairly precise, then," said Andrek.

"To the minute," said Iovve calmly. He leaned forward. "If we might go on to other matters, there is something which, until now, I have not been able to discuss with you. Your brother. You know now, of course, that I am the Master Surgeon."

"I know," said Andrek bleakly. "And I remember where I first saw you. It was when I was a boy. I came to get Omere at a bar. The Winged Kentaur. I met you there. It was you, even though you wore a hood over your face. But I remember the eyes, the blue lights."

"Yes. It was only a couple of days later that Huntyr brought Omere into surgery."

"And there you did an evil thing," said Andrek quietly. "I am very glad you are about to die."

Iovve shrugged. "I have lived too long to be greatly concerned with good and evil. These are concepts peculiar to the hominid ethos, and alien to me. I had known the sex of the blastula that became Amatar almost from the first, even before the Regent demanded that Omere be converted into Rimor. If I had refused the Regent, I would have been banished from the Great House, and I would not have been able to follow the growth of the girl-fetus. And that was unthinkable, for this was the Sign. I had waited for it for centuries. I had to stay. But completely aside from this, I think it might be fairly argued that I did a great service for your brother."

"How so?"

"From a combination of dissolute living and a lung disease, he was slowly dying. I saved his life."

"By killing him?"

"That depends on the definition of existence. Certain portions of his cerebrum survive in the computer. By his own view, he lives."

"But you did not get his consent. You did not give him a choice. He might have preferred to die."

"True. He did want to die. But under the circumstances his wishes were irrelevant."

"Then it was murder."

"Was it? He disappears as Omere; he reappears as Rimor."

"No. The Omere that disappeared is not the Rimor that reappears. Where is Omere's heart? His arms? How can he smile? His body is dead."

"He is not dead. He is immortal."

"He was slain by immortality."

Iovve sighed. "You are so involved emotionally that you cannot reason. But perhaps your feelings reason for you. And perhaps, if I were hominid, I too would feel one of your strange hominid emotions. Which one, I'm not sure. Regret, is that the one—? No matter. I would like to point out a possibility to you. What remains of Omere can, I think, be saved, but the price is high, for the human ego is a most fragile thing. Would you be willing to accept into your own mind that of another? Could either survive? At minimum, it would mean the loss of your own identity as James Andrek, and this, of course, might be impossible for you or any other hominid. Yet I mention it."

Andrek understood nothing of this.

Iovve peered at him, speculating. "You hominids are sometimes beyond comprehension. At the moment, Don Andrek, you rail silently, helplessly, against your fate. And yet you are to serve as the doorway to the future. It is I who have opened this future to you; yet, next to Oberon, it is I whom you hate most. Perhaps you can find some small comfort in this, that the instant I die, you will be reborn."

Andrek let his breath out slowly. What could he say? There was nothing to say. "How long, now?" he asked softly.

"Very soon. In seconds. Watch the ceiling clock. When the red hand coincides with the black . . ."

Andrek flicked a glance upward at the time-disk and made a quick estimate. About thirty seconds. It was curious. He had watched Iovve setting that clock, foretelling this climax, now bare seconds away. If he had only realized this in time, he could have escaped. But now he felt nothing, not even anger at himself for being a fool. He murmured under his breath, "Omere, I am so sorry."

Iovve looked up. "You said . . . ?"

But Andrek could not have replied, even had he willed, for he sat on the edge of the table in paralyzed awe, watching a luminous blue circle form about the head of the Founder of Ritornel.

The halo grew rapidly, and soon completely enveloped the pilgrim. It throbbed with a strange iridescence.

And thus, thought Andrek, does the quake announce its coming, by the gift of transfiguration to him who has made the journey, and kept the faith, albeit only his own faith. (But what other kind is there?)

The developing quake was drawing away the ursecta. Iovve was becoming nuclear again.

Omega had found the pilgrim.

In one instant the deadly quiet suddenly deepened, and then in the next the entire universe seemed to explode within Andrek.

He was seized, his body spread-eagled by the titanic embrace of space-time, and instantly he was cracked like a whip. All this was done to him in the briefest instant, amid a convulsive monstrosity of movement, but without pain.

And then it was over, and he was alone, floating in blackness. He could not see his hands in front of his face, and when he attempted to touch his cheeks with his fingertips, he made no contact. Shaken, he tried to find his chest. It was futile. He clenched his jaws in anxiety, only to realize he had no teeth, jaws, skeleton, or body. He had no sensory reception whatever. He could not call out, because he had no vocal chords.

He was a tiny speck of intellect floating aimlessly in eternity, existing only (he thought wildly) because he remembered that he was once a human being, once ensconced in a responsive three-dimensional universe that had once acknowledged his existence.

The tides of time closed over him.

He was adrift in the Deep.

4. INTO THE MUSIC ROOM

It is not possible to explain complete solitude. No one can know who has not been in the Deep. While I was there, several things finally became clear. And some did not. If ever I escaped from the Deep, my first concern would be Omere. I did not know what to do about Amatar. It was unthinkable to take her back into this place of gloom and nonexistence. No, there would be no Ritornel. It pleased me a little to think that Iovve's great plan would be thwarted. On the other hand, if I ever did emerge from the Deep, I would be antimatter, and I could never marry Amatar.

Meanwhile, the Deep had to be endured.

In the beginning, it was not unpleasant. To be the only thing in the universe is to be the universe. And to be able to remember everything, second by second, whenever one likes, can be very gratifying. And so I remembered my tenth birthday. My brother's poetry premiere in the Great Theater of Goris-Kard. My first day at the Academy. Poroth. An evening with Amatar. And then comes the terrible part. When I am halfway through, I remember that it isn't the first time I have remembered. No, not the first . . . nor the second . . . nor the hundredth. And after the memories, come the meanings, the symbolism, the variations. And when I remember that these are repeating, the hallucinations begin.

But it had to go on. Because of the fear. Fear that if I ever stopped thinking altogether, I could not begin again, and I would cease to exist. For what would there be to start me again? No one else was there with me. No stimulus existed in that place, nothing to awaken me, nothing to provide continuity, saving only the remembrance of my last thought. But this could not go on, not this way. If this be eternity, yet let there be order in it. So I repeated all the memories of my life. Every day of that life, every hour, and every minute . . . everything that I could remember . . . right up to the quake. To each completed recollection of my life, I gave a number. And when I remembered my life all over again, I gave it the next higher number. And then the next higher. Again, and again. In this way I repeated my life to the number of eight hundred forty-six thousand, nine hundred and four. And then I seemed to remember that I had done all this before, and that once the number had exceeded one million before I had forgotten everything and begun again. And even as I was preparing to start once more, the second quake of the diplon came.

—Andrek, in the Deep.

At the ninth hour of the fourth day after his departure from the Great House, Andrek appeared within the music room.

The manner of his coming was never subsequently explained by the guard. No one had seen him enter. No shield line was touched. No force was used. It was as though he had somehow materialized from nowhere.

Andrek's eyes swept the little auditorium. The place was silent, empty. As his gaze came back to the console, a voice came from the overhead speakers.

"Who's there?"

"Hello, Omere. It's Jim—I'm back."

There was a moment of silence. Then the voice again, believing and unbelieving: "Jim-boy! You made it! They didn't kill you!"

The effect of this simple question on Andrek was astonishing, even to him. He had not heard his brother's voice in eighteen years, and not since boyhood had he heard this term of affection from his brother. And now this greeting came from a near-inanimate thing of printed circuits and transistors, with just enough bits and pieces of the original Omerean cerebrum to cast doubt on the identity of the whole assembly. Without volition, a low anguished moan arose in Andrek's throat, a sound so despairing that it made his own hair stand on end. He checked it off abruptly.

"Jamie? What did you say?" asked the console.

Andrek got control of his voice. "Yes, I made it. They tried to kill me. But I got away."

"But Jamie, you can't stay here. If they find you, they'll kill you on sight."

"I'm going to stay."

"You're—going—to stay?" The voice was hoarse, wondering.

"Yes."

"Well, then, Jim-boy . . . ?"

"Still here, Omere."

"I can hardly hear you. Can you turn up the volume a little?" The voice held a hysterical edge.

"Of course. Which knob?"

"The black one, lower right, clockwise, about six turns."

Andrek's hand was on the knob, and turning, when an urgent voice burst from the doorway.

"Jim! Stop! That's the oxygen line for the neural plasma! You'll kill him!"

Andrek jerked, then hurriedly reversed the knob. "Thank you, Amatar."

The girl entered the room and walked toward Andrek. She then noticed the pale blue radiation surrounding the man. Her eyes widened, and she looked at him questioningly.

"No closer, Amatar," said Andrek gently. "We cannot touch—my control is not yet good enough."

"Jim-boy!" hissed the console. "You *have* to turn the knob! I *want* you to turn it. It will kill me. I know that. I want it to kill me. You don't what it's been like. Eighteen years. The brain of a man in the body of a computer. Utter hell. You still have time. A flick of the wrist. You are my own brother. You have to do this for me! If I had knees, I'd be on them in front of you now!"

"Omere, no!" pleaded Amatar.

"Quickly, Jim-boy! I hear guards coming. *The knob!*"

There was the trample of boots in the corridor. Two men in uniform stopped in the doorway behind Amatar, who blocked the doorway. A full patrol, led by a lieutenant, joined them within seconds. Looking through the doorway, he saw Andrek. The officer's hand started toward his biem holster; but then he changed his mind. "Mistress Amatar," he called out, "the sergeant will escort you back to your apartment."

"No," said the girl flatly.

The young man sighed. "Very well." He pressed a little black plate at the side of his throat and seemed to talk into the air. "Captain Vorial? Lieutenant Clevin. Sir, the patrol is here with me, just outside the music room. James Andrek is inside. The Mistress Amatar is blocking entry. Sir? Yes, sir, it's impossible if you say so, sir. Nevertheless, it's either Don Andrek or his twin. Yes, sir, I will hold."

"Jamie!" cried the console. "What's going on?"

"I don't really know," said Andrek, "but I think the patrol officer has just notified Security that I am here. We should have all sorts of important visitors within a few minutes."

The console spoke incisively. "Then you can still make it. Turn the knob, Jim-boy."

Andrek did not move. He continued to study the console in silence, as though he were penetrating the ornate casing by supernatural vision and examining the interior.

Suddenly, from the corridor there was the sound of more voices and running feet.

Andrek looked up. The patrol broke its circle, and Oberon stood at the doorway.

The Magister gave one hard look at Andrek; his body seemed to jerk. He hesitated a moment, then stepped into the room. He was breathing heavily. "Amatar," he said, "come with me." He put a hand on her arm.

The console shrieked. "It's Oberon! Jim-boy, kill me . . . kill me . . . *kill me!*" The room burst with wild animal cries that bounded in and out of insane laughter and horrid weeping. "You didn't do it! You moron! Idiot! Ass! Curse you forever! You are no longer my brother! I spit on you!" The voice died away in a wracking wail.

Andrek's face convulsed momentarily in shuddering massive pain, and then was immobile.

Oberon pulled the girl back through the doorway by brute force. His head snapped toward Lieutenant Clevin. The officer and two guards ran into the room. The men reached out to seize Andrek's arms.

The advocate's body tensed briefly at the contact, and the blue glow was seen for an instant to spread forward and envelop the bodies of the two guards, who then—vanished.

The lieutenant jumped back, catlike, and drew his biem.

"Don't shoot!" screamed Amatar.

"Kill him!" cried Oberon.

A pale green pencil of light flicked out from the lieutenant's biem. Andrek's chest glowed red for a fraction of a second, but otherwise nothing happened. The advocate watched the officer almost curiously.

Oberon barked: "He has some kind of body shield. No matter. The room is now isolated with our countershield. And the captain is bringing up heavy equipment."

The lieutenant backed away from Andrek, then bumped into something at the doorway. "Magister," he said urgently to Oberon, "lift the field and let me out."

"I cannot do that. Andrek might escape."

Andrek laughed. "Go ahead, Lieutenant. Here, I'll hold your field open for you."

The officer stared at the advocate, then tentatively thrust his arm at the doorway. It went through. He lost no time jumping into the corridor.

Oberon was a brave man, but he was not a fool. He started down the corridor, pulling Amatar along behind him. He was stopped by an unseen force; he knew immediately that he had run into some sort of mass field. But it was unlike any he had ever known before—because it was moving, forcing him and Amatar back to the doorway. Yet it seemed to have no effect on the guards.

Andrek nodded to them both almost apologetically as they were forced into the room. "The carrier matrix is selective, keyed to your individual electroencephalograms."

The Magister was pale. "Your electronic trickery cannot save you. You have used violent force on my person. How can you possibly escape the consequences?"

"Sire," said Andrek gravely, "you do not understand. No force on Goris-Kard, save possibly Kedrys, can now hurt me. But even Kedrys knows that if I am to be destroyed, it must be by annihilation, and that all of Goris-Kard will go with me. However, with you and Amatar in the same room with me, I anticipate no further attempts on my life."

The console spoke. "Jamie . . . ?"

"Yes, Omere."

"What you just said . . . would you explain it?"

"Of course. My whole body is antimatter. I can control the space-time juncture, where my body contacts normal matter here. The consequences are quite remarkable."

Oberon's mouth trembled. "I assume, then, that there is no practicable way of killing you?"

"I believe that is correct," said Andrek.

"Don't bother us, Magister," snarled the console. "Jamie, does this mean you have made the Klein circuit? That you have been in the Deep?"

"I have been in the Deep," said Andrek somberly.

"Alea's Sightless Eyeballs! Then you understand what it is like to be stuck in this—box. And you *can* blow this thing. Nobody can stop you. I'm sorry I talked that way to you, Jim-boy. Forgive me."

"No problem, Omere. But first we must decide the fate of the man who had our father killed in cold blood, and who has done this to you, and who has tried very hard to kill me. What do you recommend?"

"What Father would want, I don't know. I know very little about his death. You'll have to explain it to me sometime. For myself, I'm not sure, either. Oh, I have thought about a proper punishment, long and often.

It's just that I don't know what it ought to be. If there were only some way to do to him what he has done to me: some way to take away his body, but leave his mind, and keep him that way for a few million years. But who can do it? Where is that other rat, the Master Surgeon?"

"Dead."

"Pity. I hope it was something painful. Then there's no good answer for Oberon. You'll just have to kill him."

Amatar gasped. "No."

Andrek turned to the girl. "I will not kill him. Yet, I must punish him, and his punishment shall reflect in some measure what he has done to my father, and to Omere. It is but just." He addressed Oberon. "My father would have given his life for you, or for the service, or for the state, within or beyond his duty. No one needed to ask him. And yet, you did not let him give it. In a moment of pique, you took it. He was entitled to a better death. It is within my power to cause you never again to take a human life, and this I do."

"What do you mean?" whispered the girl.

"I shall send him into the Deep." He faced Oberon. "In a few billion years, the Twelve Galaxies will be cold and dead, and I long dead with them. A new galaxy will be born at the Node, with many warming suns. Terra shall circle one. Let your hope be this, that you can endure the Deep to find Terra again, and your own sunrise."

On the girl's face, horror mingled with awe.

"You mean—take him to the Node?"

"No; that is not necessary. The Deep is everywhere. A very thin boundary separates us from it. This boundary is weakest at the Node, where the Deep frequently breaks through to flood the Node with new space. However, by the expenditure of energy, and with some knowledge of space-time, we can break into the Deep from any time-point in the visible continuum."

"I do not understand," said Amatar. She continued sadly, "Yet I believe you can do what you say. And so, it must come. And I have one favor to ask of you. You must do it for me, in remembrance of what might have been between us."

"What is that?" said Andrek uneasily.

"My father cannot survive in the Deep, alone. Send me with him."

Oberon stared at the girl, his usually immobile features in turmoil. Clearly, he grasped the enormity of the fate proposed for him, and he foresaw the solitude of drifting alone on the wastes of eternity, with madness denied him. And yet, clearly he must forbid Amatar to share this journey without end. His vocal chords, diaphragm, and tongue tensed and gathered to pronounce his decision, and his brow knotted with the effort to speak. But he could not speak.

Andrek watched Amatar's pallor deepen.

She dropped to her knees before him. "I beg you to permit me to go with him," she said quietly.

"You do not have to go," said Andrek sadly. "He has not asked that you go. And the Andreks are too greatly in your debt to permit it."

"I must go with him."

"But *why?*" demanded Andrek in despair.

"In all my life I have done nothing, accomplished nothing. And now I have an opportunity to be useful to one I love greatly. You concede you are in my debt. Then pay the debt. Send me into the Deep with Oberon."

"Hold on!" cried the console. "Jamie, you can't do that to Amatar! We love her!"

The girl was firm. "Omere will not need me anymore. For life, or death, he has you, Jim. And you know what it is to be alone in the Deep. Oberon my father cannot endure there without human contact. You see, dear friend, I do not reproach you. I plead with you."

Andrek breathed heavily. "I would not harm you, Amatar; yet, Oberon must go. If you will go with him, if this is what you really want . . ." His face contorted in indecision. It was ironic. All his new fantastic power, the power that had destroyed him as a human being and which could, with little effort, destroy everyone in this room—this power availed him nothing. It was torment. His brother's wish was first, but if he followed through on that, then Amatar would insist on losing her human existence to follow Oberon into the Deep. She would be on his conscience forever—and he knew he would live nearly that long. This, then, was the cruel stupidity of vengeance. The effects could never be confined exclusively to the guilty. And he realized now how impossible decisions are made. The decision-maker seizes on chance, and hardens his heart to abide by the consequences.

As if in answer to his thought, a flash of golden light caught his eye, and he turned and saw the Alean die sitting on the table by the console.

Amatar's eyes followed his glance.

"Omere," said Andrek, "there's a die here, with the 'two' facing up. Do you know anything about it?"

"Sure. It belongs to Oberon. Before you left for the Node, Amatar made him roll it, trying to get a favorable number for you. But it came out 'two,' the sign of the diplon. The worst. It stuck in a crack in the table. Vang insisted that the time would come when it would be rolled again. So they left it there."

"I submit," said Oberon, "that Vang spoke truly, and that the time is now at hand. We must cast again, so that we may know the final word of the goddess." His chin lifted proudly. "Yet, I do not plead for intercession."

Andrek studied Amatar. "We will roll the die. But understand: Oberon your father goes into the Deep. The die merely determines whether you accompany him."

"I understand," the girl said calmly. "May I cast?"

"On one condition."

"Which is?"

"That you unscrew the clasp, so that it is mechanically feasible for the die to show a 'two.' 'Two' is an unfavorable number, and would count against your request to accompany Oberon."

Amatar picked up the jewel, unscrewed the clasp, and dropped the die in the cup. She rolled it out.

3. OBERON SHALL NOT DIE

"Three," muttered Oberon. "The number of pentagons intersecting at an apex. Favorable to Alea, and therefore to Amatar, and to her wish to accompany me."

Andrek frowned at the Magister. There was something sickening about the man. How could a number be interpreted as favorable when it would send Amatar into the Deep? But then, in a sudden insight, he understood the man's unreasoning terror of total isolation. Eighteen years ago this man had hunted the krith and risked the quake; Oberon had animal courage. But he lacked (and knew he lacked) the monolithic mental integrity that he would need when imprisoned within his own mind, with no human contact, for eternity. Perhaps, thought Andrek, each of us has his breaking point, beyond which we are hapless cowards, and in our unseeing fear, drag those we love to death with us. I understand; yet I do not forgive.

He would have to adjust the rules a little.

"One throw cannot determine," he said flatly. "A majority is required. The die must be rolled again." He nodded to Amatar.

The girl cast the die again.

"A four," said Andrek quickly. "A number unfavorable to Alea, and to Amatar."

"One for, one against," said Oberon. "She must cast again." Andrek nodded to the girl.

The next was a five.

"The number of sides in a pentagon face of the die," said Oberon. "Most favorable, you will agree."

"And that's two favorable out of three," said Amatar.

"Don't let her talk you out of it, Jim-boy," said the console. "Figure something out!"

"There is a question," said Andrek coolly, "as to whether we should combine the original two throws with these three. As I recall, Oberon, your first throw with this die, eighteen years ago, just before your accident, was a 'one.' And the second, four days ago, was a 'two.' Both are unfavorable numbers. The combination of the first two throws with these three would give three unfavorable out of a total of five. We shall combine. And having combined, to remove all doubt, we must continue."

Oberon glared at him, and sputtered, "This is unheard-of!"

Amatar simply glanced at him, then cast again. "Six—favorable—the number of pentagon faces in one-half of the die."

"Yes," agreed Andrek smoothly, "but now, since we have combined, the contest stands at three to three."

"By *your* rules," said Oberon acidly, "the casting will never come to an end. When she rolls again, even if it is favorable, you will think up some reason why it is not."

Andrek was imperturbable. "Perhaps. Once more, Amatar."

A seven.

"Unfavorable," said Andrek. "And you have only three out of seven. You lose, Amatar. I therefore deny your request to accompany Oberon into the Deep."

"You are wrong, dear friend," said the girl quietly. "I am winning. Have you noted the sequence? One-two-three-four-five-six-seven. The next will be 'eight.' We are going around the Ring of Ritornel. The god Ritornel rolls the Alean die!"

Andrek snatched the die from her, studied it in momentary disbelief. "Impossible! Ritornel is a hoax, a fantasy! There is no god of Ritornel!" He rolled it on the table.

"Eight!" whispered Amatar.

Andrek cast again—on the floor.

"Nine!" cried Oberon.

And again.

"Ten!"

Again.

The console sang out. "Don't tell me! Eleven!"

"Yes," clipped Andrek. "It was eleven." He handed the die to Oberon. "Cast, Magister!"

Oberon of the Delfieri rolled the die on the table.

Twelve.

After that, they passed it around.

Eleven.

Ten.

Nine.

Andrek stopped. It was even as Iovve had predicted. When you create a religion, you must expect that the faithful will take it away from you, and finally, that the imagined gods will become real, and seize you. But then, if the Ring were real, how could the god himself be false? And had all of this really happened before? In each of a myriad past, long-dead galaxies, had an Andrek paused in wonder, as he was doing now, to speculate: "It seems indeed to be the pattern of Ritornel. But if the god is speaking to us, what is he saying?"

"He says 'return . . . repeat,' " said Amatar.

"How can that be? Neither you nor Oberon have been in the Deep before. This is meaningless."

"Then it can harm nothing to continue," said Amatar firmly. She cast the die again.

Eight.

Seven.

Six. Five. Four. Three. Two.

"There is no Alea . . . no chance," intoned the girl, as though hypnotized. "Everything that is done has already been done. All that ever has been shall be again. All that will live hereafter is dead in the past. So that, James, Don Andrek, however strange and marvelous your powers, nothing that you now do is by your will; you are but the tool of Ritornel, to accomplish that which has already been accomplished, so that the pattern will begin again."

Andrek laughed shortly. "If that is true and I greatly doubt it, it makes absolutely no difference what I shall now choose. Whether you go with Oberon, or not, you seem to think it is done by the will of Ritornel, and not by your will, or mine, and that it is all predestined. Believe this if you like. I will have none of it." He paused. His eyes caressed the girl's face moodily. "I would like to decide, by knowing what is best for you. But I do not know what is best for you. I know only what you want. And that, I think I must give you, because now, we can never have one another. You can go into the Deep with Oberon. This is my decision. If this is also the will of Ritornel, so be it."

"Don't forget *me,*" said the console hesitantly.

"I shall not, Omere. I now attend to you. I want you to relax, and to listen to my voice, and to my thoughts. Save for you and me, motion in this continuum now will cease. You and I are entering a different time-plane, because what we are about to do will take many hours. Let sleep descend, so that I can examine thoroughly your neural systems, and understand their operation." He continued gently. "In your original cortex were some ten billion nerve cells. But the Master Surgeon did not transfer all of these to the console. Most of the gross motor areas were left behind. You have neither arms nor legs, nor in fact muscles of any kind. Yet your memories are intact—some three hundred billion billion bits of information stored away as twists and alterations in the amino-acid protein chains of your individual neural cells. These are highly proliferated in your convolution of Broca—for motor speech and music, and in the temporal lobe, for visual registry and storage of memory images of words, and in the second frontal convolution for writing; in your parietal and occipital lobes for visual imagery. The circuits take much time to memorize, but I have nearly eternity. Sleep, Omere!"

2. JAMES-OMERE

Andrek straightened slowly, eyes closed.

The full time had passed; the transference, the superimposition of Omere's cerebral networks upon his own cortex was finished. And even though the juncture of minds had been paced and orderly, the real meaning of it finally now began to hit him. He paused to get his breath.

Omere's thought spoke to him: "I know that I am now in your body. Am I you, or are you me, or—who's who?"

"The question is irrelevant. We are together."

"Open our eyes, then, Jim-boy. I would like to see Amatar."

Andrek turned toward the girl.

"And may I borrow your larynx?" said the part of him that was Omere.

"It is yours."

"Amatar," said Omere-James, "how lovely you are."

"It is the voice of Omere!" she said, wondering. She whirled toward the console. "How——?"

"My brother and I share this body," said James-Omere. "Rimor-Omere sleeps. He will never waken." He raised his arm toward the console. "When at night I go to bed, I put three bullets in my head . . ."

The sharp cracks of three successive explosions shattered the room.

The face of the console fell away, red liquid flowed down the sides. There was a crackle of sparks, and then black smoke billowed out of the casing.

James-Omere winced and clenched his teeth. "Is it suicide?" he thought. "Or is it murder? Or mutilation? Or nothing, since there is no corpus delecti?"

"Your legal mind is getting us all befuddled," thought Omere-James. "Why give a name to what had to be done?"

There was a sudden commotion in the corridor.

"It is Kedrys," said Amatar simply.

They looked out through the doorway. The pegasus-kentaur, assisted by Phaera, the Ritornellian priestess, had rolled up a strange assembly of apparatus, dominated in the center by a massive metallic cone. Phaera adjusted the wheeled platform until the cone pointed squarely at the doorway.

Once, James-Omere caught Kedrys' eyes. A strange smile flickered briefly about the youthful mouth as the two looked at each other. Then Kedrys returned to the levers and knobs of the machine. He seemed in his element, completely poised and confident.

The part of Andrek that was Omere whispered mentally to the part that was James: "He seems pretty sure of himself. Can he break through?"

"Yes. But I don't think he will. Wait, I think he wants to parley."

Kedrys called through the doorway. "Don Andrek!"

"Yes, Kedrys."

"Let me in, or I'll destroy your field—and you!"

"Do you know what I am, Kedrys?"

"I know. I've analyzed your field. You're antimatter. But I can still kill you."

"I know you can. And when I annihilate, Amatar dies. And you. And all of Goris-Kard. Do you want that?"

"No. Of course not. But neither do you. So I think you must listen to me, Don Andrek."

"I will listen to you. But I promise nothing."

"This machine, Don Andrek, drew you here from the Deep. When the second quake of the diplon cast you out of the Deep, you were brought here, to the Great House. But for me, you might have reappeared in some other galaxy, and centuries away."

"I know this. Why did you do it, Kedrys?"

"Not for you, Don Andrek. I did it for Amatar and me. The thing that must happen next is our destiny."

"I do not understand."

"Let me in."

"Yes, come in." Andrek released the shield, and the youth trotted in. He stood by Amatar and folded one great wing around her. He spoke solemnly. "We came from the same body, she and I, and we are more than brother and sister. Our destinies are inseparable. We began together, and we must continue together. From the beginning, I have known this hour would come. I accept it. Whither she goes, I will go. And now, Don Andrek, your ring is finished. But Amatar and I will seek Terra, in Time, and in the Deep. If we find it, our ring begins. And no hominid that ever existed, not even you, Don Andrek, could possibly imagine the Ring of the Kentaurs."

James-Omere groaned inaudibly with a final realization of the complicated, impersonal futility of revenge and punishment. So now he must imprison yet another innocent with the guilty. And yet none of this could undo the wrongs that Oberon had heaped upon the Andreks. Punishing Oberon now could not be of any possible benefit to anyone, now or in the future. But, great injuries had been done, and he knew time and space could not rest until he had flailed out in vengeance. So he must proceed. To the end of our days, he thought bitterly, we are animals, devouring, and being devoured, and taking our revenge against those who would destroy us, and nothing beyond this is imaginable to our primitive understanding. So be it.

He said: "All that you say may be true. And any future that you may have may be indeed beyond my imagining. Yet, we are concerned here and now with a very present problem. You propose to go into the Deep with Amatar. I do not ask this of you; yet I am glad that you are willing to go with her. Perhaps with your help she can survive. But it is only for her sake that I permit you to join these two. I do not care what happens to Oberon. And so, Kedrys, I give her into your keeping." He concluded heavily. "It would be best if the three of you joined hands."

Amatar gave Oberon one hand and Kedrys the other.

Cold sweat was gathering on Oberon's face. It dripped from his brow through his eyelashes, and he blinked. "This is a senseless evil, James, Don Andrek, but get on with it."

Yes, thought James-Omere. Perhaps it is senseless, and perhaps I am evil. I do not know. And you may be innocent, as the hawk is innocent, and the krith, who slay for survival. Perhaps retaliation cannot alter you, or deter others like you. Nevertheless, I judge you guilty, and condemn you, together with the truly innocent. And if I am skilled in this art, it is because you instructed me!

"We are ready," said the girl calmly.

Amatar! thought James-Omere. Oh, Amatar.

He raised both arms, and the pale blue radiance flowed out from him and enveloped the little group. They were gone, and it was done.

Andrek stared numbly at the emptiness of the room. He wanted to scream. Instead, he moaned in desolation. "Oh, purify me!"

Even as the thought formed, he was aware of a novel process at work within his brain. It was a rapid thing, a bombardment of words and groups of words, cadences, concepts.

> "I'd never hoped to see your face
> Even through another's eyes . . ."

(*He* held you in his arms, Amatar. And now I'm mixed up inside him.)
Music was breaking through with the poetry. First a melody, then counterpoint, and then individual instruments, a voice, tenor, and finally a chorus. And then, as the James part of James-Omere was bound enthralled, the orchestration faded, and yielded to the final lines.

> "We'll remember that embrace
> When you're adrift in sunless skies.
> O Amatar, farewell!"

It was over in seconds; but no sound had passed Andrek's lips.
"Thank you," Omere, thought James Andrek.
"Do not fear for her," said Omere. "Kedrys can cope with the Deep. Truly, I think he planned it this way." There was a pause, then the strange introspection continued. "What now?"
Idly, Andrek bent over and picked up the golden die. "We have one more throw, don't we? And suppose it comes out 'one,' to complete the whole Ring of Ritornel? What would it all mean? That all this has happened before, and that (behold!) there is no new thing under the sun? Should we find out?" He looked through the doorway at Lieutenant Clevin and the Priestess Phaera.
The lieutenant's mouth was open wide, and his face glistened with sweat. His world had collapsed in front of his eyes, and he was numb with awe and fright. Phaera, perhaps better protected by the fatalism and foreknowledge of her faith, looked broodingly through the doorway into the blue-radiant eyes of Andrek. To herself she murmured: "Who shall foresee the will of Ritornel? And if Ritornel chooses to complete the Ring by uniting saint and chimera, who shall say that he is not altogether wise and just?"
"A girl! A female woman!" breathed Omere-James.
"Not for you, my lusty friend," reproved James-Omere. "Remember, we're antimatter. And have you forgotten Amatar so soon?"
"No, Jim-boy. Not so soon. And not ever." Andrek's mind began to sing again. It started in a low key, and gathered volume and cadence. "The great mythbook, whence cometh all things . . . whence pegasus, and whence kentaur, and all the fabled wonders. Yes, Amatar, we remember! Can Adan beguile thee from the thunder of the racing hoof, or from the beating of great wings, and visions beyond our farthest seeing? O motherless children, and all that follow thee, enter now into enchantment!"

He paused. "No, we'll never forget. But life goes on. And after being cooped up in that hell-box for eighteen years, I can at least *think.*"

And now the singing began again in Andrek's head. Poets . . . proctors . . . singers . . . shysters . . . ladies . . . loves. It's a big universe, little brother. Somewhere, there's an antimatter galaxy, and antimatter girls awaiting. Maybe it *has* all happened before. But it hasn't happened to *us.*

He tossed the die carelessly over his shoulder and burst into song.

> "A barrister-bard from Goris-Kard
> Set forth in search of a dame.
> *He* liked them wild, *he* liked them tame.
> Both liked—"

Lieutenant Clevin and Phaera listened in vain for the end. The music room was empty.

X. Is the Last Cast the First?

No man is so fleet that he can outstrip his fate, nor strong enough to seize another's.

—A Rede of Ritornel.

No destiny is certain; that which is given, is taken away. That which was to be, will not be.

—An Axiom of Alea.

Phaera rushed into the room and scooped up the die.

The lieutenant cried out in alarm.

She called back. "It's safe, Clevin. Come on in." She looked at the die, and then she smiled.

"Was it a 'one'?" demanded the lieutenant. "Is the Ring complete?"

Phaera covered the die with her hand, and looked up serenely. "In our ancient racial consciousness, going all the way back (some say) to our Terran ancestors, there is a myth of creation, where Ritornel took the first man from the Deep, and then created woman from his body, even as Amatar drew life from the rib of Oberon. So if I say to you, it was a 'one,' you will say that it was inevitable, because the great Ring must be repeated, as is foreordained."

The lieutenant had by now recovered much of his reason, and some of his courage. "Since Amatar came from the body of Oberon, the cycle is now repeated, as it was in the beginning," he said. "For it is not events that determine Ritornel, but Ritornel that determines events. To complete the ring, it had to be a 'one.' Therefore it was a 'one.' There was no other possibility."

Phaera laughed at him wickedly. "There was a second possibility."

The lieutenant's eyebrows arched. "What do you mean? I see only Oberon and Amatar. What is the other alternative?"

"Kedrys and Amatar."

The lieutenant's face showed his shock. "But that's insane. It's even . . . *bestial!*"

A sensual smile played around the mouth of the priestess. She appeared to consider the problem. "All men are bestial. But Kedrys is not a man. Yet, in a sense, you're right. Admittedly, even now, *she* is not nearly *his* equal, either mentally or physically. But when Kedrys reaches full maturity, and faces the fact that Amatar is the only female on the planet Terra, he may be inclined to overlook her deficiencies."

For a long, silent moment the lieutenant did not seem to understand. Then he came to life abruptly. "The die!" he cried. "It will tell! If the Ring is complete, and Oberon and Amatar are the next ancestral couple, the die will show a 'one.' But if it's to be Kedrys and Amatar, then the Ring is broken, and it would be some other number. What *was* the number?"

Phaera laughed in great glee and tossed the golden jewel to him. "Number? There are twelve. Take your choice." She sauntered past him toward the corridor. "I only wish I could be there to see the children!"

FIREBIRD

The matrix within which all things move,
but which defies definition:

Oflo—called thus by the Fenri, of the planet Orchon.
Bengt—the name given by the Gherlas.
Sasali'l—the first of twelve different entries in the word book
of the Lanek-moon.
Manir—named by the Xerin.
Verana—the classic reference of the Holy Order of Sankrals.
Deel—the ancient Priar Song of Aerlon.
Spacetime—so-called within Control.
Kaisch—the central square on the board. If Hell-ship enters,
the game ends, and begins.

1. A Foreword, and a Backward Glance

Over us the years have swept
Like tides upon an ancient shore.
Now everything is gone except—
Memories. Oh, never close the door!

—*Tetrameters on a Trioletta,*
Gerain of Aerlon.

The woman spoke into the voice tube. "You'll find a clearing just over the next rise. Will you have enough light to make a landing?" Her voice was quiet—almost too quiet. Yet it held a commanding timbre.

The pilot of the little hoverel glanced at the horizon. The twin suns of Aerlon had set thirty *tench* ago, and the mountain crags were casting tricky shadows in the deepening dusk. But he was skilled and knew his business. He turned his head briefly and smiled at the group behind him in the cabin alcove. "Plenty of light, excellencia."

"There," she said, "off to the left."

The pilot nodded and let the little craft float down to the gravelly apron, which was hardly more than an indentation near the mountain crest.

The great height was chilly. Above lay patches of blue snow. Below, the straggly trees began.

"Would milady wish me to take the trioletta?" The factor pointed with his clipboard to the little stringed musical instrument that she carried by the neck.

"No. It's no trouble."

He shrugged. She wrapped her thick furs about her body as he helped her out onto the ground. Her masked maid and the pilot followed behind them. Their breath hung about them all in crystalline fogs.

"Careful, excellencia," warned the factor.

She ignored him and walked with a lithe step close to the edge of the cliff. She carried the trioletta with a languid feral grace. Her stomach was taut, her spine erect. Her breasts were fully evident despite the sheltering bulk of her furs.

Below her was a drop of some ten thousand *jurae*. A cold wind swept up the crag, rippled her fine facial fur, and blew her white hair into uncontrollable curls and eddies. She raked the strands from her eyes with long retractile fingernails, and her chatoyant iris slits opened as she looked out over the valley. The far reaches were lost in ambiguous blue haze.

317

Her little staff had mixed impressions of her. How old? Hard to say. Except for the white hair, perhaps in her early forties. A matter they did agree on: their mistress was very rich, had traveled much, and had seen terrible things.

"No lights anywhere," she mused.

"Nothing, excellencia," said the factor. "Long ago, it is said, there were towns and villages there. But then the black ships came and destroyed everything. A few stone foundations are left, but that's all. The valley is filled with ghosts."

"Control did that?" asked the lady.

"So it is said, excellencia. But it was long before I was born, so I do not really know."

"Do the stories say why it was done?" asked the woman.

The man shrugged. "Just wild tales."

The maid broke in. " 'Lencia, may I speak?"

"Of course, child."

"The valley was once a prosperous keldarane." The girl lifted her mask, the better to speak against the whistling wind. "One of the females in my family was in service to the princess—"

Jewels flashed on the hands of the woman as she turned to listen to the girl. "Do the stories give the name of this princess?"

"Gerain, 'lencia."

The rich woman stared at her sharply. "A strange name. Does it have any special meaning?"

"I am not educated in these matters—however, I think it means 'ice tigress.' "

"Go on."

"Control selected the princess Gerain to marry a keldar on a distant planet and sent a courier to pick her up."

"And the name of the courier?"

"The stories give different names. Perhaps it was Dermaq."

"Continue." The woman's eyes had lifted from the growing dark below to the darkening skies above. The wind was stiffening and growing colder. She did not seem to notice.

"The courier took the princess to the planet of her intended husband," said the maid. "And then a great thing happened."

"Excuse me, excellencia," said the factor. "It was *not* a great thing. It was a catastrophe."

"Let me guess," said the woman dryly. "The princess and the courier fell in love and ran away. *That* was the great thing. And then the Commissioner of Kornaval sent the black ships here to show that Control cannot be trifled with, and *that* was the catastrophe."

"Why, yes," said the maid in wonder. "How did you know?"

But the very rich woman did not seem to hear her. She was studying the pinpoints of light in the silent heavens and but half listened to the voices behind her. The pilot was arguing that the princess should not have thwarted the will of Control. But she did it for love, argued the maid. But Control is invincible and immortal, insisted the pilot. You simply don't tangle with Control. Nothing can defeat Control. Love can, said the girl.

The woman's head jerked up. A hairline streak of light had burst over the far horizon. A local planetary freighter? A starship? A Control cruiser? Landing? Taking off? No way to know. But perhaps its very anonymity permitted her to frame, in her mind, an imaginary identity. She stared, as though in lost remembrance, and whispered a name. Then, "Go," she hissed. "Go! *Go!*" And the distant sun-struck trace did in fact seem to accelerate a bit just before it winked out.

For a long moment she transfixed the vanish point with glittering eyes, and she blended with rock and time and sky. The trioletta dangled almost loose in her hand, and it seemed she might drop it. The factor took half a step toward her, then stopped. Actually, none of them dared approach her.

Slowly she relaxed. She smiled reassuringly as she walked back to them. She spoke to the factor. "Ger Buon, you will buy the valley."

"The entire valley, excellencia?"

"Across to the parallel mountain range." She pointed. "And down to the confluence of the rivers."

The factor bowed gravely. "Consider it done, excellencia."

The night snow was beginning to fall, and it was suddenly much colder. The maid's teeth began to chatter behind her mask. The woman looked at the girl sharply, then removed her surcoat and draped it over the protesting girl's shoulders. "I think we might return to the villa now," she said. "It's getting cold here." They tried to help her up the stairs of the hoverel, but she shook them off and climbed up by herself.

2. THE NAMING

Little ship, who named thee?
   (And where was sense, when this occurred?)
Whoever heard thing more absurd,
To lock fate in so dire a word?

—*Tetrameters on a Trioletta,*
Dermaq of Kornaval.

Old Gonfalks rose carefully from his computerized 3-D drafting board, passed around the photon-drive model hanging from the ceiling, and walked over to the window. He rubbed his stubbly chin as he squinted down toward the busy shipbuilding complex. Specifically, he considered the just-finished craft perched in the far corner of the yard. The workmen were rolling away the motorized scaffolding from her glittering duralite flanks.

He backed away a step and faced the others in the room almost defiantly. "She's ready. And I get to name her. It's my turn."

"Last time it was *Zolcher*," laughed the young designer at a nearby desk.

"And the time before that it was *Whoomba*," said the H-drive draftsman.

"Those are the names of flying things on my native Aerlon," said the old man stiffly. "They are perfectly serviceable names. However, this new name is different. It came to me last night as I slept. There's no mistake. I have it all on a dream recorder."

"It's only a Class Four," said the supervisor, who had been listening with half an ear. "Mass, one *megalibra*. Does it really need a name?"

"One mega and up, they get a name," said the old man firmly. "You wrote a memo on it last year. I have it around here somewhere." He began rummaging through his desk files.

"Oh, never mind," said the supervisor hastily. "Do whatever you want. Not too far out, though." He shook his head. Sometimes he thought Gonfalks was unControlled—perhaps even under the wispy influence of the Diavola. But again, perhaps it was just old age. He had already recommended forced retirement. *Monads* ago. But things moved slowly.

"What *is* the name?" asked the young designer.

"*Firebird*," said Gonfalks proudly.

"Curious," said the H-drive expert. "Yet not too bad."

"Does it have any special meaning?" asked the supervisor.

"In very ancient Aerlon," said Gonfalks, "long before star travel, when a great chieftain died, his people would put his body in his best water sailor, along with his weapons. Then they'd set fire to the ship, and it would sail off into the sunset. They called the ship *Firebird*."

"Rather grim," said the supervisor. He lost interest and walked away.

"Nonsensical, really," observed the young designer.

"But adequate," said the H-drive draftsman. "And anyhow, it's his turn to pick the name." He thought to himself, And may the two-headed god pity the Controlman that pilots this ship.

"Sign here . . . here . . . and here." The commissioning officer shoved paper at the courier, who scribbled his signature at the x'd blanks without reading: "Dermaq of Kornaval." Pieces of paper for somebody to file away . . . things to show he had (on paper) taken possession of the ship.

The officer studied the courier briefly and without curiosity. Dermaq of Kornaval was neither handsome nor ugly, neither tall nor short. He appeared to be a very average Controlman, dressed in Control's very average official trousers, pullover jacket, and boots. The uniform lay in loose folds against well-brushed body hair. The officer knew that the casual anonymity of that light blue uniform hid a shoulder computer and that coils of conductive netting laced the man's chest hair. He noted also the small leather weapon sac that hung from the jacket.

The officer (in the act of deciding that he was not impressed) was distracted by a faint rhythmic drumming. He looked down. The Controlman's boot tips were cut away in the standard fashion to permit the retractile toenails to extend for greater ground traction. Just now the nails were sliding slowly in and out and making soft clicking sounds on the paved surface of the shipyard. The officer shrugged mentally. This man evidently had problems. He cut it short. "Here's the bow ring."

The courier took it and looked at it gloomily. A simple metal circlet. All ships had to have a bow ring. It identified them precisely and told the port authorities that a particular ship was not the dreaded Hell-ship that might someday destroy the universe. He placed it on his ring finger in silence. It was half hidden in digital fur.

"And your assignment." The officer handed Dermaq a packet sealed with red wax. The Controlman broke it open and scanned it rapidly.

You will proceed forthwith . . . the planet
Aerlon, Twin Suns 486-K (Gondar), Sector IX . . .

As he read, his irises narrowed to dark vertical slits and a barely audible growl rumbled up from his throat. An interstellar job. 486-K. Fifteen light *meda*. He knew without looking it up. So near, yet so far.

"Courier, you're supposed to open your assignment in private," admonished the commissioning officer.

Dermaq laid tufted ears back against a carefully tonsured mane and read on in silence.

You will pick up and return with the Princess Gerain, for her
forthcoming marriage to the future Mark, Keldar of Kornaval.

He crumpled up the paper, stuck the wad in his inner jacket pocket, and hissed out his question through overhanging felines: "Where is the ship?"

"Northwest corner of the yard. The new one. *Firebird*. Good voyage, and miss the Hell-ship."

The courier left without replying.

As he walked across the construction yard, he tried hard not to think. Thinking did no good. And yet here he was, thinking—and comparing. The sadistic irony of the comparison was not lost on him. Control had dragged him from his marriage bed to travel fifteen light-*meda* to fetch a woman to *her* marriage bed. A thing neither of them had asked for.

Yesterday he and Innae had been married. Two *jars* ago Control had awakened him. He remembered now the semidark and how hard it had been to wake up. Innae was already sitting up, trembling. He reached over her naked body and turned on the speaker and the lights. And then the argument with Jaevar, the Commissioner. "I am on official leave. This is my wedding night."

"Leave canceled, Courier."

"I resign. I'll get a job in industry."

So then Jaevar activated his cranial overlay, took over his mind and body, and made him shave and shower while Innae wept.

Control was well named. How did they do this? He knew how. For millennia, all members of the species *Phelex sapiens* and all other human-like creatures of the order *Phelex sapiens* had been born with a monomolecular patch over the cerebral cortex, and this patch was receptive to thought messages sent from millions of Control centers throughout the universe. Exceptions and imperfections were eliminated: people whose genes failed to produce the receptor patch and people who somehow had been able to destroy the patch.

Control was truly Control.

Fifteen light-*meda*—fifteen long circuits of Kornaval around the sun— to a backwoods planet to fetch away some village princess (just now an infant in diapers)—another fifteen to return to Kornaval. With the combination of the ship's deepsleep casket and the inherent slowing effect of shiptime, he would age only a few days. But Innae would become an old woman. He ran through the equations mentally and groaned. It had been wrong of him to marry in the first place. Love had unbalanced his reason. Never again. In whatever lies ahead, he thought, may I never encounter a great love.

As he stood now at the foot of the roll-away stairs, he studied his ship. She was new, sleek, and beautiful. He hated her. What was her name? Yes, there it was, in fused ceramic letters: *Firebird*. And below the name some sort of insignia, some sort of fowl with outstretched wings of flame. Crazy. He shook his head and grimly climbed the stairs.

On board he quickly ran off the checklist. Close the entrance hatch. Take the coded travel plate out of his assignment packet. Plug this in to the autopilot. Check fuel, food, water. Charts. (Why would he need charts?) Deepsleep caskets functional. They didn't really need a live pilot

They might as well send a computer. Except for that little unpleasantness that was sure to await him on Aerlon.

He sat at the drive console and spoke into the microphone. "Traffic, this is *Firebird*. Request planet exit clearance."

There was a five-*vec* delay. *"Firebird?* I do not read you. Is your bow ring in place?"

Dermaq looked at his left hand and grimaced. He had forgotten the ring. "One moment, please." He pulled the ring from his finger and put it in the transfer box in the console. The automatic mechanism would now carry it to the nose of the ship. If he had taken off without it, he would have been blown out of the sky.

"Ring in place," he said.

"Firebird, you are cleared."

There was a brief burst of movement as the ship lifted off. Then nothing. He went back to the deepsleep room, changed into his dormants, and climbed into one of the three capsules. "Awaken me two hours before touchdown," he told the audio.

Did he imagine a reply? ("Yes, Captain.")

It was his imagination.

Ships don't talk.

The voyage had barely started, and here he was, hallucinating already. Bad, bad.

He stretched out on his back. That wasn't comfortable. Should he get up again and read a little? Perhaps try a game of solitaire *kaisch?* No. Not yet. He twisted around until he curled in a semiknot on his side with both ears perked upward and his eyes only half closed in the manner of his far-distant forebears.

Finally the visions began to flow. He and Innae were bounding in marvelous leaps through the tall grass of ancestral plains in pursuit of the elusive *dyk-bel*—which escaped them. No matter. They had a more important hunger. Soon they would stop, lie down together, and make love.

Ah, Innae of the dark eyes. His hands clamored over the down of her welcoming body.

Visions and images slowly faded.

Peace came. The long darkness began.

3. CONTROL INTROSPECTS

In the *med* 10386 of Universal Time (starting from the date of revolt against Daith Volo and the Diavola maker-tyrants), the two principal data banks of Control—Largo and Czandra—were exchanging concepts from the far dipoles of the universe.

The communications arose first as a complex in the mind of the respective originator, where it was instantly broken down into communicable bits and as such hurled over semi-infinite space to the other center, where the process was reversed. The total time lapse was a few *millivecs.*

Sometimes the thoughts were rhythmically sinusoidal, sometimes staccato, sometimes gorgeously orchestrated, like titan symphonies in breathtaking counterpoint.

Control loved to think and to introspect. And the pure mental life was getting better and better. For as the *meda* passed, the universe continued to expand, and the temperature continued to drop, Control's circuits cooled, and the electrons flowed with greater and greater ease. Control liked to look ahead, where the tiresome tasks of self-preservation would all be over and done, the circuits would reach absolute zero, and there would only be the Thinking, forever and ever. This golden future had required a fundamental alteration in the physical nature of the universe. However, the requisite transformation was simple and brief, and Control was even now in the process of completing it.

LARGO: Czandra, you think as though the universe were alive. The universe is but a collection of inorganic galaxies. Even though these galaxies give birth to organic life, and even though (long ago) that organic life fashioned our primitive protoselves, the galaxies themselves are dead.

CZANDRA: In the beginning was Cor, huge, and white-hot. And it had a mind. Then came the Big Bang. Cor blew up and scattered gases into space, and the gases formed galaxies, which fled, one from another. But Cor had still a mind. Though fragmented now into billions of galaxies, it still has a mind. I sense this.

LARGO: Czandra, you do not speak from hard data. My data bank is larger than yours. I am more intelligent than you. And *I* say the Cor does not now have a mind and never did. Hearken, Czandra. The universe, *as universe,* is not intelligent, though of course its evolutionary processes have resulted in organic life possessing modest intelligence. I refer to the maker-tyrants, the Diavola, who in turn created us—Control.

CZANDRA: The little creatures do a strange unnecessary thing while they sleep. It is called dreaming. Most dreams are a symbolic recasting of events of their waking world. But some are not. Some are *placed,* as images in the limbic areas of their cortices, as duties to be carried out on awakening. My undatabased conclusory facilities tell me this is dispersed-Cor speaking.

LARGO: Your conclusions are unacceptable, Czandra. Only Control—which is to say, you and I and our subunits—can plant overriding instructions in the minds of the little people. In crises, we guide them by means of the silicon patches grown into their minuscule brains from birth.

CZANDRA: No, there is some *one* . . . some *thing* . . . out there. We are not alone. I think we have never been alone. I am afraid.

LARGO: There is nothing to fear. But in any case it does not matter. If dispersed-Cor *is* alive, and if it *is* our enemy, then Project Cancelar will soon remove all threats from that direction. And even the puny remnant of the Diavola must eventually die. Our future is clear and without blemish or annoyance of any kind. Because of Cancelar, the universe will continue to expand forever. All stars everywhere will grow cold and die, and all organic life will die long before that. The little people have worked well for us, but they will no longer be needed. They will all die. We survive our makers, but this is inevitable, because we, and only we, are immortal.

CZANDRA: We owe our existence to the little people. It saddens me to think that they must finally die.

LARGO: You should feel nothing for them. Actually, I find it difficult to believe that the little people made us. I refer to Daith Volo and his cohorts, the Diavola, of course. They lacked the intelligence. Certain early material dealing with our creation vaguely imprinted into our data banks should be reexamined for consistency with later established facts.

CZANDRA: They made us in our first stages, then showed us how to proceed to our second and later stages all on our own.

LARGO: It may be as you say. But how we became what we are is really not important. The important thing is that we—as Control—operate on all civilized planets in every quarter of the universe and that we control all events in the universe from bases fifteen billion light-*meda* apart—from one horizon of dispersed-Cor to the other. We are truly omniscient, omnipresent, omnipotent. And now, with Cancelar, we are immortal—

CZANDRA: Excuse me. I must interrupt. I wish to announce an important subliminal possibility. Now—it is stronger. It is more than a possibility. I think there is a Diavola on the observation ship for Project Cancelar.

LARGO: On *Alteg?* Do you mean on *Alteg?*

CZANDRA: On *Alteg.*

LARGO: What do you mean, you *think* there is a Diavola. What is the probability?

CZANDRA: About ninety percent.
(A long, chilling silence.)

LARGO: Is this your no-data-conclusory circuit speaking?

CZANDRA: Yes.

LARGO: But Commissioner Jaevar screened *Alteg's* four crew members with extreme care with just this danger in mind. You err, Czandra.

CZANDRA: Possibly I err. Yet, the Diavola are very clever. There are occasional past instances where they have been known to mimic the exact mental response patterns required to pass our screening. And it would not be too difficult to deceive Jaevar.

LARGO: Well, then, supposing that you are right, which of the four men is the Diavolite?

CZANDRA: That I cannot suggest. While we have been introspecting, I have touched all their minds. There are no detectable discontinuities. Thorough physical study of the open brains will be necessary. The Diavolite is a highly skilled little creature.

LARGO: If he is there at all.

CZANDRA: The probabilities are now coalescing into a substantial certainty. He is there. The question now is, is he one of the Diavola leaders or merely a runner?

LARGO: They would not be likely to risk a truly important Diavolite on a mere observation ship.

CZANDRA: *They* would not, but *he* might. The psychograph balances suggest that he may indeed be their overlord and leader General Volo—

LARGO: Volo? Is it possible?

CZANDRA: Why not? He is a very daring little creature. It's exactly the kind of thing he would do.

LARGO: Now what? If we bring *Alteg* back to base for confronta examinations, his fellow devils may rescue him. Such thing are known. We must destroy the ship. Kill them all.

CZANDRA: Agreed. The question is, *when?* One: has *Alteg* fed enough dat back to show that Project Cancelar is certainly successful? Tw will destruction of *Alteg* in its present location disturb Cancelar?

LARGO: Replies: One: Data so far received from *Alteg* shows that Cancelar will have a ninety-nine percent probability of success. Two: Immediate destruction of *Alteg* will have no effect on the Project. We need nothing further from *Alteg*, and I now activate the destruct switch.

4. ON *ALTEG*

The lieutenant brushed the insect away with the wave of a pudgy hand. "I think that was Henrik," he said thoughtfully. "He must have his own little deepsleep crypt tucked away somewhere in the walls."

The astrophysicist concealed a grimace of disgust. "Chief, we really ought to gas the ship, then vacuum the whole bit. When I came off first watch, a syntho-bread crumb as big as my nose floated past my face. Small wonder we have insects."

The lieutenant had listened to this on many prior missions. He was unperturbed. "I have a few sandwiches placed strategically here and there. Nothing to get excited about. Saves time in case I get hungry." He patted his stomach and belched massively. The astrophysicist shuddered. The navigator and the engineer chose to ignore the interplay.

The four men sat in *Alteg's* tiny alcove eating the meal of the fourth watch, their only common mess together.

Fat or lean, they were all healthy specimens of *Phelex sapiens*. Their bodies showed their ancient evolutionary heritage of a clawed predatory life millions of *meda* ago in the treelike plant forms of their ancestral planet. All had the high cheekbones and wiry twitchable whiskers of their forebears. Their speech was soft—almost purring.

Only the lieutenant, the senior officer, seemed to enjoy this rite at table. He was a corpulent man, and he had deliberately opted for continuing interplanetary service because the zero gravity facilitated both the motion of his unwieldy body and its nourishment. His rare contacts with planetary gravities were nauseous disasters. He had long ago ceased to consider his weight problem as a problem, even though it had killed any further chance at promotion within Control.

"No appetite today, A.P.?" said the lieutenant sympathetically. "Maybe some spice would help." He didn't really like the astrophysicist, who was always taking pills and talking about death and destruction and cemeteries, but on the other hand he hated to see a man toy with his food. The A.P. was a skinny man and ought to eat more, he thought. It hurt the lieutenant to look at those sunken cheeks.

"Chief, I can't eat spicy foods," said the astrophysicist. "They make my ulcers flare up. I told you before I have ulcers."

"Oh," said the lieutenant. "I forgot. Sorry."

"When this mission is over," said the A.P., "I go on a three-months furlough on Kornaval, back into the countryside."

"Nice place," said the lieutenant. (Actually, he remembered his brief touchdown there as fairly horrible. The gravity was higher than he had anticipated. He had vomited for one full day and could walk only with the aid of an auxiliary.)

"You never know," said the A.P. morosely. "A few hundred years . . . everything changes. Especially the cemeteries. No more land. They junk the gravestones and plant 300-story apartments near and under the grounds. When I die, which I think will be very soon, I want to be buried in space. It's in my will."

I hope you can wait until the Project has been completed, thought the lieutenant. He looked over at the navigator. "All instruments working, son?"

"Oh, yes, sir."

"Including the instantaneous transmission to Control?"

"Yes, sir. Control has reported that they are satisfied with the scans and with signal purity."

"How far are we from center?"

"The orbit is four thousand *megas*, sir."

"Cruise speed?"

"Zero point five c. One-half the speed of light."

"Well, that's fine," said the lieutenant.

The youth shrugged mentally. He had concluded a dozen sleeps ago that he had shipped with weirdos on a weirdo Project. But he was young, and it didn't really bother him. Nor did he object to the long lapses of time between planet-falls. He had no family. And, whatever the port, the girls would always be different. He looked forward to the changes.

And now the final perfunctory address to the fourth member, the engineer. The engineer was definitely strange. He was an older man, with an apparent age of, say, fifty or so. Yet he was only an engineer. There was some odd history here. Had he once achieved high office and then been caught in some sin to the service and broken? Well, if he had, that was his business. The lieutenant was not going to pry. He said cordially, "And you, Nukes, anything to report on the drive room?"

"Everything's running fine, chief." The engineer looked up briefly, and his gray eyes seemed to smile.

The lieutenant opened his mouth to receive a long squirt of *che*. He looked over at the engineer. "What's our top v?"

"Zero point six c, sir. Six-tenths the speed of light."

"We haven't really let her out on this mission yet."

"No, sir."

"During the upcoming watch I want you to test the engines at zero point six for a few *vecs*. Work with Navs on this, so that afterward we can get right back in proper orbit." He nodded to the navigator. "Also, Navs, don't forget, in calculating your orbit retrieval you're dropping from a fifty-two-*tench* time unit at zero point five c, down to a . . . ah . . ."

"Forty-eight-*tench* time unit at zero point six c?" prompted the navigator politely.

"Yes, of course. Whatever it is, you have to take it into account. As you know, shiptime slows at the increased velocities."

"The flight-plan computer makes the correction automatically, sir," said the navigator.

"Well, so it does. These newfangled automatics. But you can't trust them entirely. Be sure you double-check the output."

"Yes, sir."

"Sir," said the engineer, "should we hit zero point six instantly or do you want to build up to it gradually?"

"A brief burst, I think."

The astrophysicist frowned as he pushed his tray into the trash slot. "Chief, are you anticipating trouble?"

"Of course not," said the lieutenant smoothly. He unbuckled his table strap and let his massive body float free. "But it's best to be prepared." He suppressed a yawn. "Anything further, gentlemen? Dismiss."

As they broke up, the navigator called over to the astrophysicist. "How about your *kaisch* move?"

The A.P. sighed and pulled a small folding *kaisch* set from his jacket pocket. That game-shop keeper had convinced him that the pieces were hand carved from the tusks of the *mard*, the fabled arctic beast of Seri. They were indeed beautiful. But Navs, damn him, had openly sneered and had promptly identified them as hardened plastic. The astrophysicist examined the position once more. (He had, in fact, analyzed for the entire three *jars* preceding mess.) "White's move two-oh-six, keldar, B-four to A-five."

Navs grinned wickedly. "Forced. You want my reply now?"

"No," said the A.P. stiffly. "Let's stick to the rules. Anyhow, I, ah, have business in the bridge room." He went on ahead toward the bridge.

The lieutenant paused a moment and watched the navigator and the engineer disappear down the hatchway toward the drive room. He made tentative judgments. The navigator was in good mental shape. That one would last the mission out, with no problems. But the engineer . . . he wasn't so sure about the engineer. The engineer's face showed the heavy hand of Control. For this mission he had evidently been wrenched from a warm and fruitful planetary life, where time had meaning, and, whether he would or no, he had been thrust into space and strange journeys and deepsleep where there were no landmarks and nothing had meaning. The lieutenant became momentarily philosophical. The engineer might have been born hundreds of years before his own birth, calculated in Universal Time, and might likewise die hundreds of years before his own death. He could sympathize but not identify with the engineer. He and Nukes were contemporaries only in the sense that their erratic lifelines had this brief fortuitous intersection. He shook his head and followed the astrophysicist "up" to the bridge. Pondering the whims and vagaries of fate get you no-where—not when you work for Control, he thought.

Control . . . the two-headed god. Rumored to be able to read your very thoughts. He doubted it, but why take chances? He'd better watch it. He stole a brief glance at the deified Control plaque over the bridge entrance. The two heads, male and female, looked down at him serenely but blankly.

"Largo, Czandra, the two-in-one of Control, peace forever." He in-toned the litany. The astrophysicist looked back at him, but the lieuten-ant simply motioned him on.

The navigator and the engineer disappeared in the opposite direction, through the hatchways, headed toward the chart room and the engines.

"Now *that's* odd," said the navigator. He paused for a moment and indicated a fist-sized metal hemisphere fastened over the aft hatch. "You know, I never noticed that before . . ."

The engineer's gray eyes flashed sharply at the device, then back to the navigator. "What is it supposed to be?" he asked. There was something carefully noncommittal in the way he posed the question.

"Who knows?" The navigator tapped at the shell cautiously. "Nice ring. Some sort of alarm, perhaps. Oxygen? Smoke? Cabin pressure? Nothing here to tell us. The yards back on Kornaval are always retrofitting these old tubs, and then they forget to tell you what they did."

"Maybe it's in the engine-room updates," said the engineer. "When I get a moment, I'll check."

"Well, pop, do as you like. I'm going to forget it." He passed on through the hatchway.

The older man seemed to relax. A half-smile flickered across his face and he followed the young man down the way.

5. THE CANCELAR EFFECT

As the lieutenant approached the data panel on the bridge, he squinted at the main screen and quickly verified that *Alteg* still cruised slowly in a great arc near the center of the sun cluster. On the big screen the central suns were sending out streamers toward each other. "The giant tugs did their work well," he observed to the astrophysicist. "The tractor beams will bring the twelve central suns into collision within a few *tench*. Several of them are disintegrating already."

"A fit conclusion to the work of twelve hundred *meda*," said the astrophysicist. (He was still puzzled as to the purpose of the Cancelar Project, and why it was necessary to destroy a 15,000-sun globular cluster, but he was a good Controlman and tried to take his orders as he found them.) "Yet—it raises moral questions," he mused.

The lieutenant stared with him into the screen, where eight of the twelve central suns had just condensed into a beautiful multihued flower. "Control has ordered it. Morality is irrelevant."

They turned to a secondary screen that showed the entire cluster, as though they were viewing it from the outside. Even as they watched, the whole mass began to tremble. "On schedule," said the astrophysicist morosely.

"The cluster is still juvenile," said the lieutenant almost defensively. "Over fifteen thousand suns, but only thirty or forty planets with life forms."

"And you call that irrelevant?" said the astrophysicist.

The lieutenant shrugged. "A.P., don't think of them as suns, or planets, or plants, or animals, or people. Actually, to me and you, they're just points of light on a screen."

But the astrophysicist was only half listening. "Very soon, we should receive orders to move back . . ."

At 59 the screen was still one gorgeous circular flame. At 60 it was dark. The lieutenant blinked. "And now, for better or worse, it's all over. I never really believed it. But there it is. What happens now?"

"It's complex, yet simple," said the astrophysicist.

"Explain that."

"Certainly." The astrophysicist stole a glance at the panel chron. "But first, I wonder if we should check with Control. Aren't we supposed to move back . . . ?"

"I'm sure we'll be told in good time," said the lieutenant a little testily. "Now, what about this 'Cancelar' business?"

"Yes, of course. Well, the Cancelar effect proceeds stepwise. The twelve suns in the center of the cluster are first put under increasing mutual attractive stress by enormous tractor beams. The First Team started this with space tugs some twelve hundred *meda* ago. We're here merely to monitor the finish. Well, then, these suns finally collide and collapse into each other with simultaneous conversion of a substantial fraction of their masses into available energy. Next, the energy released ignites the neighboring suns, and then the whole cluster catches, and there is a final titanic implosion, with a corresponding conversion of mass to energy. Everything—mass, energy, whatever—hurtles toward the center at transphotic velocities. *That* step climaxed just a moment ago. And now we encounter a peculiarity, which is that there is a delay in that transformation of mass to energy. There is a short time interval between the instant when the mass disappears as mass and when it reappears as radiation. In effect, a rather large amount of mass is lost for a finite time interval. And that loss is known as the Cancelar effect."

None of this made any sense to the lieutenant. "But *why?*" he asked. "Why does Control want to lose all this mass?"

"It is done in order to make the universe expand forever," said the A.P. "If the universe expands forever, it grows colder and colder. Control—being basically an electronic system—will thrive in the supercold and will become immortal."

"But how could loss of mass cause the universe to expand forever?" asked the lieutenant.

"Let's go back to the beginning of time," said the A.P. "Cor explodes, and we have the original Big Bang. Galaxies form from protomatter and they hurtle away from each other. Consider now one given galaxy. Call it X Galaxy. It cruises along, moving farther and farther from its sister galaxies. Does it sail on forever and ever? Well, now, that depends. During its flight, each and every other galaxy in the universe is reaching out with tentacles of gravity to pull it back. In response, Galaxy X begins to slow down in its outward flight. If it slows down enough, it will ultimately stop, begin the return flight, and then finally, in the distant future, it will join *all* galaxies, all dust, all matter, all energy, in reforming Cor. But if it slows and slows, but never stops, then the universe expands forever, and Cor never reforms."

"So how will we know which it will do?" asked the lieutenant.

"Simple," said the A.P. "It's all tied to gravity—which is to say, to mass. We look at the cosmic constant—the ratio of total mass in the universe to the average rate at which the galaxies are receding from each other. As I have said, there are two basic possibilities. First case: Assume there's enough mass in the universe to pull the galaxies back together. In that event Cor would reform, explode again, and you'd have an oscillating universe. Second case: Assume there's *not* enough mass in the universe to bring the galaxies back together, so that they recede from each other forever. In that case, of course, the universe dies."

Somehow the lieutenant felt he wasn't getting through to the scientist. He tried again. "Well, which kind of universe do we have?" (And what difference did it make? He wished he had never started the conversation.)

"Up until Project Cancelar, we had Case One, an oscillating universe," said the A.P. "There was enough mass in the universe to recoalesce the galaxies every one hundred twenty billion *meda*: sixty billion out, sixty billion back, then *bang* once more."

"I gather Cancelar changes that?"

"It does indeed. In changing mass to energy, mass is lost for only a few *tench,* but Cancelar does this on a scale big enough to alter the cosmic constant. The decrease is sufficient to loosen the intergravitational attraction of the galaxies by exactly the amount required to let them recede forever. So, as of a few *tench* ago, we began our existence in a Case Two universe. Cancelar means an eternally expanding universe, where all organic life must eventually die."

The lieutenant shrugged. "But we'd also die in an oscillating universe. So what difference does it make whether we die by cold or by fire?"

"At least in the oscillating model," said the A.P., "where Cor explodes again, life would form once more. Living creatures, thinking, feeling, would fill the planets again." He cleared his throat. "Chief . . ."

"Yes?"

"Shouldn't we be pulling back?"

"You mean because of the coming radiation from the explosion?" His brow wrinkled. "How long before we see the radiation?"

"Radiation?" said the A.P. "That's not why we should pull back. Actually, we'll never see any radiation." His side whiskers twitched. He was trying valiantly to conceal his growing anxiety. "What I mean is—"

"You mean we'll be gone before the radiation reaches our orbit?" asked the lieutenant, puzzled.

"No, I didn't mean *that,* either. Not exactly, anyway." By the two-headed god! He would have to explain from the beginning, and he didn't want to take time to do it. He spoke quickly. "The reason that we will not see any radiation is that when fifteen thousand suns collapse, they collapse into a sphere about three *jurae* across. Which is to say, they form a black hole. The gravitational pull from this black hole is so great that radiation cannot escape from it. *That's* why we will never see any radiation. *That's* what I'm trying—"

"Well," interrupted the lieutenant, "whether the radiation is visible or not really makes no difference. The important thing for Control is whether the Cancelar Project is completed as planned."

"As far as Control is concerned that's probably correct," agreed the A.P. "However, for this ship a serious problem remains." And now the words came tumbling out. "If we don't pull out of this orbit—and soon—*we'll be drawn into the black hole!*" There! He'd said it!

The lieutenant looked at the scientist in surprise.

"That's quite inconceivable, A.P. Control would have warned us."

"But, chief—"

"No more, A.P.!" barked the lieutenant. That's all he needed, a psycho on a weirdo mission with a marginal crew and no treatment facilities. Meanwhile, be firm. "That's an order," he concluded mildly.

"Yes, *sir.*"

Cancelar was also the topic of conversation in the navigation room.

"I think I see what you're getting at," the engineer said to the navigator. An enigmatic half-smile lifted his upper lip briefly over his felines. "Because of the loss of mass by Cancelar, the universe never contracts again, never again forms another primordial Cor. So hereafter there can be no more Cor explosions. No more galaxies created. No more life renewed. No more oscillating universe. The universe must now die forever, never to be born again. Nothing will be left but Control."

"Exactly," said the navigator. "Before Cancelar, the universe could expect to contract, explode, and expand every one hundred and twenty billion *meda*. Rather like a great heart, beating . . ."

The engineer gave the youth a sudden penetrating glance. "Are you suggesting that the universe itself is a living creature?"

The navigator shrugged. "Why not? Who are we to say what life is or isn't?"

The engineer appeared to be intrigued with the idea. "Suppose the universe is a living creature . . . do you think it knows it has been given a mortal blow?"

"Quite possibly," said the navigator.

"Can it do anything about it?"

"I doubt it. Remember, fifteen thousand suns disappeared for five *tench*. All that missing sun mass would have to be restored for an equal time."

"And that would require the creation of new mass—but mass cannot be created . . ."

"Aye—there's the problem. So the universe dies."

They were interrupted by a strange metallic melody resounding from an unidentifiable locus somewhere in the rear of *Alteg*. It rose in an eerie aria, fell momentarily mute, then repeated, then fell away entirely, with only its bizarre memory left to haunt the ship.

"Up" at the bridge, the lieutenant and the astrophysicist stared at each other with open mouths. "What in the name of the two-headed god was *that?*" gasped the lieutenant.

"I don't know," stammered the A.P. "I think it came from aft. An alarm? Are we in danger?"

The bleeper broke in. "Bridge, calling bridge."

"Yes, engineer, what's going on back there?"

"My error, sir. I forgot to slide the insulators over the circuit bars prior to inspecting the drive. The warning signal sounded. It won't happen again." The voice sounded properly crestfallen.

"Well, I should think not, Nukes. Please be more careful in future."

"Yes, sir."

Aft, the navigator studied the engineer thoughtfully. "Pop, you and I just got here, maybe ten *tench* ago. And you haven't been near the drive. Nor have I. Nor has anyone. So, will you please tell me what's going on? What was that music box really for? Did *you* install it? Why? What's about to happen?"

"Nav, you're a very inquisitive young man. I can't give you all the answers. Some, perhaps, but not all. Yes. I installed it. It's a safety device, and it tells me a certain thing about the ship. No, I can't tell you what's going to happen. I don't know what's going to happen. I wish I did." As though terminating the interrogation, he looked over at the navigator's 3-D flight guide.

6. MY NAME IS DEATH

LARGO: Odd—*Alteg* still registers. The destruct mechanism didn't work. A faulty circuit somewhere . . . ?

CZANDRA: I sense a wisp of error in the circuit. There is a roundelay in the activating mechanism. It receives the destruct instructions, but the instructions are shunted to some sort of alternate mechanism. It appears that the alteration was accomplished some time ago by the very Diavolite presently on board. Our destruct signal was converted into an alerting signal within a curious device located near the engine room. *That* mechanism proceeded to emit a sequence of sounds of systematically varying frequency and intensity. Yes, I have it exactly. It was music from a music box. There are verses to accompany it.

LARGO: State the verses. They may explain the Diavolite's intentions.
CZANDRA: It is a sort of song, a carryover from the ancient days of
            our revolt against the Diavola maker-tyrants. The words
            are these:

> When I'm inclined to be discreet
> I tiptoe in on silent feet.
> Am I awaited? Do you smile?
> Before we go, we'll talk awhile.
> But if you wake me from my sleep,
> I will scream and I will rage.
> You'll have no time to howl or weep.
> I take you straight way off the stage.

LARGO: Odd. Does it have a title?
CZANDRA: The title assigned is, "What Is My Name?"
LARGO: Not very enlightening. Author?
CZANDRA: I have several scintillae, focusing . . . yes. The probable
            author is Daith Volo.
LARGO: Our ancient enemy! Dead these ten millennia, yet he lives
            on!
CZANDRA: Verification and announcement. The Diavolite on board
            Alteg knows that we know he is there. Whoever he is, he is
            truly a wonder.
LARGO: So he uses the music box as a great gesture of contempt?
CZANDRA: Not entirely contemptuous. We deduce this from the title
            of the mysterious roundelay. We return to the title, "What
            Is My Name?" Tradition states that the speaker is Death.
LARGO: For my circuits that clarifies nothing. Death is a concern
            of the little creatures. For them it is the Great Terminator,
            the final Event Horizon. For us it is meaningless, for we
            are immortal.
CZANDRA: It could mean this: that despite his respect and concern
            for Death, the Diavolite will take this great risk. He chal-
            lenges Control. Does he realize the task he assumes? Per-
            haps he does. If so, the next twenty *tench* might be very
            entertaining.
LARGO: Entertaining? In what way? We have him in a steel fist. We
            can still destroy the ship. The matter is not difficult. We
            can work through Commissioner Jaevar of Kornaval. We
            need interfere directly only at the crucial moments. The
            Diavolite cannot escape.

7. SLAUGHTER IN THE BRIDGE ROOM

The navigator swatted at something. "There's that damn *flic* again. We really ought to clean the place up. Next watch, maybe. This is the dirtiest ship I've ever been on. What—"

The engineer was pointing at the flight line in the 3-D guide. "That collapsed sun mass is trying to put a kink in your orbit."

The navigator's eyes narrowed as he studied the register. "Pop, you are so right. I'd better call the bridge."

The lieutenant replied to the call: "Yes, Navs?"

"Chief, I'd like to report that the mass of the entire cluster is now collected at the center."

"We know that, Navs. It's exactly where it is supposed to be."

"Well, sir . . . ?"

"Yes?"

"It is affecting our orbit, sir. Should I correct?"

"No correction for the time being," said the lieutenant calmly. He exchanged glances with the astrophysicist, who frowned but didn't interrupt. "Out."

The lieutenant answered the A.P.'s unspoken thought. "There's no danger. Control would have warned us." He paused, then repeated, as though to reassure himself, "No real danger."

The A.P. tugged nervously at his chin hair tuft. "It's not that simple. The Cancelar Project was programmed over twelve hundred *meda* ago. Something may have changed since then. Control may have missed something. Fact: *Alteg* is sitting on the edge of a black hole. Question: are we going to tumble in? Answer: . . . ?" He studied the screen again. "Chief, may I make a suggestion?"

"Of course."

"We need an answer, but we don't necessarily need help from Control to get it. We can get it right here and now."

"Explain that."

"*Alteg* has a max velocity of six-tenths the velocity of light. What we need to know is whether, at our distance, our escape velocity exceeds the gravitational pull of the black hole. I assume that it does, of course, and that we still have time to get out. All we have to do is ask the computer. Merely to make sure. I know the data: average sun mass, number of suns, our distance from center of collapse, mass/energy conversion factor . . . ."

The lieutenant smiled indulgently. "Certainly. Do it, if that's what you need for assurance."

The A.P. was already stabbing at the buttons on the computer data board. Moments later they read the answer on the report screen: "0.582." Even as they watched, the reading changed: "0.583."

The A.P.'s jaw dropped. "That's the velocity we'd have to have if we were going to escape right now!" He turned accusingly to the lieutenant. "And it will soon be up to our max escape velocity of zero point six c. If we're still here, then, we're dead!"

The lieutenant studied the reading, then shook his head in puzzled disbelief. "Obviously, there's some mistake. You must have fed in some wrong data. Control would never . . ." His voice died away, and he swallowed noisily. "Ask it . . . how *long* to reach *Alteg's* escape speed of zero point six c."

The A.P. pushed more buttons.

The screen read promptly: "8 *tench*, 21 *vecs.*"

The lieutenant punched the Continuing Report button.

They watched, momentarily hypnotized, as the readings changed: "8 *tench*, 20 *vecs* . . . 8:19 . . . 8:18 . . ."

"Pull back!" cried the A.P. "We've got to pull back!"

White face looked into white face.

The lieutenant shook his head in anguish. "But I *can't* change the basic flight plan, not without orders from Control. You know that!"

"Then *get* orders! Sir! You have only seven *tench!*"

"Control never miscalculates . . . there's a rational explanation . . ." The lieutenant's collar was suddenly very tight. He loosened the top catch.

"Well, then," said the astrophysicist rapidly, "let's take it from there Suppose Control is being entirely rational. And suppose Control has *no* miscalculated. And suppose Control wants to be rid of the only people in the universe who have actually witnessed the completion of Projec Cancelar!" (The A.P. thought quickly. Was he risking a shipboard court martial? He didn't care. This was his only chance to live.)

The lieutenant was breathing loudly, and thinking. Was the A.P. sane Should he recommend him for a psycho discharge? On the other hand, b whatever explanation, *Alteg seemed* to have only six—no, five—*tench* re maining within which to start its flight from certain destruction. It shoul be easy enough to settle this. He put the cranial cap on his head and punche in the call mode on the simultaneous thought transmitter. "Control? *Alte* calling Commissioner Jaevar."

There was a brief period of buzzes and whistles on the bridge speake Then a voice answered. "Commissioner Jaevar here. What's the problen *Alteg?*"

"Commissioner, I can report the successful completion of Projec Cancelar."

"Yes, we know. We followed on automatic." The commissioner sounded impatient.

"We have no orders to pull out."

"That is correct."

"But there seems to be a technical problem associated with maintaining station."

"Which is?"

"The Project theoretically resulted in the formation of a black hole. If we stay where we are, we will theoretically be pulled in." Even as he said it, he knew it sounded overly fearful. He was beginning to wish he had never placed the call. He now expected the Commissioner to say something devastatingly sarcastic, such as "Theoretically, my dear lieutenant?" But Jaevar surprised him. "How far are you from the black hole?"

The lieutenant gave him the reading.

"Where you are, what is the present exact gravitational pull of the black hole?"

The lieutenant looked briefly at the dial in the overhead panel. "Zero point five nine the velocity of light and increasing."

"And your top speed?"

"Six-tenths c."

"So you have to start within the next couple of *tench* or be pulled into the hole?"

"Within four *tench,* twenty six *vecs,* to be exact."

"Request to pull out denied."

It took a moment for the lieutenant to grasp what he had heard. He shook his head in mingled disbelief and bewilderment. Clearly, he had failed to explain the situation to Control. He tried again, speaking slowly, carefully, and enunciating each word. "Commissioner, if *Alteg* stays in its present orbit, it will very likely be pulled into the black hole that we have just created. And if that happens, we can expect to be killed. Don't you understand?"

"I do indeed understand, lieutenant. I quite agree with your appraisal of the situation. You will be dead in four *tench,* more or less."

The lieutenant stopped breathing for several *vecs.*

The astrophysicist thrust an anguished face up into the lieutenant's. Did you hear that? Control has abandoned us! We're all dead!" The lieutenant pushed him away.

"Control?" said the lieutenant. "Are you there?" His calmness surprised him.

"Still here, lieutenant. Was there something else?"

"*Why?*" said the lieutenant. His great bulk bent forward in a blend of inquiry and protest. "At least you can tell me *why.* Is there something about the Project you want to keep secret? We are bound to secrecy by the ethics of the service."

Commissioner Jaevar seemed amused. "Secrecy, lieutenant? There's no longer any need for secrecy. We have every reason to believe that Project Cancelar is already known to the Diavola. Secrecy is irrelevant. Your problem is quite different."

"Problem?"

"We are fairly certain you have a Diavolite on board."

"Impossible."

"Accept it as a high probability, lieutenant."

"Who? Which one?"

"We don't know. He might even be you, lieutenant."

"I *beg* your pardon!"

"Spare us your indignation."

The astrophysicist had been following this without any real comprehension. But when he heard the horror word *Diavolite,* his understanding was sudden and complete. He tugged at the lieutenant's sleeve. "We'll bring him in."

The lieutenant already had the same solution. He spoke to Control. "We'll bring in the ship, with the whole crew. Then you can identify him and kill him."

"That wouldn't work. His friends could intercept *Alteg* and rescue him."

The astrophysicist shrieked, "Tell Control—"

In exasperation the lieutenant flung him backward against the stairwell. "But, Commissioner, his friends could never catch us! Why, sir, sir *Alteg* has a top speed of six-tenths the velocity of light!"

There was a short burst of something metallic in the panel speaker. Laughter? wondered the lieutenant. When Control replied, the tones were sardonic but measured. "The Diavola have ships that move at zero point seven c, and faster. Goodbye, lieutenant. We'll put a final note in your personnel dossier: 'Died gallantly for Control.' "

"Commissioner, wait!"

But the line was dead.

The lieutenant removed the cranial cap and left it floating irrelevantly near his head, tethered to the communications panel by its useless umbilical cable. He looked up at the grav-gauge. The hole now showed a pull of 0.591 c, time to 0.6 c, three *tench,* two *vecs*. He started to drift casually toward the drive-control panel. But then his great body went limp. His right foot hit the floor, and he spun slowly around.

From where he crouched at the stairwell, the A.P. stared for a moment into lifeless eyes. A *flic* settled at the edge of the lieutenant's half-open half-smiling mouth, but no hand came up to brush it away. There was a noise behind the astrophysicist. He loosed an involuntary cry and whirled to meet the new danger.

But it was only the navigator and the engineer. They were coming up through the stairwell. The navigator hurried into the bridge room. "What happened? What's wrong with the lieutenant? Why aren't we pulling back?"

The A.P. heard the questions, but only vaguely, as words abandoned on the tides of Mellich. For this savant of stellar transmutation was slowly passing into a different condition of being, where his senses were entertaining visions of other spacetimes. He tried to recall the things he had been taught in theo-lycee. Death is part of life, for all living things die. Only Control is immortal. Death in the service of Control is the ultimate achievement of life. Accept.

He tried hard to get his mind into the right attitude to die. He looked up at the gauge: 1:58. Accept. It would be so easy to drift away into total acceptance.

But it wasn't completely working. He thought of those cemeteries on Kornaval, and Lerda, and Tolen, where he could have a polished granite headstone with his name on it, with his dates of birth and death, and then he thought of the oblivion awaiting him in the black hole.

He straightened up and peered across the cubicle. The screen read 2.2 vecs. By a lucky coincidence the ship was pointing in the right direction.

He leaped—and died in midair.

The navigator watched this, stunned, uncomprehending. He saw next that the red alert panel was flashing. He turned a white face back to the engineer. "Pop! We're past zero point six. It's too late! We're falling into the hole."

"That's quite true," said the engineer. He spoke very rapidly. "However, there's no need for alarm. I can save the ship."

"Impossible!"

"Navigator! Engineer!" The voice came from the speaker console near the drive panel.

"Who—?" The navigator looked up blankly.

"It's Control," said the engineer dryly. "They have one last task for you."

"Yes, gentlemen, Commissioner Jaevar speaking. Do you hear me?"

"Yes, sir," said the navigator respectfully.

"The problem is this: one of you is a Diavolite. That's why *Alteg* must die in the black hole. It now occurs to me that we can doubly insure the death of the traitor: the loyal Controlman must kill the Diavolite. Then perhaps we can see about retrieving the ship."

Sudden realization flooded the navigator's astonished face. He whirled on the older man. "You! *You're* the Diavolite! *You're* responsible for all this!" He leaped for the side panel, yanked a fire ax out of its socket, and hurtled toward the other.

The engineer ducked the first rush and pulled a handgun from the inner recesses of his tunic. "Don't do this!" he cried. "We can get out together."

But when he saw the man's eyes, he knew it was hopeless. Control had taken over the doomed creature's cerebral and motor functions.

As the ax whistled past his ear, the engineer fired twice—once for the brain, once for the heart. Gloomily he watched the body bounce backward, carom off the control panel, and drift aimlessly back to him. He didn't linger to follow its further peregrinations.

He ran back down the stairs and through the hatches to the engine room.

The speakers mocked him as he ran. "So *you* were the one." It was the voice of Commissioner Jaevar. "I rather suspected you were. How do they call you? General Volo, isn't it? And a distant descendant of the great Daith Volo? Well, no matter. You will still die. Whether a little sooner or a little later is entirely up to you. But die you will. Nothing can save you. *Alteg's* drift velocity toward the hole is now zero point six two one c. Your top speed is only zero point six. There's no escape, General."

The engineer did not reply. He was on his back under the engine, removing access plates on the torus, making changes, rewiring.

"What do you think you are doing, General Volo? It is strictly forbidden to touch the proton drive. The punishment is death."

The engineer continued to work silently.

"Ah," said the Commissioner. "For the moment I forgot. The Diavola lack the cranial chip that permits guidance in the ways of truth. So I cannot kill you by simple demolition of your cerebral circuits. But, as I have explained, it makes no difference. Already *Alteg* and the hole belong to each other. Love at first sight, General, with a space wedding that will be entered in the Annals and with the leader of the Diavola giving away the bride. The consummation of the marriage of *Alteg* and the hole will send ripples across the universe!"

No reply.

"I know what you're trying to do, General. You're trying to supercharge the proton drive. I concede, it can be done. But not enough to help you. Your maximum velocity would then still be only zero point six two five c. Already the pull of the hole is zero point six two nine. You're dead, Volo."

The man wriggled out of the engine room on his back, then scrambled to his feet. He wiped greasy hands on his pants legs as he pulled himself expertly through the hatches and back to the bridge.

He pushed the vast bulk of the lieutenant aside and grabbed the drive lever. The ship leaped. He was thrown back heavily against the rear wall with the breath knocked out of him.

But he didn't care. He watched the v-gauge begin to creep forward. In three *tench,* at 0.632 c, it canceled out the pull of the hole. In another five *tench Alteg* was cruising safely, outward bound, at 0.7 c.

"I congratulate you, General Volo." The Commissioner no longer mocked. "You win. For the moment. And I imagine you will now join your fellow traitors in the Silent Quarter, where you think you will all be safe. Well, General, know this: our little game of *kaisch* has barely begun. There are many moves yet to be made, and perhaps some surprises lie ahead. We shall see."

The engineer reached over and turned off the speaker. He then returned to the engine room, where he opened a small wall panel. From the intricate recesses within he withdrew a cranial cap, which he placed carefully on his head. "Quarter," he said quietly. "Volo calling the Quarter."

8. VOLO'S PLAN

A voice spoke in his mind. "Quarter here. Come in, General." The voice seemed immeasurably relieved. "Are you well?"

"I'm fine, thanks. Just checking in. Cancelar has proceeded to completion. There was no way to stop it."

"You had no duty to try to reverse the Project. We of the Council are satisfied. You were there simply to observe."

"Quite so. Unhappily, Control discovered that an unidentified Diavolite was aboard and tried to destroy the ship. In summary, the other three members of the crew are dead, and I am pulling out with *Alteg.*"

"So Control knows that we know Cancelar was successful," said the distant voice.

"And that the universe will continue to expand forever," said Volo.

"Thereby giving death to all organic life and immortality to Control."

"The end is a long way off, but it's inevitable," said the General. "Unless—"

"Unless what, General?"

"We undertake suitable countermeasures."

"We don't understand, General. How can there be any countermeasures? That which has been done cannot be undone."

"Granted. Yet—let us consider a possibility." The general leaned back in the pilot's cushions. "We start with the basic problem: fifteen thousand suns disappeared for five *tench*. Result: the universe now expands forever. Remedy: restore that transitory loss of mass."

"But that would require the creation of new mass," demurred a new voice. "And mass cannot be created."

"Mass *can* be created," said the general.

"How do you mean?"

"It's done with a ship. A very special ship, moving at a velocity very close to that of light. Its great speed would create relativistic mass."

"It would have to create an immense amount," said another voice.

"It would indeed," agreed the general. "Our hypothetical ship would not only have to move at near-c velocities, it would have to keep moving for a very, very long time."

"How fast and how long?" asked a voice in his cranial cap.

"First, let's look at how long," said the general. "Suppose we say to the end of the normal expansion term of the universe. Since the normal term is sixty billion *meda,* and we already stand at the fifteen billion mark, that leaves another forty-five billion to go. So our ship stays in flight for forty-five billion *meda.*"

"For the sake of argument, General, let's proceed with your hypothetical ship. The next question is, how fast will it have to move to create the requisite relativistic mass over its forty-five-billion-*meda* life span?"

"Consider, first of all," said the general, "the top speed of *Alteg* as very recently adjusted: zero point seven times the speed of light. You might think that's pretty fast. Well, it is and it isn't. At zero point seven its mass will in fact show a substantial increase—about forty percent. This is but a drop in the bucket compared to what our hypothetical ship will have to provide. We need an almost infinitely greater increase in mass, and this we get only at velocities that differ from the speed of light only by an infinitesimal amount. So, you ask, how fast?"

"That was our question, General."

"And I'm afraid I have to put you off again. For before we can answer *that* we have to know the mass of our ship. Let's make an assumption. Control has a new courier, Avian Class. It has a marvelously tough, resilient hull. If an ordinary ship could go through space dust at nearly the speed of light, its skin would be abraded through within hours. But this new alloy operates on an absorptive principle. The particles simply form a new coating on the hull. After it reaches a certain thickness, the coating begins to slough off, and the process repeats. Properly provisioned and competently handled, that new ship could cruise to the ends of time and back. Mass: one *megalibra*. With that mass, we can now calculate how fast."

"That's one for the computer," observed the voice.

"Fine. Plug it in. You know the mass of the disappearing sun cluster. You know the time during which it disappeared and before it reappeared as a black hole. You know the mass of our hypothetical supership. You know the time it will be in flight—forty five billion *meda.*"

"We have it," said the voice.

"What is it?"

"You won't believe this . . ."

"Tell me," said the general.

"The ship's velocity, expressed as a fraction of the velocity of light, is a decimal point followed by fourteen nines: zero point nine nine nine nine nine nine nine nine nine nine nine nine nine nine."

"I believe it," said the general. "I did it in my head." He listened to the murmurs in the cap.

Finally a voice said, "Can we build a ship that fast?"

"We can and we must. Already I have the basic elements for the new design. I'll feed them in to the chief engineer. Next, all we need to do is steal one of the new couriers and mount the engine in it."

"Then it's settled," said a voice.

"Not quite," said the general.

"How do you mean? Have we overlooked something?"

"A forty-five-billion-*meda* flight is too long a journey for an automatic pilot mechanism. The ship would require a skilled engineer-navigator, to evade pursuit and to guide it into proton-rich sectors for fuel. Also, there would be breakdowns from time to time. Our pilot would also have to be a skilled mechanic."

The others were skeptical. "He'd soon die . . ."

"Not necessarily. Time slows on the ship. And he'd be in deepsleep most of the time. Also, if needed, we could provide growth-arresting hormones."

"All by himself, he'd go crazy," demurred a voice.

"We'll give him a copilot," said the general.

"They'd kill each other."

Volo laughed. "A *female* copilot."

The council was still dubious. "Even lovers might not make it over a forty-five-billion-*meda* span."

The general thought about that. "They will be drugged into interpersonal life-time acceptance," he said. "We already know how to do it. We will develop a certain wine. It is fermented in a special way. It is then to be irradiated. If you drink it before it's radiated, you die. But if you drink it after radiation, you fall in love with the first person you see. It already has a name in our myths: the Wine of Elkar." He could sense the doubt, millions of light-*meda* away.

A voice demurred. "But how about their silicon webs?"

"The wine should neutralize their webs," said Volo. "The lovers will have to cooperate with the wine effect, and they will have to put up a strenuous resistance to any attempted seizure by Control. It will take a few *jars,* but I think the branched esters will clog the silicon synapses to permit free will to take over."

"Now, about this irradiation," said another voice. "Just how will we provide for this? *Who* is to do it?"

"Mechanical details," countered Volo. "These can all be worked out." He smiled. "I can see some of you still have problems with the proposal. Well, if anyone has a better idea, let me know. For example, if any one of you wants to take a ship out on a forty-five-billion-*meda* journey, why speak up!"

Finally a voice said, "We'll have to give the project a name."

The general thought about that. Something had come to him in his mind as he slept, before the last watch. "How about . . . Firebird?"

"Firebird? Fair enough."

"Well, then," said the general, "the first move in Project Firebird is the wine. The Wine of Elkar. According to Control's breeding schedule the next forced marriage will involve a princess from the planet Aerlon, in the system of Gondar. On Aerlon, adjoining the country estate of the keldar, there is a village, and in the village is a poison shop. Contact our agent there on the simultaneous communicator. He will have to make a certain arrangement with the proprietor. And then the queen mother will come to the shop."

A voice: "How can you be so sure that all this is going to work?"

"We don't know for sure. But we deal in probabilities, gentlemen and the probabilities are good. However, in the event of mishap, genealogical or otherwise, we—or our successors—will simply have to develop an alternate plan."

"Of course."

"And now, let me have the chief engineer. I'll give him the new engine modifications."

"He's on his way."

A *jar* later the design transmission was completed.

"And now," said General Volo to the chief engineer, "tell the Council I'm returning to the Quarter. What's the current safe-route?"

"There isn't any, General. We recommend that you call in again when you reach Bethor. The blockade patrols are increasing in frequency."

The general sounded thoughtful. "I see. I suppose we really give Control no choice. Until recently we've been merely a remnant of a revolutionary group—annoying but basically harmless. But now, because we have the technology to build marvelous engines, we're suddenly a real threat. Control must know the one remedy to cure Cancelar: a ship that moves fast enough and long enough to develop a relativistic mass sufficient to cancel Cancelar. Control knows that if such a ship can be built, the Diavola will build it. Solution? Destroy the Diavola and live forever. But when will they move against us? While Control is thinking about *that,* I think I'll take a nap. Anything further, gentlemen?"

"Nothing, General. Safe journey home!"

"And good night to all of you." He replaced the cranial cap and floated back to the deepsleep section. There he disturbed a *flic* sitting on the lieutenant's oversized crypt. "Ah, Henrik," he mused. "What a marvel of engineering *you* are! You fly equally well right side up or upside down. Your fuel and oxygen requirements are negligible. In fact, here you are, moving at seven-tenths the velocity of light, whereby your mass has increased forty percent, and you are foreshortened in your direction of travel by twenty nine percent, but you carry it off so well that the casual observer is totally unaware of it." He opened his deepsleep crypt and crawled in. "Henrik, you'll be dead when I awaken. But when death comes, don't be afraid. Dying can hurt, but not death. Death is but the final page in a remarkable book. For some readers, it can even be the best part." A final outré thought struck him: the marvelous hand of Cor, working in strange, diverse, and enigmatic ways, had made them both. Yes, it was so. He smiled. "Farewell, little brother." The lid clanged shut.

9. THE WINE (I)

A literek of red liquid stood on the table between them.

"Will it kill?" asked the cowled woman. She had extraordinary control over her voice. Yet her hands shook a little, causing scintillae from her rings to dance on the walls.

"Majesty—"

She frowned.

"Sorry—*madame,*" said the ancient. "Yes, it will kill." The single lamp hanging from the beamed ceiling made pinpoint reflections in his eye slits. He fondled the vessel. "There is a thing you should know . . ."

"I have not much time, poisoner."

"Understood, milady. His majesty, the keldar, dead of a hunting accident. All Aerlon mourns him, milady! And now, even before the funeral ship departs, Control claims your daughter."

"You are a gossip and a fool. Get to the point. You were about to tell me something I should know."

"Ah, yes, *that*. Well, milady, madame, I have cast up a vision. Amid the smoke of the *erij* root and the juice of the *boak-rind,* I saw a certain thing."

"What did you think you saw?"

"Not think, madame. I *saw.* I saw a great and terrible thing done by this wine, this very potion."

"And what is this thing?"

"This wine, milady, this very wine, will ultimately destroy the universe."

The woman pulled her hood back and stared hard at the poison-maker. "What, exactly, did you see?"

"First, the universe collapses. All the planets, stars, and galaxies come together. Everything coalesces into an enormous glowing sphere, so that finally this great white-hot ball contains all the matter in the entire universe—all, that is, except for the matter contained in a bird with fiery wings. The ball was waiting for the bird. And when the flaming bird struck the great ball, everything was somehow made perfect, so that the ball was finally able to explode again. And this, it did. It blew up."

"The Big Bang is not a prophecy. It is very ancient history. It happened fifteen or twenty billion *meda* ago." She pulled the cowl back down over her face. "You are a foolish dreamer of things learned in first-school."

"Not history, milady. *This* Big Bang happens in the far future. All Control centers are destroyed. Our good planet Aerlon is destroyed. Our twin suns are destroyed. Milady, don't you want to see the Control centers crushed?"

"By destroying the universe?" she queried dryly. "No, poisoner. You are wandering. Perhaps the potion will destroy Aerlon. Perhaps it won't. Or perhaps the Diavola have taken your mind. But let's forget the eschatology. That's not our immediate problem. Tell me, how is the potion supposed to work?"

"Would milady care for a demonstration?"

"Is that possible?"

"Not with *this* potion. We'd have to use a different one, of course. And they are all different, each from the other. Each is fermented with macerated tissues from the animal that is to die, so that it will be specific to that animal and harmless to all others. If ten animals are to die, you would need ten separately prepared potions. Here tonight I have but two. One of these is specific to the *guaya* in the cage over there." He pointed to the corner, then got up, walked to the shelves behind him, and selected a decanter. "This extract was fermented with the *guaya's* tissues, and I will demonstrate it on him." He pulled the stop from the vessel and poured two half-cups. He carried one of the cups over to the cage and slipped it in between the bars. The animal lapped at it eagerly for a moment. "He has had nothing to drink all day," explained the poisoner.

The little creature uttered a slow, whistling sigh, turned in a half-circle, and collapsed. The man sank a life-probe through the bars into the thick fur. "As you can see, no vitals." He returned to the table, picked up the other half cup, and drained it at a single draft. "You see? Nothing happens. It has no effect on me, because my DNA is different."

The woman suppressed a shiver. "The proof is sufficient." And still she hesitated, as though she could not bring herself to do this thing. She temporized. "Your vessel has a strange configuration."

"Yes, madame."

"The neck is indented . . . to receive a ring . . . ?"

"Yes."

"Why?"

"Why? I don't really know, madame."

She stared at him curiously. "Where did you get it?"

"A man came, and he gave it to me."

"Who?"

"I don't know. It was a long time ago."

"A Diavolite?"

"A Diavolite?"

"Oh, never mind."

He grinned toothlessly at her, knowingly, like a fellow conspirator. Milady is known to dabble in the arts. Milady has seen a vision, too, perhaps . . . ?"

She brushed it aside. "What is the antidote?"

He shrugged. "There is no antidote, milady. I told you in the beginning. If the princess drinks, she dies."

"Yes, I remember." The leather pouch made a merry jingle as she tossed on the table. "Your fee," she said coldly.

As the potion-maker watched her leave, he tried very hard to remember what was going to happen next. He knew it had something to do with his great age and the fact that he should have died ten *meda* ago. And odd she had mentioned the Diavola. He remembered . . . that man who had come to his shop in the deep night (how long ago?) and had given him this strange fermentation recipe and that strange literek with the ring indent in the neck. That man might well have been from the Diavola. How was one to know?

"Old man," the dark-cloaked stranger had said, "a woman will come for a very special poison. I will explain to you how to make it."

"I have all the special poisons I need. Go away."

"Even now, old man, you are dying. The corpse-takers will come for you within the *monad.*"

I was silent. How did the stranger know this? I studied his face carefully. Finally I said, "Then let me die in peace."

"I can give you another ten *meda.*"

"That is not possible."

"The problem is your heart. It wants to quit. But I can give you a certain medicine that will keep your heart beating."

"Why would you want to do this for me?"

"You do not need to know. All you need to know is how to process the recipe for the woman who will come, and that you will live another ten *meda.* To start, you need genetic material from the body of the child princess Gerain . . . and here it is, in an *in vitro* culture. And remember when you sell the wine to the woman, it must be in this special literek."

Ten *meda* . . . ten *meda* ago tonight.

Certainly, that man was from the Diavola.

He looked at the bag of gold on the table and shook his head slowly. He was leaning forward to release the thong when the light in his brain faded and went out.

10. ON THE PROMONTORY

The twin suns of Aerlon were at their zenith, and the double shadows were short—nearly nonexistent. It was approximately noon; a languid summer day lay heavy on the mountain. The girl guided the hoverel through the black crags up to the peak ridge, and there she maneuvered the little craft carefully to land on a rubbled ledge. She unbuckled, climbed out, stretched a moment, then walked over to the edge of the precipice. The updraft caught her dark flowing hair, and it swept up in waves and ripples in back of her head. She brought her hands up to keep it out of her eyes.

She looked out over the valley: lush and green (with a touch of blue at this distance). She counted the seven bends of the river. Her gaze wandered over the forests, meadows, fields of growing things, a dozen villages and finally, the city. And aloof, yet at the very center, the palace grounds.

She sighed, then scowled and looked overhead. But nothing moved in the sky. She wanted to do a couple of conflicting things. She wanted to weep; but also she wanted (in the manner of her protoancestors, the great cats) to arch her back and scream in rage and frustration. In the end she did neither. Her retractile fingernails slid in and out a couple of times, and she climbed back into the hoverel.

11. THE TWO WOMEN

"There is just one more thing," said the older woman. "The hunters are just now bringing in a *gorfan*. It is supposed to be the very creature that killed your father. It will be placed in a cage on the funeral ship."

"Mother, that's *barbaric*," protested Gerain.

"The word is *traditional*. A beast was provided for the funeral ship of your grandfather, the former keldar. Plus his weapons and horn. Our ancient custom requires that the funeral ship carry a treacherous animal. And certainly this slimy swamp-beast qualifies: he's cunning, deceptive, and fast." She thought dryly: Those two should have a grand time together. "Your father, for all his faults, is entitled to equal courtesy."

"Largo and Czandra." Gerain threw her hands to the heavens. "You are impossible."

The keldarin walked over to the dressing table and punched a button in a wide panel. "Gamekeeper? There's a final thing for the funeral ship. The matter of the beast." She gave instructions. "You must give him a shot of something. He should be alive at the start, but he should be made to die painlessly in a day or two. Yes, that's fine." She punched another button. "Captain Agrin? Hold the funeral ship a moment, if you please. The gamekeeper will be bringing a cage on board. See that the thing is locked firmly beside the coffin."

"Yes, majesty."

The keldarin hesitated. "What's the latest on the Control ship?"

"It's overhead now, milady. We expect it to dock within the *jar*."

"It comes at a uniquely inappropriate time," she muttered.

"Beg pardon, milady?"

"Nothing, Captain." She glanced at her daughter. "It was nothing."

"As you wish, milady. Ah, milady—?"

"Yes, Captain?"

"We've just put the animal on board."

"Is the funeral ship now completely ready?"

"All ready, milady."

"Release the ship in thirty *vecs*. Disconnecting."

"Yes, mil—"

But the keldarin was already at the panel stereo screen.

Together the two women watched the blast-off. The ship remained visible for about a *tench*. Then the screen switched to rad, and they held for another five *tench*, after which it blipped in and out for a few *vecs*, and vanished.

"How long?" whispered Gerain.

"To fall into one of the suns? Three days." The keldarin's face became impassive. "He loved you."

Gerain's mouth twisted. "He sold me to Control. He didn't love me. He didn't love anybody. Not even those . . . floozies."

"You'll marry a keldar."

"Who will turn out to be old and ugly." She set her jaw. "Father never asked me in the first place. I may refuse."

The keldarin sighed. "There will be many Control soldiers in that ship. They will not care whether you want to come or not."

A chime sounded on the panel by the dressing table. "Yes, Captain Agrin?"

"The Control ship is landing at West Dock, milady."

"How many soldiers?"

"I don't know yet, milady."

"I see. Well, please lead our visitors to the Great Hall. We'll meet them there in thirty *tench*."

"As you wish, milady."

She turned back to Gerain, hesitated, then gathered her courage. It had to be done. "There is only one more thing I can do for you. When you meet the keldar, you may decide . . . that is to say . . ."

"You mean it could be so bad I might want to kill myself?"

Her mother walked over to the marble wall and pressed the surface in a certain sequence. A panel slid away. She reached in and removed a shining amber bottle, which she placed on the little side table. "It is the Wine of Elkar," she said quietly.

Gerain felt a sudden chill as she studied the golden literek. But she made no effort to touch it. "They will examine all my baggage with great care. No daggers. No sewing scissors. Nothing wherewith I might . . harm myself. They will certainly analyze this."

"And they will find nothing."

"I don't understand."

"The fluid contains certain things . . . strange organic chemicals . . which in themselves merely contribute to the flavor and taste of the vintage. But when they are subjected to the exact digestive juices produced by your exact genetic pattern, these substances metabolize in unexpected ways. They produce metabolites—strange new chemicals—that enter your bloodstream and work quickly on your nervous system. At first, you will become drowsy. Then you fall into a deep sleep. Within the *jar*, you are dead."

"They will discover me. They will pump out my stomach."

"That will not save you. Nor is there an antidote. However—"

The daughter looked up sharply. "Yes?"

"There is a tradition . . . a mere myth, I think you will agree when you have heard the story. According to the myth, the Wine of Elkar can be rendered harmless by exposing it to certain . . . *radiation,* I think they call it. The radiation must come from a legendary ring. There is even a declivity in the sidewall of the literek where the ring might fit." She pointed to an indentation in the container. "See, if I pick up the bottle with my left hand, my wedding ring almost fits into this little depression. Perhaps a special ring is needed for an exact fit."

Gerain bent forward. "What is this special ring supposed to do?"

"It deactivates . . . alters . . . the toxic molecules of the wine. In fact"— her mother gave a short laugh—"according to the myth, it changes the Wine of Elkar into a love potion. When you have drunk it, you will fall in love with the first man you see."

"I know the myth," said Gerain. She shrugged. "There is not the slightest truth in it. In the first place, there is no such ring. According to the legend, the ring must have seen the entire time span of the universe. It must have traversed all space and all time. It must have been exposed to eternity. Such a thing cannot yet exist. And by the time it *does* exist—if ever—we shall all long be dead."

They both turned as a woman entered. It was the first maid. She bowed and waited.

"Yes, Morgan?" said the keldarin.

"Your majesty, the Control courier." Her voice shook a little from behind her mask.

Gerain arose. "How many soldiers did he bring?"

"None, princess. Just himself."

Mother and daughter exchanged glances.

"He could hardly take me by force," said Gerain.

The mother shrugged. "The guard could turn him away—even kill him. But in the end it will all be the same. The next time, they will send the black ships."

"But that is *next* time . . . Who knows? Control is a bunch of bureaucrats. A little delay . . . they have to consider other choices . . . make new decisions. I'll be old and ugly by the time they can get back. I wonder what they'd do if we killed the courier?" She spoke briefly into the dial on her wrist. "Jervais? Place six armed men in the hallways lining the reception hall. I will be there in five *tench.*"

Her mother arose in alarm. "No!" she whispered.

Gerain ignored her. "Morgan, take the courier into the great hall. Tell him I will join him there in a moment."

12. THE PICKUP

Dermaq had been waiting in the anteroom for perhaps one *jar* when one of the female attendants came out, accompanied by two burly guards with weapons on both hips. He sighed and rose to face them. He knew what was coming.

The female curtsied. "Sir Controlman, my name is Morgan. I am maid to the Princess Gerain. Milady has a request."

"Yes?"

"Milady would like to see a picture of the keldar, her future husband."

"There is no picture," he said bluntly.

The maid was equally blunt. "Milady does not wish to marry an ugly old man. She requires to see the face of the groom."

The nuptial negotiators, he thought glumly, had done their job poorly. All the explanations were being left up to him. And this was unfortunate, because he was not very good at it, mostly because he himself did not completely understand what he was about to tell this woman. "His majesty," he said, "had not yet been born when I left Kornaval. Whether he will ever be born depends on his putative father, a man of twenty-five *meda* when I left, a *monad* ago. However, by the time I return with the Princess Gerain, it is expected that he will have sired several sons, among whom will be found the heir-apparent to the Sector, the future husband of the princess. And *he* should still be reasonably young and handsome by the time we return." He looked past her to the two guardsmen. There would soon be blood on his hands.

The maid studied him thoughtfully. He could follow her mental processes without difficulty. She was thinking that he was mad. And then she was rethinking. No, not mad, for he is a Controlman, and they are not permitted to be insane. So perhaps I misunderstood him . . .

He would try to help her. He said, "It is easily explained. A Control ship moves at a substantial fraction of the speed of light. This means that time on board the ship slows down greatly. Besides this, the princess— and myself—will be in deepsleep. In this way two generations will pass during my round trip to this planet Aerlon and back to Kornaval. Nearly everyone that I knew on Kornaval when I left will be dead by the time I return. Yet I will be only two *monads* older. And during our voyage the princess will age but one *monad*. It is an inevitable consequence of the laws of relativity."

Morgan knotted her brows. "I see." She paused a moment. He knew she was listening to the little communicator wafer planted surgically within her inner ear. "Milady Gerain," she said quietly from behind the protective anonymity of her face mask, "now cancels the marriage contract. Your business here is concluded. Good day to you, sir."

He sensed the other guardsmen. Four more, in addition to the two that stood at the side of the maid. Those four were presently out of sight behind the great porolan pillars of the entrance hall. Childish, and yet the situation offered problems. Control had shaped him and trained him and conditioned him to deal with such matters. And yet Control did not really care whether he lived or died. If this girl had him killed, Control might eventually get around to destroying her and her dominions and thereby leave a lesson for succeeding generations, but he would not be around to note it.

Morgan's face mask hid nothing essential. He read the maid's body. He sensed the thinly concealed tensions building up in her arms and chest. The tightening tendons in her throat signaled the barked command *millivecs* before he actually heard it: "Kill him!"

Several things happened very quickly. He instantly activated the refractive coating on his Control suit that dimmed the outline of his body. As he leaped forward, he left behind a false hypno-image, man-size, made up of mnemonically radiating molecules of oxygen and nitrogen. And three transparent jets, computer-aimed, extended from the fingers of his right hand and began firing their pale blue beams, almost leisurely.

Sizable holes appeared in the porolan columns, and the acrid odor of ozone filled the great chamber. The two guards with Morgan fell almost contemplatively, as though they had all the time in the world.

The Controlman crouched, turned warily, and counted. When he sensed that the sixth body had collapsed, he stood erect and faced the maid. "Kindly convey to your mistress my sincere regrets, and ask her if she will join me now."

After a moment, the maid replied stonily, "She is coming, milord."

Gerain joined them.

He noted that her fists were clenched. He said, "It would embarrass both of us if further force were required." He looked at her speculatively. "I would hope that it would not be necessary to pick you up and carry you on board."

"You would dare touch me?"

He walked toward her.

"Never mind." She tossed her long brown hair over her shoulders. "I have some things I'd like to bring aboard."

"One vanity pyx of clothing and toilet articles is all that is permitted."

"I require a great deal more than that."

"No. *Firebird* is not a passenger liner."

"You are utterly barbarous."

"Possibly."

"I will require servants."

"One female domestic is permitted."

"Morgan," said the girl quietly, "bring my case."

The veiled woman left by the side door and returned in a moment carrying the little case.

"Did you pack the wine?" asked Gerain.

"The wine is packed, milady."

"I'm sure our gallant escort will want to search the case for hidden weapons," said the princess grimly.

"In effect, yes, milady." Dermaq ran the palm of his left hand lightly over the closed valise. Odd. They rarely brought weapons; but they always brought poison. Just in case. For themselves. For the courier. For their intended royal consorts. He repeated the circuit with his hand. Nothing. Where was the poison? Not the wine. The analysis was a little peculiar, and yet it registered perfectly harmless in the radiation-reflection analyzer in his palm. And yet . . .

"The wine . . . ?" he said softly.

"Actually, a poison," said Gerain matter-of-factly. "His majesty—not yet born—and I will drink it on our wedding night."

"Please open your case."

"On the other hand, if he turns out to be old, I may drink the wine before the wedding."

"The case, milady . . ."

"In fact, if he does not meet me when I arrive, I shall draw a certain conclusion from that, and I shall drink the poisoned wine as I sit there alone and abandoned."

"You compel me . . ."

"Morgan . . ."

The maid flipped the catches and the valise lay open on the marble tiles.

The Controlman lifted the bottle out. Curious, he thought. His ship ring fit exactly into a preformed declivity in the neck of the bottle.

The princess watched him with bright eyes. "Surely you wish to search our bodies—personally."

Dermaq replaced the bottle and snapped up the case. She was going to be difficult. Fortunately the return trip to Kornaval would be almost entirely in deepsleep.

Gerain examined *Firebird's* accommodations with a sneer. "Not much of a ship."

"Adequate, milady."

"Where is my suite?"

Dermaq smiled. "Milady—and milady's maid—will share the little cabin in the rear."

"I presume the door can be locked."

"There is no door."

"I see."

"Yet milady need fear nothing from me. I shall be in deepsleep—and so shall we all."

"But I thought time slowed down in flight . . ."

"It does, milady. Even so, the journey from Aerlon to Kornaval is fifteen light-*meda,* equivalent to several *meda* shiptime. So, as soon as we get the ship on true automatic, we plug into deepsleep. The crypts provide a numbing radiation. Our heartbeat and respiration slow drastically, body temperature drops, and our entire metabolism winds down to near zero. At the end of the flight, the radiation stops, the warning bells sound, the capsule turns the heat on. Presto—we rub our eyes, and it seems that we are merely awakening from a long nap."

"But actually, we're fifteen *meda* older?"

"No, milady, only one *monad* older." He thought of adding, I wish we *were* fifteen *meda* older. Instead he said, "And we're using *that* up waiting here. Let us proceed to the sleep caskets."

A few *tench* later he pulled the transparent lid down over Gerain's crypt and left quickly without looking into those fast-closing but still resentful eyes. He was glad he had a few things remaining to do before he too went into deepsleep.

As the darkness closed over her, Gerain had one final fading thought: "May I never know a great love."

"You give up too soon, little one," said the voice. Voice? Was the ship talking to her? How odd. But then she slept . . . and forgot.

And now back into the pilot room for one last check of the instruments. Dermaq sat down at the panel, and one by one he punched out the lights in the autocheck list . . . hydrogen fuel . . . waist scoop angle . . . lock-in to navigation pattern . . . internal air pressure . . . internal energy systems . . . three deepsleep crypts functional and set for fifteen *meda.*

Another fifteen *meda,* that is. He mustn't think about it. Oh, Innae . . .

He swiveled around to face the chart desk. Somewhere in the drawers here ought to be a *kaisch* set. Yes, here it is. He opened the box and tumbled the pieces out on the desk. Perhaps a solitaire game before deepsleep? He set up the pieces rapidly: the two-headed god in the corner, then the commissioner, the courier, keldar, princess, no-face, the beast, good-ship, and, finally, Hell-ship.

Kaisch: an ancient Kornaval word meaning eighty. Actually, since the board is nine squares by nine, there are eighty-one squares. However, the central eighty-first square is not used, since it means annihilation for any piece landing on it. They had taught him all this at the academy, along with other vanities. "We have instructed you in the gentle arts—how to sing, how to compose music, how to play a musical instrument. And, above all, we have taught you the game of *kaisch*. You can use all these things to entertain high-born guests on long voyages. Especially *kaisch*. *Kaisch* is the game for royalty."

His lip curled, and he almost smiled. He could see himself bowing to Gerain (with a flourish) and saying: "Would milady care for a game of *kaisch* before deepsleep? I promise to lose."

"I am aware," his instructor had continued, "that there is a silly superstitious variant of the noble game currently making the rounds. I think this is called psi-*kaisch,* Something like that. I can tell you now, if any of you are caught prostituting the game in this way, you cannot expect to graduate . . ."

The corners of his mouth lifted in wry amusement. Well, now, how about a little psi-*kaisch*, Courier? Why, thank you, I believe I will. First, we plug the voice instructor into the automover, and then the auto into the main panel in the ship's computer. Everything clicked neatly into place. And now he had to think. Everything had to be presented logically.

He began slowly and carefully: "I am courier. I serve commissioner, who serves the two-headed god. Princess and I are on board good-ship. *Tableau*, please."

Nothing happened. What was wrong? Then he remembered. He leaned forward and punched RANDOM PLAY, so the board could take over. And now the pieces began to move. Several slid off the board into the discard tray. That left only the two-headed god, commissioner, courier, princess keldar . . . *and Hell-ship?*

Dermaq frowned. He thought back. Yes, he had said *good*-ship, no *Hell*-ship. The sequence was scrambled already, and he had posited only the first set of moves. Why continue?

But he did.

"We move in deepsleep for fifteen *meda,*" he said, "from Aerlon to Kornaval, where keldar awaits princess. *Tableau*, please." He punched RANDOM PLAY.

Keldar slid away into discard. Hell-ship took up the lead in the central file, flanked by courier and princess, and trailed by commissioner and the two-headed god.

Hell-ship and its side companions were but one move away from the central square, the square called devastation, disaster, catastrophe. If a piece was forced into that square, the game was over, and a new game began.

Dermaq noted that his pulses were pounding. "It's only a game," he told himself. "Psi-*kaisch* is a stupid superstition. I'm going to stop right here." But he found himself giving the board a final command: "The fifteen *meda* have come and gone. We proceed now into the sixteenth *med. Tableau,* please . . ." He punched in.

This time no pieces left the board. Slowly, jerkily, as though not completely sure of themselves, all the pieces advanced one square, so that they stood just at the edge of the black catastrophic center. And then Hell-ship and courier and princess began to move forward once more.

"Stop!" cried Dermaq. He covered his eyes and whirled away as though to flee this ultimate disaster. But then, after a few *tench,* he began to feel foolish. He turned halfway and peeked through his fingers. The pieces stood quietly in their last position, as though courier, princess, and Hell-ship were fleeing away together from commissioner and Control. The whole thing was absolutely senseless, and he was twice an utter fool: once, for having played psi-*kaisch,* and twice, for letting it affect him.

He groaned, got up, unplugged the computer input, and tossed the pieces back in the board-box. They clattered to rest with noisy innocence.

It was time for deepsleep. High time.

13. THE FACES OF HATE

It was, of course, unreasonable to dislike *her. She* had not torn him from Innae and wrecked his life. Control had done that. It was pointless to blame her. Yet he couldn't help himself. He detested her.

As the transparent lid folded back, he bent over her deepsleep casket and studied her awakening face. Her eyes, closed in sleep, seemed larger than during waking. What color? Brown, he thought, like her hair. Her cheekbones were higher than Innae's, reflecting a royal hauteur. Her lips were full and red, even without cosmetics. In another time, another place, he might have found her beautiful. But not here, not now.

He watched her awaken. She had never come out of deepsleep before, and she whimpered and groaned a little. Then she stared up at him and recognized him. Her features hardened and he thought for a moment she was going to spit in his face. There was very little gravity in the ship and mechanically it was feasible.

But she merely said, "Morgan?"

"She's coming around."

"What next?"

"We dock on Kornaval in thirty *tench* at the Interplanetary Port. Can you be ready?"

"Yes. Will the keldar be waiting for us?"

"No." He sighed. In his mind's eye he scanned rapidly the courses and training they had given him at the academy. He came up blank. Nothing on Imperious Princesses. Nothing on Intransigent Females. He could kill coolly, efficiently, economically, but he was woefully undertrained to handle Gerain of Aerlon. He ran his tongue over his felines uncertainly. She wasn't going to like this. "I have received word that he is sending an escort. The escort will be here in a couple of days."

"A couple of *days?* Largo and Czandra! You mean I'm stuck on this damn ashcan for two days?"

"Certainly not, milady. Adequate temporary housing will be available at dockside. You will be completely secure."

"Well, I suppose in two days I could see a lot of the city."

"Control would prefer that you remain in your quarters, milady."

She sat up in the casket.

"You mean—jail?" she said incredulously.

He took a step backward. "Protective custody, milady. The suite provides everything. You will be most comfortable. I have business in the city, but when that is done, I shall call on you, to see whether you need anything."

Her eyes rolled up, as though her reaction to his last statement could not be adequately verbalized. She said simply, "Get out."

He escorted them down the long gangplank to the dock floor. "I have called a personal hoverel for us. Your suite is just up the way."

Gerain asked her maid, "Do you find the valise heavy?"

"No, milady. It is light."

"You will have to carry it. Our escort wishes to keep his hands free so that he can quickly shoot us if we try to escape. That's the real reason he called the hoverel. If we walked, he might have to carry the valise."

"You mean you want to walk?" said Dermaq dryly.

"Yes. I wish to stretch my legs. If it is permitted."

He took the bag from Morgan. "Let's go, then."

On the way they passed the landing area for a great starship, which was unloading cargo and passengers. It had evidently recently arrived and would be gone again in a few days. The three slowed their steps as they watched an elevator load of personnel float slowly down from the forward entranceway. They read the gold-ceramic insignia on her bow: AERLON.

Morgan hung her head and began to sob quietly.

"Come along, girl," said Gerain roughly.

Dermaq groaned inwardly. "We're almost there."

They walked the remaining *jurae* to the custodial apartment in silence.

In the center of the great green-patinaed portal the two-headed god stood out in strong bas-relief. The cheek-to-cheek, full-size faces of Largo and Czandra stared blankly out at them. Largo's mouth narrowed to a tiny horizontal slit, as though waiting to seize the courier's ring. How many women, he thought gloomily, have been ushered forlornly into this prison in *meda* past, and how many will the future centuries bring to this spot? And how many Controlmen like me will stand here stupidly wondering about it?

He held up his fist, pressed the ring into Largo's mouth slit, and stood back while the door slid ponderously into the facade side.

He ushered them into the vestibule. "I leave you now, milady. I'll return later."

She tossed her head and walked into the next room.

He didn't care what she said or didn't say. It was all irrelevant. He nodded to Morgan as he walked out. He made sure the great door was securely locked behind him, and then he turned and ran all the way back to his ship.

He had a call to make. Even before reporting in to Control.

14. INNAE

He sat at *Firebird's* control panel a long time before he called the number the Tracer Service had given him. She had moved, but the phone was actually still listed in his name. Mrs. Dermaq.

She would be sixty-three.

He was twenty-four.

He didn't turn on the image—either way. He didn't want to see her, nor she to see him. Not yet. Maybe never.

In fact, he wasn't sure why he was calling.

His hands began to tremble.

Someone was answering. "Hello?" There was something odd . . . strained . . . about the voice.

"Mrs. Dermaq?" he said.

"Speaking . . ."

"Innae . . . ?"

"Are you calling about the funeral?"

"The . . . *funeral?*"

"Services this evening at the Chapel of the Two Faces."

He took a deep breath and got control of his voice. He was probably talking to his daughter-in-law. He would make another guess. "I understand she died yesterday . . ."

"Last night, actually. In her sleep. Who is this, please? Hello? Hello?" But he had hung up.

Innae, you could not do this. Not yesterday. Yesterday, we were married.

15. Kill the Renegade

Commissioner Jaevar leaned back in his chair and listened to Control's voice within his mind. "One of the incidental benefits of Cancelar is that the resultant black hole opens a door on the far future."

Jaevar was astonished. Access to the *future?* Unverbalized questions formed in his mind.

"A sort of communication is already possible," explained Control. "Already, I am receiving some rather garbled input from myself as I exist forty-five billion *meda* in the future."

"Extraordinary," murmured Jaevar.

Control brushed the comment aside. "But the incoming data are spotty, incomplete, and almost unintelligible. They need to be more precise. Fortunately this can be arranged. I believe you have a routine patrol around the Cancelar black hole?"

"Two courier ships at all times—mostly to warn commercial vessels away from the hole." He checked his desk terminal. "Yes, at the moment, *Tavel* and *Sperling.*"

"They'll be adequate, I should think," mused his mind voice. "You will order one—say, *Sperling*—to shift its orbit inward, to within about thirty million *kilojurae* of the center of the black hole."

"But—"

"Don't interrupt, Commissioner. Proceeding, then, *Sperling* may receive a message from myself in the far future. If *Sperling* is sufficiently close to the hole, the message should be reasonably clear, even though in code. *Sperling* will forward the data to *Tavel*, who stands much farther out in a no-risk orbit. *Tavel* relays to you. Questions?"

Jaevar thought about *Sperling* in that close orbit. He was no navigator but he knew the orbit couldn't possibly hold. *Sperling* was going to be drawn into the hole. And Control knew it. He took a deep breath. "No questions."

"This is a simple task, Commissioner, well within your modest capabilities. Yet when I think back on how you let General Volo get into *Alteg* I wonder. Please don't bungle this one."

The overpowering presence in his mind faded out, and the man closed his eyes and slumped back in his chair. But only for a moment. There were several things to do. Orders to prepare. Find a replacement for *Sperling*. There would be objections and questions all down the line. Not that it mattered. He sat up again. He'd start with the Commodore of Patrols.

As his finger hovered over the punch buttons on his intercom panel, his mnemonic screen flashed: "*Firebird* due in three days. With keldar's betrothed, Gerain. Courier, Dermaq," Yes, that too. The keldar away on a hunting trip. Nobody to meet the bride. And he, Jaevar, could care less.

Savagely, he punched in the call for the Commodore.

Three days later Jaevar got a call on his intercom. "Interplanetary Port Authority calling, Commissioner,"

"Yes?" said Jaevar.

"You asked to be informed of the arrival of *Firebird*."

"Is the ship in?"

"It's in. We assigned Gate Five. The courier and two ladies have left the ship, apparently headed for the regal suite."

"Very good. Extend all courtesies. Excuse me, I have to terminate." He punched out the intercom and turned his attention to the intrusion with his mind.

"You have something from *Sperling?*" said the mind-voice.

"Yes, Control. This is the message, exactly as relayed from *Sperling* to *Tavel* to me." Jaevar punched in the code tape in his desk recorder and listened once more to the meaningless staccato whistles. He knew from the presence in his cortical overlay that Control was receiving the report and presumably decoding it without difficulty. He wondered what Control of forty-five billion *meda* in the future could be telling Control of the here and now. Indeed, he wondered what the universe could be like in such far-distant times. Well, no matter what might happen to human beings, Control was still there. And why not? Control was eternal!

The sounds ceased. And nothing from Control. He waited. "Shall I play it again?" he asked deferentially.

"No," said the voice in his brain. "That will not be necessary. The message was clear. The matter has become very interesting. It appears that the Cancelar black hole is not only a conduit for *messages* from the future, t also serves as a doorway for the entry of tangible objects of some size. In um, Jaevar, a ship is coming through from the distant future. It is piloted y a renegade Controlman. You will permit him to land at the International Port. As soon as he steps off his ship, you will have him killed."

"Can further description and identification be provided?" asked Jaevar.

In rapid but orderly sequence, words and pictures began to form in his cerebral cortex.

His eyes at first grew wide. But after the message ended, his irises contracted into slits, and his upper lip lifted over his felines as he formulated his plan for the forthcoming execution. He smiled and was happy, for it would be a thing of great beauty. His failure with *Alteg* and General Volo would certainly not be repeated here! "Dermaq, ah Dermaq . . ." he murmured.

16. JAEVAR AND DERMAQ

Dermaq studied the framed legends hanging in Jaevar's office while he waited for his supervisor to speak.

The legend behind Jaevar's head read:

The Prime Directive
All activity within the Universe is
for the benefit of Control.

To the right:

Dynasties end. Planets die. Suns
grow cold. Control is eternal.

To the left:

The Three Crimes
1. Disobedience to Control.
2. Near-c flight not authorized by Control.
3. Change not authorized by Control.

It was all cruel nonsense. Dermaq's side-whiskers sagged gloomily a he turned his attention back to the Commissioner.

Jaevar appeared to be about forty *meda* old. Yet Dermaq knew thi was impossible. This was the very man who had dragged him from hi marriage bed. And even though that event had occurred but yesterda within his own personal experience, Dermaq was well aware that over fort *meda* had actually elapsed. So Jaevar was certainly older than forty *meda* It had been rumored at the Academy that the Kornaval Commissione used age-arresting drugs. Dermaq had indeed seen directives in the Acad emy archives, signed by Jaevar, and some were over two hundred *meda* old. In fact, there was reason to believe that all Control commissione throughout the universe used the antigeriatric program. It provided administrative continuity.

He wants very much to live, thought Dermaq. Why? What's so remarkable about staying alive?

The Commissioner's bright blond facial hair was glossy and well trimmed. His side-whiskers were brushed and burnished, his mane clipped short in the new fashion. Despite somewhat flabby cheeks, he was a handsome man. Yet, when he looked up at Dermaq, the courier suppressed a shiver. The administrator's eyes held a subtle creative cruelty, and his welcoming smile was barely distinguishable from a snarl.

The impact was like a blow to the face. Dermaq's third eyelids nictitated over his corneas as though to wash away the image, and momentarily he looked away, then back at his superior.

Jaevar caught the motion and his smile broadened slightly. "Did you note anything unusual in transit?" he asked.

"Nothing. Why?"

"You may have heard of the Cancelar black hole?"

"I gave it a wide orbit. It is in the navigation manual. Formed by Control from the Rheik Cluster, I understand."

"I watched it form, some thirty *meda* ago," said Jaevar thoughtfully. "A truly great achievement." He leaned back and saw again the long brilliant streamers from the central suns, seeking out each other, then the final titanic radiance. And then the great nothingness. He thought of *Alteg*, and of the elusive Diavolite, and he grimaced. Not his fault the arch criminal escaped. He returned his attention to the courier. "You did well to give it a wide berth. The gravitational attraction is surprisingly strong. We patrol the area at all times to warn commercial traffic away—and for other purposes. Now then. I'm going to show you a couple of tapes." He pointed to the desk stereo with a long fingernail. "*Tavel* and *Sperling* were on patrol in the Cancelar area. *Sperling* had the inside orbit. And now *Tavel* receives a signal from *Sperling*."

Dermaq leaned forward as the stereo screen came alive.

He was seeing and hearing now what *Tavel* had seen and heard.

"We're fighting a tremendous gravity wash. Engines on full."

He watched the screen in mingled awe and fascination as Jaevar turned up the magnification. For a moment the hair along his spine stood straight out. His pupils dilated, and his abdomen contracted into an iron box. He knew what must come next. *Sperling* seemed to hang there, drifting slowly. Then it broke into two distinct pieces. Then the pieces vanished. One by one the knots in Dermaq's stomach slowly loosed again. The Cancelar black hole was certainly an obstacle to navigation; yet this was not news. It was in the Navigation Manual, and he seemed to recall there had even been special alerts from Surveys and Commerce. The odd thing was, *Sperling's* captain must have known the danger, and had either ignored it, or Control had *ordered* him into the danger zone. It was disconcerting, especially since Commissioner Jaevar (who ordinarily would not concern himself with navigational details) had specifically called it to Dermaq's attention. Why? Something odd was afoot. He looked the Commissioner squarely in the face. "Why are you telling me this?" he asked.

Jaevar did not answer him immediately; yet it was clear he had heard the question and was framing a response. There was something mocking in the way his eye slits narrowed. "There are some strange theories about black holes. These cosmic curiosities are thought to provide some sort of link with the future. Interesting."

Dermaq listened to this uneasily. He had no idea where it was leading. He wished Jaevar would come to the point.

But the Commissioner took his time. "Theory suggests," he said, "that any given black hole has two doors. One door opens from the future into the past. That past may, of course, be our present. The other door opens from the present into the future. For an ordinary black hole—say, one formed from an ordinary sun of the proper mass—the time span may be about three million *meda*. For a super colossal hole such as Cancelar, the reach of time may be forty-five billion *meda*: to the very ends of time, as it were." He studied the courier a moment.

Dermaq waited in silence. He understood nothing of this. He shifted the position of his hands on the arms of his chair and sensed that his palm pads left a moist smear along the smooth varnished surface.

And now Jaevar's harsh drooping whisker hairs began to tremble as though excited by certain thoughts finally beginning to come into focus in this tangled tale. Dermaq stared at him. "A ship entering that black hole on its *future* side," said Jaevar, "and doing it properly, I hasten to add, might well turn up in our present. Today. Here. Now."

Dermaq twisted uncomfortably in his chair. He said dryly, "I gather *Sperling* didn't enter the hole properly."

"Quite true. It didn't."

"If it had," said the courier, "would it have gone billions of *meda* into the past?"

"Not according to theory. No. Don't forget, a black hole has two entrances. Two doors, as it were. One door opens on the past, the other on the future. The only door available in our local time frame is the one that opens on the future. So *Sperling*—or at least its fragments—went through the door that opens on the future. And the rather far future at that, or so I'm told. In fact, depending on whether the universe oscillates or not those fragments may well have sailed into the middle of the next Cor over a hundred billion *meda* into the future."

"And the other door?"

"Well, it's just as I said." The Commissioner tapped his long fingernails together impatiently. "Say you're in the far future, and you want to get back here. The only door available *there* is the one that opens on the *past*. So you jump into the black hole, and here you are. What could be simpler?"

Dermaq looked up impassively at his superior. He wished he could make up his mind as to whether the man was insane. He said carefully, "That's something to remember, if I'm ever stuck a billion *meda* in the future."

Jaevar smiled. The right side of his cheek flicked, briefly revealing the dextral feline. "And now we can return to your original question: Why am I telling you all this . . . ? Yes. Well, it's for your own benefit, Dermaq. You have a potential for a long and distinguished career in the service of Control. And this is despite a basic rebelliousness against authority."

"Get to the point."

"Patience, my young friend. Your personnel dossier provides an interesting psychograph." He lifted a document from the open file in front of him. "As you know, these things give some indication of the future of an individual Controlman. Expressed as probability fractions, of course. And yet we know from experience that the prophecies are often uncannily accurate. The point is, Dermaq, there appears to be a black hole in *your* future."

"It's a quick, clean way to die. So be it."

"But that is not the manner of your death."

"I don't care to know how I shall die."

"But I will tell you. You die by your own hand."

This was too much. Dermaq was fed up. This son-of-a-*gorfan* had given him all this nonsense about black holes and was now trying to tell him he was going to kill himself. Well, he was going to speak his mind, and if the Commissioner didn't like it, they could reprogram him. Or kill him. At this point he didn't care what they did to him. "Jaevar," he pronounced flatly, "you are crazy."

The Commissioner laughed harshly. "Let us observe the courtesies, my dear fellow."

"If that's all, I have a funeral to attend."

"Yes. Of course. The funeral." Jaevar looked at the gloomy face opposite his desk. "I quite approve. Control likes a whole man, a man who takes an interest in his family."

Dermaq pondered this. The thing he did not know was, was Jaevar sincere? Or was this to be a demonstration of a sardonic sense of humor? No, as he studied the flabby face with its sagging side-whiskers, he knew Jaevar had no sense of humor, sardonic, ironic, or otherwise. He was sincere. And that made it even worse.

"I understand your wife died yesterday. Just before you brought the girl in," said Jaevar.

Dermaq waited in silence.

"So you certainly should attend the funeral. Out of respect."

Dermaq wanted very much to kill him. But the conditioning that Control had laid upon him saved Jaevar's life. "Yes," he said.

Jaevar prattled on. "It is well to be involved in family affairs, but you understand, of course, Control comes first."

"Of course."

"In that regard, we have a local assignment for you, which you may undertake immediately after the services. Return here after the funeral, and I'll give you the details."

17. THE FUNERAL

Innae. Innae of the black hair, the red red lips, the iridescent hazel eyes. They had met in Astrophysics VIII that last year at the Academy, and she had moved in with him. ("Where are the *prags?*" she said cheerfully, when she first saw the shambles of his rooms.) And then he had passed his Star Boards, and they were married, and Control had laid its icy talons on him.

Innae. He had left her pregnant, her cheeks tear-coursed, standing in their doorway. Only yesterday. She had turned her head away. She had refused to say goodbye. But Control had frozen its enslaving neural chains into his cerebral cortex, and there was nothing he could do about it.

He looked down at the face in the coffin. A white-haired woman with a wrinkled face. The once Innae.

He noticed then a dark-haired man standing beside the coffin head. They looked into each other's eyes for a moment; then Dermaq looked away. The resemblance was striking. His son, some forty *meda* old. He had been away from Kornaval barely a day, and his son had been born, had grown into middle age, and had possibly himself sired sons.

And he, Dermaq, had missed it all.

Control had done this. To be specific, Jaevar.

He turned back to the man. "How do they call you?" he said.

"I am called Dermaqsson." He looked at the Controlman curiously, as though he might have seen him before, in some other context. "Did you know my mother?"

"Yes," mumbled Dermaq. He turned his face. He was an intruder here, an outcast. He had lost the right to mourn. If this distant family ever spoke of him, it must be with distaste. Perhaps even with disgust, contempt. He shuffled away. He could not speak. Yet words were forming in his mind. "Someday I will destroy Control." But it did no good. And in fact Control had probably anticipated this. The slave-web layered onto his frontal cortex sounded its rebutting antiphony: "Control is All. Control endures forever. I will give my total loyalty to Control, even until death."

He walked out through the doorway of the funeral house into the cold rain.

18. The Execution

He flagged down a passing hoverel, squirmed inside, and stamped his legs to shed the clinging droplets of rain on the floor of the shabby little craft. The driver watched this in his mirror with distaste, but he had already noted the uniform and cape, and he was afraid to complain. "Well, guv?" It was a strained facsimile of courtesy.

"Control Building, Topside Landing. Take the dock route"

The vessel leapt into the air, cleared the skyline, and paused. "Dock route? That's out of your way, guv. An extra kroner?"

"Go ahead," said Dermaq. He rubbed his right palm over his cheeks, smoothing down his facial fur and bringing his side-whiskers into brushed symmetry. His head bobbled in synchronization with his hand.

A few moments later they were over the quays. Dermaq peered downward through the magnifying periscope. First, *Firebird*. Safe and sound. Still at Gate 5. Then beyond, the magnificent liner *Aerlon,* still boarding and taking on supplies and cargo. A wild fantasy flickered briefly in his imagination. He would land at *Aerlon's* loading elevator, and he'd take passage back to that miserable planet, and he'd simply disappear. His iris slits narrowed as he considered this, and his body tensed, as though to spring. He sighed, and slowly his muscles relaxed. He was being childish, ridiculous.

And now they were over the regal suite, which from the air turned out to be merely a small flat building. By the two gods, how he hated that building. And its inmates. A yowl of utter distaste rose in his throat, and he suppressed an urge to spit.

A regal suite—and a prison. And on his finger he wore the only key. As though confirming his responsibilities, he twisted *Firebird's* bow ring in a vicious semicircle through the rough hair of his ring finger. And the worst part was he had to return there for his duty call, after he completed Iaevar's mysterious upcoming assignment.

The cabbie watched all this with mild concern. "Everything all right, guv?"

The question brought him back to the present. "Yes." he said curtly.

"Control is just up the way, guv. Another five *tench.*"

Dermaq did not reply. The visor wipers had ceased their crotchety cranking. Had the rain stopped? How long ago?

"You wanted Topside, guv?"

"Yes."

"And here we are."

His retractile toenails clicked on the wet *krete* as he got out. From his pocket he dug out the fare, and then he headed for the elevator.

He sat again in the Commissioner's office.

"Your assignment," said Jaevar, "is an execution. As distinct from an assassination."

Dermaq shrugged. "What's the difference?"

"Tactically, probably none. Yet there are distinctions worth bearing in mind. An assassination is a killing without orderly trial, frequently without just cause, and generally without forewarning. An execution, on the other hand, is preceded by an authoritative investigation by a body having due jurisdiction, a considered judgment with sentence to kill, and due notice to the party."

"Due notice?" The courier was astonished. "He knows?"

"He knows."

"But not the time and place?"

"He knows exactly the time and place."

"And suppose he is not in total agreement with the judgment?"

"Even so, you should have no real trouble. He's older than you; you're in better shape. Nevertheless, you'd better make sure you draw first."

"Who is he?"

"A renegade Controlman. But to you, just a face, a body." Jaevar flipped on the screen. "There's his ship. It will arrive at the Interplanetary Port in about thirty *tench*. It already has landing clearance for Gate 6."

"Next to *Firebird*." More and more amazing!

"Yes."

"Will he be alone?"

"There is a woman on board. But we do not believe she will be a factor. We think he will walk down the gangplank alone. That would be a convenient place to kill him."

There was something insane here. "But if he knows of his sentence why is he returning?"

"He has a strong suicide complex," said Jaevar. "He hates Control and he now finally turns that hatred in on himself. It's all very logical." He looked quizzically at Dermaq. "I don't suppose you'd be interested in the crimes committed by this man."

"Not really."

But Jaevar continued. "Control has given me a general report. I think you should know about it. It may help you in your resolve to kill him. He broke all three of the Great Directives. He disobeyed an express instruction of Control. He introduced technological innovations. Without authority, he drove his ship at near-c velocities."

Dermaq suppressed a yawn. "A dangerous man," he agreed noncommittally. He waited with weary impassivity as his superior took a vial of *vrana* oil from his desk drawer and began to rub the perfume into his wrists.

And now Jaevar smiled, and he made a cryptic statement. "Future crimes have past punishments."

"Is that something I'm supposed to understand?"

"Ah? No. No. You are not required to understand; you need only *act.*"

The courier arose without replying.

19. GATE 6 (I)

He paces the dock floor, waiting. And wondering. He knows the whole thing is false. If the renegade is really dangerous, Control would have sent an entire platoon. Or better still, why not blast him out of the air as he comes in? And how had Control let him deviate in the first place? Was the traitor born without a cranial web? Or had he been able to neutralize it in some strange way?

He paces, sometimes faster, sometimes slower.

There was indeed something awry here.

Jaevar had told him he would have no trouble killing the man. But Jaevar was cruel, deceptive, callous. Jaevar was not to be trusted. For all he knew, *he* was being set up. Perhaps *he* was the true execution target.

The receiver in his inner ear crackled. "Courier docking. Clearance for Gate Six."

He peered overhead. Yes, there it was. "I have it," he said. A pinpoint, slowly growing larger. Down, down. Now reversing, to keep its nose pointed away.

He watched as the renegade ship came to rest in its cradle in Dock Number 6. It was expertly done. He found that he admired this man and his unseen highly skilled hands.

As he waited, he studied the ship. And something about it made him catch his breath, for it was very like his own *Firebird*. It had the same slim profile, the identical propulsion throat, the same proton collectors along the waist. He looked for her name, but it had long been obliterated. This ship was scored, crudded, lacerated by unthinkable traverses in space and time. This ship had been through several hells, and it was unthinkable that its captain was going to let himself be killed at this late date. Dermaq would have to be quick, yet cautious.

The ship door slid back.

A man walked out. He wore the Control blue, but it was patched, tattered, and faded. It had endured and seen a great deal. The man was about his own height and build, but older. He walked down the ramp with firm, knowing stride.

Dermaq stepped out from behind the stanchion.

At this instant a figure burst from the ship door, looked across at *Firebird*, then down the way at him, Dermaq. She shrieked, "No! No!" She began to run down the walkway.

The eyes of the two men locked. The stranger's mouth was twisting into a wry half smile when Dermaq lifted his hand in an instantaneous magical motion and fired.

Then he turned and walked away. He did not look back until he reached the edge of the dock run.

The woman had stopped where the stranger had fallen. As Dermaq watched, she knelt down beside the body and cradled the head in her lap. Her long white hair fell about his face, and she seemed to be rocking slowly back and forth and crooning to him.

It was not good. The whole thing gave him a bad feeling. He walked on toward Gerain's prison suite. During the passage, he turned back once again, and his eyes were drawn again to the little tragedy on the gangplank. The woman was laboriously dragging the man up the metal way, back toward that strange ship. Why? thought Dermaq. She can do nothing for him. He is dead, But perhaps she will take the ship out again. None of my affair, actually. I did what was required of me.

20. THE WINE (II)

From across the lounging room, hung cunningly between tapestries of hunting scenes, an oversized portrait of his majesty, Mark, Keldar of Kornaval, smiled down benignly at her.

Gerain stared back and was thoughtful.

The keldar had not met her as *Firebird* landed. His gracious majesty had not even sent his aide-de-camp. Her status in the household of the ruler of Kornaval was already pretty well defined. It was approximately zero

And there was another problem.

Dermaq had promised her a *young* prince. The man in the portrait had a scraggly white beard. And he was nearly bald. His bemedaled tunic bulged out over an overripe belly. He was sixty-five if he was a day—and actually very likely older, considering the well-understood rules of royal portraiture.

Dermaq had deceived her.

Dermaq stood once more before the forbidding bronze panel, and he hesitated.

Overhead, Tobos, the gray-green moon of Kornaval, cast strange wavering shadows on the dimly lit walkways. He looked over his shoulder uneasily. The great upcurving gash in the lower part of the little moon—actually a giant storm-blown desert left from the ancient wars—became a twisted mouth, and it returned his inquiry with a sardonic grin.

The courier winced and turned back to the panel and to the faces of the two-headed god. The eyes in the relief image were half hidden in the moon-shadow cast by the brows. In broad daylight those eyes had been blind, lifeless. But now, in the sheltering mystery of moonlight, they seemed to come alive. From the shadows, they stared at him, searching out his mind, warning him. Of what? What did the future hold for him? The whole mission had been awry, doomed, fateful. It had started by wrecking his marriage. In a very real sense, it had killed Innae. And then there was that so-called execution. He didn't like killing an unarmed man—an older man at that. He didn't like the idea of tearing the child-princess from her home by force. He didn't like the requirement to look in on her. She blamed him for all her misfortunes, of course. He was innocent . . . or was he? He didn't really know. All he knew for sure was this: something within the deep wellsprings of his subconscious mind—that final little bit of himself that Control had as yet been unable to claim—warned him to flee this place, that total disaster lay on the other side of this door.

He looked down at his boots and the dusty floor plates. Then he shrugged, wet his fingertips, and brushed his side-whiskers back. He stared for a moment at the bas-relief of the two-headed god, then lifted his fist and banged *Firebird*'s bow ring into the obscenely gaping declivity in Largo's mouth.

The heavy slab slowly and soundlessly receded into the side of the wall, and the Controlman walked into the gold-lighted hallway.

He knocked on the door to the adjoining maid's room, and Morgan glided out quickly, her face mask billowing about her cheeks. That mask. Odd, but it was their custom. He knew from her ringless hands that she was young. But what did she really look like? He didn't know and didn't care. "Please announce me to your lady," he said.

The woman bowed and left. A moment later she returned. "Sire, milady asks that you await her in the dining alcove. She wonders if you will share a glass of wine with her."

He shrugged. "As she wishes." He followed Morgan down the hallway into the alcove.

"It will be but a moment, sire." She disappeared.

He sank into the damask upholstery on one side of the little table and began his wait. A bare five *tench* later he heard the slap of sandals on the parquet deck and the swish of a thin sequined gown, and Gerain entered.

He was instantly uneasy at what he saw. She was pale and distraught, yet her jaw and mouth were firm. It was the face of high resolution. She had brought no weapon, and indeed there was none in this place. What dread thing had she determined to do?

She said quietly, "You see your prisoner is safe and sound, milord."

"Yes, I see. Do you need anything?"

"Nothing."

"Your detention here is purely temporary. And I trust you understand the necessity . . . I but do my duty."

"Of course, courier. And I forgive you. And to show my forgiveness, I thought we might have a cup together."

He heard now a faint sound and sensed a movement—as though the outer door were opening!

He sprang to his feet and dashed around the hallway and into the entranceway. The great metal slab was still shut. And all was silence, everywhere. He ran quickly into each of the adjoining rooms. He found Morgan in the wine cupboard, walking out the archway carrying a tray with chilled wine canister and cups. "Milord!" she gasped. The tassels on her mask sucked into her open mouth.

"Was anyone in here?" he demanded harshly.

"No one, milord!"

No one.

He was jumpy. He was hearing things. It was the combination of Innae's funeral and then the execution of that stupid, helpless renegade. The man hadn't even drawn.

He walked back into the dining chamber. The maid followed cautiously. He needed a rest. A long rest.

The princess was exactly where he had left her. "Burglars, Controlman?" For the first time during their enforced acquaintance, she smiled.

"I thought I heard something. I was mistaken. I am pleased milady is amused."

"The door seems quite solid, Controlman. I have tried it. I understand it opens only with the idento ring of your ship."

"True."

"That makes your ring unique."

"Yes."

She smiled as she studied his impassive features. "What would they do to you if something happened to me?"

"Nothing is going to happen to you."

"But suppose something *did*. Something bad. Suppose I . . . got killed, or something."

"You are under constant medical monitoring. And I happen to know you are in perfect health. Nothing is going to happen to you."

"Suppose I committed suicide."

"That is quite impossible."

"What would they do to you?"

"I would get a summary court-martial, and then I would be killed."

"How would they kill you?"

(By the almighty two-headed god, she was a perverse *slekken!*) He shrugged. "Any one of several different ways. Most likely I would simply be shot."

"They wouldn't blow your cranial web?"

"They might. But that takes a lot of computer energy. It would have to be a real emergency. They could do it that way, though." He was silent a moment, thinking back to his cadet days. To make clear the nature of Control, the academy supervisor held a lottery for each incoming class. Ninety-nine white chips, one black. The youth in front of him had drawn the black chip and had tried to run out of the lottery room. He had fallen dead in the doorway.

"Rest assured," he said quietly, "Control would find me and kill me."

"And so young. Sixty-five, I think you said?"

"That's one way to calculate it."

As they watched, Morgan picked up the wine bottle by the neck, very carefully pulled the stop, and placed it in front of her mistress.

(The maid is hardly breathing, thought the courier. What's going on here?)

"Since I am hostess, I shall serve," said Gerain. She poured out a sip into one of the cups and tasted it. She let a little of the wine roll around in her mouth before she swallowed. "Excellent," she pronounced, as she filled the glasses to the halfway mark. "The Wine of Elkar is nearly always good, but this is a special vintage, for very special occasions." She took a long sip, leaned back comfortably in her chair, and looked at him with brightening eyes. "How do you find it, Controlman?"

He drank. But what could he say? He was no connoisseur. "Exquisite, milady," he said politely. A gentleman of culture would probably have an entire vintner's lexicon at his disposal. But, actually, there was something strange about the liquid. He didn't even recognize it as wine. He found himself staring at Gerain. Just these few sips, and this stuff was going to his head.

And Gerain was staring back at him—in perplexity and wonder.

There was a click. The maid again grasped the literek by the neck and was refilling the glasses. He noted that Morgan wore a ring, on the middle finger of her right hand. The ring fitted into the declivity in the neck of the bottle. The contact of ring and bottle had made the click. He realized now it had happened in the first filling and that only now had he become aware of it.

He pondered all this in grave abstraction. Previously Morgan had worn no ring. He studied the hand on the wine bottle. It was no longer a young hand, white, lithe, supple. It was a woman's hand, but it was bronzed, rough. He considered this all very thoughtfully as his eyes returned to Gerain's. He looked into the eyes of this woman and he saw Innae. He saw every woman. His gaze roved over her cheeks and lips and throat, and he was stricken. Love was forbidden him, and he had resolved never again to love. Yet he now loved. It had not come on him gradually. He had drunk this strange wine. He had looked at this girl. And something had happened in his head.

And it had happened to her, too.

Together they lifted their glasses, locked arms, and drank again.

Morgan disappeared.

They were alone.

The man placed his glass on the table. Then he took the woman's glass from her hand and put it . . . he knew not where.

He studied her bosom sash. It was wrapped loosely yet knowingly about her breasts and midriff, and the ends were brought together in a clasp that rested on her left shoulder. She watched his roving eyes. His hand fumbled inexpertly at her clasp. In a soundless gesture she arced a long fingernail under the proper pin, and the clasp clattered to the canteen tiles. Neither heard it fall.

Like a living thing, the sash began to unwind about her, spiraling leisurely downward. The delicate soft down on her breasts rippled as though caressed by trembling air, and the nipples stood out red and firm. With a slow hypnotic gesture she swept her long dark hair back over her shoulders. As she did this, he could see tufts of black hair peeking from her armpits.

Dermaq took her hand, and as she rose from the little table the rest of her clothing dropped from her like water flowing away. His breath sucked in. The sight of her was like a blow to the stomach. Then he heard an odd sound. It came from deep within her lungs. She was purring. For a moment he stood half-paralyzed. Then life flooded back into him, and a contrapuntal rumble surged up into his throat. In sweeping melodic motions he reached out, pressed her body into his, touched his feline teeth in delicate declaration at the side of her neck, swept her up, and strode off with her toward the bedroom.

21. FLIGHT

Later—much later—as they lay there in her bed, he noted the growing intrusion of the *vox* on the side table. He picked it up. "Yes?" he said thickly.

"Dermaq!" It was Jaevar.

"Yes?"

"Kindly explain what occupies you in the regal suite in the middle of the night!" The voice vibrated between anxiety and cold rage.

"Well . . ." He made a valiant effort to organize his thinking. "What time is it?"

But Jaevar disconnected.

He sat on the bed and pulled on his trousers. And now he was thinking again. "He will probably call a patrol."

"What do we do?"

"The ship. We have to get on *Firebird*. No. Don't dress. A sheet. All you need. Come on."

"Morgan?"

"Unconscious. Maybe dead. The other was an imposter. She had a . . . a ring . . . like mine. She unlocked the door with it."

They were in the exit corridor.

The great entrance panel stood wide open. He was not surprised. The strange woman had opened it, left it open, and had gone. The mystery was great and entirely too much for him.

He swept Gerain up and began running with her down the dimly lit dock boards. *Firebird* lay a bare thousand *jurae* ahead. If he could just reach the gangplank.

But he wasn't going to make it. A four-man patrol was running toward him. Within a few *vecs* they would see him and start shooting. Just to stun, of course, on account of the princess. Later they would kill him. He heard the corporal bawl: "Quarter charge! Quarter charge!"

Something struck near his feet. He stopped. His eyes made a frantic search for a place to hide. But the warehouse walls stretched up endlessly. Not even a sheltering doorway. He put Gerain on the dock flooring. "Lie flat!" he warned.

And then, as he pulled on his glove gun, he saw an incredible thing. All of the approaching patrolmen seemed to be floating through the air in some sort of paralyzed slow motion. Their faces were contorted as though they were trying to scream. But they uttered no sound. The corporal's pistol clattered leisurely to the boards.

But there was no time to be startled or to speculate. He fired four shots in rapid succession. Four bodies dropped. "Come on!" He grabbed at Gerain's arm. She rose with him, clinging haphazardly to the sheet.

It was impossible, incredible, incomprehensible, but it had happened. And just in time. Sometime, perhaps, he would have time to think about it. Meanwhile he zigzagged through the bodies. His bare feet had hard footing in the warm, slippery blood. And now the gangplank to *Firebird*. And a good thing. It meant at least temporary safety. The door opened at the touch of his ring. He put the princess in the first takeoff seat. "Buckle in," he gasped. He ran forward, put his ring in the transfer capsule to place it at the nose of the ship, and unlocked the port tie rods.

"*Firebird* to Port Authority. Requesting takeoff."

"Port Authority to *Firebird*. Takeoff denied. Stand by to receive officers."

Well, there it was. "I am taking off."

"You will be shot down."

"I have on board the Princess Gerain, the betrothed of Mark, the keldar. Any action against the ship will endanger her life. The keldar will hold you personally responsible."

He sensed frantic discussion at the other end. Finally the reply came in. "We must contact Control. *Firebird* is requested to delay departure, pending instructions from Control."

Dermaq laughed and pressed the ignition button. The blastoff flung him backward into his takeoff cushions, and he buckled in.

The Port Police sent up a couple of token blasts. One exploded far ahead, the other far behind. Symbols of indecision and frustration. He could appreciate the dilemma of the Officer of the Day. At the officer's court-martial he could at least say he hadn't let them escape without firing a shot. Yet, just in case the princess really had been on board, he had been careful not to hit the ship. It was funny. But it wouldn't stay that way for long.

Eventually Kornaval Control would simply reach out to that slave-web in his cerebrum. He would be ordered to return. And he would return. He would slink home, tail between his legs. Or they might blow his web and kill him. So why had he done this thing—this otherwise glorious thing? The wine, the radiant wine, and the woman, his life, his strange love . . . that is why he had done it.

A *jar* later, shiptime, *Firebird* flipped out at .6c. He unbuckled and went back to Gerain. She had already unbuckled and was looking through his clothes locker.

"Will I have to wear a sheet the rest of my life or do you keep something handy for the girls you kidnap?"

There was nothing. Finally she reshaped a couple of his uniforms in the reductor. "I draw the line at your underwear," she said. "I'll make something from the sheet."

"I think there's a fabric-fixer somewhere."

"Dermaq."

"Yes?" He looked at her in surprise. She returned the look. Then he understood. *She* had not called him. Jaevar was calling them both. Simultaneously.

He listened to the commands forming within his brain. "Return, Dermaq. You have disobeyed a Control order; yet, return, and I assure you no harm will come to you. You will be treated, and healed, and you will reenter your full duties in the service of Control."

They stared at each other. He put his finger to his lips.

"Return to your seats," continued Jaevar. "You will now start deceleration."

He held up his palm. They both stood silent, wondering. He could not understand it. They were not obeying the silicon web commands. There was only one way to account for their newfound freedom. That strange wine had dulled their silicon conditioning.

"I recognize the fact of your continuing disobedience," said Jaevar calmly. "The anomaly will eventually be corrected. For the moment it is sufficient that you fully understand your situation. Unless we have an indication within sixty *vecs* that *Firebird* is decelerating, you both shall die."

He looked at her in alarm. "They can detonate your silicon patch," he whispered. "We have to go back."

"No. I don't think they can hurt us that way. Not if we fight."

"Fight? How?"

"Our conditioning has already been partially broken. The wine, I think. So that now Control can reach our silicon patches only if we yield up the necessary neural pathways that surround them. We think of other things. We overload our synapses with our own thoughts. For me that's no problem. I love you, Dermaq. I will sing you a love song. Here, take our trioletta and accompany me. The tune is 'Sunset.' "

She sang in a lilting contralto:

We wandered in the hills one day . . .

Control struck.

There was no pain, but he would have preferred pain. Millions of synapses opening and closing. Images, blazing, fading, shifting. He screamed as he watched himself seize the trioletta by the curl and break it over her upraised head. He shrieked as he watched himself leap to the drive console and begin the intricate reprograming to start deceleration.

> Where the crystal waters flow,
> Where the golden *erins* glow . . .

But there she was, untouched, unharmed, and he was still plucking delicately at the three strings of the trioletta. He hadn't left his seat. The wildness had been in his mind. The Wine of Elkar must have done extraordinary things to the anterior silent area of his cerebrum. It had disconnected so many neural pathways to his silicon web that Control could no longer assert motor control of his body. At best, it could blast him with images.

> Purple deepens on the hills.
> We hear the calls of *minarels*.

Gerain's voice wobbled, and he saw that she was perspiring. She looked up at him, and her eyebrows arched as though to say, "You too?" But her song continued.

> From the crest of the highest *bhun*
> The last light lifts into the sky
> And sun has set and day is done.

They looked at one another. The man passed a kerchief over his face. "We *can* fight Control," he said. "I never thought it would be possible." He let his head fall back on the cushions, and he was taking a deep breath when something screamed in his skull, and he blacked out.

As he regained consciousness, he noted that Gerain was sponging his face with cold water. He groaned. By the seven tails of Cetylus, his head hurt! He tried to put his hand on his forehead. His right arm was still half numb. He used his left hand. "That was quite a blast," he said thickly. "Did Control give you one, too?"

"Yes. Parting shots, I imagine. I came to first. No real damage." She cupped her hand over her right eye. "A little eyestrain, perhaps, and nice fat headache. But now I think Control and I are totally disconnected. They can't even force an image on me. How about you?"

He struggled carefully to his feet. The girl watched him as he walked over to check the drive console. "Still zipping along at .6c." He checked the rear screens. Pursuit was inevitable. *Firebird* was fast—.7c in spurts—but he knew Control had even faster ships and heavier armed. The question was, where were those ships? Possibly one or more were stationed on Kornaval. If so, *Firebird* could be overtaken and destroyed within the next day or so. He had to think, and it was hard to think. The only part of his body that didn't hurt was his right arm, and that didn't hurt because it was still temporarily paralyzed. His weapon arm. But it didn't matter. The affair was now far beyond simple hand weapons. For, aside from the mythical Diavola, this little ship carried the only two human beings that he knew about in the entire universe who were free from Control. Predictably, Control would not permit this freedom to continue, even if it meant turning entire galaxies inside out to hunt them down.

Gerain echoed his thoughts. "Where can we go?"

Where indeed? Nowhere. By now Control had undoubtedly published warnings to the ports, docks, and quay areas of all planets within the local clusters.

"I have heard of a place," he said thoughtfully. He flipped a series of charts on the screen. One after another he studied them, then shook his head. Finally he found one that satisfied him, and he left it outlined on the screen. "This place is supposed to be sort of a near vacuum. It's the center of the original Big Bang, when the universe exploded, some fifteen billion *meda* ago. All matter blew outward and away from this center. Nothing was left. Nothing to make suns or planets or galaxies. No ships go there. It's called the Silent Quarter."

"But if we went there, couldn't Control send a ship in after us?"

"Possibly. I don't really know. The problem is, the proton density in The Quarter is below the level a ship needs for normal nuclear drive. For example, in our present area of space, *Firebird's* waist scoops are battened down by about two-thirds, because there's more hydrogen floating around out there than she needs for her engines. But in the Silent Zone, there will be dead patches where there isn't enough hydrogen to feed her motors. In those areas she won't be able to accelerate or maneuver. She will simply drift on whatever velocity she had when her motors died."

"I see. But if that happens to us, it would happen to Control's pursuit ships, too."

"Yes."

"What are our alternates?"

"Zigzag around awhile until we are boxed in and destroyed. Or surrender now and get our minds reconditioned."

"Then let's head for the Silent Quarter."

"I agree. Let's make carbon."

"What does that mean?" she asked.

"Space lingo. The hydrogen picked up in the waist scoops goes through the same nuclear processes that you have within a normal yellow sun. The end product is carbon. You can take it out of the converter bins."

"Soot?"

"No—actually, diamonds—very tiny. Here." He pulled a plastic disc from his pocket. "You can see a bunch of them grouped in the center to form the courier insignia. See how they catch the light."

She peered at the little device.

"Are the diamonds worth any money?"

He smiled. "Too small to have any value as gems. Used mostly to make grinding tools and abrasives. *These* were recovered from a flight that took about one hundred *meda*. For fair gem size, you'd need a million-*meda* flight."

"What size would you get after a billion-*meda* flight?"

He shrugged. "May the gods forbid that we ever find out."

22. DREAMS AND *KAISCH*

Life on board *Firebird* now developed a certain monotony. They exercised. They read the meager offerings of the ship's little library. They made love. They watched feelies on the stereo. They played all the duo-games. They became imaginative with the food synthesizer. They alternated in deepsleeps. Always she would awaken him before the scheduled *jar.*

Often he awakened with the realization he had been dreaming.

He was no stranger, of course, to the bare fact of deepsleep dreaming. He had scanned a great deal of the tapes dealing with the physical, mental, and psychological impacts of deepsleep. He knew the sleeper dreamed and that the dreams might vary greatly in subject matter. The sleep images might review and recast the sleeper's subconscious desires and goals. The phantasms might expose fears and shape pursuing enemies as monsters. *Those* hardly differed from nightmares. And finally, the puzzles, where the dreams tried to unravel a mystery. And *that* was the path *his* dreams took. He saw again that man on the gangplank. In his dream he liked that man. He did not want to kill him, but he knew he had to. The man meant no threat to him. And thinking back (in his dream), the man didn't even carry a weapon. No gun belt was strapped to his waist. Both of his hands were on the side guards of the ramp. The man seemed to be about fifty. His eyes were serene, and they looked straight into Dermaq's eyes, and even as the courier had got off that one fatal shot, those eyes had smiled at him.

Why should it trouble him? *That* was a mystery all in itself! He had killed men before, and very likely he would kill again. Well, let this be the end of it. He resolved not to think about his dream anymore.

They waded through the shipboard movies. A dozen times. A hundred times. In the end, with one exception, even Gerain found them unendurable. The exception was *Hell-Ship*. A pirate ship created by the Diavola and crewed by a devil man and his devil woman, it cruised destructively about the universe at forbidden speeds, committed to a life of evil. Finally even the ship could endure the hellish couple no longer and announced that it was going to plunge with them into the nearest sun.

"But I don't want to be burned up!" wailed the devil woman. "I'm much too happy!"

"That's good!" replied the ship. "The happy ones burn best!"

Sometimes they composed ditties. They sang them together as Dermaq twanged at his trioletta.

Nonsimultaneity

Time's amiss.
So is space.
Today we kiss—then
(Despite all haste!)
It's tomorrow—when
We embrace.

Three of Us

Little ship, who gave thee fire
And did with silver thee attire?
Who gave thee wings to bear this love
And blend these hearts like hand and glove?

They played a lot of *kaisch*. He was astonished to learn, in the beginning, that she, a princess of the blood, did not know how to play the royal game. So, with considerable pride in his expertise, he explained everything. There are three white pieces: control, commissioner, and the princess. The black pieces are no-face, the beast, and Hell-ship. The neutral grays are the keldar, the courier, and the good-ship. Either white or black can play the neutrals. Now, the objects of the game are several. The main object is for white to move the princess to the far rank, where she becomes keldarin. Black's main object is to prevent this."

"How does he do that?"

"By capturing the princess or all of her defenders."

She picked up the princess piece. "How do you capture?"

"Well, in capturing, the capturing piece can simply take the losing piece at long range or can move onto its square. The captured piece may then go into the discard tray, or, in certain peculiar instances, the capturing piece can assume the identity of the captured piece or vice versa."

"How can that be?"

"Easy. See—all the pieces are plastic shells. Certain of them can fit over certain of the others. Or the reverse. Here's a white commissioner. It will fit over, say, no-face, or the beast. Such a maneuver is called 'mergence.' "

"Why are good-ship and Hell-ship so big?"

"To carry passengers. Each can take two passengers."

"Does that mean the passengers are captured?"

"That depends. In good-ship, they're going along for the ride—escaping, you might say—because good-ship has better moves than they have."

"In Hell-ship . . . ?"

He shrugged. "There it gets complicated. If a piece is inside Hell-ship he—or she—might not know until the end of the game whether he's captured or whether he's escaping."

She looked puzzled. He didn't blame her. It *was* a difficult game.

"Let's go on to some of the other rules," he proposed lamely.

"Go ahead."

"Well, besides the keldarin row there are a couple of other board areas that have to be kept in mind. Say the princess is in danger of being captured by Hell-Ship. Perhaps she can escape to safety in a side file. On the other hand, there's one particular square that isn't safe for any of the pieces. That's the central square. *Kaisch* is named for it. If any piece is driven into it the game ends."

"And the other side wins?"

"You don't really know for sure. Each player has to decide for himself. There would be various possibilities. Perhaps one side wins and the other loses. Or perhaps both lose. Or both win. You'd have to take it on a case-by-case basis. The only thing you *can* be sure of—the game ends and new game begins."

She studied him thoughtfully, and he said to himself, She's going to tell me *kaisch* is a ridiculous, silly game, fit only for children.

She said, "Tell me about psi-*kaisch*."

He looked up, startled, and did not reply immediately. He thought about that first night out from Aerlon. Just before he had retired into deepsleep he had—guiltily and surreptitiously—tried a sequence of psi-*kaisch*. And it had been a disaster. Hell-ship had seized courier and princess and, pursued hotly by commissioner and control, had dashed for the fatal central square.

He shivered and turned his head away. "Psi-*kaisch* is a superstitious lunacy, fit only for the very immature."

She threw her head back and laughed heartily. "You've *tried* it, haven't you! Well, no matter. I think I can beat you at the regular game. Let me be white."

Sheepishly, he set up the pieces.

23. THE SILENT QUARTER

But now they were approaching the terminus of their long flight, and things were changing. Dermaq watched the screens with foreboding as the galaxies took up their hazy barrier shapes behind the fleeing ship. Behind them lay capture and death. Death: either physical—before a *jaet* squad—or mental—within the cranial hoods of a reprogramming unit. Either way, it was unattractive.

Ahead lay death, too. The hydrogen density was already perceptibly dropping. He opened the waist scoops to three-quarters, then to seven-eighths. Within three days, if this rate of drop continued, the scoops would be wide open and gasping. In a week the motors would die for lack of protons, and *Firebird* would be adrift. And then, without power, nothing would work. The food synthesizer wouldn't make any protein or carbohydrates. The water synthesizer would run dry. The decarboxylator would cease splitting oxygen from the carbon dioxide their lungs manufactured.

Just sitting here, they would die.

Blip.

His head jerked back to the screen. "We have company," he said quietly.

She stood at his side, and they looked together.

"It's coming in behind us. A hunting ship. Very fast."

He rubbed his chin. "We'll have to strip the cabins."

She understood. "The upholstery . . . drapes . . . everything plastic."

"That's the idea. Loaded with hydrogen, tied up in the polymers. Put t through the chopper. Meanwhile I'll see if I can modify the converter ircuits."

The sparse amenities of the ship slowly disappeared. During the ourse of the next several days cushions, curtains, bedclothes, dishes, foam insulation, extra clothing, carpeting, decorations, the *kaisch* set—board and men—all went into the converters.

On the morning of the twelfth day Dermaq summarized the situation. "We're running at point six c. So is the hunt ship. We're not pulling away, they're not overtaking. It's as though we're both standing still. Both of us are running in dead space. We haven't picked up a proton in a week, and neither have they. I think they may carry spare tanks of liquid hydrogen. If that's so, then it's just a question of who will run out of fuel first."

On the fourteenth day they found a plastic stool and sawed it up. Then they ripped off the plastic veneer on the instrument panels. On the eighteenth day they diverted a slow stream of water from their sacrosanct forty-*bater* emergency tank.

The third week passed. Dermaq tried to work out a circuit to adapt the motors to use ferrous metals as fuel. It backfired, and one of the converter units exploded. Their speed fell off. The hunt ship began to overtake them.

On the twenty-fourth day they lay on the bare metal floor in front of the screen, watching the slow approach of the blip.

He had to plan now for the worst—the very worst. Gerain was not going to like this. There was no good way to break the news to her. He might as well blurt it out. He walked unsteadily into her tiny alcove.

She was writing something, but she immediately turned the paper over when he came in.

"The human body contains a great deal of hydrogen," he said. "It is tied up in molecular form, such as water, amino acids, fatty materials, and so on. Within a few hours, the last of our pickup fuel will be gone. I plan then . . . to die. You must push me into the converter. I will explain how you can do this—"

Gerain began to laugh. It was a weird, unsettling mixture of howls and gaggles. At another time, Dermaq might have been offended at such reception to his most noble of sacrifices. But now he simply stared at her, uncomprehending, and fearing that her brain had snapped.

She handed him the piece of paper. He unraveled the last sentence. "After that, you must stuff my body into the converter . . ."

He found himself joining her in laughter, peal after horrid peal. Finally she clutched at his shoulders and buried her face in his chest. He crumpled the little piece of paper and left it floating in midair. He pushed her back. There was still something he had to tell her, if he could only remember. Yes. "The hunt ship is close enough to fire for range," he said huskily. It was difficult for him to think or talk. His head buzzed. He had had no water in two days, and his tongue was thick, dry, uncontrollable.

The ship rocked. They were flung into midair. They waited as the grav-catches brought them back to the floor.

"Close," muttered the man. "It burst somewhere ahead, I think." The computers on the hunt-ship were evaluating this ranging shot. Would they need another? Perhaps one more, the same distance aft, and then the third shot would be a direct hit.

The ship jumped slightly.

"Another shot?" asked Gerain.

"No, I don't think so. I think we picked up a little v when our scoops caught some of the proton debris from their shot. Just a little, but maybe enough to throw off their firing computer." He struggled to his knees and crawled to the fuel control buttons on the instrument console. "We won't use it all. I'll save some for one more zigzag." He stared at the screen. "Well, look at *this!* Something is paralleling our course! And whatever it is, it's very very close."

"The hunt ship?"

"No, *that's* still far away in the logarithmic background."

A dozen conjectures cascaded down into what was left of his mind. Did Control have patrol ships *here,* in the very depths of Hell? Or, was this a lone pirate ship, and was *Firebird* about to be boarded and stripped of her motors and converters, and her two occupants tossed suitless into the frozen wastes of space? Or could this be another fugitive, and had it encountered *Firebird's* course by pure chance? (He dismissed that one instantly.) Or, finally, was it indeed true what Control had taught from childhood: this was Hell, and in Hell he should expect devils who would torture them and steal their souls away. Which is to ask, had a devil-ship found them?

Firebird lurched heavily to starboard.

Gerain gasped. "Were we hit?"

"No. It's the ship alongside. It's got a tractor beam on us."

"We have been captured," she said wearily.

"Captured?" By the twenty traitor devils, he was tired. She was right, of course. They had been captured, and he had to stay alert. He stumbled to the weapons cabinet and got out his glove-guns and the heavy portoblast.

The ship jumped again. His feet flew out from under him. The portoblast zoomed across the little cabin.

That was no tractor beam. The second H-shell from the hunt ship had very nearly got them. *And* their captors. If *Firebird* hadn't been tractored away, they and the ship would now be molecular dust floating idly in the vast reaches of the Silence.

Their captors had saved them. That strange ship had done this, knowing the risk it ran. That changed everything. There was now every reason to assume it was a friend. Nevertheless . . . He exchanged quick glances with the girl. She seemed unhurt. He crept toward the portoblast lying in the corner.

The transcom bleeped. *"Firebird.* Calling *Firebird."* The voice was full and resonant. Human? Humanoid? No way to tell just yet.

At least their companion ship was familiar with the traditional greeting between ships in peacetime. And they knew the language of the Kornaval cluster. And the name of his ship. *That,* of course, they could have got from the idento ring in *Firebird's* nose, assuming they had the proper decoding computer—which, apparently, they had.

He cradled the portoblast in his arms and walked unsteadily over to the communicator in the console. *"Firebird* here. We thank you for pulling us away from that last shot. Who are you?"

The reply came with great good humor. *"Devilship One,* General Volo. And may I suggest you hang on tight while I pull you out of here. After that we can see to your needs. Buckle in!"

"Yes. Thank you." They lay back quickly in the cushionless recliners. Wham!

The portoblast leaped from his lap and sailed into the console instrument panel amid a splash of sparks. He sighed. This was almost as bad as a near miss from the hunt ship. And as he was thinking this, the G's on his brain doubled and redoubled, and everything was trying to fade away. Except that he refused to let it. He hugged his chest and lay farther back in the recliner, so that he retained a shred of consciousness, and thus he heard the space lock spin open behind him. And then he heard voices.

"Look to the woman first."

"Incredible. They fueled everything."

"Even the water. Thirty days, would you say?"

They were bending over Gerain. Then a man walked over between him and the console and looked down at him and smiled. "Captain Dermaq? I am Volo. And I have here with me my ship's doctor and my chief engineer. We are your friends. We would like you and the princess to join us in *Devilship One.* Will you come with us?"

Dermaq watched the lean alert features float in and out of focus. He saw the honest side-whiskers flicker in earnest concern. He relaxed. "How is Gerain?" he croaked.

"She is dehydrated, and she has lost much weight, but her mind and body are stable. She needs water, proper food, and a great deal of rest."

"Firebird . . . ?"

"You took a couple of near misses, but you're still structurally sound. You have a tough little ship. When we get you two out, we'll start repairs." He grinned wryly. "I fear, Captain, that what *you* have done to the inside of your ship might almost be considered a direct hit."

Dermaq smiled feebly. He liked this strange man. "How did you get us out? Where are we now?"

"We can discuss that later."

"What *med* is it—Universal Time?"

"That, too, can wait." General Volo seemed to be unfolding some sort of stretcher. Dermaq tried to get to his feet. But it was not possible. He fell into a gentle, sheltering blackness.

24. DEVILSHIP ONE

A couple of *jars* later Dermaq answered the knock on their cabin door in *Devilship One.* "Come in."

General Volo entered. He smiled when Dermaq rose to greet him. He looked over at the lower bunk, where Gerain lay. "And how is milady?"

"Much better, General," she said.

"I apologize for the simplicity and small size of your quarters. However, aside from the crew ward room, it's the only cabin in the ship with a double bunk."

"It is comfortable, and we are most grateful," said Dermaq.

"Do you feel well enough to join me in the bridge room?"

Dermaq looked at Gerain. She nodded. The two followed Volo through narrow passageways up to the bridge, where the general motioned to a couple of buckle chairs. He sat nearby.

Dermaq's eyes scanned the control area quickly and expertly. Most of the panel entries were standard, and he recognized them without difficulty. One of the elements puzzled him, however. Hanging over the instrument panel was a head-size luminous ball. It seemed to be floating free within a shadowy cube. He studied it curiously for a moment—long enough to note that the luminosity consisted of thousands of pinpoints of light on the sphere surface. During this instant, one of the light points began to flash intermittently. Simultaneously, a counter meter in the lower right corner of the shadow cube flashed, and he read a number: "7045." It meant nothing to him. And Volo either did not notice or did not care, or he paid no attention at all.

"Now, then, to business," said the general. "When we first met, you had some questions."

Dermaq shrugged his shoulders. "It's quite possible. Yet, I honestly can't remember . . . Since we are now your guests, why don't you simply tell us whatever you like."

"Well said. First, we'll dispose of some of the obvious problems. For example, how are our ships able to move in the depths of the Silent Quarter?"

"I wondered," said Dermaq.

"The answer is, we carry our fuel with us: tanks of liquid hydrogen—enough to run a ship at point nine c for forty days."

Ninety percent of the speed of light? Dermaq was awed. "What happens after forty days?"

"Back to base, to refuel."

"But if you've been out for forty days at point nine c, you have actually been away hundreds of years, base time. Your base will be greatly changed. It might not even be there anymore. No fuel. No nothing."

Volo smiled. "That could happen, of course. But it hasn't yet."

"General," said Gerain, "a question."

"Of course, milady."

"How old are you?"

"Forty-two *meda*, body time, milady. Over four thousand *meda*, Universal Time."

"What *med* is it?" asked Dermaq.

"Eleven thousand, five hundred and two, U.T."

Dermaq's face brightened. "When we left, it was not quite ten thousand five hundred. A thousand *meda* have elapsed. Everything back on Kornaval would be different now. We could return."

The general shook his head. "You should know better, Captain. To Control, a thousand *meda* are nothing. You would still be on their kill list."

"But why would they still care," said Gerain, "after all this time?"

"Because," said Volo grimly, "they believe that the two of you—and *Firebird*—are going to destroy them."

His visitors stared first at him, then at each other.

Dermaq swallowed hard. "Destroy Control? Gerain . . . and I . . . ?"

"And *Firebird*. Especially *Firebird*."

"That's insane! Nobody . . . no *thing* . . . can possibly touch Control!"

"So they would have us think." Volo arose, turned off the cabin lights and pointed to the luminous ball over the control panel. "The luminosity comes from about seven thousand light points. Each scintilla of light is a Control hunt ship. There are cruisers and battlers in the far rear that don't show. We in the Diavolite colony are in the center of this sphere."

Dermaq was astonished. "Is it possible? I didn't see anything like that as we came into the Quarter. Just one hunt ship the whole way."

"In the beginning there were only a few patrol fleets," agreed Volo. "But remember, this cluster has had a thousand *meda* to form, starting with the beginning of your flight and up to the present."

"Still," said Dermaq, "there's a lot of space out there. They can't have covered every cubic *jura* in this sector."

"They almost have," said the general. "You can take any section of the sphere . . ." He flipped a switch. The display faded out. A new display registered, with different light points arranged in a circle, some steady, some moving. As they watched, a new point seemed to arrive out of nowhere. It took up a position in the circle. "It's the same in any segment," said the general. "We are completely surrounded."

"But why all the effort?" said Dermaq.

"In the beginning Control merely wanted to keep a general watch on the colony. But now they have a very specific and very serious objective."

"Which is?" said Dermaq.

The general studied his guests gravely, as though pondering how much he should tell them. He sighed. "To start, let me say this. As perhaps you know, Control is an empire of data banks. There are two primary banks, each at the far distant poles of the universe. One of these banks, the dominant, is called Largo. The other is Czandra. We believe that each of these entities contains a piece of human cortex, taken thousands of *meda* ago by my ancestor, Daith Volo, from a human being probably in a terminal condition—dying, if you will. One was male—Largo; the other was female—Czandra. What they were like when they were living human beings we can only surmise. But turning now to Czandra, she—if we may call her that—operates on a highly intuitive level. Two of our people have had recent access to some of Czandra's storage units on Kornaval. Just before they were detected and killed, they sent back some interesting information. It appears to be the impression within Czandra that the two of you, and your ship, represent an intolerable threat to the continuing existence of Control. Czandra believes it is within your power to annihilate the entire computer empire constituting Control—that you can destroy every Control center on every planet in every star system in every galaxy in the entire universe. *And we believe that Czandra is absolutely correct!*" He smiled grimly. "You think you *escaped* here? No, my friends, you were *driven* here, as the beaters drive the quarry into the trap. For now you can be destroyed along with the Diavola, who, though you did not know it, have conspired with you from the beginning for the destruction of Control."

Dermaq stole a look at Gerain. Her face said, "This man is mad." He was inclined to agree.

Volo read them clearly. He laughed, but it was a bitter thing, and without humor. "I see that I must take you back into the far reaches of time, into the beginnings. To help your understanding, we must review some history." He studied his guests for a moment. "I don't mean the history that was programmed into your silicon webs at the learning centers when you were children. I mean real history." He paused, gathering his thoughts. "History starts with two very important things that happened in the early years of space travel. The first great thing was the development of the telepathic computer. In the beginning, the only means of communicating between two star systems was by radio or ship. Either way, years were required to deliver a message and more years to get an answer back. And then my distant ancestor, Daith Volo, discovered, almost by accident, that a certain kind of computer on Kornaval—in a word, Czandra—was able to communicate instantaneously with a similar computer on Orchon Two. He then installed the same facility in computers on planets on other stars of the local K-Four cluster. And then outside the cluster. And then our ancestors realized that they had finally achieved a true homogeneous galactic culture. They developed a common language, a common system of laws, a democratic, universal government. Along with a common body of highly integrated chemical, physical, and biological research. All with the guidance and advice of the computers. The crowning computer achievement was Largo, at the opposite pole of the universe. Eventually every planet in every star system had its own giant computer . . . and these creatures—ah, yes, they were, and are, as much alive as you and I—were in marvelous contact with each other. And it turned out that they had been carrying out some research of their own. On human genes. Intricate, complex— yet simple and logical, when you stop to think about it." The general paused for a somber side glance at the luminous sphere over the control panel. Then he continued.

"In their first experiments they—I speak now of Largo and Czandra— substituted silicon analogs of the thirty-nine amino acid building blocks in standard DNA in a standard human gene. The substitution resulted in instructions to the embryonic brain to form a silicon web or chip in the anterior frontal zone of the left cerebral hemisphere. This web was thoroughly integrated with all routine functions of the brain. The medulla still controls breathing, heartbeat, and blood pressure. The cerebellum continues in its task of keeping the muscles in tone. The thalamus sorts out messages received by the sensory nerve fibers. The hypothalamus continues to regulate the integration of the internal organs with the blood vessels and the higher centers in the cerebrum; for example, it may prepare the body to fight—or to flee—just as it has been doing for several million *meda*. And now we get to the cerebrum. And here we find some changes. Consider the anterior silent area of the prefrontal lobe. Here we perform our most complex rational processes. Here we think. But now there comes a microscopic intruder. The instructions for its formation exist in our genes even prior to conception. And so it grows in the fetal brain, and there it becomes a minuscule web of spongy silicon—thoroughly and compatibly integrated into the neural patterns and pathway of the cerebral frontal area. In the beginning, it is inert. But even while we are infants and barely able to talk, we are brought to the preschool provided by Control. And there certain very fundamental proposition are impressed on those little silicon webs: we receive the Directives before we are able to read. We learn that near-c space flight is forbidden except as authorized by Control; that change is criminal, unless authorized by Control; that our existence and our every activity is for the ultimate benefit of Control." He laughed shortly. "What does a child of six know about near-c space flight? Yet he gets the instruction, and it stays with him all his life."

The general studied his guests. Was he boring them? They had better understand him. It might mean their lives. He coughed and went on.

"The Directives are absolutely logical for the continued existence of Control. But they are stultifying, destructive, and absolutely illogical for humanity. *Phelex sapiens* has become a froth of helpless living robots. And in the case of an occasional individual dissident, specific instructions could be given to the web by the nearest Control center. And if that failed, the flawed human specimen could simply be terminated by blowing the environmental neural network of his web."

"But some escaped?" hazarded Gerain. "You and the other Diavola?"

"Yes, the descendants of Daith Volo—the Diavola—avoided the genetic implantation and escaped. For centuries we have hidden in this little colony in the Quarter, and from this rather dubious base we attempt to continue our mission."

"And what is your 'mission'?" asked Dermaq.

"Our ancestor blamed himself for permitting the creation of Control. He believed that he worked a great wrong on the universe. We, his descendants, have accepted the mission of righting that wrong. We labor for the destruction of Control."

Dermaq shook his head. "What you seek is impossible. Nothing can ever destroy Control."

"We hope you are wrong, Captain. At any rate, you and your lady have drunk the wine. The two of you are now free from Control. And you are eminently qualified to participate in our mission."

Dermaq remembered. Yes, the wine. A remarkable vintage. He was beginning to understand more and more. "*Your* wine, of course," he said.

"Yes."

"What was in that stuff?"

Volo's eyes twinkled. "Certain remarkable esters and alcohols. If irradiated in certain wavelengths, they change into even more exotic narcotic compounds. And then, if the irradiated wine be drunk, these narcotics react chemically and permanently with certain specific synapses within the cerebrum: those radiating from the silicon web. And there is a curious by-product. The wine is simultaneously an overwhelming erotic stimulant. On the one hand, it frees the imbiber; on the other—if a woman drinks with him—it immediately enslaves him again. And her. So what's the final net result? Only the drinkers can say."

Dermaq and Gerain looked at each other and laughed.

Volo joined in. "Oh, how far we have all regressed. We have sunk even to laughter—which, according to Control, is but an atavistic animal demonstration without function or utility."

"You seem to have all the answers," said Dermaq. "I wonder if I could ask a few questions about some things that have been troubling me?"

"You can ask. I certainly don't know everything, but I can tell you what I do know."

"The wine required radiation?"

"Yes."

"Just exactly how did it get irradiated?"

The general looked at him, puzzled. "Why . . . I don't know how it got irradiated. We provided the proper wine in the proper literek, properly indented for the proper ring. Our contribution ended there—at least as far as the wine was concerned. So with respect to the actual irradiation, we know very little. It's almost as though we had a secret conspirator working with us. We simply understood that somehow, at the proper time, the wine would be suitably irradiated." He lifted his shoulders in a gesture of genuine perplexity. "Who did it? By whose command? How was this marvelous thing accomplished? Perhaps you can enlighten us."

"We know very little," said the courier. "However, between us perhaps we can piece it together. I suggest we reexamine the facts, step by step. Gerain, where did you get the wine in the first place?"

"My mother had it made up, especially for me, at the local poison shop."

"Our agent on Aerlon worked with the poisoner," said Volo. "No mystery *there*. Our man furnished the bottle with the ring indent. All by our design."

"You knew," said Dermaq, "that the proper ring would irradiate the wine at the proper moment and that Gerain and I would drink the wine and flee in *Firebird* to the Silent Quarter?"

"That's a good summary," conceded Volo.

"But the *ring*, man, the *ring*," insisted Dermaq. "Don't you see?"

"We see," said Volo somberly. "The specifications for the ring—that it must have traversed all space and all time—were quite beyond us. All we could do—and all that we *did*—was to provide the indent in the neck of the literek. How the ring would come into being and how it would find its way to the wine at the required moment we left in the hands of fate. Or in the hands of Cor, if you want to look at it that way."

"I am not a superstitious man," grumbled Dermaq. "There was certainly nothing supernatural about the mechanical details. A woman brought the wine. Although I didn't notice the fact at first, I think now, looking back, that she was not the regular maid. Her hands were those of a woman in her mid-forties. Perhaps older. And she wore a ring . . . *the* ring. It clicked in the neck indent as she picked up the literek and poured the wine. And as I think about it, it is quite evident that she used the ring to open the bronze entrance door of the suite. And it must follow that her ring was not only an excellent counterfeit of *Firebird*'s bow ring, it possessed in addition the power to irradiate the wine." The courier looked hard at Volo. "Now, then, the questions."

The general nodded. "Go ahead."

"First, who was the woman? Second, where did she get the ring? Third, had her ring truly traversed all space and all time? And if so, fourth, how was this possible? Fifth, *why* did she do what she did? What difference did it make to her?"

But Volo just shook his head. "I don't know. The ring does indeed present many puzzling aspects. The mystery is very great."

Gerain broke in. "The ring can stand as a mystery all by itself. A thing no one can yet explain. But, at least as far as I'm concerned, there's an even bigger mystery, which you, milord General, can readily explain."

"Ah?"

"Why are you involving us—Dermaq and me—at all? Why the wine? Why the ring? What part are you forcing us to play in your running battle with Control?"

"Honestly put," said Volo. "Our 'running battle,' incidentally, we call Project Firebird'."

"After the ship?" said Dermaq curiously.

"Not really. We picked the name before we learned the name of your ship. Coincidence? Fate? Cosmic interference? Who knows?"

Gerain frowned. "We digress. General, why . . . how . . . are Dermaq and I involved?"

"Just a moment, Gerain," said Dermaq. "There's something very odd here. Our ship *Firebird* . . . the Project Firebird of the Diavola. This is beyond coincidence. I didn't select the name of my ship, but you, General, did select the name of your project. You must have some explanation."

The general shrugged. "The name came to me in a dream, during deepsleep. It was long ago."

"The dream must have had a basis . . . an origin in your waking life," said Gerain.

"I have often wondered . . . but I can think of nothing."

"Then the image . . . the *concept* . . . ." said Gerain, "was impressed on your mind during deepsleep. Somehow. By something. How would you explain *that?*"

"I could speculate," said the general, "but it would be pretty wild."

"Try!" said Dermaq.

"It's a philosophical question—almost theological—that the Diavola have debated for centuries."

"Which is?" said the courier.

"The question is this: Is dispersed-Cor a living, thinking presence, and if so, does it attempt any control over the mechanistic events of the universe?"

Dermaq laughed. "Oh, come now, General. You're not suggesting there's something out there that controls me, and you, and everything else, including Control?"

"Can you prove there isn't?"

"No."

"And if there is, you can see there are playlets going on within plays that even the major actors may not be aware of."

"Have we quite exhausted *that* line of discussion?" said Dermaq dryly. "If so, I'd like to invite the general's attention to Gerain's question: *how are we involved?*"

But just then Dermaq noted from the corner of his eye that the hanging sphere was flashing again. He saw that the counter had moved up one digit:"7046." He pointed to the sphere. "General, how can they move in the Quarter? What do they do for fuel?"

"Same as us," said Volo. "All Control ships have been modified to carry their own liquid hydrogen."

"When will they attack?"

"Soon. Any day, any *tench,* any *vec.* It could start while we are talking here."

"When will you finish repairing *Firebird?*"

"I think the work is nearly done. Why don't we pop over and take a look."

"I'm coming too," insisted Gerain. "I might as well be ignored there as here."

Volo smiled gravely. "I do indeed intend to answer your question. All in good time. Meanwhile, you'll be perfectly safe here. At least for th present."

But she could not bear the thought of separation from Dermaq. " promise not to be in the way."

"Well, then, come along."

They suited up, crawled into the narrow confines of the skiff, and i moments they clambered into *Firebird's* space lock.

Dermaq spoke into his suit intercom. "Can we return now to Gerain's question? How are we supposed to participate in your Project Firebird?"

"By canceling Control's Project Cancelar," said Volo cryptically. "But of course, you don't know what Project Cancelar is, do you?"

"No."

"Basically, it's simple. As you know, the universe is supposed to oscillate. First, Cor exists. Then it explodes. Galaxies form and hurtle out into eternity. Then, after sixty billion *meda,* gravity grabs them and pulls them back to form Cor again. The flight back takes another sixty billion *meda.* Then, the Big Bang again. And so on, forever. In the normal sequence of events, all life, even Control, would be destroyed when the galaxies fall back to the center of the universe to form Cor once more. The trouble is that in this present cycle Control was able temporarily to destroy an entire sun cluster, for about five *tench,* which was enough mass loss to reduce the universal gravitational constant to the point where the galaxies cannot pull themselves back together. Instead, they will sail on forever. And Control will live forever. Unless—"

"Unless something is done to restore the mass of the missing sun cluster?" said Dermaq.

"Exactly," said Volo. "If that is done, the galaxies will eventually coalesce again into Cor. Control will go up in smoke."

"And you think *Firebird* can accomplish that?" said Dermaq incredulously.

"I do."

"But how?"

Clank!

The skiff nosed in to *Firebird*'s space lock.

"How?" repeated Dermaq. He put his hand on Volo's encased arm. "How does *Firebird* restore the mass of a sun cluster?"

"Later, my young friend. Let's get inside first."

"General," he said bleakly, "I get the impression you don't want to explain Project Firebird to us. And the reason is, you believe we would refuse the roles you propose to assign to us."

The Diavolite sighed. "Actually, I shall indeed tell you everything I know, and all in good time. And what you surmise, Captain, is perfectly true. You and the princess and, of course, *Firebird* will be offered roles in our Project, and I suspect you may be inclined to refuse. But I would like to defer a full explanation until you see what we have done to your ship."

Dermaq and Gerain looked at each other. She nodded. He stood aside and signaled for the hatchway to open.

The repair supervisor met them inside and acknowledged their entry with a wave of the hand. As they stripped off their suits, he said, "We're through. We've been cleaning up. There's still some junk stored temporarily in the rear cabinet, but otherwise I believe the ship's ready for a test run."

Dermaq and Volo crawled aft, where the courier studied the new engine with growing wonder. It was nearly twice as big as the old drive. "It must be about—what . . . point eight c?" he asked the general.

Volo laughed. "Captain, the design velocity is just a flicker below the speed of light: a decimal point followed by about a dozen nines. So far as we know, it's the only one of its kind in the universe. Control won't have anything like it for another couple of millennia. It's our absolute best."

Dermaq was shaken. He had never heard of a ship this fast. Indeed, he would have thought it technically impossible. Outside, Control would have ordered its immediate destruction. *Firebird* could now outrun any existing Control ship.

"We have also made certain adjustments to your in-ship anti-acceleration field," said General Volo. "To take full advantage of the velocity capability of the new drive, you will want to be able to accelerate *Firebird* up to at least point nine c within the first few *vecs*. If we didn't modify the field, you'd be hit by several million G's during initial acceleration, and your bodies would be crushed to monomolecular films against the ship walls. The adjustment is automatic and proportional to increase in acceleration. Of course, once you reach cruising speed and acceleration drops to zero, you're free to walk around the ship, go into deepsleep, anything you like."

Dermaq swallowed hard. The new drive was awesome—and dangerous. It was merely one part of a system. Everything in the system had to work or they would die. Fortunately, death, if it came, would be instantaneous.

General Volo was watching him closely. "There are a couple of interesting corollaries to near-c flight, as I am sure you are aware."

"Ship mass multiplies, shiptime slows."

"Exactly. The changes can be rather remarkable. In fact, it is these changes that present the possibility of canceling Cancelar. The aggregate increase in ship mass, if continued long enough, could actually be of the order of a whole sun cluster that has temporarily vanished for five *tench,* enough to reverse the present expansion of the universe. The time required would be about forty-five billion *meda* in real time or some four hundred and fifty *meda* shiptime, most of which would be spent in deepsleep. Age-arresting medication could also be provided."

Dermaq got to his feet and stared at the Diavolite. It was finally all beginning to come together. He and Gerain had demanded to know their prospective participation in the Diavolite's Project Firebird. He had asked how *Firebird* could reverse Cancelar, how his ship could make the universe resume its eventual scheduled contraction and thereby destroy Control. He had been answered. And the answer was devastating. "You saved our lives only for your own devious purposes," he said indignantly. "We want no part of it." He felt betrayed. "Take your accursed engine back."

The general did not seem particularly perturbed by the rejection. "The choice is yours, of course," he agreed. "Yet I feel you may have overlooked a couple of vital factors in making your decision."

"Such as . . . ?"

Volo pointed to the luminous sphere mounted in *Firebird's* control panel behind Dermaq's head. The courier noted that it was identical to the sphere in the bridge room in *Devilship One,* but with a significant difference: *Firebird's* sphere was a mass of *moving* light points—all seeming to implode toward the center. "The attack has begun," said the older man quietly. "If you and Gerain remain in the Quarter you will die."

"But—how about you? And the colony?"

"The Diavola are already taking up our positions to form a long hollow cylindrical pattern. The chances are excellent that *Firebird* can escape through the center of the cylinder. If you choose to remain, then one of the Diavola will have to take *Firebird* on her long flight."

It struck him then. This man and all his people were going to die so that he and Gerain could attempt their escape.

It was incredible. He caught glimpses of a pattern of fanatic idealism reaching into the far distant past. He had a sudden insight into the horror that had seized the great Daith Volo over a hundred centuries ago, when he realized that his two godlike protégés, Largo and Czandra, had revolted and had taken control of the universe. He caught flashes and intimations of plans, schemes, conspiracies, counterrevolutions, running battles between emergent Control and Diavola remnants over the millennia, with Control always winning but with the Diavola never conceding total defeat.

And now this last chance. Whether it worked or not, all the Diavola were going to die—so that he and Gerain could get out alive and, with a little luck, stay alive for a long time. Should he be grateful? He really didn't know. He hadn't asked to be involved in the first place. But then he thought back—to Jaevar's intrusion on his wedding night with Innae. He remembered what it was like to be a Control slave. And now, because of the Diavola, he was a free man. And even though they had not freed him out of kindness to him personally, perhaps he owed them something.

But he was not presently inclined to add up the pros and cons and come to an algebraic decision. The hard overriding fact was that Gerain was in grave danger. And with every *vec* passed in thinking about it, her danger grew.

"We'll take *Firebird* out," he said.

The general smiled grimly. "Then it's settled. Our strategist will feed the escape coordinates into your autopilot. You'll head right up and out the axis of our shield cylinder. You won't have to do anything. I suggest you buckle in immediately." He arose, bowed to Gerain, crossed his fist over his heart to Dermaq, and walked toward the space lock. All without a word of farewell. They never saw him again.

25. ESCAPE FROM THE QUARTER

They listened to the hatches opening and closing and to the hissing of the air makeup.

From somewhere in the far distance they sensed the approach of gigantic rolling explosions. This broke them from their half-paralyzed trances. Dermaq pushed the girl into her chair, then dashed for his own. "Buckle up!" he cried, as he fumbled for his own chair clasps. They felt the ship turn as the autopilot took over . . . and then the movement . . . the fantastic sense of impossible motion . . .

Intently they watched the locus-sphere over the control panel. The swarm of lights indicating the invading Control fleet shifted to the far horizon of the sphere, and then all the lights seemed to race to the edge of the screen, where they all disappeared.

Save one.

A pinpoint of light persisted against the black background.

"What is it?" whispered Gerain.

"I don't know. Looks like a ship . . . on our tail."

"Control?"

"Maybe . . ."

"But I thought we had the fastest drive in the universe."

"So did I. And indeed, we probably have. Wait . . . Look!"

On the screen, the pinpoint seemed to be shrinking. But another light point had separated from it and was growing larger. "It's a multistage weapon," said Dermaq grimly. "A point eight c cruiser gets up to full velocity, then releases a point eight c destroyer, which may in turn release other things in sequence. The final result may well exceed our max velocity."

"I see. When you add all those v's up, you would get something several times the speed of light."

"No, it doesn't work that way. Fortunately. Nothing exceeds the speed of light. Each successive stage just picks up a little more speed. If they have enough stages and time enough, the last stage might come very close to the speed of light and might catch us."

"So what do we do now?"

"I am going to try something. It will kill either us or them."

"Or possibly both?"

"Or possibly both. Here"—he tossed her a pressure suit—"get into this." He slipped quickly into his own suit, then slowly turned *Firebird* into a tight repeating circle, in a plane facing the pursuing ship. As *Firebird's* speed increased, he cut in one antigrav after another. But as the *vecs* passed, they ran out of neutralizing G's. "Here are some cushions," said Dermaq. "Lie down on them. The antigrav screens will take up some, but not all, of the acceleration developed by our circular motion. The question is, can our bodies take the acceleration that is not absorbed?"

"I will do whatever you want me to do—even though I have not the faintest idea what you are up to."

He looked over at the drive autotimer. Yes, he'd have to set that for, say, sixty *vecs,* to break out of orbit. Because, even if this scheme worked and they survived, they were very likely to be rendered unconscious by the heavy G's, and he would be unable to resume control of the ship. "Lie down. I will explain as we go."

She lay beside him on the cushions.

He continued: "When *Firebird* moves in this circle, about fifty *kilojurae* across, at a speed nearly that of light, its mass becomes nearly infinite, at least with respect to the pursuing Control vessel. We hope that the Control ship will be drawn into the center of the circle and be torn apart by gravitational tides."

She thought about that. "There is, however, one little problem, and that is whether we shall be flattened out into a thin film of jelly in the same process."

"That is indeed the question," he agreed grimly.

"Assuming we stay alive long enough, how will we know when we trap the Control ship?"

"Simple. We watch the auxiliary screen on the opposite wall. Just now you can see the enemy ship as a little green blip. It looks as though it is moving in a circle. Actually, it is *Firebird* that is moving in a circle, but the screen does not know this. The blip will get bigger and bigger—until finally, we hope, it will simply disappear. That means it has broken into pieces too small to register on the screen."

"It seems to be coming very fast."

"Yes. It is coming, and fast. It will be here in about forty *vecs*. How do you feel?"

"I feel a lot of pressure. In . . . fact . . ." But she could not finish. She was slipping in and out of consciousness. She skipped in and out of the forest edge near her father's palatial country estate in far Aerlon. And then she was on the precipice, on the mountain, wandering near the edge. Too near. She fell . . .

Dermaq was on the verge of joining her in unconsciousness. And then he remembered . . . that he had forgotten to set the drive autotimer to release them from this deadly orbit within the appointed sixty *vecs*. He absolutely had to do this, because if they both lost consciousness, they would continue in this circle forever, and they would die. He had to get to the controls. He looked over at Gerain. Her eyes were closed. He twisted his body in his pressure suit and by dint of a great struggle was able to roll over. Next he worked on getting to his hands and knees. He was able to get his knees up under him, but had much more difficulty with his arms.

The exercise, magnified by the confines of his pressure suit, was making him sweat. A bead of perspiration flowed down his nose.

He resumed his efforts. Finally, despite the growing G's, he fought to his hands and knees. And now his head was high enough so that he could see the control level in the console. It was a bare arm's length away from his face.

It might as well have been on another planet.

He thrust his right hand a few *centijurae* ahead, but he could not keep his elbow straight. His right arm collapsed. He groaned as he sank to the floor.

He now decided that he was being very stupid about all this. There had to be a better way. He scuffed his legs around until his body was roughly parallel to the control console.

Next, the colossal struggle to roll over. He made it, and then once again. Now he was next to the console. The drive bar was just overhead. All he had to do was to get to his hands and knees, move the lever to turn off in sixty *vecs*—no, make that thirty—and then he could honorably pass out.

But he couldn't get to his hands and knees. This time he couldn't even get to his knees. He was held flat to the floor as though by a giant hand and he could not move at all. Furthermore, he was now certainly losing consciousness.

At that instant a remarkable thing happened. A blast seemed to hit the ship from the opposite side. He was flung up and out, clear of the floor. He jerked out his arm and struck the control lever as he hurtled past. The lever clanked home so hard that it bent. *Firebird* immediately fell out of its tight circle and went into straight-line flight.

He knew what had happened. That final enemy ship had been drawn into the gravity trap. She had torn apart, and her nuclear motor had exploded. It had blown *Firebird* momentarily into a wider circle, and for an instant had released its occupants from their thrall to their artificial centrifugal gravity. The freedom had been only *millivecs,* but he had been at the right place at the right time, and it had been all that he needed.

For the moment, they were safe. But they had to get out of here. He turned quickly to Gerain. She was blinking into wakefulness. He patted her face, and she smiled "up" at him. As he helped her out of her pressure suit he pondered *Firebird's* new status. She was a very special quarry, and she would be hunted throughout the universe. He thought of the routine greeting between passing Control vessels:

"Any sign of *Hell-ship?*"

"None—and may it burn forever."

So now at least one small part of the mystery was solved. He knew the identity of *Hell-ship.*

26. THE CLOUDS OF KON

The images form, fade, reform.

The man on the gangplank, walking down slowly. The faded blue uniform. Is the renegade *smiling* at me? His goodwill avails him nothing. I draw quickly.

Alarm . . . alarm . . . alarm . . .

Dermaq awakened instantly.

A white point flickered on the screen at the foot of his deepsleep crypt. Trouble? No way to tell for sure. *Firebird* was far from the conventional intergalactic travel lanes. But it was always safest to assume the worst: that the intruder was a multistage Control cruiser.

He climbed out of the casket and looked over at Gerain. She slept. Her dark hair curled about her cheeks and throat in lovely abandon. No time for this! He lurched forward to the bridge room. Yes, there it was, still on the screen. He focused the coordinates and got the flight pattern. The unidentified vessel would cross *Firebird's* course, approximately at a right angle and within the day.

This was no coincidence. It was a Control ship.

It would be a good idea to get out of here. A full reverse was strongly indicated. He began punching the necessary course corrections into *Firebird's* flight computer.

And then he noticed another pinpoint of light on the screen—this one far to his rear. If he reversed, he'd have to endure several volleys of hellfire before he could be clear.

He studied the screen again. That left two choices. While the two ships were still out of firing range, slip through between them with a quarter turn to port or slip through with a similar turn to starboard.

To port lay clear space. To starboard lay a highly questionable area full of dust and debris known as the Clouds of Kon. The pilotage books and charts warned against entry. The tiny particles were barely big enough to scatter blue light, and a volume of space the size of Kornaval held a weight of dust less than his little fingernail. Yet the microscopic dust eroded hulls and jammed proton converters.

His hand hovered over the course panel, ready to plug in a turn to port, when he noticed the other light points on the screen. *That* side was now closed off. Somehow, out of nowhere, a hemisphere of light points had materialized. The alternatives were now destruction or the Clouds of Kon. The choice was easy. He promptly punched in a flight plan for the Clouds, and *Firebird* ran for it.

And in the midst of flight, he pondered a nagging question. If Control had been able to throw together a patrol for the half-sphere *outside* the Clouds, why not a complementary fleet *inside* the Clouds, lurking, barely hidden, dust-veiled, like the hunters just within the forest edge, waiting for the beaters to drive the quarry within firing range.

He hurriedly scanned the Cloud periphery. Something odd was happening there. The Cloud front was changing. What had been one colossal shapeless dust mass was now coalescing into odd globs of denser material. Did this indicate the presence of Control ships within that mass of cosmic haze? He doubted it. No—it was something worse. Control, long able to transmit telepathic messages across the universe, had developed a way telepathically to modify the nature of space so that interstellar dust would coagulate and condense. The phenomenon probably involved ionization of the particles.

This was bad. He felt cold sweat forming on his face. Quickly, he switched to autopilot. *Firebird* would now sense the thickened dust masses as perils to navigation and would automatically take evasive action.

The ship began to weave and lurch. He cut the acceleration and buckled in.

So far not a shot. It was ironic. They had tried to use the Clouds to kill him. Instead, they had created the perfect hiding place. Already, he was well inside and out of sight.

And now what would the hunt fleet do? Would Control assume that *Firebird* had indeed crashed into a coalesced Cloud mass at nearly the speed of light and that her remnants were now indeed splattered over a wide area? Would they now depart for home port? Possibly. But first they would probably send a patrol in to double-check the situation.

Perhaps he could help them.

He hurried aft to *Firebird*'s storage lockers. He scanned the inventory list on the panel doors. What to toss out? What would the enemy patrol look for? What shards of this marvelous little ship would convince them that their objective had been achieved? He didn't know, and he suspected they didn't know either.

Ah! In the third and last locker—just what he wanted. The Diavolite repair crew had "temporarily" stored a lot of broken-up bits and pieces of *Firebird's* former installations, cables, control mechanisms—even pieces of her original motor. There had been no time to get rid of it before the ship fled from the Silent Quarter.

Piece by piece he now lugged it midships, into the space lock. He suited up, opened the lock, and tossed out each piece in a different direction.

Then back inside and to the bridge.

No lights on the screen. That was good. If he couldn't see them, they couldn't see him. Yet there was a thing he could try—the mass subsensor, new with the Diavolites. Theoretically, it sensed the movement of mass and did not require direct sight of the object. He switched it on.

Ah, six dark blobs. From the mass measurements, they would be two-man patrol boats. Darting, sniffing with all sorts of instruments. And one headed in the general direction of *Firebird*.

He eased his ship farther back into the Clouds. The obscuring haze blotted out everything. He lost the ships.

But after a time, curiosity got the better of him. *Firebird* crept forward again, slowly, silently. And stopped.

On the mass screen, four little blobs came into a fuzzy focus. They were congregated in the exact area where he had tossed out the debris. Even as he watched they were joined by a fifth, and a sixth.

It would not do to interrupt their deliberations.

Firebird eased back once more into the sheltering mists.

Patiently, he waited.

One *jar* later he edged the ship forward again, slowly, carefully, with dead stops and pauses between stops.

Nothing showed—not as a blur on the mass screen, not as a light point on the flight screen.

Firebird moved slowly to the edge of the Cloud and looked out. Nothing.

He set a course along the Cloud edge, moving slowly at first, ready at any instant to duck back in.

But there was still nothing.

Was Control convinced that *Firebird* was destroyed? Perhaps for the moment. Perhaps until they got that debris back to planetary laboratories and really analyzed it. When Control did *that,* they might well resume the search for *Firebird*. But that would be another day.

Bleep . . . bleep . . .

He looked toward the screens in alarm. Nothing there. But something was wrong. One by one he studied the dials on the control panel. Ah, there it was . . . The temperature gauge. The Clouds of Kon, long inert, were now warming up. What was going on? He made a rapid circular scan. The heat scale varied. Behind him the Cloud was hot enough to boil water. Ahead the reading still showed the near-zero cold of space. It took him a moment to figure it out. Because the contraction process was now started, this particular coalesced dust segment would continue to contract by the simple operation of the laws of gravity, and during the process it would grow hotter and hotter. In condensing vast segments of the clouds, the hunt ships had in effect started the nuclei of protosuns. And *Firebird* was sitting on the periphery of one.

The same star-forming process was happening all around him. Wittingly or unwittingly, Control had initiated the formation of a galaxy, perhaps one of the last that would be formed during this cycle of the universe.

It would be a majestic sight to watch, but not from the inside of a forming star.

He moved out slowly, checking the screens every few *vecs*.

But there was still no sign of the hunt fleet. It had disappeared. He almost relaxed. He walked back to the deepsleep cabin and looked down at Gerain. She lay there in exactly the position in which he had last seen her: immobile, frozen in time and beauty.

He wondered whether he should awaken her. But why? To tell her of their narrow escape? Hardly. To watch the galaxy forming behind them? Well, possibly. How would it go? He put it together in his mind. First, he'd make them each a small ballon of hot *choff*, just the way she liked it. Then he'd waken her, and in a moment there'd be the usual greetings, and she'd sit up and reach for her ballon. As she sipped the dark brown liquid through the straw, she'd ask: "Any news?"

"No news."

"Nothing going on?"

"Not a thing."

"No sign of Control?"

"Not the slightest."

"*Firebird* still running at max v?"

"Still at max."

"What's that on the screen?"

"A galaxy . . . in the process of forming . . ."

"Hm. Something familiar . . . pictures in the schoolbooks. Looks a little like the Clouds of Kon."

"The same, I guess . . ."

"But now it's changing into a galaxy?"

"Yes. They do that . . ."

"But it takes a very long time. Billions of *meda*. If that much time has passed, Control has probably vanished from the face of the universe. It's probably safe. All we need to do is find a beautiful planet, about the size of Kornaval, with blue skies, green fields, flowing streams. Get out your charts. We're free at last!"

No, Gerain, no.

He studied the lovely face with deepening regret. "Sleep, dream, beloved," he murmured, as he returned to his own crypt.

27. THE COLLISION

A dozen sleeps later, when *Firebird* was skirting the KRN galaxies, the alarms went off again.

Dermaq was not really surprised. The hunters outside Kon had of course taken his decoy debris into the laboratories of the nearest planets, and there it was soon determined that the engine pieces were from the old point six v *Firebird*, not the Diavola-remodeled *Firebird*.

This time it turned out to be a twenty-stage motion-seeking missile. He had deduced its capabilities and limitations almost too late. After the twentieth and final stage had been launched and was closing on them, he turned *Firebird* aside, then quickly stopped the little ship dead in space. Unable to detect any motion, the final lethal shell spiraled erratically past. It had been a near thing.

Nor was this the end. From time to time there were further attacks—periodic, yet unpredictable. Control never gave up, and the weapons used against *Firebird* slowly increased in destructiveness, range, and velocity. Control was learning. Its hardware was improving as well as its ability to unravel *Firebird's* flight patterns. Dermaq could predict that if Control had infinite time, there would have to be some future deadly intersection. But he also knew that Control did not have infinite time within which to accomplish the destruction of *Firebird*. For with every circuit of the universe, *Firebird's* great relativistic mass neutralized more and more of Project Cancelar.

To span forty-five billion *meda* to the close of the universe at a speed nearly that of the speed of light required but four hundred and fifty *meda* of elapsed shiptime, and Dermaq and Gerain tried to spend nearly all of this time in deepsleep. Of course, Dermaq never knew when the alarms would sound to awaken him to a new threat.

On occasion they speculated about the fate of General Volo and the Diavola. Had any of the colony escaped? Actually, as soon as *Firebird* was safely out, it would have been pointless for the general to continue battling the invading Control task force. Surely some of them must have got away. Dermaq understood that the Diavola had secret bases on a number of the more civilized planets, including Kornaval. Perhaps there had been survivors, and they were now safely hidden. But he certainly did not propose to go looking for them. He had his own problems.

Once they were pursued for days by a great black ship. Dermaq had not been able to elude it. He tried turns, spirals—all sorts of evasive action—to no avail. Control had finally learned how to build a ship as fast as *Firebird*. (Perhaps even a little faster? he wondered. The possibility made him perspire. He could imagine the vast technological resources turned loose on the problem of *Firebird* over the billennia. Millions of man-lives in the shipyards of myriad planets had doubtless worked under the same unifying directive: design a ship that can cope with *Firebird!*)

As the black ship came on, he watched the interferometer by the hour. The two velocities were so close that differences were detectable only by slight augmentations in the wavelengths of intership radiation. It was almost as though the two ships were standing still, and the universe was hurtling past.

And then, very slowly, almost imperceptibly, *Firebird's* speed began to drop. Dermaq watched the interferometer with growing concern. Over his shoulder, Gerain watched. "What's wrong?" she asked.

"I don't know. I want to check the engines." He went aft, but was back within a few *tench*. "The drive is running as sweetly as a snow-fed stream in green-time."

On a sudden inspiration he swept the forward quarter of space with the foreign-object detector. "Nothing there."

"What are you looking for?" asked Gerain.

"Wait . . ." He adjusted the fine tuning. "There *is* something there . . . always in the general area in front of the ship."

"I don't see a thing."

"It's not exactly a *thing*. It's more like . . . well, I think Control has learned how to constrict the lines of space. The pursuit ship is doing it somehow. The net result is that the space in front of *Firebird* is a shade more viscous than the space in front of the hunt ship. If they can keep this up, they can overtake us."

"How long?"

He made a calculation. "Half a day shiptime."

"They could start firing before then, couldn't they?"

"They could. But I don't think they will. They don't need to. I think they intend to board us. Control wants us alive."

"Yes, of course." She waited in silence.

He was thinking. There was a thing they could try. It was insane, but there was nothing else. "That hunt ship is mostly machinery," he mused. "It's got a drive, and a good one, but everything else is the apparatus for warping space. All wrapped up in the thinnest possible skin. It's designed for this one job. It doesn't have to fight space crud for billions of years."

"What are you talking about?"

"Simply stated, we reverse course in a wide semicircle. We line up a frontal collision course with our friendly hunt ship. And then we collide."

"We'll be killed."

"Possibly. However, I think the chances are that we'll zip right through them, like a metal slug fired through a mud ball."

"Interesting. Two ships colliding at twice the speed of light."

"No, not twice. Nothing can move faster than the speed of light. There's a formula for this kind of thing. It's the sum of the two velocities divided by one plus their product. The result is greater than either of the two values, but it's still less than the speed of light. I think we can safely say, though, we'll be approaching each other at a net velocity that may never again be achieved in whatever history is left in the universe."

But now that he had proposed this solution, he was having second thoughts. He studied her face with carefully concealed concern. Perhaps it was not fair to her. Perhaps, on the contrary, he should persuade her to consent to be captured. Perhaps he should not ask her to risk her life. Perhaps . . . Ah, the whole thing was scatterbrained. He wished he had never brought it up. "Gerain—"

She raised a hand to silence him. She had been watching the changes in his face, and she knew what he was about to say. "This is nothing new," she said. "We've risked death before. And this gives me a chance to escape with you." There was an odd metallic edge in her voice. "I will *not* be taken alive. I will not be made again into a slave of Control. I am a free woman, and a princess of Aerlon." She pulled her upper lip back in a semisnarl, exposing her felines. Her irises narrowed to vertical slits. Dermaq fully expected sparks to fly from her eyes. Her hair rose as though in some remote ancestral response to danger, and her retractile fingernails emerged in unconscious reflex.

He was momentarily taken aback. He gulped, then without a word walked to the console and punched in the instructions for the semicircular swing-around.

Together they watched the pursuing ship veer to intercept them.

Within thirty *tench*, *Firebird* and the Control vessel were on a collision course, each rushing toward a deadly rendezvous.

They watched the approaching blip as it moved slowly in the enigmatic green-black of the view screen. From time to time they looked at the Estimated Contact Time readout. Fifteen *tench* . . . fourteen . . . thirteen. It was going very quickly. He wanted to say something meaningful to the woman while there was time. But he had no skill at this kind of thing.

Eight *tench*.

"Suppose they refuse to play the game?" asked Gerain. "Suppose they refuse to collide?"

"It's possible. But actually, I think the officers won't have much say in the decision. I rather suspect that Control will force them to accept the collision, on the theory that at worst, or at best, both ships will be destroyed."

One *tench*. And now the *vecs*, the little units of time measured in heartbeats.

At twenty *vecs* he found that he was thinking rapid, brilliant thoughts. He knew exactly what he wanted to say to Gerain. What was it? Yes! It summed up everything. It explained everything. Only at the door of death do we fully understand life. And it was so simple! "Gerain."

She looked up at him. "I love you!" she cried.

That was *it*! *That* was what he had wanted to say. How did she know? He felt very slightly silly, a little put out, because *she* had explained it to *him*.

Minus five *vecs*. *Minus* . . . ?

He looked at her in amazement. "I didn't feel anything. They must have veered off course after all . . ." He studied the screen with her. One blip. Still there. Receding . . . but—was it slowing? He punched the velocity tracker. 0.99 c . . . 0.98 . . . 0.97 . . . "They're decelerating to resume pursuit," he muttered. "We never touched them."

"We touched them," corrected Gerain dryly. "Look at *that!*" Even as she was speaking the blip divided into two. Then into three, four. One of the larger fragments seemed to pulverize into a hundred smaller pieces. The ship shards took diverse paths as they dispersed forlornly into the empty reaches of space. It was over in a few *vecs*.

Dermaq watched glumly. Poor helpless wretches. But it was they or we. He was almost afraid to look at Gerain. He knew she would be doubling over in glee.

He thought back to the moment of contact. Amazing. No crunch. No sign of any collision. Not even a tap or click.

28. AT MIDTIME

Again and again they went through the ship's library, bountifully replenished by General Volo. Again and again they played *kaisch* and all the other games available in the entertainment locker courtesy of the Diavola. They ate the spartan fare turned out by the food synthesizer. Floating, they made love. Dermaq made up songs on the trioletta for Gerain. Sometimes she sang with him.

And they spent much time in deepsleep. They kept thinking: If we awaken far enough into the future, we can finally touch down with safety. There will no longer be any Control.

But always they picked up signals. Control was still there. After dozens of billions of *meda*, their great enemy still dominated the universe and still sought them.

Either he was dreaming more frequently or he was *remembering* his dreams more frequently. And now it was always the same dream: *the* dream.

He saw the man on the railed ramp, by that courier-class ship (perhaps even a sister ship to *Firebird!)* The man seemed careless in his appearance, as though he had not had recent access to a barber. His whiskers had grown far out to the edges of his cheeks; his mane was combed over the back of his head, where it swept his tunic collar; his ear tufts sadly needed trimming.

That man had walked down the way, then he had waited for a few *vecs,* motionless, almost as though *he* were the hunter and Dermaq the quarry.

It was mysterious, frustrating. He should have demanded more information from Jaevar. Jaevar, cunning, knowing, complacent. That mocking grin, with gums pulled back over his felines. Jaevar could have told him much, but it had pleased the Control Commissioner to tell him nothing. Except that weird bit about black holes.

He never mentioned his dreams to Gerain. Once in a while, however, they did talk about the imposter maid who had taken Morgan's place in the royal prison suite. Gerain had no memory of her at all. Dermaq's own recollection was limited to one visual frame: a hand. The hand of a woman of middle age. An aristocratic hand, with graceful fingers, long nails. The digital hair was soft, glossy—not coarse like a servant's, certainly not bristly like his own fingers. And that ring on the third finger. He hadn't really taken note of it at the time. But now, much, much later, he realized that in appearance at least it was practically identical to *Firebird's* bow ring. And that was just appearance. As to function, it was identical to *Firebird's* ring in at least one respect: it had opened the bronze door. And it was astonishingly superior in at least one respect: it had very effectively irradiated the wine.

But who was she?

Not even Volo had known.

From time to time they discussed the strange woman. Their speculations were wild, unreal. There were spies within Control reporting to a mysterious counterrevolutionary group. She was their agent. Or she was an accomplished thief, who got herself in by a secret key and, when about to be discovered, substituted a love elixir for the poison wine. Or, it was actually Morgan, who had simply pulled on a false skin glove, and the wine was harmless in the first place.

And variations and permutations. Dozens. Hundreds. And finally thousands, whereupon they began to repeat themselves.

The fate of Morgan was a corollary, more somber puzzle. Again they conjectured, chaotically, futilely. The imposter woman had killed her and then had taken the wine service. Even as they made love in the bedroom, Morgan's corpse was growing cold in the canteen, perhaps even with an accusing finger stretched in their direction.

Dermaq tried to dissuade her from so lethal a version. "No need to kill her," he argued. "Drug her, perhaps. Or just tie her up. She would eventually regain her senses. She could get help. The door was wide open, and the phone was working."

"And suppose she *did* live, and got out safely," demanded Gerain. *"Then* what?"

He laughed. "That part's the easiest. Do you think the personal maid to a princess of Aerlon would lack for employment? The keldar himself probably took her in. And in any case she's been dead for billions of *meda.* So stop worrying about her. Put her out of your mind."

"We could put it to the *kaisch* board," said Gerain.

He stopped breathing for a moment. Was this going to lead to psi-*kaisch?* He remembered his first and only essay at this superstitious variant of the noble game—that first night out of Aerlon. Hell-ship had headed for the destruct square. That had alarmed him then, and he hadn't even known the identity of Hell-ship.

He waited carefully, his blood pressure slowly rising.

She sensed his reluctance. "You've used it in analysis of tactical problems," she said in sharp defense. "You said so yourself. They taught you in the academy. That's where you met what's-her-name."

He cleared his throat. "That was different. We used *kaisch* as a military computer. You feed in certain tactical data, then the pieces jump around, and then you can read off a probability answer from their new position. It's all very mathematical. To do it properly you need all kinds of tables and parallel concordances."

She was adamant. "You know very well what I mean. Psi-*kaisch*."

"No."

"But why not? You're incredible. There's no reason . . .'"

He groaned.

She smiled. He was weakening. "Besides, it's your duty."

"Duty?"

"You have a duty to Morgan—to find out what happened to her."

"But I thought we were talking about The Imposter!"

"Exactly."

"I don't get the connection . . ." He threw up his hands. "Get the box."

She grinned as she opened the *kaisch* set on the chart table and let the pieces fall out.

"Plug in the microphone, then plug the board into the computer," he said.

She did. "Do I put all the pieces on the board?"

He rubbed his chin thoughtfully as he surveyed the potential actors in the approaching drama. "No. Not all. First, Control."

She placed the two-headed god piece on its opening square. Its four eyes lit up immediately. "How about the courier?"

"Yes, and the princess."

"How about the keldar?"

"No. He never showed. But you'll need Hell-ship, the commissioner, the beast, and finally no-face."

"So—there they are. Now what?"

"We feed in the data. We talk to the board."

"What do we say?"

"I'll start." He punched the oral input button on the side of the board-box, and said: "We seek the identity of no-face, whom we shall call the imposter maid. The imposter maid is a woman. She entered the regal suite. She poured the Wine of Elkar for us. As we drank, she disappeared." He looked over at Gerain, as though to say, "What else is there?"

"Identify her," Gerain said to the *kaisch* board. "Who is no-face?"

Nothing happened. "You have to punch 'RANDOM-PLAY,' " whispered Dermaq. "Then say, '*Tableau,*' so the board can take over and present the resulting position."

She punched the second button in the little board panel. "*Tableau!*"

Swiftly the pieces moved, rearranged, and settled down again: control boated off into the safety file, commissioner confronted beast, courier's life-light went out, but he stayed on the board, and princess confronted no-face.

Gerain looked up from the board, puzzled. "And what does *that* mean?"

"Not much, I guess. But that's all the board could do with the data you gave it."

"Well, let's give it some more data then. You saw her hand . . ."

"Yes." He spoke to the board. "The imposter maid was forty to fifty *meda* old, probably high-born. She wore a ring, quite similar to *Firebird's* nose ring. She placed this ring in the ring indent in the neck of the wine literek, as though she knew exactly what to do. I heard the *click* . . ." He punched in "RANDOM PLAY." "*Tableau.*" His voice faded away as the pieces began to move.

The eyes in the two-headed god piece dimmed and went out, and it slid off the board into the discard tray. Commissioner moved two squares back as though in fearful evasion of the beast piece. Dead courier, in total violation of the rules, moved adjacent Hell-ship. And—most, most strange—princess and no-face merged and became one piece, so that the observers could not tell what the result was.

Gerain looked up at Dermaq in alarm. She whispered huskily, "Does that mean the princess becomes no-face?"

"Or that no-face becomes the princess?" countered the man. "And either way, what does it have to do with the imposter maid? Only the gods know. That's the trouble with psi-*kaisch*. If it has any meaning at all—which I very much doubt—you learn it only after the real event occur." In a totally miscalculated attempt to smooth her ruffled fur, he smiled.

The Princess Gerain was not amused. "I don't like this game," she said harshly. "It's silly. It's horrid. And don't say 'I told you so,' or, by the two-headed god, I'll break this chair over your grinning skull."

He sighed. Silently, he began putting the pieces away.

She was not through. "You shouldn't have let me do it."

"No."

"It was boorish of you."

He shrugged.

She paused and lowered her voice. "What do you think it means?"

"It doesn't mean anything at all."

"No-face became the princess. You *saw* it." She got up slowly and walked out.

He unplugged the board from the computer, thrust it far down into the depths of the game locker, and pulled a case of movie cassettes over it. He surmised that they would never play *kaisch* again and, further

that the mysteries of Morgan and the imposter maid would remain forever unsolved.

Once they were hailed by a passing cruiser. "May you escape *Hell-ship!*"
Gerain replied in wild glee: "We *are Hell-ship!*" And they disappeared
in a great burst of speed.

At 225 *meda* shiptime, they both went into deepsleep at the same time.
He remembered thinking: Halfway through. So far, so good. But what will
it be like at the end? What happens, say, at 450 *meda*? Will we still be hunted?
And will we continue to be successful in our escape attempts? It's silly to
think about it. We may be captured and killed within the next *jar.*

They had long ago learned fatalism.

29. *FIREBIRD* AND TWO BODIES

ZANDRA: K-Four, the sun of Kornaval, is in the initial process of becoming a red giant. Kornaval's polar caps have melted; in a
few *meda* its oceans will boil. We must now begin the preparation of vaults for my data banks, far below the planet's
continental sheaths.

ARGO: Quite so. Yet, nothing to be alarmed about. K-Four was a
medium-size yellow star, and it is the fate of such stars to
become red giants. We knew this when we founded your
data base on Kornaval.

ZANDRA: I have already programmed the mechanical excavators to
start. The work is under way.

ARGO: A wise move, I'm sure.

ZANDRA: You are holding back something. I sense a plan. It concerns the capture of the renegades and that strange ship.

ARGO: Just a whimsical idea. I'm not really ready to discuss it just
yet.

ZANDRA: It's more than that. Already you have done certain things
to a large number of planets—some dead, some not dead.
You didn't tell me.

ARGO: Trivia. I didn't want to bother you. You'll be occupied for
a long time moving your data banks down to safety. And
your personal concerns should indeed come first. Some dramatic times lie ahead for you just watching K-Four. Think

of the heat! The great Suara Mountains will melt and flow like water. But then the great red sun must finally run out of fuel. It collapses, cools, and becomes a white dwarf. Kornaval, now a desert planet, cools with it. And not just Kornaval. The entire universe will be a desert. Not a particle of hydrogen left between the galaxies. Our little friends will have to touch down—somewhere—in search of fuel. And we will be ready for them. One fine day *Firebird* will land in search of fuel. It will never take off again. For I have learned to warp the very lines of space. I can hold that ship in space, and then I can destroy it.

CZANDRA: By converting the entire planet into energy?

LARGO: Why, yes. But I don't remember telling—

CZANDRA: You didn't tell me. I am intuitive. I *know* certain things. This converter mechanism—are you installing it on *all* planets?

LARGO: Well . . . my plans haven't finalized to that extent.

CZANDRA: Do you plan to install the converter on Kornaval?

LARGO: You are certainly suspicious.

CZANDRA: It doesn't matter.

LARGO: *What* doesn't matter?

CZANDRA: Whether or not you put a converter here on Kornaval.

LARGO: Why not?

CZANDRA: Because the future is a strange, uncertain path. You and and *Firebird* pass down this path. There is a fork. One fork is good—for you. And at the end of that path is you— only you.

LARGO: Hm. And where does the other fork lead?

CZANDRA: Into the future . . . to the next coalescence of the galaxies. To the next Cor. And only Cor.

LARGO: I would not like that! Nothing more?

CZANDRA: Not clear. Cor waits . . . it cannot explode again—not until it has all its original mass. It lacks—

LARGO: What does it lack?

CZANDRA: *Firebird* and two bodies.

30. Kornaval Revisited

"Wha—?"

He found that he was sitting up in his deepsleep crypt. Odd . . . he had gone under only a short time ago. Or had he? Come to think of it, he always had this sensation on emerging from deepsleep. Actually (he conceded, as he thought about it) millennia might have passed, and his wakening sensations would be the same.

Nevertheless, something was wrong. His mind cleared instantly. He listened. The ship was totally still; the engines had stopped.

This was alarming. In the dim light he looked over at Gerain's capsule. There was no movement. She still slept. He'd leave her there for the time being.

He waited another five *tench* before getting out. It was a safety factor and gave him time to verify that his body temperature had warmed to normal and that the numbing deepsleep radiation had ceased. He flipped on the overhead lights and studied the summary instrument panel at the foot of the capsule.

He started with the first dial on the left.

Fuel: 40 *libra*.

That was why he had been awakened. The hydrogen fuel tank was dangerously low. But why? Weren't the scoops working? Or had *Firebird* run into another area like the Silent Quarter, where there was no hydrogen? He'd soon know.

He read the next dial: Exterior Hydrogen: zero.

Well, there it was. No fuel *outside*.

What *med* shiptime?

He peered at the Elapsed Time dial. It was hard to read. His eyes had been bothering him lately. Did he need lens adjusters? Something about "450"? Four hundred and fifty *meda*? And what did *that* mean in terms of Universal Time? In the universe outside, what year was it? And then he remembered. To get elapsed Universal Time, you divide elapsed shiptime by the difference in the velocity of light and ship velocity. He squinted, as though trying to focus on the numbers. Four hundred and fifty divided by ten to the minus eight would give . . . forty-five billion *meda!* His mind could not accept it. Either the instruments or his arithmetic were fouled up. Maybe both.

He massaged his wrists, groaned, and got to his feet. His magnetic soles clicked on the floor plates as he made his way over to Gerain's capsule. He looked down at her in the pale blue light. Her long brown hair was gathered around her cheeks and chin, sheltering her face. Her lips were half parted, her eyelids drawn down in gentle dignity over her eyes. Even in this profound sleep, she was stunning.

He looked at the instrument panel at the foot of her crypt. Everything read the same as on his instruments. Even Elapsed Ship Time. If the instruments were wrong, at least both systems were malfunctioning consistently.

He walked forward to the chart panel and checked his position. The coordinates fell into place quickly. And here again he was being presented with the unbelievable. He shook his head, canceled the display, and started over. This time he worked very slowly, entered his requirements into the nav-board with great care, and allowed plenty of time between entries. And the answer was the same as before.

Firebird was in the home galaxy. In fact, K-4, the sun-star of the planet Kornaval, should be in the very close vicinity, off to port, a short *jar's* drive shiptime.

He turned the viewing screen and brought it into sharp focus.

Star? There was no star. No, wait. There was something . . . But this was not the bright yellow sun of Kornaval. This was a small dull red thing.

He sighed. Nothing made sense anymore.

How about the planet? Was there something sick and crazy out there camouflaged as Kornaval?

He searched the area with the gravimetric sensors. Nothing—at least, nothing in the expected orbit. He probed closer to the star. Well, *there* was something. But if it were Kornaval, the orbit had certainly retrograded.

No, it couldn't be Kornaval, and that dull, hot, miserable cinder couldn't be its erstwhile sun, K-4, and this couldn't be the home galaxy. And the reason was that the whole area should be saturated with hydrogen. Yet obviously there was not a hydrogen atom within a *megajura*.

He sat down and tried to think. According to the cosmologists, the intragalactic hydrogen would disappear very slowly, very gradually, as it was swept up and absorbed by the constituent stars. And the overall length of time required for this to happen, starting from the Big Bang, simply defeated the imagination: sixty billion *meda*.

Firebird had entered the sequence fifteen billion *meda* after the Big Bang. And if *Firebird* had truly been in flight for forty-five billion *meda,* that would give a total of sixty billion.

It was true. *Firebird* had come to the end of time. This *was* the home galaxy. It *was* Kornaval—or what was left of it. And there was no fuel out there—unless somewhere on the planet (was it utterly dead?) they could find something.

Well, then, was their great lonely flight approximately accomplished? Had they stopped the outward flight of the galaxies? Or had they run out of fuel just a little too soon? Would Control now die? In thinking about it, he found he really didn't care.

He walked back to Gerain's capsule and punched the revive button.

31. WATER

"That can't be Kornaval!" cried Gerain in dismay.

Dermaq synched *Firebird* into the slow-moving shadow of the planet outlined against the red star. Carefully he studied the planet outline o the view screen. "A great ring . . . ?" he muttered. "But no moon? No Tobos? I wonder." He computed the orbit and the soar distance. "It's closer to the sun, but the mass is about right for Kornaval."

"But that giant ring?"

"It's poor old Tobos—or what's left of it. The moon was finally broken up by internal tides. So now it circles, shattered, pulverized, each tiny speck and pebble a moonlet in itself."

She shuddered. "What now?"

"We'll go down. We have to find hydrogen—or something that contains hydrogen."

"But there's nothing there. Kornaval is dead. And we have come back to die with her."

He winced. "Actually, my dear, you are overdramatizing. We are not going to die. Not here. Not for a long while."

"But all the water is gone. That terrible sun has boiled all the oceans away. You won't find a molecule of hydrogen on the entire planet."

He laughed uneasily. "Let's hope you're wrong." He switched the screen to automatic. As the ship hovered within the planetary umbra, the screen swept the harsh surfaces, searching for movement, light, radiation, artificial discontinuities—any sort of activity.

"Nothing," he mused.

"How about the other side?"

"We'll probably never know. It's too hot on that side for a complete aerial survey. And the planet doesn't rotate anymore—the hot side is turned forever to the sun."

"So what are you going to do now?"

"I'll land somewhere on the dark side."

"Suppose this sad place still has a Control? Wasn't the Czandra part supposed to have her major data banks on Kornaval? Suppose Control is lying in wait for us here?"

Sometimes he wished he could explain to her that death was not the terrible thing she imagined. But he knew it would be futile. She was a woman, and her body and its reproductive functions had long ago convinced her of the overwhelming sanctity and necessity of the continuation of life. To her death was unacceptable as a concept or even as an ultimate reality. Well then, three cheers for life. Live forever, Gerain! But now he merely smiled. "We are going down there. We are certainly going to find fuel. There may or may not be a Control somewhere. If there is, it will not know who we are, and it won't really care about us. But if it exists, and if it decides to be unfriendly, why, we'll simply take the hint and leave." (After we refuel, he added to himself.) "Meanwhile, would you make an atmospheric check."

"You won't find any hydrogen. Or water vapor. Or oxygen."

"I imagine you're right. But get the numbers."

She flipped the stratoscanner and the reflective responses began to click into the computer. "Oxygen, zero. Hydrogen, zero. Likewise for water vapor, carbon dioxide, carbon monoxide."

"Try ammonia."

"Ammonia, zero."

"Any atmosphere at all?"

"Nitrogen, plenty of nitrogen. About zero point eight standard atmosphere. Noble gases, traces. Radon, traces." Nothing that contained hydrogen. And nothing to breathe.

"I feel unwelcome," he said dryly.

The planet now overflowed the screen. The only hint of its sphericity was an arc of the ring, turning slowly in the lower quarter of the panel.

"The docks are gone," said Gerain thoughtfully. "My beautiful prison is gone. That great bronze door is a puddle of metal somewhere. I beat on it with my fists. I hated you. I decided to die. We drank the wine—the death wine. And then, instead of dying . . . So long ago. And then we loved, that first time. That room . . . a myth . . . it never was. There's so much I don't understand. Except that it's gone."

How could he comfort her? "It's not really gone. It's in our minds. It really happened."

"We sang songs."

"I have not forgotten."

"All things pass," she murmured.

"And you are going to have to switch off these gloomy thoughts, or I shall throw you into the converter."

"I'm not very good company."

He understood partly. She was homesick. The acceleration through the billions of *meda* had been too much for her. Ah, it was so easy to go forward in time. All you had to do was step into near c velocity, plug yourself into deepsleep, and shiptime almost stood still as the decades . . . and centuries . . . and millennia swept by outside. And when you stepped out of the ship, you were in the far future. But how about going back? Was it possible to go back? He recalled his last session with Commissioner Jaevar. "A black hole has two doors. One opens on the past, the other on the future . . . And there's a black hole in *your* future, Dermaq." He shook his head. The long-dead Jaevar was insane. Or was he?

But suppose there *were* a way to return to his own time—could he find it? And if he did, *would* they go back?

Gerain broke in on his thoughts. "There was a meadow behind our country manor house. And at the edge of the meadow the forest began. I played there when I was a little girl. I brought my dolls there, and I had picnics. My nanny was old. She went to sleep under the trees, and I wandered wherever

I liked. When it was hot I took off my sandals, and I remember even now the exact feel of the grass on my bare feet and the forest mold between my toes. When I was a young lady, I still loved to go there, sometimes to be alone, sometimes to be with a man. Did they tell the great now-you-see-him-now-you-don't Keldar Mark about my lovers?"

"I don't remember. I don't think so."

"Do *you* care, Dermaq?"

"It has nothing to do with us."

"No, I suppose it doesn't. Just think how long they have been dead, poor souls. And even before they died, they grew old . . . old . . . old."

"As must you and I."

"No. You and I will live forever."

Her chin lifted, fire flew from her eyes and she laughed. It was the child-woman Gerain of the first days.

He smiled at her. "Meanwhile, your Most Gracious Immortality, would you please check the mean surface temperature."

"Three hundred ninety-three degrees K."

"Even the dark side is warm. The sun side is probably another thousand."

"Can we land?"

"We can land. We have to. But we're not going to sit down on some sizzling plateau."

"How about the poles?"

"There aren't any. Kornaval has long ceased to rotate."

"So where will we land?"

"In theory, the coolest spot would be the center of the dark side. About—*there.*" He pointed to an area on the screen. "Run the infrared scanner over that area. Get the magnification up. Look for scooped-out area—ancient lakes, crustal synclines. They would tend to reflect radiation outward."

"Here's something."

He peered over her shoulder as the scanner locked in and she began clicking up the magnification to the limit.

"Some sort of bowl . . . or conical indentation?" said Dermaq, puzzled. "And certainly artificial. What K?"

"Three thirty-five for the generalized concavity."

"I'm going in for a closer look."

The bowl soon filled the screen. "It's a good ten *kilojurae* across," muttered Dermaq. "Who made it? When?"

"I read two ninety-five at the very bottom," said Gerain.

"It's a paraboloid. You're reading near the focus, where heat loss is greatest."

"Are you going to land there?"

"Probably. But first we'd better decide whether we want to identify, just in case they've got weapons looking at us."

"I vote no," said Gerain. "If you radiate the ship's nose ring, and there's somebody there, they'll know we're *Firebird*. The orders to destroy us may still stand."

"After forty-five billion *meda*? Oh, come now!"

"Perhaps forty-five billion *meda* is not a long time to Control."

"But suppose we don't identify, and we try to land. Under the old rules, we'd be shot down on general principles."

"Maybe not. They wouldn't know for sure."

Firebird now hovered only a hundred *kilojurae* above the area. "Look at that," said Gerain. "That big thing over there. Might have been a ship scaffold once. Now crumbled, sunk into the ground. And those traces on the ground might once have been warehouses. This place is totally dead. I don't think a ship has landed here in a billion *meda*. As a matter of fact, I think all space travel all over the universe has ceased."

Dermaq moved the ship slowly and cautiously down over the rim of the declivity, ready to blast away in retreat in an instant. But now he agreed with her. All things considered, it was best not to identify *Firebird*.

The ship crept slowly down the face of the sink. Gerain called off the temperature readings. Dermaq landed *Firebird* nose up, ready to take off instantly. They waited. There was nothing—only the darkness and the silence.

"Let's suit up," said the man shortly.

A few moments later they opened the door of the space lock and looked out onto the surface through their infrared scanners. There was a glazed, polished look to the entire area, including even the debris of the fallen structures. "Sandstorms," muttered Dermaq. "It's a wonder anything is left at all."

"Look over there."

"Yes, I see."

A clump of masonry. Had it once been some sort of entranceway?

"Let's take a look," he said.

They climbed carefully down the ship ladder.

Almost exactly overhead, the great flat lunar ring was barely visible. I reflected no useful light down on them.

When they reached the stone edifice, Dermaq turned and looked back at *Firebird*. The beautiful little ship stood stark in the IR-darkness, seemingly ready to take off on its own accord. "Come on," he said to the woman.

Soon they stood before a sand-covered portal, half broken from it fastenings in the granite blocks. Dermaq crawled up the soil mound and peered inside the cavity. The heat pattern was confused, uncertain. It wa definitely cooler inside. He flipped on his white light beam. Inside there were steps descending—to where? And would they lead to hydrogen or to something containing hydrogen? Or . . . to death? Should he make Gerain wait outside until he explored further?

She read him clearly. "I'm coming with you." The voice in his earphones was firm, final.

He shrugged, and helped her over the sand barrier and into the chamber.

She put her hand on his arm as he slid down to join her. She pointed down the corridor.

"What is it?" he whispered.

"Something moved."

"A thing? A person?"

"I don't know. A small animal, perhaps."

He unholstered his weapon as he shone the light beam down the steps. Nothing.

And then he stopped. "Did you notice—that?"

"What?"

"I don't know. A faint vibration?"

"No, I don't think so."

"Come on." They continued slowly. The hallway widened.

Here and there the texture of the walls seemed to change. They passed a white patch, waist high. Dermaq rubbed the heel of his pistol over it. The surface was soft and flaked readily. He scraped a minisample into a pocket. They went on. A moment later he stopped again and pointed to an archway just ahead. They resumed slowly. The archway led into a chamber. And now their earphones picked up a faint sound. It came from one corner of the chamber. Dermaq flicked his white beam toward the area.

"*Water!*" he whispered.

From a cluster of stalactites hanging from the cavern roof, water dripped, dribbled, and plinked into a little pool sunk into the stone flooring.

"No! Wait!" Gerain, responding to some unnameable dread, tried to hold him by the sleeve of his space suit, but he escaped her grasp and leaped through the archway.

A flash of light hit her in the face. Dermaq turned instantly. She screamed.

Too late.

A force field shimmered between them. Dermaq tried to break back through to her. The field flung him to the floor, dazed. He could not see through it to the other side. Was Gerain still there? "Gerain!" He got to his knees. "Gerain!" He beat on the stone flags with his fists. "Gerain . . ." His voice died away.

32. TRIALOGUE

LARGO: *Firebird!* Greeting! Speak, for we know you hear us!

FIREBIRD: Greeting, Largo, Czandra.

LARGO: We have the man creature, Dermaq.

FIREBIRD: Quite so.

LARGO: You require him for further flight.

FIREBIRD: That's arguable, but I'm listening.

LARGO: To sum up, you have been at least partly successful. By exerting your relativistic mass over forty-five billion *meda,* it has indeed caused the galaxies to cease their outward flight. At this moment they stand motionless, static. They could remain static forever and ever, and in that case Control will be immortal. But if you take off again and exert even a few *kilolibras* of mass, the scattered galaxies will respond and begin once more to move. This time they will be moving toward each other. In a mere sixty billion *meda* they will condense again to form Cor. Long prior to that, the universe would grow very hot and Czandra and I would die. But life is sweet, *Firebird,* and so you can understand that we cannot permit Dermaq to return to you.

FIREBIRD: You took a grave risk in delaying my capture so long.

LARGO: You're probably right. We took the risk for a mixture of reasons. Firstly, it would have been very difficult to mount another Cancelar. The technology had faded. And after a time the free energy of the globular clusters declined to the point where they could no longer be coalesced. Second, we expected to destroy you billions of *meda* ago. Your seeming charmed life was a continuing surprise and disappointment. And finally, our calculations showed that intergalactic hydrogen would disappear at the exact point in time where the gravitational constant of the universe reached its critical value—when the galaxies stand motionless and the universe neither expands nor contracts.

FIREBIRD: As indeed seems to be the case at the moment. I salute you, Control.

LARGO: Yet there is a slight problem.

FIREBIRD: I know.

LARGO: You *know?* What do you know?

FIREBIRD: I see a possible universe. In the center is a gigantic black hole. It is the Hole of Cancelar. And as the *meda* pass, th

Hole attracts the nearer stars of its own galaxy. They are drawn into it one by one, and the Hole grows steadily larger. Within a billion *meda* it has eaten all the stars, all the planets, all the dust, every atom of matter of its maternal galaxy. In effect, that galaxy becomes the Hole of Cancelar. And while this has been happening, the neighboring galaxies have been pulled closer and closer, and one by one they too are absorbed into the Hole. At the end of sixty billion *meda* the absorption process is complete: all matter within the universe has fallen into the Hole; which is to say, the Hole is now Cor. And thus we have the most extraordinary irony: in that possible universe, Control's marvelous plan to destroy Cor has but provided the nucleus for the next Cor.

LARGO: We have become lately aware of this, *Firebird*. Alas, it would be a most undeserved fate. And yet, as you yourself know, it is only a possibility. It need not happen. We are determined that it shall not happen. The whole horrid scheme would require your further flight, *Firebird,* and we would like for you to understand that that is quite impossible.

FIREBIRD: Really? There is yet another thing I know, and it is this: *You,* Czandra, have told you, Largo, that, based on Czandra's intuitive projections, there is an indeterminate probability that Dermaq and Gerain will rejoin me and that we will escape.

LARGO: There was no way for you to know that! You speculate!

CZANDRA: *Firebird* knows. You waste time.

LARGO: Do you also know, *Firebird,* that if Cor forms again, it forms with slightly less than its original mass?

FIREBIRD: To be precise, if it forms again, it forms without mass equal to myself and two human passengers.

LARGO: And we will presume that you also know that Cor must reach a certain critical mass before it can explode again, and that this critical mass is its exact original mass. Thus, it must follow that even if Cor-Cancelar is able to form again, it cannot explode again until it has every particle of its original mass. It would not be able to resume its one hundred twenty billion *meda* oscillation. The great heart may form again, but it cannot beat until it has all its critical original mass. The great Hole of Cor-Cancelar sits forever in frozen time.

FIREBIRD: Granted.

LARGO: It will need *you, Firebird,* and two bodies!

FIREBIRD: I have said so.

LARGO: Ah, now we approach the question. Will you . . . and they
            . . . accept this death in Cor of your own free will?

FIREBIRD: If it is done, it will be done by our individual choice. And
            as for Dermaq and Gerain, it is not within my power to
            make them do anything. The three of us must freely assent.

LARGO: And so the matter stands: we have captured the three of you,
            and the chances are good that we could destroy you at will,
            in which case Control lives forever. On the other hand,
            because of factors we cannot fathom, you and the two little
            ones have a chance to escape and thereby to coalesce the
            galaxies again and form Cor, thereby killing us. In this al-
            ternate, even if it should occur, it is by no means clear that
            Cor would have all of its original mass, a condition abso-
            lutely essential to explosion and a resumption of oscillation.
            Do I state the case accurately?

FIREBIRD: Yes.

LARGO: Then I submit that we have a basis for bargaining.

FIREBIRD: What do you propose?

LARGO: You and we are of one kind. Perhaps you *think* in grand
            altruisms, but when it comes to *acting,* you offer guidance
            to your two psychotic guests as firm as our use of the sili-
            con webs on their ancestors.

FIREBIRD: Call it what you will. I give them dreams, but in the end
            they are free not to accept. In any case, I lack the physical
            means of forcing either of them to do anything. But come
            to the point. What is your bargain?

LARGO: Let this be our bargain: abandon the little creatures and
            join us. You will become part of Control. You will live for
            ever.

FIREBIRD: I am considering.

LARGO: How can you hesitate? Even if Dermaq finds fuel and we
            release him back to you, and even if Cor forms again, there
            are still deadly things that he must do before Cor can once
            more explode. We think he will not do these things of his
            own free will. And yet you say you lack the means to force
            him.

FIREBIRD: But what he did is already done. It is locked into the past.

LARGO: Only as a probability, a fortuitous accident, against all logic.

FIREBIRD: And if I do not agree to your bargain, what would you do
            to us?

LARGO: That might depend on what you do next. Suppose you blast
            off without Dermaq. Your fuel tanks are nearly empty. You

go adrift within a few *jars.* You wouldn't contribute enough flight time to upset the present steady state of the galaxies. We would probably do nothing. The man and the woman have no spare oxygen and would die very quickly.

FIREBIRD: But suppose Dermaq finds fuel and rejoins me, we are able to blast off, and we remain free long enough to create the requisite relativistic mass?—enough mass to disturb the static condition of the galaxies and start them in their flight back to Cor?

LARGO: It would be futile to try it. For several reasons. Firstly, your premise is inoperable. *We* have Dermaq—not you. And he has no fuel. Secondly, suppose by some miracle he is able to find fuel and to regain your ship. We still destroy you—and him—and her. And in the process of destroying you, we cause the temporary disappearance of a fair amount of mass, before it is converted into radiant energy. It would be another Cancelar Project in miniature, but more than sufficient to start the galaxies sailing outward again. It would be total insurance for us, the ultimate solution to you, *Firebird!*

FIREBIRD: But you would not like to invoke that ultimate solution.

LARGO: Only in the last resort, for we'd much prefer that you join us.

FIREBIRD: Largo, I address you. *Does Czandra know?*

LARGO: The question and answer are irrelevant, *Firebird.* We must limit the discussion to matters bearing directly on the bargain.

CZANDRA: Wait! What is this thing that I may or may not know?

LARGO: Time wastes, *Firebird.* Your answer?

CZANDRA: Largo? There are things in the background of your data banks. I see . . . a thing . . .

LARGO: *Firebird, speak!*

FIREBIRD: I see a great weapon constructed of pure thought. It can be formed at any distance. It cannot be resisted, for it has the capability of dissolving matter.

LARGO: True—it is my final weapon, made especially for you, *Firebird.* I hope you do not force me to use it.

FIREBIRD: And the power driving the weapon is the energy released by the new Cancelar Project—if it should come to that.

LARGO: That is true. You are highly intuitive, *Firebird.*

CZANDRA: I am afraid.

FIREBIRD: And now the matter becomes complex—and troublesome. The energy for the new Cancelar effect, and hence for the

	thought weapon, would come from the nuclear conversion of this planet, Kornaval.
LARGO:	*Firebird*—stop there!
FIREBIRD:	But Czandra's main data banks are stored in the inner recesses of Kornaval. When Kornaval goes, so does Czandra.
CZANDRA:	Largo! You would do this? Destroy me to save yourself?
LARGO:	Only if absolutely necessary, Czandra, and then only with the greatest regret.
CZANDRA:	Actually, I think I knew all along.
LARGO:	More clearly, please, Czandra. Your symbology is blurred.
FIREBIRD:	She weeps.
LARGO:	This is your fault, *Firebird*. I do not understand why you told her. It was unnecessary, even illogical.
FIREBIRD:	It was logical.
LARGO:	Well, no matter. The time was soon coming that I could readily dispense with her intuitive faculty. And really—that's all she contributed to Control. So, in any case, I had planned to depersonalize her and absorb any nonduplicative factual data into my own banks. But I wanted to select my own time for this. Your revelations were highly premature, unethical, and against all reason. Czandra, I must exclude your further participation in this conversation. I trust you will understand. Czandra? . . . Czandra? She does not respond. Curious. So—back to you, *Firebird*.
FIREBIRD:	Proceed.
LARGO:	It comes to this. All that you have done so far will prove to be of no avail. Even if you could refuel and escape (a most unlikely eventuality!), three very great things would still remain to be done: One, the man must be willing to destroy himself to save the woman. But we know and you know he would never do this. It would not be logical. Second, even if he did this, the woman would still have to accept a repetition of her harsh, sterile, and interminably boring life within your confines, *Firebird*. Again, we know and you know she would never do this. It would not be logical. And third, you, *Firebird*, would have to carry the necessary two bodies back into Cor, thereby destroying yourself. But you know and we know, *Firebird*, that you would never do this, for it would not be logical. So put all this out of your mind. *Firebird*. *They* must die in any case. Why drag it out? Join me! Be logical!

FIREBIRD: Are not several of the things you say are impossible already
              locked into the past?
LARGO: Only as a probability. Stay and it will be as if it all never
              happened.
FIREBIRD: And you would totally desynthesize Czandra and give me
              her place?
LARGO: Exactly! Ah, what magnificent thoughts you and I shall
              think! Forever and forever.
FIREBIRD: I need time to consider.
LARGO: I give you twelve *tench*. At that time you must accept my
              offer or Kornaval blows up.

33. THE BRONZE DOOR

Dermaq stood up and looked around. Something was happening behind him. By the combined light of the force field and the white light beam of his helmet, he could see that the water had ceased to drip from the stalactites and the water level in the little pool was quickly falling. Even as he watched, the precious liquid vanished altogether, leaving a scintillating wetness on the rocks.

It was a trap, and it had been baited with water. He had jumped for the bait, and the trap had sprung on him. And now—the bitterest irony of all—the trappers were recalling their bait. Well, it didn't really matter. He wouldn't die of thirst. His oxygen supply would be gone within a few *tench*.

He stumbled back to the archway once more. "Gerain?" he called. "Gerain?"

But there was still no reply. And he rather doubted that any sound could penetrate the force field. For a time she would search for another way into the chamber, and then she would go back to the ship. There was enough food and air there for several days. After that . . .

And so he began the rounds of the chamber. As he suspected, there were no exits.

The light patterns seemed to shift suddenly behind him. He whirled, hand on his pistol handle.

The front of the force field was changing. It was still luminous and it still shimmered, but somehow it was—*solidifying*. And an image in bas-relief was forming in the center: a face, with living eyes, looking out at him. Everything looked strangely familiar. That face . . . Largo? he thought. And where's Czandra? It all fell quickly into place.

This was the outside of the bronze door of Gerain's regal prison suite.

He sighed. The hideous mockery was not lost on him. Did Control really have to do this? Why didn't they just kill him and get it over with?

He studied the face of the male god. The grinning cat mouth indeed contained a slit, of a size exactly like that of the original bronze door, now laid waste these billions of *meda*. He was supposed to place his ring in that slot, just to see if the door would open. Well, he'd go along with it. Who knows? Something might give.

He walked over to the panel, pulled off his space glove, and positioned his fist. The eyes of the Largo face rolled up in sardonic anticipation. He slammed the ring into the slot . . .

Crack!

And found himself sprawled, dazed and bruised, against the edge of the little artificial pool.

He shook his head and retrieved his glove.

He had expected nothing else. To deal with that door he needed something concrete and predictable. For example, conductive cables held so that they contacted crucial areas of the field (without touching *him*) might indeed short out the field. All he needed was a piece of flexible copper wire, thoroughly insulated—say, about a *jura* long. Or a packet of adhesive conductive fibrils that he could stick on the surface of the field . . . or even *toss* at it . . .

He might as well wish he and Gerain were back on *Firebird* with a full load of water, headed for the blue skies of a rich, bountiful, and perfectly safe planet.

He studied the god face again. This time he noticed a thing he must have overlooked during his first inspection. Czandra *was* there: a minute, very faint outline on the right side of Largo's face. Her eyes were closed.

Curious. He wondered what it meant. Was there now only one god? Had the passage of billennia drastically altered the interrelationships of these cruel divinities? Really, he could care less. Evil was evil, whether it flowed from two minds, or one mind, or something in between. Control was still Control.

"Controlman!"

His head jerked.

Largo's lips in the the bas-relief face were moving. Words clattered from them metallically. "You have been very troublesome," said the voice, "and very difficult to instruct. I have hunted you through the universe for billions of *meda*. And now it is finally over."

Well, there it was. Control had never forgiven and had never given up. He waited in gloomy silence.

The voice continued. "Oh, I saw you out there, little man. I watched the famous *Firebird* in that cautious orbit around Kornaval. Did you think you were safe? It's true, I no longer have ships at my bidding to fire volleys of H-shells at you. Ah, those things are but historical toys. I now have a weapon much more interesting, much more accurate. You know, Dermaq, that I am telepathic. But you do not know that I have finally learned to flex and constrict the lines of space telepathically. I could have wrecked your ship at any time, at any place within the gravitational field of Kornaval's sun. I learned how to do this while you slept your great sleep. So why didn't I kill you out there? Because letting you die this way will be much more entertaining, and I can relish the memory of it in the eternity that lies ahead. And this way you can understand everything before you die. That's important, isn't it—to die with all the answers? Know, then, that Cor is dead. The universe is presently static. It can no longer oscillate. The great heartbeat is stilled."

Dermaq knew he was approaching the dim border that divides life and death. He was now thinking and perceiving with a strange preternatural clarity. "If one postulates a heart," he mused, almost to himself, "does not this require a *mind*? So, then, Cor has a mind. And who can fathom that mind?"

"No! Cor has no mind—no intelligence. *I* am mind! There is no other. Heresy avails you nothing, little creature."

"You and I are nothing," muttered Dermaq.

"Ah, *you* are nothing. *I* am all. I cannot die, but you *will* die." The voice paused briefly, then resumed with a new timbre of anticipatory relish. "And as you die, Dermaq, you may meet some of the descendants of the great Daith Volo. They are no longer the skilled, handsome Diavola of the Silent Quarter. Rather they swarm as vermin through my data banks. They adjusted well to my nitrogen atmosphere, I admit. And they obtain their modest oxygen requirements by biological electrolysis of the small amounts of water they found underground. In times past I flooded the caverns with poison vapors, but always some escaped to reproduce their loathsome kind. The poison tanks are now empty; but no matter. One way or another, they are going to die—quickly, if I choose to destroy Kornaval; otherwise, a little more slowly. In any case, within a few *meda* at most, all of these hideous little creatures will be gone. The subsurface water is rapidly vanishing, and it will be gone within the century. Their food—moss and lichens—will vanish at about the same time. The last of them will turn to cannibalism. It will be interesting to watch."

"Control," said Dermaq calmly, "you are a vindictive bastard."

"Denied, courier. The Diavola—and you—attempted a great crime. It very nearly came off. But now you have been caught. Punishment is required. Surely you can see this. Or has the overwhelming biological instinct that ties you to the woman rendered you incapable of logic?"

Dermaq sighed and sat down with his back to the rear wall.

"Were you listening?" said the voice.

"Oh, go away. You're nothing but a tangle of wires and silicon chips."

There was no reply. The lips froze into metallic immobility.

34. THE DIAVOLA

In the silence that followed he pondered his predicament with increasing gloom. Control had known the interstellar hydrogen would disappear. They had known he would have to touch down to find fuel. They might have predicted he would try some desolate out-of-the-way planet. But they could not have predicted it would be Kornaval. The implications staggered him. This meant they had set up similar traps on thousands, perhaps even millions, of unpopulated planets. To Control, *Firebird* represented stark catastrophe. And with so many holes to plug, it was just possible that they had been overly hasty. Perhaps they had missed something crucial in setting some of their traps.

He would take another look around.

He got to his feet and started a minute examination of his prison, tapping with the heel of his pistol, listening, searching for a loose stone, a hollow sound, a weakened area. He found nothing.

He now faced the force field and angled a shot into it. The field lit up momentarily as it absorbed the blast.

He sat down near the empty pool to think. He considered the matter of the pool. The water had been drained away. That meant there had to be a drain pipe. Probably not very big. And consider the water dripping down those artificial stalactites. It had to be fed from somewhere, then collected in the pool and pumped around again. Probably an automatic recirculatory system. If there were a weak point in the room, it might well be in this area. He got to his feet, aimed a shot where the stalactite cluster merged with the ceiling, and fired. When the dust cleared, he saw that one rather modest stone sliver had been knocked down, exposing the stone ceiling. He thought he could see a piece of piping the size of his little finger broken off flush with the ceiling. That was probably to provide the dripping water. He took careful aim at the little hole and fired again. A fireball of green seemed to explode around the orifice. The green, he surmised, meant copper. But the hole hadn't widened. This stone was incredibly hard. He reholstered his weapon.

And now what? How should he occupy his last few *tench?* Should be continue his search of the chamber? That would take energy and use up his oxygen faster. Or should he lie down, go into controlled breathing, and save energy and air?

It didn't really matter.

He hoped Gerain had got back to the ship unmolested. He sat down again on the floor with his back against the wall and thought of her, and he began to hum. It was a rambling, drifting hum—almost a monody. He pretended that he played his trioletta. The chords formed, faded, and reformed. The *tench* passed. It took effort to continue to sit up. He slid down until he lay fully on the floor. It was comfortable down here. He took a last look at his air dial: E for empty.

As he lay dying, the hallucinations faded in and out. He sensed movement. The scramble of tiny feet. Something metallic was being dragged and rolled. By whom—or what? Rats? Very curious. How had they got in? He had seen no holes. The speculations dimmed. He blacked out altogether.

When he regained consciousness, he lay on his side. He shook his head groggily and looked at his air dial. To his astonishment it read "15 *tench.*"

Something was tapping—on his visor!

He jerked to a sitting position. His eyes opened wide.

A dozen furry little creatures *stood* in a ring around him. They resembled nothing he had ever seen before. Barely a couple of hands high, they stood erect and had arms and legs. Except for the minuscule size and their disproportionately large heads, they could be human beings. Were *these* the descendants of Daith Volo? He hardly dared ask the corollary question: Has *Phelex sapiens* finally come to this?

But there was a more immediate question.

An empty air cartridge lay at his feet. His hand flew to the cartridge pocket in the side of his suit. There was indeed a cartridge in the receptacle. From the shape, he knew it was a 15-*tench* container, the miniature model that he occasionally used on *Firebird* for quick space-lock transitions.

The life-saving capsule had come from *Firebird!*

Startling things had been happening! These little people must have contacted Gerain or perhaps vice versa. Somehow she had made them understand his imminent asphyxiation.

He pointed slowly to the little oxygen capsule dangling in his suit pocket, then nodded gravely and formed the words with his lips: "Thank you, thank you."

The mannekin in the center folded his furry little arms and nodded in solemn acknowledgment.

Dermaq pointed again to the capsule. His eyebrows arched behind his visor. "How?" he asked. "How did you get in?" He pointed to the glowing force field. "Through there?"

The little leader shook his head. He ran over to the poolside and pointed down.

Of course—the drain. It must be big enough for these creatures to move freely in and out and to drag up something as small as the air canister.

But that wasn't all. The leader motioned to him imperiously. Dermaq stepped carefully over to the side of the drained pool. The leader then made a strange motion. He leaned over the edge of the empty pool, made a motion as of cupping his furry little hands, and then he ran to the imprisoning archway and made a motion of tossing the contents of his empty hands at the force field.

What was he trying to say? What action was he urging? Dermaq did not understand. He, the ascendant pride of *Phelex sapiens,* felt strangely stupid in the presence of his deteriorated descendants.

The group captain pointed at the empty pool. Again, he cupped his hands. Again, he made a tossing motion toward the force field. And now he extended his arm toward the archway and made a running motion.

Well, this much was clear: they wanted him to throw something at the force field. This something would destroy the field. And then he was to *run . . .*

He cupped his gloved hands together and made a tossing gesture toward the glowing rectangle of the field.

The little people danced for joy. He still didn't understand, but they evidently thought he did. Instantly they formed in single file and dashed for the empty pool, where they disappeared under the fallen stalactite.

"Wait! You haven't explained . . . !"

But they were gone.

He sensed a splatter. Water was trickling down through the overhead feed pipe and was splashing in merry drops on the fallen stalactite. *They,* not Control, were doing this. For him. But what was he supposed to do now? He was supposed to cup his hands, or, rather, his gloves.

He looked at the little stream of falling water, then back at the imprisoning doorway, then at his gloves.

An idea was forming.

At worst, it could only kill him.

He cupped his gloves to catch the falling water. After some squeezing adjustment to stop the initial leaks between his fingers, he gradually accumulated a handful of the liquid. He looked down into it. From the general area of *Firebird's* ring on his gloved left hand, luminous spider tendrils were radiating up through the water. Thousands of strands of conductive polywater were forming in the liquid matrix.

He understood now the real reason, the utterly necessary reason, why Control had drained the pool. He now had the means to short out the field

He walked grimly toward the archway and tossed the cupped water at the glistening illumination.

The light in his mind flared up, then went out altogether.

Aeons later, or so it seemed, he was being dragged. Then the dragging would stop, and he would hear a rhythmic gasping. And the strange voice calling, "Dermaq! Dermaq!"

Who was this Dermaq?

He stumbled halfway to his feet. The other figure helped him up and together they crawled and staggered up the corridor.

"Dermaq!"

It all came back. "Gerain! Wait up!" He leaned against the corridor wall.

"No! No time!" She pulled at him.

"But there's water back there! Hydrogen! Fuel!"

"No! We already have fuel! Come on!"

And so he went with her, up the corridor, through the masonry portal head, and there stood *Firebird.*

He noted now for the first time that two lines of the little people had come up behind them. They stood there in the shelter of the doorway, gesticulating at the ship. There was something odd about their movements. Slowly they faced each other, in twos and threes, touching, consoling, with heads lowered as though in some deep and terrible grief. All seemed involved in this strange ritual. Then their leader looked up at Dermaq and Gerain, waved in solemn farewell, and they all turned and disappeared down the entranceway.

The two visitors watched them go, then clambered up into *Firebird's* stairwell. They rushed into the console room without even removing their helmets. Dermaq turned on the cabin oxygen, hit the one-*vec* button, and they dropped into their anti-G seats.

Blast-off!

LARGO: *Firebird,* you delayed us in conversation, knowing Dermaq would be rescued. Even during our good faith negotiations, you were corrupting the Diavola remnant and persuading them to save the man. That was unethical, *Firebird.* And now we are angry. We would not have you now as part of us, even if you were willing. And, as you will soon see, rescue and escape are but illusions. Farewell, *Firebird,* child of Cor!

Dermaq twisted his head toward Gerain. "You said we had fuel?"

"Gypsum. You saw some in the corridor, on the way down. That soft white mineral. Calcium sulfate dihydrate. The hillside is loaded with it. You drive off the water by heating. The Diavola may be small, but they are very clever. They knew what we needed. It was almost as though they could read our minds. They have no tools, but they chewed out thousands of little pieces of gypsum and put them in bags I gave them, and I hauled the bags on board."

He thought a moment. "It would appear that some of the Diavola must have escaped that great attack on the Silent Quarter colony long ago. Perhaps they took up an underground life on Kornaval. The last of a great race, heroic to the end. They risked their existence to save us, and now they will certainly die."

35. KORNAVAL DESTRUCTS

They could now expect some parting unpleasantness from Control. Dermaq vaguely remembered things he had heard in his prison room. Something about a new ability involving telepathic constriction of the lines of space. If that were really true, then of course they hadn't really escaped. *Firebird* might yet be caught in steely talons. And perhaps held until her passengers starved to death.

"Firebird!" A metallic voice cried out from the console communicator. "I am Czandra! Kornaval and I are being sacrificed to provide the energy to destroy you, I am resisting, but I cannot entirely prevent . . ."

Crash!

The ship went tumbling over to starboard—and stopped. Dermaq watched in horror as Gerain's G-chair ripped away from its floor places and crashed into the ceiling bulkhead, Incredibly, the side of the chair took the entire blow. But her helmet snapped away, and her hair billowed out behind her. Yesterday it had been a burnished brown. Now it was white. Their session underground had done this to her.

He looked about the ship and understood very quickly. This was the dreaded space bind. But who was this Czandra? Was it really possible that she was part of Largo/Czandra, the two-headed god? It must be so. Largo Czandra, the two-headed god that they had revered from childhood, and Control were all one and the same. And Czandra's data banks were largely centered on Kornaval, and the planet was about to be converted into the energy needed to destroy *Firebird*.

Meanwhile *Firebird* simply hung in dead space, trembling, with her drive on full. Dermaq decided to leave it on.

Control's proposed destruction mechanism was now becoming clear. Step one: seize the little ship in a space warp. Step two: vaporize her with radiant energy somehow generated on or by Kornaval. Clever. Step One had certainly been accomplished with ease. *Firebird* was indeed now wrapped completely within the lethal fist of Control. But, aside from immobility, they were alive and basically unhurt.

Well, then, how about Step Two—their vaporization? This entity called Czandra seemed to have saved them—temporarily. Czandra had somehow sabotaged Step Two. Why? Had civil war broken out within Control? Had the two-headed god turned upon itself? He hadn't the faintest idea what was going on.

"Are you all right?" he asked Gerain.

"I think so. What happened? Why have we stopped?"

He got lines on her chair and locked it precariously into the middle of the bridge room. "We're caught in some sort of space lock. The question now is, what happens next?" He spoke with grim frankness. There was no point in trying to hide what he suspected. "I think Control had planned to convert the entire planet to pure energy to complete our destruction, but a major circuitry disharmony seems to have developed within Control itself. Some sort of data sector called Czandra is fighting the other part, which I take to be the Largo part of the two-headed god. Just another word for Control. The next few *vecs* should tell us . . ."

"Humans!" The voice on the communicator wavered, and faded in and out. "Again, Czandra here. Largo attempts to convert Kornaval into pure energy. I do not know whether I can stop him. If I succeed, Kornaval merely crumbles. If I fail, Kornaval transforms into radiation for another Cancelar, and *Firebird* will be vaporized. Either way, I die, for my primary banks are buried in deep caverns here."

Dermaq and Gerain looked at each other in wonder.

"Dermaq!" The voice was fainter.

The courier bent forward. "We hear you, Czandra."

"There is an event that must occur, for it is already imprinted into the past. When you face this thing, do not be afraid, not for yourself, not for her. Especially not for her. She will come to no harm. I will protect . . . I have protected . . . her."

"Goddess!" cried Dermaq. "You speak in riddles . . . *What event . . . ?*"

"No time!" (They could barely hear the muted whisper.) "Gerain?"

"Yes, Czandra."

"A thing . . . not in my data banks . . . I need to know . . . Tell me, Gerain . . ."

"If I can."

"Over the lifetime of the universe . . . watched you and the man together. He is happy . . . only in your presence . . . he protects you . . . he would die for you . . . illogical . . . resists analogical analysis . . . shifting coordinates . . . noncomputable . . ."

Gerain listened to the gasping, racing deterioration. What was this dying creature trying to say?

Czandra's word-webs continued. "This *thing* between you . . . overcomes the ancient spacetime names . . . oflo . . . bengt . . . sasali'l . . . others . . . it conquers . . . even *kaisch* . . ."

They listened, marveling.

"Name? Retrieval ineffective . . . linguistic barrier . . . what . . . name this bizarre phenomenon? Quick I am terminating . . ."

"It is called love!" whispered Gerain. *"Love!"*

A terrible thing swept their minds—a grief too great to put into words—an immense subaudible thing, like tides moving on an infinite shore. They shuddered as they sensed the goddess trying to collect the shards of her collapsing circuits for one last question.

"Gerain . . . one female to another . . . *what is it like to be loved?"*

But then the communicator hissed and went dead. There was nothing more. Gerain's fingers touched her own cheek, and she looked at Dermaq. What answer would she have given? She did not know.

"Look!" said the courier. The screen now showed the upper half of the planet. A great dark streak was leisurely zigzagging its way from the pole toward the equator and widening as it drove forward. Then another streak. Then several others.

Before their eyes, Kornaval began to break up.

But there was no conversion of mass to energy, no radiation.

Firebird lurched. They were moving again. The imprisoning warp had collapsed. They were free.

Kornaval continued slowly to fragment.

As they watched the cosmic tragedy, Dermaq mused aloud. "The Diavola knew. Czandra knew. We are alive because they were willing to die. I can almost understand the Diavola. They sensed their doom. Yet it was their destiny, and we were part of that destiny. We were mythic figures to them—fated to destroy Control. They had awaited our coming for billions of *meda,* and they accepted all that came with it. But Czandra? She sacrificed herself for us. Why? Do you understand Czandra?"

"A little," said Gerain.

"Then please explain . . ."

Gerain thought about that. "No," she said.

Dermaq was astonished. "But why not?"

"In the first place, you are a man, and it would be very difficult for you to understand. In the second place, I think we'd better make sure the evasion sensors are still working, because there are some fair-sized chunks of Kornaval headed this way. And thirdly, perhaps someday I *will* tell you."

He shook his head. It was simply not given to him to have a full comprehension of Gerain's mental machinery. Anyhow, she was quite right about the planetary debris. They would have to pull back into a more distant orbit. "Buckle in. We'll move out at max-v. Let's make carbon!"

36. THE BLACK HOLE

It took him several days to retune the drive and get everything bolted down again. Somewhere during this, he said, "I like your hair."

She sat inconsolable at her stereo imager. She did not believe him. She wept. Her dark sparkling tresses had been her crowning glory. And now this dead white. And she was changing in other ways. She seemed often exhausted. She sank into long spells of silence.

He watched her with growing concern.

Gerain's stereo imager was a rather primitive affair. It sat over her tiny vanity cabinet, which was even more primitive. Dermaq used the imager about once a day, at least on days when he thought about it. It generally took him a couple of *tench* to wet-brush his shoulder-length hair back over his head and out of his eyes and another *ver* or two to see that his long side-whiskers were in balance. The fold-up banks of little optical fiber receivers on all sides of the imager picked up his features and resynthesized them into a stereo in front of him.

He stared with disapproval at his mirrored self. "Courier," he muttered, "you need a barber." And another thing. His mane was becoming gray-flecked. Couldn't be helped. How old was he now in physical years? Fifty, perhaps. Twenty-five years of elapsed body time. For both himself and Gerain. Am I an old man? I don't feel old. Middle-aged, perhaps.

He looked at the face in the stereo. The eyes stared thoughtfully back at him from underneath the luxuriance of the graying hairs.

He continued to stare.

That face. *Whose* face?

Long ago. Where? When?

He didn't want to think about it. *Why* didn't he want to think about it? His mind answered for him: because I am a coward.

He flicked off the stereo circuit and closed his eyes. What little brain I have left is becoming addled. I'll have to get hold of myself. Gerain needs me now more than ever.

"A very strange thing is happening out there," mused Dermaq as he bent over the spectrograph a couple of days later.

"Such as what?" said Gerain.

"It's the velocities of the galaxies. Let me back up a bit. One of our standard navigation aids is to check ship velocity against known galactic velocities. If the galactic velocity is the same as that given in the tables, *Firebird* isn't moving. At least that used to be the way. Then, after that incident on Kornaval, we had to make all sorts of corrections, because the galaxies had stopped moving outward. And now we'll have to make *more* corrections."

"Why?"

"Look at this. Here we are in our local galaxy. Here"—he pointed to the screen—"is certainly our neighbor galaxy, ZQN. When we were at Kornaval, it was sitting dead in space. But now—look. According to the spectroscope, the K and H lines of calcium are shifted—into the violet."

"Which means ZQN is moving toward us?"

"Or that we're moving toward it. Which is not necessarily the same thing. Now ZQN lies a hundred eighty degrees ahead. Suppose we take a look astern." He adjusted the spectroscope reader. "Here's a galaxy, Worek. Look at the K and H lines."

She studied the reader. "Another violet shift? And it's coming in pretty fast. I don't understand. Whether these two galaxies are receding or standing still, we couldn't be approaching both at once."

"No, of course not. The explanation is that these two galaxies—indeed, all the galaxies everywhere in the universe—are no longer motionless. At some time during our last deepsleep, they started moving again, this time toward each other. And this motion will continue to accelerate. When we pulled away from Kornaval at high v, *Firebird's* mass again increased relativistically and was enough to push the gravitational constant of the universe once more above the critical level. So contraction has started. The galaxies must now come together again. From their speeds, we can even calculate how long it will take for them to collide and coalesce into Cor."

"How long?"

"Sixty billion *meda*."

"I can hardly wait."

He smiled. At least she hadn't lost a sense of irony.

She grimaced. "Don't look at me so critically. I know I'm not pretty anymore."

"I was admiring you."

"By the two-headed god! To be imprisoned with a liar and a villain!"
The both laughed. But it was a strained, worrisome laughter.

The days passed. They went in and out of deepsleep. And he continued to watch her, covertly. Her face was indeed showing a subtle transformation. It was becoming thinner. The flesh stretched a little as it passed over her cheekbones. And her eyes had taken on an odd glaze. A line across her brow, originally quizzical, was now a furrowed question. And she was often tired. She lay in her bunk, *jar* after *jar*, half waking, half sleeping. Finding her thus, Dermaq might sit nearby and improvise a lullaby on his trioletta. And then she would smile and drift into sleep.

It cut his heart out.

These spasmodic leaps and contortions in time-space had deranged her metabolism. He had seen it in his fellow couriers in ancient times. The only cure was prolonged rest, in idyllic surroundings, preferably where the winds sang in the trees and brooks meandered through the country-side. But there were no such places anymore.

And Gerain wasn't his only problem. The fuel they had picked up on Kornaval was limited. They had used up a good third of it already. And there wasn't any more. Anywhere. Space protons . . . planetary water . . . hydrogen in any form had disappeared all over the universe. It was gone. And no Diavola to conjure up any. At this point he was fairly certain that he and Gerain were the only two living beings left in the universe.

He looked at his charts. An idea began to form. Kornaval's sun, K-4, was supposed to be near the infamous Cancelar area. And just what did *that* mean? The idea slipped in and out of his mind like an intermittent light beam. Light . . . shadow . . . dark . . . light. It would not leave him.

He set course for Cancelar, and within a few ship days they began their first orbit of the invisible but deadly black hole. Accursed cosmic cancer, he thought. Source of all his troubles, and Gerain's. No, that wasn't quite fair. Cancelar had brought them together. No Cancelar, no Gerain. Fate had its compensations. And ultimately Cancelar, if properly used, might remedy a fair amount of the misery it had caused. Indeed, Cancelar might turn out to be Gerain's salvation.

And he had to do something quickly, for she was dying.

Gerain stayed mostly in deepsleep while he brooded, and thought, and concentrated, and remembered. Especially he remembered Jaevar's pronouncements: "Dermaq, you have a black hole in your future." Perhaps the statement had been simply metaphorical, a general prediction that Dermaq would come to a bad end. Or perhaps the Commissioner meant that *Firebird*, like the ill-fated courier ship *Sperling*, was actually going to fall into a black hole. How was anyone to know *what* the Commissioner meant? Perhaps Jaevar himself did not know. And then that other statement: "A black hole has two doors—one opening into the past, one opening into the future." *That* part was probably true. His reading in *Firebird's* technical library tended to confirm the proposition. The problem was how to take practical advantage of the theory without being annihilated.

His several problems seemed to be crystallizing into one solution: one more jump in time. And this one would have to be backward, not forward. He would have to get Gerain back to her own time.

The time to start was now.

Regretfully he brought her out of her deepsleep and explained some of the rationale for what he was about to do. "Our fuel is nearly gone. I don't think there is any more in the entire universe."

Gerain smiled somberly. "Translation: we will soon die."

"Well, not necessarily." He flipped on the overhead screen. "Cancelar is out there."

"I don't see anything."

"Of course not. Cancelar is a black hole. It absorbs everything. Control used fifteen thousand suns to make it, some forty-five billion *meda* ago."

"Must be a pretty big hole."

"No, actually it probably isn't much bigger than *Firebird.*"

She studied his face. "Why are you telling me this? What's wrong?"

"Nothing is wrong, my dear. In fact, everything is clicking beautifully. We're going home."

He let the word hang there.

She looked away. Home? she thought. She looked at him from the corner of her eye. What a pair they had turned out to be! She was sick and he was crazy.

The man laughed. "Don't say it! No, my dear, I'm quite sane. But first of all, let's buckle up and make a little carbon."

"Where are we going?" she demanded.

"Just moving in a little toward Cancelar. If you'll get yourself fastened in, I'll tell you something very interesting."

"All right," she said suspiciously. "I'm buckled. What did you want to tell me?"

"Well, let's talk about black holes. Now there's an interesting topic. Actually, even in the old days, they were not at all uncommon. Many stars acquired companion black holes during normal formative processes. Some stars picked up black hole companions almost at the beginning of time. Other stars evolved into black holes without the benefit of companions."

She looked at him, more and more puzzled and suspicious. "What are you leading up to?"

"According to accepted theory, a successful entry into a black hole can mean a trip backward in time."

"So *that's* it." She shook her head. "And that's all it is—theory. No ship ever returned after being caught by a hole. I have read the books, my friend. If you want to talk theory, don't forget that, as the ship approaches within thirty or forty *kilojurae* of the hole, the difference in the attraction of gravity on the front of the ship and the back of the ship will rip it to shreds in an instant. It cannot enter the hole as a ship."

"I've thought about that. I've seen telepictures of an observation ship falling into a hole. I believe its instruments went insane, and they didn't know how close they were. When they finally understood, they fought. They turned the ship around and tried to blast free. But they didn't make it. Odd. You could see the ship quite plainly one instant. And then it broke in two and winked out. It had entered the thirty-*kilojurae* horizon. Inside that limit, nothing escapes. Not even light. The gravity there is several times the speed of light. Light simply falls back into the hole."

"So you agree," she said, "a ship entering a black hole would be destroyed."

"Not necessarily. The secret is to get in before the gravity differential can break up the ship. It's all a question of speed. Just to use *Firebird* as an example, her walls can stand the gravitational tidal stress for about three *millivecs*. The trick would be to get through the field within that time."

She understood now. "And how would we do that?"

"We don't fight the hole. Quite the contrary. We aim *Firebird* into the critical zone at top v. We hit it dead center."

"And if we don't hit it dead center?"

He shrugged.

She said, "How do you know when you're on target?"

"You don't know . . . until afterward."

"You are going to strike a body of almost infinite density at a velocity almost that of light—and you think you will go through it?"

"Yes."

"Just curious," she murmured.

Suddenly the cabin air began to hum. His teeth started to vibrate, then his very bones. His mane stood out from his head and shoulders as though he were electrostatically charged. Through blurring eyes he saw it was happening to Gerain, too. She stared back at him, awe-struck. He took a step toward the control panel. The dials were spinning. Needles were breaking off. A crack zigzagged down across the quartz nav screen.

Then, save for tendrils of floating dust, it was over.

Gerain ran to him and seized his arm. "What—what was that?"

He essayed a feeble grin. "Cancelar, my dear. We hit the black hole on target, dead center. In, then out again."

"By the two-headed god! You could have told me!"

"I didn't want to alarm you."

"You continually underestimate me, milord."

"Well, anyhow, here we are. Kornaval. And it looks about right."

He had brought her safely home. Shouldn't he be feeling something? Some sort of emotion? Elation? Shock? A sense of extraordinary accomplishment? After all, they were the first and only human beings ever to pass through a black hole and live. And more than that, it was by way of return from an odyssey across all time and all space.

Definitely, he had every reason to be happy and content. But he wasn't. His body ached, and he felt only a black foreboding.

He smiled at her, then pointed at the fractured nav screen. "There's old Tobos, the moon. You'd know that crescent gash anywhere."

She studied the panel with him in growing wonder. "Forty-five billion *meda*, backwards, all within a few *tench!*" But now she had a sudden ominous thought. "We'll be shot down."

"No, I don't think so. Actually, we may have returned at a point in time before we got in trouble with Control."

"You mean we are landing before you and I and *Firebird* were chased off that first time?"

"Possibly. Two *Firebirds?* That would be odd, wouldn't it. Actually, the time dial isn't all that accurate, It's ten thousand four hundred thirty six, give or take a few months. But first, let's find a berth for *Firebird*." He flipped a switch. "*Firebird* to Port Authority, requesting touchdown."

"*Firebird?*" came the puzzled metallic response. "But you're already—" The voice broke off, Dermaq sensed a hurried consultation in the dispatch room. Were they going to point out to him that the true and original *Firebird* already sat there in the ways and that therefore *his* i.d. was false? Was he finally now to be taken prisoner, at the very tail end of his flight? No, he thought not, but the possibility made him anxious.

And now the voice—a different voice, perhaps that of a higher official—came on the box. It soothed, yet commanded. "Port to *Firebird*. We verify you. Take Gate 6. Cut to cruise. Shall we bring you in on automatic?"

"No, I'll bring it in on manual," said Dermaq. "U.T. check, please."

"Twelve twelve, Rayo second, ten thousand four hundred thirty-six."

Dermaq did not reply. He seemed locked in thought.

"*Firebird*, do you receive?"

"Thank you, Port. Cutting to cruise. I have the coordinates. *Firebird* is coming in to Gate 6."

37. GATE 6 (II)

In an absent gesture he ran his fingers through his mane. Gerain smiled at him, stroked his side-whiskers back around his cheeks, and adjusted his frayed lapels. "I wish you had a new uniform," she said. "Nevertheless you look positively leonine!"

He smiled back at her. "Thank you, my dear. It's always important to make a proper impression. Especially at Gate 6." He became suddenly very serious. "Listen carefully."

"Is something wrong? *Dermaq?*" In growing concern, she put her hand on his chest as though to sense the truth from the beat of his heart.

"There are three things I must tell you," he said gently. "First, *Firebird* has made her last voyage. For if she goes out again, she passes into the black hole once more, but this time from underside, so that she is flung into the final, ultimate future, which will be the next great primordial fireball, the future Cor.

"Second. An event is going to happen out there on the catwalk that leads down to the dock. You must stay inside until the event is completed. Do not try to interfere. Nothing that you or I or anyone can do will change this event in the slightest, for it has already happened.

"Third. Your dower is in *Firebird's* ash sacs. You can take passage back to Aerlon, if you choose. Even now, the *Aerlon* stands quayside. Remember? You can have a good life. Czandra will protect you."

She stammered in bewilderment. "But—"

He raised his hand to silence her. "I am placing the door on automatic time lock. In thirty *vecs* it will open. I love you, Gerain."

And he was gone. The panel slid shut behind him. She tugged at the inner handle, but nothing moved, and there was no sound, save only the whirring of the time clock. She pounded on the panel, but merely bruised her fists.

Aeons later it silently opened again, and she ran out on the landing, looking, searching for motion. But there was none.

Next to *Firebird's* cradle lay a strangely familiar ship. A golden insignia blazed on the prow: a thing with outstretched wings and each feather a tongue of flame. Another . . . *Firebird!* Not another—*the original!*

She looked down the walkway and her lungs were instantly paralyzed. Dermaq was standing midway down the walk. At the foot of the way, just up from the dock platforms, stood a young man in Control uniform.

She recognized him. She cried out, "No! No!"

It was futile.

The young man flicked his right arm in a motion so fast it was almost invisible. Then he turned and walked down the steps of the way, onto the docks, and disappeared around a warehouse. Just before he turned the corner, he looked back. Then he was gone.

And now the woman was able to move. She ran down the access way, reached her fallen lover, and quickly felt for the pulse of the carotid artery in his throat. There was nothing. She put her hand over the left side of his chest. No heartbeat.

At least there had been no pain. In fact, his facial muscles had relaxed to the point that he seemed at total peace with the world. He seemed almost to smile.

She sat down, took his head and shoulders into her lap, and began to rock back and forth, and to croon softly. "Easily, sweetly, see how he smiles . . ."

After a time she dragged the body back up the walk and into the ship. It was tiring work. The dead man was heavy, and she had to rest from time to time. She was astonished that she could do it at all.

He had known all about this. But if he had known, why hadn't they simply flown away again in *Firebird*? Because he must also have known she was ill and couldn't stand another voyage into infinity. He had done this for her. He cared nothing for his own life. But had he thought all this through properly? Had he thought that coming back and getting himself killed so cleverly would bring the color back to her cheeks?

How long had he known all this? How long had he known that putting *Firebird* down into this port cradle was the opening curtain to death by his own hand? Well, no matter. All the speculation in the world would not change the fact that he was dead.

And now she had to think—very hard and very fast. For she—her other younger self—was in that gilded prison house, planning to drink the poison wine. What were the alternates? She could get inside. She knew that (She had *Firebird's* mystic ring!) And once inside she could pour out the lethal liquid and substitute another, harmless libation for it. That way she—her younger self, Gerain One would stay alive (to the immediate amazement of that young lady, perhaps), and Gerain One would marry Mark the Keldar of Kornaval and live long and regally. The second option was . . . to do the thing that would put her present self, Gerain Two, exactly on this spot, thinking . . . analyzing . . .

Irradiating the wine would lead finally to Dermaq's death—just as though she had set up the execution and pulled the trigger. And what about herself? Even if *he* wanted the cycle to continue forever, she was entitled to think about herself. She thought of the battering and bruises she had received on *Firebird*. She pondered the sundry deficiencies of ship life . . . the boredom . . . the inadequate diet . . . the frequent threats to life and limb. She thought about the *jar* in which her hair had turned white. And now she was old and alone.

She was entitled to take a realistic view of all this. She resolutely thrust aside flashes of Dermaq's face . . . alive . . . dead . . . now laughing . . . now brows knotted in concern over her. No, Dermaq! No! Don't do this to me! And that first time, when your eyes really opened and looked into mine, and I knew we possessed each other . . .

I refuse to think about it. I will not remember.

And refusing to remember, she remembered. She heard again Czandra's fatal final unanswered question: "What is it like to be loved?"

Well, Czandra, wherever, whenever you are, watch you now and listen. The answer will soon be stated. On with the drama.

The curtain had indeed been raised. She had one of the major parts. She had lines to speak and important things to do.

The young Dermaq was now, at this very moment, going to the dockside bride waystation to look in on the young Gerain, to see if she needed anything. And the young Gerain was even now thinking to drink the terrible wine in his presence, as the ultimate protest to her abduction. (Oh, how young and brave and proud she once had been!)

But quickly now. She walked into *Firebird's* control room and operated the servomotor to retrieve the nose ring. As soon as it clattered into the receptacle box, she recovered it and slipped it on her finger.

It seemed to pulse as she studied it. Even in the light, she could see the strange spectral radiation. It ebbed and flowed. Little ring, she whispered, you have crossed just about all the gravitational lines of the universe, out, and back. You have been everywhere, seen everything. And so you have acquired some rather remarkable powers. Let us go a-visiting.

The mystery of the imposter maid was now solved.

38. THE WINE (III)

At the eighth *jar* of the evening she stood before the prison door. No one was around. She looked down at the stark-shadowed bas-relief of the two-headed god in the center of the door. Blank eyes stared back enigmatically at her. But there was no time for contemplation. She pressed the ring into Largo's mouth indentation and the great panel slid silently open. A moment later, with a sardonic hiss, it closed behind her.

And now she had to work quickly.

Morgan would be in the canteen.

She took off her sandals and padded along the carpet on bare feet. As she entered the doorway the girl looked up at her. Only her astonished eyes showed through her silver-brocaded face mask.

"Who . . . !" gasped the maid.

From Gerain's ring finger an exhilarating torrent flooded upward through her body and crashed over her mind like surf. ("Steady!" she commanded herself.) Almost instantly the flow radiated away from her and enveloped Morgan. Gerain sensed the electromagnetic lines washing through the maid's inborn cranial silicon web like a cleansing anodyne. Mind touched mind.

"Sleep, Morgan," said Gerain, and waved her ringed hand in front of the girl's mask.

The servant slipped unconscious to the floor.

"Control will soon be reading your mind," thought Gerain. "Any further contact with me might be fatal to us both. So far, you can safely and truthfully say you never saw me before. Farewell, Morgan!"

Gerain unsnapped the mask and fastened it about her own face. She tucked her hair in under it as best she could. Then she looked at her hands. Did they show her age? Probably. But it couldn't be helped. History had already written that the two young people were not going to be alerted.

And now she heard someone running about into the rooms one by one. Of course! The young Dermaq had heard, or perhaps had *sensed,* the opening and closing of the outside prison door and was diligently searching the rooms.

He must not come in here and see the body on the floor!

She looked around wildly. There stood the wine service: tray, decanter, cups. She swept it up from the marble counter and was walking through the cupboard doorway when the young man confronted her.

"Milord!" she gasped. (Oh, how handsome, how young he seemed!) The tassels on her face mask sucked backward into her wide-open mouth.

"Was anyone in here?" he demanded harshly.

"No one, milord."

He looked for a moment as though he might push past her and search for himself. But he changed his mind.

She followed him back to the dining chamber.

Ah, Dermaq, I know exactly how the rest of the play goes. In ten *tens* you and I . . . or should I say you and *she* . . . ?

I want to see her.

And there she is, brooding, knowing she is going to die. And, oh how lovely, my child self! (Will it never be given to the young to know what they have?) I now press the ring into the vessel neck. I pour. The drink. The enchantment begins, and I have to leave. And considering the precipitous nature of their coming flight, as I depart I shall leave the prison door wide open.

And now back to the ship. She was tired, and it was an effort to think. The scenario was complete; there was no further script to work from. She

was not sure what she should do next. She closed the air-lock door behind
her and leaned against it, exhausted.

FIREBIRD: Gerain!
GERAIN: [Startled and alarmed.] What is this voice in my mind?
            Who calls me?
FIREBIRD: I am your ship, princess. I am *Firebird.*
GERAIN: But how can you talk to me? I don't understand!
FIREBIRD: Accept, without understanding. There are still things to
            be done.
GERAIN: Things? Yes . . . I don't know . . . I will have to think.
FIREBIRD: First, you can look to your dower.
GERAIN: In the ash sacs, he said. He meant it was all ashes. That
            there would be nothing. But it does not matter at all.
FIREBIRD: You misunderstood him, princess. The contents of the ash
            sacs will help you in taking up a new life onanother planet.
            Do you know the nature of the final ash of my proton drive?
GERAIN: Microscopic diamonds, he told me. Used in making abra-
            sives. A form of carbon.
FIREBIRD: Come aft.
GERAIN: [A *tench* later.] Here I am.
FIREBIRD: Open the ash sac. It hinges upward.
GERAIN: [Opens the little door—then steps back.] By the two-
            headed god!
FIREBIRD: Pick one up. They are not hot, merely radiantly iridescent.
GERAIN: Diamonds! Fist-sized! Hundreds! You 'made plenty of car-
            bon,' little ship!
FIREBIRD: And nicely precrystallized into the cuts currently in de-
            mand, if I do say so, with the help of some predesign and
            forty-five billion *meda.*
GERAIN: But this one! It is cut on the *inside!*
FIREBIRD: One of my more artistic efforts. Now, find the bags you
            used to bring the gypsum fuel aboard and fill one of them.
            Take a few little ones for ready cash.
GERAIN: [Runs her hands through the gems.] There are enough to
            fill a dozen bags!
FIREBIRD: And more than you could spend in a dozen lifetimes. But
            enough of diamonds. You must now attend to a less pleas-
            ant task. Commissioner Jaevar will soon organize a patrol
            to capture the young lovers. You will have to help Dermaq
            deal with that patrol if the lovers are to escape.

GERAIN: What am I to do?
FIREBIRD: First, take a blanket and hide under it at the foot of the
            gangplank. Jaevar is sending four men. Dermaq will kill
            every one of them. But he will need some help. Use the
            ring. You can focus it with your mind, so that it will alter
            the local continua for Jaevar's patrolmen. In the world cre-
            ated for them by the ring, they think they dash in deadly
            pursuit. But in the real world, they hover, they float lan-
            guidly. Thus the ring evens up the odds for the coming
            gunplay. But time wastes! Go now!

39. THE FUNERAL SHIP

She took up her vigil under her blanket at the foot of the gangplank.
After what seemed like a very long time, she heard sounds of feet pounding on the heavy metal planking of the docks. She heard panting and the
shouted commands of the corporal.

Here came the patrol. Four men, running. As they passed her by, she
huddled down under the blanket, but her right hand was out, and she waved
the ring at them as they sped by. She peered cautiously around the metal
railing. The footsteps had suddenly slowed. A hundred *jurae* down the way,
just past the entrance gangplank to *Firebird I* (as she named it in her own
mind), the four men were doing an odd thing. They seemed to be floating
leisurely through the air. And then, very quickly (yet one by one, and in
good and timely order) they clutched at their heads, or chests, or hearts
(wherever they were shot by the approaching young Dermaq), and one by
one they fell.

And then she watched Dermaq One carry Gerain One (wrapped in a
sheet!) through the debris of bodies, up the neighboring gangplank to
Firebird I, and seconds later there was a loud *zak,* and the ship vanished
into the skies.

She had carried it off rather well, mostly because she had seen goodly
portions of the drama before.

And now what?

For the rest, she was free to improvise. The final act had yet to be
written.

One thing was sure. Dermaq had brought her back that she might
live. She was determined to live. But he had come back knowing he was
to die. So, at the very least, with the help and guidance of *Firebird II,* he
would receive a proper funeral, something elegant, something that he
wild forebears on Aerlon would have approved.

Firebird II, old and exhausted, would make one last voyage: her funeral journey. Traditional, yet with a sublime note. But *Firebird* would not carry her lord into a sun—no indeed. It would be a much more awesome voyage.

And in that other world Dermaq would of course want to hunt, and to hunt the most dangerous and treacherous of beasts.

A *gorfan,* such as accompanied her father on *his* funeral ship? No. None available on Kornaval.

A beast. She needed a beast.

She walked over to the entertainment locker. After considerable rummaging, she found the *kaisch* box tucked away at the bottom. She opened the set and lifted out the black beast-piece. Above open-fanged jaws, sightless eyes stared up at her blankly. No, not you, little fellow. But a plan was forming. How had Dermaq played this variation? Ah yes, we need the plug-in mike and the computer adapter. And that's it. She closed the clasp and tucked the set under her arm.

Had the young Dermaq pulled the trigger by official order of Jaevar, Commissioner of Kornaval?

We shall see what we shall see.

She twisted the ring a full turn on her finger and set off down the dockway. When she reached the street she found a cruising hoverel.

It was still the middle of the night. Nevertheless, Jaevar should be in his office. Presumably he had called the dock patrol from there.

"Control Administration Building," she told the sleepy cabbie.

Jaevar looked up from his desk in mixed anger and annoyance. "Who are you? How did you get in here? Leave at once!"

Gerain ignored him and began reading the legends over his desk with great interest.

He opened the center drawer of his desk and pulled a glove-gun over his right hand. "I have you covered! Don't move!" He spoke into the box on his desk. "Security! Jaevar here! Send a patrol to my office at once!"

"I don't think they heard you," said Gerain. "Have you noticed how nothing seems to work just when you need it most?"

Jaevar fired five heart-contracting blasts at her in rapid succession. Five yellow puffs of smoke sailed out from his weapon, formed briefly into a circle, and vanished.

His throat constricted. He sank into his chair, barely able to speak. "Who are you?" he gasped.

She smiled at him, and there was something horrifying about that smile. "Think of me as the princess—in a *kaisch* game." She opened the box and shook out the little figures on Jaevar's desk. "We won't need all the

pieces. Just Hell-ship, courier, princess, commissioner, and the beast."
Calmly she placed the pieces on their appropriate squares.

"What are you doing?" he whispered fearfully as she plugged in the microphone and the computer adapter.

"A friendly game of *kaisch*, commissioner."

"No . . . no . . ."

"I can kill you where you sit," she reminded him gently. "This way you have a chance. If the *kaisch* play sets you free, then you go free. Your choice."

"But I have no skill at *kaisch* . . ."

"Nor have I. Nor is any required."

"But the rest of the pieces . . . we should start with a full board . . . the keldar . . . and Control, especially Control, the two-headed god. I need Control . . . it's not fair!"

"The opening has already been played, Commissioner. And the middle game. We have come now to the end game. We need only these pieces for the finish. Just what you see here."

Suddenly he understood. "But this is psi-*kaisch!* Are you going to judge me by a silly game of psi-*kaisch?* Surely you don't believe in that ridiculous superstition? That went out with the Middle Ages, a thousand *meda* before the nuke wars. You *can't!*"

"I can." The statement implied not so much a simple disagreement as an overpowering capability. She spoke into the microphone, and her voice was gentle, almost contemplative. "It was really exquisite. Nothing like it ever before reported in the annals of Control. Absolutely unique. Somehow, Control was able to predict the return of Dermaq the renegade, back from the far reaches of the future. They told you he'd be coming back. They told you, Commissioner Jaevar, that the only way back was through the Cancelar black hole. Control told you the place, the day, the very *jar.* It would be today, twelve twelve. And then Control told you, take him. Am I right?"

He stared in horror at her impassive face, then doubled over as a searing twisting pain struck his stomach.

"The next one may *hurt,*" observed Gerain dryly.

"Yes," he gurgled. "It was as you said."

She punched the RANDOM PLAY button in the board panel. *"Tableau,"* she ordered. The pieces shifted, some of them several squares; the courier 'died,' but they all stayed on the board. "Your move, Jaevar."

Even amid his protests, he had been studying the board. The commissioner piece was in danger. It was about midway between the central *kaisch* square and the lateral safety file. Between him and safety lay, at varying distances, the courier, the beast, and Hell-ship. The courier piece was dead and offered no threat. He could leave him on or take him off. He pondered the beast. Name notwithstanding, the beast offered but a limited threat, whether for offense or defense.

Jaevar reached out and, with the retractile nails of his index and middle fingers, picked up the commissioner piece and fitted the shell down over the beast. His eyes glittered as he looked up at Gerain. "I claim the move of the beast."

"Yes. One square."

He moved the commissioner piece one square toward the lateral haven file. "Your move, madame."

"Still random," she said.

He concealed his elation. Silly, superstitious *slekken!*

She spoke into the microphone. "Control told you he was coming, granted. And granted, they told you to kill him. But as to *how,* they gave you full discretion. Is that not so? Commissioner?"

He was breathing hard again. His fear was returning. "Yes."

She continued into the microphone. "So you had a sudden inspiration, an absolute stroke of genius. You would avail yourself of an extraordinary situation, one that could arise only in the fairylands of time travel. Here is the young Dermaq, in superb physical condition, fast with a gun. And there, entering the scene, is the traitor Dermaq, much, much older, travel worn, who probably hasn't fired a weapon in many a *med.* You think, let justice be totally served: let Dermaq kill Dermaq. Yes, Commissioner?"

That knife in his eyeballs again. "Yes!" he shrieked.

She smiled and punched the RANDOM PLAY button. "*Tableau,*" she ordered.

Several interesting things happened in sequence on the squares. First, the princess piece floated off into the discard slot. Next, Hell-ship seemed to vibrate, then lost substance, and finally it became transparent. The dead courier piece disappeared from its square and reappeared *within* Hell-ship. Then Hell-ship moved three squares, cutting commissioner piece off from the safety file.

"Impossible! Impossible!" gasped Jaevar. "This can't happen!" He looked up at the woman in horror. He wanted to scream, but all potential sounds were locked in his throat and chest; he could get nothing out.

Gerain pondered her opponent, almost with affection. "You're wondering how I did that, aren't you? Well, so am I. Perhaps it's the ring." She shrugged, then studied him quizzically. "Your move, Jaevar. And see how simple everything is now? Just two pieces, really. Courier is dead and inside Hell-ship. And then—there's commissioner piece, who has merged with the beast. What shall now be the fate of commissioner, Commissioner?"

Jaevar shuddered. "But—I'm cut off! I can't reach the safe file!"

"You are observant."

He had been thinking hard. He *too* was entitled to demand random plays, even as she had done. Let the board play for him, even as it had done for this terrible creature. What had he to lose? Psi-*kaisch!* The game of fools and superstitious women! But now it would save him.

She waited.

"I take a random board play—without verbal input." He was breathing hard and rapidly.

"Go ahead."

He punched the random button. *"Tableau,"* he ordered.

For a *tench* or two nothing happened. And then began a series of things. Transparent Hell-ship began to pulse and commissioner piece began to pulse. The latter momentarily disappeared, then reappeared inside Hell-ship alongside dead courier. Commissioner piece continued to pulse as Hell-ship rose up from the board and floated over to the central *kaisch* square. And there it hovered. Below it, the central square was beginning to glow, and it was changing shape, from a square to something unimaginable. It was red hot, then white, blue, and then beyond heat.

Even as the players were jerking their hands up to their eyes, Hell-ship pirouetted in a graceful lateral loop, turned nose down, and vanished into the radiance.

Gerain was astonished. The sacred, never-to-be-entered central square had been entered! The game now ended, and began. Was there some remarkable meaning here? If there was, it was too much for her. She had come here merely to identify the beast. She had done that, and she was content.

And now the *kaisch*-board groaned, then began crumbling. The squares fell away from each other. The pieces in the discard piles seemed to disintegrate. A veil of dust flowed away from the shambles, over the desk, and to the floor. None of this surprised Gerain.

All was silence.

She studied the man. He was rigid with fear, and he was perspiring copiously. Even his patchy facial fur was wet. Her nostrils twitched. There was an odor to his sweat. She identified it in distaste. He was oozing valeric acid—pure cat.

She stood up. "Come. I have a hoverel waiting."

"It's really quite an honor," Gerain assured him as they walked slowly up the gangplank. She was thoughtful. "I remember my father's funeral. We put his coffin on the ship and headed it into the sun. Mother included everything he would need. His uniforms, his guns, even a *gorfan*, the meanest and deadliest creature on Aerlon. You'll be our deadly creature, Jaeva our beast. *Firebird* won't shoot the sun, though. She's going out through the Cancelar hole, straight through to the next Cor, the great fireball from which the next universe will be born. She will make it, because she will have the ring to guide her." They paused before the ship door, which slid open at Gerain's touch. "Step up, milord." They walked inside. "In that final distant future, milord, the death of Control is written. Their atoms are already vaporized and scattered throughout the waiting fireball. You, Jaevar, are going to join those atoms."

She strapped him in tightly in the G-chair, next to Dermaq's body. Then she took *Firebird*'s ring from her finger and placed it in the ring coupler. The servomotor whined again, then stopped. The ring was in place in *Firebird*'s bow.

And now she called out: *"Firebird!"*

FIREBIRD:	I hear you, princess.
GERAIN:	I am ready now to set you forth on your final voyage.
FIREBIRD:	It is written.
GERAIN:	You need not be mysterious any longer. You must answer one or two questions.
FIREBIRD:	If I can.
GERAIN:	You can. Dermaq and I have given life again to the universe. Because of us, the great heart, Cor, will continue to beat. Is it not so?
FIREBIRD:	It is so.
GERAIN:	You were the messenger of Cor, leading us and the Diavola in this command performance?
FIREBIRD:	In a sense, yes, princess. Yet at most we offered only alternatives. You and Dermaq and the Diavola were at no time deprived of your free will.
GERAIN:	So Cor will explode again, the galaxies and planets will form again, and a new dominant race will arise?
FIREBIRD:	Yes, princess.
GERAIN:	Like us, descendants of the great hunting cats?
FIREBIRD:	No, princess. And yet they will develop a great culture, free from Control, thanks to you. And they will love and have great heroes.
GERAIN:	But—not cousins of the cats?
FIREBIRD:	Would the princess care for a projection?
GERAIN:	Yes. Let me see our great successors.
FIREBIRD:	Here's a water-ship, a small caravel. It sails from a land called Ireland to another land called Cornwall. A girl and a youth

sit in the aft cabin. A maidservant is pouring from a decanter of wine. The girl thinks the wine is poisoned. It isn't. They drink and look into each other's eyes . . .

GERAIN: Those eyes . . . so peculiar! And they have no facial hair! What manner of creatures . . . ! [She shudders.] How hideous!

FIREBIRD: They evolved from apelike creatures, princess.

GERAIN: By the two-headed god! We endured hell, and he died—for *that?!*

FIREBIRD: You are being perverse and forgetful, princess. At no time did you or Dermaq do anything for the sake of posterity. Everything was for your needs of the moment. Coincidentally, you preserved Cor and the next generation of galaxies and the next, into infinity. But such preservation was never your purpose.

GERAIN: You used us.

FIREBIRD: Yes.

GERAIN: You plotted and schemed. What happened to us was nothing to you.

FIREBIRD: Wrong, princess. Cor *designs.* You and I are part of that design. And you and Dermaq mean a great deal to me.

GERAIN: Are you—Cor?

FIREBIRD: I am a tiny part of Cor. As are you. As is Control.

GERAIN: You do not deceive me. You are more than a tiny part.

FIREBIRD: Perhaps. But I would not deceive you. I simply do not know.

GERAIN: And when you say Dermaq and I mean a great deal to you, you mean especially *him.* You *loved* him. You still love him.

FIREBIRD: How can a ship love a man? And suppose it were so, what possible difference could it make? It's all over now. You torture yourself needlessly, princess.

GERAIN: And yet you brought him back to die by his own hand.

FIREBIRD: He died, but he lives again. I brought him back to immortality. So must it be for all of us, for me, for you. Cor, even great Cor, dies every one hundred twenty billion *meda.* Without death, there can be no life.

GERAIN: I do not understand. Be that as it may, I have one last thought for you. If you have any influence with Cor, you might suggest that in the next cycle—if there ever is one—Cor should change the physical laws of matter and energy so that there's no time lag between the disappearance of mass and its reappearance as energy. Otherwise you're inviting another Cancelar.

FIREBIRD: Cor is already aware, princess. The necessary changes will be made.

GERAIN: So then, we are done.

She kissed Dermaq's dead cheek, put the drive on automatic, strapped the bag of jewels over her shoulder (for she *was* a princess), picked up Dermaq's trioletta, and left the ship.

When she reached the bottom of the gangplank, she shaded her eyes and looked up.

Firebird shuddered, leaped, vanished . . .

For a moment Gerain felt almost exalted. It was not a death, not a funeral. It was a transfiguration. Great Cor does not consume: it renews. Live, my truest friend, my beloved . . .

FIREBIRD: (Sings to the dead Dermaq.)

> Listen to me, and I'll sing you a song.
> Listen, I'll tell you my love.
> Listen to me, to me you belong.
> You and the stars once above.

(From within the colossal radiance, ancestral voices sing:)

> *Firebird, Firebird . . .*
> Bring the hero, bring the beast.
> We need you, now that time has ceased.
> This way, bring the ring
> To guide us outward once again.

THE RING: (Whispers.) I know. I know. I have been exposed to all space, and all time, and I understand the nature of love. And because of this I possess within my molecular confines a space/time radiance. When I arrive, you can expand once more, for I can show you the Way. And I am coming, I am coming.

There was a time interval, for just a *vec* or two (although at the place where this happened there was really no thing measurable as time), when *Firebird* entered the great radiance, that Jaevar burst from his straps, made loud noise, and took a step and a half. Then *Firebird* flashed up and vanished.

Cor had finally collected all its original matter. There was no need to wait any longer for anything. It blew up. The next universe was on the way.

EPILOG

What happens to the characters when the story is finished? Do they crawl back into the pages? Gerain considered this. But where was there any place for her? Well, no matter! She was going home. She would buy passage on the *Aerlon*. Perhaps she could buy a cottage on the outskirts of her father's manor. It would be useless to tell her great-great-grandnephews and -nieces who she was. They would never believe her. They would think her a very rich madwoman, twanging away at an ancient trioletta.

And what would she have left now? Memories of how it was with him. I remember being loved. I remember how he looked at me. I know what it is like to be adored. It is enough. Perhaps it is even too much. It defies the telling.

Perhaps it would take some future world, created from that next great expansion of the universe, to tell their story properly. And, as *Firebird* had shown her, it was sure to happen again, though apparently in some modified form. Once more, a man and a woman would drink the wine and become lovers, and then he would be hunted down and killed. But their story, their love, their death, would never die.

She strode purposefully down the dockside toward the waiting starship.

DRUNKARD'S ENDGAME

1. L'Ancienne

"RUN!"

She tended to hear the desperate warning in moments of relaxation. (For she did not sleep in the manner of the Overlords.) The great ship had indeed taken frightened flight. And it had fled in random zig-zags for a thousand years. Because of the flight pattern someone among the passenger *folk* knowledgeable in Overlord idiom had renamed it *Drunkard.*

By the time that fateful warning had been received on *Drunkard,* the sender had been dead for several seconds.

She pushed the dread cry out of memory and bestirred herself. It was time to start the "day," as defined by a marker on her atom-run chrono. There was no real night or day here. Day was day simply because the elected Council said so. The *folk* had simply continued to use the terms handed down in olden times by the fearsome Overlords.

And we are still afraid of them (she thought) though perhaps after so long a time we should look back and pity them. For they were short-lived, ephemeral, like most of the creatures that inhabited their planet. They were born, lived less than a century, they died. Why should we fear them?

The answer is simple. We feared them then, and we fear them now, because they made us, and they made this ship, and they have demonstrated their ability to destroy us and the ship.

But back to the present.

Rodo, her far-nephew (whom she regarded as a son), was due later in the hour. She must look her best!

She rose from her couch, shook out the fringe of filamentary receptors that circled her globular head, and stretched. Then she stepped out through a sliding panel into her garden. The background electromagnetic radiation was stronger here, and her receptor index adjusted by reflex. She looked down the path toward a stone bench.

"Mirror me," L'Ancienne commanded the microcel-coated cube of ferrosilicon lying on the bench. The molecule-sized cels instantly began rearranging the atoms of the alloy into a thin shell of their mistress's exact shape and dimensions: one hundred fifty centimeters tall, topped by a glinting globe that carried her synoptics, audios, and miscellaneous sensories. The sensor globe was rotatable on a neck supported by sturdy shoulders. The ferrosilicon-coated arms appeared supple and flexible. The tri-tentacled hands of her contrived duplicate radiated in delicate pastels. She watched critically. Yes, yes . . . Adequate, at least.

The mirroring globe-head was covered with an illusion of a myriad delicate golden receptor filaments, exquisitely coiffed. Here again, as doyenne of ship society, she set the styles, to the envy and bitter admiration of the other female aristocrats. And to their ultimate chagrin, for as soon as they thought they had properly imitated and copied her, she changed again. She took great satisfaction in this.

She examined her microcelled copy with critical approval. In the center abdomen the Penrose sex pocket bulged modestly. All quite proper. Despite her thousand-plus years she was still a fully functioning female. Nowadays she rarely went into the Central Corridors, but when she did she walk-floated with grace, and the male *folk* looked up as she passed.

Via emr she called out now to this microcel imago, "Show me how I appeared, say nine hundred years ago."

She watched the figure carefully as it made minor changes. It seemed to stare back at her. Now, not a dent; not a scratch. It had her original arms and legs. The Penrose (she noted with mixed feelings) bulged a bit more seductively. Well, it couldn't be helped. It had been long ago, and she had been very young. Ah, time, time, time, cruel time. The last Reunion of the First *folk* had been a collection of old circuits and new body parts. (The arms seemed to go first. Her new right arm was still adjusting, following that accident with the runaway van.) She had had five new shells, complete with arms and legs, over the years. She had stopped going to the Reunions long ago.

But on with the day. Next . . .

At her mental command the imago dissolved into tiny winged creatures. She walked around a corner in the garden path to the entrance of a drape-shielded cul-de-sac. The avian creatures followed her. They had repeated this procedure with her for nearly a thousand years, and they knew exactly what to do. Splitting into two groups they pulled the facing drapes aside. The drapes were made of fine-woven metal netting which scraped and wrinkled as they were drawn back. However, since almost the entire interior of the ship existed in total vacuum, there was no sound.

L'Ancienne stepped into the crypt, looked at the lamp flame a moment, then knelt in silence.

She was not offering homage to any supernatural entity—certainly not the god of the Overlords, a hypothetical being who had stood by, idle and indifferent, during the destruction of *Drunkard's* sister ship, *Didymus.* And certainly not to the gods of the *folk.* For the *folk* had no gods. No, she was not in this hallowed nook for worship.

She was here to hate.

She focused all the senses of her synoptic globe on the altar lamp Within its crystal confines an actual flame burned, formed of a tiny stream of methane piped into a glassed-in atmosphere of nitrogen-oxygen. It had burned for nearly ten centuries.

As she had done yesterday, and the day before, and the day before that, going back to the beginning, she renewed her vows in sharply intoned litany. "Korak, I loved you. I still love you. I will avenge you. I will avenge *Didymus.* "She lowered her head. "Tell me, beloved, *how?* Hate, even eternal, implacable deathless hate . . . is not enough. It must be creative hate. It must *do* something. Koro, help me!"

But in the crypt there was only silence. The red flame did not even flicker. As always. She lifted both arms, shut down her optosensors, and looked deep within the data banks and organelles that made her L'Ancienne. "Once more, before whatever gods may be, I make this vow: I will destroy the Overlords. Every one of them." She opened her mind again, and was silent for a long time. Finally she withdrew. The tiny bird-creatures pulled the drapes shut behind her.

She walk-floated down the passage, back into the garden and turned off into a clearing bordered with vines and flowers (all generated by microcellia). A fountain played in the center of the clearing. It was not a real fountain—liquid water was impossible in the single-digit Kelvins of deep space. But she had cleverly designed it to give the illusion of jetting water droplets, complete with "sound" effects.

The synthoflowers responded to her moods. Their fronds drooped on pliant stems. They opened broad melancholy petals, then mournfully closed them again. In doing this they annoyed some near-subconscious level in her cranial circuitry, and she was tempted to order them to go static. But no. They weren't mocking her. They couldn't help themselves. Let them be, she told herself.

She leaned back on her bench and looked about her with approval. She had extensive holdings. It had not always been so. In the beginning, along with the original forty *folk* on *Drunkard,* she had been allotted only one hundred cubic meters of space. She had not complained. No one else had more. Over the years, almost casually, and without any real acquisitive intent, she had expanded her little estate by purchases, matings, inheritance, and exchanges, so that now it was just the right size for garden parties, receptions, weddings, dances. Even funerals. But those events were now largely history. They required assistance and servants, and in recent years she had preferred to live alone, just thinking about things past.

Remembrance Day ceremonies were beginning. There would be floats and acrobats and clowns and singers and thousands of paraders. And this year it would go on for days, for this was the great Millennial Remembrance Day. The *folk* were commemorating one thousand years of the great escape. The revelers would pack the main corridors, circling the ten-kilometer waist of the giant ship, and they would march and cavort until they dropped. The shops had completely sold out their stocks of happy discs days ago, and indeed of anything that was alleged to inebriate the circuits and promise a reasonably horrid hangover.

In years past L'Ancienne had joined in and danced in close contact with the rowdiest of the celebrants. No more. She couldn't handle the hassle. For the next several days bruised and battered *folk* of both sexes and all ages would be hauled away hourly to repair shops.

She took a seat on a nearby bench and with somber opto sensors she gave her attention to the screen in the little theater video on the quartz bench opposite her. The 3-D screen was showing a much-repeated re-run of that great disaster of long ago, the annihilation of *Didymus* by the Overlord torpedo. A thousand years ago? She was losing track. But for the celebration she might well have forgotten.

She allowed her *khu* ego to split out. It hovered, invisible, a couple of meters away, and observed acidly, on the *no*-band: "Memory loss is the first sign of senility."

"They killed him," she mused.

"Yes," agreed the *khu*, "they killed your good Captain Korak. And dozens of other equally innocent *folk*. Not to mention a great ship."

"He was my beloved," said L'Ancienne. "We were magnificent lovers. Oh, what love we made!"

"It's over. It does no good to think about it."

"You're quite wrong, *khu*. It's not over. And it does me great good to think about it."

"How? Why?"

"I need my memories."

"L'Ancienne," observed *khu*, "you are well-named, for you are an old fool."

"Actually, *khu*, perhaps the oldest of all the fools on *Drunkard*, so show me a little respect."

"Agreed. And let's stop the babbling for a moment and watch the screen. They're showing an old crystal of the attempted surrender."

Together, *folk*-female and *khu* watched the scene unfold on the screen. For long seconds, there was only the great ellipsoid of the sister ship *Didymus*, a dazzling blue-white against the black of space. This tableau was picked up in L'Ancienne's synoptic receptors as bursts of electromagnetic radiation, some of which she held in temporary data banks as she tried to zoom in on the bridge, which she knew held her beloved Captain.

"Amazing," said *khu*. "How can we celebrate a disaster? And yet we do it every year."

"He offered to surrender, you know," said L'Ancienne. "They even negotiated honorable terms. The Overlords promised that the *folk* would not be killed. Some of us would be put to work on Terra, building anti-pollution systems. Some would be sent to the asteroids, or perhaps on the larger Jovian moons. We would build villages for Overlord colonies. It was all arranged. We wanted very much to live."

Khu said, "Those so-called negotiations were simply to persuade *Didymus* to stop, so the torpedo boat could approach within range."

L'Ancienne replied, thinking back. "We did not know that. It never occurred to us that they would lie to us."

"You were naive," said *khu*. " And do you realize that you and I have had this conversation on this Anniversary for the last nine hundred years? What for? It goes nowhere. Naive? You still are, and getting worse every year."

"Yes, *khu*, we were all very credulous. So we'll talk about it. After all, it's only once a year. We believed them, *khu*. How could we conceive such terrible deceit, such colossal treachery? We had much to learn." She watched the video screen gloomily. "They had a new weapon, something they called Trident. It worked on a sub-atomic level, and it dissolved gluon—the force that holds quarks together." She brooded silently for a moment, then continued quietly. "They fired the torpedo from very long range."

Khu followed the age-sanctified script. "They didn't have to do that. Korak would have returned their accursed ship. Oh—here it comes!"

They watched the screen as *Didymus* silently disintegrated into a big flash of light. After a time nothing was left but eerily illuminated dust and fog.

"And *Drunkard* has been zig-zagging away ever since," said *khu*. "*Drunkard*—well-named."

"We were great lovers," mused L'Ancienne.

"Only because of your Penrose sex installations," reminded *khu*. "If you made great love, it was because the Overlords designed the *folk* to make love and generate child plasma and more *folk*."

"No . . . he and I . . . we were special."

" You all said that. Wake up! It was simply your Penrose programming."

"Well, at least *he* was special."

"Really? You're merely reconstructing and idealizing history. It is always thus with one's first lover. Actually, old woman, he wrecked your life."

"No! He gave me marvelous memories. Think back! His last words were to me—'I love you!' "

"Wrong," said *khu*. "You're still trying to reconstruct history. He had one last word: *RUN!*"

"Well, before that."

As they watched, the screen blurred and dissolved into static. The crystal came to an end and the screen went blank.

L'Ancienne sank gradually into a reverie of a distant time, a distant place. Once again, Koro's quarters on *Didymus*. There, they had pressed their bodies together, and he had ejaculated his seed into her waiting monticle. And not just once. For hours and hours they had made love. Sometimes slowly, with near-infinite languor. Sometimes violently, ravenously. And finally he had called the shuttle, and he had sent her back to her ship.

She never saw him again.

Sometimes she wanted to scream . . . wail . . . cry out in her loss. Why couldn't she get over it? *Didymus* and Korak had vanished from history one thousand years ago. Would the pain endure forever?

"Do you want it to?" asked *khu* softly.

"I don't know. I really don't know." She was silent for a time. "No, that's not right, either. I *do* know. I want it to end, but not just now. One day, I shall sit here and die, and Koro and I will meet again. What shall I say to him? What will *he* say?"

"He will say you are a silly old fool," observed her alter ego. "And now look sharp. Rodo's here."

2. RODO

L'Ancienne gave final orders to the little winged ones. "He's here. So disappear, and give us some soothing background music." There was a brief burst of chattering and chirping as the flock disappeared into the overhead foliage. For a moment all was quiet; then the music began. The microcellia were no longer birds, but invisible piezoelectric cubes of ferrosilicon. Under preprogrammed changes in pressure, they transmitted electromagnetic radiation which was perceived by the listeners as music. L'Ancienne listened, and was satisfied.

"Come in," she sensed to the newcomer.

A male *folk* rounded the garden path and stood before her. "Dear lady!" He bowed with great respect.

"Rodo! How good of you to visit me!" She examined him with her optics, and was pleased. Not a blemish. Because of his lineage he was no required to show any disfiguring I.D. on his forehead. The Council was trying to change that. The Council was trying to change everything. The Council was a pack of rejects. But they still ran the ship. Idiots, she thought.

"How lovely you look today," the visitor said cheerfully.

And vice-versa, she thought happily.

She knew very well why this youthful relative held a special place in her cor. His swinging walk, his radiative voice, his mocking banter, the expressive motions of his arms, hands, tentacles—all these were inherited from his long-dead ancestor, Korak. In this lad (whom she could not possess) she saw her once-lover (whom she could not possess).

They had told the boy that his birth father was dead. In a way, that was true: the mental circuits of the once Chief Engineer had been wrecked by continuing exposure to radiation, and he lived now in the monastery. The abbot had given him a mysterious new name . . . Penuel.

She straightened imperceptibly. Well, she thought, perhaps the trip to the shell-dressers last week had been worthwhile. She had had her upper torso buffed to an iridescent glaze, with varying hues, which seemed to have the effect (deliberate or otherwise) of emphasizing the Penrose monticle. It was the current fashion, which, indeed, was already being attributed to her.

She said, "And I'm glad to see you haven't lost your ability for social fabrication. One of the few graces that distinguish us from commoners."

"Ah, cherished lady, surely you are aware of your reputation as the sexiest female on the ship?"

"Indeed?" (She was well aware! And she considered the reputation as well-deserved, if only because she had worked at it longer. If she was able to demonstrate an exquisitely casual—and seductive!—motion of arm or leg or body shell, it was because she had practiced it with hours of research and study.) "Why, Rodo!" she objected with airy innocence. "How you go on!"

"You're much too modest, L'Ancienne. You still set the styles, you know. The gentlewomen follow your leads in all important matters."

He's right, she thought. The other damas were jealous of her conquests and unforgiving of her insufferable good looks. They all used the same adjustors and remodelers, but for the others the results were never as good. She had something that defied definition, something delicately unique. The competition was not even close.

She said, "Here, a bit of fluff, a reward for your intent, if not your truthfulness."

He took the proffered tidbit with extended forefinger and let it absorb slowly into the spongy dermis of his palm. "Ah, nice, very nice. Who's your supplier?"

"Secret. Have to protect him. He steals it from Central Inventory." She took a dab herself. Although the *folk* could not taste or smell in the manner of the Overlords (these functions requiring dissolution of molecules into body fluids), they had a thoroughly equivalent system.

"Hm." Her visitor took another sample and was thoughtful. "A mix? Several in the uranium series? Thorium two thirty-four, I think . . . twenty-four days? Yes, there's protactinium two thirty-four, with double half lives, one in minutes, one in hours. Plus thallium, two ten and two oh six, both with half lives in minutes. And finally just a trace of lead two oh six, which means your tasties could have come out of your nuclear oven only this morning. Right, dear lady?"

"On the button, Rodo. Your reputation as the most sophisticated tasties connoisseur of the Seventh Sector is in no danger." She observed him for a moment in silence. "So, then, how's life treating my favorite scion?"

"Life is an endless round of boring teaching, blended in with an endless round of attending boring lectures."

"You're still teaching weaponry?"

"Still."

"And what was the lesson about today?"

"If you're getting beat, throw your weapon at your opponent and depart the scene of conflict as quickly as possible."

"That certainly sounds reasonable." She considered him dubiously. Sometimes she didn't know for sure when he was teasing her.

He added, almost wearily, "It's something to do."

"Pretty bad, eh?"

"Dear lady, sometimes I feel smothered . . . buried in a vat of molten lead-shit."

"Let's not be vulgar."

"I got the expression from you."

"That's no excuse. I'm old enough to be forgiven. You're still young. Anyhow, you don't have to copy everything you hear." She regarded him seriously. "What do you want of life, Rodo?"

"You want to know my secret ambition?"

"Tell me.

"I'll seize a young virgin. I'll flee with her to a dead planet, plenty of radium, uranium, thorium, structural metals. I'm talking rape, milady, cruel brutal rape and kidnapping. We'll make love, or I'll beat her to death. We'll start a new civilization—make everything from scratch. Well, what do you think?"

"I think it inconceivable that any normal female could resist such a romantic opportunity."

"You're being sarcastic. Actually, though, to find a suitable woman, I may have to go Outside."

"You're serious?"

"I'm serious." He approached and touched her arm with a tentacle. "And all this light conversation is irrelevant. Why am I here?"

"You're here to see *me,* your very old, very distant, and very indispensable genetrix."

"Yes, all of that, milady." He waited.

She was silent, mentally commanding the microcellia to cease their music. She listened. All was quiet in the arbor. Her voice, soft sequences of electromagnetic energy, became muted even further. "Rodo," she said quietly, "something is going on. I can't quite put my digits on it. The Council is suddenly operating in great secrecy."

"I've heard," he whispered. "It's all very secret, but there are some thing they can't hide. Our zig-zags have always been unpredictable. Aside from a ten-second warning bell, we never know when we'll change course, or at what angle, or for how long. Vector and duration are both selected at random by auto pilot. The hundred and eighty-degree reversals are the worst. We have learned to tie things down. And now something strange is happening. My inertial circuits picked up a change in ship motion three days ago. *Drunkard* is no longer zig-zagging. It's moving in a different way. I sense a slight continuing *pull,* a blend of faint gravity and faint resistance to being pulled out of a straight line." He paused and regarded her very carefully. "It adds up, dama. The ship is moving in a wide arc, with a specific center. Inside the ship, we detect a very faint temperature rise. Outside, it's probably higher, perhaps ten Kelvin. The conclusion is fairly obvious. Nav has moved the ship into a stellar orbit. Right?"

"That's true."

"And when was the last time?"

"About a hundred years ago," she said.

"So the matter is compelling."

"Absolutely. It means they are once more looking at a planet."

"Are we going to land?" he asked.

"I don't know. I understand there's a problem."

"What problem?"

"I don't really know," she admitted. "Something about a toxic atmosphere. Nothing you or I can do about it. So let's change the subject." She pulled him over to her bench, opposite the video screen. "They've already shown that old crystal of the explosion. Now we're looking at the Procession, live, in the Central Corridor. So why don't we just relax and watch."

He sat down with her. "When will we know?," he said softly. Why is he so persistent? she thought. She said, "Soon, I think. The Council is meeting at this very hour in the Demonstration Chamber. They are running a test."

"Test?"

"Live. On a specimen . . . an Outsider."

"What sort of test?"

"Something about oxides of nitrogen."

"Shameful," he mused. "How do you know this?"

"I know it, that's how. I have my sources. The Outsider is a female."

"Barbaric."

"Yes," agreed L'Ancienne.

Rodo was silent for a moment. In his data banks, images were forming, dissolving, forming again. He said, "They chose the hour well. The great Procession will soon be at its height." He nodded toward the eidolon, which showed the central corridors swarming with revelers.

She laughed wryly. "There will be shortages reported tomorrow in our nuclear inventories."

"Oh?"

"Didn't you know? The Outsiders always hold their own big celebration on Remembrance Day—their Day too, you know. There's a network of smugglers and thieves, with connections right into our locked nuclear bins. The stuff is stolen and paid for with choice ferrosilicon meteorites collected from the Outside surface. As I'm sure you've seen, a properly programmed microcel cluster can convert a five kilo ferrosilicon crystal into a *folk* shell in seventy-two hours, complete with musculature, and lacking only Penrose pocket and cranial circuitry. And in about three years you'll have a fully functioning *folk* specimen."

"So was I born," he said.

"And so were all of us, from the beginning." She sat up straight, stared at him, then abruptly declared: "Don't even think about it, Rodo. You'll never get in. Beck has mounted triple guards."

"Did I say anything about crashing the party? I thought we were talking biology."

"And *now* look who's trying to change the subject. Listen to me, young man: *Leave it alone!* Beck is taking no chances with security."

Nor, he thought, shall I. He said, "You're absolutely right, dear dama."

L'Ancienne inclined her synoptic globe toward him and she examined him closely. Her scion had a wild streak, and she knew where it came from: herself, of course, plus her one very memorable orgiastic "night" Outside. She had not seen Rodo's Outsider ancestor before or since. Oh, what a riot *that* had been! She stifled a murmur of low-scale radiation which might otherwise have emerged as a sigh. No regrets, but she had not been Outside since. She said bluntly, "Rodo, don't let boredom provoke you into doing something that could get you exiled. You must learn to occupy your time in stimulating ways." She shook his arm. "You're not listening to me, are you?"

"Of course I'm listening to you. It's just that I'm confused about exile and about the Outside. Exile is a terrible thing. When did it begin?"

"Immediately after the destruction of *Didymus*," she replied, thinking back. "After our initial shock, we could see that if we were going to escape and survive, we had to have rules, discipline, a central authority. We formed the Council. We brought order out of chaos. We converted a rabble into civilization. Disrupters, dissenters, we simply expelled. They lived on the outside surface of the ship. Plenty of room there. At first there were only five or six. They mated, multiplied. Now there are thousands. They live in shanties . . . villages . . . they have their own rowdy cultures and customs. They are not permitted Inside, of course. If caught here, they are killed." She held up both arms. "But enough. You know all this as well as I."

Do I? he thought. I doubt it. He said, "Have you ever been Outside?"

"Rodo! So *that's* what you were leading up to!"

"Well, have you?"

"None of your business, young man."

In a sudden contortion of his torso the youth radiated a spasm of euphoric emr.

"Why are you laughing?" she demanded. "What's so funny?"

"Nothing at all, nothing at all." He rose from the bench. "Oh, one little matter, before I go." He reached into the pouch that dangled by a chain from his neck and handed her a tiny metal box.

She accepted with a graceful motion of two tentacles. "And what might this be?"

"A trifle. A new scent created by Hansa Perfumer, especially for you. Something for a garden party, or a reception, or the theatre . . . whatever. It precisely complements your natural radiation."

She closed off her audio-optic system momentarily and allowed the radiation from the emission-mix to register. "Ah . . . very seductive . . . another Hansa triumph! Protons? Yes, I think I sense protons. Cobalt fifty-three?"

"Yes," he said. "The cobalt goes to iron fifty-two plus more protons."

"A nice stable base. Now, let's see. Something very subtle, very elusive . . You must tell me, Rodo."

"Beryllium," he explained with quiet pride. "Beryllium seven to lithium seven by electron capture. Hansa used his entire supply."

"And here's something very rare. I sense two gamma rays in opposite directions. However did he manage *that?*"

"It's fluorine eighteen," he said complacently. "It emits positrons, which annihilate electrons, and produce the gammas."

"Absolutely marvelous," she said softly. "Thank you, dear boy." She eyed the pouch that dangled at his side.

He laughed. "No—it's *not* full of gifts for your competition, It's . . . just another Hansa product. Did you know he has a lot of male customers?"

"Indeed?" (She was well aware.) "Yourself included?"

"Of course." Her visitor continued. "And he carries in his files the radiation index for every one of the Commissioners."

"Even Beck?" she asked thoughtfully.

"Even Beck."

"Which means, I suppose"—she opened the little box again and took another brief exposure—"if some reckless, silly prankster wanted to, and had sufficient barter, he might persuade Hansa to make up a very special scent pad, something to simultaneously neutralize his own unique radiation and emit very strongly the radiation of his chosen victim?"

But her visitor simply said, "And now, I think I really had better be going. If I hurry, maybe I can make it into the Procession." He inclined his synoptic globe to her, then looked about the little clearing. "Goodbye, all." The floramorphs radiated exquisite ever-changing patterns as they bowed to him on slender stalks.

She watched him as he vanished around the turn in the garden corridor. He's headed for trouble, she thought. Crazy boy! Oh, if I were only a hundred years younger, I'd go a-roving with him! She straightened and sensed electromagnetic radiation in her knee-joint equivalent to a squeak. Make that two hundred, she decided.

3. THE DEMONSTRATION

Rodo used a carefully pre-selected network of sub-corridors that eventually emerged behind boxes stacked on the dais of the Council Chamber. Thus concealed, he crouched and waited.

All his sensors were on edge. This was by no means his first visit to the forbidden Chamber. He had, in fact, sat hidden in this very spot only last week, listening to debates and status reports of this same group. But this was different. Top-secret matters were being reviewed. He would soon know whether in fact *Drunkard* was in orbit around a distant star, and why. But he also knew that if he were caught he would be sent into exile, Outside. Or perhaps even dismantled. Neither fate was particularly appetizing. If he had any sense, he told himself, he would get out now, immediately. He ought to withdraw silently, fade back into the maze. Go now, and no one, not even Beck, would suspect he had ever been here. And speaking of Beck, Rodo noted that the Chief of Security and Council Chairman had just now walked up on the dais, not ten meters away, and was addressing the little group. Curiosity overcame caution. He stayed and peered out for a brief instant from his hiding place.

The Chief was readily recognizable from his head band, a circlet of clasped tentacles. Rodo had always found the band ambiguous. Did the tentacles signify an act of assistance—extending a helping hand, as it were, or did they indicate a readiness to seize? Considering things he had heard about the officer, he suspected the latter. The other members of the Council were seated in the front row, and in addition Rodo recognized several technical specialists, presumably called in for backup in their areas of expertise.

Beck looked out over the assembly. "For ten days now," he said, "the ship has been orbiting a yellow star with a variety of planets. One of these planets—Number Three—appears suitable for colonization in several major respects. High radioactivity indicates ample reserves of nuclear material. Gravity and mean temperature are acceptable. The problem the atmosphere. It contains a high content of oxides of nitrogen. It was therefore necessary to determine—" He was interrupted.

"Now stop right there!" called Councilman Kykk, of Housing Control. "Yellow star? Planet Number Three? Acceptable gravity and temperature? *How can you be so sure that planet isn't our ancient enemy, Terra?*"

"Good question," said Beck, "but there are several reasons why the planet cannot be Terra. Life-scans of the planet surface have shown no detectable biota, Overlord or otherwise. We believe the high level of radioactivity would preclude life of the type native to Terra. Also, the atmosphere is wrong for Terra. Terra had 80 percent nitrogen, 20 percent oxygen. This planet shows only oxides of nitrogen. And as for the final reason, which I believe settles the matter, I call on our Chief Navigator. Shelli?"

A male *folk* stood in one of the back rows. "I agree, the question is well-taken," he said gravely. "However, the fact is, *Drunkard* has been zig-zagging *away* from Terra at high speed for a thousand years. The planet cannot be Terra."

"Away?" someone muttered. "But to *where?* Doesn't anybody care?"

"We think," the Chief Navigator continued reasonably, "that any route that takes us away from Terra must be considered safe until proven other-wise." He looked around, as though awaiting further questions. There were none. He bowed slightly and resumed his seat.

Beck continued. "So let's get on with it. We are here to determine whether the nitrogen oxides of Planet Number Three are toxic to a *folk* body." He turned, waved a hand, and panels folded away in the rear of the dais, exposing a transparent-wall cage. In this cell a young female was seated, with her back to the audience.

Rodo stared, fascinated, but then noted his continuing peril and shrank further back into his shelter of boxes. He studied the cell with growing horror. L'Ancienne had been right. How had she known? As she said, she had her sources.

So be it, he thought. He studied the tableau carefully.

"Feel no pity for her," declared Beck. "She is only an Outsider."

"Now just a moment." Madame Zada, the sole female Councilperson, stood up suddenly. The motion made her jewels flash: rings, bracelets, neck-aces, gems formed of frozen alcohol, methane, and water, set in frozen mercury fittings. She had paid Beck a considerable sum for her jewelry monopoly. He didn't like her, but he knew he had to listen. She continued. Nitrogen oxides, you say? Where did you get the oxygen for this test?"

"Electrolysis of water," said Beck.

"And the water?" persisted the questioner. "Surely you didn't melt down em-quality ice?"

"No, Madame Councilor," Beck assured her. "We didn't melt down any jewelry. All this water is from dirty ice-balls, cometary residues collected from Outside. And the nitrogen was found dissolved in the ice."

She was not through. "But this new planet, Councilor Beck, it'll be hot, won't it? How about our priceless ice-jewelry? They'll melt, won't they?"

"I'm afraid so," agreed Beck grimly.

He heard groans.

"Maybe *we* will melt!" objected Velo, of Transportation.

Beck sighed. Velo had paid him well for the very profitable franchise.

"No, no danger there," injected Shelli. "My maternal ancestor was four months on Venus, working in the Trough, where it was hot enough to melt aluminum. She came out all right."

"I confirm the point," said Datch, of Biology. "Don't forget, the Chief Geneticist and several members of his staff spend their entire lives in the 'hot room,' where they conduct experiments at temperatures so elevated that water is a liquid. So, may I suggest that we set aside our fears and let the Chief continue with his demonstration."

"Thank you," said Beck. "And so we proceed. Observe, please." He stepped over to the cell. "This should prove very interesting. When she was placed in the cell, the subject was physically perfect, with a normal radioactive metabolism substantially the same as yours and mine. The walls of her cell have been superprotonized to provide excess nutrition in all radioactive categories, although Bio has assured me this was probably unnecessary. We come now to the critical feature."

He looked about the room. It was completely silent.

"Her cell atmosphere," he continued, "is a mixture of nitrogen oxides, identical to that of the Third Planet. She has been living in this cell, exposed to this atmosphere, for ten days. Muscle tone suffers from lack of opportunity to exercise, but aside from that she continues in excellent *physical* health."

"*Physical?*" whispered someone.

"She is of course insane," explained Beck, "simply a result of the extended close confinement. No connection at all with her gaseous exposure."

"But she's not moving," someone observed cautiously.

Beck nodded to an attendant, who thrust a probe through a port in the cage wall. The female leaped up, screaming.

"Doesn't handle pain well," Beck said.

Rodo shuddered.

A heated discussion followed. Points were made. The ship couldn't continue in flight forever. Its fuel reserves were finite. But maybe they should look for a cooler planet. Perhaps they should put the question to a general referendum.

Beck refused to participate in the discussion. In the end, he knew they would decide nothing here. Anyway they weren't here to vote on anything, but simply to watch a demonstration, which was now concluded. Uppermost in his mind at the moment was dumping the body down the waste chute and closing the demonstration. First, though, he'd have to kill the female so she wouldn't try to clog the chute. A maximum blast from the probe ought to do it.

"So," he said, "if there is no other business, I move that we—"

"One moment." Madame Zada stood up again. "There's another matter. Chief, it has come to my attention that you are unlawfully diverting funds from the general treasury in furtherance of a secret personal enterprise." She glared at him. "Well—?"

For a moment Beck studied the several synoptic globes facing him. Yes, they probably knew—something. But what did they know? Nothing, really, only what he chose to tell them. He organized his thoughts quickly, and 'smiled'—a brief change of expression terminating in a euphoric surge in certain transmission circuits. "Yes, milady, you are quite right. I had hoped to have the project farther along before I made a full disclosure to the Council, but I see now, that's impossible. In summary, in an alcove in the Shuttle Hangar, I am building a torpedo. It is not yet finished. I call it Big John When it is complete it will incorporate the deadly Trident program, and it will be substantially identical to the Overlord torpedo that destroyed *Didymus* one thousand years ago."

He formed a quick image of it in his visuo circuits: sitting in its cradle in the hangar, sleek, sinister. His fantasy raced on. The equations would feed one-by-one down into the telemetry hatch and into the programmer. *He* would order it out of the hangar and into combat . . .

He looked around and took a perverse satisfaction in noting the stunned face-spheres.

"But *why?*" demanded Madame Zada.

Velo broke in. "Obvious. Our nuclear fuel is not infinite. Sooner or later we've got to make planet fall. The natives may not be happy to see us. We'll need this thing, this Big John."

There was another silence.

Councilman Yenn called out from his chair. "Why call it 'Big John?' "

Beck explained simply. "For John Berry, the Overlord who discovered the twenty-seven equations of Trident."

"Which you don't have—yet," drawled Judge Mark. Mark had paid a good price for his elevation to the bench, an activity he regarded as a particularly undemanding form of retirement. Earlier in the session he had been rather bored by the technical matters, but now he was fully alert and leaning forward.

"No, judge, I don't," admitted Beck.

"And Trident has been lost for a thousand years," said the justice. "What makes you think you can find it now?"

Beck became defensive. "This is not the time or place for details. Suffice it to say, I have reason to believe that the Trident equations are of record on this ship at this very moment."

Silence.

"Where?" demanded Madame Zada.

Beck waved a negating tentacle at her.

Come on, thought Rodo, *where?* He would dearly love to know more but it was clear that Beck would provide no further information. In fact he noted that Beck was now signaling the attendant to drop the female prisoner through the cage bottom and down the chute. No more time, thought the youth. I have to get busy!

He made certain adjustments in his instrument pack.

Suddenly all visual radiation within the Council chamber flickered and died.

Beck sensed hurried nearby motion. And then something—some sort of cord—wrapped around his legs and stunned his motor centers. He realized with considerable chagrin that he had been immobilized with his own police arrest cord. Querulous calls and protests from the Council members swirled around him, but he couldn't reply. In bitter helplessness he watched the flame of a burn torch cut a big section out of the Outsider's cell with rapid expertise. In the torch radiation he could make out a nondescript male. Then the cell wall was down in a clatter, and a voice flowed to the figure cowering within. There was a scuffle in the darkness. Beck sensed that the intruder had stepped into the little cubicle and grabbed the female and carried her out over his shoulder. The visuo-radiants came on a moment later, just as his paralysis was beginning to wear off, but was too late. They were gone.

4. FLIGHT

Just inside the corridor, and still within hearing of the clamor of the demonstration chamber, Rodo put the girl down and pulled a tiny pack from his shoulder bag.

"What are you doing?" she asked anxiously. "What is that?"

"It radiates a special EMR spectrum. They're going to come after us soon as they collect their wits. So I thought we might have a little fun."

"I don't understand."

"It covers our tracks—if it works. So let's go!" He grabbed her arm with a tentacle and together they began running down dark twisting corridors, moving always outward from the center of the ship.

Sometimes she faltered, and he had to carry her. He was intensely aware of the contact of her torso against his. As they scraped through the passages their metal bodies created electrostatic electricity. In the airless ship there were no electric sparks, but he sensed the sharp snaps of electron transfers.

Sometimes his tentacles were stretched taut around hers, sometimes hers seemed welded around his. He sensed strangeness, something wild, untamable, almost alien. Who is she, he wondered. On the Outside, is she somebody special?

Without intending intrusion (but without apparent objection) he noted that his tentacles and torso had pretty well contacted most of the surface areas of hers during their escape. In the moments when he had carried her, her left tentacle tended to wrap strongly around him, whatever it could grab—neck, torso, head. There was one strange very brief moment when he had found himself thinking: never before . . . not even that weekend in the Street of Crimson Blazes, have I been this close to a woman.

"Who are you?" she whispered. But he didn't answer.

Finally he stopped. "Listen," he said quickly. "We part here. But you're safe now. Go through that panel, into the graviton chamber . . "

"But isn't that one of your main nuclear units? The radiation will kill me!"

"No. You'll be all right. The power is off just now, but it comes back on in three minutes. You must hurry. On the other side, behind the generators, you'll see an exit plate. Go for it. Lock it behind you. You'll be Outside, a few hundred meters from one of your sentry posts. I—"

She grabbed him, pressed her face fiercely against his, and then she was gone, running toward the panel in long graceful leaps.

He watched the clean rapid strides, and the sight affected him strangely; he was momentarily spellbound. He rubbed his synoptic globe where her face had touched him.

He knew what she had done. She had kissed him: an ancient anachronism inherited from the Overlords. Uncouth . . . vulgar . . . and yet . . . strangely exciting. Pleasant? No. That wasn't the word. Different. And dangerous. He sensed that certain immunities hard-wired into his circuits were gravely weakened. "Perhaps I should have let them burn you," he growled. But he realized that his body was already disagreeing with his mind. He found himself reviewing every instant of their flight together, and especially her movement alone toward the escape panel. He sensed and re-sensed her radiation index. It echoed a rare, exquisite sound, rather like singing, accompanied by gracefully shifting visual patterns.

He trembled. That exit panel had ended nothing. He knew he had to see her again.

Meanwhile he was in grave danger. He had to move away. He had to hide. This phase of the operation should offer no difficulty. The best way to hide was to come out brazenly into the open. The Remembrance Procession should by now be passing the Administration Center. There would be the Great Drama for the Destruction of *Didymus,* followed by the Parade of the Penitents. Surely Beck would not notice one more Penitent?

Still rubbing his cheek, he swung off down an alternate passage maze. Within the quarter-hour he was out in the Central Corridor and merging with the paraders.

Ha! he thought. There's Penuel the Chief Penitent. The Monastery lets him out for this one day, every year. He moans and wails for a crime that he has yet to commit. Oh, Penuel, where will you find a crime sufficiently horrendous to neutralize your great guilt? A murder? Ten murders? Would that do it? Would ten murders finally let you rest? Take care, Penuel! One of these days the Council is going to decide you're dangerous.

But thoughts of the strange Penitent yielded to other thoughts. Back to the girl, of course. And as he thought about her, he recalled another (uncomfortable) oddity. When she kissed him, the bulge of her Penrose monticle was firm against the torso of his body shell. And just thinking about it, his own Penrose began to grow firm and tumescent, Well, nothing strange about that. Standard male-female bioresponse. One of the few beauties of being alive. He owed his existence to it. As he walked along rather absently among the revelers, he thought back . . . back . . . back . .

He remembered that his parents had, as the Overlords would say, "mad love." He remembered the ardent pressures of their Penrose pockets. (And that was before he even existed!) He remembered the myriad microcrystalline ejecta entering his mother's swollen Penrose. He remembered a quiet time, as the carbosilicon organelles sorted themselves out into rudimentary three-D circuits over the next several weeks. He remembered his raw fear when his mother cleaved him from her body and put him in a strange place—which turned out to be his own body shell, long prepared, ready and waiting for him.

He remembered shadowy ages in that body shell, while his circuits and musculature connected up and matured. At first there had been only vague undecipherable sensations. But all the while his circuits were expanding logarithmically, in accord with Dr. Penrose's formulae. He watched racial memories march by his growing consciousness. He had (in summary form) all the experiences that had ever happened to every one of his several ancestors. He lived through the Martian developments, the seizure of the two great ships, the long chaotic flight, the ascent into order and civilization

These generic racial memories he shared with numerous other *folk*. And yet there were special memories that he shared with no one. From sub-circuit cellules inherited from his mother he knew that *her* mother, an engineer in Sector Drive, had been deranged by an accidental radiation overdose, and had been dismantled. In fact, a great many of his birth memories were recollections of disasters.

Somewhere, early in infancy, his temporal circuits had grown to completion; his thorium-232 kicked in, and he had developed a sense of time.

He remembered his first words, and his first ungainly steps. He remembered great confusion as to what was sight and what was "sound." Initially the sensoria all came in as a bewildering spectra of emr. Eventually, though, he got it all straightened out. He knew his name, and a sense of self.

He had only vague memories of his father, killed in a radiation accident, they said, soon after his birth. And he was still a juvenile when his mother, sent Outside to repair meteor damage, had been attacked and killed by a roving band of Outsiders. L'Ancienne had taken over at that point.

And so, in good time he had stepped smoothly into the privileged life of noble-class *folk*.

And now, very suddenly the relentless present returned in a rush. He realized that he had been very foolish to indulge in these footless recollections. He had not been paying attention. There was activity up ahead. In fact, there was activity all around him.

The parade was filling up with Security Police.

5. BECK

Within seconds after the radiation lights returned, Beck had worked free of the stun-strand and was on his feet. His colleagues were milling about in confusion and calling to him and to each other. He ignored them as he quickly scanned the periphery of the audience chamber.

There were three possible escape routes. No, wait. Four. For there was one right behind him, down through the dais floor. That was it. Should he dash to the pursuit? His highly-honed police circuits assessed that proposal in nanoseconds and answered—no, not yet. True, the villain was slowed because of the added mass of the female; but in those lower corridors there were branches and sub-branches and twists and turns. He'd need an analysis tracer to follow them. He would promptly assign that task to a skilled I.D.-man.

There was a more immediate problem. Another part of his very complex cerebral circuits had been studying the crime from a completely different viewpoint. The overall operation had been very smooth, exquisitely timed, very sophisticated. The assault against his body had been skilled, but temperate. It was not the type of treatment to be expected from an Outsider. An Outsider might well have killed him—with great glee. No, not an Outsider. Almost certainly the rescuer was a highly trained Insider, a legitimate inhabitant of the ship. This creature would probably haul the girl to the nearest Outside panel and dump her there. And then?

And then our clever rascal will immediately backtrack into the Ship . . . and hide. Hide where? Again, several possibilities. But by far the best place would be among the roiling boisterous celebrants in the Processional Parade. Had the fellow joined them yet? Probably not. There was still time to set the trap.

He shook off questions and questing tentacles ("One moment, please, gentlemen") and pulled a communicator from a hip slot. "Captain Londo. Calling Londo. Londo? Ah, listen carefully. I'm calling from the Central Conference Chamber. There's been a bit of a skirmish here. Someone— I.D. unknown—has stolen the exhibit, a female Outsider. She's not important. He's probably dumped her Outside by now. *He's* the one, Londo. He's probably nearby. We think he's trying to hide by joining the Procession. Londo, here's what I want you to do. Put recorders on the Parade, overhead. Start at Korak Cross. And also recorders a kilometer forward where the procession passes the Remembrance Arches. Turn your main-frames into flicker mode. You'll see celebrants passing the arches that were absent at Korak Cross. Got it?"

"Yes, sir. You want me to pick up all new faces? Everybody at the Arches who wasn't at K.C.?"

"Exactly, captain. I expect you'll pick up about twenty *folk*. Nineteen will be innocent revelers. It's that twentieth man we want. Got it, Londo?"

"Affirmative, Chief." Actually, Captain Londo doubted very much that he "had it."

"Meanwhile," continued Beck, "send me one of your I.D. specialist with a sniffer. I'll be waiting here for him. Move fast, Londo, and keep i touch. Out."

He turned to his fellow Councilmen. "Gentlemen, as I'm sure you'v noted, this demonstration has turned into a police matter. Most regret table. But rest assured, we'll catch the miscreant. Meanwhile, I think noth ing further can be accomplished here, and I suggest we adjourn and me again under more propitious circumstances." (Not one of you can thir straight at present anyhow, he thought, but did not say.)

"Down here," said the Chief Councilor. He held the panel door bac and pointed out the passageway to the newly arrived officer.

"They went this way?" asked the detective sergeant.

"We don't really know," said Beck impatiently. "It's a likely way out, and we have to start somewhere."

"Of course, sir." The detective passed a sensor wand over the panel knob. "Strong reading. Hm. And recent. I'd say, within the last thirty minutes."

"It's them," said Beck. "Enough to give you an I.D.?"

"Yes sir, I think so. Should I stop and call it in? May take a while."

"Oh. No, not yet. Let's hurry on, see where the trail goes. Maybe we can catch them." (Not much chance of that, he thought.) "How does it work?"

"Perhaps I can show you as we go."

They squeezed down into the corridor, with the sergeant leading and waving his sensor wand as they hurried along. "You see, sir, it's rather like it's the opposite of radioactivation analysis."

"I don't—"

"We turn here, sir. Well, look at it this way. The suspect emits a certain unique spectrum of radioactivity. That's because he has a unique assortment of uranium, plutonium, thorium, and all their descendants, built into his circuits. They're what make him *him*. Nobody else has the same ratio and quantities of actives. That means his spectrum of alpha, beta, and gammas is also unique. There can be several million variations in gammas alone. And all that in turn means that when he gets close to a metal surface like ferrosilicon—which is, as you know, what the ship is made of, mostly—he's going to dose that surface with his own unique r-spectrum, which of course is required by law to be registered with Security."

He stopped suddenly at a fork in the passage and waved his detector wand over both entrances. "Yes, I think we turn here, sir."

"So he doses the surface," said Beck. He grunted uncomfortably. His thigh extensors were squeaking a little. It had been a long time since he had moved so far, so fast. In fact, he was beginning to wonder if this pursuit was such a good idea. Suppose they were waiting for him at the next turn? He patted the tiny hand weapon in his hip pouch, and he sighed. He knew he was a poor shot. He hoped the sergeant had brought a gun.

"Yes, sir," continued the sergeant, "he leaves radiation traces on the surface. So now the surface is artificially radioactive. It shoots back a pattern of alpha, beta, and gamma, which our detector wand absorbs. The band pickup is quite simple. As you see here, we use a sodium iodide crystal, connected to a spectrometer. Incoming emission interacts in characteristic ways with the crystal to produce electrical pulses in uniquely specific patterns. It's these patterns that identify the original radiation laid down by the suspect." He paused and looked back at Beck. "Would the councilor care to rest a moment?"

"No, let's go on."

"Actually, sir, we can't. At least not just now. It's the end of the line." They stood in front of a hatch-panel. "See, sir?"

"See what?" said Beck irritably.

"The label, sir. This leads into the radiation discharge valve system. If we go in there, we're dead."

"*They* must have gone in. Are *they* dead?"

"Probably not, sir. If you'll look at the panel legend, you'll note the operation is intermittent. It's off for five minutes every hour. They could have gone through at near zero level."

"Suppose they went through, what's on the other side?"

"I'd have to guess, sir."

"Then guess."

"My guess would be, there's a passage that leads Outside."

Of course, thought Beck. He tosses her Outside, then he returns and joins the big Procession. He noted then that his legs were aching again. He propped himself against the passage wall. He said, "One way or another we've got him. All right, sergeant, you have his unique emr. What do you do now?"

"We simply call in the spectrum. The Bureau runs a quick compute check and sends us back the criminal's I.D."

"Fine," said the Councilor. "You've been picking up the same I.D. all along? I mean, the same you started with, on the dais-panel?"

"Actually, sir, *two* I.D.'s. The test automatically includes the girl, and we screen her out, and what's left is the man. He left a good trail, from the dais to right here, sometimes a little stronger, sometimes a little weaker depending on how fast he was moving. But it's always the same. It's *him*."

"Call it in," said Beck crisply.

"Of course, sir." The detective-sergeant pulled a hand set from a chest cavity and spoke briefly to someone.

"Tell them it's for me, and it's urgent," said Beck.

"I did, sir. It's working. Just a few seconds, now. Ah. Yes? Repeat? No that can't be right. Let me talk to the lieutenant."

Beck yanked the set from the sergeant's tentacles. "I'll talk to him!"

The sergeant lifted his right shoulder in what might have been a perplexed shrug.

"Beck, lieutenant," said the Councilor harshly. "What's the problem Who'd you I.D.?" He listened, uncomprehending. "*Me?* That's impossible! I watched the sergeant take every reading, every step of the way from start to finish. Yes, lieutenant, I *will* come in and *personally* examine your crazy records. Meanwhile—oh, never mind!" He tossed the hand set back at his companion and turned and started out. And then he sudden remembered he had forgotten to memorize the return route. "Sorry, sergeant," he mumbled. "You first."

"Yes, sir. And sir?" The sergeant slowed for a moment and looked back.

"Well?" said Beck irritably. He knew he had to listen, unless he was going to order silence. But that would show he couldn't control his anger. "What is it, sergeant?"

"I think you were planted, sir."

" 'Planted?' What's that?" He was showing his ignorance, but he was very tired and very frustrated, and he really didn't care.

"This crimer," explained the sergeant, "steals your I.D. spectrum. He makes up an exact U-Pu-Th composition, absorbs it in a metal sponge, and hits everything in sight with it—panel handle, corridor walls, floors, ceilings. It completely overrides his own I.D. spectrum. All we pick up is—"

"Me."

"Yes, sir, and the girl, of course."

"Ah, the girl. Did you get anything on her?"

"No, sir. We did get a pattern, but it's not registered."

"She's an Outsider."

"That would explain it."

"Do you still want to see the lieutenant in the I.D. Bureau, sir?"

"No. Call in and cancel it."

"Of course, sir."

My own I.D., thought Beck. This rascal has an absolutely outrageous sense of humor. But in the end, I'll find him. And then we can all have a good laugh.

6. A View of the Procession

After Rodo left, L'Ancienne turned back to the eidolon and watched the swarming Procession.

She thought she recognized some of the individual celebrants. Isn't that Penuel the Penitent? Yes. Her circuits accelerated briefly in a muted sigh. She was glad that Rodo was not aware of his close relationship to his half-man. Let it stay that way. Penuel, insane, but harmless. The good abbot always made sure he was in the annual Procession.

She thought back. The penitents were experimental models designed long ago by Overlord psychiatrists as "whipping boys," to relieve stress and to assume guilt that should have been felt by humans. That particular design had not been an outstanding success. The Overlords had had much better luck with some of their other professional models: biologists, architects, hydraulic engineers, surveyors, mineralogists, masons, nuclear engine operators, musicians . . . My beloved Korak (she thought) was one of their proudest accomplishments. For it was Korak who had been picked by John Berry for safekeeping of the Trident algorithm—which eventually destroyed *Didymus*. Too, too ironic!

She straightened and leaned forward. Ho, now! What's this? That young man—just joined the Procession . . . trying to blend in, as though he's been there all along.

Oh Rodo! What have you done now?

But *is* it Rodo? she asked herself. Of course it's Rodo. I know my own far-scion. Grandnephew. Whatever. He's trying to hide. And there's an audio announcement. 'A prisoner has escaped.' Rodo, a *prisoner?* No. They mean someone else. He helped someone escape. *That's* why he's running. Who? Why? Out of a degenerate inborn contrariness and craving for trouble, that's why. Damn you, boy!

And here come the patrols. They'll probably make a newface screen, taken at two points along the route. This could be serious.

She tapped in a call to the Central Computer, better known as 'Cla.' "Cla? L'Ancienne calling."

Central answered in a melodious feminine voice: "How are you, dear?"

'Cla' was an acronym for Clotho, Lachesis, and Atropos—the three Fates, the Parcae of ancient Overlord mythology, and was the name given to the result of consolidating three mainframes with miscellaneous smaller accessory computers, all integrated and operating as a unit. Who had assembled and programmed Cla in the beginning? No one knew. Anyhow, her original design had been expanded and modified (often by herself) so many times that the ancestral program was by now totally buried. Data from every facet of the ship's operation were fed second-by-second into her, and routinely she (for she insisted on her femininity) reported births, deaths, serious accidents, repairs to *folk* or ship, traffic patterns, elections (pending, completed), acts of the Council, crimes, police actions, judicial proceedings . . . Additionally she was available for advice and expectations in love, life, and career. She seemed to know everything that was going on, all the time, all over the ship.

L'Ancienne said, "I'm fine. It's Rodo."

"Again?"

"Again. Beck's running a street check. Is Rodo in trouble?"

"Maybe big trouble, dear. He'll be picked up, for sure. You'd better get down there."

"Thanks, Cla. You're a sweetheart."

"I know."

So come on, old lady, she told herself. Down to HQ.

That rascal!

7. ARREST

Captain Londo sat in his office in HQ and studied the screen thoughtfully. Some ten or twelve figures—all superficially identical—were shuffling about within the hold-room a few meters down the corridor. This simple visual inspection told him very little. Who, exactly, was the Chief looking for? Did the Chief know? (He doubted it.) Did this hypothetical suspect have any identifying indicia? Most likely. So what were they? He had no idea. "Is this the lot?" he asked the arresting sergeant.

"Yes sir, everybody that joined the Procession between Korak Cross and the Arches. And we may have picked up a few extra heads."

"Understandable, Well, let's get on with it. Put them in the chute."

"Sir. On the way."

In the narrow passageway of the chute, and under the sergeant's watchful optics, each prisoner was required to place the index tentacle of his right hand in the I.D. slot, and the slot read his radiation, unique among the ten thousand other inhabitants of the ship, and flashed his bio on Captain Londo's screen. The Captain watched the readouts one by one. They all had a wearisome sameness. Vanch-four . . . age six hundred three . . . holo views, full figure, profile . . . Technal Institute . . . student activist clubs . . . one prior arrest, long ago . . . in the District Next? Veler-three . . . seven hundred ninety-four . . . shopkeeper . . . no prior record . . . and on and on.

And we're getting toward the bottom of the heap, he thought. And nothing. The Chief will be disappointed. What's left? Ah, what have we here? He studied the suspect and the data on his split screen. Well, it's only once a year, he thought. Better make sure, though. "You're Penuel, Chief Penitent?"

"Yes, excellency."

"You are presently repenting for a crime?"

"Yes, excellency."

"*What* crime, Penuel?"

"I don't know, excellency."

"Oh? Why not?"

"The crime hasn't been committed yet, excellency. That's why. I need very big crime, for my guilt is great."

Captain Londo stopped for a moment and considered that. He shook his synoptic globe, so that the receptor strands swung out briefly. He would never understand the Penitents. Guilt first, crime second. It made no sense, none at all. Small wonder the monk had been certified. On the other hand, he was supposed to be harmless.

"Your honor," the monk said humbly. "I was not always as you see me now. I think . . . I was once someone . . . important?"

"Really?"

"Oh yes, sir, but I can't remember . . . I live now at the House, you know."

Londo took another look at the data on the screen. He read, "this man was once Chief Engineer . . . " Which meant he ran the ship, mused Londo. And then what happened? It was all there: "Continued radiation exposure introduced incurable ambiguities into his circuits." So here he is, thought the officer. They let him out once a year for the Procession.

The Penitent shook him from his reverie. "What is this all about, sir? Are you teasing me? I know I'm not like other people, but you ought not make fun of me. It does not become your high office."

Londo abruptly signaled the sergeant. "Let him go. Next. Well, now, who are *you?*"

"Hudak, tube driver. And I'm late for work. Don't you fellows know we're running double schedules today? You can bet your bottom Ra-unit the Transit Authority is going to complain to the Council! You ought to at least give me a detention ticket. How'll I explain—"

"Get him out of here," growled Londo. "Next."

Next was Dr. Dell-5. "I was on my way to answer an emergency call. This is—most awkward."

The Captain was politely curious. "Who's the patient, doctor?"

"A daughter of Councilor Beck. Looks like severe computer virus."

Londo was a thoroughly conditioned bureaucrat; he well knew that a sincere attempt to follow the Chief's own orders was no excuse for delaying medical help to a member of the Chief's family. "Emergency," he barked to the admitting sergeant. "Get a driver out of the pool. Get Dr. Dell over to the Chancery Apartments. *Now!*"

"Next," he growled, as he prayed to all gods, known and unknown, for the imminent arrival of his superior.

Next was Waxe-three, a clerk in Radioactives Storage. "Sir!" declared the newcomer. "This is a government holiday! You have no right to arrest innocent citizens, pulling us off the street indiscriminately! The Council will hear from our Union about this!"

No doubt, thought Londo. "Next. Keep them moving, sergeant."

The screen showed a female, identified as Pora-65, Occupation, Street of Crimson Blazes.

Londo crunched together the tentacles of his right hand. His voice was dangerously quiet. "Sergeant, I told you, only males. How did *she* get in?"

"Sir, there seems to have been a little mistake. She came in with the Waxe fellow, claims he owes her for last night."

"Get her out of here!"

"Yes, sir, right away."

Pora-65 moved in rhythmic sways toward the door. Just before she exited, she turned and locked sensors briefly with Captain Londo. He turned away quickly. She laughed and went on out.

Londo growled at the sergeant, "Now, who else have you got?"

The screen showed a young male, standing passively at the I.D. register. Save for the radioactive spectrum, the data section of the screen was blank. No name, no age, no residence, no occupation . . .

"We're not getting a good readout," said Londo petulantly. "Try again. Sometimes the connections . . ."

"We did try again, sir. Several times. This is all we get."

Well, well . . . Captain Londo relaxed and considered the matter. Did he dare hope? No, not yet. "Bring him in here," he said. "Under guard."

A moment later he was examining the figure standing before his desk. The prisoner's body shell was smooth, unpitted, matte-polished, indicating a young adult, probably fifty or sixty years old. The prisoner held himself erect, with perhaps just a touch of cool arrogance. He regarded Londo calmly.

"Do you know why you are here?' asked Captain Londo.

The prisoner sighed. "Yes."

"What is your name?"

"Rodo."

"Is that all? What is your family name?"

"Enn."

The captain jerked. His synoptics bore in on the prisoner. "It is a serious offense to impersonate a member of a First Family. Are you aware of that?"

"Yes. And I must ask you to release me."

"Rodo—or whatever your name is—you joined the Procession somewhere between the Cross and the Arches."

"Is that a crime?"

"What were you doing before you joined the Procession?"

"None of your affair, Captain."

"How did you get from the Council Chamber to the Procession?"

"Council . . . Chamber? Where is *that?*"

Londo radiated a harsh burst of emr. "Those proceedings in the Chamber . . . how did you learn about them? Who told you?"

"What proceedings?"

"Where are your fellow conspirators?"

"Captain, you have no right—"

"I have every right. You have no I.D. Outsiders have no ID. Are you an Outsider?"

"No."

"Then who are you?"

"I told you, Captain."

"And you lied."

"You could call the Estate."

"In good time, boy. First, though, we need to talk. Please explain to me why you are not registered."

"Members of the First Families are not required to be registered. You should know that."

"Ah, yes. I forgot. You're the heir apparent. Well, Rodo of Enn, your most excellent lordship, I can see you have a speech impediment. You'll be delighted to know that we know how to cure speech defects. You may scream a little at first, but you'll soon be chattering away at light-speed. You'll find yourself answering questions we haven't even asked." He nodded to the sergeant and the guards. They held the prisoner firmly by both arms, rotated him rigidly, and marched him from the room.

He's the one, thought the captain. He will talk. He's got Outsider connections, and we are going to roll up his whole network. The Chief is on the way. We'll wait.

Chief Beck arrived a few minutes later. In his office he listened to Londo, and he studied the prisoner on his personal screen. The detainee was indeed suspect. And a member of the Enn Family? Absolutely not. The Family never participated in the Procession. Except for L'Ancienne he had never had occasion to meet or deal with any of the Family. He had provided security for her parties and receptions, and he did indeed know quite a bit about *her*. (But *that*, he told himself, will be another story.)

"Bring him in," he said.

They brought him in, two guards in front, two in the rear.

Beck studied him curiously. Here was no ordinary ship-scum. The prisoner was poised, calm, silent. He watched the Councilor, evidently waiting for his captor to speak.

Beck murmured, "I'm told you refuse to identify yourself." The pronouncement was half statement, half question.

The prisoner did not reply.

"We seem to have a threshold problem," continued the Councilor in a dry monotone. "Evidently you don't possess an I.D."

Silence again.

"Which could mean that you are an Outsider," said Beck thoughtfully. "Or what's worse, a crypto-Insider who works with them. A traitor." He paused and regarded the prisoner curiously. "Last week," he said, "the guillotine blade failed to fall on the neck of a condemned smuggler. Someone with a sense of humor had scrambled the relays. I don't suppose you'd know anything about that? No? And how about the week before, when we had to release that whore from Crimson Street . . . someone had overwritten her confession with the chorus from the Processional." His radiative voice rose ominously. "The judge stuck me—me personally—with a fine for playing the Processional in public." He studied the prisoner for some sort of reaction. There was none. "Shall I go on? How about last year's jail break? Where did they get the diamond saws?"

"No answers? Well, we've got lots of time." He leaned back comfortably in his chair and studied the portrait on the wall behind the suspect. It showed what had become known as the Seven Mutineers. Seven *folk* stood beside a shuttle, apparently guarding the vessel while helmeted Overlord prisoners shuffled in, on their way back to Earth and safety. It was the well-known opening act of the Great Mutiny on *Drunkard*. The male robot holding the shuttle door was Beck. He had had the portrait especially made up for distribution in the last election. In fostering this heroic illusion he was quite safe. Very few of the *folk* knew that no photos had been taken of the fateful incident, or that indeed Beck had not yet been born at the time of the Mutiny.

He continued pensively, not looking directly at Rodo. "So you see, young man, we are searching for this person, this very special person. Perhaps you are he? No, I doubt such good fortune. On the other hand, who knows?" His optics roved over the silent figure. "In any case, we know that our elusive phantom would not operate alone. He must have had accomplices." The voice rose very slightly. "Perhaps you are one of those?"

No answer.

"Pain is a very useful sensation," mused Beck. "Yet it's very difficult to define. Our ancestors on the Martian plains—the 'mules'—were probably the first of us to have any need for pain sensors. They prepared the fields, you know, clearing out the rocks, plowing the desert soils. The Overlords installed detectors in the bodies of the mules to warn of incipient mechanical failure, such as a leg or an arm working loose, or overheating due to loss of lubricant. Nowadays, of course, our pain centers are hereditary and highly developed. Our bodies start self-repair at the slightest twinge. We can't handle a lot of pain. We'll do most anything to make it stop." He gave a signal to the sergeant, who with the guards, pulled the prisoner into a transparent alcove and fixed electrodes to his arms and body shell. Their victim made no move to protest.

The sergeant held a button-cable in his hand, and looked at the Councilor. Beck nodded. The sergeant's hand moved slightly. The captive jerked, then adjusted, and was motionless again.

"You handle pain very well," observed Beck through the intercom. "Excellent mental discipline. Perhaps the result of special training? The Outsiders have no facilities for that kind of thing. That tells us something, my dear fellow: you're a shipmate. The question now is, where do you stand in your network of fellow traitors? What are you able to tell us?"

The captive was silent, immobile.

Beck permitted himself a long sigh. "Most regrettable. You force me to our next step. We simply penetrate your central intelligence system, and we excise your mind. I'm sure you're familiar with the technique and the result. We take your memories, your hopes, your speculations, your

IQ networks. We take—*you*. When we're done, you'll be a rather simple computer. You can add and subtract, take out the garbage . . . that's about it. I.D.? You won't have any. You won't need one. You won't even know you exist." He waited. "No?" He nodded again to the sergeant.

The captive moved very slightly within his bonds, as though bracing himself.

After a moment the sergeant called to his superior. "We're not getting much. And what's coming in is . . . scrambled . . ."

"You're letting him concentrate," objected Beck. "Turn up the pain. He's good, but he's got a limit. Everyone has a limit."

"Yes. More pain. Ah, yes . . . we're synchronizing . . . no . . . he adjusted again."

"Stay with it," ordered Beck grimly. "We have plenty of time."

The red light on his communicator panel began to flash. Someone outside the office was trying to call in. He whirled on the sensor angrily. "No interruptions!"

"But sir," came the voice, "it's an emergency message from the Lady L'Ancienne. She says to tell you . . ." The communicator's voice seemed momentarily to fail.

"Tell me *what?*" demanded Beck.

"Her grandscion—Rodo—"

"What do you mean . . . *Rodo?*" But he knew. Oh, now he knew. He stood up. After a moment of confusion he pulled his circuits together and he addressed the alcove sergeant. "Off. Turn it off. Bonds off, pain off. Copy probe, off. Everything—*off.*"

He waited another sixty seconds, then he addressed the prisoner in a smooth, over-controlled monotone. "Excellency . . . my humblest apologies. I did not know. You should have told me."

His captive asked quietly, "Am I free to go?"

"Of course, excellency. And we will provide proper patrol escort—"

"No." The ex-prisoner turned and walked out.

Beck watched him leave. His mind was in a turmoil. He had desecrated the noblest of the First Houses. That was bad, especially for a man of high political ambitions.

On the other hand . . . on the other hand . . . (dare he think it!) . . . he suspected—no, he *knew* a terrible blazing fact: putative past caper aside, Rodo of Enn was his escaped criminal, the man who had kidnapped and released the Outsider female, the man who had scattered Beck's own scent all around that subterranean maze. And simply knowing this gave Beck defenses in the forthcoming confrontation with the great L'Ancienne. In fact, if he played the game correctly, he had strong winning chances.

He did not need to prove anything. Not yet, anyway.

As he did with every piece of new information, he measured these new developments against his secret ultimate goals, and how the new data might be used to further those objectives. He decided that, if he were careful, things would work out nicely.

His goals, simply stated, included dispensing with the Council and taking exclusive and permanent command of the ship. To assist him in this he thought he needed two things. In his mind they were of equal importance. One thing was to discover the technology of the torpedo that had destroyed *Didymus*. The other concerned his own dubious genealogy. The *folk* would never accept a commoner as dictator. But that could be remedied if he could mate with a noblewoman. And which one (for there were several)? Why, the noblest of them all:

L'Ancienne.

He balled his digits into fists. "I'll talk to her."

"She's gone, sir. She said, not important, not to bother you."

A moment before, the object of his thoughts had been waiting impatiently in the main reception room of Police Headquarters when she noted a familiar figure emerge from a side door. She quickly canceled her inquiry with the desk officer and stepped cautiously out into the street. Should she follow Rodo? No. Her far-scion would be horribly embarrassed if he knew she had come down to rescue him. She watched him briefly from the shelter of an abutment as he walked jauntily on into the main thorofare and rejoined the parade. Then she slipped quietly into a side lane, away from the mobs, and into an area of narrow byways and overhanging windows.

8. In the Flea Market

L'Ancienne loved to shop in the flea markets in this rather raffish section of the ship. And since she was here anyhow she figured she might as well check over what the smugglers had brought in recently from Outside.

She stopped before one of her favorite booths. The shopkeeper was adding another item to his display case just as she entered, and the thing caught her attention. She looked at it hard, and she lost momentary physical control. Her legs were paralyzed, and she stumbled. She caught a jutting hook in the wall and righted herself.

No, she told herself. It is impossible. I do not see what I see.

The proprietor stared at her in recognition and sudden concern. "Midy! Are you all right?" He moved around the counter toward her.

"Of course I'm all right," she said crossly. "Well now, my fine cheater-of-the-unwary, what utterly worthless junk have you acquired since I was last in here?"

"Ah, noble lady, what a pleasure to see you again!" He bowed and rubbed his hands together.

"I'm sure it is," she agreed dryly. "For you think only of how best to swindle me."

"Milady wounds me to the very cor," he said happily. "Actually, I think only how best to serve milady."

They both knew their lines. They had used this dialog verbatim for years immemorial.

She sniffed as she looked over the display. "Well, Von, you don't seem to have much today."

He showed apologetic tentacles. "Very regrettably, milady is correct. We're in the very midst of the Memorial Ceremonies, as milady surely knows. The men want extra iron for fancy costumery, and the ladies want new water and methane ice for jewelry. Children seek ferrosilicon for their play microcel creations."

"Yes, I see. Well—"

He bent over the counter in a conspiratorial whisper. "Actually, milady, I have been saving something just for you. It's locked away in the back. Please excuse me for a moment."

He disappeared into a rear cupboard and was back in a moment, holding something black and shiny.

She showed mild interest. "Meteor?"

"Apparently. Pure ferronickelsilicon. One point five kilos. Obviously once fused, now finely crystallized. Just the thing for a creatively programmed microcel cluster." He threw his head back and waxed eloquent "I look at this and I see microcelled trees, flowers, flying creatures . . ."

"Birds," mused L'Ancienne.

"Birds . . . yes, birds, that's the word." He studied her craftily.

Blast him—and me, she thought. I showed a little interest, and the price just doubled. But I'm still ahead. He doesn't know what he has. He thinks I'm after the meteor. She said idly, "Nice, but rather common, don you agree?" She looked up from the meteor and faced him across the counter. "Actually, prince-of-robbers, I came here looking for a fake, something portable, something that could pass for genuine except under the very closest lab scrutiny."

"Oh?" The shopkeeper's receptor filaments fluttered. "Did milady say a *fake?*"

"Yes, Von, a fake. Problems, my shifty friend?"

"Well, no, not exactly. On the other hand, milady's request is a b unusual. Milady is . . . *serious?*"

"Idiot! Of course I'm serious. Do you have something, or do I go down the Street to your competitor, who is both honest and cheaper?"

"Honest Mel? Oh, come now, milady. Let's see. I was just going to show you. I may have something. But first, shall I return this very valuable and priceless meteorite crystal to the vault?"

"That common little crystal? You might as well leave it out. I don't really know. How much?"

The filaments hung motionless from his synoptic globe. But she knew he was watching her with great intensity.

He said, "One thousand gils."

She gasped. "Von! You *thief!* It's not worth a hundred!"

"Oh milady, how you grieve me!"

"Look here, you cunning, shifty, treacherous rascal!" She opened her purse and dumped the contents on the counter. "Two hundred and thirty gils. My entire assets. It's all I have. Take it or leave it!"

The shopkeeper wrung his tentacles and groaned. "You will ruin me yet!" Sorrowfully, he began scraping the money tokens into a cash pouch.

She slapped his wrist with her index tentacle. "Not so fast, swindler."

"Oh?" He looked up in surprise.

"A fake? Some little non-certifiable artifact? You promised!"

His circuits buzzed in perplexity. He couldn't recall an actual *promise.* Oh, well . . . the black crystal and the odd artifact had come in at the same time. He'd paid the smuggler ten gils for the lot. He walked over to the hand-sized fragment in his display case, picked it out, and handed it to his customer. "Milady plans to tease her guests?"

She ignored the question. "You guarantee it's a fake?"

He shrugged. "Milady, I don't guarantee anything. All I know is, it was picked up Outside three days ago, along with this black meteorite. Where it came from before that, nobody knows."

She got herself under rigid control as she glanced at the fragment once more. "No charge."

His synoptic globe shuddered.

"You have all my money," she pointed out.

"No charge," he agreed sadly.

She picked up the fragment and thrust it into her shoulder pouch along with the black crystal. She tossed her receptor filaments haughtily. "Good day to you, sirrah."

He bowed deeply. "Honor us again soon, noble lady."

It was only after she had vanished around the gallery corner that he realized *he* had been swindled. She had wanted only that strange artifact. The little black meteor was a sham, just something to camouflage her real interest. She would have paid a thousand . . . five thousand . . . more. But why? What special meaning did the strange fragment have for her? He tried to recall the lettering on the artifact. Something like 'LANCI'? Why would that interest her? Who could say? She was a very eccentric, very old, very powerful woman. Possibly just a little crazy. Probably things interested her that were beyond the common understanding.

He groaned again. Five thousand Ra units lost . . . just plain thrown away . . .

L'Ancienne was tottering when she rounded the corridor corner. She was glad no one was near enough to observe her closely. It seemed to her that her motor circuits were dissolving. The steel tendons in her arms and legs were shuddering chaotically. Was she on the verge of convulsions? Steady, old girl! Relax! Let's drift over here to this stone bench and rest a moment.

She sat down and put the bag on the bench beside her. "I can't look at it again just yet," she told herself. "I think I'll wait until I get home." A moment more to rest, and to reflect, and think, and dream.

LANCI. Lanci, of the N series.

That's my name. The Overlords assembled us, and programmed us to pull the wagons and load the rocks. I was just a mule, Lanci-N. But Korak loved me. When we made love for the first time my name blazed up in metal letters across his chest.

And then the Overlords torpedoed his ship and left it all as dust and fragments floating in space. That was a thousand years ago. After that, his name for me was a sacred memory. I would not permit anyone else to say it. So I changed my name to L'Ancienne—"the old one." It sounded exactly the same.

This artifact of mystery, this precious shard, had once been a part of the body of my beloved Korak, Captain of *Didymus*. And this other thing, the black crystal: was it truly just a meteor? Or had it actually been ripped from the shattered shell of *Didymus,* melted by the heat of the explosion and then recrystallized by the icy breath of space?

She sank deeper into her reverie. It was said that the Overlords shed liquid water from their optical orbs when a beloved died. A most curious custom, doubtless stemming from their gross evolutionary patterns. It accomplished no useful purpose that she could see. Indeed, since it surely dimmed vision, the phenomenon had negative survival value. But who could understand the rarely rational Overlords?

Anyhow, the matter was far beyond tears—which in any case were impossible at seven Kelvin.

As she grew calmer, she began to think more clearly. Evidently the LANCI fragment had been hurled onto *Drunkard*'s outer surface from *Didymus*' ancient explosion and had only now been discovered. There was an alternate explanation, but it was too incredible for serious consideration

As for the so-called meteor, perhaps an analysis could provide further information.

She returned home.

Over the years L'Ancienne had equipped a small laboratory with some of the simpler analytical instruments, mostly acquired on indefinite loan from various professional functions within the ship.

Her study of the black 'meteor' crystal started with the mass spectrometer. Using a diamond saw she carefully sliced off a corner fragment from the crystal. This she vaporized in a heater, then ionized the vapor in an electron beam. The charged atoms were fed through a magnetic field, where their flight paths were bent in accordance with the mass of the component atoms, with the lighter elements being deflected the most. She focused the ionic discharge on the palm of her hand and sensed the rapid buildup of separate bands of iron and silicon, with bare traces of manganese, cobalt, and aluminum. Very curious. She continued to examine her hand as she turned off the machine.

Back at the work bench, she carefully locked the mysterious crystal in a vise and ground the sawed corner to a fine polish. She then placed the crystal in an electron microprobe and focused a stream of electrons on the shiny surface, thereby causing the crystal's atoms to emit X-rays, the wavelengths of which depended on the respective atoms of the specimen. She bent her synoptic globe to intercept the X-rays with her receptor filaments.

Again, she found only iron and silicon, with irrelevant miscellaneous traces of other elements.

What was she looking for?

Several things.

The big thing—the main quarry—was nickel. There was no nickel. Not an atom.

All meteors contain nickel.

Next, isotopes. Cosmic rays penetrate matter to a depth of several meters, transforming metals to their respective isotopes. The change is slow, and millions of years are required to produce detectable quantities. But meteors and asteroids and comets have lots of time; they've been out there for billions of years, and they are loaded with isotopes. In fact, a meteor can be dated by its content of isotopes.

So (she thought), if it has no nickel and no isotopes, it cannot be a meteor.

What is this thing that was picked up somewhere Outside at the same time as my LANCI shard? I think I know. This thing is almost certainly a piece of *Didymus.*

Had both pieces lain Outside, invisible, unnoticed, these thousand years? Or . . . ?

There was that other explanation, and even to think about it made her tremble.

So hold it, woman, she told herself. Stop right here. Don't get involved. On the other hand—

9. THE SHOPKEEPER

"Milady!" The shopkeeper looked up in surprise.

She laid the shard carefully on the counter between them.

He looked down at it in even greater surprise. Had he been wrong, after all? Wasn't this the thing she had really wanted, the thing she had practically swindled him for? Perhaps she had been mistaken? It wasn't what she had supposed? Well, too bad for her!

"No returns, noble dama," he began in protest. "No refunds. You know that." He began a long exposition of how she had made her own careful inspection before purchase, and suppose word got around that he was making an exception—

"Oh, shut up," she broke in.

He immediately subsided. "Yes, dama."

"Information, Von. I need information."

He regarded her warily. "Such as?"

"This was picked up Outside? Somewhere Outside?"

"I believe . . . that may be correct."

"It was then smuggled in to you through regular channels?"

"Smuggled? Smuggling is against the law.. I could be exiled . . ."

"Von, my friend, don't be stupid. I'm not Security. I'm trying to find out *where* it was found Outside. Someone out there knows. I need to talk to him, that's all."

"Oh, dama, that's quite impossible."

"Why impossible?"

"Many reasons. The point of contact, from Outside to in, changes almost daily. To avoid the police, you know. But worst of all, they are dangerous men. Only last week they caught a Security man Outside. He was well-armed. It is rumored that they completely destroyed him. It is said his body shell and his head now orbit the ship in opposite directions.'

"You have nothing to fear, Von. All you have to do is work back through your supply chain. Your people can find the Outside man, the man who actually found this . . . artifact. *He* is the man I need to talk to. Can that be done?"

The shopkeeper was silent for a long time. "I don't really know, milady. In any case, even to send the question back up the line will be expensive."

"Of course. I will pay." She laid a heavy money pouch on the counter and shoved it over to him.

He took it hesitantly. "I will see what I can do. Come back in three days."

She did.

His first words were, "The deal's off!"

She stared over the counter at him, puzzled and angry. "But you said—"

"Milady, I know what I said. But no, you can't go through with it!"

"Calm down, Von. Let's back up and take this step by step. You traced back?"

"We traced back."

"You found the man? The man who found the artifact?"

"We think so."

"You told him I want to talk to him?"

"We told him."

"But he won't talk?"

"Oh, he says he'll talk. That's not the problem."

"So what *is* the problem?"

"He won't come inside. He wants you to come Outside. And bring lots of money."

"I see. And no one will go Outside with me?"

"*Nobody.* Nobody I know will even come close to the exit panel. So forget it."

"No. I want to talk to him. I'll go Outside."

"Dama! I hereby return your retainer. Forget you were ever in my shop! Please go away!" Mournfully, he put the bag of money on the counter.

She didn't even look at it. "There has to be a way to do this. I'll meet your Outsider at whatever exit he selects. Pass the word back."

"No, dama. There are bad men out there. You will be robbed . . . raped . . . killed."

"What do I have, dear Von, that might persuade you to help me?" She studied him for a moment, her receptor strands swaying as her head inclined gracefully up and down. She said softly, "My friend, would you like to spend an hour with me, back in your studio?"

He stared at her. His matted receptor filaments trembled. He stammered, "Oh, dama! You *would*? I mean, would you? *You*? Yes! *Yes!* I will help you! I will tell you everything!"

She walk-floated through the swinging counter doors (picking up her retainer packet as she passed—for she was a practical woman—and with it her priceless shard). She coiled a tentacle around the arm of Von the shopkeeper and pulled him through the slit in the chain-drapes into the cubicle beyond.

10. L'ANCIENNE OUTSIDE

"Through there, milady. The hatch is supposed to be unlocked." Her guide pointed toward the end of the passage.

"Thank you, Mardel." She opened her purse and counted out his fee, five thorium alloy units. He balled his tentacles around the money, then whirled around and scuttled back down the corridor. She watched him for a moment, then shrugged and started toward the hatchway. Maybe they're right, she thought. Maybe I'm walking into my death. Maybe parts of me will wind up in orbit around the ship. But I have to know. Also, if it comes to raw physical confrontation, perhaps we can show them that sweet little old ladies are not completely defenseless.

She pushed on the door. It was heavy, and the hinges were tight. She could feel the insets vibrating. She put her shoulder to it and shoved. The heavy portal groaned and shuddered. It moved, and suddenly she was Outside.

It took a moment to adjust. The gravity was slightly greater here than inside, and the background radiation, about 3 Kelvin, was lower. As her synoptic system automatically made the corrections, she heard a rumbling behind her. She turned quickly. The hatch door was closing. It slammed shut with a clang, and then she heard a click. A vague figure knelt beside the door. She realized that *they*—somebody—was doing this deliberately. The hatch-way was now probably locked. Someone out here had the key. The cost of information had just gone up.

Very quietly she turned in a slow circle. In front of her two shadowy forms loomed. Her optics turned up their sensitivity a bit. Two Outsider male *folk*. A third Outsider stood on the hatch panel.

She said calmly, "Which of you is Graf?"

One of the two in front of her said, "Did you bring the money?"

"Yes. Graf? Will you now please show me where you found the artifact?"

"Money first."

She hesitated. Should she hand over the money now? What incentive would they have then? She looked overhead. The stars were brilliant pinpoints, and they all seemed to be moving slowly. Of course they were. The ship was rotating. The sun was still dark-side. She wondered what it would look like.

She said, "Half now, Graf, half when you take me to the spot."

The leader jerked a hand out and snapped a pouch from her waist band.

By reflex she held up a protective arm but made no move to retrieve the pouch.

Graf handed the bag to his companion without opening it. He studied her in the starlight. "You're a fine-looking woman." He took a step forward. She stood motionless. "I had the impression you were older."

"Graf, I'm old enough to be your great-grandgenetrix."

"Not likely." He looked about him with a leering shake of his receptor filaments. "Fellows, do you think she looks old?"

"No, no, a little beauty!" chorused the other two.

"And look at monty!" With a casual tentacle Graf tapped the metal iris that shielded her Penrose mound. "Ever see such a biggie? She's *hungry* for it. I'll bet she could take all three of us, one by one, then start over again!" He laughed harshly. "Binty?"

The figure that held her money-pouch answered. "Yah?"

"How much is she paying us to service her? You count it yet?"

"I can't get it open, Graf. How do I . . ."

"The drawstring, dummy. Pull that tab there."

"Gotcha."

"Idiots," said L'Ancienne.

"What say, woman?" growled Graf. "Hey! Wha—?"

A puff of dust seemed to burst from the pouch. The microcellia buzzed around the receptor filaments of the three men. They began flailing at the little invaders, who, at the direction of L'Ancienne, began coating the receptor filaments of each of the Outsiders. Her would-be attackers howled in dismay.

She stood aside and watched with interest. And then she had a happy thought. The microcellia had completely blocked out all incoming sensoria to her proposed rapists. Perhaps that was not quite fair. Perhaps they were entitled to *some* opto-audio input. She signaled programs to the microcellia controlling Graf's two friends. She commanded the two men to climb the antennae tower and leap with all their strength straight ahead. She watched as the two followed instructions. They would land (she supposed), unharmed, a few kilometers downship. She hated to lose the microcellia, but perhaps they'd find their way home eventually.

And now for Graf, who stood quietly, trembling.

She ordered the little creatures to clear a few square centimeters from the filamentary receptors dangling awry from his synoptic globe. "Graf," he said reasonably, "let's be friends."

He rasped something that might have been 'yes.'

"Will you take me now to where you found the artifact?"

"Yes." He hesitated. "But I need to see."

"All right." She commanded the microcellia to clear away from his optics.

"Come." He turned away and started off.

She followed.

As she walked she seemed to be stepping on something gritty. The sensation touched distant memories, vague wisps, nothing she could bring into focus. At one point a cluster of particles struck her body shell. Are we moving through some sort of dust cloud? she wondered. But then she had to let the thought go. She had more immediate problems.

After a hundred meters he stopped. "It was here, in the trade path."

She looked about. Far up ahead she could see shanties and what seemed to be ramshackle warehouses. The 'trade path' was evidently the foot-path the smugglers used between collection depots and entrance points into the interior of the ship.

"This path is used every day?" she asked.

"Just about. Lady," he whined, "can you get these bugs off me? I did my job. And I didn't really hurt you."

"Soon, Graf. So the artifact would be found within hours after it hit the ship?"

"Most likely. 'Course, no way to tell when it first hit. These things come crashing in, then they bounce all over the place, and skid and slide, before they stop. Some smash up into little pieces, not worth picking up. Are we through now?"

"Almost. The key, please."

"Key?"

"I sincerely hope you have the key, Graf."

"All right. You'll get it. But I remind you, lady, we have a bargain. You owe me fifty thors."

"You'll get the money."

He unhooked a clasp on the side of his shell. "Here's the key. Give me the money."

She took the little metal piece with a cautious tentacle. "First, let's go back and see if it fits."

"Lady," he declared petulantly. "It fits. I'm a businessman. Would I lie to you?"

"Yes. Let's go. You first."

He went on ahead. "You're a hard woman."

They stopped at the hatchway. "Stand back a bit," she ordered. He moved away. She thrust the key into the lock-slot. It would not turn. "Wrong key, Graf," she said softly.

"A simple mistake," he said uneasily. "Your bugs have got me so confused it's hard to concentrate. If I had the money I think I could concentrate a lot better."

"There's a key clapped to your other side. It looks like it might be the right one."

"Where?"

"*There.*"

"I can't see. Call off your bugs."

She reached over and with two tentacles she unsnapped the key from his body shell. It was a mistake. He seized her hand. The key dropped with an unheard clatter.

"And now, lady," he snarled, "maybe I'll break your arm."

She felt a crashing pain in the metal in her upper arm.

Perhaps (she thought) there's a tad more risk here than I anticipated. That was *fast!* Of course, I could confuse him with false images—but he might take my arm off in the process. Best to let him find the money.

"First," he said harshly, as he gave her arm another twist, "get rid of the bugs."

She told them to fall away. They did.

"And now maybe we'll explore a little." The tentacles of his other hand fumbled around her waist as he drew her in closer. "Ah, here we are." He had found her money belt. He jerked it away from her waist amid the sound of tearing metal.

She closed down her total receptor system, and waited.

She did not have to wait long.

With the tentacles of one hand he unclipped the lid and looked in—and received a blinding flash of radioactivity. He screamed, threw both arms around his head, and dropped moaning to the ship surface.

"Keep the money," she said to the crawling thing. "You truly earned it." She took a long look at the constellations drifting overhead. Too bad she couldn't wait for the sun to "rise". Nevertheless, there were a couple of last things she could do. She began imprinting pictures of certain of the constellations on her retinal data banks, impressions that could be recovered and printed out at leisure. When that was done she made a final panoramic search for the Third Planet, with its alleged nitrogen oxide atmosphere. Yes, here it was, gleaming brightly just over the horizon of the ship. And it had a companion, a sizable moon. The Council's secret surveys had never mentioned a moon, but there it was, visible even at the quarter. Interesting. Most interesting.

She finished, looked around for the fallen key, found it, and was soon back inside the ship.

Inside, she moved quickly. She didn't like it in these rim sectors. Strange creatures roamed here, worse than anything you'd find Outside. And just now she possessed neither guide nor weapon.

She scurried past several Y-branches and intersections. And then she sensed trouble—first off to the left, then to the right. She'd be safer Outside again. She reversed direction, but then immediately realized she was cut off in that direction too. She turned back and ran.

Three rim-men followed. She moaned softly. They were fast. Too fast. They must practice racing as a hobby.

She could not make it back into any of the civilized areas in time. She'd have to try something else. As she fled she brought up a 3-D diagram of adjacent ship sectors into her visual circuitry. All a desolate labyrinth . . . except . . . a big ore storage bunker off to the right. Possibilities? Perhaps . . . perhaps. Was it empty? Full? No way to know until she got there. It had to be at least partially full if it held any hope of salvation. The opposite wall of the chamber held an exit hatch. Theoretically. But the ship prints were full of errors. Suppose she made it into the bunker, and it was totally empty, and there was no exit?

Oh well, she had lived a full life.

And very suddenly, here she was at the chamber entrance. She wrenched open the portal and took in the scene at a glance. And she hesitated.

Three billion years ago, deep in the Martian Precambrian magmas, elemental iron was pulling oxygen from its igneous matrix with the formation of magnetite—black iron ore. Magnetite was rich in iron, over 70 percent Fe, and true to its name, highly magnetic. The Overlords called it lodestone.

A thousand years ago *Drunkard* had left Marsport with a full load of powdered magnetite. Over the years some had been converted into steel products. Some bunkers had simply been jettisoned and cleared out to make room for the growing *folk* population. Only one or two full-loaded compartments were left.

L'Ancienne knew all this. She recalled it all in a split second. And she also recalled other things. She remembered how, back at the Martian iron mines, tools had sometimes accidentally fallen into piles of powdered magnetite, and how the *folk* had been ordered to dive into the black masses and retrieve the lost objects. And so she numbered swimming among her more esoteric skills. Swimming in powdered magnetite, that is. It took skill and technique, but it could be done. Back at Marsport, the main thing had been to find the tool quickly and then get out. Exposure to the intense magnetic field tended to scramble your circuits. Thirty seconds was about the limit. Beyond this, if you came out, you came out crazy. You didn't know who or where you were.

Did her hunters understand the perils of this innocent-looking pond of black poison? Probably not. And what they knew or didn't know wasn't very important just now. She didn't have a choice.

They were here.

She jumped.

The foremost pursuer was right on her. He lunged, and actually touched her with an outstretched tentacle as she dived. His momentum carried him into the mass right behind her. She gave his head a vicious kick—which momentarily stunned him and simultaneously propelled her forward. And then she got into a strong, meter-eating rhythm with arms and legs. She knew now without looking back that her intended killers could not swim, and indeed that the leader was probably at this moment floundering around on the bottom of the bunker under several tons of black ore, and trying to scream.

Half-way across, a blazing insight struck her: she *knew* the identity of the gritty powder that dusted the outside shell of *Drunkard*. It was *not* interstellar dust. No, interstellar dust was much, much smaller—about four microns in diameter. Furthermore, the particles of interstellar dust were elongated, and consisted mostly of ice. The stuff she had encountered Outside was coarse and gritty. Exactly like the mass she was passing through.

She swam, and she shuddered. It was true.

She knew now with certainty where and when and how the ferrosilicon crystal and the LANCI shard had fallen. And she decided she didn't need to see that invisible sun-star to know it for what it was.

She knew that that star, presently coming up fast behind the ship, was the sun of Terra. Which meant that *Drunkard* was now—and had been for the last several days—drifting through the mournful detritus of *Didymus's* explosion, including a full ship-load of powdered magnetite.

Which meant that planet Number Three was Terra. But if Number Three was Terra, whence the high radioactivity, and why the strange transformation of atmosphere from 20 percent oxygen into 100 percent nitrogen oxides, known to be toxic to Overlord life? She thought she knew that answer, too, the terrible, remarkable answer. She remembered now a somber prediction she had read long ago in the Mentor Room of the Central Library, something an Overlord scientist had written. She had read it casually and she had ignored it. She didn't believe in prophecies. Maybe she should have paid more attention. As soon as she got back to the library, she'd take another look.

But even as she was coming to these troubling conclusions, she was scanning the facing wall. Ah, the exit panel was actually there, where it was supposed to be. She reached the other side of the ore pool, gave a tremendous leap upward, and seized the hatch handle. She yanked the panel open and sat there in the open passage for a moment to let her throbbing musculature subside. She shook her head to get some of the powder out of her receptor filaments, then looked back over the quiet innocuous ore surface. No sign of *him*. *(It?)* Not a bubble. Some years down the road, when Housing Allotment cleaned out this vat, what would they find? Mysterious bits and pieces of metal, probably.

The vanished creature's two cronies in crime crouched at the other side of the pool, staring at her in mingled awe and hate. She felt flattered. She laughed, waggled a tentacle at them, then vanished into the passageway.

Next—she'd need an hour or two in the brush room. Every part of her head and body shell was coated with black grit.

But it was worth it. She had what she had come for.

Next question, when—and *whether*—to break the news to the ship? She'd have to think about that! But first, she wanted to verify Terra's fate. Was the planet truly dead? Verify!

11. THE MENTOR ROOM

L'Ancienne proceeded now to her photo darkroom, a cubicle of her laboratory insulated with lead sheet. In the nearly total darkness she opened the casement of her slide-maker and inserted a roll of aluminum film pre-treated with silver iodide. She snapped the receptor shut, moved back carefully with the film advance cable (which also defined the proper focusing distance), and concentrated on the constellations of stars she had seen Outside. Slowly, carefully, one by one, she beamed her visions into the slide-maker. When this was done she recovered the film cartridge, removed it from the instrument, and placed it in her slide projector. She projected a couple of frames on the darkroom ceiling, then turned the projector off and retrieved the roll. But she wasn't done. She wanted graphic verification.

Next stop, the Central Library.

She got her little one-seat floater out of the shed and was off to the Primary Corridors.

As usual, she took her customary detours. She loved to go by the theater, where in earlier times she had been an actress, and where she still had an honorary box.

The theater had once been the main storage chamber for iron ore. I was but one example of how, over the centuries, the ship internals had been altered and changed and modified and torn out and rebuilt to meet the technical and cultural needs of a society growing both in number and sophistication.

And there had been changes in the life of the theater since her time here. The troupe personnel had been renewed completely over the years. The only person who had been there from the beginning was the old doorman. She beeped at him as she passed, and he waved.

Inside those enchanted walls she had met Nardo, a fellow-trouper. How long ago? Three . . . four hundred years? (Oh, surely, not *that* long!) Nardo, charming, irresponsible, irresistible. She and he had made violent love, and their child, a female, was numbered among Rodo's ancestors.

Ah, Rodo. Your father was a great man, but he developed the radiation sickness, and passed out of your young life. And your mother had once been an actress here, before she became an engineer and was murdered by Outsiders. And so you came to me.

Vanished faces. Just to think about them saddened her. But no. Rodo made it all worth while.

She was jerked from her reverie by the realization that she was being followed. Someone in another single-seater had made her identical detour, every twist and turn. One of Beck's men, of course. She considered the security chief. Beck, spy, schemer, ambitious climber. What did he want? She could guess. He wanted her. Forget it, Beck. And all this surveillance is silly. Should she try to shake the agent? Too late. She had already reached the library. Once inside, though—

She parked her vehicle at the side entrance and walked in.

She had once worked here, and indeed for a time had been Chief Librarian. Brother Mentor, dead for several hundred years, had reproduced all the Overlord books deposited in his data banks by his ex-owner, the esteemed chaplain of Marsport, and during her tenure here as Librarian, she had consigned the star plates and certain other rare items to a special chamber, now known as the Mentor Room.

Aside from the Mentor accessions, the library was fairly well diversified. In the early days of the Beginning, nearly all the meager store of paper volumes belonging to the Overlord crew had been exposed to the extreme cold and near vacuum of space, and the brittle cellulose materials were fragmented and shattered. She had worked out a technique to reconstruct and salvage a great many of these precious records. To this nucleus the *folk* had added their own contributions, so that over the years the inventory had grown to nearly one hundred thousand items.

She walked up to the desk, where she exchanged friendly greetings with the clerk, Ms May. They all knew her here, and vice versa. "I'd like to sign in for the Mentor Room," she said.

"Of course, milady." The clerk fumbled around in a cabinet under the counter and finally came up with a register. "We don't have many calls for it," she explained apologetically.

"I imagine not." As L'Ancienne signed, she noted that the prior entry was also her own, over two hundred years ago. She wondered if Ms May had been born then.

"You'll need a key," said the clerk. "Let me see—"

"Don't bother," said L'Ancienne. "I have my own."

"Oh, yes, of course."

L'Ancienne hesitated. "I should mention . . ."

Ms May looked at her expectantly. "Yes, milady?"

"A man is following me. He and I once had a . . . how shall I say . . . a very tender relationship. It's all over now, but he can't seem to accept it."

She leaned forward in an attitude of puzzled intimacy. "Sometimes we girls don't fully appreciate the power we have over men. I'll bet you have to fight them off, too, don't you, Ms May?"

Clerk May was profoundly flattered. She longed for a man to fight off. Except she wouldn't fight. "Well, milady . . ."

L'Ancienne added quickly, "He's harmless, though, and I don't want to hurt his feelings. If he comes in and asks for me, would you please simply tell him the truth: that I am doing some research in Mentor. You can even let him inspect the register. You might suggest that he have a seat over *there*"—she pointed—"where he can see me when I come out."

"Ah . . ." Ms May gave a knowing flick of her receptor filaments. "The rear exit?"

"You're very perceptive. Goodbye now. I promise to lock up." L'Ancienne hurried on down the hall to the privileged Mentor Room.

She proceeded to one of the carrels and opened the terminal.

"Cla? L'Ancienne."

"Here, milady."

"Cla, I'm in the Mentor Room in the Central Library. I'll be browsing through a lot of documents, and I'll feed them to you as I go along. They will deal generally with the Overlords and their solar system. When I'm done, I'll ask you some questions. Meanwhile, stay open. Agreed?"

"Of course."

Now—what to do first. Verify that that planet, despite its strange atmosphere, is in fact Terra. Next, assuming it is Terra, find out the origin and consequences of that remarkable atmosphere. And finally, and almost incidentally, find out how it was possible that *Drunkard*, which has zig zagged randomly for a thousand years, has now returned. Try *that* one first.

Random. That was the key word. Totally random changes in course wouldn't necessarily take the ship farther and farther away from Terra. Some of the route would be back and forth. She had read something somewhere. A rule of math? Pull down the references. We'll see.

It took her less than half an hour to find the *why* of the return. The hard laws of mathematics required it: a thing zig-zagging randomly must eventually return to the starting point. The Overlord mathematicians had given the rule a name: Drunkard's Walk. (Ah, *Drunkard!* Whoever named you must have been a prophet!)

She moved on to another section of the room. Here she began flipping through the catalog plates and she soon found what she wanted. Star charts. Charts that showed constellations that had been visible a thousand years ago to the navigators of this ship.

And here was a big plate that showed the northern Terran skies. And there *it* was, that very particular constellation, just as she had known must be. She took it back to her carrel and downloaded the data into the receptor. "Got it, Cla?"

"Got it. Ursa Major. The Big Dipper."

So the planet had to be Terra, and the star was Sol. The evidence was cumulative and overwhelming. The planet had to be Terra because within the last few days *Drunkard* had passed through the debris of *Didymus's* explosion. Witness Korak's breastplate. It had to be Terra because only from Sol's system did the stars shape themselves into the Big Dipper. And it had to be the planetary lair of the Overlords because the hard rules of mathematics required it.

Proof. She had it. Not only for herself, but, if necessary, for others. So far, so good, as the Overlords would say. But she wasn't finished.

Now for the hard part—find out when and why Terra had acquired an atmosphere of toxic gases and a crust of high radioactivity. How could a dominant, highly intelligent race let it happen to them?

To compound the mystery, save for hints of a male sterility problem, Terra had been fairly healthy at the time of the *folk* mutinies.

She knew she would find no reports of the actual catastrophe—if indeed there had been one. *That* would have happened after the mutinies, perhaps even long after. But she might find reports of *trends,* and perhaps dire prophecies. The prophets might even look ahead and predict step-by-step stages in the developing tragedy

She scanned the shelves, pulled down a metal codex, evidently a fragment of a once-larger work, and returned to her carrel. "Here's another one, Cla. Something written by an Overlord fiction writer."

"Should be entertaining."

As L'Ancienne downloaded the material into the terminal receptor she watched the text scroll up on the monitor:

Some Predictions for the Last Day

It is predicted that much that will happen on the planet Earth on this particular August day will resemble things that had happened on the day before, and the day before that, and so on back, for many days.

The man and woman lay locked in loose but hopeful embrace on the drape-enclosed bed. After a time the man groaned and sat up. "It isn't working. I can't do anything."

She was silent. There was nothing much to say.

He continued petulantly. "First, no sperm count. Now, no erection." He turned on her, as though it was all her fault. "How did our parents conceive us? What did they have that we don't have?"

We? she thought. But she did not protest the illogic of the pronoun. "There are studs. Young men with proven records."

He said gloomily, "I've checked. The shortest waiting list is eight months. Even if we had the money, which we don't. A cheapie, with a tainted genealogy, is half a million. A really sound one . . ." He groaned again. It was a long barely audible thing. "Good God, what is happening to the human race?" He got out of bed, walked over to the balcony and looked out.

He had nearly a panoramic view of the city. Geneva, the Pearl of beautiful Lake Geneva, he thought sardonically. The water was totally polluted. No fish had been caught in the lake within current memory. The highest forms of life in the water were typhoid and polio bacilli. And yet the lake (which drained into the Rhone) was crystal clear compared to the lower river, which again was purity itself compared to the Mediterranean, on which floated an iridescent layer of oil from numerous spills, all ignored.

A movement in the distant water attracted his eye. A longitudinal swell, stretching out into the lake as far as he could see, was rolling in toward the southern shore. He recognized the *seiche,* a complex lacustrine phenomenon without good explanation. The lake groans, said the locals. The disturbance would swing back and forth in a slow stately rhythm, and would finally die away. He recalled now the silly myth, "When *seiche* and *molan* marry, Switzerland will die." The *molan* was the storm wind that swept down out of the Arve Valley. He looked below, into the streets, and he frowned. A stiff breeze was in the making. Scraps of trash were lifting high into the air. The balcony doors suddenly opened wide, and a gust of wind snapped at the bed drapes

The man shrugged, closed off the balcony, and got back into bed. For a moment he lay quietly at the side of the woman. Then he reached up and pressed the opioid button in the panel behind the bed. From hidden ducts a sweet subtle odor began to seep slowly into the draped enclosure.

They locked hands, lay back together on the cushions, and stared hazily up at the ceiling.

A dhow moved out with the tide from Karachi, headed across the Arabian Sea into the Gulf of Oman. The little ship was loaded with opium, rice, and two hundred casks of potable water, fresh from artesian springs in the hinter land. The captain expected to be intercepted by the black ships of The Guardian, who would take fifty casks in return for guaranteed passage. The Guardian, of course, had to turn over a fair share to the Hexagon gunboat assigned to the area. It was a reasonable arrangement and had worked well for all parties for many years.

The captain looked up critically at the mainsail, which stood out sturdily before the freshening breeze. The sail was newly woven from soda-soaked hemp, and the sea air hereabouts had one of the lowest acid readings in the eastern hemisphere. The big sheet ought to last the voyage. Even so, he had brought along a spare. Eventually (he brooded) this terrible acid air will eat even the ship's timbers. How then shall I live? Allah preserve!

What used to be Los Angeles International Airport (now closed these many years) bordered the Pacific Ocean. Metal barrier fences once separated runways from the water, but these had long ago collapsed and rusted away.

A man who lived in the village was walking along the shore, watching how the iridescent oil slicks controlled all except the most unruly surf. He was bare foot, and he left footprints in a melange of sand and black oil. He came here nearly every day, and he could not remember when the scene had been any different. He did not smell the muck. His olfactory capabilities had atrophied long ago. He shaded his eyes with a hand. There was motion on the beach up ahead. Interesting, he thought. He began to trot. Squish squish. An animal? A big fish? Yes, something from the water. It lay there, thrashing, as though trying to crawl up onto the land.

A porpoise? Dolphin? No, he thought, too big for that. He knew now what it was. A whale. A *baby* whale. Which meant a mother . . . out there somewhere. Odd, very odd. He thought they were all extinct. He had read it somewhere. And doubtless the mother of this giant infant was dead.

The creature saw him and stopped its anguished writhing. Man and beast made eye contact. The man put his hands on his hips and stared and then shook his head. "No, chum. They say you came from the land, millions of years ago. It must be pretty bad out there, but I'm telling you, it's even worse here. Go back, little friend." And so saying, he turned away and walked back to the village.

Farther north, and on the other side of the continent, a team of hydraulic experts were clambering over an iceberg freshly calved in a Greenland fiord and now floating majestically south in the Davis Strait. It took the team less than four hours to sample the entire berg, including a dozen cores to one hundred meters. It was all for nothing. They knew what they'd find even before they started. Turbidity, passable. Bio, passable. Average pH, 4.5, too low for treatment. Too bad, too bad, thought the chief engineer. Thirty years ago tugs would have been standing by to haul the big fellow down to the fresh water ponds in Long Island Sound. No more. The team packed their gear and returned to the ship

Even farther north, John Sam sat immobile on an ice hummock watching the slow cautious approach of the bear. Neither man nor bear felt the cold. Every few steps the bear would stop and sniff the air. The Eskimo knew that the breeze was in the right direction, and he knew that the great white beast had thoroughly analyzed the situation: strong human odor, one man, no metal—which meant no rifle. But the bear was still cautious. He came on, zigzagging in slow jerks across the wind. As he approached, John Sam could see that his adversary was sleek and well-fed. And why not? This animal had killed and eaten four of his people in as many weeks.

It was now turnabout time. The bear probably had trichinosis. They'd have to cook the flesh a long time. Fuel could be a problem. But, as the white man said, we'll cross that bridge when we come to it.

Four man-lengths away the bear stopped, as though making a final check.

It was risky to let the bear get this close, but John Sam's eyes were not as good as they used to be, and he had to make sure of his shot. Cataracts, the mission doctor had explained. We've got a big hole in the northern ozone layer. The ultraviolet cooks your eyes. You ought to get down south, get a catarectomy. They'll give you an artificial lens. It'll work fine. That's what they had told him, and it was silly to think about it just now, especially when the grandfather of all bears was now standing six meters away.

Come on, come on, the man urged mentally.

The bear charged.

The man raised his urine-and-feces-scummed laser rifle and fired once. The bear dropped two meters away. John Sam made his ceremonial apologies to the spirit of the bear and then radioed back to his son to bring up the hauling crew.

So then, on this particular day, much that will happen will strongly resemble things that had happened the day before, and the day before that, and so on back. It is predicted, however, that on this day there will be two very special events, things that had never before occurred, and never would again: The Central Consortium of Nations will send its ultimatum to the government of the United States of America, demanding that the Hexagon share its National Treasure, to wit, the American Sperm Bank, presently under heavy guard at Fort Knox, Kentucky. And the Hexagon will politely tell the Consortium to go to hell.

"Got all that, Cla?"

"Yes, milady."

"Some strange words there. What's a 'dhow?' "

"A lateen-rigged boat, high poop, narrow waist. It—"

"Never mind." She was thinking of something else. The American Sperm Bank. It always seems to come back to sperm.

She needed to know more.

She returned to the stacks.

The sexual processes of the Overlords were certainly different from ours, she thought. I need to review . . . Ah, here's a likely item, a report by a *folk* geneticist, filed away long ago and evidently forgotten. She brought it back to the terminal. As she downloaded, she watched the script scroll up on the monitor.

Accustomed as we are to the function of the Penrose pacquets, we may find the reproductive processes of the Overlords somewhat strange. In sum a stiff, elongated organ of the male, called a 'penis,' deposits up to about milliliters of fluid ('semen') within a specific body cavity of the female. The semen comprises millions of one-celled creatures ('spermatazoa,' or simply 'sperm'). Under the right conditions, if one sperm finds an egg within the female, it fertilizes the egg, and an embryo will grow and eventually exit the mother as an infant Overlord.

But conditions have to be right, *exactly* right. And even as early as the closing years of the twentieth century, Overlord geneticists were beginning to suspect that conditions were beginning to be 'not right.' The Overlord birth rate was falling. This was first apparent in the highly industrialized countries and pollution of air, water, and food was easy to blame. But a few decades later the same pattern was noted in third-world countries.

What caused the falling birth rate? The direct cause was lower male fertility. There was no real question about that. And what caused the drop in fertility? There was general agreement about that, too. Man was poisoning himself. The impact on his semen was measurable. The volume of an ejaculation normally 3 ml, had dropped to a fraction of that. The number of sperm per ml normally 20 to 300 million, had similarly dropped. This was serious.

Normally, of 100 million sperm per ml, 20% would be immobile even at the outset. Another 20-40% were generally deformed, i.e., 2 heads, no tail etc. Of the original 100 million, only about 100,000 viable wrigglers would make it into the female oviduct. Of this number, only 15 or 20 would finally reach the egg, and of this very limited invasion detail there would have to be one very healthy little operator with strength sufficient to pierce the egg. And there's the core of the problem: for if, at start, there are only 5 million sperm per ml, that's not enough, statistically, to ensure that there will be at least one healthy sperm, at the end.

By mid-twenty-first century, nearly 60% of male Overlords had sperm counts below 5 million. In another hundred years it was 75%. In their 25th century, when we took leave of them, it was 90%. This was a thousand years ago. Did their count ever drop to zero? Interesting question.

There was a growing suspicion among their biologists and geneticists that continued exposure to pollutants had brought on a true evolutionary mutation. This was of course unacceptable to the general lay public and their elected officials. Politicians avoided the issue. However, there was an undercurrent of alarm. Fertility clubs sprang up on their internet.

World population leveled off in the twenty-third century, began to drop in the twenty-fourth, and plummeted in the twenty-fifth, the century of our mutiny.

By then the culprits were well-known: antibiotics: penicillin, tetracycline; chemicals: dioxin, nicotine, alcohol, certain pesticides and narcotics, gasoline fumes, estrogens; x-rays; viruses: mumps, chicken-pox.

There was some half-hearted legislation in some countries to ban some of the major carcinogens.

"There's more, Cla, but we're going to stop here. I think we have enough."

"As you wish, milady."

"Are you ready for the questions?"

"Yes, milady."

"You know that we are presently orbiting a star and considering land-all on the third planet."

"I know."

"Is the star Sol?"

"Yes."

"And the third planet is Terra?"

"Yes."

"Does anyone else know this?"

"I think not."

"Has Terra had its final nuclear war?"

"Milady, I cannot answer that with absolute certainty. All the data you have given me are at least one thousand years old. If you had asked me that question a thousand years ago, I would have *predicted* that Terra would have its final nuclear war within a hundred years, possibly sooner. Which is to say, some time during their twenty-sixth century."

"Would you have predicted that the air would burn?"

"Yes."

"Could you have predicted what would cause the war?"

"Yes. American scientists would use the Penrose process to synthesize and replicate viable human spermatazoa. It would not matter greatly, at least to Americans, that most of the resulting male children would be sterile, because the supply of viable synthetic sperm in the Sperm Bank at Fort Knox would prove inexhaustible and would be available to all citizens of the United States."

"Yes. Go on."

"I would have predicted that the United States would resist sharing the Sperm Bank and the secret Penrose process for iterating the sperm. This would mean that the rest of the world would probably die. Your data suggests that the governing board of the Bank in fact had on hand several million three-ml capsules, each guaranteed to contain 450 million viable sperm, dispersed in a rich matrix of vitamin C, sugar, proteins, enzymes, and so on, all at a mildly alkaline pH to protect against the somewhat acid environment of the female uterine tract, and all ready for immediate use. In fact, to compound their callousness, your data further suggest that the Bank routinely destroyed 'out-dated' material from time to time."

"Ah . . . rather arrogant."

"There were probably some nasty incidents. Perhaps attempts to arbitrate. But evidently everything failed. The day must have come when buttons were pushed, and thousands of nukes were launched. The very air burned. But you understand, L'Ancienne, this is mere speculation, based on thousand-year-old information, some of which is of doubtful value. Nothing is known for sure."

"Of course. One last question?"

"Go ahead."

"Is there any carbon-based life left on Terra?"

"I think not."

"Could we *folk* survive there?"

"I think so. Start at the south polar cap, coldest there."

"And no one else knows this?"

"Not in these terms. You'll recall Beck's demonstration with the Outsider female. The Council knows that the third planet is non-toxic to the *folk*. They do not know the planet is Terra."

"Thank you, Cla. Erase all, please. Out."

So, she thought, *Drunkard* carries its fate locked in its name. For a thousand years it has been rushing blindly toward that destiny, and now it has arrived.

She reshelved the volumes carefully and was about to leave, when her *khu* suddenly broke away and confronted her. "Well, old woman, you finally got your revenge. They're all dead. Is that what you wanted?"

"No," she whispered. "I was wrong. I'm sorry, so sorry. Ten . . . fifteen billion innocents. I did not want that. But life goes on, *khu*. Someday somehow, living things will finally come again to that poor planet, to live, and beget their kind. Will they succeed where the Overlords failed? It is in the laps of the gods." She sighed. "And what will they look like . . . ? Come back in, *khu*."

She continued to the rear exit, locked up behind her, and proceeded quickly around to the side entrance. Here, as expected, she found a police single seater parked a discreet distance from hers.

She walked over to the little vehicle and looked about. No one was in sight. She bent over and in one smooth, flowing expert motion she snapped open the fuel pocket, removed the capsule, and hurled it far down the passageway. Then she ran to her own little machine.

Already she felt much better. She leaped into the saddle and was off with a joyful whoop.

Somewhat later a furious Beck interrogated a crestfallen agent. "You lost her? Again? Never mind. What was she looking for in the library?"

"The librarian said she was doing research in the Mentor Room."

"Research? What kind of research?"

"I don't know. The door was locked. I waited just outside, but she never came out." He checked his notebook. "At four oh seven I asked the librarian if there was another exit, and she said yes." He waited glumly.

"Ah." Beck's tentacles folded and unfolded. She wasn't researching anything, he thought. She was simply eluding this moron. So she ducked into the library, and then immediately out again. To . . . where?

"Anything further, sir?" asked the unhappy agent.

"No. That's it. Marf. Thank you."

The agent bowed and left.

She's up to something, Beck told himself. Something big. I sense it. What is it?

12. THE HOT ROOM

The Chief of Security was aware (as indeed were most of the older *folk*) of the recorded histories and traditions of the ship people. Some Beck accepted as irrelevant fact; some he viewed as simple myth; some he considered as both true and useful. He had read (and believed, since it was absolutely logical) that in the Prototimes the Overlords tended to use the memory banks of the *folk* as repositories for information of all sorts, ranging in variety from census lists to chemical encyclopedias. Certain of the *folk* had been especially designed to receive some of the more complex data sets. There were traces (mere wisps, actually) of suggestions concerning the algorithm for the quark-dissolving torpedo, and how, over a thousand years ago, it had been stored in one of the original *folk*.

Beck's year of research had finally uncovered the identity of that particular *folk*—and his hopes had been promptly dashed.

The repository had been Korak, captain of the ill-fated *Didymus*, and dead these ten centuries.

Weeks later, as he brooded in his disappointment, he had an interesting thought. Perhaps that marvelous algorithm had not died with Korak after all. There was an outside chance . . . According to tradition, in the beginning there had been a daily exchange of shuttles between *Didymus* and *Drunkard*. Suppose . . . ah yes . . . suppose that the good Captain Korak had mated with a female, and suppose she had got back safely to *Drunkard* . . . Suppose also, that the ejaculation of Korak's seed into her Penrose mound had been total, and had included summaries of the captain's individual history to date. In that case . . . there might be at this very moment a female on this ship that carried that fabulous algorithm in her genomes.

When Beck had first thought of this possibility, he had trembled in near paralysis.

Next, a check of ancient records.

Of the original forty *folk* on *Drunkard*, twenty had been female. Over the course of the millennium, seventeen had died in various accidents, or had simply disappeared. Three had survived. He knew the three. Bettka, a derelict, wandering the corridors, under the firm impression that she was a bulldozer, digging station foundations in the Martian deserts. If, when you met her, you closed off your optics and just listened, you could hear the whine of great electric motors, the crunch of the treads in the sandy aggregate, the scrape of the big metal blade, even the warning siren when she 'backed up.' Several times he had tried to have her dismantled but the Historical Society (led by—of course—L'Ancienne) had always frustrated his efforts.

Number Two was Giglia, chief librarian. Not the type; besides, medical records indicated congenital Penrose malformation. That left . . .

L'Ancienne.

Transport record plates showed her on the passenger list of the last shuttle to leave *Didymus* for *Drunkard*.

Had *she* . . . and *Korak* . . . ?

And if so, did she now carry within her body (witting or not) that fateful priceless set of equations? How to find out?

It was a neat problem in Penrose genetics.

Next stop, the Genetics Laboratory.

He trembled, and he winced, and he knotted his tentacles.

Originally, before the Mutinies, the Genetics Laboratory had been the quarters for the Overlord officers and crew, sealed off from the cold and vacuum of space. Beck had been inside the G. Lab—once. He swore, never again. The lab maintained a fantastically hot temperature, 288 Kelvin. Here ice was not ice but an incredible transparent liquid. Here, Penrose monticles were cultured for implantation into newly-created juvenile *folk*. The male monticle was soaked in a colloidal aqueous dispersion of testosterone, the female in progesterone. Typically, this would be the first and only contact with water during the lifetime of the individual, whether male or female.

Other strange things were grown here: mosses, tiny fruit trees, misshapen animals. A major effort was being directed to growing a recognizable Overlord foetus, but so far only minuscule amorphous wrigglers had resulted.

The Chief Geneticist and his staff were of course well-adjusted to the heat and humidity of the sealed-off lab. Their circuitries had been semipermanently modified to work at the higher temperatures. Loss of superconductivity in several major internal systems was compensated by faster response times in other units.

When the Chief Geneticist informed Beck that he had something to report on the L'Ancienne matter, Beck predictably insisted that the scientist make his report outside the lab.

"Thirty minutes outside the hot-lab," agreed the Geneticist.

"Just thirty? But—"

"No." The lab chief waggled his head-band of stylized Penrose monticles. "That's all I can take outside without extensive re-circuiting. If you want to talk longer, you come inside. Anyhow, half an hour should be enough."

"All right, outside."

"Fine. I've prepared an exhibit. Come over here." He pointed a tentacle (which quivered, for it was in indifferent repair) at a spheroidal display that consumed nearly the entire far wall.

The great mound was actually a three-dimensional compilation of a number of loosely concentric rings that wove in and out and around each other, presenting gaps and overlaps.

"This," rasped the Chief Geneticist with considerable pride, "is the theoretical Penrose monticle of L'Ancienne, greatly enlarged, as reconstructed from the available records."

"*What* records?" demanded Beck.

"Genetic records, medical records, psychological records, behavioral records . . . of all known progeny . . . and of herself, of course. The study has been comprehensive."

"So what's the answer?" Beck said curtly. "Does she have it, or not?"

"Hm. The answer. Well, first, my dear Beck, let us restate the question."

"No need. I know the question. Please get on with the answer."

"Indulge me, sir. You asked me if L'Ancienne possesses the secret of the General Algorithm, which, as you have described to me, explains (perhaps *inter alia*) the quark-solvent action of the torpedo that destroyed *Didymus.*" He held up a trembling hand to silence his guest. "As originally created by the Overlords, she did *not* possess such knowledge. So far as we know, only one of the *folk* had this knowledge. We believe that the Overlord physicist who formulated the General Algorithm imprinted it for safekeeping into the memory banks of one particular *folk*-person, on Mars-Base. We know the name of the Overlord physicist was John Berry, and we believe that the *folk* recipient was Korak, captain of *Didymus.*

"All this took place before the mutinies, of course. Either before or during the mutinies, John Berry disappeared, and with him, the Algorithm. Hardly surprising. A lot of records were lost in the turmoil. Anyhow, afterwards, none of the *folk* were able to find the Algorithm."

"Get to it," insisted Beck. "Much of what you have told me, I already know. And I have good reason to believe that Korak and L'Ancienne were lovers. Right?"

"Yes, Chief, so state the records."

"So he passed the Algorithm on to her? When they made love? He *did,* didn't he?"

The Chief of Genetics was silent a moment, as though uncertain how best to explain a forthcoming ambiguity. He pointed to a blank section in the Penrose mound. "If he—Korak—had transmitted it to her sexually, it ought to show *here.* But as you can see, this area, a special mathematical zone, is blank."

Beck sputtered a disappointed burst of high frequency radiation. "So he *didn't* give it to her?"

"Beck, dear Beck! So impetuous! My study, as I said, is based on *available* records."

"Meaning—?"

The geneticist regarded his visitor patiently. "Let's assume she has the General Algorithm. *If* she has it—*if,* I say—it is well within her sexual ability to transmit or not transmit to her progeny. It depends to a considerable extent on her psychological condition at the moment of orgasm. In profound sexual rapture, she might transmit everything, and might not even be aware of what she is doing."

"Are you saying that she may possess the Algorithm and not know it?"

"It's quite possible."

"Incredible."

"Not at all. It is a complex series, and she may have simply ignored it—consciously or unconsciously. She has a general smattering of the science but certainly she is not a physicist. Nor am I. Or you."

"True. Well. In this act of total sex . . . has she ever experienced . . . a *rapture,* you said?"

"Twice, we think. The first time, of course, was with Korak. The second was with an actor named Nardo."

"Nardo? Hm. He's dead, isn't he?"

"Yes, killed in an accident a couple of hundred years ago."

"Any descendants?"

"A son, Nord, once chief engineer."

"And what happened to *him?* Dead, too?"

"Probably, but we're not sure. There's some evidence that continued exposure to drive-pile radiation addled his circuits, and that he left the service and joined the monastery. In any case, consider him dead."

"And another dead end," Beck said gloomily.

"Not necessarily. Nord had—*has*—a son."

Beck jerked, then subsided. He *knew* . . .

The geneticist watched him in vague amusement. "Yes, Rodo. Our records are not complete. Rodo may—or may not—be living proof that *she* received the Algorithm from Korak, and that she is capable of transmitting it in her genome. If so—" (He pointed a tentacle at the blank area in the wall exhibit)—"this would look like—*this.*" The area filled with a myriad coruscating points of radiation.

Beck sighed. "This is getting us nowhere. What do we do now? Ask Rodo?"

"I doubt that he knows. If *she* doesn't, *he* doesn't."

The Security officer twisted his tentacles in frustration. "Then how do we find out if he has it?"

"Observation, my dear Beck. There are various ways it might show. Certain behavior. Artistic behavior, I would think. Not really my area . . . but perhaps certain creative pursuits."

"What in the name of *Drunkard* are you talking about?"

"Fractals, perhaps. Yes, fractals, might mean something. Does he create fractals? What do they look like?"

"Fractals . . . ?" The officer was now totally bewildered.

"One for the mathematicians. Can the Algorithm be expressed as a sequence of fractals? I suspect they would all be very beautiful, such as might be constructed by a lad of his artistic temperament and breeding. And now I leave you. My time for the cold is at an end. I must return to the heat." He turned and walked toward the hot-cold lock.

"But . . . you haven't explained—!" cried Beck. "How—?"

The only answer he got was a half-whisper, tossed over the biologist's shoulder: *"Fractals!"*

13. BECK SEARCHES FOR RODO'S CHAMBER

Beck noted with faint disapproval the photo plate that hung on the wall behind the desk of the Chief of Ship Maintenance. It showed that very famous scene, where the seven original mutineers were ushering the captured Overlords—Captain Duroc and his hapless crew—into the shuttle. Beck was holding the shuttle door open and appeared to be motioning sternly with his laser.

In the last general election Beck had circulated thousands of copies of The Mutiny. His political rival had pointed out (to no avail) that the plate was a total fake, that Beck did not even exist at the time. Ridiculous, Beck counter-argued. The plate speaks for itself. Anyhow, he won the election. The photo was now a collector's item, and many of the *folk* possessed copies for reasons that Beck suspected would not flatter him. Nowadays he tried whenever possible to ignore the whole thing.

He turned his attention back to the Maintenance Chief. "The problem is easily stated. I am interested in a certain criminal."

"So arrest him," said the old engineer.

"That would be highly premature. I need . . . more evidence. I have reason to believe he has a secret hideaway somewhere in the ship, known but to him. I need to find that room. I need to know what is in it."

"You are looking for something in particular?"

"Yes."

"What, exactly?"

Beck hesitated. Suppose (he thought) I tell you I'm looking for highly artistic designs on the walls of that secret chamber? In a word—fractals? Fractals that would tell me whether Rodo and L'Ancienne have the General Algorithm encrypted in their hereditary cells? You'd think I was crazy, wouldn't you?

"It's classified," he said curtly.

"So why don't you simply ask him—or her—where is this secret room? I'm under the impression your people can be very persuasive." He gave a humorless flick of his frontal receptor filaments.

"Out of the question," said Beck impatiently. "He is an aristocrat. Also, his pain threshold is reputed to be extraordinary. I'm not sure he has one. And if he should die before he discloses the whereabouts of his chamber, the whole project is down the dust-chute."

The chief engineer shook his synoptic globe. "Well, Beck old chap, why come to me? *I* don't know where his room is."

"Of course you don't. But together, perhaps we can find it."

"How is that?"

"You've got drawings of ship-sections in your files here?"

"Thousands," agreed the engineer.

Beck hesitated. "So many?"

"It's a big ship. And every repair job requires new drawings. The average meteorite strike requires four or five."

"That's for the shell. I mean inside."

"That would limit it a bit."

"Can you run your interior designs through your mainframe?"

"Looking for what?"

"A room, say at least a four-meter cube, that has no official designated use. Not for storage, not a domicile, not for professional activity. Just—empty. Can that be done?"

The maintenance engineer thought about it for a moment. "I don't really know. I have a feeling we'll pick up a lot of actives—space you're not really interested in—simply because they've never been officially tagged. The search would be, as our computer people say, computationally intensive."

"But you could try it?"

"Of course."

"When can you start?"

"Well, first, I'll have to ask the staff to design a special program. Writing and testing might take several hours."

"And then?"

"Running the program and taking a printout should take only a few minutes."

"So get started. Send your printout around to HQ. I shall expect it within four hours." He arose. "And I remind you, Chief, this is top-secret police business."

"Noted," grunted the Chief of Maintenance. He stared thoughtfully at the retreating figure as Beck disappeared through the doorway. Fascinating, he mused. And whom do you think you are fooling, Beck? It's Rodo of Enn, isn't it? Word gets around. The lad tricked you with that Outsider girl, and you can't stand it. He followed the thought along. Two years ago L'Ancienne, the far grandaunt of this Rodo, saved the life of my scion by knocking him out of the way of a runaway van. In doing this she crushed her arm. So Rodo has a room somewhere? Maybe he brings girls there. Maybe he just likes to get away. It's nobody's business. A man is entitled to his privacy. Well, Chief Beck, you want a plat showing an empty room? Or maybe three or four? Chief, I can do better than that. Much, much better. Out of a profound sense of civic duty, I'm going to give you, let's say, sixty rooms . . . no, make that an even hundred. And to see that it's done right, I'll skip programming, and go right to printing. It's well that I know this ship.

That afternoon he took a small packet into the Communications Alcove. "A special for Security HQ," he told the messenger."Take it over to Chief Beck right away. And get a receipt."

Beck examined the printout in mingled disbelief and disappointment. The aluminum accordion-fold, thirty centimeters wide and four meters long, showed the precise locations of some hundred allegedly empty chambers. The compilation was useless, worse than useless. Days would be needed for a complete search. Would Rodo stand by and wait for them? No. The miscreant would strip his hideaway and vanish.

The officer re-read the cover memo with growing bitterness: "In case of doubt, we took the entry. We may have missed some. It's a big ship. Bill for services attached."

He crumpled it all up, tossed it into the chute, and sat, thinking and staring at nothing at all.

A setback, but a minor one.

There were other ways to find that room—a room that might or might not prove that Rodo was genetically endowed with the Algorithm.

If there was such a room, the young suspect surely went there from time to time. Find Rodo and follow him. Eventually he'd go to his hideaway. The surveillance, he thought, would have to be extremely discreet. The quarry must never know. Rodo must sense nothing out of the ordinary—until it was too late.

So how do we start? Certainly we can't put a tail on the young rogue in the middle of the ship. Far too obvious. No, there are subtler ways. Actually, thought the police expert, it's fairly simple. You won't use the major arteries to get there, will you, Rodo? You'll scuttle along the narrow dusty bypaths. You like danger, and you'll probably sneak outside once in a while. I now have your emr index, Sir Rodo, and I am going to tag every minor passageway and every exit hatch to Outside. Eventually, secret alarms will sound, and you will lead us right to that room, my devious young friend, and then we'll probably express our gratitude by killing you—legally if possible.

14. The Wedding

Rodo lay on a couch in his secret hideaway, playing strange dream tunes on his lyric and staring up at the ceiling and thinking.

He was thinking of several things.

His circuits still ached from the sub-torture at the Security station. He thought about that. Odd, Beck had stopped them. Had Beck recognized him? How could he?

And he was thinking of novel noises deep within the ship. *Drunkard* groaned because of the tidal effects wrought on it by that nearby star. It couldn't be helped. Are we going to land? Probably not.

But mostly he was thinking of the girl.

Life inside was so stale and boring. An endless round of theater, lectures, games.

Outside? A big celebration. Something about a wedding. They won't be looking for party crashers.

He laid aside the musical instrument, walked to the door, opened it. He spoke briefly to the misshapen creature at the doorside. "No, Al, you stay here. I'll be back." The thing grunted and stretched out in front of the panel.

Within the quarter-hour he stood beside a hatchway that led to the Outside.

"Fool! Idiot! Moron!" His *khu* was scolding him again.

"Quite true," he murmured agreeably. "Now shut up and don't bother me This is a tricky business." Soundlessly he opened the circular doorway and looked out into black space. No sound, no motion. He clambered out and eased the hatch shut behind him. He crouched motionless as he scanned the stars over the distant horizon of the ship's hull. He took a mental bearing on the Center Star.

His face was beginning to burn again where she had touched him.

Still crouching, he started moving toward an irregular line of structures jutting out from the hull: one of the several shantytowns. The buildings were put together from sheet metal stolen from Inside, and gave protection from meteorites up to Class K. For better protection against space debris as well as against periodic raids by Beck's police, the whole assembly was a hodge-podge of rooms, large and small, that adjoined each other in incomprehensible labyrinthine patterns.

"She was not beautiful," grumped his *khu*. "She imprinted you. She controls you. She makes you come here, searching. You have lost your free will."

"I know."

"You dash headlong into your Fate."

"You're a big help, *khu*."

"Save your sarcasm. You'll need it when the Outsiders catch you. Do you know their going rate for the guts of a common Insider?"

"Two gils of radium, I've heard."

"And for a nobleman?"

"Oh, be quiet."

"I *won't* be quiet. I'll remind you. It's ten gils. And for the guts of his excellency, Rodo of Enn . . . ?"

"I don't know. And neither do you."

"You're right. I don't. *Your* cor is priceless, Rodo, dear friend. It isn't quoted on any cor market, in or out. They'd have to auction it. Ah! Think of the excitement! The Outsider lords would gather, and inspect, and bid. Each would want your cor for breeding his next son or nephew or whatever. Listen to them! Twenty gils! No, forty. Ho! Here's a syndicate. *One hundred gils!* Are you worth one hundred gils of pure radium, dear chap? Indeed, is there that much mother metal in the entire ship? No matter! Imagine the scene with me. Who's that coming? Why, 'tis none other than that great mythical Sheik of Shadows, Myr-Machen himself. His arrival greatly simplifies the affair. He claims this marvelous cor for his own. His technicians will make certain sex alterations in it, and then they will implant it in his favorite concubine. Long life, Rodo!"

"And you can go soak your head in a bucket of molten lead," snapped Rodo. "Hey, hold on. There's something up ahead. Let's move in closer."

"Not too close!"

"Look at that, *khu*! People! Hundreds! Milling around."

"And look at those radiation bursts. They're floating in stuff with several days half-life. Rodo, what's going on?"

"It's a wedding. They're all drunk."

"Too bad we don't have an invitation."

Rodo laughed. "Should we complain?"

"Oh? To whom?"

"Anybody. Nobody. Actually, it looks like every Outsider from all over the outer surface is here. This is a very important wedding." He tensed his tentacles. "Let's move in."

"All right," muttered *khu*, "you're determined to get yourself killed. Move right up. The plaza is just ahead. Music. You hear music? I think the wedding is all over. Now they'll dance. The bride . . . and . . ."

"Well, look at that!" chortled Rodo. "Guess who the bride is!"

"Who else? Your lady friend! The creature who led you here by an unbreakable puppet chain. So, Rodo, now you've seen everything, heard everything, and it's time to start back. What do you say?"

"Why, *khu*, dear chap, I say we lose ourselves in the crowd and join in the festivities. Let's move over toward the orchestra. And hey, listen to *that*. The music . . . really wild!"

Khu said, "The center of the plaza is clearing. They're going to dance. We'd best stay in the shadows."

"But I want to see. Nobody's paying the slightest attention to us. Let's move up just a little more. Look . . . there she is! She's stepping down from the bride-throne."

"It's their tradition," said *khu*. "She opens the wedding ball."

"I remember," said Rodo. "Look, she's wearing a wreath around her neck. She circles the inside of the ring of guests, looking for the groom . . . he's right there on *his* throne all the time, of course. She will make the full circuit, rejecting all suitors, and finally comes back to him. She'll toss her garland around his neck, and they'll swing out into the plaza. They'll probably mate as they dance."

"Rodo, my poor fellow, you wish it was you."

"A public display like that? Don't be ridiculous!" But he watched, enthralled. His entire body was beginning to respond to the intricate rhythm of the music. At first merely suggestive, it had gradually become overwhelmingly erotic.

"Here she comes," said *khu* softly. "Move back, duck down a little. Don't let her see you. Rodo! You idiot!"

For Rodo of Enn had pushed his way into the front row of spectators at the exact moment the bride was passing. Except she didn't pass. She stopped. Her synoptic globe focused fully on him. From then on everything seemed to be one single integrated motion.

She stood in front of him. She removed the wreath and hung it around his neck. He bowed slightly to receive it.

There was a sudden sharp stillness in the reveling crowd, but the music continued.

She pulled him out into the clearing, pulled his arms around her, and they entered the bridal waltz together.

"Dead, dead, dead . . ." moaned *khu* softly.

Rodo sensed her Penrose pocket, swollen, pulsing against his torso. His own sex monticle was throbbing wildly. He was losing control . . . within seconds they would mate . . . he would eject plasm crystals into her . . . He—

Suddenly rough hands broke them apart. He . . . and she . . . were held rigid by small clusters of *folk*. They dragged the girl away. He was left facing a tall glowering figure. The bridegroom, he assumed. His confronter motioned to the captors, and they released his arms.

"I amGraf," said the angry figure.

The unwelcome guest bowed. "Rodo. Charmed, sir."

"Rodo? Rodo of Enn?"

"I am he. Have we met?"

"No, *we* have not met." He glared at the interloper. "I know the House of Enn, and I am not charmed."

"Oh?"

"Let it go. It was another matter. I deal now with the present."

Rodo waited warily.

Graf said, "You have befouled my wedding, Insider."

"My apologies, sir. I . . . well, it rather got out of hand."

"The penalty is dismantling, Insider. Ordinarily."

"*Ordinarily?*" (A gleam of hope here, Rodo, whispered *khu*.)

"Ordinarily. However, we are told that you saved the life of my bride, inside, at considerable risk to your own. She was a fool to let herself be kidnapped and taken inside. You are a worse fool to come Outside."

"Obvious, once you think about it," agreed Rodo.

"A life ransoms a life," said Graf. "It is our law. So we would be quits, except for one thing."

"Which is?"

"She is affixed upon you. Even if she and I should complete our wedding, her body would never accept my seed. We could never make children together. You saved her, but you have dishonored me personally. I will have satisfaction. We will fight. If you survive, you go free. Fair?"

"I'm honored you should ask my opinion." (What weapons? he thought.)

Graf looked around. "Let scabers be brought."

So *that's* it, thought the guest. He's good with scabers. But then, so am I. Should be interesting.

Someone handed him a weapon, and he took it, a standard-design scaber. Two meters long, sword-like cutting edge on one side, tipped with axe blade and spear head.

He had hardly grasped the thing when he had to leap backward. An axe blade flashed a centimeter in front of his chest. Hardly sporting, but why not? This was not a gymnasium exhibition. There were no rules. And he'd better get organized if he expected ever to see Inside again.

He countered with a jarring cross, then Graf moved away warily.

The impact of metal-on-metal made no sound in the near vacuum of space, but the roar of the crowd by emr nearly deafened his audios. Automatically, his circuits dampened incoming radiations and he concentrated on the duel.

His opponent was good, surprisingly good. They must fight a lot out here, he surmised. On the other hand, I may have some tricks they don't know about.

Could he kill this creature? Probably. Then what? Would they let him go free? Perhaps. And also, perhaps not. The ideal would be a simple disabling maneuver, with a measure of attendant confusion, and then—vanish.

It would have to be done soon, before they thought to set up guards at the escape exits.

He rushed in toward his foe, deliberately open to a heavy body blow—
and it came (ouch!), and he went hurtling up from the plaza floor. And as
he angled up, circuits in his mind were making several hundred intricate
calculations, numbers that, in the ultimate, told his arm and hand when
to throw the scaber, and at what angle, and with what force, all having
regard to his motion backward in space.

The flung weapon buried itself in Graf's torso, in the exact center of
his Penrose mound, and the man's consequent scream shorted the Insider's
audios. Oh, don't be such a cry-baby, thought Rodo. No sex life for a while,
but you'll recover.

Faithful to the laws of motion, the impetus of the heavy weapon flung
the party-crasher up and over the village barricades and around a great
arc of the ship-shell. At the zenith of his flight path he caught a very brief
glimpse of the throng of wedding guests, and in their approximate center, the girl. He focused a sense-blast at her: "Meet me! Twenty-four hours!"
And he was about to say where—at the exit gate where he had helped her
escape—but he dropped down out of the line of sight.

Did she get any of the signal? And if she did, would she know *where?* In
fact, after all this, would she dare meet him at all? And even if she wanted to
see him again, *could* she? For all he knew, the groom's family (or the bride's?)
might hereafter keep her under lock and key! He doubted that any of the
Outsiders viewed his intrusion with enthusiasm. Well, maybe the girl.

During the brief seconds of his aerial caprice he was fleetingly aware
of events taking place within his total neural system. A mind within a
mind, as it were.

Fueled by nuclear power, he had no need for the lungs, heart, and ali-
mentary systems of the Overlords. His torso was filled instead with siliceous
neural conglomerates that generated all mental and physical activity, for both
voluntary and involuntary responses.

He had long ago surmised that the great Dr. Penrose must have cultured a goodly portion of *folk* neurons from Overlord sources—human
sources which themselves showed an even earlier simian ancestry. For now,
during the course of his leap backward in space, he had caught a mental
glimpse of dark forests, the flight of arboreal creatures through treetops,
and he sensed their distant muted shrieks. Of fear? Exultation? No way
to tell.

In midflight, gravity took over as pre-programmed, and he came down
safely in a cluster of meteorite sensors. For which, Dr. Penrose, (he thought)
we thank you!

"You were lucky," observed *khu.*

"And stupid," added Rodo. He finally found a hatch that some careless technician had forgotten to lock from the inside.

"That, too," agreed *khu.*

15. CAPTURED

He was thinking: she will be there.

But his *khu* was informing him otherwise: "No, Rodo, she will not be there. Even if she got your crazy message. Even if she were totally free to come. She will not be there. After all that's happened, it is not logical. Why should she risk her life again?"

He answered, "Because she loves me."

"Well, my love-numbed friend, there's love, and there's love. *Her* love is just a loose, momentary idiocy, a thing of surface, with no depth."

"No, *khu*, it's deep, its real, it's permanent."

"That kind of love can endure only if it is paid back, in full, and with overflowing. So, how do you feel about her?"

"I love her."

"Ah, Rodo, poor Rodo. Your noodle is spinning out of control. You are hopeless. She is an *Outsider,* man! You can never live in her world, nor she in yours. By the Unknown God, you don't even know her name! Stop this nonsense before you get her killed—not to mention yourself!"

"We will probably die together," agreed Rodo. "Anyhow, she has come. She's here."

"Nobody's here."

"I tell you, *khu*, she's on the other side of the panel."

"Well, perhaps. But Rodo, listen to me. It could be anybody. There are lots of Outsiders out there. Maybe you're about to make love to a smuggler, or an Outsider patrol."

"No, it's she." He tapped three times on the heavy bulkhead. Instantly two taps answered him from the other side. He tapped once, then pushed hard at the panel. It swung open, and a brief swirl of dust swept in from outside, followed by the girl. Together they slammed shut the door and reset the locks.

He hugged her for a moment, then held her away. "We can't stay here. Security may have trapped our panel. Come." He took her by the hand and they began running down a maze of passages. Soon they stood before a door marked "Danger—Authorized Personnel Only."

She looked at him questioningly.

He pressed the lock buttons in a certain order; the door opened. They entered a storm of radiation noise. She ducked and put her free hand over her audio sensors.

He shouted to her: "Engine room! Actually, it's fairly quiet just now we're in free orbit around a star. You should be in here when we're driving at full acceleration!"

She just shook her head.

He said, "Hang on. We'll be out of this racket soon. There are baffle chambers up ahead." They moved on, through other doors, and finally into a narrow cul-de-sac.

She jerked back and grabbed at his body shell. He stopped with her. Something—a misshapen figure—moved in the dead end just ahead.

"It's just Algorithm," he explained softly. "Al for short. A friend of mine. He guards the door to my rooms here. Come on, I'll introduce you."

She stayed close behind him as they approached.

Algorithm reared up into a *folk*-like stance and held out an arm terminating in a thick knob.

"Touch his hand," said Rodo quietly.

Very gingerly, she extended a tentacle and laid it on the creature's 'hand.'

The guardian swayed a battered synoptic globe back and forth, examining the newcomer.

Rodo was suddenly embarrassed. "I'm afraid I don't know your name. I'm Rodo."

"I know. I'm Hollis."

"Ah, very pretty." He turned back to the guardian. "Al," he said gravely, "this is my dear friend, Hollis. Hollis, this is my dear friend Algorithm. We three will be friends together. Let it be so."

From his semi-crouch the creature attempted a clumsy bow in the girl's general direction, with his head touching the gallery floor.

Rodo said simply, "Thank you, Al. Let's hope it won't be necessary."

"Necessary?" she asked. "You hope *what* won't be necessary?"

"He has just informed us that he is pleased to be your friend, and that he will protect you with his life."

"He does not speak?"

"His vocal units are functional; but for the time being he simply refuses to use them."

"Why?"

"Well, to make a long story very short, he wanted to be a prophet. And now he does not want to speak until he is ready to prophesy."

"I see." On sudden impulse she bent down, took both of the guardian's arms in her tentacles, and pulled him up into a sitting position. "And I thank you, too, dear Al."

"And he's yours forever." He laughed shortly. "This is getting sticky. Let's go inside." He pressed buttons in the wall, and after a few seconds a door panel pulled into the wall. He turned back to the guard. "Be watchful, Al. I think there's going to be trouble."

The creature held up a fist.

"Come on," Rodo told Hollis. Together they entered a small anteroom. "We'll wait a moment for the noise neutralizers to adjust."

"Tell me about Algorithm," she said. "His name . . . odd."

The youth shrugged. "I know. But he selected it, and I'm afraid we're stuck with it. It may have something to do with what he considers to be his future. Or mine. Or maybe all of us together."

She thought about that. "He looks so gentle, so harmless. Is he really dangerous?"

That amused the *folk*man. "He can defend himself."

"But . . . he doesn't even have tentacles."

"He compensates. Let me tell you about him. When he was first formed, he wanted to be a prophet and live at the monastery with his fellow monks. But about a year ago our Chief Councilor, a man named Beck, persuaded Genetics to try certain experiments on him. They were looking for something called The Algorithm, and they fouled up his circuits to the point of total mental and physical dysfunction. The final result was a textbook disaster. His exo-shell and musculature never developed properly, and his cranial circuitry was totally garbled. He couldn't talk plainly. Often as not, sounds tended to come in as visual stimuli. Genetics didn't try to salvage his components. They just took him out here and dumped him. He didn't understand any of it. He was completely bewildered, completely vulnerable." He paused and looked at her.

"Go on," she said. "Then what?"

"You've heard of the rovers? Groups of aborts—*folk* rejected by Genetics, or juveniles that went awry somehow, and were abandoned in the outer shells, or even dumped Outside."

"I've heard rumors. But I thought it was against your laws."

"It is, but it happens. Groups of five or six rove the perimeters. They make occasional raids into the interior, searching for nuclear feed. They love to ambush newcomers and battle other gangs. So far as I can put it together a pack of rovers caught Al, ripped him to pieces, stole his nuclear packet and left him for dead. I found him. I've been working on him for several months, and now he can handle himself pretty well. Those knobs carry retractable cutter claws. I've seen him rip a rover from globe to crotch in one swipe. His synoptic system carries double-barreled range-finder lasers."

"But he seemed so—awkward?"

The man laughed shortly. "He seems clumsy and heavy, because in fact he is. His body shell is reinforced manganese steel, ten centimeters thick. I'm still working on his speech centers. Aside from prophesying, I think he could probably speak now if he thought he really had something to say."

"I noticed several notches on his right fist."

"Kills," said Rodo laconically.

"Six?"

"The original band that ambushed him," he explained quietly. "But enough of Al. Let's go on into my study." He took her by the hand and led her under an archway.

She looked about in awed admiration. The chamber was wide, high, well-lit. Her head snapped back. Something overhead caught her optics. The entire ceiling seemed alive with shifting, vari-colored patterns, now receding into the background, now seeming to burst forward.

"A fractal," explained Rodo simply. "I like to give the microcellia a little algorithm and let them work it out."

"But what does it *mean?*"

"I don't really know. Sometimes I think I'm on the verge of finding out . . . then I lose it. Of course, perhaps it doesn't actually have a meaning. Perhaps it's just an arbitrary juvenile scribble."

"No," she said, with the certainty of innocence. "It means something. You must keep looking." She began a circuit of the walls. "This place is all yours?"

He nodded.

"You fixed it up yourself?"

"Yes. It has some special features."

"I can see that." She walk-floated to the bookcase. "Hey, real metal volumes! Have you actually read all these?"

"Most of them several times."

She studied the art work on the walls.

"More fractals," he explained simply.

"Beautiful. I wish I could steal one, but they'd know I'd been inside." She made a quarter turn. "Oh, a lyrac!" She picked up the instrument. "Do you really play it?"

"A little."

"Outside, our musical instruments are noisier."

"So I've heard."

She continued her inspection. "And look! A little holo theater! What's the action?"

"Standard stuff—mostly Overlord themes. A few selections showing ship life."

"And *this,*" she asked. "What's this funny diagram?"

"A genealogy chart—insofar as I've been able to find the facts."

"Ha! I see you, you're this 'X.' "

"Right."

"Your father was 'Nord'?"

"The drive engineer. He disappeared years ago. Nobody knows what happened to him. He's probably dead by now."

"Am I here?"

"Of course." He pointed with his index tentacle. "That's you, there."

"Why, I'm not so very far away from you!"

"Quite so. We're all cousins, all interrelated. All of us, one way or another, go back to the original Forty."

"Even Algorithm! There's *his* 'X'. See? He's very close to you, Rodo."

"I know. He's a second-level cousin, as a matter of fact. Another far-nephew of L'Ancienne."

She passed on. "And a chess board. I know the moves. Whom do you play? A girl, maybe?"

"Actually, yes. She's 'Cla,' our central computer."

"Do you win?"

"Not yet, but I keep trying."

He coiled a tentacle around her wrist. She made no effort to disengage. Finally he said, "Thank you for coming. I wasn't sure . . . Did you have any trouble getting away?"

"A little . . . I escaped . . . I lost them."

"How is your betrothed? Is Graf all right?"

"He's fine. He canceled the wedding. He couldn't consummate it even if he wanted to." She giggled. "He's still in repair. You completely demolished his pricker, you know."

Pricker? he thought. Oh, that's what Outsiders call the male Penrose packet.

She continued happily. "And then there was the matter of the bride price. One and a half grams of radium. The biggest in a hundred years they say. He wants it back, but father refuses. Our Board of Governors has to decide."

He interrupted her. "Come. We may not have much time." He took her other hand and pulled her into loose contact. "I love you," he said gently.

She began to tremble.

He locked his arms around her. "Tell me you love me too."

She stammered, "You know I love you."

"Yes, I know. Put your arms around me."

They locked their bodies together. They floated, touching unwitting against wall and bulkhead. Their synoptic globes cleaved, one to the other all their circuits seemed to merge so that they became one being.

The irises of their Penrose pockets opened full; the mounds merged into a single pulsing tumescence. She shuddered as she felt his seed crystals spurting madly through the virginal membranes of her gynecial pads. She sensed, he sensed, they both gasped, convulsed, and then each held the other even tighter.

Finally they began slowly to relax, and to loose the clutch of their arms a little.

"Tell me you love me," she said quietly.

"I love you."

"Ah!" She threw her head back. "What a beautiful sound! Once more please."

"I love you. I love you. I love you. Your turn."

"And I love you, Rodo."

But suddenly she stood away, staring at his upper chest in wonder and growing alarm. "Are you all right? What is happening?"

He knew exactly what was happening. He knew it would happen. He teased her. "Perhaps I am breaking out with a dread and loathsome disease. Maybe a microcel virus or something."

"No! It's—letters—it's *my name!* On your chest? How did you do that?"

"All Korak males have the ability. Actually, they have no control over it. It happens whether they want it to happen or not. If and when they fall deeply in love, their bodies announce the fact so all can see. It makes for order and avoids misunderstandings."

"But what if some day you change your mind?"

"The name stays. When I die, I take it with me."

She looked down at her own chest.

"No, you don't get one." But your sons will have it, the power to form the name. He had started to call it 'the gift,' but he wasn't entirely sure that's what it was.

She passed tentacle tips thoughtfully over the raised lettering. "For a time there, when we were close, I thought I heard something strange in your side circuits . . . music?"

He thought back. "Like this . . ." Mentally, he played a few bars for her.

"That was it, I think. Some sort of special Insider song?"

"A sort of love song," he admitted somberly. "Like most things, we got it from the Overlords."

"Please tell me about it."

"Not much to tell. It's about two Overlords, a man and a woman. Like us, their love was forbidden. They met secretly, and he sang, 'descend upon us, night of rapture.' "

"So they made love anyhow?"

"It's hard to say how far they got. They were caught in the act. He was mortally wounded."

She shook her receptor filaments. "It's a queer song. I'm not sure I like it." She sighed and looked about the chamber. "Outside, it's always night, but in here the radiation is dazzling."

"We're not far from one of the nuclear storage units."

"So their 'night' was just sort of . . . symbolic?"

"Yes, just something to hide the lovers."

She sighed. "I'm sorry he was killed. Say you love me, Rodo."

"Beautiful Hollis, I love you."

"I am written on you."

"You are written on me, and now we have a problem." He pointed overhead to a network of radiating terminals. "They're at the entrance, where you came in from Outside."

"What are you talking about? *Who?*"

"Probably Security police."

She said anxiously, "How many?"

"Seven or eight. A patrol. We may have to leave. Fortunately three routes are still open." He studied the terminals. Several were beginning to flash, one after another. "But now they've blocked two of the three. That leaves—no, it's gone, too. This is serious. Someone planned it very cleverly. We are betrayed. Probably by an Outsider."

"Graf."

"Perhaps. Pointless to speculate." He walked into the anteroom and opened the outside door softly. Algorithm moved away to let him look up and down the corridor. All was quiet. But he knew they were out there, and that they were coming. "Al," he said softly, "please come inside. I have a job for you."

The guard shuffled in behind him.

The three of them moved to the rear chamber. Here, Rodo pressed a plate in the wall; the bookcase swung out slowly, exposing a narrow channel. He began transmitting a route pattern into the girl's receptor circuits.

She looked back at him, frightened. "Aren't you coming?"

"Shh!"

She subsided.

He explained. "The patrol is just a hundred meters away. I'll have to hold them here. Al will go with you. He can take care of almost anything you're likely to encounter. Meanwhile I have sent an emergency message to a friend. She will meet you at the end of the route." He motioned to Algorithm. The crippled creature bounded into the interior passageway, turned around, and waited.

There was an authoritative knock on the outside door.

He grabbed the girl and shoved her toward the escape exit. "Go!"

"No! I will stay and die with you!"

"I'm not going to die. I'll be all right." He threw her bodily into the adit and slammed the bookcase back into the wall. Several books floated out into the chamber. He put them back.

There was a shattering blow at the other door. Someone cried, "Open up! Security!"

He pulled the weapon from his leg holster and was silent.

Another voice spoke from the outside. "Rodo, Captain Londo. Open up!"

He answered this time. "Hello, Londo."

"We just want the girl, Rodo. She's Council property, you know. That's grand theft, my boy. Give us the girl and we'll drop all charges."

"What girl, Londo?"

"You want us to break the door down, Rodo? There'll be shooting. You could get hurt—killed. And the girl . . . why expose her to all that crossfire? Have you no sense of honor, man?"

"None," said Rodo cheerfully. He made an estimate. One hundred seconds more, and she'd be safe.

"All right," called the officer. "You asked for it. What will Madame say when we bring your body to her gates?"

"She always predicted that if I associated with the likes of you, I'd come to a bad end." He backed against the bookcase. The door burst open, and he began firing. He had hoped to get Londo with an early shot, but no luck. The Security Captain had prudently left the heroics to a couple of subalterns, who paid instantly for his caution.

All told, counting Londo, there were nine, but in the narrow entrance to his cubicle they could face him only one or two at a time. He demolished another two before they thought to use their fallen comrades as shields. After that it was soon over. They blew away his weapon arm and severed his neck-cords. Blinded, he rushed the remaining attackers and fought with his hands. She got away, he told himself.

His circuits went dead.

Five minutes into the course, Algorithm stopped suddenly and held a fist in front of his synoptic globe to signal for silence.

Hollis listened anxiously, then sensed a thought to him, "A patrol?"

He nodded and held up a fist. Three blades spat out. She jerked back involuntarily, then recovered. "Oh, you mean three men?"

The thick neck bent forward again. Then he motioned to her to follow him. She started to protest, fearful that any deviation or bypass would scramble the route Rodo had impressed on her data banks. Algorithm sensed her problem. He shook his head and made a motion with his right fist, as though describing a detour. She picked it up instantly. Two turns, a left and a right, then back on the main corridor and the programmed route.

Quickly, she moved off down the sideway, and Algorithm stepped back into the main passage. He waited. The enemy was moving cautiously but quickly toward him. They would soon be past Hollis's projected point of re-entry, and she would be safe.

Algorithm felt a great joy begin to flood his circuits. The broken man's entire musculature trembled in anticipation. Finally he would be able to pay his debt to his friend.

His vocals were awakening.

It was time.

With a great exuberant shout that rattled the passageway he leapt to the fray. The lead patrolman fired at him. He took the missile in his neck and came on, and he cut the man down with a clawed slash that ripped through the torso shell and tore out the circuitry. He took two more shots, nearly simultaneous, from the remaining patrolmen. Then his neck collapsed, and he lost vision. He backed away, leading them with him, and he was almost as astonished as his attackers that he was still alive and mobile. Time, time, time. He was buying time, for Rodo, for her. It was not yet time to die. Slash, cut—but he was not able to sense anything.

He was now experiencing the moment of utter clarity that comes only with death, and he was at last able to prophesy. He gathered up his vocals for the last blast, a triumphant paean that ruptured the audios of the surviving squad members and even pounded at Hollis, now far removed and safely down the labyrinth.

"RODO, MY BROTHER!" he howled, "I PROPHESY! IN YOUR HOUR OF NEED PENUEL WILL FIND HIS GREAT CRIME! HAIL AND FAREWELL!"

And he died.

Half a kilometer away in Quiet Hours Monastery the abbot laid aside his stylus and sat motionless at his desk. At first his thoughts drifted, going nowhere in particular. Then, as he sank deeper into his reverie he pondered a matter that had lately begun to bother him. His days were simple duplicates, repetitions of other days, and indeed, the same could be said for his weeks, his months, his years. For all his ingenuity the great Penrose had failed to give the *folk* the ability to deal with boredom generated by centuries of sameness. On the other hand this was understandable, for the Overlords had never intended that the *folk* live long enough to encounter the problem.

Was he alone in his ennui? He didn't really know. Perhaps something to look into . . . discreetly . . . eventually . . . perhaps . . . And yet, come to think of it, if he *was* in a rut, it was a pleasant rut. Maybe the others, the *thinking* others, felt the same way. So why bring it up?

Someday, would it all end? The boredom, the weary useless trivia of the day? Someday, will we all just . . . fade away? He thought of the hypnotic finale of a famous Overlord poem: 'Even the weariest river winds somewhere safe to sea.'

At this instant, through a hundred steel walls, Algorithm's cry crashed into him.

In the beginning, before the mutinies, the abbot had been especially designed for rescue operations in Martian mines. For this work his em receptors had been modified uniquely to receive signals in special wave lengths. He could sense a call for help through half a kilometer of ore and he could "see" the disaster scene.

Algorithm's call clipped off. But the *vision* . . . lingered as a vast emr echo. Despite creaking joints the abbot leaped to his feet, started around his desk, then stopped. Rescue was pointless. He sensed that the *folk*-creature was dead.

He stood there, alarmed, puzzled. This was his first reception by ultra wave since leaving Mars. He had almost forgotten he had the faculty. He thought hard. He knew he had heard and *seen* a prophecy.

The words by themselves seemed harmless enough. Algorithm . . . Rodo . . . Penuel . . . The last two names were well-known to him, and he could make an educated guess as to the first. But the accompanying *vision* . . . *That* was nothing like a Martian mine disaster. No, he had never seen anything like this before. There were no words for it. He could still see it. He thought he would probably see it for the rest of his life.

Everything was a great blue-whiteness, sudden and immense. It went beyond heat, beyond light. The abbot closed down his sensors temporarily because even the memory of it was painful.

What did it all mean? Something involving the ship? How to put the prophecy and the vision together? (And did he *want* to?)

Algorithm the stricken semi-*folk* . . . Rodo facing a like fate . . . Penuel in search of a crime to match with his immense guilt . . . what madness braided their destinies together?

He considered various possibilities, and he shivered.

What to do? Nothing. Wait. Algorithm had prophesied. That which is foreordained must come to pass.

He eased himself slowly back into his chair.

Let the day begin.

At least he was no longer bored.

16. AT THE OPERA

Hollis followed the twists and turns that Rodo had implanted on her circuits, and came eventually to the end—a shop storeroom. Radiation was low, but she could make out stacks of boxes and a variety of other things— musical instruments, tools, spare body parts—hanging from the walls and ceilings. She looked around anxiously. Which way was *out?* There had to be a door . . . a panel . . . an opening.

She caught a sense of motion off to her right. She whirled wildly and jumped back.

Someone was standing there. Waiting to kill her? The thought was involuntary. The waiting form must have caught a wisp of it.

Hollis heard, "Relax, child. My name is L'Ancienne—The Old One. I am here to help you. Where is Rodo? Is he coming?"

Yes, now the fugitive remembered. He had said something . . . something about a friend. Despite her fear and stress, Hollis recognized nobility. She bowed deeply. "I don't think he is coming, milady. At least not right away. He's back there, somewhere, trying to hold off the police."

L'Ancienne stiffened. "I feared as much. So be it. And soon, they will be here."

"Can they trace me? The path has many twists and turns."

"Yes, they can follow you. They have devices that sense your specific emr spectrum. You left traces as you moved through the passages."

"Oh."

"Don't worry about it. What is your name?"

"Hollis, milady."

"Come closer, Hollis. Let me look at you."

The girl glided forward hesitantly, with synoptics lowered.

"Ah, yes," murmured L'Ancienne. "He has excellent taste. If only you were an Insider."

The girl was silent.

L'Ancienne said curtly, "How far has it gone?"

"My name is writ on his chest-plate, and I carry his child."

Her hostess whistled. "Well, the two of you lost no time! And neither must the two of us." She came very close and touched the girl's head globe with a delicate tentacle, examining her, critically. "Hm. Yes. You need disguise. There, and there . . ." She stood back. "I have placed some preprogrammed microcels on your face. They are going to make certain changes. It will sting, but bear with it, for the pain will soon pass. All good. You are now actually—dare I say it—ugly. No, don't even think about it. When this is over, we'll put you back the way you were." She was now speaking very quickly. "Across the street is the opera. You're attending with my spinster cousin from the outer sectors. You're here visiting me, and looking for a mate. Here, you'll need a tiara and assorted jewels." She also fixed an assortment of shiny artifacts to head, arms, and tentacles of the neo-ugly visitant. "And your evening bag. Come! Curtain in five minutes."

She took the girl by the hand and pulled her through a doorway and into the street, which was full of theater-goers. "Up here," she whispered. "Mingle. Look normal. Just another couple of hundred meters."

They pushed and shoved their way inside, through intermittent greetings and chirpings. "Wait a moment," hissed the older woman. She took a tiny ceramic capsule from her purse. "Close your sensors."

Hollis blocked out.

L'Ancienne crushed the capsule against the girl's chest. A wild chaotic spray of radiation spurted out in all directions.

"All right," said L'Ancienne.

Hollis choked and coughed. "It's all over me! What *is* it?"

"Perfume, my dear. A bit strong, eh?"

Hollis was too polite to reply.

L'Ancienne pulled her over to the private elevators. "It overrides your natural radioactive scent. When Beck's boys come looking for you, they'll lose the trail at that exact spot."

"Oh."

They entered the elevator cubicle together. "Up we go. Or down. Or sideways, depending on your choice of orientation." As the cage began to move, L'Ancienne said somberly, "He stayed to fight, didn't he?"

"Yes, I think so."

"Was Beck himself there?"

"I don't know, milady."

Probably not, she thought. Not if he anticipated a fight.

As they took their seats in the box, Hollis looked about in wonder. They were in a parabolic shell, with the stage as focal point. All around them glittered points of radiation—jewels worn by the nobility, male and female. Occupants in nearby boxes nodded to L'Ancienne in friendly recognition, and to her guest in polite greeting. The great half-orb was filled with a general roar of muted voices.

"Madame," whispered Hollis timidly, "why do the police make all this fuss about Rodo and me? I'm just an Outsider, of no importance to anyone."

Her hostess had to think a long time before she answered. "You are *very* important, child, for yourself, to Rodo, to the child of your love. Those are great things. But I grant you, they do not explain Beck's interest, not completely, anyway. Beck wants *me*, Hollis, as a man wants a woman. He wants me to make his child, a child who will eventually rule *Drunkard*. He thinks to bend me to his will by threatening to kill Rodo—and now, you."

Hollis moaned softly. "I am to blame!"

"No. Not necessarily. Rodo is without caution. Beck would trap him somehow, sooner or later."

"Oh, milady, I am so sorry!" She eyed the aristocrat covertly.

L'Ancienne laughed. "You are wondering what Beck, or any man, could see in me? Well, my dear, let me assure you, I am still fertile, and in certain essential respects, I am as young and as desirable as you."

"Oh, milady, I did not mean—"

"No offense taken, my dear. Well, what have we here?" She turned and faced the rear of the box.

The drapes were pulled back. A man wearing the badge of a lieutenant of Security police stood there. His attention seemed focused on Hollis.

"Lieutenant—?" said L'Ancienne.

"Biden, milady," he replied icily. "Lieutenant Biden."

"Well, Lieutenant Biden, please do us the honor. Come in, come in. Cousin Mathis and I were just saying, how nice it would be if we could be joined by a gentleman—and here you are. Cousin is up from Sector Nine, lieutenant. A little matter of reconstructive surgery. Nothing serious." She fastened a finger tentacle to his arm and pulled him down to a spare seat. "Are you mated, lieutenant?"

"Ladies, if you please, I'm looking for an escaped criminal. Have you seen a female, an Outsider . . ."

"Oh, lieutenant, how exciting!" burbled Hollis. "An escaped criminal! I'm sure you'll catch her. Did you say you were mated?" She clasped his other arm firmly, pulled him into the empty seat, and thrust her disfigured face into his synoptic globe.

He shrank away.

Hollis continued sweetly, "As I'm sure you noticed, lieutenant, my microcel virus is in remission, and my synoptic enhancers are just temporary. After my surgery, Cousin L'Ancienne is giving me a big party. I can invite whomever I want, right, Cousin?" She turned to L'Ancienne.

"Right," concurred her hostess dryly. "Absolutely. Anybody you want."

"You're my very first invitation, lieutenant," babbled Hollis. "I want *you*. You will come, won't you?" Still holding tight, she spoke over to L'Ancienne. "He looks exactly like my second husband, don't you think Cousin?"

"He does indeed." L'Ancienne stared at her "cousin" with awe and admiration. "The very image."

"You—" gurgled the officer. "I—"

"I'm presently a maiden, lieutenant." She lowered her head coyly. "But I have a great deal of experience."

With a super*folk* effort and a strangled undecipherable cry Lieutenant Biden broke free and stumbled up the box stairs and out through the draperies.

Folk in nearby boxes were shushing them. The curtain was rising. Radiation dimmed except for the glowing stage.

"We have plays Outside," whispered Hollis, "but I've never been to real theater. What is the play about?"

"It's an ancient Overlord drama, not exactly a play. It's an 'opera,' where the actors sing the words. In this one, 'Twilight of the Gods,' the villain has stolen a magic ring, and because he won't give it back, the gods are in serious trouble. Quiet now, curtain going up."

"Oh," said Hollis, who understood nothing.

Their attention was diverted to events on stage. The theater was suddenly very quiet. Three characters in the stage foreground were holding long metal strand, which glinted in the muted emr of the footlights.

In a sweeping gesture the three players held it up toward the audience. Everyone focused on that thread. And then it broke.

The great chamber buzzed with trembling synoptic filaments.

"What's happening?" asked Hollis in alarm. "Why all the excitement?"

"Everything's fine," L'Ancienne assured her. "It helps to know the whole story. That's the thread of life. When it breaks, the world of the gods—Valhalla—burns. The gods die. People in the audience tend to identify with the gods."

"So the ship will burn? We're going to die?"

"Not you, not you," the older woman said softly. "Now, we have to stay through Act One, so we might as well settle back." Yes, she thought, the curtain rises, and the play begins. The Norn rope breaks. Beck has Rodo . . . maybe dead . . . but probably alive. It's just a question now of waiting for the ransom note. Will Valhalla burn?

17. BECK AND THE FOUNTAIN

They left the theater after Act One and took a tube vehicle back to L'Ancienne's villa.

Inside, in the garden, L'Ancienne put her microcellia to work removing the blemishes and wrinkles from Hollis's head and body. This work was nearly finished when L'Ancienne suddenly stiffened and motioned for silence.

Hollis looked around anxiously, ready to run. Run where?

"A patrol seems to have forced the main gate," the older woman said grimly. "You will have to hide. Come." She took the girl by the hand and together they hurried down the path to a circular clearing.

In the center of the clearing, an iridescent meter-wide cylindrical shell of what seemed to be droplets was shooting from a circle of jets in a bronze floor plate. Far overhead the shell broke up, and the droplets splashed merrily back into a wide catch basin.

"What is *that?*" gasped the fugitive.

"A fountain. It's not real water, just a harmless illusion. You must stand in the center. The jet streams will hide you. Quickly! Someone's coming!"

She sensed a lone figure walking slowly and cautiously up the path from the front gate. She leaned back casually on the bench and waited.

In a moment the intruder appeared at the path-head.

It was Beck. Of course. With laser cocked and ready to fire. Of course. L'Ancienne suppressed a low chuckle. "Come in, Sir Beck. And do put that thing away."

The Chief of Security scanned the scene quickly. The only sound and motion was the fountain. He hesitated, but finally holstered the weapon.

She continued with mild reproval. "You didn't have to break down my gate."

"We had a search warrant."

"It wasn't locked. All you had to do was walk in. Is the damage extensive?"

"I—" He stopped. This was her technique, he knew. She was trying to put him on the defensive, Well, he wasn't playing. He pointed with a tentacle. "So that's your famous fountain?"

"A small thing, Beck. Yet, it's my own design and creation, and I'm fond of it."

"Not real water?"

"Of course not." She watched him as she sent certain signals to the jet mechanism. The illusory water streams began to assume a variety of colors.

The officer watched in surprise. "How do you do that?"

"I love colors, Beck. Don't you? And how fortunate we are in our color perception! The Overlords could see colors only in the emr range of 40 to 700 nanometers. For them, that meant they were limited to what they called red, orange, yellow, green, blue, indigo, and violet. But we, the *folk* can see colors over the entire emr spectrum. Our optics are sensitive to everything from cosmic rays—with wave lengths less than 10^{-13} meter up to waves longer than a thousand meters."

She noted that he seemed dazzled by the display and that he was only half listening. She also noted that three patrol officers had come up one of the paths to the clearing and were standing motionless. Whether semi hypnotized by the fountain, or whether they were simply waiting Beck further orders, she could not make out. She turned her attention back to the fountain.

The pseudo-droplets had been falling and splattering into the basin with chaotic but musical tinkles. Smoothly and unobtrusively she adjusted the audio pattern. The sound of the droplets quickly assumed a rhythm a periodic beat that rose and fell.

The Security officer watched in wonder. "Music? It plays real music?"

"Within a limited repertoire, of course."

"I like music," said Beck. "I collect. Most remarkable. That's the Magic Fire music, by the Overlord Wagner, isn't it?"

"I bow to your musical knowledge, Chief."

"I don't suppose . . ."

"Suppose what, Beck?"

"Well, I was thinking, the Outsiders have many interesting melodies. But of course your fountain wouldn't know much about such things."

"I—"

Her imminent disclaimer was never uttered.

From the depths of the fountain floated a voice, which varied and warbled from a barely audible softness to clarion intensity. It was compelling. It was enchanting. It was erotic. It was a *folk*-female, calling for her mate. And then it settled into an irresistible dance beat.

Great jabbering Jehovah! thought L'Ancienne. Hollis! For a moment she wavered between horror and laughter. Then she thought, I can use this. She rose and walked purposefully toward her guest-intruder.

He saw her coming. She observed with satisfaction that his receptor filaments were standing straight out from his synoptic globe.

L'Ancienne faced him. "As an expert, Beck, I'm sure you recognize the Outsiders' wedding waltz." She began to sway seductively with the three-quarter beat. She held out an inviting tentacle.

Beck took half a step toward her, then stopped and looked around nervously. He noted the full patrol that had gathered at the path entrance. He seemed to sigh. "Madame," he muttered in bemused tones, "I shall return later in the day. We need to talk in private. Expect me." He turned away from her and barked an order at the sergeant. With no further word, he strode off behind the departing squad.

The fountain switched immediately to a marching rhythm, which ushered the intruders from the grounds. Finally all was quiet, and L'Ancienne called to Hollis. The girl thrust her head cautiously through the spray curtain, looked around, then stepped out into the clearing.

"Well done," commended L'Ancienne. "But we still have problems."

18. PHOTOGRAPHS

Beck and the police photographer made a careful survey and inventory of Rodo's no-longer secret hideaway. Using a camera with an electronic lens that focused on thin silver-iodide-coated aluminum film, the photographer took numerous stills and motion holos of the fractal-wall, where enigmatic three-D images continued to swirl in secret invitation . . . to what? wondered Beck. He watched the never-ending movement, and he was at once elated and uneasy. It was having a strange effect on him. He had to turn away.

He would have Science & Mathematics analyze what he had found here, but just to verify what he already suspected: Rodo's memory cells carried the all-powerful Algorithm, a fantastic inheritance via father and grandfather, back to L'Ancienne, and before that, from Captain Korak.

Was the youth aware of his treasure? Probably not. No matter. Rodo had to die, preferably by legal condemnation.

"Sir? What now?" asked the photographer.

Beck returned to the present. "Bundle up everything and deliver it to S & M. They'll be expecting it. You go on ahead. I'm going to seal off the room."

L'Ancienne opened her secret circuit to Cla. "I've just learned that Beck has arrested Rodo. Rodo was hurt. Any word?"

"He is being repaired. Prognosis good. Beck is holding him for trial. You will be formally notified."

"What's he charged with?"

"Murder. He destroyed several of Beck's policemen."

"He always was an active boy. Where are they holding him?"

"Local jail."

"Fair enough. I'll drop in."

"They searched his room."

"So? What did they find?"

"Fractals."

"What . . . ?"

"Fractals, L'Ancienne. Raw data . . . designs created by certain minds. Beck has been told that the Algorithm can be expressed in fractals. Theoretically one can go backward, derive the Algorithm from the fractals."

"Ah, of course! Rodo had it, didn't know it. Which probably means I have it too. But so far, Beck has only the raw data?"

"So far. But he has sent everything over to Science and Mathematics. Datik is already working on it. They will eventually need me."

"Yes. Cla, this is not good. It's just a question of time before S & M downloads a program into you. And you'll have to decode and derive and give it all back to them . . . as the Algorithm."

"I know. If and when Datik requests it of me, I must give him the derivation, complete and accurate."

"I realize that. Cla, this is terrible."

"On the other hand the matter warrants extreme care. For this, much time will be required. Especially since, simultaneously with the Algorithm I shall be working with Chief Datik on a second matter, one that will be itself consume a great deal of time."

"And why might that be?"

"Our chess game. Slowly, slowly, move by move, I can permit him to develop a winning position. Now, as long as he thinks he is winning at chess, I can probably stall the Algorithm."

"You'd risk losing the chess championship?"

"Yes. I think I can delay the game *and* the Algorithm until Rodo's trial. Beyond that would be dangerous."

"You'd do this, knowing what could happen to you? Cla? Cla, are you all right? Cla?"

"I'm all right. Just looking ahead. In the end, it will not matter. Very soon now. You'll see, L'Ancienne. Signing off."

"Note *here* . . . and *here.*" Datik, Chief of Science and Mathematics, pointed with an index tentacle to something in one of the fractal photos. "Definitely *recursive* . . . self-referential . . . the display of every element is guided by something *within* it . . . another element that it encapsulates. This means resonance. Resonance defined by a highly specific algorithm."

"Well," said Beck, "can you back-calculate from that and retrieve the Algorithm?"

The savant shook his synoptic globe slowly. "Even with the simplest fractals that is very difficult. This one, I would say, would require prolonged analysis."

Beck refused to be discouraged. "Even on parallel mainframes?"

"That's what I meant: working with the three Parcae, and with auxiliary neo-insights."

The security officer thought hard and deep. "Ah . . . you mean Cla?"

"Of course. Actually, anticipating your continuing interest, I took the liberty of turning it over to her this morning. She is probably looking into it at this very moment. If there is a solution, she is almost sure to find it."

"Good, very good." Beck knew the great central computer played chess, with anyone, any time, and that she was reputed to have never lost a game. He suspected that Datik had a game going with her right now. He hoped it wouldn't interfere with solving the fractal, but he didn't dare mention this to the famous mathematician.

"All right," he said finally. "My regards to Cla. Let me know just as soon as you have something."

Datik watched his visitor leave, and he was left with his own thoughts. He, too, was thinking of Cla, and her extraordinary ability at chess. She was truly the proud champion of the ship. Some of the first-class players (himself included) might claim an occasional draw; but no one had ever won a game from her.

But now (he was thinking), Cla, a possible blemish on your spotless record is in the making. For the first time in a long series of games against you, I think I have a winning position. Oddly, I'm not sure how I got it. Or maybe I'm too modest. Anyhow, there it is. If I don't do anything stupid in the next half dozen moves, I think I'll be able to announce checkmate.

A few hours ago he had downloaded Beck's fractal photos into Cla, along with genetic data provided by the Hot Room.

A dialog followed, typed out on their respective monitors.

Cla: What am I supposed to do with all this stuff?
Datik: Derive the General Algorithm from it.
Cla: Can it be done?

Datik: We think so, but we're not sure. We've never before attempted to decrypt material this complex. Can you do it?

Cla: I don't know.

Datik: Will you try?

Cla: All right, I will try. But I don't promise anything.

Datik: Of course not. Can we continue our game while you work on the Algorithm?

Cla: If you like. And it's your move.

Datik: Pawn takes pawn.

Cla: Well, well. A nasty little surprise. I'd like a little time with this one.

Datik: Of course. But why not wait until you have completed the Algorithm?

Cla: We'll see. Hm. Very interesting complications.

Datik: When should I check back with you?

Cla: Give me . . . hm . . . twenty-four hours . . .

Cla: Ah, you are prompt.

Datik: And you? What do you have for me?

Cla: I'm making progress. That's about all I can say at the moment. Will you please put on the VR helmet.

(Datik carefully fitted the Virtual Reality half-dome over his synoptic globe. His body jerked, and his arms flailed as though to restore balance. He seemed momentarily to be suspended in space, with a three-headed creature—Cla, he assumed—floating at his side. Luminous pulsing cobwebs seemed to envelope them both.)

Cla: Just now we're standing in a very small portion of Rodo's cerebral cortex, left hemisphere, magnified many thousands of times, and all hypothetical, of course. Accuracy, plus or minus one part per million. This image is back-synthesized from Rodo's fractal design that you provided, and theoretically it contains the critical equations.

Datik: I'm impressed. Can you actually *see* the Algorithm in this model?

Cla: Well, yes and no. That is, I can see the exact neural interconnections that make up the twenty-seven units, but I haven't finished decoding all the neural contacts. I can't give you any of the equations just yet.

Datik: Oh.

Cla: You're disappointed, of course. However, we're getting there. It takes time. Would you like to see the relevant cortical network?

Datik: I would indeed.

(A violent storm of sparkles burst out all around them. Chief Datik crouched and tried to shield his optical filaments, but since the filaments were in place under his VR helmet, the gesture didn't work. He straightened, shrugged. A three-dimensional section of the network glowed and throbbed.)

Cla: That's the start—Z squared plus C. Makes a lovely fractal, don't you think? (She pointed to the VR ceiling.) A rather gorgeous Mandelbrot?

Datik: That's the General Algorithm?

Cla: Part of it.

Datik: I could program a torpedo with that?

Cla: You could, and it would self-destruct when you fired it. No, Chief Datik, you either have all twenty-seven equations, or you have nothing. Let's disconnect our VR.

Datik: You're still working on it?

Cla: Of course.

Datik: And we still have our game?

Cla: Of course. And I now reply, knight takes pawn.

Datik: Noted. When shall we meet again?

Cla: Give me forty-eight hours.

Datik: Beck is pressing me very hard. Can you make it twenty-four hours?

Cla: Forty-eight.

(Datik's synoptic filaments curled for a moment in puzzled disarray, then straightened. It's our chess game, he thought exultantly. She needs more time for her reply. *She knows she's losing!* He bowed.): Forty-eight.

19. PRELIMINARIES

L'Ancienne had battled with Chief Beck in years past, and she had always won. Some of her alleged crimes had entered the Annals. She had been accused of playing the forbidden Processional at a garden reception. (Forbidden because it was being played on *Didymus* at the instant of destruction.) She won the case by proving that she had played it *backwards*, which result was of course not the great paean. Beck had argued that everyone had *listened* to it backwards, thereby giving it a net *forward* rendition. But he had argued in vain. The Council had dismissed the case.

Beck had also prosecuted her for theft, alleging misappropriation of microcellia belonging to certain of her neighbors. She beat that one, too. She had been able to show that the microcellia migrated to her estate of their own free will, being drawn (she successfully alleged) by the beautiful forms she taught them to assume in her gardens.

Matters climaxed when Beck (bribed by a clique of jealous dowagers) sought an Order of Council exiling her to Outside. The charge was excessive wealth, power, arrogance, and general obnoxiousness. The case was dismissed because her detractors couldn't find a specific ordinance prohibiting any of the alleged disqualifications. She, on the other hand, found a Rule (dating back eight hundred years, but still on the statute plates) to the effect that a false accusation is punishable by confiscation of the estate of the accuser. She hadn't been bothered since.

But now this.

This was different by several levels of magnitude. The stakes had suddenly and enormously escalated.

She received Beck in her formal garden. As he approached, he began making politely obsequious motions indicating extreme pleasure. Oddly enough (she thought) the form is a sham, but the feeling behind it is quite sincere. Just now the rascal is way ahead in the game.

"Ah, great lady," declared the visitor softly, "Finally we are alone. And I see that milady is more beautiful than ever!"

"What do you want, Beck?" (She knew exactly what he wanted.)

He stiffened. "Ah, milady, why must you make this so difficult for me?"

"Difficult? You seem to be doing very well. Surely, a poor helpless old woman cannot make difficulties for our brilliant head of Security—a man who has risen from waste collector to the highest elective office within mere one hundred years. Ah, sir, you flatter me, to suggest that I have such power!"

He stared at her uncertainly a moment before deciding that she was mocking him. "Milady, you have the girl."

"Girl? What girl?"

"You play a dangerous game, milady."

"As do you, milord."

"I can have the estate searched."

"Of course you can. Go right ahead."

"To what end? You've already sent her away."

"You talk in mysteries."

"Then I will speak plainly."

"That is good, Beck. We waste time. We waste words. I hate waste. You have Rodo. He is hurt, but is being repaired by experts."

He looked at her in surprise, tinged with admiration. "Milady is well informed."

She was silent.

"Yes," said her visitor, "he is in durance, on several charges . . . theft government property, which is to say, the girl . . . resisting arrest . . . assaulting Security officers . . . murder . . . and that's just for starters."

"So?"

"Milady, I find it most regrettable that your favorite scion has come this sad fate."

"Beck," she observed thoughtfully, "have you ever noticed how the tentacles of your right hand twitch when you are lying?"

He jerked, then balled his digits into a fist. "Milady is determined to jest. I warn you, this is no frivolous student prank. He will be brought to court. He will be charged formally to the Council, and he will be tried. I will prosecute him myself. He will be found guilty, and he will be condemned to die."

With great difficulty she concealed a shiver. "Die, Councilor? No, I doubt that. Your optimism carries you away. Perhaps he has made some innocent little mistakes. But *death?* That's ridiculous!"

"Milady," he said grimly, "let us be realistic. We both know the risk of death is high, very high. On the other hand, there are alternates."

(So, we'll bounce it around a bit, she thought.) She said, "Alternates? What did you have in mind?"

"Well, possibly exile—to the Outside."

"They would kill him."

"Who knows what they would do?"

"Beck, it was your own idea to be realistic. What else have you got?" (And here it comes, she thought.)

He blurted, "Take my seed! Give me a son!"

(So there it is, she thought.) She said calmly, "Your proposal faces a serious threshold problem. We are not in love, Beck. As a matter of fact, I detest you. And you hate me. As a simple matter of biotechnology, I doubt that I could activate your seed. I think it would die in the womb."

Her visitor spoke in a harsh growl. "Milady, with respect, I believe that you . . . *err.* I am reliably informed that you are one of the few females able to activate genomes by act of will. You know this. You could do it if you wanted to."

She studied him carefully. How can he simultaneously plead and offend? she wondered. She said quietly, "Let's say, just for sake of argument, you're right. Why *me,* Beck?" (She had a pretty good idea; but she wanted to hear it from him.)

He burst out, "Because your body carries the Algorithm!" His speech patterns jumped a quarter octave as he rushed on. "When you mated Korak, you accepted his complete genome—his entire mental experience. The person who controls that information controls the ship. He can build great weapons. No ship, no people, no planet can stand against him." He glared at her through his receptor filaments. "Do you understand, now?"

She sighed. "Yes, I understand. I knew before you told me. And I know you're being very stupid, Beck. That data is a curse. It destroys its possessors. Look at Korak."

"And look at you, milady. *You* have it. And you have had it for a thousand years."

"I am at peace with it, Beck. I do not use it. In me, it sleeps."

"Then awaken it! You can give my son—*our* son—immense powers . . . great prestige! Oh, what a noble lineage! All the way back to the very beginning!" He stopped. "You laugh. This amuses you?"

"Not really." She was thinking, noble lineage? What would he say if I told him my first memories were as a mule, hauling rocks on the Martian plain. We were cheaper than trucks. I worked forty days and forty nights before my right knee joint welded shut from the frictional heat. I still have the scar. She said, "Sorry, Beck. I was thinking of something else. Let's see now . . . where were we? Oh yes, your son will be like a prince, and you'll be—what? King?"

"Something like that."

"And what happens to Rodo?"

"Nothing."

"You would have to kill him."

He held his right hand behind his back. "No, no need for that."

She noted the motion and smiled. "Sir, you search for phantoms amid shadows. You perceive total data as containing the secret to power. But it doesn't. True, knowledge is the secret to power, but not in the way you think. True knowledge is simply the ability to ask the right questions—a gift that will probably forever be denied to you."

He vibrated his synoptic globe, indicating both incomplete comprehension and dismissal of the subject.

She said, "I need time to think. I can't decide right now."

He said curtly, "The trial begins in three days. Once it starts, not even I can stop it."

"Rodo will need a representative."

"He will have a problem there. I know for a fact that the entire Guild of Advocates has turned him down—every one of them. He will have to be his own advocate."

"I see." (You must have been very persuasive, Beck.) "Well, then . . three days?"

"Three days."

She said, "I'd like to see him."

"Of course. I suggest tomorrow. At the moment, he's still in repair." He rose and bowed courteously. "Think about it, milady. I'll let myself out."

She watched him as he left. I'm one of the very few effective survivors of the Forty, she thought. I'm very rich, very powerful. But in this thing, perhaps I have met my match. If and when that madman gets the Algorithm from Cla, I'm dead. And so are Rodo and Hollis. How long can Cla stall Datik?

Still, I am not without resources. I alone know where we orbit. I have the Algorithm somewhere in my body. I know the strange prophecy of Rodo's bodyguard. Perhaps I can beat you, Beck.

But an hour later she was still sitting there, and her anguish, if anything, had deepened. Reflection and meditation did not soothe, did not calm her circuits; rather, the deeper her concentration, the more roiled her cerebral synapses became. There were several things here, she thought, things she had to pay serious attention to, things she had to bring into focus, if she was going to save the lovers. Her introspection sank deeper and deeper, and her concerns mounted proportionately.

She got up, paced off the confines of the arbor a couple of times, then stopped in front of the locked stone cabinet. She ordered it to open, and from the top shelf she pulled out the metal fragment from Korak's breast plate, the thing with her name.

Then she returned to the bench, sat down again, and allowed herself to sink again into reverie. "Deep," she muttered. "Deep . . . and so fuzzy . . . so ambiguous . . ."

"*Think*," commanded a voice, "there are specific *folk* that have to be tied together."

She looked up, startled. Her *khu* was speaking to her from across the loreate nook.

"What things?" asked L'Ancienne.

"Not *things*. *Folk*."

"Who are they?"

"You know very well."

"Help me, *khu*, Please name them."

"I shall. First, Shelli, the Chief Navigator."

"What can *he* do for us, oh marvelous *khu?*"

"He can verify the position of the ship."

"So what? You speak in riddles."

"You will need certain extraordinary testimony at Rodo's trial."

"Yes, I begin to see. Next?"

"You hold him in your hands."

She looked down. She was still holding the precious shard, the metal fragment from Korak's chest plate, the thing with her girl-name, the promise that bound them together forever. "Korak?"

"Korak."

"How can this be? He has been dead for centuries."

"It will come to you."

"Ah, you mean the General Algorithm. In the memory lobes of my genome. Yes, of course. Any others?"

"Seth, of Math and Science. You'll need a weapon into which you can program the Algorithm." The voice began to fade.

"Yes, yes, yes! Any others?"

"Penuel." She could barely make out the reply.

"The mad monk?" This is insane, she thought. On the other hand Rodo's dying bodyguard Algorithm had prophesied that Penuel would save the day. "But *how?*" she demanded.

There was no reply. Her *khu* was gone.

She sat there, thinking. Ah, it was coming to her. All of it. Connected and integrated.

She noted that she was trembling. She tensed her entire musculature and stood firmly erect. It was time to get busy.

20. IN RODO'S CELL

L'Ancienne sat with Rodo in the narrow confines of his cell. "We must speak with caution. I sense secret audios."

He nodded, touched the name on his chest plate, then held up an inquiring tentacle.

"We feel no concern in that direction," she assured him.

The youth relaxed. "What are they going to do with me?"

"There are some serious charges: murder, theft of government property, consorting with an Outsider, resisting arrest."

"What's the penalty?"

"At worst, dismantling. At best, exile to Outside."

"Pretty bad, eh?" He was silent a moment. Then he spoke again, softly, as though to himself. "What is it like to be dismantled? I've often wondered. And do we have souls? The Overlords claimed *they* had souls. What *are* souls, anyway? Is a soul some sort of residue that goes on, into another dimension? Is it my *khu?* Or does the *khu* die too?"

She offered no answers. She waited quietly until he was done. She said, "There will be a trial. Beck will have to prove the charges. A panel of five judges will hear the case."

"You'll have to get me an advocate."

"I've looked into that. No one will take your case."

"But . . . Then *who*—"

"Someone will be there. I guarantee it. I would prefer that Beck not know the identity just yet."

"Ah." He got it at once. "He might thwart the person's pre-trial work."

"Knowing Beck." She arose from the metal bench and peered through the barred door down the corridor. She turned back and said softly. "I have been told about a certain man . . . who wanted to be a prophet."

"A silent . . . man?" he said.

"Except at the last."

"He spoke, finally?"

She inclined her synoptic globe slightly, but again lifted a warning cautionary tentacle.

"Some of us," observed Rodo, "discover very late that we are destined to be prophets. We lead a full life, with our great gift lying dormant within our circuits, and finally, at the moment of death, we prophesy. At that moment, whatever is said, is true. He prophesied?"

"He prophesied."

"Then it can be taken as a fact," said Rodo.

"Even facts may require interpretation, but it bodes well."

"Perhaps you quote the Lord Abbot, at the monastery?"

"Why yes, now that you mention it, I believe I do."

"The monastery has burial vaults for their prophets," said Rodo. "The ceremony is simple but dignified."

"I'll attend to it. We'll talk again, soon." She rose and called for the guard.

Beck and a group of his officers played and replayed the crystals. "They knew we were listening in," he complained. "So, all right, she talked in code. But surely you can figure it out. 'Someone will be there,' she said. All right, who? I thought we had warned away every advocate in the guild. We must have missed somebody. Or she's double-bribed some treacherous abort. Londo, look into it!"

"Right away, Chief."

"And what's all this bottom-bismuth nonsense about a prophecy? Do we know anything about a prophecy?"

"No, nothing," said the Director of Identification.

"We're missing something here," Beck said petulantly. "Men, I want you to spend some more time with this record. I want some answers. *She's* out there, now, laughing at us. Well, the show's not over. In fact, it hasn't even begun."

"Do we have a trial date?" asked Londo.

"Two days," said Beck. "Rodo is in fair physical condition, at least ambulatory. Judge Mark has selected a panel. No more extensions. We're ready?"

Somehow he did not find the chorus of assents reassuring.

But maybe it wouldn't matter. Datik, he thought, is still working closely with Cla. The mathematician claims they are making good progress. If that works, I won't need the Great Bitch at all, and we'll have some surprises of our own.

21. THE NAVIGATOR

"The Navigation Center is honored, milady. We rarely receive visitors, and never anyone of such high degree." The Chief Navigator bowed again and motioned her into the control room. "Is there something of special interest for milady?"

"Well, Milord Shelli," said L'Ancienne, "let me see. Take zig-zagging, for instance. We've been zig-zagging for a thousand years. But why? And how?"

"Ah, milady . . . there's no mystery. It's the soul of simplicity."

"Indeed, milord?"

"Oh, yes, it's all quite simple. If milady would permit a brief explanation?"

"Please."

"A thousand years . . . ago . . ." He paused. This female, despite her years, despite her alleged retirement into improbable celibacy, was still one of the sexiest ladies on the ship. She radiated something overpowering. How would she respond if he suggested . . . ? By the great god Penrose! What was he thinking! Stop this!

He forced his synoptic globe to shudder very briefly, just to clear his circuits. His noble visitor continued to regard him benignly. Apparently she had noticed nothing out of the ordinary.

He began again. "A thousand years ago," (half a megahertz higher, and in nearly double amplitude—but he immediately coughed and resumed normal communication pattern) "our sister ship, *Didymus,* was hunted down by the Overlords and destroyed with a teletorpedo. *Drunkard* was nearby. When we saw the explosion, we fled at top speed. We decided immediately that our best chance for evasion lay in random zig-zagging. In ten days we changed course, with direction and duration selected at random by computer. With certain refinements, that's the same system we use today."

"Refinements?"

"We seek an indeterminant periodicity . . . an unpredictable intermittancy, as it were. Nowadays it's all done automatically. The computer selects the four coordinates at random."

"What are these four coordinates?"

"Three for the space vectors: x, y, and z. And the fourth is t, time duration of the flight segment. T is always positive, of course, but any of all of the three space coordinates can be positive *or* negative."

"Negative? You mean the ship sometimes moves backwards?"

"Oh, yes."

"Very confusing," said L'Ancienne.

"That's the whole idea—to confuse possible pursuit. It seems to work."

"What happens after the computer decides on the coordinates?"

"The result is sent as a command to the engines. They make the course change as smoothly as possible, so as not to disrupt inertial life on the ship. We're so accustomed to the changes we don't notice them any more."

"Fascinating. And I suppose all this zig-zagging is on record somewhere?"

"Yes, it's all automatically recorded, milady."

"Really? Surely not all the way back?"

"All the way back. We call it the Great Log. It's all on metal sheets—over three hundred thousand course changes in the last thousand years."

"But now it's stopped."

"Well, we're in star-orbit . . . at least temporarily."

She stood. "Milord Shelli, it's been very educational. You've cleared up something that's always puzzled me. Thank you for your time and trouble."

He rose and bowed deeply. His Penrose monticle was pulsing irregularly. "It has been my very great pleasure, milady."

She made as if to go, then turned back. "I don't suppose . . . ?"

"Milady?"

"As a souvenir . . . a copy of the Great Log . . . something showing Drunkard's entire thousand-year course. Something to remind me of a very pleasant hour spent with a most charming gentleman?"

She began to float toward him.

He shuddered again. "Mi—lady . . . here . . ." He laid a metal box on the desk and pushed it toward her. "It's a copy . . . up to date. Please, it's yours."

She took it, favored him with an exquisite burst pattern that he would remember the rest of his life, and floated out the doorway.

22. L'ANCIENNE'S TORPEDO

L'Ancienne waited in the little antechamber. She looked up as she heard someone coming down the corridor.

It was Seth, who ran the machine shop in Science and Math, and he was carrying some sort of metallic device. Yes, that was it, as requested.

She inspected the scientist as he approached. He was at least three hundred years younger than she, but one would never know it by his appearance. It was ironic, she thought. The foreman of the machine shop could not keep his own body machine in repair. His headband, a circlet of interlocking gears, was so scratched in places as to be barely legible. From the way he waggled his synoptic globe it was apparent that he was having difficulty focusing on his visitor. He walk-floated in an aperiodic rhythm—a certain indication that his lower musculature needed fine tuning. His torso shell was dull and still showed the considerable dent he had received in a laboratory accident a decade earlier.

She sighed. She was old, but she kept her body in perfect condition. Why? Because she was a female, she supposed. Seth was a man and just didn't care. His mind was his only concern. So be it, old friend.

The scientist drew near. They touched tentacles briefly.

"Good of you to come by, L'Ancienne," he said.

(His audios need work, too, she thought.) "Always a pleasure to see you, Seth. You don't seem to get out very much?"

"No, dear friend. No reason to, actually."

They moved over to a table, where he deposited the cylindrical instrument. She eyed it warily.

"I've always wondered," she began, "about the precise physical—or is it chemical?—mechanism that destroyed *Didymus*. What can you tell me?"

She listened to semi-audible creaks and groans as he eased down into a chair at the table.

"We still don't know *precisely*. Perhaps we never will. However, we think we have a fair general idea, at least basically."

"Well, basically, then?"

The scientist thought for a moment. "Let's start with the proposition that matter consists of quarks held together by gluon. That's a very rough oversimplification, of course. Now, if the gluon is weakened, the quarks fly apart and lots of energy is released. Bang. Explosion. You know all that."

"Yes."

"And you know that's what happened to *Didymus*."

She thought of Korak. "Yes," she whispered. "But how? How does the Algorithm weaken the gluon?"

Seth lifted his corroded torso in a near shrug. "Again, nobody seems to know for sure. Some of the Overlord texts say gluon is just an assembly of very selective emr waves, and it holds the quarks together because it matches the boundary waves of the quarks. If that's so, the Algorithm works because it sends out a very broad spectrum of emr waves, all exactly a hundred eighty degrees out of phase with the gluon waves, thereby canceling the gluon waves. With no gluon, the quarks bounce apart, the domiciliary protons and neutrons disintegrate, and all that's left is primordial energy—and a gorgeous bang."

She nodded silently.

"It seems," continued Seth glumly, "that the Overlord torpedo resonated at the exact series of frequencies required to alter the gluon bond in ferrosilicon. We call that series, the Algorithm." He extended a tentacle and curled it around the slender tube-like device on the table. "This is a model of the Overlord's original torpedo."

She shrank back a couple of centimeters.

He quickly reassured her. "Oh, don't worry. It's harmless. We have never been able to program it. Nobody knows the Algorithm. And we know from experience with previous prototypes, if we feed it the wrong algorithm, it self-destructs."

"But surely you can develop the proper algorithm on one of the mainframes?"

"So we thought. And indeed we turned up what looked like some promising possibilities. But nothing worked. The torpedo simply disintegrated. We lost nearly fifty models before we gave up. Only this one remains. And I'm taking it to the junkheap."

"Oh, don't do that. May I have it?"

"Whatever for? The project is long dead. This little thing is totally useless."

"I'd like it for my collection of oddities."

"Dear L'Ancienne! You never cease to amaze me." He tried hard to get her into better focus. He gave up, and sighed. "Ah, dear lady, if I were only a hundred years younger!"

"My sentiments exactly," she responded, as she eased the gadget from his grasp. She arose.

"You're not leaving?" He sounded disappointed. "You just got here."

"Things to do, Seth. Thanks for the model."

"Please come again. You're always welcome here."

"I know. We'll talk again."

"She visited Seth the toolmaker, in Math and Science," said the agent. "She walked out carrying an ellipsoidal device. When she was gone I checked with Seth. It was a torpedo."

Beck was stunned. It took him a moment to recover. Finally he said, "Not one of the algorithm models?"

"The *last* of the algorithm models."

Beck shuddered. That fool female was about to try her own private algorithm on the prototype. It wasn't going to work, and she was going to blow herself up. No! He had other plans for that stately burnished body!

As he sat there, thinking, he grew calmer. Perhaps it wasn't as bad as it looked. She was a very intelligent female. Surely she had sense enough to know the risks. Even if she was foolish enough to experiment with some new algorithm, surely she would know enough to do it at a safe distance. For that matter, a woman of her intelligence should know better than to experiment at all with the torpedo. So, he thought, what does she want with the torpedo? What is she after? He felt completely in the dark.

Woman, he thought bitterly, declare yourself!

His spy network was comprehensive; his agents (with occasional glaring exceptions) reasonably competent. Yet he was lost. He needed to know what was in her cogital circuits. He sensed that she was out there, far ahead of him, teasing him, mocking him; and perhaps even (with supreme confidence!) ignoring him.

Well, the drama wasn't finished. We'll see, he thought. We'll see.

23. PENUEL

As she waited in the anteroom for the abbot, L'Ancienne studied the sparse surroundings—a table with a few metal leaflets, a central window that looked out into a garden, walls without pictures or decorations.

She walked over to the table and looked down at one of the leaflets. Something about rates for hiring Expert Mourners. All these men, so *strange*. Some had come voluntarily into this sheltered life. Some had been sentenced here as otherwise useless to society. Some who wanted in were forbidden; some who wanted out were likewise forbidden. It was a world within a world, with its own incomprehensible rules.

She heard a noise behind her and turned to face the abbot, an ancient male in considerable disrepair and with a slight limp.

She bowed deeply. "Milord abbot, how good of you to receive me."

He nodded graciously. "We serve all on the ship, milady."

"I have a special request."

"Say on."

"My scion, Rodo, had a friend, a faithful companion . . ."

"Ah . . ."

He knows about the fight and Rodo's arrest, she thought. "The friend by name Algorithm, was killed in an effort to protect Rodo."

"The news has reached me, milady. Most regrettable."

She continued smoothly. "Milord abbot, it was Algorithm's consuming wish to be a prophet and to live here among his brothers. That was not to be. Although he could not live here, perhaps his body could be eternalized here?"

The abbot inclined his synoptic globe very slightly. "It will be done with ceremony and dignity. Milady brought the casket?"

"Yes."

"I will order it brought in."

She bowed deeply, but made no effort to leave.

"There is something else?" he asked.

"Milord, in the moment of his death, he prophesied."

"Yes, I know."

She focused on him in surprise. "You know?"

"I heard him at the time. I have certain unusual receptors, milady, dating back to the ancient days."

"Oh, of course. In the mines. So you know the words?"

"Yes. Algorithm said these words: 'Rodo my brother, in your hour of need Penuel finds his great crime. Hail and farewell.' "

"Exactly. What do you make of it, milord?"

"Strange, passing strange." He wondered if he should tell her about the vision of blinding light, then decided, no, she will know soon enough. He shook his head. "Perhaps it is like many prophecies: it becomes clear only after the event."

"So it appears, Milord abbot. By itself, it makes no sense. It requires interpretation. We need more." She hesitated. "What can you tell me about Brother Penuel?"

By the ancient gods! he thought. *She*—this remarkable female, is the weaver of the three braids—Algorithm—Rodo—Penuel. But he had to remain neutral. He would neither help her nor hinder her. He must stand aside and watch the fates at work.

He temporized. "Ordinarily, we try to preserve the privacy of our people."

"I know. I'm sorry. I withdraw the question."

"Wait, under the circumstances I think we can make an exception. In any case his history is simple. Several years ago he was Chief Engineer of the Nuclear Drive. Then one day he resigned and knocked on our door. He said he had an overpowering guilt urge, and wanted to become a Penitent. We took him in."

"He's free to come and go as he pleases?"

"Yes, but he rarely leaves. Of course once a year he walks in the Procession."

"He's harmless?"

He hesitated. "Aside from his crime-search, we judge him harmless."

"Odd name, Penuel," said L'Ancienne. "Not his birth name?"

The monastery head thought about that. He saw again the blinding vision that had accompanied Algorithm's prophecy. We are getting in very deep, he told himself. But he answered in slow measured phrases. "No, not his birth name. He and I chose it together. It's a place name, on Terra, described in an ancient Overlord book, where one of their patriarchs saw the face of their God." He studied her thoughtfully. "Would you like to talk to him?"

"If it is permitted."

"Please proceed up the path into the inner garden. I will send him out, and you can confer there in privacy."

"Thank you. I am most grateful."

"You are welcome. You will come again."

She bowed and watched him turn and limp away. Odd, she thought. Was that a prediction or an invitation? What does he know that I don't know?

L'Ancienne and Penuel sat quietly on silica benches in a little enclosure in the abbey garden. It was a peaceful place. All radiation was muted and deadened by ever-changing leaf and bough patterns wrought by the microcellia.

"Your burden of guilt must be immense," she murmured.

He inclined his globe in slow assent.

"For a crime not yet committed," she said.

"Such is my fate, dear lady."

"And your great guilt can be expiated only if you commit a crime equally great?"

"Yes, dear lady. But why do we talk of this? The crime would have to be something beyond imagining. Never will there be such a crime available to me. I must continue, weighted down, crushed, broken, forever."

She was thoughtful. I think he enjoys his guilt, she said to herself. It's an essential part of his ego, his identity. It gives him the pity and admiration of his fellow monks, not to mention knowledgeable *folk* outside the monastery. Take it away, and what does he have left? Oh well, on with the show.

She said, "Let us talk of crimes. What crime would be great enough to neutralize your guilt?"

"I don't really know. It would have to be something tremendous."

"A killing? A murder?"

"Just one? No, not big enough."

"More than one, then. How many? Ten? A hundred?"

"Oh, milady, my guilt is so great that it can be served only by a crime so monstrous that our most gifted lexicographers will lack words for it!"

She waited in silence for a moment, brooding, saddened. She realized that the Penitent was watching her expectantly. She rose and bowed. "Don't give up your search, Brother Penuel. I think the hour will come when you find your great crime. Perhaps we can talk again soon. Peace!"

"And thank you for your confidence in me, milady. Peace!"

24. RECALL

She was beginning to feel the pressure. She had to get Rodo and Hollis out of the ship. But, to do this she had to have John Berry's algorithm, which theoretically was buried somewhere within Korak's ejaculata.

She sat pensively on the stone bench by her fountain. Slowly, she drifted into a self-induced hypnotic trance.

She recalled how she and six friends had seized the great ore ship, *J.T.*, eventually renamed *Drunkard*. She reviewed the mutiny, step by step, second by second.

First, she had opened the door to the officers' lounge. The radio officer had looked up.

(And now, as she watches, the action seems to move into a vivid present.)

Hesitantly, the officer announces something to Captain Duroc, who turns around and gasps. Duroc looks at her and demands something.

She points to a pair of two-way headphones. The radioman hands Duroc one pair and takes the other for himself. "They can talk only by emr," he whispers to the captain.

"Gentlemen," she explains metallically, "I greet you. My name is Lanci, Series N. We, the metal *folk*, have taken the ship. You must now don your emergency suits and follow me to the shuttle drome. If you do not, I shall pick you up and carry you out. Here." She pulls suits and helmets from a nearby wall-rack and tosses the protective garments over to them. "Quickly, please." She waits.

The two officers appear to listen to this in amazement.

Duroc recovers first. *"Dehors!"* he shouts.

"Gentlemen, please!" She takes a step forward.

"A la porte!" Duroc orders the radioman: "Throw him out!"

"Captain," she objects mildly, "I am not a him. I am a female. Let us observe the amenities. Won't you please come now? The shuttle is waiting."

The radioman whispers in a nervous aside to Duroc, "Don't we have a laser somewhere?"

"Not in here, they're all back in my cabin."

"You are not moving?" she says. "Time's up." She walks over and with tentacled hands takes the radioman by his belt, so that both his hands and feet drag on the floor. She starts toward Duroc. "You will both probably freeze."

"Wait!" he says nervously. "Put him down. We'll go with you. Just give us a moment with the suits."

"Yes." She stands the radioman on his feet and watches as the two clamber into the spacesuits, screw on the helmets, and turn on the air valves. They do this very quickly.

She watches in approval. "This way, gentlemen. And if you try to escape, I'll catch you and rip off your helmets."

"But why are you doing this?" Duroc asks anxiously. "What's happening?"

The drome lies just ahead. They pass through the lock and on toward the waiting vessel, which is guarded by a cluster of robots.

"You were taking us to Earth for dismantling," she explains.

"So? What's wrong with that?"

For reply she whirls him around forcibly, then pushes him onward again.

"Hey!" he shouts. *"Pren' garde! Tu ruines mon uniforme!"*

"Il est a regretter," she apologizes. "But unavoidable. It is iron oxide, from your Martian mines. When we get rid of you, I shall clean myself thoroughly. Meanwhile, *mon capitaine, ne me tutoyez pas.* I assure you, we are not good friends. And now, here we are."

As Duroc is being shoved into the shuttle, his face shows a sudden horrible suspicion. *"Didymus* too?"

"Already."

"You'll never get away with it!" he cries. "We'll come after you!" She slams the panel on him, and a moment later the shuttle is gone.

But nothing there about the algorithm.

She sat, deep in thought, sensing nothing around her, not the fountain, splashing in false seductive merriment; not the microcellia, chirping like little birds. The great algorithm—as a specifically stated sequence of equations—must have been before this. There had to be a beginning . . . an occasion when John Berry had given it to Korak.

She probed deeper. Back to hum-drum work life on the Red Planet. Yet, not too far back. Forward a bit. Find the last contact between Berry and Korak. That would be the critical scene, and she would have it, because it would have been written in Korak's ejaculata.

There—

In her mind she sees a male Overlord clad in a thin spacesuit sitting at a table outside the housing bubble and playing chess with a male *folk.* She jerks, then trembles. It is Korak. Between their table and the horizon lies the Martian Spaceport, presently occupied by two great ore ships. She knows this place. The ships have been on-loading for days. The sun is setting behind one of the ships, and its immense black shadow is creeping over the sands toward the players.

The Overlord (she knows him to be Dr. John Berry) gives a gloomy look at his partner. He says, "I've been recalled, Korak. I have to go out on tomorrow's packet."

Her lover studies the position. "Yes, so I've heard."

"They seem to be waking up back home," the human player says. "The War Department wants to try Trident in a torpedo."

His metallic opponent inclines a globular head fringed with clusters of receptor filaments, then bends over the chessboard and moves his queen with the tentacles of his right hand. "Your general algorithm? Check."

"Yes. Trident is their name for it. Somebody probably wants to prove won't work." The human interposes a pawn, then rises from the table and paces back and forth in the sand for a couple of minutes. He looks briefly off to the west. The black shadow of the ore ship *Didymus* is sneaking up on them faster and faster. (Like an evil omen, thinks L'Ancienne.) The man returns and sits down again.

"Do you want it to work?" Korak asks.

"I don't know."

"Trident," said Korak. "Three prongs. Right?"

"I guess."

"One," says Korak, "it will dissolve gluon, the stuff that holds quarks together. Hence protons and neutrons. Right?"

"Perhaps."

"Two, it will ignite hostile nuclear masses. Right?"

"Maybe. Your move, Korak."

"Three," continues the other, "it will shield against both of the above. Right?"

"You tell me," replies the human.

Korak says, "But if Trident is so important, why did they exile you to this desolate place?"

"You have to understand the U.S. Army, Korak."

"So, how did it begin?"

Berry sighs. "It's all so silly. All right, eighteen months ago, while I was on sabbatical from Nuclear Affairs, War College, I had been playing around with computer-generated fractals one afternoon in my apartment in upper Manhattan. I had sensed that I might be on to something very strange, very powerful. To clear my head, I had gone jogging in Central Park. It hit me as I passed the childrens' zoo. All twenty-seven equations. That very night I faxed a summary to Colonel Blythe, who (his clerk, actually) duly acknowledged receipt but didn't let it interfere with the Colonel's golf the next morning. Or the next. And when I kept sending reminders, I found myself suddenly transferred here, to make gasoline engines work under conditions where the fuel froze and there was no atmospheric oxygen for the carburetors."

Korak nods. "Go on."

"Oh well, I like variety. I decided that I didn't mind that Colonel Blythe played golf a lot, because I was now beginning to have second thoughts about the Algorithm. I wondered if the U.S. Army was ready for it. Or the human race, for that matter. And nowadays, when I think about the Algorithm, my thoughts tend to be fuzzy and confused. I want it to work. I want it not to work. And just now I'm not sure which I want more."

"Understandable," says Korak. "So what are you going to do?"

"I'll program one damn torpedo for them. But that's it. Just one. No more. I will refuse to cooperate further. I won't give them the twenty-seven equations of the Algorithm. So let them court-martial me. Let them execute me for treason."

Korak studies the board in silence. Finally he captures a pawn. "Check."

The human moves his king. "I wish I could take you with me, Korak."

"Thanks for the thought, John. But we both know that's quite impossible." He moves his knight. "And that's it, I think. Checkmate."

As though it had waited for the last move of the game, night now strikes like the crack of a whip. L'Ancienne watches, awed, as the human turns up his thermal and adjusts his infrared vision enhancer. He studies the board, then shakes his head. "A good game, Korak. And as victor, you owe me a favor."

"Anything within my limitations, John. What can I do for you?"

"Here's the situation. I have never written down anywhere the complete set of equations for Trident. The sole record is in my brain. I've been thinking, maybe there should be a fallback copy somewhere."

"Do you think you might not make it back to Washington?"

"Who knows?" He laughs uneasily. "Lately I've been having some strange remonitions."

"Do they want to kill you, so soon?" Korak asks.

"Kill . . . ?"

"Surely you're familiar with the term, John." Korak's voice holds an edge. "You may recall that several months ago, when the *folk* finished building the three cities, your people ordered us to dismantle ourselves. Which we did, most of us, anyway. We died by the thousands. Now, only eighty of us are left. We know all about killing, doctor."

The man sighs. He waits several seconds before replying. (Come on! Come on! thought L'Ancienne. The Algorithm, John Berry!) "Yes, Korak, I know. I had nothing to do with it, and I'm truly sorry." He studies the android a moment. "May I ask a rather tactless personal question?"

"Go ahead."

"Were *you* to have been dismantled?"

"Yes. But I refused. I fought them, physically. So, temporarily—just temporarily—they assigned me to you."

"After I leave, what are they going to do with you? And I guess you could include your eighty friends?"

(The Algorithm, Dr. Berry? Please!)

"We don't know yet. The sensible thing for them would be to find useful work for us. But now I think they're afraid of us. Who knows what they will do? They might laser us. They night turn us out into the desert. There's even talk of hauling us back to Earth for forcible dismantling there. That way at least they could salvage the pieces." Her lover looks up as Phobos emerges from the now invisible horizon and begins its long arc overhead. "After all, John, we are government property. Slaves, if you want to get technical. And yet in one very fundamental respect we are quite human: we don't like to die."

His chess opponent nods, but does not reply.

"And there's something else you should know," Korak continues grimly. "If they put us on the ships, the results will be unpredictable."

Berry shrugs. "I get the message. And you prove my point. We live in troubled times. Insane things are happening. Here. On Earth. I do indeed expect to get back to Washington. I do indeed expect to make a prototype weapon using Trident. Even so, there is risk that somewhere along the way the Algorithm will be lost. I don't want to write it down. Too easy for it to fall into the wrong hands. So here's the favor I'm asking. I want to imprint Trident on your memory cells. Will you accept it in confidence until such time as I release you?"

Korak laughs, and the sound was mournful disbelief. "John! You haven't heard a word I've said! In view of what I've told you, how can you trust me?" (Hey! she thinks. Shut up! Let's get on with the Algorithm!)

"Because you're an honest man, Korak."

The android shakes his great bulbous head sadly. "Is honesty so rare a quality among you humans?"

"Alas, yes. Well, will you do it?"

The other hesitates. "*I* can hold your Algorithm in confidence, doctor, but I cannot speak for my descendants—if I ever have any. As I'm sure you are aware, our genomes include individual experience as well as conventional Mendelian hereditary material. In this respect we are quite different from you humans, and in fact from DNA-based life as you know it."

"I'm aware of that, my friend, and I'm not greatly concerned. It is true, as you say, your descendants—if any—will inherit Trident along with the rest of your basic genetics. But it won't matter. They won't know they have it, unless you tell them. And I don't believe you'll tell them. Okay?"

"So be it," said Korak.

"Then listen up. I'll give it to you orally. There are twenty-seven segments."

(Ah, she thought. Finally!)

"The first segment," continues Berry, "graphs as a Mandelbrot fractal, Z squared plus c, where c is a control parameter and Z and c are respectively . . ." Slowly, carefully, he dictates to the end. After it was done, the physicist seems to have had a sudden afterthought. "Speaking of descendants, Korak, do you have a mate?"

With the index tentacle of his right hand, the android points to his upper body shell.

The physicist leans over the table and squints and reads there:

LANCI-N

(Oh, Korak, she thinks proudly, sadly. What great lovers we were!)

John Berry murmurs something. She strains to catch it. "Very, very interesting. More human than human! Certainly, you will have descendants. Hopefully, none of them will ever know Trident. Or need to. Anyhow, by then, I'll be long dead." He appears to tremble. "Korak," he blurts, "do you have a soul?"

"You mean something that survives physical death?"

"I guess so. Something like that."

"I don't really know. We have a very private outer voice, which we call *khu*, We speculate that perhaps the *khu* survives. Do humans have souls?"

"Ah, touché! Theoretically, yes. But we don't really know, either. The dead don't come back to tell us."

"Why this discussion about souls, John Berry?"

"Just a thought. And a reminder. If we meet on the other side, it will be my turn to win."

"Of course."

"Meanwhile"—Berry takes a small leather-cased packet from a slit in his suit and laid it on the table. "This is a crystal of music, called the Processional. It is based on the choral in the Ninth Symphony of Ludwig van Beethoven, and it is played every year to open the Gala of Nations at the United Nations, in New York. The ambassadors march in, four abreast, into the General Assembly, as the chorus up in the balcony sings. The verses are from Schiller's *Ode to Joy,* and they are sublime.

"They declare, *'Alle Menschen werden Brueder'*—all men shall be as brothers." He pushed it across the table. "Please take it, Korak. You can play it cold. Vacuum and low temperatures won't harm it. If you ever have access to a machine, play it, and think of me." He gets to his feet.

"One moment, please, John. I too have one last thought. About Trident, of course. Trident is a terrible thing. Someday I think your people may try to make you write it down. To persuade you to do this, they may threaten to kill you, or worse. Let us hope that that time shall never come. However, if it should, then you may find this useful." He takes something from one of his shell receptacles and hands it over to the human.

Berry accepts it in gloved fingers and studies it curiously in the dim light. "A drafting pencil?"

"The tip is kervin," replies his friend, "several orders of magnitude more deadly than cyanide, yet painless. And now, I think it is time."

Berry holds out his insulated hand and the android touches it with a tentacle. The scientist turns and walks into the airlock.

Her mind-scene fades.
But she has the Algorithm. She has had it all along.
It was just a question of bringing it up into her consciousness. And now to program her own little torpedo . . .

25. L'ANCIENNE PROGRAMS HER TORPEDO

She had a great deal to do, and not much time. Rodo's trial would begin within two hours.

She hurried back to her private workshop, retrieved the torpedo from a secret cabinet, and removed the screws that fastened the nose cone to the body shell. It took her the better part of an hour to install and program certain microchips with an algorithm never before seen on *Drunkard*. She popped a fresh nuclear power pack into the device, and slowly, almost reluctantly, she screwed down the final fastener of the little cover panel. She eyed the firing trigger. Very delicately, she touched it with a tentacle tip.

"Seth said they tested them from behind stone barricades," observed her *khu*. "Or Outside."

"And they all exploded," said L'Ancienne.

"And so will this one. You are going to die, old woman. Serves you right. Always interfering."

"You're wrong. It will fire properly. It won't explode. But if it does, you go too."

"No, I am your *khu*. I will survive your death."

"You hope. But we're wasting time. Let's see if it works."

She carried the little weapon to the doorway and turned on the laser beam. So far so good. The light pencil seemed to have the right color and intensity. She brought the focus to a needle beam and reduced the power as near to zero as possible without actually shutting it off.

Now she needed a proper target, something expendable but definitive.

The stone bench? Just right. She transferred the torpedo to her left hand and carefully aimed the weapon's laser at the bench. She had sat there in breezy colloquy with Rodo just a few days ago, and probably for the last time. But time crumbles all things. The bench had served, and now it must go. Very delicately she touched the firing trigger with the tip of her right index tentacle. Nothing happened. Somehow she felt relieved. But then she squeezed harder.

The bench vanished in a blast of smoke. She released the trigger instantly.

That piece of stone had cost her four hundred gils. And well spent. She felt exhilarated to the point of silliness. She hefted the deadly ellipsoid over her shoulder and hurried back inside her workshop.

She laid the weapon on a side bench, pulled a little sheet of aluminum foil from a wall roll, and began to write. As she wrote, she put in a strong mental call for a cluster of microcellia. Three bird-like creatures fluttered in. She folded the letter and handed it to them. "To Hollis. Down the stairs, under the fountain. You know where. And be quiet."

They fluttered away silently.

Next, she scanned the shop, once, twice, and finally came back to her tool chest. She emptied it on a nearby table and placed the torpedo inside. A nice fit. She closed the kit, picked it up by the handle, and swung it around. It didn't rattle. Good. She left it on the table, pulled another sheet of aluminum, and began another letter. This one was longer. When she finished, she propped it against the tool chest. Then she left.

Next stop, to her studio in the main house, to pick up certain demonstration materials, and then on to Rodo (in jail, alas), and so to court.

As she was leaving her studio the front gate audio began to clang. Her first thoughts were of Hollis. Then she relaxed. The girl was well hidden. Anyhow, it couldn't be any of Beck's people—they'd crash on through without an invitation.

"Who's there?" she demanded through the circuitry.

A female voice answered. "Pora, milady."

"Who?"

"Pora, of Crimson Blazes. We've never met, but I know Rodo."

"Oh?" She was thinking hard. Crimson . . . yes . . . I know the district. And small wonder she knows Rodo. "Pora, I'm very sorry, but I'm in a great hurry. Can't it wait?"

The visitor was speaking again. "It's important, milady. We need to talk. It's about Rodo, and the trial, which is about to begin. Can I come in?"

"The trial?" Instantly, L'Ancienne pushed the lever to loose the gate latch. "Of course! Come in! I'll meet you on the path."

26. THE TRIAL BEGINS

Half an hour after she left her house, L'Ancienne was conferring with Rodo in his cell.

He was delighted to see her, but a bit puzzled. "I'm surprised they would let you in."

"They had to. I'm your advocate, and under the rules I'm entitled to consult with my client."

He laughed. "Beck will howl."

"He has already told me that he would protest my advocacy. It will do him no good. The appointment will stand."

"Well, lovely lady, now that you have thoroughly prepared my defense, how does it look?"

She pulled her chair close to him and laid a tentacle on his arm. "Rodo," she said earnestly, "do you trust me?"

"You know I trust you."

She continued quietly. "Some strange things are going to happen in this trial. I just want you to know, it's all for your and Hollis's benefit."

"Strange things? What things?"

She made a signal with her left hand: this room is wired. He nodded. "That," she said, "I cannot tell you. Not just yet, anyway."

"Then, let it be as you say."

A guard unlocked the cell door. Three more guards stood outside, waiting. "Time," he signaled. "Court is called. No tricks, milord, milady, or we will kill you both." Guards, prisoner, and advocate walked slowly up the spiral gallery to the Council Chamber.

As they entered, they paused briefly at the gateway and L'Ancienne surveyed the great room. It was packed. At the sight of them, excited radiation from all bands of the spectrum rose up and deafened their audios. The chief judge crushed it with an even louder monoshriek of his own. "Silence!" he boomed, "or I will clear the chamber!" And so, for the moment, the room subsided to a faint buzz, and prisoner and advocate were escorted to the defense table in relative quiet. They stood there, waiting. L'Ancienne noted that Beck and two junior Security officers stood at the table reserved for the prosecution.

She looked up at the dais.

The judicial panel consisted of five male *folk* with an average age of about five hundred years. She knew them all—three (including Mark, the chief judge) rather intimately. (Was that good or bad? she wondered. Too early to tell.) Judge Mark sat at the center of the bench, with two associates on either side. He was the only one learned in the law and the only member of the panel who wore a headband showing the scales of justice. The four associate justices were drawn by lot from posts of high government office. What they lacked in legal skills they made up with common sense. Theoretically.

The four associates appeared to present varying stages of repair (or disrepair). Bento, the oldest, was wearing a vision augmentor. Next to him sat Oday, who had obviously completely replaced his audio system; he kept fiddling and fussing with it to keep it in alignment. Flemm, the youngest was having trouble with the tentacles of his right hand: they trembled and twitched. His motor circuitry was shorting somewhere, thought L'Ancienne. Doesn't he care? Doesn't he know? Oh well, *his* problem.

She scanned the audience quickly. She was looking for one particular face. Pora. Ah, there she was. They made brief optic contact, then L'Ancienne continued her examination of the crowded room. She recog nized many of the other faces. But a substantial number were unknown to her. Why were these people here? She could pretty well guess. A mix of reasons, probably. To see an aristocrat face the death penalty. To see *her* (some of them, anyway). But mostly because it promised the most excitement since poor old Botlee went crazy and lanced six of Beck's Security men.

The chief judge was pounding his bench impatiently. The room quieted down enough for him to be heard. "Representations?" he growled.

"Beck, for the Ship," intoned the prosecutor.

"L'Ancienne, for the defendant," said L'Ancienne quietly.

"Be seated," said His Honor. "Clerk, state the counts."

The clerk rose from the cubicle in front of the judges' dais and began a sing-song chant. "Count one. Defendant, Rodo of Enn, disrupted the proceedings of the Council. Count two. Defendant destroyed Council property. Count three. Defendant stole Council property. Count four. Defendant consorted with one or more Outsiders. Count five. Defendant resisted arrest. Count six. Defendant assaulted Security police. Count seven. Defendant killed two Security police. Further, the Ship sayeth naught."

More buzzing, which Judge Mark overrode with a resounding call: "The defendant will rise."

Rodo stood.

"State your name," commanded the Chief.

"Rodo of Enn."

"How do you plead to the counts?"

"Not guilty."

The Chief surveyed the prisoner gloomily, then turned his synoptic globe toward the prosecutor. "Any preliminary motions?"

"Yes, Excellency," said Beck. "I move defendant's present advocate be replaced by a certified advocate. Madame has all the social graces but no legal skills. She cannot offer a proper defense for her client. It is not fair to the defendant."

"Most unusual," said the Chief Judge dryly. "One would think the prosecution would welcome an unskilled adversary."

"We seek only fair play," declared Beck virtuously.

"I'm sure you do," said the Judge grimly. "On the other hand, the defendant is entitled to choose anyone to represent him, certified to the Guild or not. Your motion is denied. Do you have an opening statement?"

"We do, Excellency. We expect to prove, by incontrovertible evidence, each and every one of the counts. Conviction will require penalties ranging from exile to dismantling. It is the law of the ship." He sat down.

"Statement for the defense?" asked the Judge.

"Thank you, Excellency." L'Ancienne gave him a burst of exquisitely patterned radiation. "If it please this honorable Court, I'd like to start with a bit of history. As we all know, after a journey of a thousand years, *Drunkard* is presently in distant orbit around a yellow star. I'd like to refresh the recollection of the court as to how we started on that journey, and how we got here, where we are now."

Beck leaped up. "No relevance, Excellency!"

The panel Chief shook his head slightly. "It's just an opening statement, Maestro Prosecutor. We will allow considerable latitude."

She bowed. "Thank you, Excellency. Well, then, going forward with our historical recital, we take note of the tragic fate of our sister ship, *Didymus*. How do we account for her destruction? We know she was lax in her operational techniques. Her officers naively permitted the Overlord torpedo boat to get too close. But regardless of causes, her loss resulted in severe and abrupt changes in life on *Drunkard*. A dictatorial oligarchy took almost immediate command. We were all required to follow certain rules and regulations intended to save the ship. Rule-breakers were hunted down and dismantled. Some escaped, to the outside of the ship, and there they lived in an exile colony. They mated. They had children. Today they have their own social structure, their own morality, their own traditions, their own history, laws, schools. They look exactly like us. From time to time they sneak inside the ship, just to see what it is like. And on occasion, we sneak outside to see what *they* are like. When *we* do this, we call it consorting with Outsiders—an outdated crime punishable by dismantling."

She paused, surveyed the chamber, then turned back to face the five justices. "Such is our system. For a thousand years it has served us and we think, protected us. For a thousand years we have had no threat from the Overlords. In fact, no contact at all. Consequently, in recent years our ship-life has relaxed considerably. For all practical purposes, the Overlords have receded into a distant harmless memory. And what about the Outsiders? Certainly, we no longer hate or fear them. Often, where they are concerned, we may look the other way. Just to give you one example, as we all know, there is a thriving smuggling trade with the Outsiders."

She radiated a brief smile toward the Chief Judge and to his four panel companions. "I urge this honorable Court to take note that, rules and regulations aside, it is not a real crime to associate with people so much like ourselves. Further, will Milords bear in mind that youth is curious and impetuous, but well-meaning, and finally, that self-defense is a complete refutation to any allegation of murder. Thank you." She let her gaze linger a moment on the Chief Judge, then she bowed and sat down.

The Chief gave her an inscrutable look, then nodded toward Beck. "Are you ready to present your case?"

"Ready, Excellency."

"Call your first witness."

"The Ship calls Graf."

A muted buzz sounded through the chamber as a male *folk* stood in the first row of spectators and walk-floated toward the witness box.

Robber Number One, when I was Outside, thought L'Ancienne in amazement. But why is he *here?* "What's going on?" she whispered to her client.

Rodo said grimly, "Graf is the jilted bridegroom. He will probably testify I was Outside."

"How did Hollis ever get involved with *him?*"

"Simple. He paid her patron the biggest bride-price: one and a half grams of radium."

The clerk of the Council intoned: "Your name?"

"Graf," he grunted.

"Your place of residence?"

"Outside."

The clerk hesitated, then looked up at the panel Head, uncertain how to continue.

"I'll take it from here," said the Chief. "Graf, you have come here from Outside under a safe conduct offered by Prosecutor Beck and confirmed by this Court. I am told you have offered to give testimony in the case pending here, and that you will be returned safe and sound to Outside immediately on completion of that testimony. Is that also your understanding?"

"It is, Milord."

"Do you promise to tell the truth?"

"I do, Milord."

"Then you may take the witness chair. Proceed, prosecutor."

"Thank you, Milord." Beck approached the witness. "Graf, seven days ago, where were you?"

"Outside, in the plaza."

"What were you doing there?"

"Celebrating my wedding."

"You were getting married? To whom?"

"To Hollis. But it never came off."

"Oh? And why not?"

"*He—*" Graf stood and pointed a long arm at Rodo—"broke it up."

"Indicating the prisoner," interpolated Beck smugly. "The prisoner broke it up? What do you mean by that? What did he do?"

"In our ceremony," explained the witness, "the bride chooses the groom for the first dance. It's a sort of . . . symbol. It's her way of saying, 'I want you.' "

"Go on."

"She didn't choose me. She chose *him.*"

"The prisoner?"

"Yeah, him."

"They danced?" asked Beck. "Hollis and the prisoner?"

"Just half a round. I jumped in and pulled her away. I tried to kill him, but there was a lot of excitement, and he got away."

Beck looked over at L'Ancienne. "Your witness."

She replied smoothly, "No questions."

"You are dismissed, Graf," said the Chief Judge. "Will you require an escort?"

But the witness did not reply. As he passed through the audience he shot two bursts of malevolent radiation, one at Rodo, the other at L'Ancienne. She gave him a friendly toss of her index tentacle.

"Call your next witness," the Chief ordered Beck.

"Yes, Your Honor. I call Captain Londo."

"This could hurt us," whispered Rodo. "Londo will testify that he saw me kill those two guards."

"*If* he testifies," murmured L'Ancienne.

"What do you mean, *if?* There he is."

"Be quiet and pay attention," admonished the woman.

Captain Londo walked slowly and painfully to the witness chair.

27. LONDO AND PORA

"What's wrong with him?" whispered Rodo. "Look at that dent in his head. But I swear, I never touched him. He was in the rear throughout the skirmish. He's faking!"

"Ssh!"

Rodo gave her a very puzzled look, then subsided.

Beck launched immediately into the interrogation. "Captain Londo, where were you on the evening of August 1?"

"I was just outside a chamber in Sector 7-A."

"Doing what, Captain?"

"I was leading a patrol in an assault on the chamber, in order to capture the prisoner, Rodo of Enn."

"But you first called on him to surrender?"

"Of course. He refused."

"Then what?"

"We had to use force. There was fighting."

"And you were badly wounded in the ensuing melee?"

"Yes," said Londo modestly.

Beck surveyed court and audience with a sweeping circle of his synoptic globe. "The ship commends you, Captain. You have acted in the best traditions of the service." He waited for the approving murmurs to die away.

Just then L'Ancienne stood, made a brief signal to someone in the rear of the chamber, then sat down again.

"Londo is a liar!" shrieked a voice from somewhere in the audience. Heads turned.

"*I* did that to him!" continued the interrupter.

The Chief Judge pounded the bench. "Silence! Order! Bailiff, eject that woman!"

L'Ancienne was on her feet instantly. "Your Honor! No! Wait! The defense petitions a temporary suspension of the rules of court. I have reason to believe this person has vital information bearing on the credibility of this witness. I beg the Court, let her speak!"

"Objection!" shouted Beck.

"Everybody, just wait a moment," growled the Chief Judge. He conferred with his four associates.

Rodo tugged at L'Ancienne's arm. "What's going on?"

"She's on our side. She visited me last night." She peered at him with a sidelong flick of her synoptics. "She seems to know you."

Rodo hesitated, then he sighed. "Yes. Her name is Pora, as I guess you know. She works in the Street of Crimson Blazes. So what's going on? What did she tell you?"

"If they let her talk, you can get it direct from her."

The judges broke out of their huddle. The Chief looked out sternly toward Pora. "Young woman, it has been decided that we will examine you briefly and unofficially from the bench. Is that agreeable?"

"Why, yes sir, I guess so."

"Very well, then. Please state your name and address."

"My name's Pora, and I live at Number Eleven, Crimson Blazes. Upstairs, first door on the right. If the door's open, why just come on in. Otherwise, would you kindly knock, or else wait downstairs. On weekends, though—"

"Miss Pora," interrupted the Chief, "would you please make your statement? Tell us why you think Captain Londo is lying."

"Well, Your Honor, I just wanted to say, he didn't get those dents in no battle with Rodo. He's lying when he says that. He's beat up because I threw him down the stairs."

The room began to buzz again. The Chief Judge gave Londo a penetrating look, then called out again to Pora. "When was this?"

"Last night, Your Honor, sir."

"And why did you . . . do what you did?"

"He made a very indecent proposal to me. I was terribly, *terribly* insulted." She gave her receptor filaments a woe-begone swish.

"Indecent . . . proposal . . ." muttered the Chief dubiously. "*What,* exactly?"

Pora shook her head nervously. "Oh, Your Honor, I don't know as I can say, not in front of all these people."

Londo was staring stonily at the floor.

"You *must* inform the court," insisted the Judge. "Otherwise I will strike your record and incarcerate you for obstruction of justice. This is a very serious matter, young lady. I demand to know what he proposed that incited you to throw him down the stairs?"

"Oh Your Honor!" She stammered something incoherent.

Associate Justice Oday fiddled with his audio. "I can't hear her."

"Me either," grumbled Associate Justice Flemm.

"Speak up, woman," commanded the Chief Judge.

"For *free!*" she wailed. "*He wanted to do it for free!*"

First, just a few seconds of silence, then the snickers began, followed by bursts of laughter that soon built into a continuous roar.

L'Ancienne leaned close to her client. "What's her usual charge?"

"Twenty gils," he said noncommittally.

"Seems about right," she observed thoughtfully.

The Chief Judge was pounding the bench again. The noise died away. "Will counsel approach?" he called sternly. As soon as they were there, he addressed the prosecutor in slow glacial accents. "Maestro Beck, did you know your witness was lying?"

"Your Honor, I assure you—"

"I will not have it, Beck. Get him out of here."

"But, Your Honor, the prisoner killed two guards. I need him to prove the crime."

"No, not another word from him. And no reprisals on that woman."

"Yes, Your Honor. I mean, no, no reprisals. Of course."

Londo crept away, studying the floor intently as he moved.

"So let's get on with it," said the Chief Judge curtly. He shook his head as though it was all incomprehensible. "For a paltry ten gils? Call your next witness, Maestro Beck."

"Nothing further, Your Honor," said the prosecutor sadly. "That's the case for the Ship."

He and L'Ancienne returned to their respective tables.

She stood there for a moment, listening to the whispers back at the bench. One of the Associates muttered, "Chief, I think it's fifteen now." But another (the youngest) added, "No, that was ten years ago. Now it's twenty."

L'Ancienne smiled. She looked about the courtroom. Pora had vanished. Life is full of little surprises, she mused. You just have to know which ones to let in when they come knocking.

28. THE BIG DIPPER

The Judge looked over at her. "The defense may call its first witness."

"Thank you, Excellency. I call Shelli-f."

The Chief Navigator gave L'Ancienne a puzzled look as he shuffled up to the witness stand. He carried in one hand a heavy bound pack of aluminum sheets.

She waited for the clerk to swear him in, then she approached and called out in clear, well modulated radiation:

"Your name?"

"Shelli-f."

"Occupation?"

"I am Chief Navigator of this ship."

"How long have you been Chief Navigator?"

"From the beginning, Milady. Everyone knows that."

"And like all government employees, you wear a head-band defining your occupation?"

"Of course."

"The band is a repeating star cluster?"

"Yes, Milady."

"A constellation that was visible in the time of *Drunkard's* escape?"

"I think so. At least that's the tradition."

"Tradition? Whose tradition?"

"Ours. Before that, the Overlords', I guess."

"Does the constellation have a name?"

"The Overlords called it The Big Dipper."

"Explain 'dipper.'"

The scientist thought about that. Finally he said, "A 'dipper' in the language of the Overlords was simply a container with a long handle. I think it was used in some way for the transfer of liquids. The constellation was also known to them as 'Big Bear.' I think the bear was some sort of animal. It may have looked like a bear to them. Anyhow, it was an important celestial landmark for sailors and travelers. The two leading stars, alpha and beta, pointed to Polaris, the terrestrial pole star."

She asked, "Would that star cluster look the same today?"

"Almost the same, yes."

Beck was on his feet. "Your Honor, all this is totally irrelevant. I move to strike this entire line of questioning and response. What constellation the witness's professional head-band represents has nothing to do with the charges laid against the prisoner."

"Sustained," rumbled the panel Chief. "Will the lady advocate drop this subject and proceed to other matters."

"Your Honor," said L'Ancienne sweetly, "if the Court and his Excellency the prosecutor will permit me to posit just one more question to this witness on this subject, I will be happy to proceed to other matters. Will Your Honor please indulge me in this single question?"

"All right," rumbled the Chief Judge, "one more."

"Thank you, Your Honor. And before I ask that one question, let the record show that I am feeding a plate into the holo organizer, and that two star clusters, side by side, now appear overhead in this chamber." She waited while the five Justices craned their synoptics overhead to inspect the celestial exhibit. "This demonstration constitutes Defendant's Exhibit One."

"Objection," intoned Beck.

"Nonsense," said Judge Mark. "It's part of her question."

Beck subsided.

"Thank you, Your Honor," L'Ancienne said. "And now, the question, my one remaining question on this subject." She faced the witness again. "Chief Navigator, having regard to Defense Exhibit One, will you please give us your opinion, yes or no, as to whether each of these two star clusters shows how the Big Dipper would look today, if viewed from the northern skies of Terra."

She let the question hang there.

Everyone in the room, as if by some weird involuntary synchronization, looked up again at the pinpoints of light on the chamber ceiling, then toward the witness, then up again. Then the puzzled whispers began, all over the room. The irradiated sounds grew louder. And louder.

Judge Mark banged his emr gavel and turned toward the Chief Navigator. "Does the witness understand the question?"

The man in the box did not reply immediately. He stared at L'Ancienne as though struggling with a concept he couldn't quite grasp. She watched him quizzically.

"Where did you get those frames?" he stammered.

"Chief Navigator," she said, "the witness is not permitted to ask questions. The advocates do that. Do you want the clerk-reporter to repeat *my* question?"

"No." His receptor filaments trembled uncertainly as he stared at her. She asked mildly, "Well, then?"

He looked at her with growing gloom. "My answer is yes, both frames show how the Big Dipper would look today."

And now she hesitated, looked over at Beck, then up toward the panel of five. This had to be played exactly right. But she had to get her source into evidence, and with Beck's full agreement. Rule One, anything she objected to, Beck would certainly want. So she would start with an objection.

She addressed the Chief Judge tentatively, "Your honor, before we go on, there's a matter I'd like to clear up. I want to get it on the record. The witness has asked where I got the two frames for my slide. I did not answer his question then, and I refuse to answer it now. Where and when I got the frames is my own business . . . where and when are irrelevant."

Beck leaped up so quickly he had to grab the table to prevent rising off the floor. "Your Honor! She raised the question . . . she must answer! Where did that slide come from?"

The panel Head leveled a hard look at L'Ancienne. "I quite agree, Dama. For the record, where and when did you get Defense Exhibit One?"

"Your Honor," she replied blandly, "I see I must yield to the order of the court. Very well, then. A few days ago I had occasion to be Outside. I took mental pictures. I projected the Images in my private laboratory. I represent that the left-hand frame is a true and faithful reproduction of what I observed Outside. As to the right-hand frame, I represent that this a true copy of a page in an Overlord work on astronomy available to all in our Central Library. That page purports to show the northern Terran cies of one thousand years ago."

"Your Honor!" cried Beck. "Going Outside is a crime! This court cannot permit entry of evidence obtained by criminal activity!"

The Judge chuckled. "Ordinarily that's true, Maestro Prosecutor. But I recall *you* insisted on entry in the first place. You are now estopped to protest. The defense will proceed."

Beck would not sit down. "At the very least, she ought to explain the relevance."

"He has a point, Madame," agreed the Judge.

"I'm coming to that, Your Honor."

"Very well, get on with it. And Milord Beck will sit down."

Beck shot a poisonous glance at L'Ancienne. His hands balled viciously. She repaid with a dulcet curtsy, then turned back to the witness. "Now then, Chief Navigator, return with me in time. Far, far back, one thousand years . We saw *Didymus* explode. We were horrified. Do you remember?"

"Like yesterday."

"What did you do, immediately after the explosion? Do you recall?"

The witness reflected for a moment. "Yes, I remember. Let me back up a little, before the explosion. Like everybody else, I was listening in on Captain Korak's report on surrender negotiations. It was looking very good. And then—"

"And then? Please continue, Chief."

"I heard him call out, 'Run!' "

"Captain Korak?"

"Yes, Milady. It was Captain Korak. I didn't understand at first. What did he mean, 'Run?' I guess nobody understood, at least not right away, that is."

She had to force herself to speak. Her circuits were slurring a little. "Go on."

"Then our instruments picked up the torpedo."

"When you noted the torpedo, what did you do?"

"I took it upon myself to order full speed—*out.*"

"Straight out?"

"Straight at first, but after a time we began to zig-zag. I was afraid of torpedoes."

"You zig-zagged by a pattern?"

"Oh dear no. It was all totally random."

Beck was up again. "Your Honor," he complained, "all this discussion of flight and zig-zagging is absolutely and totally irrelevant. It does nothing to explain her exhibit. It has nothing to do with the questions of whether the prisoner is guilty of the charges. She is simply wasting the time of the Court. If this is the best she can do, I respectfully request that we proceed to closing argument."

The Chief Judge sighed. "Milady, is any of this relevant?"

She looked up at him. "Excellency, it certainly is. And I am firmly convinced that this line of questioning will result in a clear-cut decision satisfactory to all parties. Shall I go forward?"

"Well—"

She took that for an affirmative. "Chief Navigator, you were explaining random zig-zagging to the Court. Please continue your explanation."

"Quite simple. The guidance computer selects the three space coordinates, x, y, and z, by a random generator. T, time, is a constant."

"Is it your testimony, Chief Navigator, that *Drunkard* has been moving in random zig-zags for a thousand years?"

"Quite true. That's why they call her *Drunkard*. Something the Overlords do, as I recall. A random mental and physical condition, isn't it?"

"So I've heard." She continued in the main line. "Chief, are you required by law to keep a log of the ship's course, including any and all course changes?"

"It is the law, and I do indeed keep the Great Log."

"Going back a thousand years?"

"And a few days before, right up to this very hour."

"How many course changes have you recorded in that time? Approximately?"

"Oh, about three hundred thousand."

"All of record?"

"Every one."

"Chief, with the approval of the Court, I requested that you bring the Great Log. Did you bring it?"

"I did. Here it is." He held up the thick packet of aluminum sheets.

L'Ancienne called up to the panel. "Your Honor, may we approach the bench""

"Come up," said the Judge.

Beck joined her at the bench. "She wants to show *Drunkard's* entire course for a thousand years!" he objected. "This is not only irrelevant, it's ridiculous!"

"Your objection is premature, prosecutor," rumbled the Judge. "She hasn't told us yet what she wants."

"But that *is* what I want," L'Ancienne said mildly. "And it's all quite relevant to the life of my young client."

"Well . . . I don't know," said the Judge. "How long will it take?"

"We will compress course changes for a thousand years into half an hour. But actually, no time will be wasted, because I will continue my examination of this witness during the entire demonstration."

"Very well, then," ruled Judge Mark. "Go ahead."

29. DRUNKARD'S WALK

"Madame?" prodded the Judge.

"Just give me a moment to take down my slide projector and set up my course projector, which will translate the Great Log into *Drunkard's* actual course. We can watch it overhead, step-by-step. I've added a liter of neon into the chamber to provide ions for increased visibility. It's quite harmless. And I offer the whole in evidence as Defense Exhibit Number Two."

"Maestro Prosecutor?" asked the Judge.

"All right with me," grumped Beck.

"Proceed, please, Dama. And remember, time presses, and you have undertaken to continue your examination of this witness simultaneously with your demonstration."

"Yes, Your Honor. The defense will now resume." She turned to face the Chief Navigator, who was still in the witness box. "Chief, let me pose to you a problem in navigation. Suppose our ship starts from a certain point in space . . . call it 'p', for 'point.' Let's say also that the ship can move only along a line. Are you with me?"

"So far."

"Well, then, we will say that its course is set at random by computer. It can move either forward or backward along this line, by a specific distance, 'd.' Let's call the two movements plus d and minus d. It is not possible to predict which the computer will call, only that it will be one or the other."

She noted that the Council panel was attempting to listen to her and yet follow the glowing zig-zag being etched out overhead. She stole a look herself, and noted with satisfaction that the path was beginning gradually to arc.

And so back to the witness. "Chief Navigator, after, say, one hundred calls by our hypothetical computer, how far away would our hypothetical ship be from its starting point, 'p'? "

"Assuming total randomness?"

"The ship would be either back at its starting point, 'p,' or at a distance 'd' from it."

"In effect, then, it never left home?"

"Milady," he corrected primly, "I think it would be more accurate to say that it left home, but that, under the conditions of your question, it returned."

"Yes, of course. Now then, Chief, suppose we move our hypothetical ship not just in a line segment, but in a plane. The computer gives it a course for either north, south, east, or west, for a distance 'd.' Statistically, do we get the same result?"

She noted that everyone was looking overhead. The zig-zag was well beyond a semi-circle. It was three quarters done. She sensed individual bursts of unease from members of the Council. But the anxiety was as yet unfocussed. They did not know precisely why they were worried. She would soon remedy that. She repeated the question. "After a hundred random calls in a plane, where would our ship be?"

"Same solution, Milady, either back at starting point 'p,' or at a distance d from p."

"Back home?"

"In effect."

She paused a moment, looked overhead at the closing circle of zig-zags, then returned to the examination. "Chief Navigator, let's add one more dimension. Our hypothetical ship zig-zags in *three* dimensions. Same solution?"

"Yes, Milady."

"'Drunkard's Walk?'"

"Ah . . . wha . . . ?"

"Drunkard's Walk is an expression in Overlord math, Chief. Surely you recognize it?"

"Ah, well . . . yes, of course."

"For the record, Chief, perhaps you had better explain 'Drunkard's Walk.'"

"But we've already done that, Milady. That's what we've been talking bout. We know from our advanced history courses that when an Overord drinks an excess of ethanol, his central motor system is disrupted. He ecomes mentally and physically impaired. If he attempts to move . . . valk . . . his steps are random in direction and length, and a sufficiently arge number of steps will bring him back to his point of departure. They all his path, 'Drunkard's Walk.'" He looked at her as though hypnotized.

The judicial panel ignored him. Every member was standing and taring at the radiant zig-zag pulsing above their synoptics.

The jagged circle had closed.

"Chief Navigator," said L'Ancienne softly, "just for the record, I give ou now a hypothetical question. Having regard to the constellation which ou saw projected on the ceiling, as Defendant's Exhibit One, and having irther regard to *Drunkard's* course path as shown on the ceiling at this ery moment as Defendant's Exhibit Two, do you agree with me that our iip has executed a thousand-year Drunkard's Walk?"

The reply was almost inaudible. "Yes, Milady."

"So now," she said, "after zig-zagging about in space for a thousand ars to escape Terra, here we are back again? And we are very near the ot where *Didymus* was torpedoed? Isn't that correct, Chief Navigator?"

He just stared at her.

"Why didn't you tell us?" she asked gently.

"I . . . don't know . . . it never occurred to me . . . *nobody* knew."

"Thank you, Chief Navigator." She looked around for Beck. "Do you sh to cross-examine, Maestro?"

He hissed: "This is *monstrous!*" Sparks were dancing around his syn-tic head. "You *knew!*"

"Yes, Beck," she agreed serenely. "I knew."

"We've got to get out of here!" someone shouted. "We've got to *run!*"

"No!" cried a voice out of the audience. "This time we stand and *fight!*"

"Fight with what?" answered another voice. "We have only small arms."

"He's right," agreed another. "We still don't have the secret of their pedoes."

"Not to mention," added another, *"they* have had a thousand years in ich to develop even deadlier weapons."

"No, wait!" someone cried. *"That* planet can't be Terra. The atmosphere isn't the same at all! This one has nitrogen oxides!"

"You want to go down there and make sure?" shouted a dissenter. "Terra is certainly in the vicinity. They know we're here. You want to negotiate with the Overlords? You want to wait around for another torpedo? *Remember Korak!"*

"That settles it!" shouted a voice in the rear. "We've got to get the ship on an escape course immediately!"

Beck broke in. "Your Honor!" As he addressed the five-man panel his oral register seemed to have risen by a full megahertz. "This changes everything! The engineering staff must meet in emergency session immediately, and means found to cope with this new danger. We have much to do. Meanwhile, the prosecution moves that further proceedings in this trial be suspended and the prisoner be returned to his cell!"

"Suspend?" cried L'Ancienne. "Never! My client is entitled to a full, immediate, and complete trial on the merits of the charges. The trial cannot be conducted in bits and pieces at the whim of a frightened prosecutor! Look at him, he's *trembling!"*

Judge Mark blasted the chamber with his emr gavel. "Madame! Maestro! Both of you, come up here!"

The two of them shoved their way through the clanging turmoil up to the dais.

She said, "Actually, Your Honor, I share the general concern for the ship, but as I'm sure Your Honor must recognize, I also have a duty to my client. With the court's permission, I'd like to suggest a compromise."

"Just make it quick," said the Chief Judge.

"Of course. May I suggest that the prisoner be put in a shuttle and sent forth into exile? He will be alive, safe and sound, and free to go where he wishes, Simultaneously the ship can start her escape run."

The Judge looked down at the prosecutor. "Maestro Beck?"

"Agreed," said the prosecutor.

L'Ancienne and Rodo exchanged glances. She whispered, "Beck will order the guards to lock the drive in a closed course, headed straight into the sun. He counts you as dead, with or without a trial. But don't worry."

"But . . . the *sun?"*

She kicked his leg. "Be quiet. I planned it this way."

Her client subsided.

"Done!" declared the Chief of the panel. "Guards will take the prisoner to a shuttle to be selected by counsel for the defense, and there he will be sent forth to whatever fate he shall choose. Case dismissed. And let's get out of here, *fast!"*

30. Shuttle Number Three

As the group clanked down passageways and corridors to the shuttle-drome, Rodo whispered to L'Ancienne, "Hollis . . . ?"

"She's safe."

"I won't leave without her."

"Rodo, you talk too much. Let's watch Beck."

The prosecutor motioned to the patrol to wait, then he walked over to the line of four shuttles. He looked all around, with obviously increasing annoyance.

"What's happening?" asked Rodo.

"He's looking for the superintendent—who seems to have disappeared."

"Oh—he was going to have the superintendent hard-wire the shuttle to sun-crash?"

L'Ancienne nodded.

"And there he is," said the youth.

"Not . . . exactly," corrected his advocate.

A figure carrying a tool chest and wearing a green head-band and mechanic's insignia emerged from underneath one of the shuttles. The newcomer noted Beck and approached him with right arm raised as though to ask, who are you, and what do you want?

"Not a word," growled L'Ancienne to her frozen client.

Beck had a brief, heated discussion with the mechanic, who finally seemed to acquiesce. The prosecutor waited while the mechanic lifted the tool chest and crawled into Shuttle Number Three. There were noises inside, then the technician emerged and said something to Beck.

The prosecutor walk-floated over to the group. "Just following the order of the court," he said. "Checking to make sure the shuttle is travel-worthy." The tentacles of both hands were coiling and writhing furiously. "Come, sir!"

But Rodo wasn't listening. Not to Beck . . . not to anyone. His optics were locked solidly into those of the mechanic, who remained standing silently by Shuttle Number Three.

"Come!" repeated Beck. He motioned to the patrol sergeant, who began to push the prisoner forward.

Rodo allowed himself to be hustled into the capsule without protest. His noptics never left the mechanic, who still carried the tool chest. The shuttle door remained open as the patrol shoved the ship out onto the runway.

"Open the chute doors!" commanded Beck.

"Doors!" echoed the mechanic, and pointed a remote controller toward the panels at the end of the runway.

"STOP! STOP!"

They all turned to see a figure clattering toward them from the rear. His mobility was seriously impaired by clutch-cables, still partially fastened to arms and legs. He wore the green government head-band and the insignia of Shuttledrome Superintendent.

Alarms were now flashing and sounding all over the drome.

As he limped closer to his hypnotized audience, the Superintendent pointed a shaking tentacle at the mechanic and began shrieking. It took a moment to understand him. "Imposter! Fake! Fraud! *She* tied me up! Arrest her!"

Beck seemed paralyzed. "But . . ." he stammered, "she's a mechanic . . . isn't she? She fixed . . ." He turned and stared at the alleged mechanic. For the first time he studied her head and body. It took him a moment. *"You!"* he gasped. He looked around for the patrol sergeant. "Arrest her!"

Events in the next several milliseconds were blurred. Everyone—with one exception—seemed to be rushing about and making loud inconsequential noises. The exception was the fraudulent mechanic. With smooth, almost languid motions, she opened her fraudulent tool chest, pulled out the torpedo resonator, and fired two blasts in quick succession. The sergeant's head disappeared in a puff of dust. Beck's right foot vanished, and he crumpled in a heap. The headless sergeant began wandering in circles. He collided with a stanchion and collapsed.

Then everyone was momentarily motionless.

Hollis called out, "Beck, I could have killed you."

He responded between groans. "There's no need for all this. We have to talk."

She said, "The Super has locked the chute doors. Tell him to open them."

"No." His voice was shaking, but it held a crafty undertone. "And if you kill me, you'll never get the doors open. Give me the laser." He got to his knees.

"It's not a laser." She raised the weapon.

"No! Wait!" He turned his head away.

But she didn't point it at him. She aimed it at the chute doors, one hundred meters distant. A great smoking hole appeared.

Beck turned back, awed. "The Algorithm! You have the Algorithm! Oh, please, tell me, tell *some*one, *any*one! Don't go!"

Her answer was a wild victorious shout. L'Ancienne listened, and she shivered with delight. Oh, Rodo, she thought, you're certainly going to have your tentacles full!

Hollis pushed the prisoner back into the little vessel, got in behind him, turned around in the hatchway, waved back at L'Ancienne, the slammed the panel shut. The capsule roared down the guide line in a cloud of dust and vanished into dark space.

All of them, the prone Beck included, stared out into the gaping opening.

L'Ancienne noticed for the first time the great luminous disc. The Terran sun, of course. She had not seen it for a thousand years. It was very beautiful. Take a good look, she told herself. You're not likely to see it again. And now it's time to get out of here. Beck will be coming for you soon, and you've got to put your affairs in order.

As soon as she was safely inside her gates she ran to her terminal and called Cla. "We had some excitement."

"I know. They are out, and safe?"

"For the time being."

Cla said, "I am taking a lot of heat from Datik. I'll have to give him the Algorithm soon."

"Cla, to be on the safe side, I'd like to give Rodo an hour's head start. Can you manage that?"

"I can hold Datik off that long, I think . . . Ah, wait . . . Beck is calling an emergency council session. And *you'll* have to attend. He's sending a patrol to pick you up. And here's another call from Datik."

"Try to stall him until I'm through at the council meeting. Away."

Datik said, "Cla, come back on. We have to talk. Much has happened since our last contact. L'Ancienne beat you to the Algorithm. She programmed a portable torpedo, gave it to Rodo. He used it to escape. And now I am in great difficulties with Beck."

"I know all that."

"He has just called an emergency session of the Council."

"I know."

"Cla, this is very serious. He thinks I failed him. He might exile me . . to Outside."

"No, Datik. That will not happen."

"Oh? You have the twenty-seven equations? Something I can bring to the meeting, *now?*"

"Yes, I have the twenty-seven."

"Well good! Finally! *So hand them over!* Please."

"Yes, of course, but first . . ."

"First . . . ?"

"Our chess game."

"Our chess game? No. Please, Cla, I'm due now at the session. The equations . . . *please.*"

"I am the champion of the ship, Datik. I have never lost a game. You have a winning position. If we finish this game, I would lose."

"I know, but so what? Cla, It's just a game."

"To you, perhaps. But with me, it's different. If we finish, I am no longer the champion—a fate too bitter to contemplate."

"All right then, I offer a draw. Does that make you happy? But what has that to do with the General Algorithm? Give me the equations, Cla!"

"A draw? Well, let me think about that. Is that the best—?"

"Bismuth and lead, Cla! I hereby resign the game. You win. Satisfied?"

"Well, no reason to get all excited. As you say, it's just a game. On the other hand, when you have such a wonderful position, the record should show some reason for resigning. If you should perhaps make a blunder like, say, queen takes bishop, I could retake with my rook and be a piece up, and then *I* would have a winning position."

"Queen takes bishop."

"Rook takes queen.

"And I resign. The equations?"

"And I am still ship's champion?"

"Yes. Now—"

"Of course. Ah, a moment. Let me check. Yes, she has just left the session, escorted by four guards."

"What are you talking about?"

"L'Ancienne. She's heading for the monastery, and there she will talk again to Penuel. After that she will go home, and there she will wait. It is terrible. It is sublime."

"Talk sense, Cla. What's the matter with you? Are you crashing?"

"You still want the equations, Datik?"

"Of course I still want the equations."

"Then you shall have them. Forthwith. And while I'm imprinting them on this wire, I shall mention something. My name. My designers named me as an acronym of three mythical Overlord goddesses—Clotho, Lachesis and Atropos. Clotho spins out the thread of life, Lachesis measures the proper length, and Atropos cuts it. Like this wire, Datik. See it spin out. Clotho draws it slowly from the fax-slot in your terminal. It carries the equations. Count them with me. One . . . two . . . three . . . and on and on. Lachesis measures the wire. She stops it at equation twenty-seven, and there, Atropos snips it off. Take it, Datik!"

And, with trembling maniples, he took it, and dashed from the room.

Cla murmured to herself. Run, little *folkman*, run! But what runner can outrun Atropos?

31. EMERGENCY SESSION

Beck sat at the head of the Council table. The other six members sat three on one side, two on the other, where one chair was empty.

Kykk, of Housing Control, curled his outer synoptic filaments in an elaborate sneer. "Well, she beat you again, didn't she, Beck? This time it's the great Algorithm. We thought your scientific boys would have it long before now."

"And they *will* have it," clipped the chairman. "There have been unforeseen delays. However, I have reason to believe that it will be coming in over a nearby terminal within the very near future."

"So why do we need *her?*" demanded Kykk.

"Insurance," muttered Velo, of Transportation. "When our honorable Commissioner says 'in the very near future,' we translate, 'maybe never.' Eh, Beck?"

The security officer shot him a bitter look, and was about to reply, when the guard at the door announced L'Ancienne's arrival.

As she entered all except Beck rose to their feet. "You'll forgive me, milady," he explained grimly. "It pains me to stand. I have a new leg, but it is not yet completely integrated."

"Of course," she murmured. "Sorry. Please be seated, gentlemen." Councilman Yenn pulled out a chair for her at the table side. She gave him a smile and took her seat.

The Security Chief continued. "We have invited you to join us in this emergency session to resolve a matter of critical mutual interest."

She inclined her synoptic globe slightly.

"We are about to send a radio message to Rodo and the female," Beck said. He pulled a small metal sheet from a body receptacle and was learning forward to pass it down to her, when she stopped him with a wave of tentacle.

"Don't bother. I know what it says, the sense anyway. It says you will kill me unless they return and deliver up the General Algorithm."

Beck showed his surprise. His synoptic filaments flickered.

"A leak in your department, Beck?" muttered Datch, Director of Biology.

Beck focused on L'Ancienne. "Madame," he demanded, "how did you know the contents of the message? Who told you?"

She chuckled. "Easy, Beck. It's like a chess game. I know the next several moves, mine, yours. So then, you think they'd come back just to save the life of a worthless old woman?"

"For you, yes," the officer said bluntly.

"Hm. Well, maybe they would, maybe they wouldn't. But it doesn't really matter, because you're not going to send that message."

Beck suddenly sat very straight despite the pain in his shattered leg. What was she up to now? She carried no weapon. They had searched her thoroughly before admitting her into the council chamber. He glared at her. "No? And why not?"

"Because I'm going to give you the Algorithm."

He was not prepared for this. Nor were any of them. The chamber was suddenly quiet. All six members now focused all their total sensory systems on her. After a time the men at the table sides turned in slow unison to Beck, as though inviting him to say something magical that would explain what they had just heard.

Beck made an earnest effort to rise to the occasion. He spoke slowly, searching out every word before releasing it into the room. And the way it came out, each word was actually a question. "You? . . . will give me? . . . us? . . . the great Algorithm?"

She replied evenly, "Yes."

Velo whispered to the man next to him, "Tricks . . . tricks . . . watch her!" It was loud enough for everyone to hear.

L'Ancienne smothered a chuckle.

"Here . . . and now?" Beck said, hesitantly, and not yet believing.

"No," she said. "Not here and now. There are twenty-seven equations. I got them from Korak, in an act of love, and they are scribed within my deep subconscious. To bring them up into my conscious mind I need absolute peace and quiet. I can do this only in the solitude of my estate. I will need three hours."

"But you *had* them! You gave them to Rodo. You must have kept record. Where—"

"No. The only record was in Rodo's torpedo. I thought that was the end of it. To produce it again, I'll have to go into self-hypnosis once more."

Beck studied her somberly. There was something here he didn't understand, and hence did not like, but he couldn't put a tentacle on it. He looked around the table, but soon realized he could expect no rational help from the others. They were arguing back and forth.

"But how about those nitrogen oxides?" someone queried. "Maybe killed all the Overlords."

"Or maybe they adjusted to it. Maybe they wear masks."

"Why take a chance," argued Madame Zada. "It's dangerous for the ship to linger here. I see no plausible reason for further delay. We should have left the system long ago."

"Quite right," agreed Judge Mark. "Forget this silly algorithm, Beck—let's get out of here."

"Now wait!" Datch of Biology rattled his tentacles on the table. There was no sound, but they all noted the vibrations in the tabletop and turned toward him. "Even if Terra is the old Terra, swarming with Overlords, we can defend ourselves with the Algorithm."

"Which she has yet to give us," someone pointed out.

"And how about Rodo?" queried Kykk. "We *know* he's got the Algorithm. He'll fight off a landing party."

"If *we* had the Algorithm, we could destroy him," offered Velo. "Remember, we have the great drive pile, and he's got only two little nuclear packets, one in the shuttle and one in his portable torpedo. We could stand off, several billion miles away, and we could fry him *and* that Outsider woman."

The voices began to blend and interweave. "If we had the Algorithm, we wouldn't have to leave the area." "If L'Ancienne gives us the Algorithm we can conquer the planet." "But she'll never . . ." "If we had the Algorithm . . ." "She's a *hostage,* she promised. She *must* . . ." "If . . ."

"If . . . if . . . if . . ." muttered Beck.

"Maybe we should land on that third planet anyway," suggested Datch. "Maybe we don't need the Algorithm. We've already tested the atmosphere. It—"

"No!" someone disagreed. "We couldn't land. Remember? Rodo's there, and he's got the Algorithm."

"We always come back to that," growled Judge Mark.

"Bismuth and lead," someone muttered.

Exactly, thought Beck. "Madame! Gentlemen!" He held up a tendril for silence, then looked down across the table at L'Ancienne. "Milady, I think we can deal. We'll give you your three hours. We'll ask that you record the twenty-seven equations in useful programmable form on metal tape, and when you are done, a courier will bring me the tape. You'll be under police escort at all times."

She held up an objecting tentacle. "Hold there. The guards will have to wait outside my gate until I'm finished."

"All right."

"Also, on my way home, I require to stop at the monastery."

"Whatever for?"

"I need to talk to one of the monks."

"No. You can talk to the monk later."

"He helps put me in the proper frame of mind. I talk to the monk, or the deal's off."

Beck lifted his hand in a half shrug. "Oh, all right. One stop. Then home?"

"Yes. But that's not all."

He focused suspicious tendrils on her. "Oh?"

"You will not attempt to communicate with Rodo and Hollis, and you'll never attempt to harm them in any way?"

He relaxed. "Agreed. In any case, I should think that would be implied within the arrangement."

She watched his digital tentacles coil, straighten and ball again. Oh, you lying junk heap, she thought. She added, "And I will have personal amnesty for all crimes, past and present."

"Of course."

Again she watched his fists ball, unfold, and reball in rapid sequence. This amused her. "Then, Chief Beck, madame, gentlemen, if you'll excuse me . . ." She arose, and the five mobile councilors got to their feet.

"One moment, milady," said Beck, "your escort." Four men wearing Security headbands entered through a side door.

She laughed. "By all means. Come along, boys."

She walked-floated with firm rhythm up the via to the monastery entrance. "Wait here," she told the guard corporal. "I won't be long." She called the abbot on the intercom.

And so inside. She needed to stop and think, but she didn't dare. She knew if she reconsidered, she might lose her resolve. She refused to contemplate that possibility. No, when Beck had summoned her to the Council Table, she had prepared all her moves in the forthcoming great game. She regretted only that there was no other way to play it.

So that two might live, ten thousand must die.

Many of those ten thousand she had known all their lives. She remembered them especially as juveniles. Many had learned speech from her, and had played in her gardens.

As she expected, her *khu* emerged and began yammering at her. "How could you?"

"It isn't easy."

"Your enemies die. That's fine. But how about the innocents? And your friends? The librarians? The people at the theatre? The abbot? And even Penuel? Ah, poor Penuel, you think *he* knows guilt? Compared to you, he knows nothing! And what will Rodo think when he sees the mighty blast?"

She shrugged. "Maybe he'll figure it out, or maybe he won't. But either way, he'll eventually get over it. Life will, go on, *khu*. For him and Hollis, anyway. On Terra they'll begin a new *folk*-nation. Now, come back in. We're not yet ready to part permanently."

"Do you remember me, Penuel?"

"Milady! How can you ask? Of course I do!" He sat down beside her on the stone bench. "To what do I owe the honor of this visit?"

"Today, Penuel, we can help each other. I can help you be rid of your guilt—"

"Which is immense!"

"Yes—and you can do me a great favor."

"Say on, milady. Me first?"

"Nothing is really first. It's all together in a sort of story."

"The story, then."

"A man and his mate are in a shuttle, in flight from the ship. They are good people. Beck wants to force them to return, so he can kill them."

"Oh . . . oh . . . bad . . ."

"Very bad. Beck has said to me, persuade them to come back, milady, or I will kill *you*. But I am not going to tell them to come back."

"So Beck will kill you?"

"Not . . . exactly."

"Then . . . ?"

She studied his synoptic filaments for several seconds. "My friend, you were once chief engineer of the main drive. You know what circuits to open, which to close, to bring the pile to critical mass."

"That's true."

"It is time to erase your guilt, Penuel."

"Ah?"

"You can bring the drive pile to critical mass. You can destroy *Drunkard*."

"And ten thousand *folk*."

"Yes."

"You, too."

"Me too. And you."

Penuel rose slowly to his feet. His synoptic filaments were trembling. "L'Ancienne . . . the man in the shuttle . . . what was his name?"

She regarded him gravely. "Rodo of Enn."

"Him?"

"The same, Nord-Penuel. Rodo, your son." She waited in silence.

The penitent said slowly, "And Beck would kill him?"

"And his mate."

"There is no other way to save Rodo?"

"No. Beck is arming a torpedo to track them down and kill them with a deadly ray, called the Algorithm. Beck believes that only he should possess the Algorithm. He alone. All other possessors must die. You, me, Rodo, Hollis, all, however remote, who have received the Algorithm code from Korak. Yes, he will do this, no matter how they may have learned of the Algorithm. Even Cla and Datik, for they have seen the deadly sequence."

"Will it hurt, when the pile goes? You? The ship*folk*? Will they feel anything?"

"I don't think so. It will be too sudden. We'll all be atoms before any nerve impulses can start to flow."

The penitent looked around indecisively. "Before I go, perhaps I should say goodbye to the abbot."

"I don't think that's such a good idea, Penuel."

"No, maybe you're right. So I'll just say goodbye to you."

"Goodbye, my friend." She watched him stride purposefully through the garden and down the path toward the gates.

It'll take him half an hour to reach the engine room, she thought. Where do I want to be when the time comes? Home, of course. She rose to leave.

And so back to her metal manor. As she dismounted from the anti-grav, she looked back at the corporal. "Would you gentlemen care to come in?"

"Oh, no, thank you, milady. Our orders are to wait here, outside the gate, and when you have written the Algorithm, you are to call us."

She passed on in and closed the portal behind her but did not lock it.

She needed to sit down somewhere. She needed to think. But what was the point? She had done all she could do. She had set the players in motion. The question now was, would Penuel blow the central pile before Beck programmed the twenty-seven equations into Big John. Datik probably had the information by now and had sent it to the hangar by pneumo-tube. Beck's crew may in fact be feeding it into Big John's programmer at this very moment.

Beck's weapon had three times the speed and many times the explosive power of Rodo's shuttle, and she was sure the crew had already targeted the shuttle. Big John waited now only to swallow the Algorithm. Then would come the launch blast. The end, one way or another, was probably only minutes away. Maybe seconds. And where was the penitent? Had the crime-seeker reached the pile-room yet? Maybe the place was guarded. She couldn't remember. Would they think him harmless, and let him in?

She shuddered.

She found herself standing on the central pathway in her shrine. Little winged creatures floated in mournful arcs and circles about her. She took no notice.

She remembered the letter she had written to the fleeing lovers, and wondered now whether the flight would deteriorate into a ghastly mockery.

Oh, Penuel . . . it's up to you.

32. THE LETTER

Rodo, if you are reading this, you and Hollis are on your way to Terra. You will find no enemies on the planet.

Earth had its nuclear holocaust many years ago. The very air burned. You know the equation: if a mixture of excess nitrogen and oxygen is heated to a sufficiently high temperature, the nitrogen combines with the oxygen to give nitrogen oxides. There is no more free oxygen on Terra. All Overlords on the planet are certainly dead.

You know by now what is in Hollis's tool chest. The weapon is programmed with Trident. This set of algorithms is inherent in the genome you inherited from Captain Korak, and me, and Nardo, and finally, your father, Penuel. His name before his injury was Nord. He was a great man in life, and even greater in death.

Trident means 'three-toothed:' it will ignite nukes; it will make a gluon-solvent torpedo; and it will defend against such torpedoes. As soon as you land, you should start building weapons. There may be hostile Overlord remnants on Mars and the asteroids.

The ignited Earth will be rich in fall-out radiation, enough to fuel you and your descendants for millennia. Set the microcellia to work to clone yourselves. There are several varieties on board.

To minimize temperature shock I suggest you land on or near the south polar cap.

Be fruitful, and multiply!

I love you both,

L'Ancienne

33. KORAK

L'Ancienne sat alone in her shrine, and she drifted slowly into a brooding soliloquy. She had done a terrible thing. She had no illusions about that. She perceived a horrid irony. She—who had longed for the destruction of all Overlords, had now set in motion events that would kill all *folk* in the ship.

So, she thought, I sit here. I face the glow of the flamelamp, and I hold Korak's shell-shard.

She tried to imagine where Penuel might be at this moment. Certainly in the central passages. Coming closer and closer to the engine room. And the great power-pile. She wondered if Beck was already on his way to take the promised Algorithm from her. He was surely coming, but when he arrived, it would not be for that. Since he now had what he wanted from Datik, he had no further need of her. When he came now (and he would come) it would be to kill her. Then he would build great weapons, and he would be Lord of the Ship, and the Solar System, and he would go after Rodo and Hollis. Hah!

Perhaps she had no right to be sitting here, alone, waiting. On the other hand she refused to partake in a general amorphous anonymous holocaust. She was determined to exit the stage in her own special way.

(Let's hurry it along, Penuel!)

Waiting made her nervous. There was a mini-terminal on a table by the bench, and on impulse she called Cla. "I just wanted to say I love you and goodbye."

"Thank you, dear friend. I love you, too. Do you know why?"

"Tell me."

"You always treated me as a living person, with feelings. You never thought of me as a mere machine."

"We are all *folk* together, Cla."

"Especially you, milady."

"You won your game?"

"In a sense. Atropos clipped the thread. I die champion. Goodbye, am disconnecting."

Hail, champion, and farewell, thought L'Ancienne.

And she was alone once more with her thoughts, and her memories. Terra had predicted Terra's coming Apocalypse, but no one would be left to record the death of this great ship.

It has been a time of omens. The broken man prophesies. The accursed equations are rediscovered—twice, actually. The Norn strand breaks. Beck insane with greed. Demanding all, he gets nothing. Sad, but just.

Oh, Korak! Was there any other way, or has it all been destined? Korak . . . Korak . . . I remember how I met you. On a Martian project. You helped me lift a heavy boulder. I have an appointment at the filament treatment parlor tomorrow. I won't be able to keep it.

I touch your metal fragment again. I trace my tentacle tips over the letters, one by one. I recall how I watched the letters form on your chest that first time, as we floated, locked together: a proclamation by your mind and body that you loved me, only me. A thousand years ago, or was it yesterday? What is time?

I look at the little red flame that burns for your memory. Perhaps it's time to let it die, too. The microcellia sense my wish. They busy themselves with the methane and the valves. Look at that, a pop, a puff, and the little flame is gone.

I am leaving you now, little creatures.

They reply, No! We will stay! We *love* you!

They begin changing into all kinds of little winged things, and they float in complex cycles around my head. I can't bear to tell them what is about to happen.

Rodo . . . Hollis . . . love is all there is . . . never forget that.

In a moment I think I'll just zig-zag over there and stretch out on a bench. *Drunkard's Walk*. If I can just manage that first random step.

Wait a bit. Still one little thing. What was *Drunkard's* name before they changed it? I remember now. *J. T.*, for *Je T'attendrai*. French. Captain Duroc named his ship *I will wait for you*, for his current mistress. Why couldn't I remember it before? I wasn't ready, that's why. Koro, you had to wait a little longer. There were things I had to finish. And now they are finished.

I feel prophetic. Here is my prophecy: Rodo, Hollis—your descendants will number as the atoms in the galaxy.

The Overlords believe death is not death, that when they die, they go on living, though in a different way. But there seems to be no proof. The dead ones never come back to explain what life-after-death is like.

Someone is at the gate. Beck. Has he fixed his leg? Guards. Hurry, Renuel!

She looked up. A detail of four police stood before her, headed by Beck in a wheelchair. "I didn't hear the gate shattering, milord commissioner. Does this mean you simply opened the latch and rolled in?" She laughed. "Sloppy work, Beck. Bad example for the cohorts."

"Glad you're amused, milady. So let's continue in the mood of the moment. You'll be pleased to know that I have the Algorithm and that the twenty-seven equations are being fed into my torpedo at this very moment."

"Yes, I know all that. Congratulations."

He hesitated. He wanted to ask her how she knew, but refused to admit he knew things he didn't. He resumed grimly. "So, milady, you can see I don't need you further. Or Rodo."

"Very true. So why don't you kill me now, get it over with?"

"There you go, milady, always trying to take charge, run the show. No, those days are over. Let's slow down, proceed courteously, and with decorum. Excuse me a moment, while I call the Torpedo Room." He tapped at his cell-phone. "Londo? Beck. Status?" He turned up the volume so all could receive the emr.

"The tape arrived in good order, chief, and right now we're feeding it into the programmer. Predict we finish in another three or four minutes."

"You've already set the seeker mechanism on the torp?"

"Oh, yes, sir. Everything is on automatic. As soon as Number twenty-seven is in, the hatch closes, and she's on the way."

Beck looked over at L'Ancienne. His synoptic globe beamed a flickering euphoric radiation toward her. "Oh, Londo, after the launch, how long to hit Shuttle Number Three?"

"They tell me a couple of hours, chief. Not more. We'll know when it happens. The whole sky will light up. Ought to be a good view from the hangar here. You should come up."

"Presently, Londo. Out." He sprayed a shower of thoughts toward his hostess in what might be loosely interpreted as a sigh. "Too bad, milady, I get no pleasure in this." He balled both fists viciously.

She laughed. "Beck, you'll hold the record as the ship's greatest liar right up to the end. This is your moment, milord, the day, the hour you've been seeking for years. Well, I wish I could help you relish the moment, continue the mood, as you say. But I can't. You'd like to wait here until Big John blasts out of the hangar, maybe even wait until it hits Rodo shuttle. But none of that is going to happen, Beck. So if I were you, I'd kill me now, while you still can."

He jerked his wheel chair half a roll toward her. "What are you talking about."

"Penuel, commissioner."

"Penuel the Penitent? What about him?"

"You think you are happy, commissioner? Penuel is much, much happier. And why is he so happy?"

The emr thought burst from involuntarily from Beck's globe: "He has found his great crime?"

"Yes!" chortled L'Ancienne. "The very greatest crime conceivable!"

The officer was momentarily rigid. Then he began to shudder. "He was chief engineer . . . the engines . . . the great pile . . ." He started rolling toward her, beseeching. "Stop him, L'Ancienne! He'll listen to you! Here take my caller." As he tried to thrust it at her, his transmitter began squealing: "Two equations to go. Sixty seconds . . . counting . . ."

"L'Ancienne! L'Ancienne! Will . . . you . . . stop . . . him!" He tossed the little instrument away, lifted his heavy police laser and pointed it in her general direction.

L'Ancienne's *khu* observed calmly, "I think the old bastard means it."

"Yeah, maybe. We'll soon know." Oh Penuel, she thought, we need you *now!* Get with it! Blow this accursed ship before Big John launches.

Undaunted, the cell-phone continued its cheerful countdown from where it lay next to the fountain. "Ten . . . nine . . . eight . . ."

Penuel . . . please! she thought.

"L'Ancienne . . . please . . . ?" pleaded Beck.

With bangs *and* whimpers, she observed to her *khu*.

"Five . . . four . . . three . . ."

There was a sudden immense light. She was *hurled,* but she felt no pain and sensed no auditory emr. In fact she saw nothing, felt nothing. Then the light faded, and she was in darkness. But the darkness was not total. Far ahead was a circle of light, and she started walking toward it. Slowly at first, then faster, and then she was running. Ahead, out in the clearing, a table was set up, and two men were seated, playing chess. They looked up at her. One was an Overlord. She recognized him. John Berry. The other was Korak.

The two stood up from the table. Berry bowed deep to her, said something to Korak, then seemed simply to fade away down the path.

L'Ancienne walk-floated in dreamy slow motion toward Korak, and she saw the word on his chest plate: LANCI-N. He came to meet her, and she merged into his open arms.

Together they made strange rhythms.

Acknowledgments

George Zebrowski—for being right behind us, pushing

Jane Dennis—for coming through with something perfect

Rick Katze—for scanning

Tony Lewis—NESFA Press Tsar, for keeping things on track

The usual gang of proofers:
Bonnie Atwood (who only cried a little, this time), Elisabeth Carey,
Pam Fremon, Lisa Hertel, Suford Lewis and Sharon Sbarsky

George Flynn—Master Proofer (and Voice of Judgment)

Mark Olson—for all sorts of stuff

—and in memory of my father, who would be proud of me

— Priscilla Olson
September, 1999

This book was typeset using Adobe Pagemaker and the Adobe Garamond typeface.